A TREASURY OF
FANTASY

"A Phantasy"

PATTEN WILSON

A TREASURY OF FANTASY

Heroic Adventures in Imaginary Lands

REVISED EDITION

Edited by Cary Wilkins

ILLUSTRATED

Chatham River Press
New York

A NOTE TO THE READER:

"The Master Key," a work first published in 1903, contains some
racial and ethnic references that may be offensive to modern readers.
Readers should be aware, however, that these do not reflect the
attitudes of the publisher of this edition and that they merely reflect
the language, and its usage, of the early twentieth century.

This 1984 edition of *A Treasury of Fantasy* was published earlier
in a slightly different form.

ACKNOWLEDGMENTS

The illustrations for *Phantastes* are reproduced by permission of
the Rare Book & Manuscripts Division, the New York Public
Library, Astor, Lenox and Tilden Foundations.

"The Doom That Came to Sarnath" Copyright 1939, 1943 by
August Derleth and Donald Wandrei. Reprinted by permission of
the author's Estate and the agents for the Estate, Scott Meredith
Literary Agency, Inc., 845 Third Avenue, New York, NY 10022.

"Swords of the Purple Kingdom" Copyright © 1967 by Glenn
Lord for *King Kull*. Reprinted by permission of Glenn Lord, agent
for the Robert E. Howard heirs.

"The Rule of Names" Copyright © 1964, 1975 by Ursula K. Le Guin;
reprinted by permission of the author and the author's agent, Virginia Kidd.

This 1984 edition is published by Chatham River Press,
a division of Arlington House, distributed by Crown Publishers, Inc.,
One Park Avenue, New York, New York 10016

Manufactured in the United States of America

Library of Congress Cataloging in Publication Data
Main entry under title:
A Treasury of fantasy.
   Contents: The story of Sigurd/translated from the Icelandic by Eiríkr
Magnússon and William Morris—The quest of the Holy Graal/Mrs. Andrew
Lang—The enchantment of Lionarda/Francisco de Moraes—[etc.]
   1. Fantastic fiction.   I. Wilkins, Cary, 1954–
PN6120.95.F25T7   1984   808.83'876   84-11325
ISBN: 0-517-453711 (pbk.)
h g f e d c b a

Contents

PATTEN WILSON

Foreword

Good fantastic literature not only provides us with an enjoyable escape into a land of dreams and adventure, but also frees our imagination from the world around us. Too many of us are content with our everyday lives, even though other lands may be at our back door.

Fantasy has been with us ever since man began inventing stories. The world is just not big enough for our imagination, so we invent new worlds of our own, with new laws and new beings.

The early myths of man helped him confront his fears, desires, joys, and sorrows. They were filled with gods and heroes of unearthly proportions, and horrible monsters and creatures of death and destruction. For these peoples, myths were ways of dealing with their mysterious, unknowable world; for us they are fascinating stories of fantasy that still speak to our basic natures. "The Story of Sigurd," which opens this collection, is from the myths of the Viking age. From the later myths of Great Britain comes a story from the Arthurian legends, "The Quest of the Holy Graal." Influenced by legends of this kind were the later medieval romances, such as *Palmerin of England.* An excerpt from this work reveals a courteous knight battling dragons and overcoming magic spells to rescue his lady Lionarda.

Fantasy plays a large part in German Romantic literature of the late eighteenth and early nineteenth centuries, especially in the tales of E.T.A. Hoffmann and Johann Ludwig Tieck. In "The Elves," a haunting story by Tieck, the protagonist is a seven-year-old girl who wanders into a land of enchantment and unimaginable happiness. The German Romantics influenced many writers, including nineteenth-century British author John Ruskin, whose delightful fairy tale, "The King of the Golden River," is in this collection.

The three novels of this anthology represent the beginnings of modern fantasy. Nearly one hundred years before Tolkien published his great trilogy *The Lord of the Rings,* George Mac Donald was writing brilliant stories of adult fantasy. His novel *Phantastes* is a richly imaginative story of a quest through Fairy Land—a quest for truth and goodness. Through an enchanted forest, a magnificent palace of black and white marble, a gray rocky shore at the end of the world—we go from one dreamscape to another in a celebration of life and ourselves. The hero, Anodos, finds a fairy book of wondrous stories: "It glowed and flashed the thoughts upon the soul. . . ." So it is with *Phantastes*.

Some fantasy scholars consider William Morris to be the father of modern fantasy. Artist, illustrator, designer, poet, novelist, social reformer—Morris rebelled against the dehumanizing aspects of the industrial revolution and created a romanticized view of medieval times. In *The Wood Beyond the World*, the hero, Golden Walter, is haunted by a vision. He leaves the known world to pursue that vision. "Here in this land be strange adventures toward, and . . . if we, and I in especial, were to turn our backs on them, and go home with nothing done, it were the pity of our lives," says Walter.

These great works of early fantasy influenced in their turn the great fantasy writers of the twentieth century. The four works here show the diverging paths the genre has taken. L. Frank Baum's speculative fantasy "The Master Key" explores what happens when mysterious secrets of nature are revealed before mankind is ready to receive them. H. P. Lovecraft's chilling tale "The Doom That Came to Sarnath" describes the horrible fate of a race of conquerors. Kull emerges from the pen of Robert E. Howard as a savage warrior king of Valusia, the mightiest of seven empires. A comic tale by Ursula K. Le Guin reminds us that even fantastic worlds have rules and laws. When they are broken, the consequences for all may be disastrous.

The unbounded world of fantasy takes many shapes and forms. It is a world that transports us "beyond the fields we know" so that we may hear the faraway call of other lives, in other lands.

The Story of Sigurd

from The Völsunga Saga

Translated from the Icelandic
by Eiríkr Magnússon and
William Morris

The worm Fafnir.

LANCELOT SPEED

The Story of Sigurd

I

Of the Birth and Waxing of Sigurd Fafnir's-Bane

THE TALE TELLS that Hjordis brought forth a man-child, who was straightly borne before King Hjalprek, and then was the king glad thereof, when he saw the keen eyes in the head of him, and he said that few men would be equal to him or like unto him in any wise. So he was sprinkled with water, and had to name Sigurd, of whom all men speak with one speech and say that none was ever his like for growth and goodliness. He was brought up in the house of King Hjalprek in great love and honour; and so it is, that whenso all the noblest men and greatest kings are named in the olden tales, Sigurd is ever put before them all, for might and prowess, for high mind and stout heart, wherewith he was far more abundantly gifted than any man of the northern parts of the wide world.

So Sigurd waxed in King Hjalprek's house, and there was no child but loved him; through him was Hjordis betrothed to King Alf, and jointure meted to her.

Now Sigurd's foster-father was hight Regin, the son of Hreidmar; he taught him all manner of arts, the chess play, and the lore of runes, and the talking of many tongues, even as the wont was with kings' sons in those days. But on a day when they were together, Regin asked Sigurd, if he knew how much wealth his father had owned, and who had the ward thereof; Sigurd answered, and said that the kings kept the ward thereof.

Said Regin, "Dost thou trust them all utterly?"

Sigurd said, "It is seemly that they keep it till I may do somewhat therewith, for better they wot how to guard it than I do."

Another time came Regin to talk to Sigurd, and said,

"A marvellous thing truly that thou must needs be a horse-boy to the kings, and go about like a running knave."

"Nay," said Sigurd, "it is not so, for in all things I have my will, and whatso thing I desire is granted me with good will."

"Well, then," said Regin, "ask for a horse of them."

3

"Yea," quoth Sigurd, "and that shall I have, whenso I have need thereof."

Thereafter Sigurd went to the king, and the king said,

"What wilt thou have of us?"

Then said Sigurd, "I would even a horse of thee for my disport."

Then said the king, "Choose for thyself a horse, and whatso thing else thou desirest among my matters."

So the next day went Sigurd to the wood, and met on the way an old man, long-bearded, that he knew not, who asked him whither away.

Sigurd said, "I am minded to choose me a horse; come thou, and counsel me thereon."

"Well then," said he, "go we and drive them to the river which is called Busil-tarn."

They did so, and drave the horses down into the deeps of the river, and all swam back to land but one horse; and that horse Sigurd chose for himself; grey he was of hue, and young of years, great of growth, and fair to look on, nor had any man yet crossed his back.

Then spake the grey-beard, "From Sleipnir's kin is this horse come, and he must be nourished heedfully, for it will be the best of all horses;" and therewithal he vanished away.

So Sigurd called the horse Grani, the best of all the horses of the world; nor was the man he met other than Odin himself.

Now yet again spake Regin to Sigurd, and said,

"Not enough is thy wealth, and I grieve right sore that thou must needs run here and there like a churl's son; but I can tell thee where there is much wealth for the winning, and great name and honour to be won in the getting of it."

Sigurd asked where that might be, and who had watch and ward over it.

Regin answered, "Fafnir is his name, and but a little way hence he lies, on the waste of Gnita-heath; and when thou comest there thou mayest well say that thou hast never seen more gold heaped together in one place, and that none might desire more treasure, though he were the most ancient and famed of all kings."

"Young am I," says Sigurd, "yet know I the fashion of this worm, and how that none durst go against him, so huge and evil is he."

Regin said, "Nay it is not so; the fashion and the growth of him is even as of other lingworms, and an over great tale men make of it; and even so would thy forefathers have deemed; but thou, though thou be of the kin of the Volsungs, shalt scarce have the heart and mind of those, who are told of as the first in all deeds of fame."

Sigurd said, "Yea, belike I have little of their hardihood and prowess, but thou hast naught to do to lay a coward's name upon me, when I am scarce out of my childish years. Why dost thou egg me on hereto so busily?"

Regin said, "Therein lies a tale which I must needs tell thee."

"Let me hear the same," said Sigurd.

II

Regin's Tale of His Brothers, and the Gold Called Andvari's Hoard

"THUS THE TALE begins," said Regin. "Hreidmar was my father's name, a mighty man and a wealthy: and his first son was named Fafnir, his second Otter, and I was the third, and the least of them all both for prowess and good conditions, but I was cunning to work in iron, and silver, and gold, whereof I could make matters that availed somewhat. Other skill my brother Otter followed, and had another nature withal, for he was a great fisher, and above other men herein; in that he had the likeness of an otter by day, and dwelt ever in the river, and bare fish to bank in his mouth, and his prey would he ever bring to our father, and that availed him much: for the most part he kept him in his otter-gear, and then he would come home and eat alone, and slumbering, for on the dry land he might see naught. But Fafnir was by far the greatest and grimmest, and would have all things about called his.

"Now," says Regin, "there was a dwarf called Andvari, who ever abode in that force, which was called Andvari's force, in the likeness of a pike, and got meat for himself, for many fish there were in the force; now Otter, my brother, was ever wont to enter into the force, and bring fish aland, and lay them one by one on the bank. And so it befell that Odin, Loki, and Hœnir, as they went their ways, came to Andvari's force, and Otter had taken a salmon, and ate it slumbering upon the river bank; then Loki took a stone and cast it at Otter, so that he gat his death thereby; the gods were well content with their prey, and fell to flaying off the otter's skin; and in the evening they came to Hreidmar's house, and showed him what they had taken: thereon he laid hands on them, and doomed them to such ransom, as that they should fill the otter skin with gold, and cover it over without with red gold; so they sent Loki to gather gold together for them; he came to Ran, and got her net, and went therewith to Andvari's force, and cast the net before the pike, and the pike ran into the net and was taken. Then said Loki:

> "'What fish of all fishes,
>   Swims strong in the flood,
> But hath learnt little wit to beware?
>   Thine head must thou buy,
>   From abiding in hell,
> And find me the wan waters' flame.'

"He answered:

> "'Andvari folk call me,
>   Call Oinn my father,
> Over many a force have I fared;
>   For a Norn of ill-luck,
>   This life on me lay
> Through wet ways ever to wade.'

"So Loki beheld the gold of Andvari, and when he had given up the gold, he had but one ring left, and that also Loki took from him; then the dwarf went into a hollow of the rocks, and cried out that that gold-ring, yea and all the gold withal, should be the bane of every man who should own it thereafter.

"Now the gods rode with the treasure to Hreidmar, and fulfilled the otter-skin, and set it on its feet, and they must cover it over utterly with gold: but when this was done then Hreidmar came forth, and beheld yet one of the muzzle hairs, and bade them cover that withal; then Odin drew the ring, Andvari's-loom, from his hand, and covered up the hair therewith; then sang Loki:

> "'Gold enow, good enow,
>   A great weregild, thou hast,
> That my head in good hap I may hold;
>   But thou and thy son
>   Are naught fated to thrive,
> The bane shall it be of you both.'

"Thereafter," says Regin, "Fafnir slew his father and murdered him, nor got I aught of the treasure, and so evil he grew, that he fell to lying abroad, and begrudged any share in the wealth to any man, and so became the worst of all worms, and ever now lies brooding upon that treasure: but for me, I went to the king and became his master-smith; and thus is the tale told of how I lost the heritage of my father, and the weregild for my brother."

So spake Regin; but since that time gold is called Ottergild, and for no other cause than this.

But Sigurd answered, "Much hast thou lost, and exceeding evil have thy kinsmen been! but now, make a sword by thy craft, such a sword as that none can be made like unto it; so that I may do great deeds therewith, if my heart avail thereto, and thou wouldst have me slay this mighty dragon."

Regin says, "Trust me well herein; and with that same sword shalt thou slay Fafnir."

III

Of the Welding Together of the Shards of the Sword Gram

So REGIN MAKES a sword, and gives it into Sigurd's hands. He took the sword and said,

"Behold thy smithying, Regin!" and therewith smote it into the anvil, and the sword brake; so he cast down the brand, and bade him forge a better.

Then Regin forged another sword, and brought it to Sigurd, who looked thereon.

Then said Regin, "Belike thou art well content therewith, hard master though thou be in smithying."

So Sigurd proved the sword, and brake it even as the first; then he said to Regin,

"Ah, art thou, mayhappen, a traitor and a liar like to those former kin of thine?"

Therewith he went to his mother, and she welcomed him in seemly wise, and they talked and drank together.

Then spake Sigurd, "Have I heard aright, that King Sigmund gave thee the good sword Gram in two pieces?"

"True enough," she said.

So Sigurd said, "Deliver them into my hands, for I would have them."

She said he looked like to win great fame, and gave him the sword. Therewith went Sigurd to Regin, and bade him make a good sword thereof as he best might; Regin grew wroth thereat, but went into the smithy with the pieces of the sword, thinking well meanwhile that Sigurd pushed his head far enow into the matter of smithying. So he made a sword, and as he bore it forth from the forge, it seemed to the smiths as though fire burned along the edges thereof. Now he bade Sigurd take the sword, and said he knew not how to make a sword if this one failed. Then Sigurd smote it into the anvil, and cleft it down to the stock thereof, and neither burst the sword nor brake it. Then he praised the sword much, and thereafter went to the river with a lock of wool, and threw it up against the stream, and it fell asunder when it met the sword. Then was Sigurd glad, and went home.

But Regin said, "Now whereas I have made the sword for thee, belike thou wilt hold to thy troth given, and wilt go meet Fafnir?"

"Surely will I hold thereto," said Sigurd, "yet first must I avenge my father."

Now Sigurd the older he grew, the more he grew in the love of all men, so that every child loved him well.

IV

The Prophecy of Grifir

THERE WAS A man hight Grifir, who was Sigurd's mother's brother, and a little after the forging of the sword Sigurd went to Grifir, because he was a man who knew things to come, and what was fated to men: of him Sigurd asked diligently how his life should go; but Grifir was long or he spake, yet at the last, by reason of Sigurd's exceeding great prayers, he told him all his life and the fate thereof, even as afterwards came to pass. So when Grifir had told him all even as he would, he went back home; and a little after he and Regin met.

Then said Regin, "Go thou and slay Fafnir, even as thou hast given thy word."

Sigurd said, "That work shall be wrought; but another is first to be done, the avenging of Sigmund the King and the other of my kinsmen who fell in that their last fight."

V

Of Sigurd's Avenging of Sigmund His Father

NOW SIGURD WENT to the king and spake thus:

"Here have I abode a space with you, and I owe you thanks and reward, for great love and many gifts and all due honour; but now will I away from the land and go meet the sons of Hunding, and do them to wit that the Volsungs are not all dead; and your might would I have to strengthen me therein."

So the kings said that they would give him all things soever that he desired, and therewith was a great army got ready, and all things wrought in the most heedful wise, ships and all war-gear, so that his journey might be of the stateliest: but Sigurd himself steered the dragon-keel which was the greatest and noblest; richly wrought were their sails, and glorious to look on.

So they sail and have wind at will; but when a few days were overpast, there arose a great storm on the sea, and the waves were to behold even as the foam of men's blood; but Sigurd bade take in no sail, howsoever they might be riven, but rather to lay on higher than heretofore. But as they sailed past the rocks of a ness, a certain man hailed the ships, and asked who was captain over that navy; then was it told him that the chief and lord was Sigurd, the son of Sigmund, the most famed of all the young men who now are.

Then said the man, "Naught but one thing, certes, do all say of him, that none among the sons of kings may be likened unto him; now fain were I that ye would shorten sail on some of the ships, and take me aboard."

Then they asked him of his name, and he sang:

> "Hnikar I hight,
> When I gladdened Huginn,
> And went to battle,
> Bright son of Volsung;
> Now may ye call
> The carl on the cliff top,
> Feng or Fjolnir:
> Fain would I with you."

They made for land therewith, and took that man aboard. Then quoth Sigurd, as the song says:

> "Tell me this, O Hnikar,
> Since full well thou knowest
> Fate of Gods, good and ill of mankind,
> What best our hap foresheweth,
> When amid the battle
> About us sweeps the sword edge."

Quoth Hnikar:

"Good are many tokens
If thereof men wotted
When the swords are sweeping:
Fair fellow deem I
The dark-winged raven,
In war, to weapon-wielder.

"The second good thing:
When abroad thou goest
For the long road well arrayed,
Good if thou seest
Two men standing,
Fain of fame within the forecourt.

"A third thing:
Good hearing,
The wolf a howling
Abroad under ash boughs;
Good hap shalt thou have
Dealing with helm-staves,
If thou seest these fare before thee.

"No man in fight
His face shall turn
Against the moon's sister
Low, late-shining,
For he winneth battle
Who best beholdeth
Through the midmost sword-play,
And the sloping ranks best shapeth.

"Great is the trouble
Of foot ill-tripping,
When arrayed for fight thou farest,
For on both sides about
Are the Dísir by thee,
Guileful, wishful of thy wounding,

"Fair-combed, well-washen
Let each warrior be,
Nor lack meat in the morning,
For who can rule
The eve's returning,
And base to fall before fate grovelling."

Then the storm abated, and on they fared till they came aland in the
realm of Hunding's sons, and then Fjolnir vanished away.

Then they let loose fire and sword, and slew men and burnt their
abodes, and did waste all before them: a great company of folk fled
before the face of them to Lyngi the King, and tell him that men of war
are in the land, and are faring with such rage and fury that the like has
never been heard of; and that the sons of King Hunding had no great

forecast in that they said they would never fear the Volsungs more, for here was come Sigurd, the son of Sigmund, as captain over this army.

So King Lyngi let sent the war-message all throughout his realm, and has no will to flee, but summons to him all such as would give him aid. So he came against Sigurd with a great army, he and his brothers with him, and an exceeding fierce fight befell; many a spear and many an arrow might men see there raised aloft, axes hard driven, shields cleft and byrnies torn, helmets were shivered, skulls split atwain, and many a man felled to the cold earth.

And now when the fight has long dured in such wise, Sigurd goes forth before the banners, and has the good sword Gram in his hand, and smites down both men and horses, and goes through the thickest of the throng with both arms red with blood to the shoulder; and folk shrank aback before him wheresoever he went, nor would either helm or byrny hold before him, and no man deemed he had ever seen his like. So a long while the battle lasted, and many a man was slain, and furious was the onset; till at last it befell, even as seldom comes to hand, when a land army falls on, that, do whatso they might, naught was brought about; but so many men fell of the sons of Hunding that the tale of them may not be told; and now whenas Sigurd was among the foremost, came the sons of Hunding against him, and Sigurd smote therewith at Lyngi the King, and clave him down, both helm and head, and mail-clad body, and thereafter he smote Hjorward his brother atwain, and then slew all the other sons of Hunding who were yet alive, and the more part of their folk withal.

Now home goes Sigurd with fair victory won, and plenteous wealth and great honour, which he had gotten to him in this journey, and feasts were made for him against he came back to the realm.

But when Sigurd had been at home but a little, came Regin to talk with him, and said:

"Belike thou wilt now have good will to bow down Fafnir's crest according to thy word plighted, since thou hast thus revenged thy father and the others of thy kin."

Sigurd answered, "That will we hold to, even as we have promised, nor did it ever fall from our memory."

VI

Of the Slaying of the Worm Fafnir

Now SIGURD AND Regin ride up the heath along that same way wherein Fafnir was wont to creep when he fared to the water; and folk say that thirty fathoms was the height of that cliff along which he lay when he drank of the water below. Then Sigurd spake:

"How sayedst thou, Regin, that this drake was no greater than other lingworms; methinks the track of him is marvellous great?"

Then said Regin, "Make thee a hole, and sit down therein, and whenas the worm comes to the water, smite him into the heart, and so do him to death, and win for thee great fame thereby."

But Sigurd said, "What will betide me if I be before the blood of the worm?"

Says Regin, "Of what avail to counsel thee if thou art still afeard of everything? Little art thou like thy kin in stoutness of heart."

Then Sigurd rides right over the heath; but Regin gets him gone, sore afeard.

But Sigurd fell to digging him a pit, and whiles he was at that work, there came to him an old man with a long beard, and asked what he wrought there, and he told him.

Then answered the old man and said, "Thou doest after sorry counsel: rather dig thee many pits, and let the blood run therein; but sit thee down in one thereof, and so thrust the worm's heart through."

And therewithal he vanished away; but Sigurd made the pits even as it was shown to him.

Now crept the worm down to his place of watering, and the earth shook all about him, and he snorted forth venom on all the way before him as he went; but Sigurd neither trembled nor was adrad at the roaring of him. So whenas the worm crept over the pits, Sigurd thrust his sword under his left shoulder, so that it sank in up to the hilts; then up leapt Sigurd from the pit and drew the sword back again unto him, and therewith was his arm all bloody, up to the very shoulder.

Now when that mighty worm was ware that he had his death-wound, then he lashed out head and tail, so that all things soever that were before him were broken to pieces.

So whenas Fafnir had his death-wound, he asked, "Who art thou? and who is thy father? and what thy kin, that thou wert so hardy as to bear weapons against me?"

Sigurd answered, "Unknown to men is my kind. I am called a noble beast: neither father have I nor mother, and all alone have I fared hither."

Said Fafnir, "Whereas thou hast neither father nor mother, of what wonder wert thou born then? But now, though thou tellest me not thy name on this my death-day, yet thou knowest verily that thou liest unto me."

He answered, "Sigurd am I called, and my father was Sigmund."

Says Fafnir, "Who egged thee on to this deed, and why wouldst thou be driven to it? Hadst thou never heard how that all folk were adrad of me, and of the awe of my countenance? But an eager father thou hadst, O bright-eyed swain!"

Sigurd answered, "A hardy heart urged me on hereto; and a strong hand and this sharp sword, which well thou knowest now, stood me in stead in the doing of the deed; *Seldom hath hardy eld a faint-heart youth.*"

Fafnir said, "Well, I wot that hadst thou waxed amid thy kin, thou mightest have good skill to slay folk in thine anger; but more of a marvel is it, that thou, a bondsman taken in war, shouldst have the heart to set on me, *for few among bondsmen have heart for the fight.*"

Said Sigurd, "Wilt thou then cast it in my teeth that I am far away from my kin? Albeit I was a bondsman, yet was I never shackled. God wot thou hast found me free enow."

Fafnir answered, "In angry wise dost thou take my speech; but hearken, for that same gold which I have owned shall be thy bane too."

Quoth Sigurd, "Fain would we keep all our wealth till that day of days; yet shall each man die once for all."

Said Fafnir, "Few things wilt thou do after my counsel; but take heed that thou shalt be drowned if thou farest unwarily over the sea; so bide thou rather on the dry land, for the coming of the calm tide."

Then said Sigurd, "Speak, Fafnir, and say, if thou art so exceeding wise, who are the Norns who rule the lot of all mothers' sons."

Fafnir answers, "Many they be and wide apart; for some are of the kin of the Æsir, and some are of Elfin kin, and some there are who are daughters of Dvalin."

Said Sigurd, "How namest thou the holm whereon Surt and the Æsir mix and mingle the water of the sword?"

"Unshapen is that holm hight," said Fafnir.

And yet again he said, "Regin, my brother, has brought about my end, and it gladdens my heart that thine too he bringeth about; for thus will things be according to his will."

And once again he spake, "A countenance of terror I bore up before all folk, after that I brooded over the heritage of my brother, and on every side did I spout out poison, so that none durst come anigh me, and of no weapon was I adrad, nor ever had I so many men before me, as that I deemed myself not stronger than all; for all men were sore afeard of me."

Sigurd answered and said, "Few may have victory by means of that same countenance of terror, for whoso comes amongst many shall one day find that no one man is by so far the mightiest of all."

Then says Fafnir, "Such counsel I give thee that thou take thy horse and ride away at thy speediest, for ofttimes it falls out so, that he who gets a death-wound avenges himself none the less."

Sigurd answered, "Such as thy redes are I will nowise do after them; nay I will ride now to thy lair and take to me that great treasure of thy kin."

"Ride there then," said Fafnir, "and thou shalt find gold enow to suffice thee for all thy life-days; yet shall that gold be thy bane, and the bane of everyone soever who owns it."

Then up stood Sigurd, and said, "Home would I ride and lose all that wealth, if I deemed that by the losing thereof I should never die; but every brave and true man will fain have his hand on wealth till that last day; but thou, Fafnir, wallow in the death-pain till Death and Hell have thee."

And therewithal Fafnir died.

VII

Of the Slaying of Regin, Son of Hreidmar

THEREAFTER CAME REGIN to Sigurd, and said, "Hail, lord and master, a noble victory hast thou won in the slaying of Fafnir, whereas none durst heretofore abide in the path of him; and now shall this deed of fame be of renown while the world stands fast."

"Now crept the worm down to his place of watering."

LANCELOT SPEED

Then stood Regin staring on the earth a long while, and presently thereafter spake from heavy mood: "Mine own brother hast thou slain, and scarce may I be called sackless of the deed."

Then Sigurd took his sword Gram and dried it on the earth, and spake to Regin:

"Afar thou faredst when I wrought this deed and tried this sharp sword with the hand and the might of me; with all the might and main of a dragon must I strive, while thou wert laid alow in the heather-bush, wotting not if it were earth and heaven."

Said Regin, "Long might this worm have lain in his lair, if the sharp sword I forged with my hand had not been good at need to thee; had that not been, neither thou nor any man would have prevailed against him as at this time."

Sigurd answers, "Whenas men meet foes in fight, better is stout heart than sharp sword."

Then said Regin, exceeding heavily, "Thou hast slain my brother, and scarce may I be sackless of the deed."

Therewith Sigurd cut out the heart of the worm with the sword called Ridil; but Regin drank of Fafnir's blood, and spake, "Grant me a boon, and do a thing little for thee to do. Bear the heart to the fire, and roast it, and give me thereof to eat."

Then Sigurd went his ways and roasted it on a rod; and when the blood bubbled out he laid his finger thereon to essay it, if it were fully done; and then he set his finger in his mouth, and lo, when the heart-blood of the worm touched his tongue, straightway he knew the voice of all fowls, and heard withal how the wood-peckers chattered in the brake beside him:

"There sittest thou, Sigurd, roasting Fafnir's heart for another, that thou shouldest eat thine own self, and then thou shouldest become the wisest of all men."

And another spake: "There lies Regin, minded to beguile the man who trusts in him."

But yet again said the third, "Let him smite the head from off him then, and be only lord of all that gold."

And once more the fourth spake and said, "Ah, the wiser were he if he followed after that good counsel, and rode thereafter to Fafnir's lair, and took to him that mighty treasure that lieth there, and then rode over Hindfell, whereas sleeps Brynhild; for there would he get great wisdom. Ah, wise he were, if he did after your redes, and bethought him of his own weal; *for where wolf's ears are, wolf's teeth are near.*"

Then cried the fifth: "Yea, yea, not so wise is he as I deem him, if he spareth him, whose brother he hath slain already."

At last spake the sixth: "Handy and good rede to slay him, if he spareth him , whose brother he hath slain already."

At last spake the sixth: "Handy and good rede to slay him, and be lord of the treasure!"

Then said Sigurd, "The time is unborn wherein Regin shall be my bane; nay, rather one road shall both these brothers bare."

And therewith he drew his sword Gram and struck off Regin's head.

Then heard Sigurd the wood-peckers a-singing, even as the song says.

For the first sang:

"Bind thou, Sigurd,
The bright red rings!
Not meet it is
Many things to fear.
A fair may know I,
Fair of all the fairest,
Girt about with gold,
Good for thy getting."

And the second:

"Green go the ways
Toward the hall of Giuki,
that the fates show forth
To those who fare thither;
There the rich king
Reareth a daughter;
Thou shalt deal, Sigurd,
With gold for that sweetling."

And the third:

"A high hall is there
Reared upon Hindfell,
Without all around it
Sweeps the red flame aloft;
Wise men wrought
That wonder of halls
With the unhidden gleam
Of the glory of gold."

Then the fourth sang:

"Soft on the fell
A shield-may sleepeth,
The lime-trees' red plague
Playing about her:
The sleep-thorn set Odin
Into that maiden
For her choosing in war
The one he willed not."

"Go, son, behold
That may under helm
Whom from battle
Vinskornir bore,
From her may not turn
The torment of sleep,
Dear offspring of kings,
In the dread Norns' despite."

Then Sigurd ate some deal of Fafnir's heart, and the remnant he kept. Then he leapt on his horse and rode along the the trail of the worm Fafnir, and so right unto his abiding-place; and he found it open, and beheld all the doors and the gear of them that they were wrought of iron: yea, and all the beams of the house; and it was dug down deep into the earth: there found Sigurd gold exceeding plenteous, and the sword Rotti; and thence he took the Helm of Awe, and the Gold Byrny, and many things fair and good. So much gold he found there, that he thought verily that scarce might two horses, or three belike, bear it thence. So he took all the gold and laid it in two great chests, and set them on the horse Grani, and took the reins of him, but nowise will he stir, neither will he abide smiting. Then Sigurd knows the mind of the horse, and leaps on the back of him, and smites the spurs into him, and off the horse goes even as if he were unladen.

VIII

Of Sigurd's Meeting with Brynhild on the Mountain

By LONG ROADS rides Sigurd, till he comes at the last up on to Hindfell, and wends his way south to the land of the Franks; and he sees before him on the fell a great light, as of fire burning, and flaming up even unto the heavens; and when he came thereto, lo, a shield-hung castle before him, and a banner on the topmost thereof: into the castle went Sigurd, and saw one lying there asleep, and all-armed. Therewith he takes the helm from off the head of him, and sees that it is no man, but a woman; and she was clad in a byrny as closely set on her as though it had grown to her flesh; so he rent it from the collar downwards, and then the sleeves thereof, and ever the sword bit on it as if it were cloth. Then said Sigurd that over-long had she lain asleep; but she asked,

"What thing of great might is that has prevailed to rend my byrny, and draw me from my sleep?"

Even as sings the song:

> What bit on the byrny,
> Why breaks my sleep away,
> Who has turned from me
> My wan tormenting?

"Ah, is it so, that here is come Sigurd Sigmundson, bearing Fafnir's helm on his head and Fafnir's bane in his hand?"

Then answered Sigurd:

> "Sigmund's son
> With Sigurd's sword
> E'en now rent down
> The raven's wall.

Sigurd comes upon the castle.

LANCELOT SPEED

"Of the Volsungs' kin is he who has done the deed; but now I have heard that thou art daughter of a mighty king, and folk have told us that thou wert lovely and full of lore, and now I will try the same."

Then Brynhild sang:

> "Long have I slept
> And slumbered long,
> Many and long are the woes of mankind,
> By the might of Odin
> Must I bide helpless
> To shake from off me the spells of slumber.

> "Hail to the day come back!
> Hail, sons of the daylight!
> Hail to thee, dark night, and thy daughter!
> Look with kind eyes a-down,
> On us sitting here lonely,
> And give unto us the gain that we long for.

> "Hall to the Æsir,
> And the sweet Asyniur!
> Hail to the fair earth fulfilled of plenty!
> Fair words, wise hearts,
> Would we win from you,
> And healing hands while life we hold."

Then Brynhild speaks again and says, "Two kings fought, one hight Helm-Gunnar, an old man, and the greatest of warriors, and Odin had promised the victory unto him; but his foe was Agnar, or Audi's brother: and so I smote down Helm-Gunnar in the fight; and Odin, in vengeance for that deed, stuck the sleep-thorn into me, and said that I should never again have the victory, but should be given away in marriage; but thereagainst I vowed a vow, that never would I wed one who knew the name of fear."

Then said Sigurd, "Teach us the lore of mighty matters!"

She said, "Belike thou cannest more skill in all than I; yet will I teach thee; yea, and with thanks, if there be aught of my cunning that will in anywise pleasure thee, either of runes or of other matters that are the root of things; but now let us drink together, and may the Gods give to us twain a good day, that thou mayst win good help and fame from my wisdom, and that thou mayst hereafter mind thee of that which we twain speak together."

Then Brynhild filled a beaker and bore it to Sigurd, and gave him the drink of love, and spake:

> "Beer bring I to thee,
> Fair fruit of the byrnies' clash,
> Mixed is it mightily,
> Mingled with fame,
> Brimming with bright lays
> And pitiful runes,

Wise words, sweet words,
Speech of great game.

"Runes of war know thou,
If great thou wilt be!
Cut them on hilt of hardened sword,
Some on the brand's back,
Some on its shining side,
Twice name Tyr therein.

"Sea-runes good at need,
Learnt for ship's saving,
For the good health of the swimming horse;
On the stern cut them,
Cut them on the rudder-blade
And set flame to shaven oar:
Howso big be the sea-hills,
Howso blue beneath,
Hail from the main then comest thou home.

"Word-runes learn well
If thou wilt that no man
Pay back grief for the grief thou gavest;
Wind thou these,
Weave thou these,
Cast thou these all about thee,
At the Thing,
Where folk throng,
Unto the full doom faring.

"Of ale-runes know the wisdom
If thou wilt that another's wife
Should not bewray thine heart that trusteth;
Cut them on the mead-horn,
On the back of each hand,
And nick an N upon thy nail.

"Ale have thou heed
To sign from all harm,
Leek lay thou in the liquor,
Then I know for sure
Never cometh to thee
Mead with hurtful matters mingled.

"Help-runes shalt thou gather
If skill thou wouldst gain
To loosen child from low-laid mother;
Cut be they in hands hollow,
Wrapped the joints round about;
Call for the Good-folks' gainsome helping.

"Learn the bough-runes' wisdom
If leech-lore thou lovest;
And wilt wot about wounds' searching
On the bark be they scored;

On the buds of trees
Whose boughs look eastward ever.

"Thought-runes shalt thou deal with
   If thou wilt be of all men
Fairest-souled wight, and wisest;
      These areded,
      These first cut,
These first took to heart high Hropt.

"On the shield were they scored
   That stands before the shining God,
On Early-waking's ear,
On All-knowing's hoof,
On the wheel which runneth
Under Rognir's chariot;
On Sleipnir's jaw-teeth,
On the sleigh's traces.

"On the rough bear's paws,
And on Bragi's tongue,
On the wolf's claws,
And on eagle's bill,
On bloody wings,
And bridge's end;
On loosing palms,
And pity's path:

"On glass, and on gold,
And on goodly silver,
In wine and in wort,
And the seat of the witch-wife;
On Gungnir's point,
And Grani's bosom;
On the Norn's nail,
And the neb of the night-owl.

"All these so cut,
   Were shaven and sheared,
And mingled in with holy mead,
And sent upon wide ways enow;
      Some abide with the Elves,
      Some abide with the Æsir,
Or with the wise Vanir,
Some still hold the songs of mankind.

"These be the book-runes,
   And the runes of good help,
And all the ale-runes,
And the runes of much might;
      To whomso they may avail,
      Unbewildered unspoilt;
They are wholesome to have:
Thrive thou with these then,
When thou hast learnt their lore,
Till the Gods end thy life-days.

"Now shalt thou choose thee
E'en as choice is bidden,
Sharp steel's root and stem,
Choose song or silence;
See to each in thy heart
All hurt has been heeded."

Then answered Sigurd:

"Ne'er shall I flee,
Though thou wottest me fey;
Never was I born for blenching,
Thy loved rede will I
Hold aright in my heart
Even as long as I may live."

IX

More Wise Words of Brynhild

Sigurd spake now, "Sure no wiser woman than thou art one may be found in the wide world; yea, yea, teach me more yet of thy wisdom!"

She answers, "Seemly is it that I do according to thy will, and show thee forth more redes of great avail, for thy prayer's sake and thy wisdom;" and she spake withal:

"Be kindly to friend and kin, and reward not their trespasses against thee; bear and forbear, and win for thee thereby long enduring praise of men.

"Take good heed of evil things: a may's love, and a man's wife; full oft thereof doth ill befall!

"Let not thy mind be overmuch crossed by unwise men at thronged meetings of folk; for oft these speak worse than they wot of; lest thou be called a dastard, and art minded to think that thou art even as is said; slay such an one on another day, and so reward his ugly talk.

"If thou farest by the way whereas bide evil things, be well ware of thyself; take not harbour near the highway, though thou be benighted, for oft abide there ill wights for men's bewilderment.

"Let not fair women beguile thee, such as thou mayst meet at the feast, so that the thought thereof stand thee in stead of sleep, and a quiet mind; yea, draw them not to thee with kisses or other sweet things of love.

"If thou hearest the fool's word of a drunken man, strive not with him being drunk with drink and witless; many a grief, yea, and the very death, groweth from out such things.

"Fight thy foes in the field, nor be burnt in thine house.

"Never swear thou wrongsome oath; great and grim is the reward for the breaking of plighted troth.

"Give kind heed to dead men,—sick-dead, sea-dead, or sword-dead; deal heedfully with their dead corpses.

"Trow never in him for whom thou hast slain father, brother, or whatso near kin, yea, though young he be; *for oft waxes wolf in youngling.*

"Look thou with good heed to the wiles of thy friends; but little skill is given to me, that I should foresee the ways of thy life; yet good it were that hate fell not on thee from those of thy wife's house."

Sigurd spake, "None among the sons of men can be found wiser than thou; and thereby swear I, that thee will I have as my own, for near to my heart thou liest."

She answers, "Thee would I fainest choose, though I had all men's sons to choose from."

And thereto they plighted troth both of them.

X

Of the Semblance and Array of Sigurd Fafnir's-Bane

NOW SIGURD RIDES away; many-folded is his shield, and blazing with red gold, and the image of a dragon is drawn thereon; and this same was dark brown above, and bright red below; and with even such-like image was adorned helm, and saddle, and coat-armour; and he was clad in the golden byrny, and all his weapons were gold-wrought.

Now for this cause was the drake drawn on all his weapons, that when he was seen of men, all folk might know who went there; yea, all those who had heard of his slaying of that great dragon, that the Værings call Fafnir; and for that cause are his weapons gold-wrought, and brown of hue, and that he was by far above other men in courtesy and goodly manners, and well-nigh in all things else; and whenas folk tell of all the mightiest champions, and the noblest chiefs, then ever is he named the foremost, and his name goes wide about on all tongues north of the sea of the Greek-lands, and even so shall it be while the world endures.

Now the hair of this Sigurd was golden-red of hue, fair of fashion, and falling down in great locks; thick and short was his beard, and of no other colour; high-nosed he was, broad and high-boned of face; so keen were his eyes, that few durst gaze up under the brows of him; his shoulders were as broad to look on as the shoulders of two; most duly was his body fashioned betwixt height and breadth, and in such wise as was seemliest; and this is the sign told of his height, that when he was girt with his sword Gram, which same was seven spans long, as he went through the full-grown rye-fields, the dew-shoe of the said sword smote the ears of the standing corn; and, for all that, greater was his strength than his growth: well could he wield sword, and cast forth spear, shoot shaft, and hold shield, bend bow, back horse, and do all the goodly deeds that he learned in his youth's days.

Wise he was to know things yet undone; and the voice of all fowls he knew, wherefore few things fell on him unawares.

Of many words he was, and so fair of speech withal, that whensoever he made it his business to speak, he never left speaking before that to all men it seemed full sure, that no otherwise must the matter be than as he said.

His sport and pleasure it was to give aid to his own folk, and to prove himself in mighty matters, to take wealth from his unfriends, and give the same to his friends.

Never did he lose heart, and of naught was he adrad.

XI

Sigurd Comes to Hlymdale

FORTH SIGURD RIDES till he comes to a great and goodly dwelling, the lord whereof was a might chief called Heimir; he had to wife a sister of Brynhild, who was hight Bekkhild, because she had bidden at home, and learned handicraft, whereas Brynhild fared with helm and byrny unto the wars, wherefore was she called Brynhild.

Heimir and Bekkhild had a son called Alswid, the most courteous of men.

Now at this stead were men disporting them abroad, but when they see the man riding thereto, they leave their play to wonder at him, for none such had they ever seen erst; so they went to meet him, and gave him good welcome; Alswid bade him abide and have such things at his hands as he would; and he takes his bidding blithesomely; due service withal was established for him; four men bore the treasure of gold from off the horse, and the fifth took it to him to guard the same; therein were many things to behold, things of great price, and seldom seen; and great game and joy men had to look on byrnies and helms, and mighty rings, and wondrous great golden stoups, and all kinds of war weapons.

So there dwelt Sigurd long in great honour holden; and tidings of that deed of fame spread wide through all lands, of how he had slain that hideous and fearful dragon. So good joyance had they there together, and each was leal to other; and their sport was in the arraying of their weapons, and the shafting of their arrows, and the flying of their falcons.

XII

Sigurd Sees Brynhild at Hlymdale

IN THOSE DAYS came home to Heimir, Brynhild, his foster-daughter, and she sat in her bower with her maidens, and could more skill in handycraft than other women; she sat, overlaying cloth with gold, and sewing therein the great deeds which Sigurd had wrought, the slaying of the Worm, and the taking of the wealth of him, and the death of Regin withal.

Now tells the tale, that on a day Sigurd rode into the wood with hawk, and hound, and men thronging; and whenas he came home his hawk flew up to a high tower, and sat him down on a certain window. Then fared Sigurd after his hawk, and he saw where sat a fair woman, and he knew that it was Brynhild, and he deems all things he sees there to be worthy together, both her fairness, and the fair things she wrought: and therewith he goes into the hall, but has no more joyance in the games of the men folk.

Then spake Alswid, "Why art thou so bare of bliss? this manner of thine grieveth us thy friends; why then wilt thou not hold to thy gleesome ways? Lo, thy hawks pine now, and thy horse Grani droops; and long will it be ere we are booted thereof?"

Sigurd answered, "Good friend, hearken to what lies on my mind; for my hawk flew up into a certain tower; and when I came thereto and took him, lo there I saw a fair woman, and she sat by a needlework of gold, and did thereon my deeds that are passed, and my deeds that are to come."

Then said Alswid, "Thou hast seen Brynhild, Budli's daughter, the greatest of great women."

"Yea, verily," said Sigurd; "but how came she hither?"

Alswid answered, "Short space there was betwixt the coming hither of the twain of you."

Says Sigurd, "Yea, but a few days agone I knew her for the best of the world's women."

Alswid said, "Give not all thine heed to one woman, being such a man as thou art; ill life to sit lamenting for what we may not have."

"I shall go meet her," says Sigurd, "and get from her love like my love, and give her a gold ring in token thereof."

Alswid answered. "None has ever yet been known whom she would let sit beside her, or to whom she would give drink; for ever will she hold to warfare and to the winning of all kinds of fame."

Sigurd said, "We know not for sure whether she will give us answer or not, or grant us a seat beside her."

So the next day after, Sigurd went to the bower, but Alswid stood outside the bower door, fitting shafts to his arrows.

Now Sigurd spake, "Abide, fair and hale lady,—how farest thou?"

She answered, "Well it fares; my kin and my friends live yet: but who shall say what goodhap folk may bear to their life's end?"

He sat him down by her, and there came in four damsels with great golden beakers, and the best of wine therein; and these stood before the twain.

Then said Brynhild, "This seat is for few, but and if my father come."

He answered, "Yet is it granted to one that likes me well."

Now that chamber was hung with the best and fairest of hangings, and the floor thereof was all covered with cloth.

Sigurd spake, "Now has it come to pass even as thou didst promise."

"O be thou welcome here!" said she, and arose therewith, and the four damsels with her, and bore the golden beaker to him, and bade him drink; he stretched out his hand to the beaker, and took it, and her hand withal, and drew her down beside him; and cast his arms round about her neck and kissed her, and said:

"Thou art the fairest that was ever born!"

But Brynhild said, "Ah, wiser is it not to cast faith and troth into a woman's power, for ever shall they break that they have promised."

He said, "That day would dawn the best of days over our heads whereon each of each should be made happy."

Brynhild answered, "It is not fated that we should abide together; I am a shield-may, and wear helm on head even as the kings of war, and them full oft I help, neither is the battle become loathsome to me."

Sigurd answered, "What fruit shall be of our life if we live not together: harder to bear this pain that lies hereunder, than the stroke of sharp sword."

Brynhild answers, "I shall gaze on the hosts of the war-kings, but thou shalt wed Gudrun, the daughter of Giuki."

Sigurd answered, "What king's daughter lives to beguile me? neither am I double-hearted herein; and now I swear by the Gods that thee shall I have for mine own, or no woman else."

And even suchlike wise spake she.

Sigurd thanked her for her speech, and gave her a gold ring, and now they swore oath anew, and so he went his ways to his men, and is with them awhile in great bliss.

XIII

Of the Dream of Gudrun, Giuki's Daughter

THERE WAS A king hight Giuki, who ruled a realm south of the Rhine; three sons he had, thus named: Gunnar, Hogni, and Guttorm, and Gudrun was the name of his daughter, the fairest of maidens; and all these children were far before all other kings' children in all prowess, and in goodliness and growth withal; ever were his sons at the wars and wrought many a deed of fame. But Giuki had wedded Grimhild the Wise-wife.

Now Budli was the name of a king, mightier than Giuki, mighty though they both were: and Atli was the brother of Brynhild: Atli was a fierce man and a grim, great and black to look on, yet noble of mien withal, and the greatest of warriors. Grimhild was a fierce-hearted woman.

Now the days of the Giukings bloomed fair, chiefly because of those children, so far before the sons of men.

On a day Gudrun says to her mays that she may have no joy of heart; then a certain woman asked her wherefore her joy was departed.

She answered, "Grief came to me in my dreams, therefore is there sorrow in my heart, since thou must needs ask thereof."

"Tell it me, then, thy dream," said the woman, "for dreams oft forecast but the weather."

Gudrun answers, "Nay, nay, no weather is this; I dreamed that I had a fair hawk on my wrist, feathered with feathers of gold."

Says the woman, "Many have heard tell of thy beauty, thy wisdom, and thy courtesy; some king's son abides thee, then."

Gudrun answers, "I dreamed that naught was so dear to me as this hawk, and all my wealth had I cast aside rather than him."

The woman said, "Well, then, the man thou shalt have will be of the goodliest, and well shalt thou love him."

Gudrun answered, "It grieves me that I know not who he shall be; let us go seek Brynhild, for she belike will wot thereof."

So they arrayed them in gold and many a fair thing, and she went with her damsels till they came to the hall of Brynhild, and that hall was dight with gold, and stood on a high hill; and whenas their goings were seen, it was told Brynhild, that a company of woman drove toward the burg in gilded waggons.

"That shall be Gudrun, Giuki's daughter," says she: "I dreamed of her last night; let us go meet her; no fairer woman may come to our house."

So they went abroad to meet them, and gave them good greeting, and they went into the goodly hall together; fairly painted it was within, and well adorned with silver vessel; cloths were spread under the feet of them, and all folk served them, and in many wise they sported.

But Gudrun was somewhat silent.

Then said Brynhild, "Ill to abash folk of their mirth; prithee do not so; let us talk together for our disport of mighty kings and their great deeds."

"Good talk," says Gudrun, "let us do even so; what kings deemest thou to have been the first of all men?"

Brynhild says, "The sons of Haki, and Hagbard withal; they brought to pass many a deed of fame in their warfare."

Gudrun answers, "Great men certes, and of noble fame! Yet Sigar took their one sister, and burned the other, house and all; and they may be called slow to revenge the deed; why didst thou not name my brethren, who are held to be the first of men as at this time?"

Brynhild says, "Men of good hope are they surely, though but little proven hitherto; but one I know far before them, Sigurd, the son of Sigmund the King; a youngling was he in the days when he slew the sons of Hunding, and revenged his father, and Eylimi, his mother's father."

Said Gudrun, "By what token tellest thou that?"

Brynhild answered, "His mother went amid the dead, and found Sigmund the King sore wounded, and would bind up his hurts; but he said he grew over old for war, and bade her lay this comfort to her heart, that she should bear the most famed of sons; and wise was the wise man's word therein: for after the death of King Sigmund, she went to King Alf, and there was Sigurd nourished in great honour, and day by day he wrought some deed of fame, and is the man most renowned of all the wide world."

Gudrun says, "From love hast thou gained these tidings of him; but for this cause came I here, to tell thee dreams of mine which have brought me great grief."

Says Brynhild, "Let not such matters sadden thee; abide with thy friends who wish thee blithesome, all of them!"

"This I dreamed," said Gudrun, "that we went, a many of us in company, from the bower, and we saw an exceeding great hart, that far excelled all other deer ever seen, and the hair of him was golden; and this deer we were all fain to take, but I alone got him; and he seemed to me better than all things else; but sithence thou, Brynhild, didst shoot and slay my deer even at my very knees, and such grief was that to me that scarce might I bear it: and then afterwards thou gavest me a wolf-cub, which besprinkled me with the blood of my brethren."

Brynhild answers, "I will arede thy dream, even as things shall come to pass hereafter; for Sigurd shall come to thee, even he whom I have chosen for my well-beloved; and Grimhild shall give him mead mingled with hurtful things, which shall cast us all into mighty strife. Him shalt thou have, and him shalt thou quickly miss; and Atli the King shalt thou wed; and thy brethren shalt thou lose, and slay Atli withal in the end."

Gudrun answers, "Grief and woe to know that such things shall be!"

And therewith she and hers get them gone home to King Giuki.

XIV

Sigurd Comes to the Giukings and Is Wedded to Gudrun

NOW SIGURD GOES his ways with all that great treasure, and in friendly wise he departs from them; and on Grani he rides with all his war-gear and the burden withal; and thus he rides until he comes to the hall of King Giuki; there he rides into the burg, and that sees one of the king's men, and he spake withal:

"Sure it may be deemed that here is come one of the Gods, for his array is all done with gold, and his horse is far mightier than other horses, and the manner of his weapons is most exceedingly goodly, and most of all the man himself far excels all other men ever seen."

So the king goes out with his court and greets the man, and asks,

"Who art thou who thus ridest into my burg, as none has durst hitherto without the leave of my sons?"

He answered, "I am called Sigurd, son of King Sigmund."

Then said King Giuki, "Be thou welcome here, then, and take at our hands whatso thou willest."

So he went into the king's hall, and all men seemed little beside him, and all men served him, and there he abode in great joyance.

Now oft they all ride abroad together, Sigurd and Gunnar and Hogni, and ever is Sigurd far the foremost of them, mighty men of their hands though they were.

But Grimhild finds how heartily Sigurd loved Brynhild, and how oft he talks of her; and she falls to thinking how well it were, if he might abide there and wed the daughter of King Giuki, for she saw that none might come anigh to his goodliness, and what faith and goodhelp there was in him, and how that he had more wealth withal than folk might tell of any man; and the king did to him even as unto his own sons, and they for their parts held him of more worth than themselves.

So on a night as they sat at the drink, the Queen arose, and went before Sigurd, and said:

"Great joy we have in thine abiding here, and all good things will we put before thee to take of us; lo now, take this horn and drink thereof."

So he took it and drank, and therewithal she said, "Thy father shall be Guiki the King, and I shall be thy mother, and Gunnar and Hogni shall be thy brethren, and all this shall be sworn with oaths each to each; and then surely shall the like of you never be found on earth."

Sigurd took her speech well, for with the drinking of that drink all memory of Brynhild departed from him. So there he abode awhile.

And on a day went Grimhild to Giuki the King, and cast her arms around his neck, and spake:

"Behold, there has now come to us the greatest of great hearts that the world holds; and needs must he be trusty and of great avail; give him thy daughter then, with plenteous wealth, and as much of rule as he will; perchance thereby he will be well content to abide here ever."

The king answered, "Seldom does it befall that kings offer their daughters to any, yet in higher wise will it be done to offer her this man, than to take lowly prayers for her from others."

On a night Gudrun pours out the drink, and Sigurd beholds her how fair she is and how full of all courtesy.

Five seasons Sigurd abode there, and ever they passed their days together in good honour and friendship.

And so it befell that the kings held talk together, and Giuki said,

"Great good thou givest us, Sigurd, and with an exceeding strength thou strengthenest our realm."

Then Gunnar said, "All things that may be will we do for thee, so thou abidest here long; both dominion shalt thou have, and our sister freely and unprayed for, whom another man would not get for all his prayers."

Sigurd says, "Thanks have ye for this wherewith ye honour me, and gladly will I take the same."

Therewith they swore brotherhood together, and to be even as if they were children of one father and one mother; and a noble feast was holden, and endured many days, and Sigurd drank at the wedding of him and Gudrun; and there might men behold all manner of game and glee, and each day they feast better and better.

Now fare these folk wide over the world, and do many great deeds, and slay many kings' sons, and no man has ever done such works of prowess as did they; then home they come again with much wealth won in war.

Sigurd gave of the serpent's heart to Gudrun, and she ate thereof, and became greater-hearted, and wiser than e'er before: and the son of these twain was called Sigmund.

Now on a time went Grimhild to Gunnar her son, and spake:

"Fair blooms the life and fortune of thee, but for one thing only, and namely whereas thou art unwedded; go woo Brynhild; good rede is this, and Sigurd will ride with thee."

Gunnar answered, "Fair is she certes, and I am fain enow to win her";

"With the drinking of that drink all memory of Brynhild
departed from him."

and therewith he tells his father, and his brethren, and Sigurd, and they all prick him on to that wooing.

XVI

The Wooing of Brynhild

NOW THEY ARRAY them joyously for their journey and ride over hill and dale to the house of King Budli, and woo his daughter of him; in a good wise he took their speech, if so be that she herself would not deny them; but he said withal that so high-minded was she, that that man only might wed her whom she would.

Then they ride to Hlymdale, and there Heimir gave them good welcome; so Gunnar tells his errand; Heimer says, that she must needs wed but him whom she herself chose freely; and tells them how her abode was but a little way thence, and that he deemed that him only would she have who should ride through the flaming fire that was drawn round about her hall; so they depart and come to the hall and the fire, and see there a castle with a gold roof-ridge, and all round about a fire roaring up.

Now Gunnar rode on Goti, but Hogni on Holkvi, and Gunnar smote his horse to face the fire, but he shrank aback.

Then said Sigurd, "Why givest thou back, Gunnar?"

He answered, "The horse will not tread this fire; but lend me thy horse Grani."

"Yeah, with all my good will," says Sigurd.

Then Gunnar rides him at the fire, and yet nowise will Grani stir, nor may Gunnar any the more ride through that fire. So now they change semblance, Gunnar and Sigurd, even as Grimhild had taught them; then Sigurd in the likeness of Gunnar mounts and rides, Gram in his hand and golden spurs on his heels; then leapt Grani in to the fire when he felt the spurs; and a mighty roar arose as the fire burned ever madder, and the earth trembled, and the flames went up even unto the heavens, nor had any dared to ride as he rode, even as it were through the deep mirk.

But now the fire sank withal, and he leapt from his horse and went into the hall, even as the song says:

> The flame flared at its maddest,
> Earth's fields fell a-quaking
> As the red flame aloft
> Licked the lowest of heaven.
> Few had been fain,
> Of the rulers of folk,
> To ride through that flame,
> Or athwart it to tread.
>
> Then Sigurd smote
> Grani with sword,
> And the flame was slaked
> Before the king;

> Low lay the flames
> Before the fain of fame;
> Bright gleamed the array
> That Regin erst owned.

Now when Sigurd had passed through the fire, he came into a certain fair dwelling, and therein sat Brynhild.

She asked, "What man is it?"

Then he named himself Gunnar, son of Giuki, and said:

"Thou art awarded to me as my wife, by the good-will and word of thy father and thy foster-father, and I have ridden through the flames of thy fire, according to thy word that thou hast set forth."

"I wot not clearly," said she, "how I shall answer thee."

Now Sigurd stood upright on the hall floor, and leaned on the hilt of his sword, and he spake to Brynhild:

"In reward thereof, shall I pay thee a great dower in gold and goodly things?"

She answered in heavy mood from her seat, whereas she sat like unto swan on billow, having a sword in her hand, and a helm on her head, and being clad in a byrny, "O Gunnar," she says, "speak not to me of such things; unless thou be the first and best of all men; for then shalt thou slay those my wooers, if thou hast heart thereto; I have been in battles with the king of the Greeks, and our weapons were stained with red blood, and for such things still I yearn."

He answered, "Yeah, certes many great deeds hast thou done; but yet call thou to mind thine oath, concerning the riding through of this fire, wherein thou didst swear that thou wouldest go with the man who should do this deed."

So she found that he spake but the sooth, and she paid heed to his words, and arose, and greeted him meetly, and he abode there three nights, and they lay in one bed together; but he took the sword Gram and laid it betwixt them, that in that wise must he needs wed his wife or else get his bane.

Then she took from off her the ring Andvari's-loom which he had given her aforetime, and gave it to him, but he gave her another ring out of Fafnir's hoard.

Thereafter he rode away through the same fire unto his fellows, and he and Gunnar changed semblances again, and rode unto Hlymdale, and told how it had gone with them.

That same day went Brynhild home to her foster-father, and tells him as one whom she trusted, how that there had come a king to her; "And he rode through my flaming fire, and said he was come to woo me, and named himself Gunnar; but I said that such a deed might Sigurd alone have done, with whom I plighted troth on the mountain; and he is my first troth-plight, and my well-beloved."

Heimir said that things must needs abide even as now they had come to pass.

Brynhild said, "Aslaug the daughter of me and Sigurd shall be nourished here with thee."

Now the kings fare home, but Brynhild goes to her father; Grimhild welcomes the kings meetly, and thanks Sigurd for his fellowship; and withal is a great feast made, and many were the guests thereat; and thither came Budli the King with his daughter Brynhild, and his son Atli, and for many days did the feast endure: and at that feast was Gunnar wedded to Brynhild: but when it was brought to an end, once more has Sigurd memory of all the oaths that he sware unto Brynhild, yet withal he let all things abide in rest and peace.

Brynhild and Gunnar sat together in great game and glee, and drank goodly wine.

XVII

How the Queens Held Angry Converse Together at the Bathing

ON A DAY as the Queens went to the river to bathe them, Brynhild waded the farthest out into the river; then asked Gudrun what that deed might signify.

Brynhild said, "Yeah, and why then should I be equal to thee in this matter more than in others? I am minded to think that my father is mightier than thine, and my true-love has wrought many wondrous works of fame, and hath ridden the flaming fire withal, while thy husband was but the thrall of King Hjalprek."

Gudrun answered full of wrath, "Thou wouldst be wise if thou shouldst hold thy peace rather than revile my husband: lo now, the talk of all men it is, that none has ever abode in this world like unto him in all matters soever; and little it beseems thee of all folk to mock him who was thy first beloved: and Fafnir he slew, yea, and he rode thy flaming fire, whereas thou didst deem that he was Gunnar the King, and by thy side he lay, and took from thine hand the ring Andvari's-loom;—here mayst thou well behold it!"

Then Brynhild saw the ring and knew it, and waxed as wan as a dead woman, and she went home and spake no word the evening long.

So when Sigurd came to bed to Gudrun she asked him why Brynhild's joy was so departed.

He answered, "I know not, but sore I misdoubt me that soon we shall know thereof overwell."

Gudrun said, "Why may she not love her life, having wealth and bliss, and the praise of all men, and the man withal that she would have?"

"Ah, yea!" said Sigurd, "and where in all the world was she then, when she said that she deemed she had the noblest of all men, and the dearest to her heart of all?"

Gudrun answers, "Tomorn will I ask her concerning this, who is the liefest to her of all men for a husband."

Sigurd said, "Needs must I forbid thee this, and full surely wilt thou rue the deed if thou doest it."

Now the next morning they sat in the bower, and Brynhild was silent; then spake Gudrun:

"Be merry, Brynhild! Grievest thou because of that speech of ours together, or what other thing slayeth thy bliss?"

Brynhild answers, "With naught but evil intent thou sayest this, for a cruel heart thou hast."

"Say not so," said Gudrun; "but rather tell me all the tale."

Brynhild answers, "Ask such things only are good for thee to know— matters meet for mighty dames. Good to love good things when all goes according to thy heart's desire!"

Gudrun says, "Early days for me to glory in that; but this word of thine lookest toward some foreseeing. What ill dost thou thrust at us? I did naught to grieve thee."

Brynhild answers, "For this shalt thou pay, in that thou hast got Sigurd to thee,—nowise can I see thee living in the bliss thereof, whereas thou hast him, and the wealth and the might of him."

But Gudrun answered, "Naught knew I of your words and vows together; and well might my father look to the mating of me without dealing with thee first."

"No secret speech had we," quoth Brynhild, "though we swore oath together; and full well didst thou know that thou wentest about to beguile me; verily thou shalt have thy reward!"

Says Gudrun, "Thou art mated better than thou art worthy of; but thy pride and rage shall be hard to slake belike, and therefor shall many a man pay."

"Ah, I should be well content," said Brynhild, "if thou hadst not the nobler man!"

Gudrun answers, "So noble a husband hast thou, that who knows of a greater king or a lord of more wealth and might?"

Says Brynhild, "Sigurd slew Fafnir, and that only deed is of more worth than all the might of King Gunnar."

(Even as the song says):

> The worm Sigurd slew,
> Nor e'er shall that deed
> Be worsened by age
> While the world is alive:
> But thy brother the King
> Never durst, never bore
> The flame to ride down,
> Through the fire to fare.

Gudrun answers, "Grani would not abide the fire under Gunnar the King, but Sigurd durst the deed, and thy heart may well abide without mocking him."

Brynhild answers, "Nowise will I hide from thee that I deem no good of Grimhild."

Says Gudrun, "Nay, lay no ill words on her, for in all things she is to thee as to her own daughter."

"Ah," says Brynhild, "she is the beginning of all this bale that biteth so; an evil drink she bare to Sigurd, so that he had no more memory of my very name."

"All wrong thou talkest; a lie without measure is this," quoth Gudrun.

Brynhild answered, "Have thou joy of Sigurd according to the measure of the wiles wherewith ye have beguiled me! unworthily have ye conspired against me; may all things go with you as my heart hopes!"

Gudrun says, "More joy shall I have of him than thy wish would give unto me: but to no man's mind it came, that he had aforetime his pleasure of me; nay not once."

"Evil speech thou speakest," says Brynhild; "when thy wrath runs off thou wilt rue it; but come now, let us no more cast angry words one at the other!"

Says Gudrun, "Thou wert the first to cast such words at me, and now thou makest as if thou wouldst amend it, but a cruel and hard heart abides behind."

"Let us lay aside vain babble," says Brynhild. "Long did I hold my peace concerning my sorrow of heart, and, lo now, thy brother alone do I love; let us fall to other talk."

Gudrun said, "Far beyond all this doth thine heart look."

And so ugly ill befell from that going to the river, and that knowing of the ring, wherefrom did all their talk arise.

XVIII

Of Brynhild's Great Grief and Mourning

AFTER THIS TALK Brynhild lay a-bed, and tidings were brought to King Gunnar that Brynhild was sick; he goes to see her thereon, and asks what ails her; but she answered him naught, but lay there as one dead: and when he was hard on her for an answer, she said,

"What didst thou with that ring that I gave thee, even the one which King Budli gave me at our last parting, when thou and King Giuki came to him and threatened fire and the sword, unless he had me to wife? Yea, at that time he led me apart, and asked me which I had chosen of those who were come; but I prayed him that I might abide to ward the land and be chief over the third part of his men; then were there two choices for me to deal betwixt, either that I should be wedded to him whom he would, or lose all my weal and friendship at his hands; and he said withal that his friendship would be better to me than his wrath: then I bethought me whether I should yield to his will, or slay many a man; and therewithal I deemed that it would avail little to strive with him, and so it fell out, that I promised to wed whomsoever should ride the horse Grani with Fafnir's Hoard, and ride through my flaming fire, and slay those men whom I called on him to slay, and now so it was, that none durst ride, save Sigurd only, because he lacked no heart thereto; yeah, and the Worm he slew, and Regin, and five kings beside; but thou, Gunnar, durst do naught; as pale as a dead man didst thou wax, and no king thou art, and no champion, so whereas I made a vow unto my father, that him alone would I love who was the noblest man alive, and that this is none save Sigurd, lo, now have I broken my oath and brought it to naught, since he is none of mine, and for this cause shall I compass thy death; and a great reward of evil things have I wherewith to reward Grimhild;—never, I wot, has woman lived eviler or of lesser heart than she."

Gunnar answered in such wise that few might hear him, "Many a vile word hast thou spoken, and an evil-hearted woman art thou, whereas thou revilest a woman far better than thou; never would she curse her life as thou dost; nay, nor has she tormented dead folk or murdered any; but lives her life well praised of all."

Brynhild answered, "Never have I dealt with evil things privily, or done loathsome deeds;—yet most fain I am to slay thee."

And therewith would she slay King Gunnar, but Hogni laid her in fetters; but then Gunnar spake withal:

"Nay, I will not that she abide in fetters."

Then said she, "Heed it not! for never again seest thou me glad in thine hall, never drinking, never at the chess-play, never speaking the words of kindness, never overlaying the fair cloths with gold, never giving thee good counsel;—ah, my sorrow of heart that I might not get Sigurd to me!"

Then she sat up and smote her needlework, and rent it asunder, and bade set open her bower doors, that far away might the wailings of her sorrow be heard; then great mourning and lamentation there was, so that folk heard it far and wide through that abode.

Now Gudrun asked her bower-maidens why they sat so joyless and downcast. "What has come to you, that ye fare ye as witless women, or what unheard-of wonders have befallen you?"

Then answered a waiting-lady, hight Swaflod, "An untimely, an evil day it is, and our hall is fulfilled of lamentation."

Then spake Gudrun to one of her handmaids, "Arise, for we have slept long; go, wake Brynhild, and let us fall to our needlework and be merry."

"Nay, nay," she says, "nowise may I wake her, or talk with her; for many days has she drunk neither mead nor wine; surely the wrath of the Gods has fallen upon her."

Then spake Gudrun to Gunnar, "Go and see her," she says, "and bid her know that I am grieved with her grief."

"Nay," says Gunnar, "I am forbid to see her or to share her weal."

Nevertheless he went unto her, and strives in many wise to have speech of her, but gets no answer whatsoever: therefore he gets him gone and finds Hogni, and bids him go see her: he said he was loth thereto, but went, and gat no more of her.

Then they go and find Sigurd, and pray him to visit her; he answered naught thereto, and so matters abode for that night.

But the next day, when he came home from hunting, Sigurd went to Gudrun, and spake:

"In such wise do matters show to me, as though great and evil things will betide from this trouble and upheaving, and that Brynhild will surely die."

Gudrun answers, "O my lord, by great wonders is she encompassed, seven days and seven nights has she slept, and none has dared wake her."

"Nay, she sleeps not," said Sigurd, "her heart is dealing rather with dreadful intent against me."

Then said Gudrun, weeping, "Woe worth the while for thy death! go and see her; and wot if her fury may not be abated; give her gold, and smother up her grief and anger therewith!"

Then Sigurd went out, and found the door of Brynhild's chamber open; he deemed she slept, and drew the clothes from off her, and said,

"Awake, Brynhild! the sun shineth now over all the house, and thou has slept enough; cast off grief from thee, and take up gladness!"

She said, "And how then hast thou dared to come to me? in this treason none was worse to me than thou."

Said Sigurd, "Why wilt thou not speak to folk? for what cause sorrowest thou?"

Brynhild answers, "Ah, to thee will I tell of my wrath!"

Sigurd said, "As one under a spell art thou, if thou deemest that there is aught cruel in my heart against thee; but thou hast him for husband whom thou didst choose."

"Ah, nay," she said, "never did Gunnar ride through the fire to me, nor did he give me to dower the host of the slain: I wondered at the man who came into my hall; for I deemed indeed that I knew thine eyes; but I might not see clearly, or divide the good from the evil, because of the veil that lay heavy on my fortune."

Says Sigurd, "No nobler men are there than the sons of Giuki, they slew the king of the Danes, and that great chief, the brother of King Budli."

Brynhild answered, "Surely for many an ill deed must I reward them; mind me not of my griefs against them! But thou, Sigurd, slewest the Worm, and rodest the fire through; yea, and for my sake, and not one of the sons of King Giuki."

Sigurd answers,"I am not thy husband, and thou art not my wife; yet did a farfamed king pay dower to thee."

Says Brynhild, "Never looked I at Gunnar in such a wise that my heart smiled on him; and hard and fell am I to him, though I hide it from others."

"A marvelous thing," says Sigurd, "not to love such a king; what angers thee most? for surely his love should be better to thee than gold."

"This is the sorest sorrow to me," she said, "that the bitter sword is not reddened in thy blood."

"Have no fear thereof!" says he; "no long while to wait or the bitter sword stand deep in my heart; and no worse needest thou to pray for thyself, for thou wilt not live when I am dead; the days of our two lives shall be few enough from henceforth."

Brynhild answers, "Enough and to spare of bale is in thy speech, since thou bewrayedst me, and didst twin me and all bliss;—naught do I heed my life or death."

Sigurd answers, "Ah, live, and love King Gunnar and me withal! and all my wealth will I give thee if thou die not."

Brynhild answers, "Thou knowest me not, nor the heart that is in me;

for thou art the first and best of all men, and I am becoming the most loathsome of all women to thee."

"This is truer," says Sigurd, "that I loved thee better than myself, though I fell into the wiles from whence our lives may not escape; for whenso my own heart and mind availed me, then I sorrowed sore that thou wert not my wife; but as I might I put my trouble from me, for in a king's dwelling was I; and withal and in spite of all I was well content that we were all together. Well may it be, that that shall come to pass which is foretold; neither shall I fear the fulfilment thereof."

Brynhild answered and said, "Too late thou tellest me that my grief grieved thee: little pity shall I find now."

Sigurd said, "This my heart would, that thou and I should go into one bed together; even so wouldst thou be my wife."

Said Brynhild, "Such words may nowise be spoken, nor will I have two kings in one hall; I will lay my life down rather than beguile Gunnar the King."

And therewith she calls to mind how they met, they two, on the mountain, and swore oath each to each.

"But now is all changed, and I will not live."

"I might not call to mind thy name," said Sigurd, "or know thee again, before the time of thy wedding; the greatest of all griefs is that."

Then said Brynhild, "I swore an oath to wed the man who should ride my flaming fire, and that oath will I hold to, or die."

"Rather than thou die, I will wed thee, and put away Gudrun," said Sigurd.

But therewithal so swelled the heart betwixt the sides of him, that the rings of his byrny burst asunder.

"I will not have thee," says Brynhild, "nay, nor any other!"

Then Sigurd got him gone.

So saith the song of Sigurd:

> Out then went Sigurd,
> The great kings' well-loved
> From the speech and the sorrow,
> Sore drooping, so grieving,
> That the shirt round about him
> Of iron rings woven,
> From the sides brake asunder
> Of the brave in the battle.

So when Sigurd came into the hall, Gunnar asked if he had come to a knowledge of what great grief lay heavy on her, or if she had power of speech: and Sigurd said that she lacked it not. So now Gunnar goes to her again, and asked her, what wrought her woe, or if there were anything that might amend it.

"I will not live," says Brynhild, "for Sigurd has bewrayed me, yea, and thee no less, whereas thou didst suffer him to come into my bed: lo thou, two men in one dwelling I will not have; and this shall be Sigurd's death, or thy death, or my death;—for now has he told Gudrun all, and she is mocking me even now!"

XIX

Of the Slaying of Sigurd Fafnir's-Bane

THEREAFTER BRYNHILD WENT out, and sat under her bower-wall, and had many words of wailing to say, and still she cried that all things were loathsome to her, both land and lordship alike, so she might not have Sigurd.

But therewith came Gunnar to her again, and Brynhild spake, "Thou shalt lose both realm and wealth, and thy life and me, for I shall fare home to my kin, and abide there in sorrow, unless thou slayest Sigurd and his son; never nourish thou a wolfcub."

Gunnar grew sick at heart thereat, and might nowise see what fearful thing lay beneath it all; he was bound to Sigurd by oath, and this way and that way swung the heart within him; but at the last he bethought him of the measureless shame if his wife went from him, and he said within himself, "Brynhild is better to me than all things else, and the fairest woman of all women, and I will lay down my life rather than lose the love of her." And herewith he called to him his brother and spake:

"Trouble is heavy on me," and he tells him that he must needs slay Sigurd, for that he has failed him wherein he trusted him; "so let us be lords of the gold and the realm withal."

Hogni answers, "Ill it behoves us to break our oaths with wrack and wrong, and withal great aid we have in him; no kings shall be as great as we, if so be the King of the Hunfolk may live; such another brother-in-law never may we get again; bethink thee how good it is to have such a brother-in-law, and such sons to our sister! But well I see how things stand, for this has Brynhild stirred thee up to, and surely shall her counsel drag us into huge shame and scathe."

Gunnar says, "Yet shall it be brought about: and, lo, a rede thereto;— let us egg on our brother Guttorm to the deed; he is young, and of little knowledge, and is clean out of all the oaths moreover."

"Ah, set about in ill wise," says Hogni, "and though indeed it may well be compassed, a due reward shall we gain for the betrayal of such a man as is Sigurd."

Gunnar says, "Sigurd shall die, or I shall die."

And therewith he bids Brynhild arise and be glad at heart: so she arose, and still ever she said that Gunnar should come no more into her bed till the deed was done.

So the brothers fall to talk, and Gunnar says that it is a deed well worthy of death, that taking of Brynhild's maiden-head; "So come now, let us prick on Guttorm to do the deed."

Therewith they call him to them, and offer him gold and great dominion, as they well have might to do. Yea, and they took a certain worm and somewhat of wolf's flesh and let seethe them together, and gave him to eat of the same, even as the singer sings:

> Fish of the wild-wood,
> Worms smooth crawling,

> With wolf-meat mingled,
> They minced for Guttorm;
> Then in the beaker,
> In the wine his mouth knew,
> They set it, still doing
> More deeds of wizards.

Wherefore with the eating of this meat he grew so wild and eager, and with all things about him, and with the heavy words of Grimhild, that he gave his word to do the deed; and mighty honour they promised him reward thereof.

But of these evil wiles naught at all knew Sigurd, for he might not deal with this shapen fate, nor the measure of his life-days, neither deemed he that he was worthy of such things at their hands.

So Guttorm went in to Sigurd the next morning as he lay upon his bed, yet durst he not do aught against him, but shrank back out again; yea, and even so he fared a second time, for so bright and eager were the eyes of Sigurd that few durst look upon him. But the third time he went in, and there lay Sigurd asleep; then Guttorm drew his sword and thrust Sigurd through in such wise that the sword-point smote into the bed beneath him; then Sigurd awoke with that wound, and Guttorm gat him unto the door; but therewith Sigurd caught up the sword Gram, and cast it after him, and it smote him on the back, and struck him asunder in the midst so that the feet of him fell one way, and the head and hands back into the chamber.

Now Gudrun lay asleep on Sigurd's bosom, but she woke up unto woe that may not be told of, all swimming in the blood of him, and in such wise did she bewail her with weeping and words of sorrow, that Sigurd rose up on the bolster, and spake:

"Weep not," said he, "for thy brothers live for thy delight; but a young son have I, too young to beware of his foes; and an ill turn have these played against their own fortune; for never will they get a mightier brother-in-law to ride abroad with them; nay, nor a better son to their sister, than this one, if he may grow to man's estate. Lo, now is that come to pass which was foretold me long ago, but from mine eyes has it been hidden, for none may fight against his fate and prevail. Behold, this has Brynhild brought to pass, even she who loves me before all men; but this I may swear, that never have I wrought ill to Gunnar, but rather have ever held fast to my oath with him, nor was I ever too much a friend to his wife. And now if I had been forewarned, and had been afoot with my weapons, then should many a man have lost his life or ever I had fallen, and all those brethren should have been slain, and a harder work would the slaying of me have been than the slaying of the mightiest bull or the mightiest boar of the wild-wood."

And even therewithal life left the King; but Gudrun moaned and drew a weary breath, and Brynhild heard it, and laughed when she heard her moaning.

Then said Gunnar, "thou laughest not because thy heart-roots are gladded, or else why doth thy visage wax so wan? Such an evil creature thou art; most like thou art nigh to thy death! Lo now, how meet would it be for thee to behold thy brother Atli slain before thine eyes, and that thou shouldst stand over him dead; whereas we must needs now stand over our brother-in-law in such a case—our brother-in-law and our brother's bane."

She answered, "None need mock at the measure of slaughter being unfulfilled; yet heedeth not Atli your wrath or your threats; yea, he shall live longer than ye, and be a mightier man."

Hogni spake and said, "Now hath come to pass the soothsaying of Brynhild, an ill work not to be atoned for."

And Gudrun said, "My kinsmen have slain my husband but ye, when ye next ride to the war and are come into the battle, then shall ye look about and see that Sigurd is neither on your right hand nor the left, and ye shall know that he was your good-hap and your strength; and if he had lived and had sons, then should ye have been strengthened by his offspring and his kin."

XX

Of the Lamentation of Gudrun Over Sigurd Dead, As It Is Told in the Ancient Songs

Gudrun of old days
Drew near to dying
As she sat in sorrow
Over Sigurd;
Yet she sighed not
Nor smote hand on hand,
Nor wailed she aught
As other women.

Then went earls to her,
Full of all wisdom,
Fain help to deal
To her dreadful heart:
Hushed was Gudrun
Of wail or greeting,
But with heavy woe
Was her heart a-breaking.

Bright and fair
Sat the great earls' brides,
Gold arrayed
Before Gudrun;
Each told the tale
Of her great trouble,
The bitterest bale
She erst abode.

Then spake Giaflaug,
Giuki's sister:
"Lo upon earth

"Sigurd caught up the sword Gram, and cast it after him,
and it smote him on the back."

LANCELOT SPEED

I live most loveless
Who of five mates
Must see the ending,
Of daughters twain
And three sisters,
Of brethren eight,
And abide behind lonely."

Naught gat Gudrun
Of wail or greeting,
So heavy was she
For her dead husband,
So dreadful-hearted
For the King laid dead there.

Then spake Herborg
Queen of Hunland:
"Crueller tale
Have I to tell of,
Of my seven sons
Down in the Southlands,
And the eighth man, my mate,
Felled in the death-mead.

"Father and mother,
And four brothers,
On the wide sea
The winds and death played with:
The billows beat
On the bulwark boards.

"Alone must I sing o'er them,
Alone must I array them,
Alone must my hands deal with
Their departing;
And all this was
In one season's wearing,
And none was left
For love or solace.

"Then was I bound
A prey of the battle,
When that same season
Wore to its ending;
As a tiring may
Must I bind the shoon
Of the duke's high dame,
Every day at dawning.

"From her jealous hate
Gat I heavy mocking,
Cruel lashes
She laid upon me,
Never met I
Better master

Or mistress worser
In all the wide world."

Naught gat Gudrun
Of wail or greeting,
So heavy was she
For her dead husband,
So dreadful-hearted
For the King laid dead there.

Then spake Gullrond,
Guiki's daughter:
"O foster-mother,
Wise as thou mayst be,
Naught canst thou better
The young wife's bale."
And she bade uncover
The dead King's corpse.

She swept the sheet
Away from Sigurd,
And turned his cheek
Towards his wife's knees—
"Look on thy loved one
Lay lips to his lips,
E'en as thou wert clinging
To thy king alive yet!"

Once looked Gudrun—
One look only,
And saw her lord's locks
Lying all bloody,
The great man's eyes
Glazed and deadly,
And his heart's bulwark
Broken by sword-edge.

Back then sank Gudrun,
Back on the bolster,
Loosed was her head array,
Red did her cheeks grow,
And the rain-drops ran
Down over her knees.

Then wept Gudrun,
Giuki's daughter,
So that the tears flowed
Through the pillow;
As the geese withal
That were in the homefield,
The fair fowls the may owned,
Fell a-screaming.

Then spake Gullrond,
Giuki's daughter:

"Surely knew I
No love like your love
Among all men,
On the mould abiding;
Naught wouldst thou joy in
Without or within doors,
O my sister,
Save beside Sigurd."

Then spoke Gudrun
Giuki's daughter:
"Such was my Sigurd
Among the sons of Giuki,
As is the king leek
O'er the low grass waxing,
Or a bright stone
Strung on band,
Or a pearl of price
On a prince's brow.

"Once I was counted
By the king's warriors
Higher than any
Of Herjan's mays;
Now am I as little
As the leaf may be,
Amid wind-swept wood
Now when dead he lieth.

"I miss from my seat,
I miss from my bed,
My darling of sweet speech.
Wrought the sons of Giuki,
Wrought the sons of Giuki,
This sore sorrow,
Yea, for their sister,
Most sore sorrow.

"So may your lands
Lie waste on all sides,
As ye have broken
Your bounden oaths!
N'er shalt thou, Gunnar,
The gold have joy of,
The dear-bought rings
Shall drag thee to death,
Whereon thou swarest
Oath unto Sigurd.

"Ah, in the days by-gone
Great mirth in the homefield
When my Sigurd
Set saddle on Grani,
And they went their ways
For the wooing of Brynhild!

An ill day, an ill woman,
And most ill hap!"

Then spake Brynhild,
Budli's daughter:
"May the woman lack
Both love and children,
Who gained greeting
For thee, O Gudrun!
Who gave thee this morning
Many words!"

Then spake Gullrond,
Guiki's daughter:
"Hold peace of such words
Thou hated of all folk!
The bane of brave men
Hast thou been ever,
All waves of ill
Wash over thy mind,
To seven great kings
Hast thou been a sore sorrow
And the death of good will
To wives and women."

Then spake Brynhild,
Budli's daughter:
"None but Atli
Brought bale upon us,
My very brother
Born of Budli.

"When we saw in the hall
Of the Hunnish people
The gold a-gleaming
On the kingly Giukings;
I have paid for that faring
Oft and full,
And for the sight
That then I saw."

By a pillar she stood
And strained its wood to her;
From the eyes of Brynhild,
Budli's daughter,
Flashed out fire,
And she snorted forth venom,
As the sore wounds she gazed on
Of the dead-slain Sigurd.

XXI

Of the Ending of Brynhild

AND NOW NONE might know for what cause Brynhild must bewail with weeping for what she had prayed for with laughter: but she spake:

"Such a dream I had, Gunnar, as that my bed was acold, and that thou didst ride into the hands of thy foes: lo now, ill shall it go with thee and all thy kin, O ye breakers of oaths; for on the day thou slayedst him, dimly didst thou remember how thou didst blend thy blood with the blood of Sigurd, and with an ill reward hast thou rewarded him for all that he did well to thee; whereas he gave unto thee to be the mightiest of men; and well was it proven how fast he held to his oath sworn, when he came to me and laid betwixt us the sharp-edged sword that in venom had been made hard. All too soon did ye fall to working wrong against him and against me, whenas I abode at home with my father, and had all that I would, and had no will that anyone of you should be any of mine, as ye rode into our garth, ye three kings together; but then Atli led me apart privily, and asked me if I would not have him who rode Grani;—yea, a man nowise like unto you; but in those days I plighted myself to the son of King Sigmund and no other; and lo, now, no better shall ye fare for the death of me."

Then rose up Gunnar, and laid his arms about her neck, and besought her to live and have wealth from him; and all others in likewise letted her from dying; but she thrust them all from her, and said that it was not the part of any to let her in that which was her will.

Then Gunnar called to Hogni, and prayed him for counsel, and bade him go to her, and see if he might perchance soften her dreadful heart, saying withal, that now they had need enough on their hands in the slaking of her grief, till time might get over.

But Hogni answered, "Nay, let no man hinder her from dying, for no gain will she be to us, nor has she been gainsome since she came hither!"

Now she bade bring forth much gold, and bade all those come thither who would have wealth: then she caught up a sword, and thrust it under her armpit, and sank aside upon the pillows, and said, "Come, take gold whoso will!"

But all held their peace, and she said, "Take the gold, and be glad thereof!"

And therewith she spake unto Gunnar, "Now for a little while will I tell of that which shall come to pass hereafter; for speedily shall ye be at one again with Gudrun by the rede of Grimhild, the Wise-wife; and the daughter of Gudrun and Sigurd shall be called Swanhild, the fairest of all women born. Gudrun shall be given to Atli, yet not with her good will. Thou shalt be fain to get Oddrun, but that shall Atli forbid thee; but privily shall ye meet, and much shall she love thee. Atli shall bewray thee, and cast thee into a worm-close, and thereafter shall Atli and his sons be slain, and Gudrun shall be their slayer; and afterwards shall the great waves bear her to the burg of King Jonakr, to whom she shall bear sons of great fame: Swanhild shall be sent from the land and given to King Jormunrek; and her shall bite the rede of Bikki, and therewithal is the kin of you clean gone; and more sorrows therewith for Gudrun.

"And now I pray thee, Gunnar, one last boon.—Let make a great bale on the plain meads for all of us; for me, and for Sigurd, and for those who were slain with him, and let that be covered over with cloth dyed red by the folk of the Gauls, and burn me thereon on one side of the King of the Huns, and on the other those men of mine, two at the head and two at the feet, and two hawks withal; and even so is all shared equally; and lay there betwixt us a drawn sword, as in the other days when we twain stepped into one bed together; and then may we have the name of man and wife, nor shall the door swing to the heel of him as I go behind him. Nor shall that be a niggard company if there follow him those five bondwomen and eight bondmen, whom my father gave me, and those burn there withal who were slain with Sigurd.

"Now more yet would I say, but for my wounds, but my life-breath flits; the wounds open—yet have I said sooth."

Now is the dead corpse of Sigurd arrayed in an olden wise, and a mighty bale is raised, and when it was somewhat kindled there was laid thereon the dead corpse of Sigurd Fafnir's-bane, and his son of three winters whom Brynhild had let slay, and Guttorm withal; and when the bale was all ablaze, thereunto was Brynhild borne out, when she had spoken with her bower-maidens, and bid them take the gold that she would give; and then died Brynhild, and was burned there by the side of Sigurd, and thus their life-days ended.

The Quest of the Holy Graal

By Mrs. Andrew Lang

King Arthur

DAN BEARD

The Quest of the Holy Graal

I

How the King Went on Pilgrimage, and His Squire Was Slain in a Dream

NOW THE KING was minded to go on a pilgrimage, and he agreed with the Queen that he would set forth to seek the holy chapel of St. Augustine, which is in the White Forest, and may only be found by adventure. Much he wished to undertake the quest alone, but this the Queen would not suffer, and to do her pleasure he consented that a youth, tall and strong of limb, should ride with him as his squire. Chaus was the youth's name, and he was son to Gwain li Aoutres. "Lie within to-night," commanded the King, "and take heed that my horse be saddled at break of day, and my arms ready." "At your pleasure, Sir," answered the youth, whose heart rejoiced because he was going alone with the King.

As night came on, all the Knights quitted the hall, but Chaus the squire stayed where he was, and would not take off his clothes or his shoes, lest sleep should fall on him and he might not be ready when the King called him. So he sat himself down by the great fire, but in spite of his will sleep fell heavily on him, and he dreamed a strange dream.

In his dream it seemed that the King had ridden away to the quest, and had left his squire behind him, which filled the young man with fear. And in his dream he set the saddle and bridle on his horse, and fastened his spurs, and girt on his sword, and galloped out of the castle after the King. He rode on a long space, till he entered a thick forest, and there before him lay traces of the King's horse, and he followed till the marks of the hoofs ceased suddenly at some open ground and he thought that the King had alighted there. On the right stood a chapel, and about it was a graveyard, and in the graveyard many coffins, and in his dream it seemed as if the King had entered the chapel, so the young man entered also. But no man did he behold save a Knight that lay dead upon a bier in the midst of the chapel, covered with a pall of rich silk, and four tapers in golden candlesticks were burning round him. The squire marvelled to see the body lying there so lonely, with no one near it, and likewise that the King was nowhere to be seen. Then he took out one of the tall tapers, and hid the candlestick under his cloak, and rode away until he should find the King.

On his journey through the forest he was stopped by a man black and ill-favoured, holding a large knife in his hand.

"Ho! you that stand there, have you seen King Arthur?" asked the squire.

"No, but I have met you, and I am glad thereof, for you have under your cloak one of the candlesticks of gold that was placed in honour of the Knight who lies dead in the chapel. Give it to me, and I will carry it back; and if you do not this of your own will, I will make you."

"By my faith!" cried the squire, "I will never yield it to you! Rather, will I carry it off and make a present of it to King Arthur."

"You will pay for it dearly," answered the man, "if you yield it not up forthwith."

To this the squire did not make answer, but dashed forward, thinking to pass him by; but the man thrust at him with his knife, and it entered his body up to the hilt. And when the squire dreamed this, he cried, "Help! help! for I am a dead man!"

As soon as the King and the Queen heard that cry they awoke from their sleep, and the Chamberlain said, "Sir, you must be moving, for it is day"; and the King rose and dressed himself, and put on his shoes. Then the cry came again: "Fetch me a priest, for I die!" and the King ran at great speed into the hall, while the Queen and the Chamberlain followed him with torches and candles. "What aileth you?" asked the King of his squire, and the squire told him of all that he had dreamed. "Ha," said the King. "is it, then, a dream?" "Yes, Sir," answered the squire, "but it is a right foul dream for me, for right foully it hath come true," and he lifted his left arm, and said, "Sir, look you here! Lo, here is the knife that was struck in my side up to the haft." After that, he drew forth the candlestick, and showed it to the King. "Sir, for this candlestick that I present to you was I wounded to the death!" The King took the candlestick in his hands and looked at it, and none so rich had he seen before, and he bade the Queen look also. "Sir," said the squire again, "draw not forth the knife out of my body till I be shriven of the priest." So the King commanded that a priest should be sent for, and when the squire had confessed his sins, the King drew the knife out of the body and the soul departed forthwith. Then the King grieved that the young man had come to his death in such strange wise, and ordered him a fair burial, and desired that the golden candlestick should be sent to the Church of Saint Paul in London, which at that time was newly built.

After this King Arthur would have none to go with him on his quest, and many strange adventures he achieved before he reached the chapel of St. Augustine, which was in the midst of the White Forest. There he alighted from his horse, and sought to enter, but though there was neither door nor bar he might not pass the threshold. But from without he heard wondrous voices singing, and saw a light shining brighter than any that he had seen before, and visions such as he scarcely dared to look upon. And he resolved greatly to amend his sins, and to bring peace and order into his kingdom. So he set forth, strengthened and comforted, and after divers more adventures returned to his Court.

II

The Coming of the Holy Graal

IT WAS ON the eve of Pentecost that all the Knights of the Table Round met together at Camelot, and a great feast was made ready for them. And as they sat at supper they heard a loud noise, as of the crashing of thunder, and it seemed as if the roof would fall on them. Then, in the midst of the thunder, there entered a sunbeam, brighter by seven times than the brightest day, and its brightness was not of this world. The Knights held their peace, but every man looked at his neighbour, and his countenance shone fairer than ever it had done before. As they sat dumb, for their tongues felt as if they could speak nothing, there floated in the hall the Holy Graal, and over it a veil of white samite, so that none might see it nor who bare it. But sweet odours filled the place, and every Knight had set before him the food he loved best; and after that the Holy Vessel departed suddenly, they wist not where. When it had gone their tongues were loosened, and the King gave thanks for the wonders that they had been permitted to see. After that he had finished, Sir Gawaine stood up and vowed to depart the next morning in quest of the Holy Graal, and not to return until he had seen it. "But if after a year and a day I may not speed in my quest," said he, "I shall come again, for I shall know that the sight of it is not for me." And many of the Knights there sitting swore a like vow.

But King Arthur, when he heard this, was sore displeased. "Alas!" cried he unto Sir Gawaine, "you have undone me by your vow. For through you is broken up the fairest fellowship, and the truest of knighthood, that ever the world saw, and when they have once departed they shall meet no more at the Table Round, for many shall die in the quest. It grieves me sore, for I have loved them as well as my own life." So he spoke, and paused, and tears came into his eyes. "Ah, Gawaine, Gawaine! you have set me in great sorrow."

"Comfort yourself," said Sir Lancelot, "for we shall win for ourselves great honour, and much more than if we had died in any other wise, since die we must." But the King would not be comforted, and the Queen and all the Court were troubled also for the love which they had to these Knights. Then the Queen came to Sir Galahad, who was sitting among those Knights though younger he was than any of them, and asked him whence he came, and of what country, and if he was son to Sir Lancelot. And King Arthur did him great honour, and he rested him in his own bed. And next morning the King and Queen went into the Minster, and the Knights followed them, dressed all in armour, save only their shields and their helmets. When the service was finished the King would know how many of the fellowship had sworn to undertake the quest of the Graal, and they were counted, and found to number a hundred and fifty. They bade farewell, and mounted their horses, and rode through the streets of Camelot, and there was weeping of both rich and poor, and the King could not speak for weeping. And at sunrise they all parted company with each other, and every Knight took the way he best liked.

III

The Adventure of Sir Galahad

NOW SIR GALAHAD had as yet no shield, and he rode four days without meeting any adventure, till at last he came to a White Abbey, where he dismounted and asked if he might sleep there that night. The brethren received him with great reverence, and led him to a chamber, where he took off his armour, and then saw that he was in the presence of two Knights. "Sirs," said Sir Galahad, "what adventure brought you hither?" "Sir," replied they, "we heard that within this Abbey is a shield that no man may hang round his neck without being dead within three days, or some mischief befalling him. And if we fail in the adventure, you shall take it upon you." "Sirs," replied Sir Galahad, "I agree well thereto, for as yet I have no shield."

So on the morn they arose and heard Mass, and then a monk led them behind an altar where hung a shield white as snow, with a red cross in the middle of it. "Sirs," said the monk, "this shield cannot be hung round no Knight's neck, unless he be the worthiest Knight in the world, and therefore I counsel you to be well advised."

"Well," answered one of the Knights, whose name was King Bagdemagus, "I know truly that I am not the best Knight in the world, but yet shall I try to bear it," and he bare it out of the Abbey. Then he said to Sir Galahad, "I pray you abide here still, till you know how I shall speed," and he rode away, taking with him a squire to send tidings back to Sir Galahad.

After King Bagdemagus had ridden two miles he entered a fair valley, and there met him a goodly Knight seated on a white horse and clad in white armour. And they came together with their spears, and Sir Bagdemagus was borne from his horse, for the shield covered him not at all. Therewith the strange Knight alighted and took the white shield from him, and gave it to the squire, saying, "Bear this shield to the good Knight Sir Galahad that thou hast left in the Abbey, and greet him well from me."

"Sir," said the squire, "what is your name?"

"Take thou no heed of my name," answered the Knight, "for it is not for thee to know, nor for any earthly man."

"Now, fair Sir," said the squire, "tell me for what cause this shield may not be borne lest ill befalls him who bears it."

"Since you have asked me," answered the Knight, "know that no man shall bear this shield, save Sir Galahad only."

Then the squire turned to Bagdemagus, and asked him whether he were wounded or not. "Yes, truly," said he, "and I shall hardly escape from death"; and scarcely could he climb on to his horse's back when the squire brought it near him. But the squire led him to a monastery that lay in the valley, and there he was treated of his wounds, and after long lying came back to life. After the squire had given the Knight into the care of the monks, he rode back to the Abbey, bearing with him the shield. "Sir Galahad," said he, alighting before him, "the Knight that wounded Bagdemagus sends you greeting, and bids you bear this shield, which shall bring you many adventures."

"Now blessed be God and fortune," answered Sir Galahad, and called for his arms, and mounted his horse, hanging the shield about his neck. Then, followed by the squire, he set out. They rode straight to the hermitage, where they saw the White Knight who had sent the shield to Sir Galahad. The two Knights saluted each other courteously, and then the White Knight told Sir Galahad the story of the shield, and how it had been given into his charge. Afterwards they parted, and Sir Galahad and his squire returned unto the Abbey whence they came.

The monks made great joy at seeing Sir Galahad again, for they feared he was gone for ever; and as soon as he was alighted from his horse they brought him unto a tomb in the churchyard where there was night and day such a noise that any man who heard it should be driven nigh mad, or else lose his strength. "Sir," they said, "we deem it a fiend." Sir Galahad drew near, all armed save his helmet, and stood by the tomb. "Lift up the stone," said a monk, and Galahad lifted it, and a voice cried, "Come thou not nigh me, Sir Galahad, for thou shalt make me go again where I have been so long." But Galahad took no heed of him, and lifted the stone yet higher, and there rushed from the tomb a foul smoke, and in the midst of it leaped out the foulest figure that ever was seen in the likeness of a man. "Galahad," said the figure, "I see about thee so many angels that my power dare not touch thee." Then Galahad, stooping down, looked into the tomb, and he saw a body all armed lying there, with a sword by his side. "Fair brother," said Galahad, "let us remove this body, for he is not worthy to be in this churchyard, being a false Christian man."

This being done they all departed and returned unto the monastery, where they lay that night, and the next morning Sir Galahad knighted Melias his squire, as he had promised him aforetime. So Sir Galahad and Sir Melias departed thence, in quest of the Holy Graal, but they soon went their different ways and fell upon different adventures. In his first encounter Sir Melias was sore wounded, and Sir Galahad came to his help, and left him to an old monk who said that he would heal him of his wounds in the space of seven weeks, and that he was thus wounded because he had not come clean to the quest of the Graal, as Sir Galahad had done. Sir Galahad left him there, and rode on till he came to the Castle of the Maidens, which he alone might enter who was free from sin. There he chased away the Knights who had seized the castle seven years agone, and restored all to the Duke's daughter, who owned it of right. Besides this he set free the maidens who were kept in prison, and summoned all those Knights in the country round who had held their lands of the Duke, bidding them do homage to his daughter. And in the morning one came to him and told him that as the seven Knights fled from the Castle of Maidens they fell upon the path of Sir Gawaine, Sir Gareth, and Sir Lewaine, who were seeking Sir Galahad, and they gave battle; and the seven Knights were slain by the three Knights. "It is well," said Galahad, and he took his armour and his horse and rode away.

So when Sir Galahad left the Castle of Maidens he rode till he came to a waste forest, and there he met with Sir Lancelot and Sir Percivale; but they knew him not, for he was now disguised. And they fought together, and the two Knights were smitten down out of the saddle. "God be with thee, thou best Knight in the world," cried a nun who dwelt in a hermitage close by; and she said it in a loud voice, so that Lancelot and Percivale might hear. But Sir Galahad feared that she would make known who he was, so he spurred his horse and struck deep into the forest before Sir Lancelot and Sir Percivale could mount again. They knew not which path he had taken, so Sir Percivale turned back to ask advice of the nun, and Sir Lancelot pressed forward.

IV

How Sir Lancelot Saw a Vision, and Repented of His Sins

HE HALTED WHEN he came to a stone cross, which had by it a block of marble, while nigh at hand stood an old chapel. He tied his horse to a tree, and hung his shield on a branch, and looked into the chapel, for the door was waste and broken. And he saw there a fair altar covered with a silken cloth, and a candlestick which had six branches, all of shining silver. A great light streamed from it, and at this sight Sir Lancelot would fain have entered in, but he could not. So he turned back sorrowful and dismayed, and took the saddle and bridle off his horse, and let him pasture where he would, while he himself unlaced his helm, and ungirded his sword, and lay down to sleep upon his shield, at the foot of the cross.

As he lay there, half waking and half sleeping, he saw two white palfreys come by, drawing a litter, wherein lay a sick Knight. When they reached the cross they paused, and Sir Lancelot heard the Knight say, "O sweet Lord, when shall this sorrow leave me, and when shall the Holy Vessel come by me, through which I shall be blessed? For I have endured long, though my ill deeds were few." Thus he spoke, and Sir Lancelot heard it, and of a sudden the great candlestick stood before the cross, though no man had brought it. And with it was a table of silver and the Holy Vessel of the Graal, which Lancelot had seen aforetime. Then the Knight rose up, and on his hands and knees he approached the Holy Vessel, and prayed, and was made whole of his sickness. After that the Graal went back into the chapel, and the light and the candlestick also, and Sir Lancelot would fain have followed, but could not, so heavy was the weight of his sins upon him. And the sick Knight arose and kissed the cross, and saw Sir Lancelot lying at the foot with his eyes shut. "I marvel greatly at this sleeping Knight," he said to his squire, "that he had no power to wake when the Holy Vessel was brought hither." "I dare right well say," answered the squire, "that he dwelleth in some deadly sin, whereof he was never confessed." "By my faith," said the Knight, "he is unhappy, whoever he is, for he is of the fellowship of the Round Table, which have undertaken the quest of the Graal." "Sir," replied the squire, "you have all your arms here, save only your sword and your helm. Take therefore those of this strange Knight,

"There rushed from the tomb a foul smoke, and in the
midst of it leaped out the foulest figure that ever was seen
in the likeness of a man."

H. J. FORD

who has just put them off." And the Knight did as his squire said, and
took Sir Lancelot's horse also, for it was better than his own.

After they had gone Sir Lancelot waked up wholly, and thought of
what he had seen, wondering if he were in a dream or not. Suddenly a
voice spoke to him, and it said, "Sir Lancelot, more hard than is the
stone, more bitter than is the wood, more naked and barren than is the
leaf of the fig tree, art thou; therefore go from hence and withdraw
thee from this holy place." When Sir Lancelot heard this, his heart was
passing heavy, and he wept, cursing the day when he had been born.
But his helm and sword had gone from the spot where he had lain them
at the foot of the cross, and his horse was gone also. And he smote
himself and cried, "My sin and my wickedness have done me this
dishonour; for when I sought wordly adventures for worldly desires I
ever achieved them and had the better in every place, and never was I
discomfited in any quarrel, were it right or wrong. And now I take
upon me the adventures of holy things, I see and understand that my
old sin hinders me, so that I could not move nor speak when the Holy
Graal passed by." Thus he sorrowed till it was day, and he heard the
birds sing, and at that he felt comforted. And as his horse was gone
also, he departed on foot with a heavy heart.

V

The Adventure of Sir Percivale

ALL THIS WHILE Sir Percivale had pursued adventures of his own, and
came nigh unto losing his life, but he was saved from his enemies by the
good Knight, Sir Galahad, whom he did not know, although he was
seeking him, for Sir Galahad now bore a red shield, and not a white
one. And at last the foes fled deep into the forest, and Sir Galahad
followed; but Sir Percivale had no horse and was forced to stay behind.
Then his eyes were opened, and he knew it was Sir Galahad who had
come to his help, and he sat down under a tree and grieved sore.

While he was sitting there a Knight passed by riding a black horse,
and when he was out of sight a yeoman came pricking after as fast as he
might, and, seeing Sir Percivale, asked if he had seen a Knight mounted
on a black horse. "Yes, Sir, forsooth," answered Sir Percivale, "why do
you want to know?" "Ah, Sir, that is my steed which he has taken from
me, and wherever my lord shall find me, he is sure to slay me." "Well,"
said Sir Percivale, "thou seest that I am on foot, but had I a good horse I
would soon come up with him." "Take my hackney," said the yeoman,
"and do the best you can, and I shall follow you on foot to watch how
you speed." Sir Percivale rode as fast as he might, and at last he saw that
Knight, and he hailed him. The Knight turned and set his spear against
Sir Percivale, and smote the hackney in the breast, so that he fell dead
to the earth, and Sir Percivale fell with him; then the Knight rode away.
But Sir Percivale was mad with wrath, and cried to the Knight to return
and fight with him on foot, and the Knight answered not and went on
his way. When Sir Percivale saw that he would not turn, he threw

himself on the ground, and cast away his helm and sword, and bemoaned himself for the most unhappy of all Knights; and there he abode the whole day, and being faint and weary, slept till it was midnight. And at midnight he waked and saw before him a woman, who said to him right fiercely, "Sir Percivale, what doest thou here?" "Neither good nor great ill," answered he. "If thou wilt promise to do my will when I call upon you," said she, "I will lend you my own horse, and he shall bear thee whither thou shalt choose." This Sir Percivale promised gladly, and the woman went and returned with a black horse, so large and well-apparelled that Sir Percivale marvelled. But he mounted him gladly, and drove in his spurs, and within an hour and less the horse bare him four days' journey hence, and would have borne him into a rough water that roared, had not Sir Percivale pulled at his bridle. The Knight stood doubting, for the water made a great noise, and he feared lest his horse could not get through it. Still, wishing greatly to pass over, he made himself ready, and signed the sign of the cross upon his forehead.

At that the fiend which had taken the shape of a horse shook off Sir Percivale and dashed into the water, crying and making great sorrow; and it seemed to him that the water burned. Then Sir Percivale knew that it was not a horse but a fiend, which would have brought him to perdition, and he gave thanks and prayed all that night long. As soon as it was day he looked about him, and saw he was in a wild mountain, girt round with the sea and filled with wild beasts. Then he rose and went into a valley, and there he saw a young serpent bring a young lion by the neck, and after that there passed a great lion, crying and roaring after the serpent, and a fierce battle began between them. Sir Percivale thought to help the lion, as he was the more natural beast of the twain, and he drew his sword and set his shield before him, and gave the serpent a deadly buffet. When the lion saw that, he made him all the cheer that a beast might make a man, and fawned about him like a spaniel, and stroked him with his paws. And about noon the lion took his little whelp, and placed him on his back, and bare him home again, and Sir Percivale, being left alone, prayed till he was comforted. But at eventide the lion returned, and couched down at his feet, and all night long he and the lion slept together.

VI

An Adventure of Sir Lancelot

As LANCELOT WENT his way through the forest he met with many hermits who dwelled therein, and had adventure with the Knight who stole his horse and his helm, and got them back again. And he learned from one of the hermits that Sir Galahad was his son, and that it was he who at the Feast of Pentecost had sat in the Siege Perilous, which it was ordained by Merlin that none should sit in save the best Knight in the world. All that night Sir Lancelot abode with the hermit and laid him to rest, a hair shirt always on his body, and it pricked him sorely, but he bore it meekly and suffered the pain. When the day dawned he bade the hermit farewell. As he rode he came to a fair plain, in which was a great castle set about with tents and pavilions of divers hues. Here were full five hundred Knights riding on horseback, and those near the castle were mounted on black horses with black trappings, and they that were without were on white horses and their trappings white. And the two sides fought together, and Sir Lancelot looked on.

At last it seemed to him that the black Knights nearest the castle fared the worst, so, as he ever took the part of the weaker, he rode to their help and smote many of the white Knights to the earth and did marvellous deeds of arms. But always the white Knights held round Sir Lancelot to tire him out. And as no man may endure for ever, in the end Sir Lancelot waxed so faint of fighting that his arms would not lift themselves to deal a stroke; then they took him, and led him away into the forest and made him alight from his horse and rest, and when he was taken the fellowship of the castle were overcome for want of him. "Never ere now was I at tournament or jousts but I had the best," moaned Sir Lancelot to himself, as soon as the Knights had left him and he was alone. "But now am I shamed, and I am persuaded that I am more sinful than ever I was." Sorrowfully he rode on till he passed a chapel, where stood a nun, who called to him and asked him his name and what he was seeking.

So he told her who he was, and what had befallen him at the tournament, and the vision that had come to him in his sleep. "Ah, Lancelot," said she, "as long as you were a knight of earthly knighthood you were the most wonderful man in the world and the most adventurous. But now, since you are set among Knights of heavenly adventures, if you were worsted at that tournament it is no marvel. For the tournament was meant for a sign, and the earthly Knights were they who were clothed in black in token of the sins of which they were not yet purged. And the white Knights were they who had chosen the way of holiness, and in them the quest has already begun. Thus you beheld both the sinners and the good men, and when you saw the sinners over-come you went to their help, as they were your fellows in boasting and pride of the world, and all that must be left in that quest. And that caused your misadventure. Now that I have warned you of your vain-glory and your pride, beware of everlasting pain, for of all earthly Knights I have pity of you, for I know well that among earthly sinful Knights you are without peer."

VII

An Adventure of Sir Gawaine

SIR GAWAINE RODE long without meeting any adventure, and from Pentecost to Michaelmas found none that pleased him. But at Michaelmas he met Sir Ector de Maris and rejoiced greatly.

As they sat talking there appeared before them a hand showing unto the elbow covered with red samite, and holding a great candle that

"He drew his sword and set his shield before him, and
gave the serpent a deadly buffet."

H. J. FORD

burned right clear; and the hand passed into the chapel and vanished, they knew not where. Then they heard a voice which said, "Knights full of evil faith and poor belief, these two things have failed you, and therefore you may not come to the adventure of the Holy Graal." And this same told them a holy man to whom they confessed their sins, "for," said he, "you have failed in three things, charity, fasting, and truth, and have been great murderers. But sinful as Sir Lancelot was, since he went into the quest he never slew man, nor shall, till he come into Camelot again. For he has taken upon him to forsake sin. And were he not so unstable, he should be the next to achieve it, after Galahad his son. Yet shall he die an holy man, and in earthly sinful men he has no fellow."

"Sir," said Gawaine, "by your words it seems that our sins will not let us labour in that quest?" "Truly," answered the hermit, "there be an hundred such as you to whom it will bring naught but shame." So Gawaine departed and followed Sir Ector, who had ridden on before.

VIII

The Adventure of Sir Bors

WHEN SIR BORS left Camelot on his quest he met a holy man riding on an ass, and Sir Bors saluted him. Then the good man knew him to be one of the Knights who were in quest of the Holy Graal. "What are you?" said he, and Sir Bors answered, "I am a Knight that fain would be counselled in the quest of the Graal, for he shall have much earthly worship that brings it to an end." "That is true," said the good man, "for he will be the best Knight in the world, but know well that there shall none attain it but by holiness and by confession of sin." So they rode together till they came to the hermitage, and the good man led Sir Bors into the chapel, where he made confession of his sins, and they ate bread and drank water together. "Now," said the hermit, "I pray you that you eat none other till you sit at the table where the Holy Graal shall be." "Sir," answered Sir Bors, "I agree thereto, but how know you that I shall sit there?" "That know I," said the holy man, "but there will be but few of your fellows with you. Also instead of a shirt you shall wear this garment until you have achieved your quest," and Sir Bors took off his clothes, and put on instead a scarlet coat. Then the good man questioned him, and marvelled to find him pure in life, and he armed him and bade him go. After this Sir Bors rode through many lands, and had many adventures, and was often sore tempted, but remembered the words of the holy man and kept his life clean of wrong. And once he had by mischance almost slain his own brother, but a voice cried, "Flee, Bors, and touch him not," and he hearkened and stayed his hand. And there fell between them a fiery cloud, which burned up both their shields, and they two fell to the earth in a great swoon; but when they awakened out of it Bors saw that his brother had no harm. With that the voice spoke to him saying, "Bors, go hence and bear your brother fellowship no longer; but take your way to the sea,

HJF.

HOW SIR BORS WAS SAVED
FROM KILLING HIS BROTHER

"And there fell between them a fiery cloud, which burned
up both their shields."

H. J. FORD

where Sir Percivale abides till you come." Then Sir Bors prayed his brother to forgive him all he had unknowingly done, and rode straight to the sea. On the shore he found a vessel covered with white samite, and as soon as he stepped in the vessel it set sail so fast it might have been flying, and Sir Bors lay down and slept till it was day. When he waked he saw a Knight lying in the midst of the ship, all armed save for his helm, and he knew him for Sir Percivale, and welcomed him with great joy; and they told each other of their adventures and of their temptations, and had great happiness in each other's company. "We lack nothing but Galahad, the good Knight," Sir Percivale said.

IX

Adventure of Sir Galahad

Sir Galahad rested one evening at a hermitage. And while he was resting, there came a gentlewoman and asked leave of the hermit to speak with Sir Galahad, and would not be denied, though she was told he was weary and asleep. Then the hermit waked Sir Galahad and bade him rise, as a gentlewoman had great need of him, so Sir Galahad rose and asked her what she wished. "Galahad," said she, "I will that you arm yourself, and mount your horse and follow me, and I will show you the highest adventure that ever any Knight saw." And Sir Galahad bade her go, and he would follow wherever she led. In three days they reached the sea, where they found the ship where Sir Bors and Sir Percivale were lying. And the lady bade him leave his horse behind and said she would leave hers also, but their saddles and bridles they would take on board the ship. This they did, and were received with great joy by the two Knights; then the sails were spread, and the ship was driven before the wind at a marvellous pace till they reached the land of Logris, the entrance to which lies between two great rocks with a whirlpool in the middle.

Their own ship might not get safely through; but they left it and went into another ship that lay there, which had neither man nor woman in it. At the end of the ship was written these words: "Thou man which shalt enter this ship beware thou be in steadfast belief; if thou fail, I shall not help thee." Then the gentlewoman turned and said, "Percivale, do you know who I am?" "No, truly," answered he. "I am your sister, and therefore you are the man in the world that I most love. If you are without faith, or have any hidden sin, beware how you enter, else you will perish." "Fair sister," answered he, "I shall enter therein, for if I am an untrue Knight then shall I perish." So they entered the ship, and it was rich and well adorned, that they all marvelled.

In the midst of it was a fair bed, and Sir Galahad went thereto and found on it a crown of silk, and a sword drawn out of its sheath half a foot and more. The sword was of divers fashions, and the pommel of stone, wrought about with colours, and every colour with its own virtue, and the handle was of the ribs of two beasts. The one was the bone of a serpent, and no hand that handles it shall ever become weary or hurt;

and the other is a bone of a fish that swims in Euphrates, and whoso handles it shall not think on joy or sorrow that he has had, but only on that which he beholds before him. And no man shall grip this sword but one that is better than other men. So first Sir Percivale stepped forward and set his hand to the sword, but he might not grasp it. Next Sir Bors tried to seize it, but he also failed. When Sir Galahad beheld the sword, he saw that there was written on it, in letters of blood, that he who tried to draw it should never fail of shame in his body or be wounded to the death. "By my faith," said Galahad, "I would draw this sword out of its sheath, but the offending is so great I shall not lay my hand thereto." "Sir," answered the gentlewoman, "know that no man can draw this sword save you alone"; and she told him many tales of the Knights who had set their hands to it, and of the evil things that had befallen them. And they all begged Sir Galahad to grip the sword, as it was ordained that he should. "I will grip it," said Galahad, "to give you courage, but it belongs no more to me than it does to you." Then he gripped it tight with his fingers, and the gentlewoman girt him about the middle with the sword, and after that they left that ship and went into another, which brought them to land, where they fell upon many strange adventures. And when they had wrought many great deeds, they departed from each other. But first Sir Percivale's sister died, being bled to death, so that another lady might live, and she prayed them to lay her body in a boat and leave the boat to go as the winds and waves carried it. And so it was done, and Sir Percivale wrote a letter telling how she had helped them in all their adventures; and he put it in her right hand, and laid her in a barge, and covered it with black silk. And the wind arose and drove it from their sight.

X

Sir Lancelot Meets Sir Galahad, and They Part for Ever

NOW WE MUST tell what happened to Sir Lancelot.

When he was come to a water called Mortoise he fell asleep, awaiting for the adventure that should be sent to him, and in his sleep a voice spoke to him, and bade him rise and take his armour, and enter the first ship he should find. So he started up and took his arms and made him ready, and on the strand he found a ship that was without sail or oar. As soon as he was within the ship, he felt himself wrapped round with a sweetness such as he had never known before, as if all that he could desire was fulfilled. And with this joy and peace about him he fell asleep. When he woke he found near him a fair bed, with a dead lady lying on it, whom he knew to be Sir Percivale's sister, and in her hand was the tale of her adventures, which Sir Lancelot took and read. For a month or more they dwelt in that ship together, and one day, when it had drifted near the shore, he heard a sound as of a horse; and when the steps came nearer he saw that a Knight was riding him. At the sight of the ship the Knight alighted and took the saddle and bridle, and the

Knight saluted him and said, "What is your name? for my heart goeth out to you."

"Truly," answered he, "my name is Sir Lancelot du Lake."

"Sir," said the new Knight, "you are welcome, for you were the beginner of me in the world."

"Ah," cried Sir Lancelot, "is it you, then, Galahad?"

"Yes, in sooth," said he, and kneeled down and asked Lancelot's blessing, and then took off his helm and kissed him. And there was great joy between them, and they told each other all that had befallen them since they left King Arthur's Court. Then Galahad saw the gentlewoman dead on the bed, and he knew her, and said he held her in great worship, and that she was the best maid in the world, and how it was great pity that she had come to her death. But when Lancelot heard that Galahad had won the marvellous sword he prayed that he might see it, and kissed the pommel and the hilt, and the scabbard. "In truth," he said, "never did I know of adventures so wonderful and strange." So dwelled Lancelot and Galahad in that ship for half a year, and served God daily and nightly with all their power. And after six months had gone it befell that on a Monday they drifted to the edge of the forest, where they saw a Knight with white armour bestriding one horse and holding another all white, by the bridle. And he came to the ship, and saluted the two Knights and said, "Galahad, you have been long enough with your father, therefore leave that ship and start upon this horse, and go on the quest of the Holy Graal." So Galahad went to his father and kissed him, saying, "Fair sweet father, I know not if I shall see you more till I have beheld the Holy Graal." Then they heard a voice which said, "The one shall never see the other till the day of doom." "Now, Galahad," said Lancelot, "since we are to bid farewell for ever now, I pray to the great Father to preserve me and you both." "Sir," answered Galahad, "no prayer availeth so much as yours."

The next day Sir Lancelot made his way back to Camelot, where he found King Arthur and Guenevere; but many of the Knights of the Round Table were slain and destroyed, more than the half. All the Court was passing glad to see Sir Lancelot, and the King asked many things of his son Sir Galahad.

XI

How Sir Galahad Found the Graal and Died of That Finding

SIR GALAHAD RODE on till he met Sir Percivale and afterwards Sir Bors, whom they greeted most gladly, and they bare each other company. First they came to the Castle of Carbonek, where dwelled King Pelles, who welcomed them with joy, for he knew by their coming that they had fulfilled the quest of the Graal. They then departed on other adventures, and with the blood out of the Holy Lance Galahad anointed the maimed King and healed him. That same night at midnight a voice bade them arise and quit the castle, which they did, followed by three

Knights of Gaul. Then Galahad prayed every one of them that if they reached King Arthur's Court they should salute Sir Lancelot his father, and those Knights of the Round Table that were present, and with that he left them, and Sir Bors and Sir Percivale with him. For three days they rode till they came to a shore, and found a ship awaiting them. And in the midst of it was the table of silver, and the Holy Graal which was covered with red samite. Then were their hearts right glad, and they made great reverence thereto, and Galahad prayed that at what time he asked, he might depart out of this world. So long he prayed that at length a voice said to him, "Galahad, thou shalt have thy desire, and when thou askest the death of the body thou shalt have it, and shalt find the life of the soul." Percivale likewise heard the voice, and besought Galahad to tell him why he asked such things. And Galahad answered, "The other day when we saw a part of the adventures of the Holy Graal, I was in such a joy of heart that never did man feel before, and I knew well that when my body is dead my soul shall be in joy of which the other was but a shadow."

Some time were the three Knights in that ship, till at length they saw before them the city of Sarras. Then they took from the ship the table of silver, and Sir Percivale and Sir Bors went first, and Sir Galahad followed after to the gate of the city, where sat an old man that was crooked. At the sight of the old man Sir Galahad called to him to help them carry the table, for it was heavy. "Truly," answered the old man, "it is ten years since I have gone without crutches." "Care not for that," said Galahad, "but rise up and show your good will." So he arose and found himself as whole as ever he was, and he ran to the table and held up the side next Galahad. And there was much noise in the city that a cripple was healed by three Knights newly entered in. This reached the ears of the King, who sent for the Knights and questioned them. And they told him the truth, and of the Holy Graal; but the King listened nothing to all they said, but put them into a deep hole in the prison. Even here they were not without comfort, for a vision of the Holy Graal sustained them. And at the end of a year the King lay sick and felt he should die, and he called the three Knights and asked forgiveness of the evil he had done to them, which they gave gladly. Then he died, and the whole city was afraid and knew not what to do, till while they were in counsel a voice came to them and bade them choose the youngest of the three strange Knights for their King. And they did so. After Galahad was proclaimed King, he ordered that a coffer of gold and precious stones should be made to encompass the table of silver, and every day he and the two Knights would kneel before it and make their prayers.

Now at the year's end, and on the selfsame day that Galahad had been crowned King, he arose up early and came with the two Knights to the Palace; and he saw a man in the likeness of a Bishop, encircled by a great crowd of angels, kneeling before the Holy Vessel. And he called to Galahad and said to him, "Come forth, thou servant of Christ, and thou shalt see what thou hast much desired to see." Then Galahad began to tremble right hard, when the flesh first beheld the things of the spirit, and he held up his hands to heaven and said, "Lord, I thank thee, for now I see that which hath been my desire for many a day.

Now, blessed Lord, I would no longer live, if it might please Thee."
Then Galahad went to Percivale and kissed him, and commended him
to God; and he went to Sir Bors and kissed him, and commended him
to God, and said, "Fair lord, salute me to my lord Sir Lancelot, my
father, and bid him remember this unstable world." Therewith he
kneeled down before the table and made his prayers, and while he was
praying his soul suddenly left the body and was carried by angels up
into heaven, which the two Knights right well beheld. Also they saw
come from heaven a hand, but no body behind it, and it came unto the
Vessel, and took it and the spear, and bare them back to heaven. And
since then no man has dared to say that he has seen the Holy Graal.

When Percivale and Bors saw Galahad lying dead they made as much
sorrow as ever two men did, and the people of the country and of the
city were right heavy. And they buried him as befitted their King. As
soon as Galahad was buried, Sir Percivale sought a hermitage outside
the city, and put on the dress of a hermit, and Sir Bors was always with
him, but kept the dress that he wore at Court. When a year and two
months had passed Sir Percivale died also, and was buried by the side of
Galahad; and Sir Bors left that land, and after long riding came to
Camelot. Then was there great joy made of him in the Court, for they
had held him as dead; and the King ordered great clerks to attend him,
and to write down all his adventures and those of Sir Percivale and Sir
Galahad. Next, Sir Lancelot told the adventures of the Graal which he
had seen, and this likewise was written and placed with the other in
almonries at Salisbury. And by and by Sir Bors said to Sir Lancelot,
"Galahad your son saluteth you by me, and after you King Arthur and
all the Court, and so did Sir Percivale; for I buried them with mine own
hands in the City of Sarras. Also, Sir Lancelot, Galahad prayeth you to
remember of this uncertain world, as you promised when you were
together!" "That is true," said Sir Lancelot, "and I trust his prayer may
avail me." But the prayer but little availed Sir Lancelot, for he fell to his
old sins again. And now the Knights were few that survived the search
for the Graal, and the evil days of Arthur began.

The Enchantment of Lionarda

from Palmerin of England

PALMERIN IN THE ADVENTURE OF THE ENCHANTMENT OF LIONARDA PRINCESS OF THRACE AND HOW HER ENCHANTMENT WAS ENDED

By Francisco de Moraes

Corrected by Robert Southey from the original Portuguese

"He saw some damsels seated, so fair that they seemed worthy to be in so fair a place; and amongst them was Lionarda."

H. J. FORD

The Enchantment of Lionarda

THE LORDS OF the kingdom of Thrace led Palmerin to a hill, from whence they showed him the place where Lionarda remained enchanted. Now as the day was clear, at the foot of the hill he beheld in a pleasant valley some brave and stately towers among the green trees, a goodly sight to behold; for not only was the valley wherein they were edified as fresh and delightful a place as nature could make, but also the edifices and palaces displayed such numerous pinnacles and sumptuous varandas of marble, so white and lofty, that they seemed to touch the sky; with other surpassing devices and inventions, so worthy of admiration that he thought them to be framed by the celestial powers rather than by any earthly creatures.

Well was Palmerin pleased to see a thing so pleasant; and though at that time his spirit was as it were dead with the longing remembrances which tormented it, yet the beauty of the place stirred in him a certain lively joy, and he thought how fair a lot would be his who should enjoy it, together with Lionarda; a lot which, however fair, he wished not for himself, nothing sufficing for him, but only the hope he had of his services and merits with Polinarda. After he had stayed awhile, beholding the manner of the valley, and thinking of the dangers which had been menaced, holding them in little, seeing that the place rather promised to delight the senses than to dismay the heart, he began to think lightly of the enterprize, which in truth a wise man ought not to have done, because that divers times the doubtfullest things have the pleasantest issue; and that which seemeth most pleasant at the beginning, doth prove to be the sharpest danger in the ending. But as in Palmerin this contempt of the danger arose from his surpassing hardihood, and from the many dangers which he had happily gone through, and this seemed to threaten none, he is the less worthy of blame.

One of the knights that kept him company then advanced from among the others; he was a man of great authority, for his grey hairs, and the quality of his person, and the experience of things which many years had shewn him. "Sir knight," said he to Palmerin, "to whom fortune hath alway been so great a friend, that in no danger or distress hath she ever played you false, not for this, your accustomed prosperity, should you cease to fear dangers, which to appearance may seem little; for she who in great things hath been willing to forward you, may peradventure in lesser ones forsake you, for the greater proof of her power: moreover, nothing should be judged of by its first appearance, seeing from such judgment errors arise for which afterwards there is no remedy. This I say, because the adventure which you are about to essay seemeth in its beginning more made for contentment than to be feared. But I would have you know, that this contentment is to be gained by danger, and perchance when you find yourself in it, you will find it greater than you thought for."

"Sir," answered Palmerin, "your counsel, shewing so great good will, deserves a guerdon which I cannot now bestow; and indeed your words are full of truth. I am right thankful that you have given me so good a lesson to bear in mind hereafter; God grant that this may have the end which we all desire, and if I speed to my wish, I will not be unmindful of your friendly warning." This promise, presented with so great humanity, inflamed a sudden envy in the hearts of some there present, who for the hope they had to see him king, began to enter into more praises than any true or faithful subject would offer. For they began to persuade him, that no adventure, how dangerous soever it proved, might astonish his person: but he declining from such praise as was the daily gift and work of flatterers, set spurs to his horse, and rode down the hill.

An example surely worthy of great praise to all princes and rulers living on the earth, that they should not incline and lean to such, who only study with sweet words, flattering tales, and false reports, to rest and bring them asleep in so vile an exercise. Which painted faces if they would surpass, their subjects, friends, and servants, should be equally regarded, their renown plentifully increased, and accordingly honoured; yea, the virtuous should be richly rewarded, and the vicious rightfully for ever reproached; then would not the plain dealer be governed by such as have been noted, but the good should be openly discerned from the evil, and all enjoy one hope for a continual quiet: but to our matter. As soon as Palmerin pricked forward, the light began to darken, the air to be marvellously troubled, and misty, so that the lords of Thrace lost sight of him, and could not even see one another; and there was loud thundering, and great earthquakes, and other fearful signs, so they were overcome with such fear, that some fell before their horses, being astounded; others lost their stirrups and clung to the horses' necks, and thus they made their way to the city, tearing their cloaks in the thickets, neither remembering the road nor any thing else. But as the signs that day were different from what they had been at any former time when this adventure had been essayed, the city itself was overspread with so thick and black a cloud, and filled with sounds so dolorous and dismayful, that no one had either judgment so free, or heart so strong, as to be exempt from the fear which these terrors occasioned.

Selviam, whom Palmerin had ordered to stay upon the hill, seeing his master as he deemed in such danger, forgot all fear, and being guided by the love with which he served him, spurred his horse to follow him. But as the nature of the enchantment was, that no one could enter the forbidden ground, except by great prowess and force of arms, he found himself suddenly in the city, without knowing how he came there, in company with the rest, and at such time as the cloud was beginning to disperse: Palmerin, meantime, remembering the words of the old knight, perceived the error of his first opinion; for he knew not whither he went in that thick darkness, nor could he resist an inward pain, which seemed as if it would have rent his heart; wherat he greatly marvelled, thinking that nothing but his own passion could have touched him there. And now, certain invisible bodies approached him, and by force plucked him from the saddle, and threw him down; and though to defend himself he drew his sword, and struck on all sides, he found that his blows did no harm, for they were smitten against the air. Then he thought to mount on horseback again, but his labour was in vain; it was not possible for him to find his horse, which was far enough away, and presently, not only his sword was taken from him, but likewise all his armour was caught away on a sudden; whereat he began to stand in some fear, as knowing that strength hath need of arms to execute its purpose. Finding himself thus disarmed, and weary with striving to seize these bodies which were without souls, he sate himself down, not knowing what to do, and holding that the adventure was impossible to be achieved, for he could see none with whom to fight; and even if he had seen any, he was spoiled of all implement of offence or defence. The darkness became every minute more and more; he could neither go forward nor return; wherefore he said to himself, "Certes, there are more adventures in the world than men suspect; and let not him who is without mishap wish to enter into them, for he who fears it least will find it, and they who have longest avoided it cannot escape at last."

The history saith that Palmerin remained some time sitting upon the ground, deliberating with himself what he should do; and seeing that in these cases there was no room for counsels, he rose without any determination, committing himself to the difficulties which fortune might ordain, and careless what might happen, even if it were the end of his life, which he was resolved to sell as dearly as he could, believing that he who does what he can when dying, satisfies with his life what he owes to honour. Still it troubled him to see himself without arms, fearing that for lack of them he could not fulfil his intention. But what most dismayed him was, to feel his soul so depressed within him, that his limbs seemed to be almost deprived of their wonted virtue. And now there came from the hill above, a mighty and terrible thundering, that he expected the earth would have opened under him. With this he heard fearful hollow voices, and when the rolling sounds reached him, then was he snatched up a mighty height, and presently let fall, so that he thought himself descending to the abyss. These fears, however, he underwent as one who expected worse; what he most grieved at being that they were of such a nature that resistance could not be made. At this time the darkness began to clear away, when he found himself to be in the midst of a little island, enclosed round about with a water so black and deep, that it seemed as if it came from the centre of the earth. In the midst of this islet Palmerin espied an old withered tree, and underneath it stood a knight armed in his own lost armour, with his sword likewise in his hand, who said unto him, "Now, O thou valiant knight, I would fain see what thy courage will avail, or by what means thou canst defend thyself from the wrath of my hands, which with the edge of thy own sword will mangle thy flesh and bones, whereon the wild beasts of the country shall feed: so that thy renown, famed over all the whole earth, shall here take full end, where none can approach to bear witness of thy death."

Of a truth, he who should say that Palmerin was at this time free from the fears which such a danger might well bring upon him, might say what he pleased; for his heart, though it were always accompanied with all virtue and all courage, at that hour was not so, in that he was destitute of any thing for his defence in this extremity; and seeing that he had to defend himself with nothing but the limbs which nature had given him, against an armed enemy, who, according to his proportions and semblance, was no little to be feared, committing himself to the will of fortune, though things of honour ought not to be committed to her, yet being in such a state that there was no other remedy, he approached the knight, who with all fierceness advanced to meet him with his lifted sword. A dark cloud suddenly overshadowed them; but in the cloud, though he saw him not, Palmerin seized him in his arms, and the other thrust his sword into his breast up to the hilt, he feeling such pain as if he had indeed received so deadly a thrust; and though against such a fear no courage could suffice, yet was his such that it never forsook him, and he grappled with that phantom, till by fine force at length he overthrew; then meaning to cut off his head, at the instant when he drew the sword out of his own body, the cloud dispersed, and he found himself with it in his hand, and his armour under the tree, but the knight was gone.

Amazed at these things, but seeing that what was at first so fearful proved at last to be fantastic and vain, he began to recover confidence, and donned his armour, wherewith he felt his strength increased, and a lively hope of more wonders, being now disposed to be delighted with them. Presently the day cleared, and he could see every thing as far as the eye could reach, and then on the other side beyond the island, in the midst of a green field and among goodly trees, he saw the edifices which he had seen from the hill; but there was no way of crossing to them, because of that great water which hath been spoken of, except by swimming; and this he feared to attempt, having no skill therein. Moreover, the bank on both sides was so steep that its height appeared immeasurable. Now seeing that he had this precipice to descend, and neither knowing how he could get up on the opposite side, nor how he could get to it, for the weight of his armour would drown him, he was so confounded, that neither was his courage sufficient to induce him to attempt it, nor his understanding to console him. There seemed to be no remedy, and for his more dismay, on the other side of the water he espied a company of monstrous and misshapen beasts, who seemed to be waiting there to devour him; and as if they were quarrelling who should be the first to fall on him, they began a furious battle, some helping others, so that it looked like a challenge and pitched battle, party against party. This Palmerin judged to be one of the most notable things that ever he had seen: for while the battle continued many of them spoiled and killed one another, howling the while so loudly, that it was heard in the city as though they were in the midst of it, so that the fear there was greatly increased, for they thought that Palmerin was surely in some great danger. He who resented the most fear was Selviam, grieving that he was not present with his lord, to go through the same dangers, with that true love of a faithful servant, which masters for the most part understand so well, and so ill requite. The fury of this battle was so great, that at last all who were engaged in it lay dead upon the field.

Their grievous fight being thus ended, Palmerin went about the island, to see where he might have passage to the other side. At last, in one part where the waters made a resting-place, he espied a boat, having four oars in it, which were handled and governed by four beasts of marvellous bigness, each one tied with a mighty chain, and at the poop sate a mighty lion, all imbrued in blood, as though he were master of the passage, who fed himself with nothing else but the flesh of his passengers.

While Palmerin was beholding this fearful boat, he espied a man on the farther side, crying to the beasts to carry him over with them; whereat he was much amazed, as thinking no man to be so foolish as to hazard himself in so perilous a river with such boatmen, and under such a pilot. The boat put off to take him in, and the man was no sooner entered, but the lion seized him in his paws, and with his mighty claws straightway rent him in pieces, and devoured him, giving part to his companions, the rowers; for this was their ordinary food. Any one may conceive in what state was Palmerin's heart, when he beheld all this, for he saw no way to pass but the terror of death was both before and behind him; but seeing there was no remedy, for if he remained in the islet he must needs die for want of food, so as a last resolution, he concluded to put himself to the rigour of the beasts, and shift with them by strength of arms; for he saw himself wholly destitute of any other hope. Hereupon he looked how he might descend, but there was no other way except by a rock which reached down to the water side, and which was so slippery and steep, that there was nothing on which he could lay hold, or stay himself; and he thought that he must needs be dashed to pieces before he could reach the bottom. This made him demur a little; and as this extreme danger was so greatly to be dreaded, he addressed himself to the remedy which he alway reserved for the worst perils, that is, to the remembrance of his lady, with which he was accustomed to surmount all, how great and terrible soever they might be. And having invoked her, he felt his fear gone, and without farther dread or delay let himself slide down the rock; but as all those dangers were in truth no otherwise dangerous than in appearance, he attained the river-side without any harm: the lion and his fellows pushed off from the opposite shore to receive him into the boat; and he perceiving this, drew his sword, and with shield advanced, made ready for the adventure. But for this adventure such readiness, which is elsewhere so profitable, was nothing needed, for all were but phantasms and unreal shapes; and as soon as the prow was run ashore, and he had leapt in, he saw none to attack, for forthwith that strange pilot and his boatmen were gone, he knew not how, and he found himself alone in the boat: then taking the oars, he rowed himself to the farther side; but when he had crost the river, the opposite bank was so steep and overhanging, that he could by no possible means climb up; so that he was again utterly at a loss how to proceed. Being thus confounded, presently he saw an old and broken basket lowered down to him from the top of the rock, by a rope which was so weak and slender, that he thought the mere weight of the basket would have broken it. When Palmerin perceived that there was no other means of ascending that great height, once more trusting in the remembrance of her whom he served, he thought to lay aside his arms, that he might be less heavy; and disarming himself he was about to get into the basket with nothing but his sword. But as many times the heart feels within itself foreboding doubts of what is to come, a fear came upon him which made him put them on again, thinking they might still be necessary. Then, trusting to fortune and abiding the chance, he got into the basket, and without seeing any one to hoist him, was raised into the air, but with so slow and swaying a motion, that the delay doubled his fear. And now when he was at a great height, he saw that the basket began to break, and the cord give way with the weight, and untwist itself, so that at last nothing but a single thread was left, which was almost invisibly small. Certes, though he had already suffered many fears, this was the worst of all, for he saw himself in the last extremity, being suspended in heaven by a single hair. This made him again betake himself to his lady for help, as the only one in whom he trusted in such need; and as it is by faith alone that we must stand or fall, so this faith which he had in his lady was of such avail, that overcoming the slowness of the enchantment, in one moment it brought him up, and landed him above in the field where the battle of the beasts had been, of which he could now see no sign, neither of the water below. The disappearance of these things which had caused him such fear, giving him now a new joy, which dissipated all his sorrows, as joy when it is unexpected is ever wont to do.

The day was now spent, and the moon, which was then full and in her strength, having no clouds to oppose or obscure her, began to rise in the East with a splendour which seemed almost unnaturally bright. The nightingales and other birds with which that land abounded began to welcome the night with such variety of songs and rejoicing, that Palmerin forgot all his past troubles. And laying himself down under a tree, intending to listen to them, fatigue so overpowered him, that he fell asleep, not having eaten all that day, food indeed being little needed by him: for though without it nature cannot be sustained, yet, when the spirits are roused by difficulties, the very occasion administers strength to the limbs, provided it be not over long; for of long want nature is incapable, and thereby in course becomes weak and broken down, and finally perishes. Palmerin past as peaceful a night as he had painful a day. When the dawn appeared, the birds awoke him with a song so joyous to hear, and so delightful to muse upon, that he wished the day had tarried longer, to have let him longer enjoy so sweet contentment. But as these follow their appointed order, it was not long before they forsook him, bright day-light, and their custom of seeking food, making them disperse. Palmerin rose, and looking round the field, well pleased at its beauty, beheld towards the East the towers and edifices which he had seen from the hill yesterday, surrounded with the same goodly trees; and though in this there was no show of danger, what he had already witnessed taught him still to apprehend it; on the other hand, the same experience taught him to have little fear. He had not advanced far towards them, before he espied his horse tied to a tree, saddled and bridled, and in such case as when he left him; at which he little marvelled, being now accustomed to the wonders of this land. So mounting upon him, he rode a little further, where he met with two knights, who were of great stature, and clad in the brightest and richest armour that he had ever seen; and they, without any words, couched their spears against him. He encountered the first full upon his shield, and the knight presently vanished away: the second burst his lance upon him. Palmerin veered round to requite him with a blow of his sword, but he vanished in like manner as the other.

Then Palmerin looking about, espied some men about to draw up a bridge, which was the passage over a moat of one of the towers: at this he clapt spurs to his horse, and galloped thither apace, so that he crossed the bridge before they could raise it, and before they could fasten the gate forced his way with them into a court, which was surrounded with fair apartments. But though the manner of this was worthy to be admired, two giants who came out with huge maces in their hands did not give him leisure for this. This danger was more welcome to Palmerin than the others which he had past; so leaping from his horse, he advanced on foot to attack them with his wonted courage. The battle was soon finished, for all that they were designed to do was in appearance, and as soon as he touched them they dissolved into air, of which they were made. Then seeing that all the dangers which had threatened him were illusions, he determined all which might yet present themselves to him as nothing more.

And now looking to see how he might ascend into the building, he perceived a little gate under some arches, and from thence a flight of steps ascended so steep, that it was a labour to climb them, so narrow that it was with difficulty a man could get up between the walls, and so long, that the top of them was out of sight. Palmerin, desirous to see the end of his labours, adventured to go up, and when he was a little way up the walls about him began to shake vehemently, so that sometimes he thought the vaulted roof would fall in and crush him; at other times he was so squeezed between the sides that he could not move. Long it was before he could gain the top, but then the shaking ceased, and he found himself in a long open gallery, which was of marvellous workmanship. At the end thereof there was a great door, made fast with three great locks and bolts of iron, and before the door lay a mighty serpent, whose horrible bigness not only filled up the door-way, but likewise great part of the gallery; the countenance of this serpent was such, that the very sight of it struck fear to the heart; and his eye above all was so watchful, that it seemed hopeless to attempt aught against him by slight, if it could not be obtained by force. About his neck, upon a string, were hanged the keys that should open the three locks. Then Palmerin perceived that whoever would enter must use these keys; and seeing the porter was so unsociable that he would give them to no one, and that to take them from him against his will would be a hopeless endeavour, he stood awhile in doubt what he should do; but calling to mind the illusions of this place, he determined to attack him, and advanced to strike. The serpent rose in anger, glowing with fire, and breathing out flames from his mouth. But the danger quickened Palmerin's courage, and seeing himself so engaged, he thrust his sword into one of his huge nostrils. At this he snorted out such volumes of smoke as blackened the whole air, and fled out of the gallery with terrible roarings, which seemed to shake the very earth.

The people seeing him fly over the city, and how fearful a monster he was, well judged that Palmerin had been in some great danger; and though they were in great trouble for him, it was far greater pain to Selviam, who, though he was free from bodily dangers, felt in his soul those of his master.

When Palmerin saw himself delivered from this danger, and the smoke had dispersed, he found the keys on the ground, wherewith he opened the locks, and entered into so fair a hall, and so marvellously wrought, that neither those in the island which he had won from Eutropa, nor the abode of Daliarte in the Dark Valley, might compare with this.

Entering then into other apartments, for there was none to oppose him, he saw that they were all of the same cunning workmanship, which made him highly account the rare knowledge of the king of Thrace, by whom such a work had been devised. Now, as the serpent was the last of these vain perils, nothing more hindered him from approaching the true danger, which was the sight of Lionarda, from which no human wisdom could secure him. So proceeding from one apartment to another, at last he heard the voices of women in one of the rooms, who as soon as they perceived him, being terrified at such a novelty as the sight of an armed man, fled from the apartment, leaping from some varandas into a garden. Palmerin followed them into this garden, which seemed to him yet more worthy of admiration that all which he had seen within. He had not proceeded far, when, under the shade of some thick and green laurels, round about a fountain of rarer and more marvellous fashion than he had ever beheld, he saw some damsels seated, so fair that they seemed worthy to be in so fair a place; and among them was Lionarda, who in form and feature was more beautiful than the rest, beyond comparison. They, when they saw him approach, rose up to receive him, knowing that by him they were released from that enchantment. Lionarda welcomed him with that graceful courtesy which nature had imparted to her. "Sir Knight," said she, "though certes the obligation which of so great a debt as you have laid me under, cannot be discharged with words, yet I beseech you accept now the wish I have to requite you, in satisfaction for your

"The people seeing him fly over the city, and how fearful
a monster he was, well judged that Palmerin had been in
some great danger."

H. J. FORD

deeds; and hereafter, if time shall give me room to requite you better, standing with mine honour, then shall you see the desire I have to recompense you what is due."

"Lady," he replied, "abundant recompense for any achievement, how great soever, is this sight, and this beauty, for one who should have a heart free enough to let him understand so great a happiness. The things of this place are all so wonderful, that the present put the past out of remembrance;—I intreat you tell me, if I have any greater danger to pass, than this which you present before me, for if there be I shall despair to accomplish it. The hope of such great things ought to be reserved for a greater heart than mine."

Now, though Lionarda of a truth was so fair that fairer might not be, what she felt at these words sent up so modest a colour into her countenance as made her appear yet fairer, for they seemed to have in them that meaning which might well be suspected. She replied, "I know not, sir Knight, what danger you sustain at this present; all the dangers of this place were ended at such time as you came into this garden." But then to break off their talk, there came in the lords and governors of the city, who seeing the serpent fly over the city, which they knew to be the end of the enchantment, came with full speed riding to the castle, where coming into the garden, they humbled themselves on their knees before the princess Lionarda, offering likewise to kiss the hand of Palmerin as their king; but he, whose resolution was otherwise, would not suffer this, but received them with equal courtesy. It was not long before a letter arrived, sent by queen Carmelia, for the princess. She was received in the city, with all the feasts and rejoicing which the people could devise in so short a time. Palmerin was amazed, as he returned, not to find that water which he had crost: for though he knew the other things to have been only visionary, this he thought had certainly been real. As soon as they reached the palace, Lionarda was received by her grand-mother Carmelia, with as much joy as a thing so long desired, deserved. Palmerin was lodged in the same apartment as before, when Selviam disarmed him, being full joyful to have his lord again, returned from so many dangers with such honour. This faithful love arose in him from that which Palmerin bore to him in like manner; for when it is otherwise the ingratitude of the lord makes the servant faithless. The damsel of Thrace brought him food, which is a necessary thing after labour; for only with this and with repose can the wearied limbs support themselves. In the city they began to prepare feasts for the ensuing day; every one expending according as his means permitted in different devices, after the fancy of each, different people, as is natural, devising different things.

The Elves

By Johann Ludwig Tieck

Translated from the German by Thomas Carlyle

"'Thou art aware Zerina,' said the lady, 'that she can be
here but for a little while.'"

JOHN D. BATTEN

The Elves

"WHERE IS OUR little Mary?" said the father.

"She is playing out upon the green there, with our neighbour's boy," replied the mother.

"I wish they may not run away and lose themselves," said he; "they are so thoughtless."

The mother looked for the little ones, and brought them their evening luncheon. "It is warm," said the boy; "and Mary had a longing for the red cherries."

"Have a care, children," said the mother, "and do not run too far from home, and not into the wood; father and I are going to the fields."

Little Andres answered, "Never fear, the wood frightens us; we shall sit here by the house, where there are people near us."

The mother went in, and soon came out again with her husband. They locked the door, and turned towards the fields to look after their labourers, and see their hay-harvest in the meadow. Their house lay upon a little green height, encircled by a pretty ring of paling, which likewise enclosed their fruit and flower garden. The hamlet stretched somewhat deeper down, and on the other side lay the castle of the count. Martin rented the large farm from this nobleman, and was living in contentment with his wife and only child; for he yearly saved some money, and had the prospect of becoming a man of substance by his industry, for the ground was productive, and the count not illiberal.

As he walked with his wife to the fields, he gazed cheerfully round, and said, "What a different look this quarter has, Brigitta, from the place we lived in formerly! Here it is all so green; the whole village is bedecked with thick-spreading fruit-trees; the ground is full of beautiful herbs and flowers; all the houses are cheerful and cleanly, the inhabitants are at their ease: nay, I could almost fancy that the woods are greener here than elsewhere, and the sky bluer; and, so far as the eye can reach, you have pleasure and delight in beholding the bountiful earth."

"And, whenever you cross the stream," said Brigitta, "you are, as it were, in another world, all is so dreary and withered; but every traveller declares that our village is the fairest in the country far and near."

"All but that fir-ground," said her husband; "do but look back to it, how dark and dismal that solitary spot is lying in the gay scene; the dingy fir-trees with the smoky huts behind them, the ruined stalls, the brook flowing past with a sluggish melancholy."

"It is true," replied Brigitta; "if you but approach that spot, you grow disconsolate and sad, you know not why. What sort of people can they be that live there, and keep themselves so separate from the rest of us, as if they had an evil conscience?"

"A miserable crew," replied the young farmer: "gipsies, seemingly, that steal and cheat in other quarters, and have their hoard and hiding-place here. I wonder only that his lordship suffers them."

"Who knows," said the wife, with an accent of pity, "but perhaps they may be poor people, wishing, out of shame, to conceal their poverty; for, after all, no one can say aught ill of them; the only thing is, that they do not go to church, and none knows how they live; for the little garden, which indeed seems altogether waste, cannot possibly support them; and fields they have none."

"God knows," said Martin, as they went along, "what trade they follow; no mortal comes to them, for the place they live in is as if bewitched and excommunicated, so that even our wildest fellows will not venture into it."

Such conversation they pursued while walking to the fields. That gloomy spot they spoke of lay aside from the hamlet. In a dell, begirt with firs, you might behold a hut, and various ruined office-houses; rarely was smoke seen to mount from it, still more rarely did men appear there; though at times curious people venturing somewhat nearer, had perceived upon the bench before the hut some hideous women, in ragged clothes, dandling in their arms some children equally dirty and ill-favoured; black dogs were running up and down upon the boundary; and of an evening, a man of monstrous size was seen to cross the foot-bridge of the brook, and disappear in the hut; and in the darkness, various shapes were observed, moving like shadows round a fire in the open air. This piece of ground, the firs, and the ruined huts, formed, in truth, a strange contrast with the bright green landscape, the white houses of the hamlet, and the stately new-built castle.

The two little ones had now eaten their fruit: it came into their heads to run races; and the little nimble Mary always got the start of the less active Andres. "It is not fair," cried Andres, at last; "let us try it for some length, then we shall see who wins."

"As thou wilt," said Mary; "only to the brook we must not run."

"No," said Andres; "but there, on the hill, stands the large pear-tree, a quarter of a mile from this. I shall run by the left, round past the fir-ground; thou canst try it by the right, over the fields; so we do not meet till we get up, and then we shall see which of us is swifter."

"Done," cried Mary, and began to run; "for we shall not mar one another by the way; and my father says it is as far to the hill by that side of the gipsies' house as by this."

Andres had already started, and Mary, turning to the right, could no longer see him. "It is very silly," said she to herself: "I have only to take heart, and run along the bridge, past the hut, and through the yard, and I shall certainly be first." She was already standing by the brook and the clump of firs. "Shall I? No: it is too frightful," said she. A little white dog was standing on the farther side, and barking with might and main. In her terror, Mary thought the dog some monster, and sprang back. "Fy! fy!" said she: "the dolt is gone half way by this time, while I stand here considering." The little dog kept barking, and, as she looked at it more narrowly, it seemed no longer frightful, but, on the contrary, quite pretty: it had a red collar round its neck, with a glittering bell; and as it raised its head, and shook itself in barking, the little bell sounded with the finest tinkle. "Well, I must risk it!" cried she: "I will run for life; quick, quick, I am through; certainly to Heaven! they cannot eat me up alive in half a minute!" And with this, the gay, courageous little Mary sprang along the foot-bridge, passed the dog, which ceased its barking and began to fawn on her, and in a moment she was standing on the other bank, and the black firs all round concealed from view her father's house and the rest of the landscape.

But what was her astonishment when here! The loveliest, most variegated flower-garden lay round her; tulips, roses, and lilies were glittering in the fairest colours; blue and gold-red butterflies were wavering in the blossoms; cages of shining wire were hung on the espaliers, with many-coloured birds in them, singing beautiful songs; and children, in short white frocks, with flowing yellow hair and brilliant eyes, were frolicking about: some playing with lambkins, some feeding the birds or gathering flowers, and giving them to one another; some, again, were eating cherries, grapes, and ruddy apricots. No hut was to be seen; but instead of it, a large fair house, with a brazen door and lofty statutes, stood glancing in the middle of the space. Mary was confounded with surprise, and knew not what to think; but, not being bashful, she went right up to the first of the children, held out her hand, and wished the little creature good even.

"Art thou come to visit us,then?" said the glittering child; "I saw thee running, playing on the other side, but thou wert frightened for our little dog."

"So you are not gipsies and rogues," said Mary, "as Andres always told me! He is a stupid thing, and talks of much he does not understand."

"Stay with us," said the strange little girl; "thou wilt like it well."

"But we are running a race."

"Thou wilt find thy comrade soon enough. There, take and eat."

Mary ate, and found the fruit more sweet than any she had ever tasted in her life before; and Andres, and the race, and the prohibition of her parents were entirely forgotten.

A stately woman, in a shining robe, came towards them, and asked about the stranger child. "Fairest lady," said Mary, "I came running hither by chance, and now they wish to keep me."

"Thou art aware, Zerina," said the lady, "that she can be here but for a little while; besides, thou shouldst have asked my leave."

"I thought," said Zerina, "when I saw her admitted across the bridge, that I might do it; we have often seen her running in the fields, and thou thyself hast taken pleasure in her lively temper. She will have to leave us soon enough."

"No, I will stay here," said the little stranger; "for here it is so beautiful, and here I shall find the prettiest playthings, and stores of berries and cherries to boot. On the other side it is not half so grand."

The gold-robed lady went away with a smile; and many of the children now came bounding round the happy Mary in their mirth, and twitched her, and incited her to dance; others brought her lambs, or curious playthings; others made music on instruments, and sang to it.

She kept, however, by the playmate who had first met her; for Zerina was the kindest and loveliest of them all. Little Mary cried and cried again: "I will stay with you forever; I will stay with you, and you shall be my sisters"; at which the children all laughed and embraced her. "Now we shall have a royal sport," said Zerina. She ran into the palace, and returned with a little golden box, in which lay a quantity of seeds, like glittering dust. She lifted of it with her little hand, and scattered some grains on the green earth. Instantly the grass began to move, as in waves; and, after a few moments, bright rose-bushes started from the ground, shot rapidly up, and budded all at once, while the sweetest perfume filled the place. Mary also took a little of the dust, and, having scattered it, she saw white lilies, and the most variegated pinks, pushing up. At a signal from Zerina, the flowers disappeared, and others rose in their room. "Now," said Zerina, "look for something greater." She laid two pine-seeds in the ground, and stamped them in sharply with her foot. Two green bushes stood before them. "Grasp me fast," said she; and Mary threw her arms about the slender form. She felt herself borne upward; for the trees were springing under them with the greatest speed; the tall pines waved to and fro, and the two children held each other fast embraced, swinging this way and that in the red clouds of the twilight, and kissed each other; while the rest were climbing up and down the trunks with quick dexterity, pushing and teasing one another with loud laughter when they met; if any one fell down in the press, it flew through the air, and sank slowly and surely to the ground. At length Mary was beginning to feel frightened; and the other little child sang a few loud tones, and the trees again sank down, and set them on the ground as gradually as they had lifted them before to the clouds.

They next went through the brazen door of the palace. Here many fair women, elderly and young, were sitting in the round hall, partaking of the fairest fruits, and listening to glorious invisible music. In the vaulting of the ceiling, palms, flowers, and groves stood painted, among which little figures of children were sporting and winding in every graceful posture; and with the tones of the music, the images altered and glowed with the most burning colours; now the blue and green were sparkling like radiant light, now these tints faded back in paleness, the purple flamed up, and the gold took fire; and then the naked children seemed to be alive among the flower-garlands, and to draw breath, and emit it through their ruby-coloured lips, so that by fits you could see the glance of their little white teeth, and the lighting up of their azure eyes.

From the hall, a stair of brass led down to a subterranean chamber. Here lay much gold and silver, and precious stones of every hue shone out between them. Strange vessels stood along the walls, and all seemed filled with costly things. The gold was worked into many forms, and glittered with the friendliest red. Many little dwarfs were busied sorting the pieces from the heap, and putting them in the vessels; others, hunch-backed and bandy-legged, with long red noses, were tottering slowly along, half bent to the ground, under full sacks, which they bore as millers do their grain; and, with much panting, shaking out the gold-dust on the ground. Then they darted awkwardly to the right and left, and caught the rolling balls that were like to run away; and it happened now and then that one in his eagerness overset the other, so that both fell heavily and clumsily to the ground. They made angry faces, and looked askance, as Mary laughed at their gestures and their ugliness. Behind them sat an old, crumpled little man, whom Zerina reverently greeted; he thanked her with a grave inclination of his head. He held a sceptre in his hand, and wore a crown upon his brow, and all the other dwarfs appeared to regard him as their master, and obey his nod.

"What! more wanted?" asked he, with a surly voice, as the children came a little nearer. Mary was afraid, and did not speak; but her companion answered, they were only come to look about them in the chambers. "Still your old child's tricks!" replied the dwarf; "will there never be an end to idleness?" With this, he turned again to his employment, kept his people weighting and sorting the ingots; some he sent away on errands, some he chid with angry tones.

"Who is the gentleman?" said Mary.

"Our Metal-Prince," replied Zerina, as they walked along.

They seemed once more to reach the open air, for they were standing by a lake, yet no sun appeared, and they saw no sky above their heads. A little boat received them, and Zerina steered it diligently forward. It shot rapidly along. On gaining the middle of the lake, the strangers saw that multitudes of pipes, channels, and brooks were spreading from the sea in every direction. "These waters to the right," said Zerina, "flow beneath your garden, and this is why it blooms so freshly; by the other side we get down into the great stream." On a sudden, out of all the channels, and from every quarter of the lake, came a crowd of little children swimming up: some wore garlands of sedge and water-lily; some had red stems of coral; others were blowing on crooked shells; a tumultuous noise echoed merrily from the dark shoes; among the children might be seen the fairest women sporting in the waters, and often several of the children sprang about some one of them, and with kisses hung upon her neck and shoulders. All saluted the strangers; and these steered onward through the revelry out of the lake into a little river, which grew narrower and narrower. At last the boat came aground. The strangers took their leave, and Zerina knocked against the cliff. This opened like a door, and a female form, all red, assisted them to mount. "Are you all brisk here?" inquired Zerina.

"They are just at work," replied the other, "and happy as they could wish; indeed, the heat is very pleasant."

They went up a winding stair, and on a sudden Mary found herself in a most resplendent hall, so that, as she entered, her eyes were dazzled by the radiance. Flame-coloured tapestry covered the walls with a purple glow; and when her eye had grown a little used to it, the stranger saw, to her astonishment, that in the tapestry there were figures moving up and down in dancing joyfulness; in form so beautiful, and of so fair proportions, that nothing could be seen more graceful; their bodies were as of red crystals, so that it appeared as if the blood were visible within them, flowing and playing in its courses. They smiled on the stranger, and saluted her with various bows; but as Mary was about approaching nearer them, Zerina plucked her sharply back, crying, "Thou wilt burn thyself, my little Mary, for the whole of it is fire."

Mary felt the heat. "Why do the pretty creatures not come out," said she, "and play with us?"

"As thou livest in the Air," replied the other, "so are they obliged to stay continually in Fire, and would faint and languish if they left it. Look, now how glad they are, how they laugh and shout; those down below spread out the fire-floods everywhere beneath the earth, and thereby the flowers, and fruits, and vine are made to flourish; these red streams, again, are to run beside the brooks of water; and thus the fiery creatures are kept ever busy and glad. But for thee it is too hot here; let us return to the garden."

In the garden the scene had changed since they left it. The moonshine was lying on every flower; the birds were silent, and the children were asleep in complicated groups among the green groves. Mary and her friend, however, did not feel fatigue, but walked about in the warm summer night, in abundant talk, till morning.

When the day dawned they refreshed themselves on fruit and milk, and Mary said, "Suppose we go, by way of change, to the firs, and see how things look there?"

"With all my heart," replied Zerina; "thou wilt see our watchmen, too, and they will surely please thee; they are standing up among the trees on the mound." The two proceeded through the flower garden by pleasant groves full of nightingales; then they ascended a vine-hill; and at last, after long following the windings of a clear brook, arrived at the firs, and the height which bounded the domain. "How does it come," said Mary, "that we have to walk so far here, when, without, the circuit is so narrow?"

"I know not," said her friend; "but so it is."

They mounted to the dark firs, and a chill wind blew from without in their faces; a haze seemed lying far and wide over the landscape. On the top were many strange forms standing, with mealy, dusty faces, their misshapen heads not unlike those of white owls; they were clad in folded cloaks of shaggy wool; they held umbrellas of curious skins stretched out above them; and they waved and fanned themselves incessantly with large bat's wings, which flared out curiously beside the woollen roquelaures.

"I could laugh, yet I am frightened," cried Mary.

"These are our good, trusty watchmen," said her playmate; "they stand here and wave their fans, that cold anxiety and inexplicable fear may fall on every one that attempts to approach us. They are covered so, because without it is now cold and rainy, which they cannot bear. But snow, or wind, or cold air never reaches down to us—here is an everlasting spring and summer; yet, if these poor people on the top were not frequently relieved, they would certainly perish."

"But who are you, then?" said Mary, while again descending to the flowery fragrance; "or have you no name at all?"

"We are called the Elves," replied the friendly child; "people talk about us in the Earth, as I have heard."

They now perceived a mighty bustle on the green. "The fair bird is come!" cried the children to them. All hastened to the hall. Here, as they approached, young and old were crowding over the threshold, all shouting for joy, and from within resounded a triumphant peal of music. Having entered, they perceived the vast circuit filled with the most varied forms, and all were looking upward to a large bird with glancing plumage, that was sweeping slowly round in the dome, and in its stately flight describing many a circle. The music sounded more gayly than before; the colours and lights alternated more rapidly. At last the music ceased; and the bird, with a rustling noise, floated down upon a glittering crown that hung hovering in air under the high window, by which the hall was lighted from above. His plumage was purple and green, and shining golden streaks played through it; on his head there waved a diadem of feathers, so resplendent that they glanced like jewels. His bill was red, and his legs of a glancing blue. As he moved, the tints gleamed through each other, and the eye was charmed with their radiance. His size was as that of an eagle. But now he opened his glittering beak, and sweetest melodies came pouring from his moved breast, in finer tones than the lovesick nightingale gives forth; still stronger rose the song, and streamed like floods of light, so that all, the very children themselves, were moved by it to tears of joy and rapture. When he ceased, all bowed before him; he again flew round the dome in circles, then darted through the door, and soared into the light heaven, where he shone far up like a red point, and then soon vanished from their eyes.

"Why are ye all so glad?" inquired Mary, bending to her fair playmate, who seemed smaller than yesterday.

"The king is coming!" said the little one; "many of us have never seen him, and whithersoever he turns his face, there is happiness and mirth; we have long looked for him, more anxiously than you look for spring when winter lingers with you; and now he has announced, by his fair herald, that he is at hand. This wise and glorious bird, that has been sent to us by the king, is called Phœnix; he dwells far off in Arabia, on a tree, which there is no other that resembles on earth, as in like manner there is no second Phœnix. When he feels himself grown old, he builds a pile of balm and incense, kindles it, and dies singing; and then from the fragrant ashes soars up the renewed Phœnix, with unlessened beauty. It is seldom he so wings his course that men behold him; and when once in centuries this does occur, they note it in their annals, and expect remarkable events. But now, my friend, thou and I must part; for the sight of the king is not permitted thee."

Then the lady with the golden robe came through the throng, and beckoning Mary to her, led her into a sequestered walk. "Thou must leave us, my dear child," said she; "the king is to hold his court here for twenty years, perhaps longer; and fruitfulness and blessings will spread far over the land, but chiefly here beside us; all the brooks and rivulets will become more bountiful, all the fields and gardens richer, the wine more generous, the meadows more fertile, and the woods more fresh and green; a milder air will blow, no hail shall hurt, no flood shall threaten. Take this ring, and think of us; but beware of telling any one of our existence; or we must fly this land, and thou and all around will lose the happiness and blessing of our neighbourhood. Once more kiss thy playmate, and farewell." They issued from the walk: Zerina wept, Mary stooped to embrace her, and they parted. Already she was on the narrow bridge; the cold air was blowing on her back from the firs; the little dog barked with all its might, and rang its little bell; she looked round, then hastened over, for the darkness of the firs, the bleakness of the ruined huts, the shadows of the twilight, were filling her with terror.

"What a night my parents must have had on my account!" said she to herself, as she stepped on the green; "and I dare not tell them where I have been, or what wonders I have witnessed, nor indeed would they believe me." Two men passing by saluted her, and as they went along, she heard them say, "What a pretty girl! Where can she come from?" With quickened steps she approached the house; but the trees which were hanging last night loaded with fruit, were now standing dry and leafless; the house was differently painted, and a new barn had been built beside it. Mary was amazed, and thought she must be dreaming. In this perplexity she opened the door, and behind the table sat her father, between an unknown woman and a stranger youth. "Good God! father," cried she, "where is my mother?"

"Thy mother!" said the woman, with a forecasting tone, and sprang towards her: "Ha! thou surely canst not—Yes, indeed, indeed thou art my lost, long-lost, dear, only Mary!" She had recognised her by a little brown mole beneath the chin, as well as by her eyes and shape. All embraced her, all were moved with joy, and the parents wept. Mary was astonished that she almost reached to her father's stature; and she could not understand how her mother had become so changed and faded. She asked the name of the stranger youth. "It is our neighbour's Andres," said Martin. "How comest thou to us again, so unexpectedly, after seven long years? Where hast thou been? Why didst thou never send us tidings of thee?"

"Seven years!" said Mary, and could not order her ideas and recollections. "Seven whole years?"

"Yes, yes," said Andres, laughing, and shaking her trustfully by the hand; "I have won the race, good Mary; I was at the pear-tree and back again seven years ago, and thou, sluggish creature, art but just returned!"

They again asked, they pressed her; but remembering her instruction, she could answer nothing. It was they themselves chiefly that, by degrees, shaped a story for her: How, having lost her way, she had been taken up by a coach, and carried to a strange, remote part, where she could not give the people any notion of her parents' residence; how she was conducted to a distant town, where certain worthy persons brought her up, and loved her; how they had lately died, and at length she had recollected her birthplace, and so returned. "No matter how it is!" exclaimed her mother; "enough that we have thee again, my little daughter, my own, my all!"

Andres waited supper, and Mary could not be at home in anything she saw. The house seemed small and dark; she was astonished at her dress, which was clean and simple, but appeared quite foreign; she looked at the ring on her finger, and the gold of it glittered strangely, enclosing a stone of burning red. To her father's question, she replied that the ring also was a present from her benefactors.

She was glad when the hour of sleep arrived, and she hastened to her bed. Next morning she felt much more collected; she had now arranged her thoughts a little, and could better stand the questions of the people in the village, all of whom came in to bid her welcome. Andres was there too with the earliest, active, glad, and serviceable beyond all others. The blooming maiden of fifteen had made a deep impression on him: he had passed a sleepless night. The people of the castle likewise sent for Mary, and she had once more to tell her story to them, which was now grown quite familiar to her. The old count and his lady were surprised at her good breeding; she was modest, but not embarrassed; she made answer courteously in good phrases to all their questions; all fear of noble persons and their equipage had passed away from her; for when she measured these halls and forms by the wonders and the high beauty she had seen with the Elves in their hidden abode, this earthly splendour seemed dim to her; the presence of men was almost mean. The young lords were charmed with her beauty.

It was now February. The trees were budding earlier than usual; the nightingale had never come so soon; the spring rose fairer in the land than the oldest men could recollect it. In every quarter, little brooks gushed out to irrigate the pastures and meadows; the hills seemed heaving, the vines rose higher and higher, the fruit-trees blossomed as they had never done, and a swelling, fragrant blessedness hung suspended heavily in rosy clouds over the scene. All prospered beyond expectation; no rude day, no tempest injured the fruits; the vine flowed blushing in immense grapes; and the inhabitants of the place felt astonished, and were captivated as in a sweet dream. The next year was like its forerunner; but the men had become accustomed to the marvellous. In autumn, Mary yielded to the pressing entreaties of Andres and her parents; she was betrothed to him, and in winter they were married.

She often thought with inward longing of her residence beyond the fir-trees; she continued serious and still. Beautiful as all that lay around her was, she knew of something yet more beautiful; and from the remembrance of this, a faint regret attuned her nature to soft melancholy. It smote her painfully when her father and mother talked about the gipsies and vagabonds that dwelt in the dark spot of the ground. Often she was on the point of speaking out in defence of those good beings, whom she knew to be the benefactors of the land, especially to Andres, who appeared to take delight in zealously abusing them; yet still she repressed the word that was struggling to escape her bosom. So passed this year; in the next she was solaced by a little daughter, whom she named Elfrida, thinking of the designation of her friendly Elves.

The young people lived with Martin and Brigitta, the house being large enough for all, and helped their parents in conducting their now extended husbandry. The little Elfrida soon displayed peculiar faculties and gifts, for she could walk at a very early age, and could speak perfectly before she was a twelvemonth old; and after some few years, she had become so wise and clever, and of such wondrous beauty, that all people regarded her with astonishment; and her mother could not keep away the thought that her child resembled one of those shining little ones in the space behind the firs. Elfrida cared not to be with other children, but seemed to avoid, with a sort of horror, their tumultuous amusements, and liked best to be alone. She would then retire into a corner of the garden, and read, or work diligently with her needle; often, also, you might see her sitting, as if deep sunk in thought, or violently walking up and down the alleys, speaking to herself. Her parents readily allowed her to have her will in these things, for she was healthy, and waxed apace; only her strange, sagacious answers and observations often made them anxious. "Such wise children do not grow to age," her grandmother Brigitta many times observed; "they are too good for this world; the child, besides, is beautiful beyond nature, and will never find its proper place on earth."

The little girl had this peculiarity, that she was very loath to let herself be served by any one, but endeavoured to do everything herself. She was almost the earliest riser in the house; she washed herself carefully, and dressed without assistance. At night she was equally careful; she took special heed to pack up her clothes and washes with her own hands, allowing no one, not even her mother, to meddle with her articles. The mother humoured her in this caprice, not thinking it of any consequence. But what was her astonishment when, happening one holyday to insist, regardless of Elfrida's tears and screams, on dressing her out for a visit to the castle, she found upon her breast, suspended by a string, a piece of gold of a strange form, which she directly recognised as one of that sort she had seen in such abundance in the subterranean vault! The little thing was greatly frightened, and at last confessed that she had found it in the garden, and as she liked it much, had kept it carefully; she at the same time prayed so earnestly and pressingly to have it back, that Mary fastened it again on its former place, and, full of thoughts, went out with her in silence to the castle.

Sideward from the farmhouse lay some offices for the storing of produce and implements, and behind these there was a little green, with an old grove, now visited by no one, as, from the new arrangement of the buildings, it lay too far from the garden. In this solitude Elfrida delighted most; and it occurred to nobody to interrupt her there, so that frequently her parents did not see her for half a day. One afternoon her mother chanced to be in these buildings, seeking for some lost article among the lumber, and she noticed that a beam of light was coming in, through a chink in the wall. She took a thought of looking through this aperture, and seeing what her child was busied with; and it happened that a stone was lying loose, and could be pushed aside, so that she obtained a view right into the grove. Elfrida was sitting there on a little bench, and beside her the well-known Zerina; and the children were playing and amusing one another in the kindliest unity. The Elf embraced her beautiful companion, and said mournfully, "Ah! dear little creature, as I sport with thee, so have I sported with thy mother, when she was a child; but you mortals so soon grow tall and thoughtful! It is very hard; wert thou but to be a child as long as I!"

"Willingly would I do it," said Elfrida; "but they all say I shall come to sense, and give over playing altogether; for I have great gifts, as they think, for growing wise. Ah! and then I shall see thee no more, thou dear Zerina! Yet it is with us as with the fruit-tree flowers: how glorious the blossoming apple-tree, with its red bursting buds! It looks so stately and broad, and every one that passes under it thinks, surely something great will come of it; then the sun grows hot, and the buds come joyfully forth; but the wicked kernel is already there, which pushes off and casts away the fair flower's dress; and now, in pain and waxing, it can do nothing more, but must grow to fruit in harvest. An apple, to be sure, is pretty and refreshing, yet nothing to the blossom of spring. So is it with us mortals: I am not glad in the least at growing to be a tall girl. Ah! could I but once visit you!"

"Since the king is with us," said Zerina, "it is quite impossible; but I will come to thee, my darling, often, often, and none shall see me either here or there. I will pass invisible through the air, or fly over to thee like a bird: oh! we will be much, much together, while thou art still little. What can I do to please thee?"

"Thou must like me very dearly," said Elfrida, "as I like thee in my heart: but come, let us make another rose."

Zerina took the well-known box from her bosom, threw two grains from it on the ground, and instantly a green bush stood before them, with two deep-red roses, bending their heads as if to kiss each other. The children plucked them, smiling, and the bush disappeared. "Oh that it would not die so soon!" said Elfrida; "this red child, this wonder of the earth!"

"Give it me here," said the little Elf; then breathed thrice upon the budding rose, and kissed it thrice. "Now," said she, giving back the rose, "it will continue fresh and blooming till winter."

"I will keep it," said Elfrida, "as an image of thee; I will guard it in my little room, and kiss it night and morning, as it were thyself."

"The sun is setting," said the other; "I must home." They embraced again, and Zerina vanished.

In the evening Mary clasped her child to her breast with a feeling of alarm and veneration. She henceforth allowed the good little girl more liberty than formerly, and often calmed her husband, when he came to search for the child, which for some time he was wont to do, as her retiredness did not please him, and he feared that, in the end, it might make her silly, or even pervert her understanding. The mother often glided to the chink, and almost always found the bright Elf beside her child, employed in sport or in earnest conversation.

"Wouldst thou like to fly?" inquired Zerina, once.

"Oh, well! How well!" replied Elfrida; and the fairy clasped her mortal playmate in her arms, and mounted with her from the ground, till they hovered above the grove. The mother, in alarm, forgot herself, and pushed out her head in terror to look after them; when Zerina, from the air, held up her finger, and threatened, yet smiled; then descended with the child, embraced her, and disappeared. After this it happened more than once that Mary was observed by her; and every time, the shining little creature shook her head, or threatened, yet with friendly looks.

Often, in disputing with her husband, Mary had said in her zeal,

"Thou dost injustice to the poor people in the hut!" But when Andres pressed her to explain why she differed in opinion from the whole village, nay, from his lordship himself, and how she could understand it better than the whole of them, she still broke off embarrassed, and became silent. One day, after dinner, Andres grew more violent than ever, and maintained that, by one means or another, the crew must be packed away, as a nuisance to the country; when his wife in anger said to him, "Hush! for they are benefactors to thee and to every one of us."

"Benefactors!" cried the other, in astonishment: "these rogues and vagabonds!"

In her indignation, she was now at last tempted to relate to him, under promise of the strictest secrecy, the history of her youth; and as Andres at every word grew more incredulous, and shook his head in mockery, she took him by the hand and led him to the chink, where, to his amazement, he beheld the glittering Elf sporting with his child, and caressing her in the grove. He knew not what to say; an exclamation of astonishment escaped him, and Zerina raised her eyes. On the instant she grew pale and trembled violently; not with friendly, but with indignant looks, she made the sign of threatening, and then said to Elfrida, "Thou canst not help it, dearest heart; but they will never learn sense, wise as they believe themselves." She embraced the little one with stormy haste; and then, in the shape of a raven, flew with hoarse cries over the garden towards the firs.

In the evening the little one was very still: she kissed her rose with tears. Mary felt depressed and frightened, Andres scarcely spoke. It grew dark. Suddenly there went a rustling through the trees; birds flew to and fro with wild screaming; thunder was heard to roll, the earth shook, and tones of lamentation moaned in the air. Andres and his wife had not courage to rise; they shrouded themslves within the curtains, and with fear and trembling awaited the day. Towards morning it grew calmer; and all was silent when the sun, with his cheerful light, rose over the wood.

Andres dressed himself, and Mary now observed that the stone of the ring upon her finger had become quite pale. On opening the door, the sun shone clear on their faces, but the scene around them they could scarcely recognise. The freshness of the wood was gone; the hills were shrunk, the brooks were flowing languidly with scanty streams, the sky seemed gray; and when you turned to the firs, they were standing there, no darker or more dreary than the other trees. The huts behind them were no longer frightful; and several inhabitants of the village came and told about the fearful night, and how they had been across the spot where the gipsies had lived; how these people must have left the place at last, for their huts were standing empty, and within had quite a common look, just like the dwellings of other poor people: some of their household gear was left behind.

Elfrida, in secret, said to her mother, "I could not sleep last night; and in my fright at the noise, I was praying from the bottom of my heart, when the door suddenly opened, and my playmate entered to take leave of me. She had a travelling-pouch slung round her, a hat on her head, and a very large staff in her hand. She was very angry at thee, since on thy account she had now to suffer the severest and most painful punishments, as she had always been so fond of thee; for all of them, she said, were very loath to leave this quarter."

Mary forbade her to speak of this; and now the ferryman came across the river, and told them new wonders. As it was growing dark, a stranger man of large size had come to him, and hired his boat till sunrise; and with this condition, that the boatman should remain quiet in his house—at least, not cross the threshold of his door. "I was frightened," continued the old man, "and the strange bargain would not let me sleep. I slipped softly to the window, and looked towards the river. Great clouds were driving restlessly through the sky, and the distant woods were rustling fearfully; it was as if my cottage shook, and moans and lamentations glided round it. On a sudden I perceived a white, streaming light, that grew broader and broader, like many thousands of falling stars: sparkling and waving, it proceeded forward from the dark fir-ground, moved over the fields, and spread itself along towards the river. Then I heard a trampling, a jingling, a bustling and rushing, nearer and nearer; it went forward to my boat, and all stepped into it, men and women, as it seemed, and children; and the tall stranger ferried them over. In the river were by the boat swimming many thousands of glittering forms; in the air, white clouds and lights were wavering; and all lamented and bewailed that they must travel forth so far, far away, and leave their beloved dwelling. The noise of the rudder and the water creaked and gurgled between whiles, and then suddenly there would be silence. Many a time the boat landed, and went back, and was again laden; many heavy casks, too, they took along with them, which multitudes of horrid-looking little fellows carried and rolled; whether they were devils or goblins, Heaven only knows. Then came, in waving brightness, a stately freight: it seemed an old man mounted on a small, white horse, and all were crowding round him. I saw nothing of the horse but its head, for the rest of it was covered with costly glittering cloths and trappings. On his brow the old man had a crown so bright, that as he came across I thought the sun was rising there, and the redness of the dawn was glimmering in my eyes. Thus it went on all night. I at last fell asleep in the tumult, half in joy, half in terror. In the morning all was still; but the river is, as it were, run off, and I know not how I am to steer my boat in it now."

The same year there came a blight; the woods died away, the springs ran dry; and the scene, which had once been the joy of every traveller, was in autumn standing waste, naked, and bald, scarcely showing here and there, in the sea of sand, a spot or two where grass, with a dingy greenness, still grew up. The fruit-trees all withered, the vines faded away, and the aspect of the place became so melancholy, that the count, with his people, next year left the castle, which in time decayed and fell to ruins.

Elfrida gazed on her rose day and night with deep longing, and thought of her kind playmate; and as it drooped and withered, so did she also hang her head; and before the spring, the little maiden had herself faded away. Mary often stood upon the spot before the hut, and wept for the happiness that had departed. She wasted herself away like her child, and in a few years she too was gone. Old Martin, with his son-in-law, returned to the quarter where he had lived before.

The King of the Golden River

or The Black Brothers

A Legend of Stiria

By John Ruskin

"It was the most extraordinary looking gentleman he had ever seen in his life."

RICHARD DOYLE

The King of the Golden River

or

The Black Brothers

CHAPTER I

How the Agricultural System of the Black Brothers Was Interfered With By South-West Wind, Esquire

IN A SECLUDED and mountainous part of Stiria there was, in old time, a valley of the most surprising and luxuriant fertility. It was surrounded, on all sides, by steep and rocky mountains, rising into peaks, which were always covered with snow, and from which a number of torrents descended in constant cataracts. One of these fell westward, over the face of a crag so high, that, when the sun had set to everything else, and all below was darkness, his beams still shone full upon this waterfall, so that it looked like a shower of gold. It was, therefore, called by the people of the neighbourhood, the Golden River. It was strange that none of these streams fell into the valley itself. They all descended on the other side of the mountains, and wound away through broad plains and by populous cities. But the clouds were drawn so constantly to the snowy hills, and rested so softly in the circular hollow, that in time of drought and heat, when all the country round was burnt up, there was still rain in the little valley; and its crops were so heavy, and its hay so high, and its apples so red, and its grapes so blue, and its wine so rich, and its honey so sweet, that it was a marvel to every one who beheld it, and was commonly called the Treasure Valley.

The whole of this little valley belonged to three brothers, called Schwartz, Hans, and Gluck. Schwartz and Hans, the two elder brothers, were very ugly men, with over-hanging eyebrows and small dull eyes, which were always half shut, so that you couldn't see into *them,* and always fancied they saw very far into *you.* They lived by farming the Treasure Valley, and very good farmers they were. They killed everything that did not pay for its eating. They shot the blackbirds, because they pecked the fruit; and killed the hedgehogs, lest they should suck the cows; they poisoned the crickets for eating the crumbs in the kitchen; and smothered the cicadas, which used to sing all summer in the lime trees. They worked their servants without any wages, till they would not work any more, and then quarrelled with them, and turned them out of doors without paying them. It would have been very odd, if with such a farm, and such a system of farming, they hadn't got very rich; and very rich they *did* get. They generally contrived to keep their corn by them till it was very dear, and then sell it for twice its value; they had heaps of gold lying about on their floors, yet it was never known that they had given so much as a penny or a crust in charity; they never went to mass; grumbled perpetually at paying tithes; and were, in a word, of so cruel and grinding a temper, as to receive from all those with whom they had any dealings, the nick-name of the "Black Brothers."

The youngest brother, Gluck, was so completely opposed, in both appearance and character, to his seniors as could possibly be imagined or desired. He was not above twelve years old, fair, blue-eyed, and kind in temper to every living thing. He did not, of course, agree particularly well with his brothers, or rather, they did not agree with *him*. He was usually appointed to the honourable office of turnspit, when there was anything to roast, which was not often; for, to do the brothers justice, they were hardly less sparing upon themselves than upon other people. At other times he used to clean the shoes, floors, and sometimes the plates, occasionally getting what was left on them, by way of encourage-ment, and a wholesome quantity of dry blows, by way of education.

Things went on in this manner for a long time. At last came a very wet summer, and everything went wrong in the country around. The hay had hardly been got in, when the haystacks were floated bodily down to the sea by an innundation; the vines were cut to pieces with the hail; the corn was all killed by the black blight; only in the Treasure Valley, as usual, all was safe. As it had rain when there was rain nowhere else, so it had sun when there was sun nowhere else. Everybody came to buy corn at the farm, and went away pouring maledictions on the Black Brothers. They asked what they liked, and got it, except from the poor people, who could only beg, and several of whom were starved at their very door, without the slightest regard or notice.

It was drawing towards winter, and very cold weather, when one day the two elder brothers had gone out, with their usual warning to little Gluck, who was left to mind the roast, that he was to let nobody in, and give nothing out. Gluck sat down quite close to the fire, for it was raining very hard, and the kitchen walls were by no means dry or comfortable looking. He turned and turned, and the roast got nice and brown. "What a pity," thought Gluck, "my brothers never ask anybody to dinner. I'm sure, when they've got such a nice piece of mutton as this, and nobody else has got so much as a piece of dry bread, it would do their hearts good to have somebody to eat it with them."

Just as he spoke, there came a double knock at the house door, yet heavy and dull, as though the knocker had been tied up—more like a puff than a knock.

"It must be the wind," said Gluck; "nobody else would venture to knock double knocks at our door."

No, it wasn't the wind: there it came again very hard, and what was particularly astounding, the knocker seemed to be in a hurry, and not to be in the least afraid of the consequences. Gluck went to the window, opened it, and put his head out to see who it was.

It was the most extraordinary looking little gentleman he had ever seen in his life. He had a very large nose, slightly brass-colored; his cheeks were very round, and very red, and might have warranted a supposition that he had been blowing a refractory fire for the last eight-and-forty hours; his eyes twinkled merrily through long silky eyelashes, his moustaches curled twice round like a corkscrew on each side of his mouth, and his hair, of a curious mixed pepper-and-salt colour, descended far over his shoulders. He was about four-feet-six in height, and wore a conical pointed cap of nearly the same altitude, decorated with a black feather some three feet long. His doublet was prolonged behind into something resembling a violent exaggeration of what is now termed a "swallow tail," but was much obscured by the swelling folds of an enormous black, glossy-looking cloak, which must have been very much too long in calm weather, as the wind, whistling round the old house, carried it clear out from the wearer's shoulders to about four times his own length.

Gluck was so perfectly paralyzed by the singular appearance of his visitor, that he remained fixed without uttering a word, until the old gentleman, having performed another, and a more energetic concerto on the knocker, turned round to look after his fly-away cloak. In so doing he caught sight of Gluck's little yellow head jammed in the window, with its mouth and eyes very wide open indeed.

"Hollo!" said the little gentleman, "that's not the way to answer the door: I'm wet, let me in."

To do the little gentleman justice, he *was* wet. His feather hung down between his legs like a beaten puppy's tail, dripping like an umbrella; and from the ends of his moustaches the water was running into his waistcoat pockets, and out again like a mill stream.

"I beg pardon, sir," said Gluck, "I'm very sorry, but I really can't."

"Can't what?" said the old gentleman.

"I can't let you in, sir,—I can't indeed; my brothers would beat me to death, sir, if I thought of such a thing. What do you want, sir?"

"Want?" said the old gentleman, petulantly. "I want fire, and shelter; and there's your great fire there blazing, crackling, and dancing on the walls, with nobody to feel it. Let me in, I say; I only want to warm myself."

Gluck had had his head, by this time, so long out of the window, that he began to feel it was really unpleasantly cold, and when he turned, and saw the beautiful fire rustling and roaring, and throwing long bright tongues up the chimney, as if it were licking its chops at the savoury smell of the leg of mutton, his heart melted within him that it should be burning away for nothing. "He does look *very* wet," said little Gluck; "I'll just let him in for a quarter of an hour." Round he went to the door, and opened it; and as the little gentleman walked in, there came a gust of wind through the house, that made the old chimneys totter.

"That's a good boy," said the little gentleman. "Never mind your brothers. I'll talk to them."

"Pray, sir, don't do any such thing," said Gluck. "I can't let you stay here till they come; they'd be the death of me."

"Dear me," said the old gentleman, "I'm very sorry to hear that. How long may I stay?"

"Only till the mutton's done, sir," replied Gluck, "and it's very brown."

Then the old gentleman walked into the kitchen, and sat himself down on the hob, with the top of his cap accommodated up the chimney, for it was a great deal too high for the roof.

"You'll soon dry there, sir," said Gluck, and sat down again to turn the mutton. But the old gentleman did *not* dry there, but went on drip, drip, dripping among the cinders, and the fire fizzed, and sputtered, and began to look very black, and uncomfortable; never was such a cloak; every fold in it ran like a gutter.

"I beg pardon, sir," said Gluck at length, after watching the water spreading in long, quicksilver-like streams over the floor for a quarter of an hour; "mayn't I take your cloak?"

"No, thank you," said the old gentleman.

"Your cap, sir?"

"I am all right, thank you" said the old gentleman rather gruffly.

"But,—sir,—I'm very sorry," said Gluck, hesitatingly, "but—really, sir—you're—putting the fire out."

"It'll take longer to do the mutton, then," replied his visitor drily.

Gluck was very much puzzled by the behaviour of his guest; it was such a strange mixture of coolness and humility. He turned away at the string meditatively for another five minutes.

"That mutton looks very nice," said the old gentleman at length. "Can't you give me a little bit?"

"Impossible, sir," said Gluck.

"I'm very hungry," continued the old gentleman: "I've had nothing to eat yesterday, nor to-day. They surely couldn't miss a bit from the knuckle!"

He spoke in so very melancholy a tone, that it quite melted Gluck's heart. "They promised me one slice to-day, sir," said he; "I can give you that, but not a bit more."

"That's a good boy," said the old gentleman again.

Then Gluck warmed a plate, and sharpened a knife. "I don't care if I do get beaten for it," thought he. Just as he had cut a large slice out of the mutton, there came a tremendous rap at the door. The old gentleman jumped off the hob, as if it had suddenly become inconveniently warm. Gluck fitted the slice into the mutton again, with desperate efforts at exactitude, and ran to open the door.

"What did you keep us waiting in the rain for?" said Schwartz, as he walked in, throwing his umbrella in Gluck's face. "Ay! what for, indeed, you little vagabond?" said Hans, administering an educational box on the ear, as he followed his brother into the kitchen.

"Bless my soul!" said Schwartz when he opened the door.

"Amen," said the little gentleman, who had taken his cap off, and was standing in the middle of the kitchen, bowing with the utmost possible velocity.

"Who's that?" said Schwartz, catching up a rolling-pin, and turning to Gluck with a fierce frown.

"I don't know, indeed, brother," said Gluck in great terror.

"How did he get in?" roared Schwartz.

"My dear brother," said Gluck, deprecatingly, "he was so *very* wet!"

The rolling-pin was descending on Gluck's head; but, at the instant, the old gentleman interposed his conical cap, on which it crashed with a

"'You'll soon dry there, sir,' said Gluck."

RICHARD DOYLE

shock that shook the water out of it all over the room. What was very odd, the rolling-pin no sooner touched the cap, than it flew out of Schwartz's hand, spinning like a straw in a high wind, and fell into the corner at the further end of the room.

"Who are you, sir?" demanded Schwartz, turning upon him.

"What's your business?" snarled Hans.

"I'm a poor old man, sir," the little gentleman began very modestly, "and I saw your fire through the window, and begged shelter for a quarter of an hour."

"Have the goodness to walk out again, then," said Schwartz. "We've quite enough water in our kitchen, without making it a drying-house."

"It is a cold day to turn an old man out in, sir; look at my grey hairs." They hung down to his shoulders, as I told you before.

"Ay!" said Hans, "there are enough of them to keep you warm. Walk!"

"I'm very, very hungry, sir; couldn't you spare me a bit of bread before I go?"

"Bread, indeed!" said Schwartz; "do you suppose we've nothing to do with our bread but to give it to such red-nosed fellows as you?"

"Why don't you sell your feather?" said Hans, sneeringly. "Out with you!"

"A little bit," said the old gentleman.

"Be off!" said Schwartz.

"Pray, gentlemen——"

"Off, and be hanged!" cried Hans, seizing him by the collar. But he had no sooner touched the old gentleman's collar, than away he went after the rolling-pin, spinning round and round, till he fell into the corner on the top of it. Then Schwartz was very angry, and ran at the old gentleman to turn him out; but he also had hardly touched him, when away he went against the wall as he tumbled into the corner. And so there they lay, all three.

Then the old gentleman spun himself round with velocity in the opposite direction; continued to spin until his long cloak was all wound neatly about him; clapped his cap on his head, very much on one side (for it could not stand upright without going through the ceiling), gave an additional twist to his corkscrew moustaches, and replied with perfect coolness: "Gentlemen, I wish you a very good morning. At twelve o'clock to-night I'll call again; after such a refusal of hospitality as I have just experienced, you will not be surprised if that visit is the last I ever pay you."

"If I ever catch you here again," muttered Schwartz, coming, half-frightened, out of the corner—but, before he could finish his sentence, the old gentleman had shut the house door behind him with a great bang: and there drove past the window, at the same instant, a wreath of ragged cloud, that whirled and rolled away down the valley in all manner of shapes; turning over and over in the air, and melting away at last in a gush of rain.

"A very pretty business, indeed, Mr. Gluck!" said Schwartz. "Dish the mutton, sir. If ever I catch you at such a trick again—bless me, why, the mutton's been cut!"

"You promised me one slice, brother, you know," said Gluck.

"'Out with you!'"

RICHARD DOYLE

"Oh! and you were cutting it hot, I suppose, and going to catch all the gravy. It'll be long before I promise you such a thing again. Leave the room, sir; and have the kindness to wait in the coal-cellar till I call you."

Gluck left the room melancholy enough. The brothers ate as much mutton as they could, locked the rest in the cupboard, and proceeded to get very drunk after dinner.

Such a night as it was! Howling wind, and rushing rain, without intermission. The brothers had just sense enough left to put up all the shutters, and double bar the door, before they went to bed. They usually slept in the same room. As the clock struck twelve, they were both awakened by a tremendous crash. Their door burst open with a violence that shook the house from top to bottom.

"What's that?" cried Schwartz, starting up in his bed.

"Only I," said the little gentleman.

The two brothers sat up on their bolster, and stared into the darkness. The room was full of water, and by a misty moonbeam, which found its way through a hole in the shutter, they could see in the midst of it an enormous foam globe, spinning round, and bobbing up and down like a cork, on which, as on a most luxurious cushion, reclined the little old gentleman, cap and all. There was plenty of room for it now, for the roof was off.

"Sorry to incommode you," said their visitor ironically. "I'm afraid your beds are dampish; perhaps you had better go to your brother's room: I've left the ceiling on, there."

They required no second admonition, but rushed into Gluck's room, wet through, and in an agony of terror.

"You'll find my card on the kitchen table," the old gentleman called after them. "Remember, the *last* visit."

"Pray Heaven it may!" said Schwartz, shuddering. And the foam globe disappeared.

Dawn came at last, and the two brothers looked out of Gluck's little window in the morning. The Treasure Valley was one mass of ruin and desolation. The inundation had swept away trees, crops, and cattle, and left in their stead a waste of red sand and grey mud. The two brothers crept shivering and horror-struck into the kitchen. The water had gutted the whole first floor; corn, money, almost every movable thing had been swept away, and there was only a small white card on the kitchen table. On it, in large, breezy, long-legged letters, were engraved the words:—

CHAPTER II

Of the Proceedings of the Three Brothers after the Visit of South-West Wind, Esquire; and How Little Gluck Had an Interview with the King of the Golden River

SOUTH-WEST WIND, Esquire, was as good as his word. After the momentous visit above related, he entered the Treasure Valley no more; and, what was worse, he had so much influence with his relations, the West Winds in general, and used it so effectually, that they all adopted a similar line of conduct. So no rain fell in the valley from one year's end to another. Though everything remained green and flourishing in the plains below, the inheritance of the Three Brothers was a desert. What had once been the richest soil in the kingdom, became a shifting heap of red sand; and the brothers, unable longer to contend with the adverse skies, abandoned their valueless patrimony in despair, to seek some means of gaining a livelihood along the cities and people of the plains. All their money was gone, and they had nothing left but some curious old-fashioned pieces of gold plate, the last remnants of their ill-gotten wealth.

"Suppose we turn goldsmiths?" said Schwartz to Hans, as they entered the large city. "It is a good knave's trade; we can put a great deal of copper into the gold, without any one's finding it out."

The thought was agreed to be a very good one; they hired a furnace, and turned goldsmiths. But two slight circumstances affected their trade: the first, that people did not approve of the coppered gold; the second, that the two elder brothers, whenever they had sold anything, used to leave little Gluck to mind the furnace, and go and drink out the money in the ale-house next door. So they melted all their gold, without making enough money to buy more, and were at last reduced to one large drinking mug, which an uncle of his had given to little Gluck, and which he was very fond it, and would not have parted with for the world; though he never drank anything out of it but milk and water. The mug was a very odd mug to look at. The handle was formed of two wreaths of flowing golden hair, so finely spun that it looked more like silk than metal, and these wreaths descended into, and mixed with, a beard and whiskers of the same exquisite workmanship, which surrounded and decorated a very fierce little face, of the reddest gold imaginable, right in the front of the mug, with a pair of eyes in it which seemed to command its whole circumference. It was impossible to drink out of the mug without being subjected to an intense gaze out of the side of these eyes; and Schwartz positively averred, that once, after emptying it, full of Rhenish, seventeen times, he had seen them wink! When it came to the mug's turn to be made into spoons, it half broke poor little Gluck's heart; but the brothers only laughed at him, tossed the mug into the melting-pot, and staggered out to the ale-house: leaving him, as usual, to pour the gold into bars, when it was all ready.

When they were gone, Gluck took a farewell look at his old friend in the melting-pot. The flowing hair was all gone; nothing remained but the red nose, and the sparkling eyes, which looked more malicious than ever. "And no wonder," thought Gluck, "after being treated in that way." He sauntered disconsolately to the window, and sat himself down to catch the fresh evening air, and escape the hot breath of the furnace. Now this window commanded a direct view of the range of mountains, which, as I told you before, overhung the Treasure Valley, and more especially of the peak from which fell the Golden River. It was just at the close of the day, and when Gluck sat down at the window, he saw the rocks of the mountain tops, all crimson, and purple with the sunset; and there were bright tongues of fiery cloud burning and quivering about them; and the river, brighter than all, fell, in a waving column of pure gold, from precipice to precipice, with the double arch of a broad purple rainbow stretched across it, flushing and fading alternately in the wreaths of spray.

"Ah!" said Gluck aloud, after he had looked at if for a while, "if that river were really all gold, what a nice thing it would be."

"No it wouldn't, Gluck," said a clear metallic voice, close as his ear.

"Bless me! what's that?" exclaimed Gluck, jumping up. There was nobody there. He looked round the room, and under the table, and a great many times behind him, but there was certainly nobody there, and he sat down again at the window. This time he didn't speak, but he couldn't help thinking again that it would be very convenient if the river were really all gold.

"Not at all, my boy," said the same voice, louder than before.

"Bless me!" said Gluck again, "what *is* that?" He looked again into all the corners and cupboards, and then began turning round, and round, as fast as he could in the middle of the room, thinking there was somebody behind him, when the same voice struck again on his ear. It was singing now very merrily. "Lala-lira-la;" no words, only a soft running effervescent melody, something like that of a kettle on the boil. Gluck looked out of the window. No, it was certainly in the house. Upstairs, and downstairs. No, it was certainly in that very room, coming in quicker time, and clearer notes, every moment. "Lala-lira-la." All at once it struck Gluck that it sounded louder and louder near the furnace. He ran to the opening, and looked in: yes, he saw right, it seemed to be coming, not only out of the furnace, but out of the pot. He uncovered it, and ran back in a great fright, for the pot was certainly singing! He stood in the farthest corner of the room, with his hands up, and his mouth open, for a minute or two, when the singing stopped, and the voice became clear, and pronunciative.

"Hollo!" said the voice.

Gluck made no answer.

"Hollo! Gluck, my boy," said the pot again.

Gluck summoned all his energies, walked straight up to the crucible, drew it out of the furnace, and looked in. The gold was all melted, and its surface as smooth and polished as a river; but instead of reflecting little Gluck's head, as he looked in, he saw meeting his glance from beneath the gold the red nose and sharp eyes of his old friend of the mug, a thousand times redder and sharper than ever he had seen them in his life.

"The two elder brothers . . . used to leave little Gluck to
mind the furnace, and go and drink out the money in the
ale-house next door."

RICHARD DOYLE

"Come, Gluck, my boy," said the voice out of the pot again, "I'm all right; pour me out."

But Gluck was too much astonished to do anything of the kind.

"Pour me out, I say," said the voice rather gruffly.

Still Gluck couldn't move.

"Will you pour me out?" said the voice passionately, "I'm too hot."

By a violent effort, Gluck recovered the use of his limbs, took hold of the crucible, and sloped it so as to pour out the gold. But instead of a liquid stream, there came out, first a pair of pretty little yellow legs, then some coat tails, then a pair of arms stuck a-kimbo, and, finally, the well-known head of his friend the mug; all which articles, uniting as they rolled out, stood up energetically on the floor, in the shape of a little golden dwarf, about a foot and a half high.

"That's right!" said the dwarf, stretching out first his legs, and then his arms, and then shaking his head up and down, and as far round as it would go, for five minutes, without stopping; apparently with the view of ascertaining if he were quite correctly put together, while Gluck stood contemplating him in speechless amazement. He was dressed in a slashed doublet of spun gold, so fine in its texture, that the prismatic colours gleamed over it, as if on a surface of mother of pearl; and, over this brilliant doublet, his hair and beard fell full halfway to the gound, in waving curls, so exquisitely delicate, that Gluck could hardly tell where they ended; they seemed to melt into air. The features of the face, however, were by no means finished with the same delicacy; they were rather coarse, slightly inclining to coppery in complexion, and indicative, in expression, of a very pertinacious and intractable disposition in their small proprietor. When the dwarf had finished his self-examination, he turned his small sharp eyes full on Gluck, and stared at him deliberately for a minute or two. "No, it wouldn't, Gluck, my boy," said the little man.

This was certainly rather an abrupt and unconnected mode of commencing conversation. It might indeed be supposed to refer to the course of Gluck's thoughts, which had first produced the dwarf's observations out of the pot; but whatever it referred to, Gluck had no inclination to dispute the dictum.

"Wouldn't it, sir?" said Gluck, very mildly and submissively indeed.

"No," said the dwarf, conclusively. "No, it wouldn't." And with that, the dwarf pulled his cap hard over his brows, and took two turns, of three feet long, up and down the room, lifting his legs up very high, and setting them down very hard. This pause gave time for Gluck to collect his thoughts a little, and, seeing no great reason to view his diminutive visitor with dread, and feeling his curiosity overcome his amazement, he ventured on a question of peculiar delicacy.

"Pray, sir," said Gluck, rather hesitatingly, "were you my mug?"

On which the little man turned sharp round, walked straight up to Gluck, and drew himself up to his full height. "I," said the little man, "am the King of the Golden River." Whereupon he turned about again, and took two more turns, some six feet long, in order to allow time for the consternation which this announcement produced in his auditor to evaporate. After which, he again walked up to Gluck and stood still, as if expecting some comment on his communication.

"Gluck stood contemplating him in speechless
amazement."

RICHARD DOYLE

Gluck determined to say something at all events. "I hope your Majesty is very well," said Gluck.

"Listen!" said the little man, deigning no reply to this polite inquiry. "I am the King of what you mortals call the Golden River. The shape you saw me in was owing to the malice of a stronger king, from whose enchantments you have this instant freed me. What I have seen of you, and your conduct to your wicked brothers, renders me willing to serve you; therefore, attend to what I tell you. Whoever shall climb to the top of that mountain from which you see the Golden River issue, and shall cast into the stream at its source three drops of holy water, for him, and for him only, the river shall turn to gold. But no one failing in his first, can succeed in a second attempt; and if any one shall cast unholy water into the river, it will overwhelm him, and he will become a black stone." So saying, the King of the Golden River turned away and deliberately walked into the centre of the hottest flame of the furnace. His figure became red, white, transparent, dazzling,—a blaze of intense light— rose, trembled, and disappeared. The King of the Golden River had evaporated.

"Oh!" cried poor Gluck, running to look up the chimney after him; "oh dear, dear, dear me! My mug! my mug! my mug!"

CHAPTER III

How Mr. Hans Set Off on an Expedition to the Golden River, and How He Prospered Therein

THE KING OF the Golden River had hardly made the extraordinary exit related in the last chapter, before Hans and Schwartz came roaring into the house, very savagely drunk. The discovery of the total loss of their last piece of plate had the effect of sobering them just enough to enable them to stand over Gluck, beating him very steadily for a quarter of an hour; at the expiration of which period they dropped into a couple of chairs, and requested to know what he had got to say for himself. Gluck told them his story, of which, of course, they did not believe a word. They beat him again, till their arms were tired, and staggered to bed. In the morning, however, the steadiness with which he adhered to his story obtained him some degree of credence; the immediate consequence of which was, that the two brothers, after wrangling a long time on the knotty question, which of them should try his fortune first, drew their swords and began fighting. The noise of the fray alarmed the neighbours, who finding they could not pacify the combatants, sent for the constable.

Hans, on hearing this, contrived to escape, and hid himself; but Schwartz was taken before the magistrate, fined for breaking the peace, and, having drunk out his last penny the evening before, was thrown into prison till he should pay.

When Hans heard this, he was much delighted, and determined to set out immediately for the Golden River. How to get the holy water was the question. He went to the priest, but the priest could not give any holy water to so abandoned a character. So Hans went to vespers in the evening for the first time in his life, and, under pretence of crossing himself, stole a cupful, and returned home in triumph.

Next morning he got up before the sun rose, put the holy water into a strong flask, and two bottles of wine and some meat in a basket, slung them over his back, took his alpine staff in his hand, and set off for the mountains.

On his way out of the town he had to pass the prison, and as he looked in at the windows, whom should he see but Schwartz himself peeping out of the bars, and looking very disconsolate.

"Good morning, brother," said Hans; "have you any message for the King of the Golden River?"

Schwartz gnashed his teeth with rage, and shook the bars with all his strength; but Hans only laughed at him, and advising him to make himself comfortable till he came back again, shouldered his basket, shook the bottle of holy water in Schwartz's face till it frothed again, and marched off in the highest spirits in the world.

It was, indeed, a morning that might have made any one happy, even with no Golden River to seek for. Level lines of dewy mist lay stretched along the valley, out of which rose the massy mountains—their lower cliffs in pale grey shadow, hardly distinguishable from the floating vapour, but gradually ascending till they caught the sunlight, which ran in sharp touches of ruddy colour along the angular crags, and pierced, in long level rays, through their fringes of spear-like pine. Far above, shot up red splintered masses of castellated rock, jagged and shivered into myriads of fantastic forms, with here and there a streak of sunlit snow, traced down their chasms like a line of forged lightning; and, far beyond, and far above all these, fainter than the morning cloud, but purer and changeless, slept, in the blue sky, the utmost peaks of the eternal snow.

The Golden River, which sprang from one of the lower and snowless elevations, was now nearly in shadow; all but the uppermost jets of spray, which rose like snow above the undulating line of the cataract, and floated away in feeble wreaths upon the morning wind.

On this object, and on this alone, Hans' eyes and thoughts were fixed; forgetting the distance he had to traverse, he set off at an imprudent rate of walking, which greatly exhausted him before he had scaled the first range of the green and low hills. He was, moreover, surprised, on surmounting them, to find that a large glacier, of whose existence, notwithstanding his previous knowledge of the mountains, he had been absolutely ignorant, lay between him and the source of the Golden River. He entered on it with the boldness of a practised mountaineer; yet he thought he had never transversed so strange or so dangerous a glacier in his life. The ice was excessively slippery, and out of all its chasms came wild sounds of gushing water; not monotonous or low, but changeful and loud, rising occasionally into drifting passages of wild melody, then breaking off into short melancholy tones, or sudden shrieks, resembling those of human voices in distress or pain. The ice was broken into thousands of confused shapes, but none, Hans thought, like the ordinary forms of splintered ice. There seemed a curious *expression* about all their outlines—a perpetual resemblance to living features, distorted and scornful. Myriads of deceitful shadows, and lurid lights, played and floated about and through the pale blue pinnacles, dazzling and confusing the sight of the traveller; while his ears grew dull and his head giddy with the constant gush and roar of the concealed waters. These painful circumstances increased upon him as he advanced; the ice crashed and yawned into fresh chasms at his feet, tottering spires nodded around him, and fell thundering across his path; and though he had repeatedly faced these dangers on the most terrific glaciers, and in the wildest weather, it was with a new and oppressive feeling of panic terror that he leaped the last chasm, and flung himself, exhausted and shuddering, on the firm turf of the mountain.

He had been compelled to abandon his basket of food, which became a perilous incumbrance on the glacier, and had now no means of refreshing himself but by breaking off and eating some of the pieces of ice. This, however, relieved his thirst; an hour's repose recruited his hardy frame, and with the indomitable spirit of avarice, he resumed his laborious journey.

His way now lay straight up a ridge of bare red rocks, without a blade of grass to ease the foot, or a projecting angle to afford an inch of shade from the south sun. It was past noon, and the rays beat intensely upon the steep path, while the whole atmosphere was motionless, and penetrated with heat. Intense thirst was soon added to the bodily fatigue with which Hans was now afflicted; glance after glance he cast on the flask of water which hung at his belt. "Three drops are enough," at last thought he; "I may, at least, cool my lips with it."

He opened the flask, and was raising it to his lips, when his eye fell on an object lying on the rock beside him; he thought it moved. It was a small dog, apparently in the last agony of death from thirst. Its tongue was out, its jaws dry, its limbs extended lifelessly, and a swarm of black ants were crawling about its lips and throat. Its eye moved to the bottle which Hans held in his hand. He raised it, drank, spurned the animal with his foot, and passed on. And he did not know how it was, but he thought that a strange shadow had suddenly come across the blue sky.

The path became steeper and more rugged every moment; and the high hill air, instead of refreshing him, seemed to throw his blood into a fever. The noise of the hill cataracts sounded like mockery in his ears; they were all distant, and his thirst increased every moment. Another hour passed, and he again looked down to the flask at his side; it was half empty; but there was much more than three drops in it. He stopped to open it, and again, as he did so, something moved in the path above him. It was a fair child, stretched nearly lifeless on the rock, its breast heaving with thirst, its eyes closed, and its lips parched and burning. Hans eyed it deliberately, drank, and passed on. And a dark grey cloud came over the sun, and long, snake-like shadows crept up along the mountain sides. Hans struggled on. The sun was sinking, but its descent seemed to bring no coolness; the leaden weight of the dead air pressed upon his brow and heart, but the goal was near. He saw the cataract of the Golden River springing from the hill-side, scarcely five hundred feet above him. He paused for a moment to breathe, and sprang on to complete his task.

At this instant a faint cry fell on his ear. He turned, and saw a grey-haired old man extended on the rocks. His eyes were sunk, his features deadly pale, and gathered into an expression of despair. "Water!" he stretched his arms to Hans, and cried feebly, "Water! I am dying."

"I have none," replied Hans; "thou hast had thy share of life." He strode over the prostrate body, and darted on. And a flash of blue lightning rose out of the East, shaped like a sword; it shook thrice over the whole heaven, and left it dark with one heavy, impenetrable shade. The sun was setting; it plunged towards the horizon like a red-hot ball.

The roar of the Golden River rose on Hans' ear. He stood at the brink of the chasm through which it ran. Its waves were filled with the red glory of the sunset: they shook their crests like tongues of fire, and flashes of bloody light gleamed along their foam. Their sound came mightier and mightier on his senses; his brain grew giddy with the prolonged thunder. Shuddering he drew the flask from his girdle, and hurled it into the centre of the torrent. As he did so, an icy chill shot through his limbs: he staggered, shrieked, and fell. The waters closed over his cry. And the moaning of the river rose wildly into the night, as it gushed over THE BLACK STONE.

CHAPTER IV

HOW MR. SCHWARTZ SET OFF ON AN EXPEDITION TO THE GOLDEN RIVER, AND HOW HE PROSPERED THEREIN

POOR LITTLE GLUCK waited very anxiously alone in the house for Hans' return. Finding he did not come back, he was terribly frightened, and went and told Schwartz in the prison all that had happened. Then Schwartz was very much pleased, and said that Hans must certainly have been turned into a black stone, and he should have all the gold to himself. But Gluck was very sorry, and cried all night. When he got up in the morning there was no bread in the house, nor any money; so Gluck went and hired himself to another goldsmith, and he worked so hard, and so neatly, and so long every day, that he soon got money enough together to pay his brother's fine, and he went and gave it all to Schwartz, and Schwartz got out of prison. Then Schwartz was quite pleased, and said he should have some of the gold of the river. But Gluck only begged he would go and see what had become of Hans.

Now when Schwartz had heard that Hans had stolen the holy water, he thought to himself that such a proceeding might not be considered altogether correct by the King of the Golden River, and determined to manage matters better. So he took some more of Gluck's money, and went to a bad priest, who gave him some holy water very readily for it. Then Schwartz was sure it was all quite right. So Schwartz got up early in the morning before the sun rose, and took some bread and wine in a basket, and put his holy water in a flask, and set off for the mountains. Like his brother, he was much surprised at the sight of the glacier, and had great difficulty in crossing it, even after leavingg his basket behind him. The day was cloudless, but not bright: there was a heavy purple haze hanging over the sky, and the hills looked lowering and gloomy. And as Schwartz climbed the steep rock path, the thirst came upon him, as it had upon his brother, until he lifted his flask to his lips to drink. Then he saw the fair child lying near him on the rocks, and it cried to him, and moaned for water.

"Water indeed," said Schwartz; "I haven't half enough for myself," and passed on. And as he went he thought the sunbeams grew more dim, and he saw a low bank of black cloud rising out of the West; and, when he had climbed for another hour the thirst overcame him again, and he would have drunk. Then he saw the old man lying before him on the path, and heard him cry out for water. "Water, indeed," said Schwartz, "I haven't half enough for myself," and on he went.

Then again the light seemed to fade from before his eyes, and he looked up, and, behold, a mist, of the colour of blood, had come over the sun; and the bank of black cloud had risen very high, and its edges were tossing and tumbling like the waves of the angry sea. And they cast long shadows, which flickered over Schwartz's path.

Then Schwartz climbed for another hour, and again his thirst returned; and as he lifted his flask to his lips, he thought he saw his brother Hans lying exhausted on the path before him, and, as he gazed, the figure stretched its arms to him, and cried for water. "Ha ha," laughed Schwartz, "are you there? remember the prison bars, my boy. Water, indeed! do you suppose I carried it all the way up here for *you!*" And he strode over the figure; yet, as he passed, he thought he saw a strange expression of mockery about its lips. And, when he had gone a few yards farther, he looked back; but the figure was not there.

And a sudden horror came over Schwartz, he knew not why; but the thirst for gold prevailed over his fear, and he rushed on. And the bank of black cloud rose to the zenith, and out of it came bursts of spiry lightning, and waves of darkness seemed to heave and float between their flashes over the whole heavens. And the sky where the sun was setting was all level, and like a lake of blood; and a strong wind came out of that sky, tearing its crimson clouds into fragments, and scattering them far into the darkness. And when Schwartz stood by the brink of the Golden River, its waves were black, like thunder clouds, but their foam was like fire; and the roar of the waters below, and the thunder above, met, as he cast the flask into the stream. And, as he did so, the lightning glared into his eyes, and the earth gave way beneath him, and the waters closed over his cry. And the moaning of the river rose wildly into the night, as it gushed over the Two Black Stones.

CHAPTER V

How Little Gluck Set Off on an Expedition to the Golden River, and How He Prospered Therein; with Other Matters of Interest

When Gluck found that Schwartz did not come back he was very sorry, and did not know what to do. He had no money, and was obliged to go and hire himself again to the goldsmith, who worked him very hard, and gave him very little money. So, after a month or two, Gluck grew tired, and made up his mind to go and try his fortune with the Golden River. "The little king looked very kind," thought he. "I don't think he will turn me into a black stone." So he went to the priest, and the priest gave him some holy water as soon as he asked for it. Then Gluck took some bread in his basket, and the bottle of water, and set off very early for the mountains.

If the glacier had occasioned a great deal of fatigue to his brothers, it was twenty times worse for him, who was neither so strong nor so practised on the mountains. He had several very bad falls, lost his basket and bread, and was very much frightened at the strange noises under the ice. He lay a long time to rest on the grass, after he had got over, and began to climb the hill just in the hottest part of the day. When he had climbed for an hour, he got dreadfully thirsty, and was going to drink like his brothers, when he saw an old man coming down the path above him, looking very feeble, and leaning on a staff. "My son," said the old man, "I am faint with thirst, give me some of that water." Then Gluck looked at him, and when he saw that he was pale and weary, he gave him the water; "Only pray don't drink it all," said Gluck. But the old man drank a great deal, and gave him back the bottle two-thirds empty. Then he bade him good speed, and Gluck went on again merrily. And the path became easier to his feet, and two or three blades of grass appeared upon it, and some grasshoppers began singing on the bank beside it; and Gluck thought he had never heard such merry singing.

Then he went on for another hour, and the thirst increased on him so that he thought he should be forced to drink. But, as he raised the flask, he saw a little child lying panting by the roadside, and it cried out piteously for water. Then Gluck struggled with himself, and determined to bear the thirst a little longer; and he put the bottle to the child's lips, and it drank it all but a few drops. Then it smiled on him, and got up, and ran down the hill; and Gluck looked after it, till it became as small as a little star, and then turned and began climbing again. And then there were all kinds of sweet flowers growing on the rocks, bright green moss, with pale pink starry flowers, and soft belled gentians, more blue than the sky at its deepest, and pure white transparent lilies. And crimson and purple butterflies darted hither and thither, and the sky sent down such pure light, that Gluck had never felt so happy in his life.

Yet, when he had climbed for another hour, his thirst became intolerable again; and, when he looked at his bottle, he saw that there were only five or six drops left in it, and he could not venture to drink. And, as he was hanging the flask on his belt again, he saw a little dog lying on the rocks, gasping for breath—just as Hans had seen it on the day of his ascent. And Gluck stopped and looked at it, and then at the Golden River, not five hundred yards above him; and he thought of the dwarf's words, "that no one could succeed, except in his first attempt"; and he tried to pass the dog, but it whined piteously, and Gluck stopped again. "Poor beastie," said Gluck, "it'll be dead when I come down again, if I don't help it." Then he looked closer and closer at it, and its eye turned on him so mournfully, that he could not stand it. "Confound the King and his gold too," said Gluck; and he opened the flask, and poured all the water into the dog's mouth.

The dog sprang up and and stood on its hind legs. Its tail disappeared, its ears became long, longer, silky, golden; its nose became very red, its eyes became very twinkling; in three seconds the dog was gone, and before Gluck stood his old acquaintance, the King of the Golden River.

"Thank you," said the monarch; "but don't be frightened, it's all right"; for Gluck showed manifest symptoms of his consternation at this unlooked-for reply to his last observation. "Why didn't you come before," continued the dwarf, "instead of sending me those rascally brothers of yours, for me to have the trouble of turning into stones? Very hard stones they make too."

"Oh dear me!" said Gluck, "have you really been so cruel?"

"Cruel!" said the dwarf, "they poured unholy water into my stream: do you suppose I'm going to allow that?"

"Why," said Gluck, "I am sure, sir—your majesty, I mean—they got the water out of the church font."

"Very probably," replied the dwarf; "but," and his countenance grew very stern as he spoke, "the water which has been refused to the cry of the weary and dying, is unholy, though it had been blessed by every saint in heaven; and the water which is found in the vessel of mercy is holy, though it had been defiled with corpses."

So saying, the dwarf stopped and plucked a lily that grew at his feet. On its white leaves there hung three drops of clear dew. And the dwarf shook them into the flask which Gluck held in his hand. "Cast these into the river," he said, "and descend on the other side of the mountains into the Treasure Valley. And so good speed."

As he spoke, the figure of the dwarf became indistinct. The playing colours of his robe formed themselves into a prismatic mist of dewy light; he stood for an instant veiled with them as with the belt of a broad rainbow. The colours grew faint, the mist rose into the air; the monarch had evaporated.

And Gluck climbed to the brink of the Golden River, and its waves were as clear as crystal, and as brilliant as the sun. And, when he cast the three drops of dew into the stream, there opened where they fell a small circular whirlpool, into which the waters descended with a musical noise.

Gluck stood watching it for some time, very much disappointed, because not only the river was not turned into gold, but its waters seemed much diminished in quality. Yet he obeyed his friend the dwarf, and descended the other side of the mountains towards the Treasure Valley; and, as he went, he thought he heard the noise of water working its way under the ground. And, when he came in sight of the Treasure Valley, behold, a river, like the Golden River, was springing from a new cleft of the rocks above it, and was flowing in innumerable streams among the dry heaps of red sand.

And as Gluck gazed, fresh grass sprang beside the new streams, and creeping plants grew, and climbed among the moistening soil. Young

"Then it smiled on him, and got up, and ran down the hill."

Richard Doyle

flowers opened suddenly along the river sides, as stars leap out when twilight is deepening, and thickets of myrtle, and tendrils of vine, cast lengthening shadows over the valley as they grew. And thus the Treasure Valley became a garden again, and the inheritance, which had been lost by cruelty, was regained by love.

And Gluck went, and dwelt in the valley, and the poor were never driven from his door: so that his barns became full of corn, and his house of treasure. And, for him, the river had, according to the dwarf's promise, become a River of Gold.

And, to this day, the inhabitants of the valley point out the place where the three drops of holy dew were cast into the stream, and trace the course of the Golden River under the ground, until it emerges in the Treasure Valley. And at the top of the cataract of the Golden River, are still to be seen two BLACK STONES, round which the waters howl mournfully every day at sunset; and these stones are still called by the people of the valley THE BLACK BROTHERS.

Phantastes

A Faerie Romance for Men and Women

Phantastes from "their fount" all shapes deriving,
In new habiliments can quickly dight.
FLETCHER'S *Purple Island*

Es lassen sich Erzählungen ohne Zusammenhang, jedoch mit Association, wie Träume, denken; Gedichte, die bloss wohlklingend und voll schöner Worte sind, aber auch ohne allen Sinn und Zusammenhang, höchstens einzelne Strophen verständlich, wie Bruchstücke aus den verschiedenartigsten Dingen. Diese wahre Poesie kann höchstens einen allegorischen Sinn im Grossen, und eine indirecte Wirkung, wie Musik haben. Darum ist die Natur so rein poetisch, wie die Stube eines Zauberers, eines Physikers, eine Kinderstube, eine Polter-und Vorrathskammer.   *   *

Ein Mährchen ist wie ein Traumbild ohne Zusammenhang. Ein Ensemble wunderbarer Dinge und Begebenheiten, z, B. eine Musikalische Phantasie, die harmonischen Folgen einer Aeolsharfe, die Natur selbst.

    *   *   *   *   *

In einem echten Mährchen muss alles wunderbar, geheimnissvoll und zusammenhängend sein; alles belebt, jeder auf eine andere Art. Die ganze Natur muss wunderlich mit der ganzen Geisterwelt gemischt sein; hier tritt die Zeit der Anarchie, der Gesetzlosigkeit, Freiheit, der Naturstand der Natur, die Zeit vor der Welt ein. . . . Die Welt des Mährchens ist die, der Welt der Wahrheit durchaus entgegengesetzte, und eben darum ihr so durchaus ähnlich, wie das Chaos der vollendeten Schöpfung ähnlich ist.—NOVALIS.

Phantastes

A Faerie Romance for Men and Women

By George MacDonald

In good sooth, my masters, this is no door. Yet is it a little window, that
looketh upon a great world.

"Here it chaunced that upon their quest Sir Galahad and Sir Percivale rencountered in the depths of a great forest."

ARTHUR HUGHES

Phantastes

CHAPTER I

A spirit   *   *   *
*   *   *   *
The undulating woods, and silent well,
And rippling rivulet, and evening gloom,
Now deepening the dark shades, for speech assuming,
Held commune with him; as if he and it
Were all that was.

SHELLEY'S Alastor.

I AWOKE ONE morning with the usual perplexity of mind which accompanies the return of consciousness. As I lay and looked through the eastern window of my room, a faint streak of peach-colour, dividing a cloud that just rose above the low swell of the horizon, announced the approach of the sun. As my thoughts, which a deep and apparently dreamless sleep had dissolved, began again to assume crystalline forms, the strange events of the foregoing night presented themselves anew to my wondering consciousness. The day before had been my one-and-twentieth birthday. Among other ceremonies investing me with my legal rights, the keys of an old secretary, in which my father had kept his private papers, had been delivered up to me. As soon as I was left alone, I ordered lights in the chamber where the secretary stood, the first lights that had been there for many a year; for, since my father's death, the room had been left undisturbed. But, as if the darkness had been too long an inmate to be easily expelled, and had dyed with blackness the walls to which, bat-like, it had clung, these tapers served but ill to light up the gloomy hangings, and seemed to throw yet darker shadows into the hollows of the deep-wrought cornice. All the further portions of the room lay shrouded in a mystery whose deepest folds were gathered around the dark oak cabinet which I now approached with a strange mingling of reverence and curiosity. Perhaps, like a geologist, I was about to turn up to the light some of the buried strata of the human world, with its fossil remains charred by passion and petrified by tears. Perhaps I was to learn how my father, whose personal history was unknown to me, had woven his web of story; how he had found the world, and how the world had left him. Perhaps I was to find only the records of lands and moneys, how gotten and how secured; coming down from strange men, and through troublous times, to me who knew little or nothing of them all.

To solve my speculations, and to dispel the awe which was fast gathering around me as if the dead were drawing near, I approached the secretary; and having found the key that fitted the upper portion, I opened it with some difficulty, drew near it a heavy high-backed chair, and sat down before a multitude of little drawers and slides and pigeon-holes. But the door of a little cupboard in the centre especially attracted my interest, as if there lay the secret of this long hidden world. Its key I found. One of the rusty hinges cracked and broke as I opened the door: it revealed a number of small pigeon-holes. These, however, being but shallow compared with the depth of those around the little cupboard, the outer ones reaching to the back of the desk, I concluded that there must be some accessible space behind; and found, indeed, that they were formed in a separate framework, which admitted of the whole being pulled out in one piece. Behind, I found a sort of flexible portcullis of small bars of wood laid close together horizontally. After long search, and trying many ways to move it, I discovered at last a scarcely projecting point of steel on one side. I pressed this repeatedly and hard with the point of an old tool that was lying near, till at length it yielded inwards; and the little slide, flying up suddenly, disclosed a chamber—empty, except that in one corner lay a little heap of withered rose-leaves, whose long-lived scent had long since departed; and, in another, a small packet of papers, tied with a bit of ribbon, whose colour had gone with the rose-scent. Almost fearing to touch them, they witnessed so mutely to the law of oblivion, I leaned back in my chair, and regarded them for a moment; when suddenly there stood on the threshold of the little chamber, as though she had just emerged from its depth, a tiny woman-form, as perfect in shape as if she had been a small Greek statuette roused to life and motion. Her dress was of a kind that could never grow old-fashioned, because it was simply natural: a robe plaited in a band around the neck, and confined by a belt about the waist, descended to her feet. It was only afterwards, however, that I took notice of her dress, although my surprise was by no means of so overpowering a degree as such an apparition might naturally be expected to excite. Seeing, however, as I suppose, some astonishment in my countenance, she came forward within a yard of me, and said, in a voice that strangely recalled a sensation of twilight, and reedy river banks, and a low wind, even in this deathly room,

"Anodos, you never saw such a little creature before, did you?"

"No," said I; "and indeed I hardly believe I do now."

"Ah! that is always the way with you men; you believe nothing the first time; and it is foolish enough to let mere repetition convince you of what you consider in itself unbelievable. I am not going to argue with you, however, but to grant you a wish."

Here I could not help interrupting her with the foolish speech, of which, however, I had no cause to repent:

"How can such a very little creature as you grant or refuse anything?"

"Is that all the philosophy you have gained in one-and twenty years?" said she. "Form is much, but size is nothing. It is a mere matter of relation. I suppose your six-foot lordship does not feel altogether insignificant, though to others you do look small beside your old Uncle Ralph, who rises above you a great half-foot at least. But size is of so little consequence with me, that I may as well accommodate myself to your foolish prejudices."

So saying, she leapt from the desk upon the floor; where she stood a tall, gracious lady, with pale face and large blue eyes. Her dark hair flowed behind, wavy but uncurled, down to her waist, and against it her form stood clear in its robe of white.

"Now," said she, "you will believe me."

Overcome with the presence of a beauty which I could now perceive, and drawn towards her by an attraction irresistible as incomprehensible, I suppose I stretched out my arms towards her, for she drew back a step or two, and said:

"Foolish boy, if you could touch me, I should hurt you. Besides, I was two hundred and thirty-seven years old, last Midsummer eve; and a man must not fall in love with his grandmother, you know."

"But you are not my grandmother," said I.

"How do you know that?" she retorted. "I dare say you know something of your great grandfathers a good deal further back than that; but you know very little about your great grandmothers on either side. Now, to the point. Your little sister was reading a fairy-tale to you last night."

"She was."

"When she had finished, she said, as she closed the book, 'Is there a fairy-country, brother?' You replied with a sigh, 'I suppose there is, if one could find the way into it.'"

"I did; but I meant something quite different from what you seem to think."

"Never mind what I seem to think. You shall find the way into Fairy Land to-morrow. Now look in my eyes."

Eagerly I did so. They filled me with an unknown longing. I remembered somehow that my mother died when I was a baby. I looked deeper and deeper, till they spread around me like seas, and I sank in their waters. I forgot all the rest, till I found myself at the window, whose gloomy curtains were withdrawn, and where I stood gazing on a whole heaven of stars, small and sparkling in the moonlight. Below lay a sea, still as death and hoary in the moon, sweeping into bays and around capes and islands, away, away, I knew not whither. Alas! it was no sea, but a low fog burnished by the moon. "Surely there is such a sea somewhere!" said I to myself. A low sweet voice beside me replied—

"In Fairy Land, Anodos."

I turned, but saw no one. I closed the secretary, and went to my own room, and to bed.

All this I recalled as I lay with half-closed eyes. I was soon to find the truth of the lady's promise that this day I should discover the road into Fairy Land.

CHAPTER II

"Wo ist der Strom?" rief er mit Thränen. "Siehst du nicht seine blauen Wellen
über uns?" Er sah hinauf, und der blaue Strom floss leise über ihrem
Haupte.—NOVALIS. *Heinrich von Ofterdingen.*

"Where is the stream?" cried he, with tears. "Seest thou not its blue waves above
us?" He looked up, and lo! the blue stream was flowing gently over their
heads.

WHILE THESE STRANGE events were passing through my mind, I
suddenly, as one awakes to the consciousness that the sea has been
moaning by him for hours, or that the storm has been howling about his
window all night, became aware of the sound of running water near
me; and looking out of bed, I saw that a large green marble basin, in
which I was wont to wash, and which stood on a low pedestal of the
same material in a corner of my room, was overflowing like a spring;
and that a stream of clear water was running over the carpet, all the
length of the room, finding its outlet I knew not where. And, stranger
still, where this carpet, which I had myself designed to imitate a field of
grass and daisies, bordered the course of the little stream, the grass-
blades and daisies seemed to wave in a tiny breeze that followed the
water's flow; while under the rivulet they bent and swayed with every
motion of the changeful current, as if they were about to dissolve with
it, and, forsaking their fixed form, become fluent as the waters.

My dressing-table was an old-fashioned piece of furniture of black
oak, with drawers all down the front. These were elaborately carved in
foliage, of which ivy formed the chief part. The nearer end of this table
remained just as it had been, but on the further end a singular change
had commenced. I happened to fix my eye on a little cluster of ivy-
leaves. The first of these was evidently the work of the carver; the next
looked curious; the third was unmistakeable ivy; and just beyond it a
tendril of clematis had twined itself about the gilt handle of one of the
drawers. Hearing next a slight motion above me, I looked up, and saw
that the branches and leaves designed upon the curtains of my bed
were slightly in motion. Not knowing what change might follow next, I
thought it high time to get up; and, springing from the bed, my bare
feet alighted upon a cool green sward; and although I dressed in all
haste, I found myself completing my toilet under the boughs of a great
tree, whose top waved in the golden stream of the sunrise with many
interchanging lights, and with shadows of leaf and branch gliding over
leaf and branch, as the cool morning wind swung it to and fro, like a
sinking sea-wave.

After washing as well as I could in the clear stream, I rose and looked
around me. The tree under which I seemed to have lain all night, was
one of the advanced guard of a dense forest, towards which the rivulet
ran. Faint traces of a footpath, much overgrown with grass and moss,
and with here and there a pimpernel even, were discernible along the
right bank. "This," thought I, "must surely be the path into Fairy Land,
which the lady of last night promised I should so soon find." I crossed

the rivulet, and accompanied it, keeping the footpath on its right bank, until it led me, as I expected, into the wood. Here I left it, without any good reason, and with a vague feeling that I ought to have followed its course: I took a more southerly direction.

CHAPTER III

Man doth usurp all space,
Stares thee, in rock, bush, river, in the face.
Never yet thine eyes behold a tree;
'Tis no sea thou seest in the sea,
'Tis but a disguised humanity.
To avoid thy fellow, vain thy plan;
All that interests a man, is man."
HENRY SUTTON.

THE TREES, WHICH were far apart where I entered, giving free passage to the level rays of the sun, closed rapidly as I advanced, so that ere long their crowded stems barred the sunlight out, forming as it were a thick grating betwccn me and the East. I seemed to be advancing towards a second midnight. In the midst of the intervening twilight, however, before I entered what appeared to be the darkest portion of the forest, I saw a country maiden coming towards me from its very depths. She did not seem to observe me, for she was apparently intent upon a bunch of wild flowers which she carried in her hand. I could hardly see her face; for, though she came right towards me, she never looked up. But when we met, instead of passing, she turned and walked alongside of me for a few yards, still keeping her face downwards, and busied with her flowers. She spoke rapidly, however, all the time, in a low tone, as if talking to herself, but evidently addressing the purport of her words to me. She seemed afraid of being observed by some lurking foe. "Trust the Oak," said she; "trust the Oak, and the Elm, and the great Beech. Take care of the Birch, for though she is honest, she is too young not to be changeable. But shun the Ash and the Alder; for the Ash is an ogre—you will know him by his thick fingers; and the Alder will smother you with her web of hair, if you let her near you at night." All this was uttered without pause or alteration of tone. Then she turned suddenly and left me, walking still with the same unchanging gait. I could not conjecture what she meant, but satisfied myself with thinking that it would be time enough to find out her meaning when there was need to make use of her warning; and that the occasion would reveal the admonition. I concluded from the flowers that she carried, that the forest could not be everywhere so dense as it appeared from where I was now walking; and I was right in this conclusion. For soon I came to a more open part, and by and by crossed a wide grassy glade, on which were several circles of brighter green. But even here I was struck with the utter stillness. No bird sang. No insect hummed. Not a living creature crossed my way. Yet somehow the whole environment seemed only asleep, and to wear even in sleep an air of expectation. The trees seemed all to have an expression of conscious mystery, as if they said to themselves, "We could, an' if we would." They had all a meaning look about them. Then I remembered that night is the fairies' day, and the moon their sun; and I thought—Everything sleeps and dreams now: when the night comes, it will be different. At the same time I, being a man and a child of the day, felt some anxiety as to how I should fare among the elves and other children of the night who wake when mortals dream, and find their common life in those wondrous hours that flow noiselessly over the moveless death-like forms of men and women and children, lying strewn and parted beneath the weight of the heavy waves of night, which flow on and beat them down, and hold them drowned and senseless, until the ebb-tide comes, and the waves sink away, back into the ocean of the dark. But I took courage and went on. Soon, however, I became again anxious, though from another cause. I had eaten nothing that day, and for an hour past had been feeling the want of food. So I grew afraid lest I should find nothing to meet my human necessities in this strange place; but once more I comforted myself with hope and went on.

Before noon, I fancied I saw a thin blue smoke rising amongst the stems of larger trees in front of me; and soon I came to an open spot of ground in which stood a little cottage, so built that the stems of four great trees formed its corners, while their branches met and intertwined over its roof, heaping a great cloud of leaves over it, up towards the heavens. I wondered at finding a human dwelling in this neighbourhood; and yet it did not look altogether human, though sufficiently so to encourage me to expect some sort of food. Seeing no door, I went round to the other side, and there I found one, wide open. A woman sat beside it, preparing some vegetables for dinner. This was homely and comforting. As I came near, she looked up, and seeing me, showed no surprise, but bent her head again over her work, and said in a low tone:

"Did you see my daughter?"

"I believe I did," said I. "Can you give me something to eat, for I am very hungry."

"With pleasure," she replied, in the same tone; "but do not say anything more, till you come into the house, for the Ash is watching us."

Having said this, she rose and led the way into the cottage; which, I now saw, was built of the stems of small trees set closely together, and was furnished with rough chairs and tables, from which even the bark had not been removed. As soon as she had shut the door and set a chair:

"You have fairy blood in you," said she, looking hard at me.

"How do you know that?"

"You could not have got so far into this wood if it were not so; and I am trying to find out some trace of it in your countenance. I think I see it."

"What do you see?"

"Oh, never mind: I may be mistaken in that."

"But how then do you come to live here?"

"Because I too have fairy-blood in me."

Here I, in my turn, looked hard at her; and thought I could perceive, notwithstanding the coarseness of her features, and especially the heaviness of her eyebrows, a something unusual—I could hardly call it grace, and yet it was an expression that strangely contrasted with the form of her features. I noticed too that her hands were delicately formed, though brown with work and exposure.

"I should be ill," she continued, "if I did not live on the borders of the fairies' country, and now and then eat of their food. And I see by your eyes that you are not quite free of the same need; though, from your education and the activity of your mind, you have felt it less than I. You may be further removed too from the fairy race."

I remembered what the lady had said about my grandmothers.

Here she placed some bread and some milk before me, with a kindly apology for the homeliness of the fare, with which, however, I was in no humour to quarrel. I now thought it time to try to get some explanation of the strange words both of her daughter and herself.

"What did you mean by speaking so about the Ash?"

She rose and looked out of the little window. My eyes followed her; but as the window was too small to allow anything to be seen from where I was sitting, I rose and looked over her shoulder. I had just time to see, across the open space, on the edge of the denser forest, a single large ash-tree, whose foliage showed bluish, amidst the truer green of the other trees around it; when she pushed me back with an expression of impatience and terror, and then almost shut out the light from the window by setting up a large old book in it.

"In general," said she, recovering her composure, "there is no danger in the daytime, for then he is sound asleep; but there is something unusual going on in the woods; there must be some solemnity among the fairies to-night, for all the trees are restless, and although they cannot come awake, they see and hear in their sleep."

"But what danger is to be dreaded from him?"

Instead of answering the question, she went again to the window and looked out, saying she feared the fairies would be interrupted by foul weather, for a storm was brewing in the west.

"And the sooner it grows dark, the sooner the Ash will be awake," added she.

I asked her how she knew that there was any unusual excitement in the woods. She replied:

"Besides the look of the trees, the dog there is unhappy; and the eyes and ears of the white rabbit are redder than usual, and he frisks about as if he expected some fun. If the cat were at home, she would have her back up; for the young fairies pull the sparks out of her tail with bramble thorns, and she knows when they are coming. So do I, in another way."

At this instant, a grey cat rushed in like a demon, and disappeared in a hole in the wall.

"There, I told you!" said the woman.

"But what of the ash-tree?" said I, returning once more to the subject. Here, however, the young woman, whom I had met in the morning, entered. A smile passed between the mother and daughter; and then the latter began to help her mother in little household duties.

"I should like to stay here till the evening," I said; "and then go on my journey, if you will allow me."

"You are welcome to do as you please; only it might be better to stay all night, than risk the dangers of the wood then. Where are you going?"

"Nay, that I do not know," I replied; "but I wish to see all that is to be seen, and therefore I should like to start just at sundown."

"You are a bold youth, if you have any idea of what you are daring; but a rash one, if you know nothing about it; and, excuse me, you do not seem very well informed about the country and its manners. However, no one comes here but for some reason, either known to himself or to those who have charge of him; so you shall do just as you wish."

Accordingly I sat down, and feeling rather tired, and disinclined for further talk, I asked leave to look at the old book which still screened the window. The woman brought it to me directly, but not before taking another look towards the forest, and then drawing a white blind over the window. I sat down opposite to it by the table, on which I laid the great old volume, and read. It contained many wondrous tales of Fairy Land, and olden times, and the Knights of King Arthur's table. I read on and on, till the shades of the afternoon began to deepen; for in the midst of the forest it gloomed earlier than in the open country. At length I came to this passage:

"Here it chaunced, that upon their quest, Sir Galahad and Sir Percivale rencountered in the depths of a great forest. Now Sir Galahad was dight all in harness of silver, clear and shining; the which is a delight to look upon, but full hasty to tarnish, and, withouten the labour of a ready squire, uneath to be kept fair and clean. And yet withouten squire or page, Sir Galahad's armour shone like the moon. And he rode a great white mare, whose bases and other housings were black, but all besprent with fair lilys of silver sheen. Whereas Sir Percivale bestrode a red horse, with a tawny mane and tail; whose trappings were all to-smirched with mud and mire; and his armour was wondrous rosty to behold, ne could he by any art furbish it again; so that as the sun in his going down shone twixt the bare trunks of the trees, full upon the knights twain, the one did seem all shining with light, and the other all to glow with ruddy fire. Now it came about in this wise. For Sir Percivale, after his escape from the demon lady, whenas the cross on the handle of his sword smote him to the heart, and he rove himself through the thigh, and escaped away, he came to a great wood; and, in nowise cured of his fault, yet bemoaning the same, the damosel of the alder-tree encountered him, right fair to see; and with her fair words and false countenance she comforted him and beguiled him, until he followed her where she led him to a——"

Here a low hurried cry from my hostess caused me to look up from the book, and I read no more.

"Look there!" she said; "look at his fingers!"

Just as I had been reading in the book, the setting sun was shining through a cleft in the clouds piled up in the west; and a shadow as of a large distorted hand, with thick knobs and humps on the fingers, so that it was much wider across the fingers than across the undivided part of the hand, passed slowly over the little blind, and then as slowly returned in the opposite direction.

"He is almost awake, mother; and greedier than usual to-night."

"Hush, child; you need not make him more angry with us than he is; for you do not know how soon something may happen to oblige us to be in the forest after nightfall."

"But you are in the forest," said I; "how is it that you are safe here?"

"He dares not come nearer than he is now," she replied; "for any of those four oaks, at the corners of our cottage, would tear him to pieces: they are our friends. But he stands there and makes awful faces at us sometimes, and stretches out his long arms and fingers, and tries to kill us with fright; for, indeed, that is his favourite way of doing. Pray, keep out of his way to-night."

"Shall I be able to see these beings?" said I.

"That I cannot tell yet, not knowing how much of the fairy nature there is in you. But we shall soon see whether you can discern the fairies in my little garden, and that will be some guide to us."

"Are the trees fairies too, as well as the flowers?" I asked.

"They are of the same race," she replied; "though those you call fairies in your country are chiefly the young children of the flower fairies. They are very fond of having fun with the thick people, as they call you; for, like most children, they like fun better than anything else."

"Why do you have flowers so near you then? Do they not annoy you?"

"Oh no, they are very amusing, with their mimicries of grown people, and mock solemnities. Sometimes they will act a whole play through before my eyes, with perfect composure and assurance, for they are not afraid of me. Only as soon as they have done, they burst into peals of tiny laughter, as if it were such a joke to have been serious over anything. These I speak of, however, are the fairies of the garden. They are more staid and educated than those of the fields and woods. Of course they have near relations amongst the wild flower, but they patronize them, and treat them as country cousins, who know nothing of life, and very little of manners. Now and then, however, they are compelled to envy the grace and simplicity of the natural flowers."

"Do they live *in* the flowers?" I said.

"I cannot tell," she replied. "There is something in it I do not understand. Sometimes they disappear altogether, even from me, though I know they are near. They seem to die always with the flowers they resemble, and by whose names they are called; but whether they return to life with the fresh flowers, or, whether it be new flowers, new fairies, I cannot tell. They have as many sorts of dispositions as men and women, while their moods are yet more variable: twenty different expressions will cross their little faces in half-a-minute. I often amuse myself with watching them, but I have never been able to make personal acquaintance with any of them. If I speak to one, he or she looks up in my face, as if I were not worth heeding, gives a little laugh, and runs away." Here the woman started, as if suddenly recollecting herself, and said in a low voice to her daughter, "Make haste—go and watch him, and see in what direction he goes."

I may as well mention here, that the conclusion I arrived at from the observations I was afterwards able to make, was, that the flowers die because the fairies go away; not that the fairies disappear because the flowers die. The flowers seem a sort of houses for them, or outer bodies, which they can put on or off when they please. Just as you could form some idea of the nature of a man from the kind of house he built, if he followed his own taste, so you could, without seeing the fairies, tell what any one of them is like, by looking at the flower till you feel that you understand it. For just what the flower says to you, would the face and form of the fairy say; only so much more plainly as a face and human figure can express more than a flower. For the house or the clothes, though like the inhabitant or the wearer, cannot be wrought into an equal power of utterance. Yet you would see a strange resemblance, almost oneness, between the flower and the fairy, which you could not describe, but which described itself to you. Whether all the flowers have fairies, I cannot determine, any more than I can be sure whether all men and women have souls.

The woman and I continued the conversation for a few minutes longer. I was much interested by the information she gave me, and astonished at the language in which she was able to convey it. It seemed that intercourse with the fairies was no bad education in itself. But now the daughter returned with the news, that the Ash had just gone away in a southwesterly direction; and, as my course seemed to lie eastward, she hoped I should be in no danger of meeting him if I departed at once. I looked out of the little window, and there stood the ash-tree, to my eyes the same as before; but I believed that they knew better than I did, and prepared to go. I pulled out my purse, but to my dismay there was nothing in it. The woman with a smile begged me not to trouble myself, for money was not of the slightest use there; and as I might meet with people in my journeys whom I could not recognise to be fairies, it was well I had no money to offer, for nothing offended them so much.

"They would think," she added, "that you were making game of them; and that is their peculiar privilege with regard to us." So we went together into the little garden which sloped down towards a lower part of the wood.

Here, to my great pleasure, all was life and bustle. There was still light enough from the day to see a little; and the pale half-moon, half-way to the zenith, was reviving every moment. The whole garden was like a carnival, with tiny, gaily decorated forms, in groups, assemblies, processions, pairs or trios, moving stately on, running about wildly, or sauntering hither and thither. From the cups or bells of tall flowers, as from balconies, some looked down on the masses below, now bursting with laughter, now grave as owls; but even in their deepest solemnity, seeming only to be waiting for the arrival of the next laugh. Some were launched on a little marshy stream at the bottom, in boats chosen from the heaps of last year's leaves that lay about, curled and withered. These soon sank with them; whereupon they swam ashore and got others.

Those who took fresh rose-leaves for their boats floated the longest; but for these they had to fight; for the fairy of the rose-tree complained bitterly that they were stealing her clothes, and defended her property bravely.

"You can't wear half you've got," said some.

"Never you mind; I don't choose you to have them; they are my property."

"All for the good of the community!" said one, and ran off with a great hollow leaf. But the rose-fairy sprang after him (what a beauty she was! only too like a drawing-room young lady), knocked him heels-over-head as he ran, and recovered her great red leaf. But in the meantime twenty had hurried off in different directions with others just as good; and the little creature sat down and cried, and then, in a pet, sent a perfect pink snow-storm of petals from her tree, leaping from branch to branch, and stamping and shaking and pulling. At last, after another good cry, she chose the biggest she could find, and ran away laughing, to launch her boat amongst the rest.

But my attention was first and chiefly attracted by a group of fairies near the cottage, who were talking together around what seemed a last dying primrose. They talked singing, and their talk made a song, something like this:

> "Sister Snowdrop died
>   Before we were born."
> "She came like a bride
>   In a snowy morn."
> "What's a bride?"
>   "What is snow?"
> "Never tried."
>   "Do not know."
>
> "Who told you about her?"
>   "Little Primrose there
> Cannot do without her."
>   "Oh, so sweetly fair!"
> "Never fear,
>   She will come,
> Primrose dear."
>   "Is she dumb?
>
> "She'll come by and by."
>   "You will never see her."
> "She went home to die,
>   Till the new year."
> "Snowdrop!" "'Tis no good
>   To invite her."
> "Primrose is very rude,"
>   "I will bite her."
>
> "Oh, you naughty Pocket!
>   Look, she drops her head."
> "She deserved it, Rocket,
>   And she was nearly dead."

"To your hammock—off with you!"
"And swing alone."
"No one will laugh with you."
"No not one."

"Now let us moan."
"And cover her o'er."
"Primrose is gone."
"All but the flower."
"Here is a leaf."
"Lay her upon it."
"Follow in grief."
"Pocket has done it."

"Deeper, poor creature!
Winter may come."
"He cannot reach her—
That is a hum."
"She is buried, the beauty!"
"Now she is done."
"That was the duty."
"Now for the fun."

And with a wild laugh they sprang away, most of them towards the cottage. During the latter part of the song-talk, they had formed themselves into a funeral procession, two of them bearing poor Primrose, whose death Pocket had hastened by biting her stalk, upon one of her own great leaves. They bore her solemnly along some distance, and then buried her under a tree. Although I say *her,* I saw nothing but the withered primrose-flower on its long stalk. Pocket, who had been expelled from the company by common consent, went sulkily away towards her hammock, for she was the fairy of the calceolaria, and looked rather wicked. When she reached its stem, she stopped and looked round. I could not help speaking to her, for I stood near her. I said: "Pocket, how could you be so naughty?"

"I am never naughty," she said, half-crossly, half-defiantly; "only if you come near my hammock, I will bite you, and then you will go away."

"Why did you bite poor Primrose?"

"Because she said we should never see Snowdrop; as if we were not good enough to look at her, and she was, the proud thing!—served her right!"

"Oh, Pocket, Pocket," said I; but by this time the party which had gone towards the house, rushed out again, shouting and screaming with laughter. Half of them were on the cat's back, and half held on by her fur and tail, or ran beside her; till, more coming to their help, the furious cat was held fast: and they proceeded to pick the sparks out of her with thorns and pins, which they handled like harpoons. Indeed, there were more instruments at work about her than there could have been sparks in her. One little fellow who held on hard by the tip of the tail, with his feet planted on the ground at an angle of forty-five degrees, helping to keep her fast, administered a continuous flow of admonitions to Pussy.

"Now, Pussy, be patient. You know quite well it is all for your good. You cannot be comfortable with all those sparks in you; and, indeed, I am charitably disposed to believe" (here he became very pompous) "that they are the cause of all your bad temper; so we must have them all out, every one; else we shall be reduced to the painful necessity of cutting your claws, and pulling out your eye-teeth. Quiet! Pussy, quiet!"

But with a perfect hurricane of feline curses, the poor animal broke loose, and dashed across the garden and through the hedge, faster than even the fairies could follow. "Never mind, never mind, we shall find her again; and by that time she will have laid in a fresh stock of sparks. Hooray!" And off they set, after some new mischief.

But I will not linger to enlarge on the amusing displays of these frolicsome creatures. Their manners and habits are now so well known to the world, having been so often described by eye-witnesses, that it would be only indulging self-conceit, to add my account in full to the rest. I cannot help wishing, however, that my readers could see them for themselves. Especially do I desire that they should see the fairy of the daisy; a little, chubby, round-eyed child, with such innocent trust in his look! Even the most mischievous of the fairies would not tease him, although he did not belong to their set at all, but was quite a little country bumpkin. He wandered about alone, and looked at everything, with his hands in his little pockets, and a white nightcap on, the darling! He was not so beautiful as many other wild flowers I saw afterwards, but so dear and loving in his looks and little confident ways.

CHAPTER IV

When bale is att hyest, boote is nyest.
Ballad of Sir Aldingar.

BY THIS TIME, my hostess was quite anxious that I should be gone. So, with warm thanks for their hospitality, I took my leave, and went my way through the little garden towards the forest. Some of the garden flowers had wandered into the wood, and were growing here and there along the path, but the trees soon became too thick and shadowy for them. I particularly noticed some tall lilies, which grew on both sides of the way, with large, dazzlingly white flowers, set off by the universal green. It was now dark enough for me to see that every flower was shining with a light of its own. Indeed it was by this light that I saw them, an internal, peculiar light, proceeding from each, and not reflected from a common source of light as in the day-time. This light sufficed only for the plant itself, and was not strong enough to cast any but the faintest shadows around it, or to illuminate any of the neighboring objects with other than the faintest tinge of its own individual hue. From the lilies above mentioned, from the campanulas, from the foxgloves, and every bell-shaped flower, curious little figures shot up their heads, peeped at me, and drew back. They seemed to inhabit them, as snails their shells; but I was sure some of them were intruders, and belonged to the gnomes or goblin-fairies, who inhabit the ground and earthy creeping plants. From the cups of Arum lilies, creatures with great heads and grotesque faces shot up like Jack-in-the-box, and made grimaces at me; or rose slowly and shyly over the edge of the cup, and spouted water at me, slipping suddenly back, like those little soldier-crabs that inhabit the shells of sea-snails. Passing a row of tall thistles, I saw them crowded with little faces, which peeped every one from behind its flower, and drew back as quickly; and I heard them saying to each other, evidently intending me to hear, but the speaker always hiding behind his tuft, when I looked in his direction, "Look at him! Look at him! He has begun a story without a beginning, and it will never have any end. He! he! he! Look at him!"

But as I went further into the wood, these sights and sounds became fewer, giving way to others of a different character. A little forest of wild hyacinths was alive with exquisite creatures, who stood nearly motionless, with drooping necks, holding each by the stem of her flower, and swaying gently with it, whenever a low breath of wind swung the crowded floral belfry. In like manner, though differing of course in form and meaning, stood a group of harebells, like little angels waiting, ready, till they were wanted to go on some yet unknown message. In darker nooks, by the mossy roots of the trees, or in little tufts of grass, each dwelling in a globe of its own green light, weaving a network of grass and its shadows, glowed the glowworms. They were just like the glowworms of our own land, for they are fairies every-where; worms in the day, and glowworms at night, when their own can appear, and they can be themselves to others as well as themselves. But they had their enemies here. For I saw great strong-armed beetles, hurrying about with most unwieldy haste, awkward as elephant-calves, looking apparently for glowworms; for the moment a beetle espied one, through what to it was a forest of grass, or an underwood of moss, it pounced upon it, and bore it away, in spite of its feeble resistance. Wondering what their object could be, I watched one of the beetles, and then I discovered a thing I could not account for. But it is no use trying to account for things in fairy land; and one who travels there soon learns to forget the very idea of doing so, and takes everything as it comes; like a child, who, being in a chronic condition of wonder, is surprised at nothing. What I saw was this. Everywhere, here and there over the ground, lay little, dark-looking lumps of something more like earth than anything else, and about the size of a chestnut. The beetles hunted in couples for these; and having found one, one of them stayed to watch it, while the other hurried to find a glowworm. By signals, I presume, between them, the latter soon found his companion again; they then took the glowworm and held its luminous tail to the dark earthy pallet; when lo! it shot up into the air like a sky-rocket, seldom however reaching the height of the highest tree. Just like a rocket too, it burst in the air, and fell in a shower of the most gorgeously coloured sparks of every variety of hue; golden and red, and purple and green, and blue and rosy fires crossed and intercrossed each other, beneath the shadowy heads, and between the columnar stems of the forest trees. They never used the same glowworm twice, I observed; but let him go, apparently uninjured by the use they had made of him.

In other parts, the whole of the immediately surrounding foliage was illuminated by the interwoven dances in the air of splendidly coloured fireflies, which sped hither and thither, turned, twisted, crossed, and re-crossed, entwining every complexity of intervolved motion. Here and there, whole mighty trees glowed with an emitted phosphorescent light. You could trace the very course of the great roots in the earth by the faint light that came through; and every twig, and every vein on every leaf was a streak of pale fire.

All this time, as I went on through the wood, I was haunted with the feeling that other shapes, more like my own in size and mien, were moving about at a little distance on all sides of me. But as yet I could discern none of them, although the moon was high enough to send a great many of her rays down between the trees, and these rays were unusually bright, and sight-giving, notwithstanding she was only a half-moon. I constantly imagined, however, that forms were visible in all directions except that to which my gaze was turned; and that they only became invisible, or resolved themselves into other woodland shapes, the moment my looks were directed towards them. However this may have been, except for this feeling of presence, the woods seemed utterly bare of anything like human companionship, although my glance often fell on some object which I fancied to be a human form; for I soon found that I was quite deceived; as, the moment I fixed my regard on it, it showed plainly that it was a bush, or a tree, or a rock.

Soon a vague sense of discomfort possessed me. With variations of relief, this gradually increased; as if some evil thing were wandering about in my neighborhood, sometimes nearer and sometimes further off, but still approaching. The feeling continued and deepened, until all my pleasure in the shows of various kinds that everywhere betokened the presence of the merry fairies, vanished by degrees, and left me full of anxiety and fear, which I was unable to associate with any definite object whatever. At length the thought crossed my mind with horror: "Can it be possible that the Ash is looking for me? or that, in his nightly wanderings, his path is gradually verging towards mine?" I comforted myself, however, by remembering that he had started quite in another direction; one that would lead him, if he kept it, far apart from me; especially as, for the last two or three hours, I had been diligently journeying eastward. I kept on my way, therefore, striving by direct effort of the will against the encroaching fear; and to this end occupying my mind, as much as I could, with other thoughts. I was so far successful that, although I was conscious, if I yielded for a moment, I should be almost overwhelmed with horror, I was yet able to walk right on for an hour or more. What I feared I could not tell. Indeed, I was left in a state of the vaguest uncertainty as regarded the nature of my enemy, and knew not the mode or object of his attacks; for, somehow or other, none of my questions had succeeded in drawing a definite answer from the dame in the cottage. How then to defend myself I knew not; nor even by what sign I might with certainty recognise the presence of my foe; for as yet this vague though powerful fear was all the indication of danger I had. To add to my distress, the clouds in the west had risen nearly to the top of the skies, and they and

the moon were travelling slowly towards each other. Indeed, some of
their advanced guard had already met her, and she had begun to wade
through a filmy vapour that gradually deepened. At length she was for
a moment almost entirely obscured. When she shone out again, with a
brilliancy increased by the contrast, I saw plainly on the path before
me—from around which at this spot the trees receded, leaving a small
space of green sward—the shadow of a large hand, with knotty joints
and protuberances here and there. Especially I remarked, even in the
midst of my fear, the bulbous points of the fingers. I looked hurriedly
all round, but could see nothing from which such a shadow should fall.
Now, however, that I had a direction, however undetermined, in which
to project my apprehension, the very sense of danger and need of
action overcame that stifling which is the worst property of fear. I
reflected in a moment, that if this were indeed a shadow, it was useless
to look for the object that cast it in any other direction than between the
shadow and the moon. I looked, and peered, and intensified my vision,
all to no purpose. I could see nothing of that kind, not even an ash-tree
in the neighborhood. Still the shadow remained; not steady, but moving
to and fro; and once I saw the fingers close, and grind themselves close,
like the claws of a wild animal, as if in uncontrollable longing for some
anticipated prey. There seemed but one mode left of discovering the
substance of this shadow. I went forward boldly, though with an inward
shudder which I would not heed, to the spot where the shadow lay,
threw myself on the ground, laid my head within the form of the hand,
and turned my eyes towards the moon. Good heavens! what did I see? I
wonder that ever I arose, and that the very shadow of the hand did not
hold me where I lay until fear had frozen my brain. I saw the strangest
figure; vague, shadowy, almost transparent, in the central parts, and
gradually deepening in substance towards the outside, until it ended in
extremities capable of casting such a shadow as fell from the hand
through the awful fingers of which I now saw the moon. The hand was
uplifted in the attitude of a paw about to strike its prey. But the face,
which throbbed with fluctuating and pulsatory visibility—not from
changes in the light it reflected, but from changes in its own conditions
of reflecting power, the alterations being from within, not from
without—it was horrible. I do not know how to describe it. It caused a
new sensation. Just as one cannot translate a horrible odour, or a
ghastly pain, or a fearful sound, into words, so I cannot describe this
new form of awful hideousness. I can only try to describe something
that is not it, but seems somewhat parallel to it; or at least is suggested
by it. It reminded me of what I had heard of vampires; for the face
resembled that of a corpse more than anything else I can think of;
especially when I can conceive such a face in motion, but not suggesting
any life as the source of the motion. The features were rather
handsome than otherwise, except the mouth, which had scarcely a
curve in it. The lips were of equal thickness; but the thickness was not at
all remarkable, even although they looked slightly swollen. They
seemed fixedly open, but were not wide apart. Of course I did not
remark these lineaments at the time: I was too horrified for that. I noted
them afterwards, when the form returned on my inward sight with a

vividness too intense to admit of my doubting the accuracy of the reflex. But the most awful of the features were the eyes. These were alive, yet not with life. They seemed lighted up with an infinite greed. A gnawing voracity, which devoured the devourer, seemed to be the indwelling and propelling power of the whole ghastly apparition. I lay for a few moments simply imbruted with terror; when another cloud, obscuring the moon, delivered me from the immediately paralysing effects of the presence to the vision of the object of horror, while it added the force of imagination to the power of fear within me; inasmuch as, knowing far worse cause for apprehension than before, I remained equally ignorant from what I had to defend myself, or how to take my precautions: he might be upon me in the darkness any moment. I sprang to my feet, and sped I knew not whither, only away from the spectre. I thought no longer of the path, and often narrowly escaped dashing myself against a tree, in my headlong flight of fear.

Great drops of rain began to patter on the leaves. Thunder began to mutter, then growl in the distance. I ran on. The rain fell heavier. At length the thick leaves could hold it up no longer; and, like a second firmament, they poured their torrents on the earth. I was soon drenched, but that was nothing. I came to a small swollen stream that rushed through the woods. I had a vague hope that if I crossed this stream, I should be in safety from my pursuer; but I soon found that my hope was as false as it was vague. I dashed across the stream, ascended a rising ground, and reached a more open space, where stood only great trees. Through them I directed my way, holding eastward as nearly as I could guess, but not at all certain that I was not moving in an opposite direction. My mind was just reviving a little from its extreme terror, when, suddenly, a flash of lightning, or rather a cataract of successive flashes, behind me, seemed to throw on the ground in front of me, but far more faintly than before, from the extent of the source of the light, the shadow of the same horrible hand. I sprang forward, stung to yet wilder speed; but had not run many steps before my foot slipped, and, vainly attempting to recover myself, I fell at the foot of one of the large trees. Half-stunned, I yet raised myself, and almost involuntarily looked back. All I saw was the hand within three feet of my face. But, at the same moment, I felt two large soft arms thrown round me from behind; and a voice like a woman's said: "Do not fear the goblin; he dares not hurt you now." With that, the hand was suddenly withdrawn as from a fire, and disappeared in the darkness and the rain. Overcome with the mingling of terror and joy, I lay for some time almost insensible. The first thing I remember is the sound of a voice above me, full and low, and strangely reminding me of the sound of a gentle wind amidst the leaves of a great tree. It murmured over and over again: "I may love him, I may love him, for he is a man, and I am only a beech-tree." I found I was seated on the ground, leaning against a human form, and supported still by the arms around me, which I knew to be those of a woman who must be rather above the human size, and largely proportioned. I turned my head, but without moving otherwise, for I feared lest the arms should untwine them-selves; and clear, somewhat mournful eyes met mine. At least that is how they impressed me; but I could see very little of colour or outline as we sat in the dark and rainy shadow of the tree. The face seemed very lovely, and solemn from its stillness; with the aspect of one who is quite content, but waiting for something. I saw my conjecture from her arms was correct: she was above the human scale throughout, but not greatly.

"Why do you call yourself a beech-tree?" I said.

"Because I am one," she replied, in the same low, musical, murmuring voice.

"You are a woman," I returned.

"Do you think so? Am I very like a woman then?"

"You are a very beautiful woman. Is it possible you should not know it?"

"I am very glad you think so. I fancy I feel like a woman sometimes. I do so to-night—and always when the rain drips from my hair. For there is an old prophecy in our woods that one day we shall all be men and women like you. Do you know anything about it in your region? Shall I be very happy when I am a woman? I fear not; for it is always in nights like these that I feel like one. But I long to be a woman for all that."

I had to let her talk on, for her voice was like a solution of all musical sounds. I now told her that I could hardly say whether women were happy or not. I knew one who had not been happy; and for my part, I had often longed for Fairyland, as she now longed for the world of men. But then neither of us had lived long, and perhaps people grew happier as they grew older. Only I doubted it. I could not help sighing. She felt the sigh, for her arms were still round me. She asked me how old I was.

"Twenty-one," said I.

"Why, you baby!" said she; and kissed me with the sweetest kiss of winds and odours. There was a cool faithfulness in the kiss that revived my heart wonderfully. I felt that I feared the dreadful Ash no more.

"What did the horrible Ash want with me?" I said.

"I am not quite sure, but I think he wants to bury you at the foot of his tree. But he shall not touch you, my child."

"Are all the ash-trees as dreadful as he?"

"Oh, no. They are all disagreeable selfish creatures—(what horrid men they will make, if it be true!) but this one has a hole in his heart that nobody knows of but one or two; and he is always trying to fill it up, but he cannot. That must be what he wanted you for. I wonder if he will ever be a man. If he is, I hope they will kill him."

"How kind of you to save me from him!"

"I will take care that he shall not come near you again. But there are some in the wood more like me, from whom, alas! I cannot protect you. Only if you see any of them very beautiful, try to walk round them."

"What then?"

"I cannot tell you more. But now I must tie some of my hair about you, and then the Ash will not touch you. Here, cut some off. You men have strange cutting things about you."

She shook her long hair loose over me, never moving her arms.

"I cannot cut your beautiful hair. It would be a shame."

"Not cut my hair! It will have grown long enough before any is

"I felt two large soft arms thrown round me from behind."

ARTHUR HUGHES

wanted again in this wild forest. Perhaps it may never be of any use again—not till I am a woman." And she sighed.

As gently as I could, I cut with a knife a long tress of flowing, dark hair, she hanging her beautiful head over me. When I had finished, she shuddered and breathed deep, as one does when an acute pain, steadfastly endured without sign of suffering, is at length relaxed. She then took the hair and tied it round me, singing a strange sweet song, which I could not understand, but which left in me a feeling like this—

> "I saw thee ne'er before;
> I see thee never more;
> But love, and help, and pain, beautiful one,
> Have made thee mine, till all my years are done."

I cannot put more of it into words. She closed her arms about me again, and went on singing. The rain in the leaves, and a light wind that had arisen, kept her song company. I was wrapt in a trance of still delight. It told me the secret of the woods, and the flowers, and the birds. At one time I felt as if I was wandering in childhood through sunny spring forests, over carpets of primroses, anemones, and little white starry things—I had almost said, creatures, and finding new wonderful flowers at every turn. At another, I lay half dreaming in the hot summer noon, with a book of old tales beside me, beneath a great beech; or, in autumn, grew sad because I trod on the leaves that had sheltered me, and received their last blessing in the sweet odours of decay; or, in a winter evening, frozen-still, looked up, as I went home to a warm fire-side, through the netted boughs and twigs to the cold, snowy moon, with her opal zone around her. At last I had fallen asleep; for I know nothing more that passed, till I found myself lying under a superb beech-tree, in the clear light of the morning, just before sunrise. Around me was a girdle of fresh beech-leaves. Alas! I brought nothing with me out of fairy-land, but memories—memories. The great boughs of the beech hung drooping around me. At my head rose its smooth stem, with its great sweeps of curving surface that swelled like undeveloped limbs. The leaves and branches above kept on the song which had sung me asleep; only now, to my mind, it sounded like a farewell and a speedwell. I sat a long time, unwilling to go; but my unfinished story urged me on. I must act and wander. With the sun well risen, I rose, and put my arms as far as they would reach around the beech-tree, and kissed it, and said goodbye. A trembling went through the leaves; a few of the last drops of the night's rain fell from off them at my feet; and as I walked slowly away, I seemed to hear in a whisper once more the words: "I may love him, I may love him; for he is a man, and I am only a beech-tree."

CHAPTER V

AND SHE WAS SMOOTH AND FULL, AS IF ONE GUSH
OF LIFE HAD WASHED HER, OR AS IF A SLEEP

Lay on her eyelid, easier to sweep
Than bee from daisy.
                    Beddoes' *Pygmalion.*

Sche was as whyt as lylye yn May,
Or snow that sneweth yn wynterys day.
                    Romance of Sir Launfal.

I walked on, in the fresh morning air, as if new-born. The only thing that damped my pleasure, was a cloud of something between sorrow and delight, that crossed my mind with the frequently returning thought of my last night's hostess. "But then," thought I, "if she is sorry, I could not help it; and she has all the pleasures she ever had. Such a day as this, is surely a joy to her, as much at least as to me. And her life will perhaps be the richer, for holding now within it the memory of what came, but could not stay. And if ever she is a woman, who knows but we may meet somewhere? there is plenty of room for meeting in the universe." Comforting myself thus, yet with a vague compunction, as if I ought not to have left her, I went on. There was little to distinguish the woods to-day from those of my own land; except that all the wild things, rabbits, birds, squirrels, mice, and the numberless other inhabitants, were very tame; that is, they did not run away from me, but gazed at me as I passed, frequently coming nearer, as if to examine me more closely. Whether this came from utter ignorance, or from familiarity with the human appearance of beings who never hurt them, I could not tell. As I stood once, looking up to the splendid flower of a parasite, which hung from the branch of a tree over my head, a large white rabbit cantered slowly up, put one of its little feet on one of mine, and looked up at me with its red eyes, just as I had been looking up at the flower above me. I stooped and stroked it; but when I attempted to lift it, it banged the ground with its hind feet, and scampered off at a great rate, turning, however, to look at me, several times before I lost sight of it. Now and then, too, a dim human figure would appear and disappear, at some distance, amongst the trees, moving like a sleep-walker. But no one ever came near me.

This day I found plenty of food in the forest—strange nuts and fruits I had never seen before. I hesitated to eat them; but argued that, if I could live on the air of fairy-land, I could live on its food also. I found my reasoning correct, and the result was better than I had hoped; for it not only satisfied ny hunger, but operated in such a way upon my senses, that I was brought into far more complete relationship with the things around me. The human forms appeared much more dense and defined; more tangibly visible, if I may say so. I seemed to know better which direction to choose when any doubt arose. I began to feel in some degree what the birds meant in their songs, though I could not express it in words, any more than you can some landscapes. At times, to my surprise, I found myself listening attentively, and as if it were no unusual thing with me, to a conversation between two squirrels or monkeys. The subjects were not very interesting, except as associated with the individual life and necessities of the little creatures: where the best nuts were to be found in the neighborhood, and who could crack them best, or who had most laid up for the winter, and such like; only they never said where the store was. There was no great difference in kind between their talk and our ordinary human conversation. Some of the creatures I never heard speak at all, and believe they never do so, except under the impulse of some great excitement. The mice talked; but the hedgehogs seemed very phlegmatic; and though I met a couple of moles above ground several times, they never said a word to each other in my hearing. There were no wild beasts in the forest; at least, I did not see one larger than a wild cat, There were plenty of snakes, however, and I do not think they were all harmless; but none ever bit me.

Soon after mid-day, I arrived at a bare rocky hill, of no great size, but very steep; and, having no trees—scarcely even a bush—upon it, entirely exposed to the heat of the sun. Over this my way seemed to lie, and I immediately began the ascent. On reaching the top, hot and weary, I looked around me, and saw that the forest still stretched as far as the sight could reach on every side of me. I observed that the trees, in the direction which I was about to descend, did not come so near the foot of the hill as on the other side, and was especially regretting the unexpected postponement of shelter, because this side of the hill seemed more difficult to descend than the other had been to climb, when my eye caught the appearance of a natural path, winding down through broken rocks and along the course of a tiny stream, which I hoped would lead me more easily to the foot. I tried it, and found the descent not at all laborious; nevertheless, when I reached the bottom, I was very tired, and exhausted with the heat. But just where the path seemed to end, rose a great rock, quite overgrown with shrubs and creeping plants, some of them in full and splendid blossom: these almost concealed an opening in the rock, into which the path appeared to lead. I entered, thirsting for the shade which it promised. What was my delight to find a rocky cell, all the angles rounded away with rich moss, and every ledge and projection crowded with lovely ferns, the variety of whose forms, and groupings, and shades wrought in me like a poem; for such a harmony could not exist, except they all consented to some one end! A little well of the clearest water filled a mossy hollow in one corner. I drank, and felt as if I knew what the elixir of life must be; then threw myself on a mossy mound that lay like a couch along the inner end. Here I lay in a delicious reverie for some time; during which all lovely forms, and colours, and sounds seemed to use my brain as a common hall, where they could come and go, unbidden and unex-cused. I had never imagined that such capacity for simple happiness lay in me, as was now awakened by this assembly of forms and spiritual sensations, which yet were far too vague to admit of being translated into any shape common to my own and another mind. I had lain for an hour, I should suppose, though it may have been far longer, when, the harmonious tumult in my mind having somewhat relaxed. I became aware that my eyes were fixed on a strange, time-worn bas-relief on the rock opposite to me. This, after some pondering, I concluded to represent Pygmalion, as he awaited the quickening of his statue. The sculptor sat more rigid than the figure to which his eyes were turned. That seemed about to step from its pedestal and embrace the man, who waited rather than expected.

"A lovely story," I said to myself. "This cave, now, with the bushes cut away from the entrance to let the light in, might be such a place as he would choose, withdrawn from the notice of men, to set up his block of marble, and mould into a visible body the thought already clothed with form in the unseen hall of the sculptor's brain. And, indeed, if I mistake not," I said, starting up, as a sudden ray of light arrived at that moment through a crevice in the roof, and lighted up a small portion of the rock, bare of vegetation, "this very rock is marble, white enough and delicate enough for any statue, even if destined to become an ideal woman in the arms of the sculptor."

I took my knife and removed the moss from a part of the block on which I had been lying; when, to my surprise, I found it more like alabaster than ordinary marble, and soft to the edge of the knife. In fact, it was alabaster. By an inexplicable, though by no means unusual kind of impulse, I went on removing the moss from the surface of the stone; and soon saw that it was polished, or at least smooth, throughout. I continued my labour; and after clearing a space of about a couple of square feet, I observed what caused me to prosecute the work with more interest and care than before. For the ray of sunlight had now reached the spot I had cleared, and under its lustre the alabaster revealed its usual slight transparency when polished, except where my knife had scratched the surface; and I observed that the transparency seemed to have a definite limit, and to end upon an opaque body like the more solid, white marble. I was careful to scratch no more. And first, a vague anticipation gave way to a startling sense of possibility; then, as I proceeded, one revelation after another produced the entrancing conviction, that under the crust of alabaster, lay a dimly visible form in marble, but whether of man or woman I could not yet tell. I worked on as rapidly as the necessary care would permit; and when I had uncovered the whole mass, and, rising from my knews, had retreated a little way, so that the effect of the whole might fall on me, I saw before me with sufficient plainness—though at the same time with considerable indistinctness, arising from the limited amount of light the place admitted, as well as from the nature of the object itself—a block of pure alabaster enclosing the form, apparently in marble, of a reposing woman. She lay on one side, with her hand under her cheek, and her face towards me; but her hair had fallen partly over her face, so that I could not see the expression of the whole. What I did see, appeared to me perfectly lovely; more near the face that had been born with me in my soul, than anything I had seen before in nature or art. The actual outlines of the rest of the form were so indistinct, that the more than semi-opacity of the alabaster seemed insufficient to account for the fact; and I conjectured that a night robe added its obscurity. Numberless histories passed through my mind of change of substance from enchantment and other causes, and of imprisonments such as this before me. I thought of the Prince of the Enchanted City, half marble and half a living man; of Ariel; of Niobe; of the Sleeping Beauty in the

Wood; of the bleeding trees; and many other histories. Even my adventure of the preceding evening with the lady of the beech-tree contributed to arouse the wild hope, that by some means life might be given to this form also, and that, breaking from her alabaster tomb, she might glorify my eyes with her presence. "For," I argued, "who can tell but this cave may be the home of Marble, and this, essential Marble— that spirit of marble which, present throughout, makes it capable of being moulded into any form? Then if she should awake! But how to awake her? A kiss awoke the Sleeping Beauty: a kiss cannot reach her through the incrusting alabaster." I kneeled, however, and kissed the pale coffin; but she slept on. I bethought me of Orpheus, and the following stones;—that trees should follow his music seemed nothing surprising now. Might not a song awake this form, that the glory of motion might for a time displace the loveliness of rest? Sweet sounds can go where kisses may not enter. I sat and thought.

Now, although always delighting in music, I had never been gifted with the power of song, until I entered the fairy-forest. I had a voice, and I had a true sense of sound; but when I tried to sing, the one would not content the other, and so I remained silent. This morning, however, I had found myself, ere I was aware, rejoicing in a song; but whether it was before or after I had eaten of the fruits of the forest, I could not satisfy myself. I concluded it was after, however; and that the increased impulse to sing I now felt, was in part owing to having drunk of the little well, which shone like a brilliant eye in a corner of the cave. I sat down on the ground by the "antenatal tomb," leaned upon it with my face towards the head of the figure within, and sang—the words and tones coming together, and inseparably connected, as if word and tone formed one thing; or, as if each word could be uttered only in that tone, and was incapable of distinction from it, except in idea, by an acute analysis. I sang something like this: but the words are only a dull representation of a state whose very elevation precluded the possibility of remembrance; and in which I presume the words really employed were as far above these, as that state transcended this wherein I recall it:

"Marble woman, vainly sleeping
In the very death of dreams!
Wilt thou—slumber from thee sweeping,
All but what with vision teems—
Hear my voice come through the golden
Mist of memory and hope;
And with shadowy smile embolden
Me with primal Death to cope?

"Thee the sculptors all pursuing,
Have embodied but their own;
Round their visions, form induing,
Marble vestments thou hast thrown;
But thyself, in silence winding,
Thou hast kept eternally;
Thee they found not, many finding—
I have found thee: wake for me."

As I sang, I looked earnestly at the face so vaguely revealed before me. I fancied, yet believed it to be but fancy, that through the dim veil of the alabaster, I saw a motion of the head as if caused by a sinking sigh. I gazed more earnestly, and concluded that it was but fancy. Nevertheless I could not help singing again:

> "Rest is now filled full of beauty,
> And can give thee up, I ween;
> Come thou forth, for other duty:
> Motion pineth for her queen.
>
> "Or, if needing years to wake thee
> From thy slumbrous solitudes,
> Come, sleep-walking, and betake thee
> To the friendly, sleeping woods.
>
> "Sweeter dreams are in the forest;
> Round thee storms would never rave;
> And when need of rest is sorest,
> Glide thou then into thy cave.
>
> "Or, if still thou choosest rather
> Marble, be its spell on me;
> Let thy slumber round me gather,
> Let another dream with thee!"

Again I paused, and gazed through the stony shroud, as if, by very force of penetrative sight, I would clear every lineament of the lovely face. And now I thought the hand that had lain under the cheek, had slipped a little downward. But then I could not be sure that I had at first observed its position accurately. So I sang again; for the longing had grown into a passionate need of seeing her alive:

> "Or art thou Death, O woman? for since I
> Have set me singing by thy side,
> Life hath forsook the upper sky,
> And all the outer world hath died.
>
> "Yes, I am dead; for thou hast drawn
> My life all downward unto thee.
> Dead moon of love! let twilight dawn;
> Awake! and let the darkness flee.
>
> "Cold lady of the lovely stone!
> Awake! or I shall perish here;
> And thou be never more alone,
> My form and I for ages near.
>
> "But words are vain; reject them all—
> They utter but a feeble part:
> Hear thou the depths from which they call,
> The voiceless longing of my heart."

There arose a slightly crashing sound. Like a sudden apparition that comes and is gone, a white form, veiled in a light robe of whiteness, burst upwards from the stone, stood, glided forth, and gleamed away towards the woods. For I followed to the mouth of the cave, as soon as the amazement and concentration of delight permitted the nerves of motion again to act; and saw the white form amidst the trees, as it crossed a little glade on the edge of the forest where the sunlight fell full, seeming to gather with intenser radiance on the one object that floated rather than flitted through its lake of beams. I gazed after her in a kind of despair; found, freed, lost! It seemed useless to follow, yet follow I must. I marked the direction she took; and without once looking round to the forsaken cave, I hastened towards the forest.

CHAPTER VI

Ach, hüte sich doch ein Mensch, wenn seine erfüllten Wünsche auf ihn herad regnen, und er so über alle Maasse fröhlich ist!
—FOUQUÉ, *Der Zauberring.*
Ah, let a man beware, when his wishes, fulfilled, rain down upon him, and his happiness is unbounded.

Thy red lips, like worms,
Travel over my cheek.
MOTHERWELL (?)

BUT AS I crossed the space between the foot of the hill and the forest, a vision of another kind delayed my steps. Through an opening to the westward flowed, like a stream, the rays of the setting sun, and overflowed with a ruddy splendour the open place where I was. And riding as it were down this stream towards me, came a horseman in what appeared red armour. From frontlet to tail, the horse likewise shone red in the sun-set. I felt as if I must have seen the knight before; but as he drew near, I could recall no feature of his countenance. Ere he came up to me, however, I remembered the legend of Sir Percival in the rusty armour, which I had left unfinished in the old book in the cottage: it was of Sir Percival that he reminded me. And no wonder; for when he came close up to me, I saw that, from crest to heel, the whole surface of his armour was covered with a light rust. The golden spurs shone, but the iron greaves glowed in the sunlight. The *morning star,* which hung from his wrist, glittered and glowed with its silver and bronze. His whole appearance was terrible; but his face did not answer to this appearance. It was sad, even to gloominess; and something of now is the time shame seemed to cover it. Yet it was noble and high, though thus beclouded; and the form looked lofty, although the head drooped, and the whole frame was bowed as with an inward grief. The horse seemed to share in his master's dejection, and walked spiritless and slow. I noticed, too, that the white plume on his helmet was discoloured and drooping. "He has fallen in a joust with spears," I said to myself; "yet it becomes not a noble knight to be conquered in spirit

"I gazed after her in a kind of despair."

ARTHUR HUGHES

because his body hath fallen." He appeared not to observe me, for he was riding past without looking up, and started into a warlike attitude the moment the first sound of my voice reached him. Then a flush, as of shame, covered all of his face that the lifted beaver disclosed. He returned my greeting with distant courtesy, and passed on. But suddenly, he reined up, sat a moment still, and then turning his horse, rode back to where I stood looking after him.

"I am ashamed," he said, "to appear a knight, and in such a guise, but it behoves me to tell you to take warning from me, lest the same evil, in his kind, overtake the singer that has befallen the knight. Hast thou ever read the story of Sir Percival and the" (here he shuddered, that his armour rang)—"Maiden of the Alder-tree?"

"In part, I have," said I; "for yesterday, at the entrance of this forest, I found in a cottage the volume wherein it is recorded."

"Then take heed," he rejoined; "for, see my armour;—I put it off; and as it befel to him, so has it befallen to me. I that was proud am humble now. Yet is she terribly beautiful—beware. Never," he added, raising his head, "shall this armour be furbished, but by the blows of knightly encounter, until the last speck has disappeared from every spot where the battle-axe and sword of evil-doers, or noble foes, might fall; when I shall again lift my head, and say to my squire, 'Do thy duty once more, and make this armour shine.'"

Before I could inquire further, he had struck spurs into his horse and galloped away, shrouded from my voice in the noise of his armour. For I called after him, anxious to know more about this fearful enchantress; but in vain—he heard me not. "Yet," I said to myself, "I have now been often warned; surely I shall be well on my guard; and I am fully resolved I shall not be ensnared by any beauty, however beautiful. Doubtless, some one man may escape, and I shall be he." So I went on into the wood, still hoping to find, in some one of its mysterious recesses, my lost lady of the marble. The sunny afternoon died into the loveliest twilight. Great bats began to flit about with their own noiseless flight, seemingly purposeless, because its objects are unseen. The monotonous music of the owl issued from all unexpected quarters in the half-darkness around me. The glow-worm was alight here and there, burning out into the great universe. The night-hawk heightened all the harmony and stillness with his oft-recurring, discordant jar. Numberless unknown sounds came out of the unknown dusk; but all were of twilight-kind, oppressing the heart as with a condensed atmosphere of dreamy undefined love and longing. The odours of night arose, and bathed me in that luxurious mournfulness peculiar to them, as if the plants whence they floated had been watered with bygone tears. Earth drew me towards her bosom; I felt as if I could fall down and kiss her. I forgot I was in Fairy Land, and seemed to be walking in a perfect night of our own old nursing earth. Great stems rose about me, uplifting a thick multitudinous roof above me of branches, and twigs, and leaves—the bird and insect world uplifted over mine, with its own landscapes, its own thickets, and paths, and glades, and dwellings; its own bird-ways and insect-delights. Great boughs crossed my path; great roots based the tree-columns, and mightily clasped the earth, strong to lift and strong to uphold. It seemed an old, old forest, perfect in forest ways and pleasures. And when, in the midst of this ecstasy, I remembered that under some close canopy of leaves, by some giant stem, or in some mossy cave, or beside some leafy well, sat the lady of the marble, whom my songs had called forth into the outer world, waiting (might it not be?) to meet and thank her deliverer in a twilight which would veil her confusion, the whole night became one dream-realm of joy, the central form of which was everywhere present, although unbeheld. Then, remembering how my songs seemed to have called her from the marble, piercing through the pearly shroud of alabaster—"Why," thought I, "should not my voice reach her now, through the ebon night that inwraps her." My voice burst into song so spontaneously that it seemed involuntarily.

"Not a sound
But, echoing in me,
Vibrates all around
With a blind delight,
Till it breaks on thee,
Queen of Night!

"Every tree,
O'ershadowing with gloom,
Seems to cover thee
Secret, dark, love-still'd,
In a holy room
Silence-filled

"Let no moon
Creep up the heaven to-night.
I in darksome noon
Walking hopefully,
Seek my shrouded light—
Grope for thee!

"Darker grow
The borders of the dark!
Through the branches glow!
From the roof above,
Star and diamond-spark,
Light for love."

Scarcely had the last sounds floated away from the hearing of my own ears, when I heard instead a low delicious laugh near me. It was not the laugh of one who would not be heard, but the laugh of one who has just received something long and patiently desired—a laugh that ends in a low musical moan. I started, and, turning sideways, saw a dim white figure seated beside an intertwining thicket of smaller trees and underwood.

"It is my white lady!" I said, and flung myself on the ground beside her; striving, through the gathering darkness, to get a glimpse of the form which had broken its marble prison at my call.

"It is your white lady," said the sweetest voice, in reply, sending a thrill of speechless delight through a heart which all the love charms of the preceding day and evening had been tempering for this culminating hour. Yet, if I would have confessed it, there was something either in the sound of the voice, although it seemed sweetness itself, or else in this yielding which awaited no gradation of gentle approaches, that did not vibrate harmoniously with the beat of my inward music. And likewise, when, taking her hand in mine, I drew closer to her, looking for the beauty of her face, which, indeed, I found too plenteously, a cold shiver ran through me; but "it is the marble," I said to myself, and heeded it not.

She withdrew her hand from mine, and after that would scarce allow me to touch her. It seemed strange, after the fulness of her first greeting, that she could not trust me to come close to her. Though her words were those of a lover, she kept herself withdrawn as if a mile of space interposed between us.

"Why did you run away from me when you woke in the cave?" I said.

"Did I?" she returned. "That was very unkind of me; but I did not know better."

"I wish I could see you. The night is very dark."

"So it is. Come to my grotto. There is light there."

"Have you another cave, then?"

"Come and see."

But she did not move until I rose first, and then she was on her feet before I could offer my hand to help her. She came close to my side, and conducted me through the wood. But once or twice, when, involuntarily almost, I was about to put my arm around her as we walked on through the warm gloom, she sprang away several paces, always keeping her face full towards me, and then stood looking at me, slightly stooping, in the attitude of one who fears some half-seen enemy. It was too dark to discern the expression of her face. Then she would return and walk close beside me again, as if nothing had happened. I thought this strange; but, besides that I had almost, as I said before, given up the attempt to account for appearances in fairy land, I judged that it would be very unfair to expect from one who had slept so long and had been so suddenly awakened, a behaviour correspondent to what I might unreflectingly look for. I knew not what she might have been dreaming about. Besides, it was possible that, while her words were free, her sense of touch might be exquisitely delicate.

At length, after walking a long way in the woods, we arrived at another thicket, through the intertexture of which was glimmering a pale rosy light.

"Push aside the branches," she said, "and make room for us to enter."

I did as she told me.

"Go in," she said; "I will follow you."

I did as she desired, and found myself in a little cave, not very unlike the marble cave. It was festooned and draperied with all kinds of green that cling to shady rocks. In the furthest corner, half-hidden in leaves, through which it glowed, mingling lovely shadows between them, burned a bright rosy flame on a little earthen lamp. The lady glided round by the wall from behind me, still keeping her face towards me, and seated herself in the furthest corner, with her back to the lamp, which she hid completely from my view. I then saw indeed a form of perfect loveliness before me. Almost it seemed as if the light of the rose-lamp shone through her (for it could not be reflected from her); such a delicate shade of pink seemed to shadow what in itself must be a marbly whiteness of hue. I discovered afterwards, however, that there was one thing in it I did not like; which was, that the white part of the eye was tinged with the same slight roseate hue as the rest of the form. It is strange that I cannot recall her features; but they, as well as her somewhat girlish figure, left on me simply and only the impression of intense loveliness. I lay down at her feet, and gazed up into her face as I lay.

She began, and told me a strange tale, which, likewise, I cannot recollect; but which, at every turn and every pause, somehow or other fixed my eyes and thoughts upon her extreme beauty; seeming always to culminate in something that had a relation, revealed or hidden, but always operative, with her own loveliness. I lay entranced. It was a tale which brings back a feeling as of snows and tempests; torrents and water-sprites; lovers parted for long, and meeting at last; with a gorgeous summer night to close up the whole. I listened till she and I were blended with the tale; till she and I were the whole history. And we had met at last in this same cave of greenery, while the summer night hung round us heavy with love, and the odours that crept through the silence from the sleeping woods were the only signs of an outer world that invaded our solitude. What followed I cannot clearly remember. The succeeding horror almost obliterated it. I woke as a grey dawn stole into the cave. The damsel had disappeared; but in the shrubbery at the mouth of the cave, stood a strange horrible object. It looked like an open coffin set up on one end; only that the part for the head and neck was defined from the shoulder-part. In fact it was a rough representation of the human frame, only hollow, as if made of decaying bark torn from a tree. It had arms, which were only slightly seamed, down from the shoulder-blade by the elbow, as if the bark had healed again from the cut of a knife. But the arms moved, and the hands and fingers were tearing asunder a long silky tress of hair. The thing turned round—it had for a face and front those of my enchant-ress, but now of a pale greenish hue in the light of the morning, and with dead lustreless eyes. In the horror of the moment, another fear invaded me. I put my hand to my waist, and found indeed that my girdle of beech-leaves was gone. Hair again in her hands, she was tearing it fiercely. Once more, as she turned, she laughed a low laugh, but now full of scorn and derision; and then she said, as if to a companion with whom she had been talking while I slept, "There he is; you can take him now." I lay still, petrified with dismay and fear; for I now saw another figure beside her, which, although vague and indistinct, I yet recognised but too well. It was the Ash-tree. My beauty was the Maid of the Alder! and she was giving me, spoiled of my only availing defence, into the hands of my awful foe. The Ash bent his

Gorgon-head, and entered the cave. I could not stir. He drew near me. His ghoul-eyes and his ghastly face fascinated me. He came stooping, with the hideous hand outstretched, like a beast of prey. I had given myself up to a death of unfathomable horror, when, suddenly, and just as he was on the point of seizing me, the dull, heavy blow of an axe echoed through the wood, followed by others in quick repetition. The Ash shuddered and groaned, withdrew the outstretched hand, retreated backwards to the mouth of the cave, then turned and disappeared amongst the trees. The other walking Death looked at me once, with a careless dislike on her beautifully moulded features; then, heedless any more to conceal her hollow deformity, turned her frightful back and likewise vanished amid the green obscurity without. I lay and wept. The Maid of the Alder-tree had befooled me—nearly slain me—in spite of all the warnings I had received from those who knew my danger.

CHAPTER VII

Fight on, my men, Sir Andrew sayes,
    A little Ime hurt, but yett not slaine;
Ile but lye downe and bleede awhile,
    And then Ile rise and fight againe.
                    Ballad of Sir Andrew Barton.

BUT I COULD not remain where I was any longer, though the daylight was hateful to me, and the thought of the great, innocent, bold sunrise unendurable. Here there was no well to cool my face, smarting with the bitterness of my own tears. Now would I have washed in the well of that grotto, had it flowed clear as the rivers of Paradise. I rose, and feebly left the sepulchral cave. I took my way I knew not whither, but still towards the sunrise. The birds were singing; but not for me. All the creatures spoke a language of their own, with which I had nothing to do, and to which I cared not to find the key any more. I walked listlessly along. What distressed me most—more even than my own folly—was the perplexing question—How can beauty and ugliness dwell so near? Even with her altered complexion and her face of dislike; disenchanted of the belief that clung around her; known for a living, walking sepulchre, faithless, deluding, traitorous; I felt, notwithstanding all this, that she was beautiful. Upon this I pondered with undiminished perplexity, though not without some gain. Then I began to make surmises as to the mode of my deliverance; and concluded that some hero, wandering in search of adventure, had heard how the forest was infested; and, knowing it was useless to attack the evil thing in person, had assailed with his battle-axe the body in which he dwelt, and on which he was dependent for his power of mischief in the wood. "Very likely," I thought, "the repentant knight, who warned me of the evil which has befallen me, was busy retrieving his lost honor, while I was sinking into the same sorrow with himself; and, hearing of the dangerous and mysterious being, arrived at his tree in time to save me from being dragged to its roots, and buried like carrion, to nourish him for yet deeper insatiableness." I found afterwards that my conjecture was correct. I wondered how he had fared when his blows recalled the Ash himself, and that too I learned afterwards.

I walked on the whole day, with intervals of rest, but without food; for I could not have eaten, had any been offered me; till, in the afternoon, I seemed to approach the outskirts of the forest, and at length arrived at a farm-house. An unspeakable joy arose in my heart at beholding an abode of human beings once more, and I hastened up to the door, and knocked. A kind-looking, matronly woman, still handsome, made her appearance; who, as soon as she saw me, said kindly, "Ah, my poor boy, you have come from the wood! Were you in it last night?"

I should have ill endured, the day before, to be called *boy;* but now the motherly kindness of the word went to my heart; and, like a boy indeed, I burst into tears. She soothed me right gently; and, leading me into a room, made me lie down on a settle, while she went to find me some refreshment. She soon returned with food, but I could not eat. She almost compelled me to swallow some wine, when I revived sufficiently to be able to answer some of her questions. I told her the whole story.

"It is just as I feared," she said; "but you are now for the night beyond the reach of any of these dreadful creatures. It is no wonder they could delude a child like you. But I must beg you, when my husband comes in, not to say a word about these things; for he thinks me even half crazy for believing anything of the sort. But I must believe my senses, as he cannot believe beyond his, which give him no intimations of this kind. I think he could spend the whole of Midsummer-eve in the wood and come back with the report that he saw nothing worse than himself. Indeed, good man, he would hardly find anything better than himself, if he had seven more senses given him."

"But tell me how it is that she could be so beautiful without any heart at all—without any place even for a heart to live in."

"I cannot quite tell," she said; "but I am sure she would not look so beautiful if she did not take means to make herself look more beautiful than she is. And then, you know, you began by being in love with her before you saw her beauty, mistaking her for the lady of the marble— another kind altogether, I should think. But the chief thing that makes her beautiful is this: that, although she loves no man, she loves the love of any man; and when she finds one in her power, her desire to bewitch him and gain his love, (not for the sake of his love either, but that she may be conscious anew of her own beauty, through the admiration he manifests) makes her very lovely—with a self-destructive beauty, though; for it is that which is constantly wearing her away within, till, at last, the decay will reach her face, and her whole front, when all the lovely mask of nothing will fall to pieces, and she be vanished for ever. So a wise man, whom she met in the wood some years ago, and who, I think, for all his wisdom, fared no better than you, told me, when, like you, he spent the next night here, and recounted to me his adventures."

I thanked her very warmly for her solution, though it was but partial; wondering much that in her, as in the woman I met on my first entering the forest, there should be such superiority to her apparent condition. Here she left me to take some rest; though, indeed, I was much too agitated to rest in any other way than by simply ceasing to move.

In half an hour, I heard a heavy step approach and enter the house. A jolly voice, whose slight huskiness appeared to proceed from overmuch laughter, called out: "Betsy, the pigs' trough is quite empty, and that is a pity. Let them swill, lass! They're of no use but to get fat. Ha! ha! ha! Gluttony is not forbidden in their commandments. Ha! ha! ha!" The very voice, kind and jovial, seemed to disrobe the room of the strange look which all new places wear—to disenchant it out of the realm of the ideal into that of the actual. It began to look as if I had known every corner of it for twenty years; and when, soon after, the dame came and fetched me to partake of their early supper, the grasp of his great hand, and the harvest-moon of his benevolent face, which was needed to light up the rotundity of the globe beneath it, produced such a reaction in me, that, for a moment, I could hardly believe that there was a Fairy Land; and that all I had passed through since I left home, had not been the wandering dream of a diseased imagination, operating on a too mobile frame, not merely causing me indeed to travel, but peopling for me with vague phantoms the regions through which my actual steps had led me. But the next moment, my eye fell upon a little girl who was sitting in the chimney corner, with a little book open on her knee, from which she had apprently just looked up to fix great inquiring eyes upon me. I believed in Fairy Land again. She went on with her reading, as soon as she saw that I observed her looking at me. I went near, and peeping over her shoulder, saw that she was reading *The History of Graciosa and Percinet*.

"Very improving book, sir," remarked the old farmer, with a good-humoured laugh. "We are in the very hottest corner of Fairy Land here. Ha! ha! Stormy night, last night, sir."

"Was it, indeed?" I rejoined. "It was not so with me. A lovelier night I never saw."

"Indeed! Where were you last night?"

"I spent it in the forest. I had lost my way."

"Ah! then, perhaps, you will be able to convince my good woman, that there is nothing very remarkable about the forest; for, to tell the truth, it bears but a bad name in these parts. I dare say you saw nothing worse than yourself there?"

"I hope I did," was my inward reply; but, for an audible one, I contented myself with saying, "Why, I certainly did see some appearances I could hardly account for; but that is nothing to be wondered at in an unknown wild forest, and with the uncertain light of the moon alone to go by."

"Very true! you speak like a sensible man, sir. We have but few sensible folks round about us. Now, you would hardly credit it, but my wife believes every fairy-tale that ever was written. I cannot account for it. She is a most sensible woman in everything else."

"But should not that make you treat her belief with something of respect, though you cannot share in it yourself?"

"Yes, that is all very well in theory; but when you come to live every day in the midst of absurdity, it is far less easy to behave respectfully to it. Why, my wife actually believes the story of the 'White Cat.' You know it, I dare say."

"I read all these tales when a child, and know that one especially well."

"But, father," interposed the little girl in the chimney-corner, "you know quite well that mother is descended from that very princess who was changed by the wicked fairy into a white cat. Mother has told me so many times, and you ought to believe everything she says."

"I can easily believe that," rejoined the farmer, with another fit of laughter; "for, the other night, a mouse came gnawing and scratching beneath the floor, and would not let us go to sleep. Your mother sprang out of bed, and going as near as she could, mewed so infernally like a great cat, that the noise ceased instantly. I believe the poor mouse died of the fright, for we have never heard it again. Ha! ha! ha!"

The son, an ill-looking youth, who had entered during the conversation, joined in his father's laugh; but his laugh was very different from the old man's: it was polluted with a sneer. I watched him, and saw that, as soon as it was over, he looked scared, as if he dreaded some evil consequences to follow his presumption. The woman stood near, waiting till we should seat ourselves at the table, and listening to it all with an amused air, which had something in it of the look with which one listens to the sententious remarks of a pompous child. We sat down to supper, and I ate heartily. My bygone distress began already to look far off.

"In what direction are you going?" asked the old man.

"Eastward," I replied; nor could I have given a more definite answer. "Does the forest extend much further in that direction?"

"Oh! for miles and miles; I do not know how far. For although I have lived on the borders of it all my life, I have been too busy to make journeys of discovery into it. Nor do I see what I could discover. It is only trees and trees, till one is sick of them. By the way, if you follow the eastward track from here, you will pass close to what the children say is the very house of the ogre that Hop-o'-my-Thumb visited, and ate his little daughters with the crowns of gold."

"Oh, father! ate his little daughters! No; he only changed their gold crowns for nightcaps; and the great long-toothed ogre killed them in mistake; but I do not think even he ate them, for you know they were his own little ogresses."

"Well, well, child; you know all about it a great deal better than I do. However, the house has, of course, in such a foolish neighbourhood as this, a bad enough name; and I must confess there is a woman living in it, with teeth long enough and white enough too for the lineal descendant of the greatest ogre that ever was made. I think you had better not go near her."

In such talk as this the night wore on. When supper was finished, which lasted some time, my hostess conducted me to my chamber.

"If you had not had enough of it already," she said, "I would have put you in another room, which looks towards the forest; and where you would most likely have seen something more of its inhabitants. For they frequently pass the window, and even enter the room sometimes. Strange creatures spend whole nights in it, at certain seasons of the year. I am used to it, and do not mind it. No more does my little girl, who sleeps in it always. But this room looks southward towards the open country, and they never show themselves here; at least I never saw any."

I was somewhat sorry not to gather any experience that I might have, of the inhabitants of Fairy Land; but the effect of the farmer's company, and of my own later adventures, was such, that I chose an undisturbed night in my more human quarters; which, with their clean white curtains and white linen, were very inviting to my weariness.

In the morning, I awoke refreshed, after a profound and dreamless sleep. The sun was high, when I looked out of the window, shining over a wide, undulating, cultivated country. Various garden-vegetables were growing beneath my window. Everything was radiant with clear sunlight. The dew-drops were sparkling their busiest; the cows in a near-by field were eating as if they had not been at it all day yesterday; the maids were singing at their work as they passed two and fro between the out-houses: I did not believe in Fairy Land. I went down, and found the family already at breakfast. But before I entered the room where they sat, the little girl came to me, and looked up in my face, as though she wanted to say something to me. I stooped towards her; she put her arms round my neck, and her mouth to my ear, and whispered:—

"A white lady has been flitting about the house all night."

"No whispering behind doors!" cried the farmer; as we entered together. "Well, how have you slept? No bogies, eh?"

"Not one, thank you; I slept uncommonly well."

"I am glad to hear it. Come and breakfast."

After breakfast, the farmer and his son went out; and I was left alone with the mother and daughter.

"When I looked out of the window this morning," I said, "I felt almost certain that Fairy Land was all a delusion of my brain; but whenever I come near you or your little daughter, I feel differently. Yet I could persuade myself, after my last adventures, to go back, and have nothing more to do with such strange beings."

"How will you go back?" said the woman.

"Nay, that I do not know."

"Because I have heard that, for those who enter Fairy Land, there is no way of going back. They must go on, and go through it. How, I do not in the least know."

"That is quite the impression on my own mind. Something compels me to go on, as if my only path was onward; but I feel less inclined this morning to continue my adventures."

"Will you come and see my little child's room? She sleeps in the one I told you of, looking towards the forest."

"Willingly," I said.

So we went together, the little girl running before to open the door for us. It was a large room, full of old-fashioned furniture, that seemed to have once belonged to some great house. The window was built with a low arch, and filled with lozenge-shaped panes. The wall was very thick, and built of solid stone. I could see that part of the house had been erected against the remains of some old castle or abbey, or other great building; the fallen stones of which had probably served to complete it. But as soon as I looked out of the window, a gush of wonderment and longing flowed over my soul like the tide of a great sea. Fairy Land lay before me, and drew me towards it with an irresistible attraction. The trees bathed their great heads in the waves of the morning, while their roots were planted deep in gloom; save where on the borders the sunshine broke against their stems, or swept in long streams through their avenues, washing with brighter hue all the leaves over which it flowed; revealing the rich brown of the decayed leaves and fallen pine-cones, and the delicate greens of the long grasses and tiny forests of moss that covered the channel over which it passed in motionless rivers of light. I turned hurriedly to bid my hostess farewell without further delay. She smiled at my haste, but with an anxious look.

"You had better not go near the house of the ogre, I think. My son will show you into another path, which will join the first beyond it."

Not wishing to be headstrong or too confident any more, I agreed; and having taken leave of my kind entertainers, went into the wood, accompanied by the youth. He scarcely spoke as we went along; but he led me through the trees till we struck upon a path. He told me to follow it, and, with a muttered "good morning," left me.

CHAPTER VIII

Ich bin ein Theil des Theils, der anfangs alles war.
GOETHE.—*Mephistopheles* in *Faust*.
I am a part of the part, which at first was the whole.

MY SPIRITS ROSE as I went deeper into the forest; but I could not regain my former elasticity of mind. I found cheerfulness to be like life itself—not to be created by an argument. Afterwards I learned, that the best way to manage some kinds of painful thoughts, is to dare them to do their worst; to let them lie and gnaw at your heart till they are tired; and you find you still have a residue of life they cannot kill. So, better and worse, I went on, till I came to a little clearing in the forest. In the middle of this clearing stood a long, low hut, built with one end against a single tall cypress, which rose like a spire to the building. A vague misgiving crossed my mind when I saw it; but I must needs go closer, and look through a little half-open door, near the opposite end from the cypress. Window I saw none. On peeping in, and looking towards the further end, I saw a lamp burning, with a dim, reddish flame, and the head of a woman, bent downwards, as if reading by its light. I could see nothing more for a few moments. At length, as my eyes got used to the dimness of the place, I saw that the part of the rude building near me was used for household purposes; for several rough utensils lay here and there, and a bed stood in the corner. An irresistible attraction caused me to enter. The woman never raised her face, the upper part of which alone I could see distinctly; but, as soon as I stepped within the threshold, she began to read aloud, in a low and now altogether unpleasant voice, from an ancient little volume which she held open with one hand on the table upon which stood the lamp. What she read was something like this:

"So, then, as darkness had no beginning, neither will it ever have an end. So, then, is it eternal. The negation of aught else, is its affirmation. Where the light cannot come, there abideth the darkness. The light doth but hollow a mine out of the infinite extension of the darkness. And ever upon the steps of the light treadeth the darkness; yea, springeth in fountains and wells amidst it, from the secret channels of its mighty sea. Truly, man is but a passing flame, moving unquietly amid the surrounding rest of night; without which he yet could not be, and whereof he is in part compounded."

As I drew nearer, and she read on, she moved a little to turn a leaf of the dark old volume, and I saw that her face was sallow and slightly forbidding. Her forehead was high, and her black eyes repressedly quiet. But she took no notice of me. This end of the cottage, if cottage it could be called, was destitute of furniture, except the table with the lamp, and the chair on which the woman sat. In one corner was a door, apparently of a cupboard in the wall, but which might lead to a room beyond. Still the irresistible desire which had made me enter the building, urged me: I must open that door, and see what was beyond it. I approached, and laid my hand on the rude latch. Then the woman spoke, but without lifting her head or looking at me: "You had better not open that door." This was uttered quite quietly; and she went on with her reading, partly in silence, partly aloud; but both modes seemed equally intended for herself alone. The prohibition, however, only increased my desire to see; and as she took no further notice, I gently opened the door to its full width, and looked in. At first, I saw nothing worthy of attention. It seemed a common closet, with shelves on each hand, on which stood various little necessaries for the humble uses of a cottage. In one corner stood one or two brooms, in another a hatchet and other common tools; showing that it was in use every hour of the day for household purposes. But, as I looked, I saw that there were no shelves at the back, and that an empty space went in further; its termination appearing to be a faintly glimmering wall or curtain, somewhat less, however, than the width and height of the doorway where I stood. But, as I continued looking, for a few seconds, towards this faintly-luminous limit, my eyes came into true relation with their object. All at once, with such a shiver as when one is suddenly conscious of the presence of another in a room where he has, for hours, considered himself alone, I saw that the seemingly luminous extremity was a sky, as of night, beheld through the long perspective of a narrow, dark passage, through what, or built of what, I could not tell. As I gazed, I clearly discerned two or three stars glimmering faintly in the distant blue. But, suddenly, and as if it had been running fast from a far distance for this very point, and had turned the corner without abating its swiftness, a dark figure sped into and along the passage from the blue opening at the remote end. I started back and shuddered, but kept looking, for I could not help it. On and on it came, with a speedy approach but delayed arrival; till, at last, through the many gradations of approach, it seemed to come within the sphere of myself, rushed up to me, and passed me into the cottage. All I could tell of its appearance was, that it seemed to be a dark human figure. Its motion was entirely noiseless, and it might be called a gliding, were it not that it appeared that of a runner, but with ghostly feet. I had moved back yet a little to let him pass me, and looked round after him instantly. I could not see him.

"Where is he?" I said, in some alarm, to the woman, who still sat reading.

"There, on the floor, behind you," she said, pointing with her arm half-outstretched, but not lifting her eyes. I turned and looked, but saw nothing. Then with a feeling that there was yet something behind me, I looked round over my shoulder; and there, on the ground, lay a black shadow, the size of a man. It was so dark, that I could see it in the dim light of the lamp, which shone full upon it, apparently without thinning at all the intensity of its hue.

"I told you," said the woman, "you had better not look into that closet."

"What is it?" I said, with a growing sense of horror.

"It is only your shadow that has found you," she replied. "Everybody's shadow is ranging up and down looking for him. I believe you call it by a different name in your world: yours has found you, as every person's is almost certain to do who looks into that closet, especially after meeting one in the forest, whom I dare say you have met."

Here, for the first time, she lifted her head, and looked full at me: her mouth was full of long, white, shining teeth; and I knew that I was in the house of the ogre. I could not speak, but turned and left the house, with the shadow at my heels. "A nice sort of valet to have," I said to myself bitterly, as I stepped into the sunshine, and, looking over my shoulder, saw that it lay yet blacker in the full blaze of the sunlight. Indeed, only when I stood between it and the sun, was the blackness at all diminished. I was so bewildered—stunned—both by the event itself and its suddenness, that I could not at all realize to myself what it would be to have such a constant and strange attendance; but with a dim conviction that my present dislike would soon grow to loathing, I took my dreary way through the wood.

CHAPTER IX

O Lady! we receive but what we give,
And in our life alone does nature live:
Ours is her wedding garment, ours her shroud!

*   *   *

Ah! from the soul itself must issue forth,
A light, a glory, a fair luminous cloud,
Enveloping the Earth—
And from the soul itself must there be sent
A sweet and potent voice, of its own birth,
Of all sweet sounds the life and element!
COLERIDGE.

FROM THIS TIME, until I arrived at the palace of Fairy Land, I can attempt no consecutive account of my wanderings and adventures. Everything, henceforward, existed for me in its relation to my attendant. What influence he exercised upon everything into contact with which I was brought, may be understood from a few detached instances. To begin with this very day on which he first joined me: after I had walked heartlessly along for two or three hours, I was very weary, and lay down to rest in a most delightful part of the forest, carpeted with wild-flowers. I lay for half an hour in a dull repose, and then got up to pursue my way. The flowers on the spot where I had lain were crushed to the earth; but I saw that they would soon lift their heads and rejoice again in the sun and air. Not so those on which my shadow had lain. The very outline of it could be traced in the withered lifeless grass, and the scorched and shrivelled flowers which stood there, dead, and hopeless of any resurrection. I shuddered, and hastened away with sad forebodings.

In a few days, I had reason to dread an extension of its baleful influences from the fact, that it was no longer confined to one position in regard to myself. Hitherto, when seized with an irresistible desire to look on my evil demon (which longing would unaccountably seize me at any moment, returning at longer or shorter intervals, sometimes every minute), I had to turn my head backwards, and look over my shoulder; in which position, as long as I could retain it, I was fascinated. But one day, having come out on a clear grassy hill, which commanded a glorious prospect, though of what I cannot now tell, my shadow moved round, and came in front of me. And, presently, a new manifestation increased my distress. For it began to coruscate, and shoot out on all sides a radiation of dim shadow. These rays of gloom issued from the central shadow as from a black sun, lengthening and shortening with continual change. But wherever a ray struck, that part of earth, or sea, or sky, became void, and desert, and sad to my heart. On this, the first development of its new power, one ray shot out beyond the rest, seeming to lengthen infinitely, until it smote the great sun on the face, which withered and darkened beneath the blow. I turned away and went on. The shadow retreated to its former position; and when I looked again, it had drawn in all its spears of darkness, and followed like a dog at my heels.

Once, as I passed by a cottage, there came out a lovely fairy child, with two wondrous toys, one in each hand. The one was the tube through which the fairy-gifted poet looks when he beholds the same thing everywhere; the other that through which he looks when he combines into new forms of loveliness those images of beauty which his

"A runner . . . with ghostly feet."

ARTHUR HUGHES

own choice has gathered from all regions wherein he has travelled. Round the child's head was an aureole of emanating rays. As I looked at him in wonder and delight, round crept from behind me the something dark, and the child stood in my shadow. Straightway he was a commonplace boy, with a rough broad-brimmed straw hat, through which brim the sun shone from behind. The toys he carried were a multiplying glass and a kaleidoscope. I sighed and departed.

One evening, as a great silent flood of western gold flowed through an avenue in the woods, down the stream, just as when I saw him first, came the sad knight, riding on his chestnut steed. But his armour did not shine half so red as when I saw him first. Many a blow of mighty sword and axe, turned aside by the strength of his mail, and glancing adown the surface, had swept from its path the fretted rust, and the glorious steel had answered the kindly blow with the thanks of returning light. These streaks and spots made his armour look like the floor of a forest in the sunlight. His forehead was higher than before, for the contracting wrinkles were nearly gone; and the sadness that remained on his face was the sadness of a dewy summer twilight, not that of a frosty autumn morn. He, too, had met the Alder-maiden as I, but he had plunged into the torrent of mighty deeds, and the stain was nearly washed away. No shadow followed him. He had not entered the dark house; he had not had time to open the closet door. "Will he ever look in?" I said to myself. "*Must* his shadow find him some day?" But I could not answer my own questions.

We travelled together for two days, and I began to love him. It was plain that he suspected my story in some degree; and I saw him once or twice looking curiously and anxiously at my attendant gloom, which all this time had remained very obsequiously behind me; but I offered no explanation, and he asked none. Shame at my neglect of his warning, and a horror which shrunk from even alluding to its cause, kept me silent; till, on the evening of the second day, some noble words from my companion roused all my heart; and I was at the point of falling on his neck, and telling him the whole story; seeking, if not for helpful advice, for of that I was hopeless, yet for the comfort of sympathy—when round slid the shadow and inwrapt my friend; and I could not trust him. The glory of his brow vanished; the light of his eye grew cold; and I held my peace. The next morning we parted.

But the most dreadful thing of all was, that I now began to feel something like satisfaction in the presence of the shadow. I began to be rather vain of my attendant, saying to myself; "In a land like this, with so many illusions everywhere, I need his aid to disenchant the things around me. He does away with all appearances, and shows me things in their true color and form. And I am not one to be fooled with the vanities of the common crowd. I will not see beauty where there is none. I will dare to behold things as they are. And if I live in a waste instead of a paradise, I will live knowing where I live." But of this a certain exercise of his power which soon followed quite cured me, turning my feeling towards him once more into loathing and distrust. It was thus:—

One bright noon, a little maiden joined me, coming through the wood in a direction at right angles to my path. She came along singing and dancing, happy as a child, though she seemed almost a woman. In her hands—now in one, now in another—she carried a small globe, bright and clear as the purest crystal. This seemed at once her plaything and her greatest treasure. At one moment, you would have thought her utterly careless of it, and at another, overwhelmed with anxiety for its safety. But I believe she was taking care of it all the time, perhaps not least when least occupied about it. She stopped by me with a smile, and bade me good day with the sweetest voice. I felt a wonderful liking to the child—for she produced on me more the impression of a child, though my understanding told me differently. We talked a little, and then walked on together in the direction I had been pursuing. I asked her about the globe she carried, but getting no definite answer, I held out my hand to take it. She drew back, and said, but smiling almost invitingly the while, "You must not touch it;"—then, after a moment's pause—"Or if you do, it must be very gently." I touched it with a finger. A slight vibratory motion arose in it, accompanied, or perhaps manifested, by a faint sweet sound. I touched it again, and the sound increased. I touched it the third time: a tiny torrent of harmony rolled out of the little globe. She would not let me touch it any more.

We travelled on together all that day. She left me when twilight came on; but next day, at noon, she met me as before, and again we travelled till evening. The third day she came once more at noon, and we walked on together. Now, though we had talked about a great many things connected with Fairy Land, and the life she had led hitherto, I had never been able to learn anything about the globe. This day, however, as we went on, the shadow glided round and inwrapt the maiden. It could not change her. But my desire to know about the globe, which in his gloom began to waver as with an inward light, and to shoot out flashes of many-coloured flame, grew irresistible. I put out both my hands and laid hold of it. It began to sound as before. The sound rapidly increased, till it grew a low tempest of harmony, and the globe trembled, and quivered, and throbbed between my hands. I had not the heart to pull it away from the maiden, though I held it in spite of her attempts to take it from me; yes, I shame to say, in spite of her prayers, and, at last, her tears. The music went on growing in intensity and complication of tones, and the globe vibrated and heaved; till at last it burst in our hands, and a black vapour broke upwards from out of it; then turned, as if blown sideways, and enveloped the maiden, hiding even the shadow in its blackness. She held fast the fragments, which I abandoned, and fled from me into the forest in the direction whence she had come, wailing like a child, and crying, "You have broken my globe; my globe is broken—my globe is broken!" I followed her, in the hope of comforting her; but had not pursued her far, before a sudden cold gust of wind bowed the tree-tops above us, and swept through their stems around us; a great cloud overspread the day, and a fierce tempest came on, in which I lost sight of her. It lies heavy on my heart to this hour. At night, ere I fall asleep, often, whatever I may be thinking about, I suddenly hear her voice, crying out, "You have broken my globe; my globe is broken; ah, my globe!"

Here I will mention one more strange thing; but whether this peculiarity was owing to my shadow at all, I am not able to assure myself. I came to a village, the inhabitants of which could not at first sight be distinguished from the dwellers in our own land. They rather avoided than sought my company, though they were very pleasant when I addressed them. But at last I observed, that whenever I came within a certain distance of any one of them, which distance, however, varied with different individuals, the whole appearance of the person began to change; and this change increased in degree as I approached. When I receded to the former distance, the former appearance was restored. The nature of the change was grotesque, following no fixed rule. The nearest resemblance to it that I know, is the distortion produced in your countenance when you look at it as reflected in a concave or convex surface—say, either side of a bright spoon. Of this phenomenon I first became aware in a rather ludicrous way. My host's daughter was a very pleasant pretty girl, who made herself more agreeable to me than most of those about me. For some days my companion-shadow had been less obtrusive than usual; and such was the reaction of spirits occasioned by the simple mitigation of torment, that, although I had cause enough besides to be gloomy, I felt light and comparatively happy. My impression is, that she was quite aware of the law of appearances that existed between the people of the place and myself, and had resolved to amuse herself at my expense; for one evening, after some jesting and raillery, she, somehow or other, provoked me to attempt to kiss her. But she was well defended from any assault of the kind. Her countenance became, of a sudden, absurdly hideous; the pretty mouth was elongated and otherwise amplified sufficiently to have allowed of six simultaneous kisses. I started back in bewildered dismay; she burst into the merriest fit of laughter, and ran from the room. I soon found that the same undefinable law of change operated between me and all the other villagers; and that, to feel I was in pleasant company, it was absolutely necessary for me to discover and observe the right focal distance between myself and each one with whom I had to do. This done, all went pleasantly enough. Whether, when I happened to neglect this precaution, I presented to them an equally ridiculous appearance, I did not ascertain; but I presume that the alteration was common to the approximating parties. I was likewise unable to determine whether I was a necessary party to the production of this strange transformation, or whether it took place as well, under the given circumstances, between the inhabitants themselves.

CHAPTER X

From Eden's bowers the full-fed rivers flow,
To guide the outcasts to the land of woe:
Our Earth one little toiling streamlet yields,
To guide the wanderers to the happy fields.

AFTER LEAVING THIS village, where I had rested for nearly a week, I travelled through a desert region of dry sand and glittering rocks, peopled principally by goblin-fairies. When I first entered their domains, and, indeed, whenever I fell in with another tribe of them, they began mocking me with offered handfuls of gold and jewels, making hideous grimaces at me, and performing the most antic homage, as if they thought I expected reverence, and meant to humour me like a maniac. But ever, as soon as one cast his eye on the shadow behind me, he made a wry face, partly of pity, partly of contempt, and looked ashamed, as if he had been caught doing something inhuman; then, throwing down his handful of gold, and ceasing all his grimaces, he stood aside to let me pass in peace, and made signs to his companions to do the like. I had no inclination to observe them much, for the shadow was in my heart as well as at my heels. I walked listlessly and almost hopelessly along, till I arrived one day at a small spring; which, bursting cool from the heart of a sun-heated rock, flowed somewhat southwards from the direction I had been taking. I drank of this spring, and found myself wonderfully refreshed. A kind of love to the cheerful little stream arose in my heart. It was born in a desert; but it seemed to say to itself, "I will flow, and sing, and lave my banks, till I make my desert a paradise." I thought I could not do better than follow it, and see what it made of it. So down with the stream I went, over rocky lands, burning with sunbeams. But the rivulet flowed not far, before a few blades of grass appeared on its banks, and then, here and there, a stunted bush. Sometimes it disappeared altogether under ground; and after I had wandered some distance, as near as I could guess, in the direction it seemed to take, I would suddenly hear it again, singing, sometimes far away to my right or left, amongst new rocks, over which it made new cataracts of watery melodies. The verdure on its banks increased as it flowed; other streams joined it; and at last, after many days' travel, I found myself, one gorgeous summer evening, resting by the side of a broad river, with a glorious horse-chestnut tree towering above me, and dropping its blossoms, milk-white and rosy-red all about me. As I sat, a gush of joy sprang forth in my heart, and overflowed at my eyes. Through my tears, the whole landscape glimmered in such bewitching loveliness, that I felt as if I were entering Fairy Land for the first time, and some loving hand were waiting to cool my head, and a loving word to warm my heart. Roses, wild roses, everywhere! So plentiful were they, they not only perfumed the air, they seemed to dye it a faint rose-hue. The colour floated abroad with the scent, and clomb, and spread, until the whole west blushed and glowed with the gathered incense of roses. And my heart fainted with longing in my bosom. Could I but see the Spirit of the Earth, as I saw once the indwelling woman of the beech-tree, and my beauty of the pale marble, I should be content. Content!—Oh, how gladly would I die of the light of her eyes! Yea, I would cease to be, if that would bring me one word of love from the one mouth. The twilight sank around, and infolded me with sleep. I slept as I had not slept for months. I did not awake till late in the morning; when, refreshed in body and mind, I rose as from the death that wipes out the sadness of life, and then dies itself in the new morrow. Again I followed the stream; now climbing a steep rocky bank that hemmed it in; now wading through long grasses and wild flowers in its path; now through meadows; and anon through woods that crowded down to the very lip of the water.

At length, in a nook of the river, gloomy with the weight of overhanging foliage, and still and deep as a soul in which the torrent eddies of pain have hollowed a great gulf, and then, subsiding in violence, have left it full of a motionless, fathomless sorrow—I saw a little boat lying. So still was the water here, that the boat needed no fastening. It lay as if some one had just stepped ashore, and would in a moment return. But as there were no signs of presence, and no track through the thick bushes; and, moreover, as I was in Fairy Land, where one does very much as he pleases, I forced my way to the brink, stepped into the boat, pushed it, with the help of the tree-branches, out into the stream, lay down in the bottom, and let my boat and me float whither the stream would carry us. I seemed to lose myself in the great flow of sky above me, unbroken in its infinitude, except when, now and then, coming nearer the shore at a bend in the river, a tree would sweep its mighty head silently above mine, and glide away back into the past, never more to fling its shadow over me. I fell asleep in this cradle, in which mother Nature was rocking her weary child; and while I slept, the sun slept not, but went round his arched way. When I awoke, he slept in the waters, and I went on my silent path beneath a round silvery moon. And a pale moon looked up from the floor of the great blue cave that lay in the abysmal silence beneath.

Why are all reflections lovelier than what we call the reality?—not so grand or so strong, it may be, but always lovelier? Fair as is the gliding sloop on the shining sea, the wavering, trembling, unresting sail below, is fairer still. Yea, the reflecting ocean itself reflected in the mirror, has a wondrousness about its waters that somewhat vanishes when I turn towards itself. All mirrors are magic mirrors. The commonest room is a room in a poem when I turn to the glass. (And this reminds me, while I write, of a strange story which I read in the fairy palace, and of which I will try to make a feeble memorial in its place). In whatever way it may be accounted for, of one thing we may be sure, that this feeling is no cheat; for there is no cheating in nature and the simple unsought feelings of the soul. There must be a truth involved in it, though we may but in part lay hold of the meaning. Even the memories of past pain are beautiful; and past delights, though beheld only through clefts in the grey clouds of sorrow, are lovely as Fairy Land. But how have I wandered into the deeper fairy-land of the soul, while as yet I only float towards the fairy palace of Fairy Land! The moon, which is the lovelier memory or reflex of the down-gone sun, the joyous day seen in the faint mirror of the brooding night, had rapt me away.

I sat up in the boat. Gigantic forest trees were about me; through which, like a silver snake, twisted and twined the great river. The little waves, when I moved in the boat, heaved and fell with a plash as of molten silver, breaking the image of the moon into a thousand morsels, fusing again into one, as the ripples of laughter die into the still face of joy. The sleeping woods, in undefined massiveness; the water that flowed in its sleep; and, above all, the enchantress moon, which had cast them all, with her pale eye, into the charmed slumber, sank into my soul, and I felt as if I had died in a dream, and should never more awake.

From this I was partly aroused by a glimmering of white, that, through the trees on the left, vaguely crossed my vision, as I gazed upwards. But the trees again hid the object; and at the moment, some strange melodious bird took up its song, and sang, not an ordinary bird-song, with constant repetitions of the same melody, but what sounded like a continuous strain, in which one thought was expressed, deepening in intensity as evolved in progress. It sounded like a welcome already overshadowed with the coming farewell. As in all sweetest music, a tinge of sadness was in every note. Nor do we know how much of the pleasures even of life we owe to the intermingled sorrows. Joy cannot unfold the deepest truths, although deepest truth must be deepest joy. Cometh white-robed Sorrow, stooping and wan, and flingeth wide the doors she may not enter. Almost we linger with Sorrow for very love.

As the song concluded, the stream bore my little boat with a gentle sweep round a bend of the river; and lo! on a broad lawn, which rose from the water's edge with a long green slope to a clear elevation from which the trees receded on all sides, stood a stately palace glimmering ghostly in the moonshine: it seemed to be built throughout of the whitest marble. There was no reflection of moonlight from windows— there seemed to be none; so there was no cold glitter; only, as I said, a ghostly shimmer. Numberless shadows tempered the shine, from column and balcony and tower. For everywhere galleries ran along the face of the buildings; wings were extended in many directions; and numberless openings, through which the moonbeams vanished into the interior, and which served both for doors and windows, had their separate balconies in front, communicating with a common gallery that rose on its own pillars. Of course, I did not discover all this from the river, and in the moonlight. But, though I was there for many days, I did not succeed in mastering the inner topography of the building, so extensive and complicated was it.

Here I wished to land, but the boat had no oars on board. However, I found that a plank, serving for a seat, was unfastened, and with that I brought the boat to the bank, and scrambled on shore. Deep soft turf sank beneath my feet, as I went up the ascent towards the palace. When I reached it, I saw that it stood on a great platform of marble, with an ascent, by broad stairs of the same, all round it. Arrived on the platform, I found there was an extensive outlook over the forest, which, however, was rather veiled than revealed by the moonlight. Entering by a wide gateway, but without gates, into an inner court, surrounded on all sides by great marble pillars supporting galleries above, I saw a large fountain of porphyry in the middle, throwing up a lofty column of water, which fell, with a noise as of the fusion of all sweet sounds, into a basin beneath; overflowing which, it ran in a single channel towards the interior of the building. Although the moon was by this time so low in the west, that not a ray of her light fell into the court, over the height of the surrounding buildings; yet was the court lighted by a second reflex from the sun of other lands. For the top of the column of water, just as it spread to fall, caught the moonbeams; and like a great pale lamp, hung high in the night air, threw a dim memory of light (as it were) over the court below. This court was paved in diamonds of white and red marble. According to my custom since I entered Fairy Land, of taking for a guide whatever I first found moving in any direction, I followed the stream from the basin of the fountain. It led me to a great open door, beneath the ascending steps of which it ran through a low arch, and disappeared. Entering here, I found myself in a great hall, surrounded with white pillars, and paved with black and white. This I could see by the moonlight, which, from the other side, streamed through open windows into the hall. Its height I could not distinctly see. As soon as I entered, I had the feeling so common to me in the woods, that there were others there besides myself, though I could see no one, and heard no sound to indicate a presence. Since my visit to the Church of Darkness, my power of seeing the fairies of the higher orders had gradually diminished, until it had almost ceased. But I could frequently believe in their presence while unable to see them. Still, although I had company, and doubtless of a safe kind, it seemed rather dreary to spend the night in an empty marble hall, however beautiful; especially as the moon was near the going down, and it would soon be dark. So I began at the place where I entered, and walked round the hall, looking for some door or passage that might lead me to a more hospitable chamber. As I walked, I was deliciously haunted with the feeling that behind some one of the seemingly innumerable pillars, one who loved me was waiting for me. Then I thought she was following me from pillar to pillar as I went along; but no arms came out of the faint moonlight, and no sigh assured me of her presence.

At length I came to an open corridor, into which I turned; notwithstanding that, in doing so, I left the light behind. Along this I walked with outstretched hands, groping my way; till, arriving at another corridor, which seemed to strike off at right angles to that in which I was, I saw at the end a faintly glimmering light, too pale even for moonshine, resembling rather a stray phosphorescence. However, where everything was white, a little light went a great way. So I walked on to the end, and a long corridor it was. When I came up to the light, I found that it proceeded from what looked like silver letters upon a door of ebony; and, to my surprise even in the home of wonder itself, the letters formed the words, *The Chamber of Sir Anodos.* Although I had as yet no right to the honours of a knight, I ventured to conclude that the chamber was indeed intended for me; and, opening the door without hesitation, I entered. Any doubt as to whether I was right in so doing, was soon dispelled. What to my dark eyes seemed a blaze of light, burst upon me. A fire of large pieces of some sweet-scented wood, supported by dogs of silver, was burning on the hearth, and a bright lamp stood on a table, in the midst of a plentiful meal, apparently awaiting my arrival. But what surprised me more than all, was, that the room was in every respect a copy of my own room, the room whence the little stream from my basin had led me into Fairy Land. There was the very carpet of grass and moss and daisies, which I had myself designed; the curtains of pale blue silk, that fell like a cataract over the windows; the old-fashioned bed, with the chintz furniture, on which I had slept from boyhood. "Now I shall sleep," I said to myself. "My shadow dares not come here."

I sat down to the table, and began to help myself to the good things before me with confidence. And now I found, as in many instances before, how true the fairy tales are; for I was waited on, all the time of my meal, by invisible hands. I had scarcely to do more than look towards anything I wanted, when it was brought me, just as if it had come to me of itself. My glass was kept filled with the wine I had chosen, until I looked towards another bottle or decanter; when a fresh glass was substituted, and the other wine supplied. When I had eaten and drunk more heartily and joyfully than ever since I entered Fairy Land, the whole was removed by several attendants, of whom some were male and some female, as I thought I could distinguish from the way the dishes were lifted from the table, and the motion with which they were carried out of the room. As soon as they were all taken away, I heard a sound as of the shutting of a door; and knew that I was left alone. I sat long by the fire, meditating, and wondering how it would all end; and when at length, wearied with thinking, I betook myself to my own old bed, it was half with a hope that, when I awoke in the morning, I should awake not only in my own room, but in my own castle also; and that I should walk out upon my own native soil; and find that Fairy Land was, after all, only a vision of the night. The sound of the falling waters of the fountain floated me into oblivion.

CHAPTER XI

A wilderness of building, sinking far
And self-withdrawn into a wondrous depth,
Far sinking into splendour—without end!
Fabric it seemed of diamond and of gold,
With alabaster domes, and silver spires,
And blazing terrace upon terrace, high
Uplifted.
WORDSWORTH.

BUT WHEN, AFTER a sleep, which, although dreamless, yet left behind it a sense of past blessedness, I awoke in the full morning, I found, indeed, that the room was still my own; but that it looked abroad upon an unknown landscape of forest and hill and dale on the one side—and on the other, upon the marble court, with the great fountain, the crest of which now flashed glorious in the sun, and cast on the pavement beneath, a shower of faint shadows from the waters that fell from it into the marble basin below.

Agreeably to all authentic accounts of the treatment of travellers in Fairy Land, I found by my bedside a complete suit of fresh clothing, just such as I was in the habit of wearing; for, though varied sufficiently from the one removed, it was yet in complete accordance with my tastes. I dressed myself in this, and went out. The whole palace shone like silver in the sun. The marble was partly dull and partly polished; and every pinnacle, dome, and turret ended in a ball, or cone, or cusp of silver. It was like frost-work, and too dazzling, in the sun, for earthly eyes like mine. I will not attempt to describe the environs, save by saying, that all the pleasures to be found in the most varied and artistic arrangement of wood and river, lawn and wild forest, garden and shrubbery, rocky hill and luxurious vale; in living creatures wild and tame, in gorgeous birds, scattered fountains, little streams, and reedy lakes—all were here. Some parts of the palace itself I shall have occasion to describe more minutely.

For this whole morning, I never thought of my demon shadow; and not till the weariness which supervened on delight brought it again to my memory, did I look round to see if it was behind me: it was scarcely discernible. But its presence, however faintly revealed, sent a pang to my heart, for the pain of which, not all the beauties around me could compensate. It was followed, however, by the comforting reflection that, peradventure, I might here find the magic word of power to banish the demon and set me free, so that I should no longer be a man beside myself. The Queen of Fairy Land, thought I, must dwell here: surely she will put forth her power to deliver me, and send me singing through the further gates of her country back to my own land. "Shadow of me!" I said; "which art not me, but which representest thyself to me as me; here I may find a shadow of light which will devour thee, the shadow of darkness! Here I may find a blessing which will fall on thee as a curse, and damn thee to the blackness whence thou hast emerged unbidden." I said this, stretched at length on the slope of the lawn above the river; and as the hope arose within me, the sun came forth from a light fleecy cloud that swept across his face; and hill and dale, and the great river winding on through the still mysterious forest, flashed back his rays as with a silent shout of joy; all nature lived and glowed; the very earth grew warm beneath me; a magnificent dragon-fly went past me like an arrow from a bow, and a whole concert of birds burst into choral song.

The heat of the sun soon became too intense even for passive support. I therefore rose, and sought the shelter of one of the arcades. Wandering along from one to another of these, wherever my heedless steps led me, and wondering everywhere at the simple magnificence of the building, I arrived at another hall, the roof of which was of a pale blue, spangled with constellations of silver stars, and supported by porphyry pillars of a paler red than ordinary.—In this house (I may remark in passing), silver seemed everywhere preferred to gold; and such was the purity of the air, that it showed nowhere signs of tarnishing.—The whole of the floor of this hall, except a narrow path behind the pillars, paved with black, was hollowed into a huge basin, many feet deep, and filled with the purest, most liquid and radiant water. The sides of the basin were white marble, and the bottom was paved with all kinds of refulgent stones, of every shape and hue. In their arrangement, you would have supposed, at first sight, that there was no design, for they seemed to lie as if cast there from careless and playful hands; but it was a most harmonious confusion; and as I looked at the play of their colours, especially when the waters were in motion, I came at last to feel as if not one little pebble could be displaced, without injuring the effect of the whole. Beneath this floor of the water, lay the reflection of the blue inverted roof, fretted with its silver stars, like a second deeper sea, clasping and upholding the first. This fairy bath was probably fed from the fountain in the court. Led by an irresistible desire, I undressed, and plunged into the water. It clothed me as with a new sense and its object both in one. The waters lay so close to me, they seemed to enter and revive my heart. I rose to the surface, shook the water from my hair, and swam as in a rainbow, amid the coruscations of the gems below seen through the agitation caused by my motion. Then, with open eyes, I dived, and swam beneath the surface. And here was a new wonder. For the basin, thus beheld, appeared to extend on all sides like a sea, with here and there groups as of ocean rocks, hollowed by ceaseless billows into wondrous caves and grotesque pinnacles. Around the caves grew sea-weeds of all hues, and the corals glowed between; while far off, I saw the glimmer of what seemed to be creatures of human form at home in the waters. I thought I had been enchanted; and that when I rose to the surface, I should find myself miles from land, swimming alone upon a heaving sea; but when my eyes emerged from the waters, I saw above me the blue spangled vault, and the red pillars around. I dived again, and found myself once more in the heart of a great sea. I then arose, and swam to the edge, where I got out easily, for the water reached the very brim, and, as I drew near, washed in tiny waves over the black marble border. I dressed, and went out, deeply refreshed.

And now I began to discern faint, gracious forms, here and there throughout the building. Some walked together in earnest conversation. Others strayed alone. Some stood in groups, as if looking at and talking about a picture or a statue. None of them heeded me. Nor were they plainly visible to my eyes. Sometimes a group, or single individual, would fade entirely out of the realm of my vision as I gazed. When evening came, and the moon arose, clear as the round of a horizon-sea when the sun hangs over it in the west, I began to see them all more plainly; especially when they came between me and the moon; and yet more especially, when I myself was in the shade. But, even then, I sometimes saw only the passing wave of a white robe; or a lovely arm or neck gleamed by in the moonshine; or white feet went walking alone over the moony sward. Nor, I grieve to say, did I ever come much nearer to these glorious beings, or ever look upon the Queen of the Fairies herself. My destiny ordered otherwise.

In this palace of marble and silver, and fountains and moonshine, I spent many days; waited upon constantly in my own room with everything desirable, and bathing daily in the fairy bath. All this time I was little troubled with my demon shadow. I had a vague feeling that he was somewhere about the palace; but it seemed as if the hope that I should in this place be finally freed from his hated presence, had

sufficed to banish him for a time. How and where I found him, I shall
soon have to relate.

The third day after my arrival, I found the library of the palace; and
here, all the time I remained, I spent most of the middle of the day. For
it was, not to mention far greater attractions, a luxurious retreat from
the noontide sun. During the mornings and afternoons, I wandered
about the lovely neighbourhood, or lay, lost in delicious day-dreams,
beneath some mighty tree on the open lawn. My evenings were by and
by spent in a part of the palace, the account of which, and of my
adventures in connection with it, I must yet postpone for a little.

The library was a mighty hall, lighted from the roof, which was
formed of something like glass, vaulted over in a single piece, and
stained throughout with a great mysterious picture in gorgeous colouring. The walls were lined from floor to roof with books and books; most
of them in ancient bindings, but some in strange new fashions which I
had never seen, and which, were I to make the attempt, I could ill
describe. All around the walls, in front of the books, ran galleries in
rows, communicating by stairs. These galleries were built of all kinds of
coloured stones; all sorts of marble and granite, with porphyry, jasper,
lapis lazuli, agate, and various others, were ranged in wonderful
melody of successive colours. Although the material, then, of which
these galleries and stairs were built, rendered necessary a certain
degree of massiveness in the construction, yet such was the size of the
place, that they seemed to run along the walls like cords. Over some
part of the library descended curtains of silk of various dyes, none of
which I ever saw lifted while I was there; and I felt somehow that it
would be presumptuous in me to venture to look within them. But the
use of the other books seemed free; and day after day I came to the
library, threw myself on one of the many sumptuous eastern carpets,
which lay here and there on the floor, and read, and read, until weary;
if that can be designated as weariness, which was rather the faintness of
rapturous delight; or until, sometimes, the failing of the light invited
me to go abroad, in the hope that a cool gentle breeze might have arisen
to bathe, with an airy invigorating bath, the limbs which the glow of the
burning spirit within had withered no less than the glow of the blazing
sun without.

One peculiarity of these books, or at least most of those I looked into,
I must make a somewhat vain attempt to describe.

If, for instance, it was a book of metaphysics I opened, I had scarcely
read two pages before I seemed to myself to be pondering over
discovered truth, and constructing the intellectual machine whereby to
communicate the discovery to my fellow men. With some books,
however, of this nature, it seemed rather as if the process was removed
yet a great way further back; and I was trying to find the root of a
manifestation, the spiritual truth whence a material vision sprang; or to
combine two propositions, both apparently true, either at once or in
different remembered moods, and to find the point in which their
invisibly converging lines would unite in one, revealing a truth higher
than either and differing from both; though so far from being opposed
to either, that it was that whence each derived its life and power. Or if

the book was one of travels, I found myself the traveller. New lands, fresh experiences, novel customs, rose around me. I walked, I discovered, I fought, I suffered, I rejoiced in my success. Was it a history? I was the chief actor therein. I suffered my own blame; I was glad in my own praise. With a fiction it was the same. Mine was the whole story. For I took the place of the character who was most like myself, and his story was mine; until, grown weary with the life of years condensed in an hour, or arrived at my death-bed, or the end of the volume, I would awake, with a sudden bewilderment, to the consciousness of my present life, recognising the walls and roof around me, and finding I joyed or sorrowed only in a book. If the book was a poem, the words disappeared, or took the subordinate position of an accompaniment to the succession of forms and images that rose and vanished with a soundless rhythm, and a hidden rhyme.

In one, with a mystical title, which I cannot recall, I read of a world that is not like ours. The wondrous account, in such a feeble, fragmentary way as is possible to me, I would willingly impart. Whether or not it was all a poem, I cannot tell; but, from the impulse I felt, when I first contemplated writing it, to break into rhyme, to which impulse I shall give way if it comes upon me again, I think it must have been, partly at least, in verse.

CHAPTER XII

Chained is the Spring. The night-wind bold
  Blows over the hard earth;
Time is not more confused and cold,
  Nor keeps more wintry mirth.

Yet blow, and roll the world about;
  Blow, Time—blow, winter's Wind!
Through chinks of Time, heaven peepeth out,
  And Spring the frost behind.

               G.E.M.

THEY WHO BELIEVE in the influences of the stars over the fates of men, are, in feeling at least, nearer the truth than they who regard the heavenly bodies as related to them merely by a common obedience to an external law. All that man sees has to do with man. Worlds cannot be without an intermundane relationship. The community of the centre of all creation suggests an interradiating connexion and dependence of the parts. Else a grander idea is conceivable than that which is already imbodied. The blank, which is only a forgotten life, lying behind the consciousness, and the misty splendour, which is an undeveloped life, lying before it, may be full of mysterious revelations of other connexions with the worlds around us, than those of science and poetry. No shining belt or gleaming moon, no red and green glory in a self-encircling twin-star, but has a relation with the hidden things of a man's soul, and, it may be, with the secret history of his body as well. They are portions of the living house wherein he abides.

Through the realms of the monarch Sun
Creeps a world, whose course had begun,
On a weary path with a weary pace,
Before the Earth sprang forth on her race:
But many a time the Earth had sped
Around the path she still must tread,
Ere the elder planet, on leaden wing,
Once circled the court of the planet's king.

There, in that lonely and distant star,
The seasons are not as our seasons are;
But many a year hath Autumn to dress
The trees in their matron loveliness;
As long hath old Winter in triumph to go
O'er beauties dead in his vaults below;
And many a year the Spring doth wear
Combing the icicles from her hair;
And Summer, dear Summer, hath years of June,
With large white clouds, and cool showers at noon;
And a beauty that grows to a weight like grief,
Till a burst of tears is the heart's relief.

Children, born when Winter is king,
May never rejoice in the hoping Spring;
Though their own heart-buds are bursting with joy,
And the child hath grown to the girl or boy;
But may die with cold and icy hours
Watching them ever in place of flowers.
And some who awake from their primal sleep,
When the sighs of Summer through forests creep,
Live, and love and are loved again;
Seek for pleasure, and find its pain;
Sink to their last, their forsaken sleeping,
With the same sweet odours around them creeping.

Now the children, there, are not born as the children are born in
worlds nearer to the sun. For they arrive no one knows how. A maiden,
walking alone, hears a cry: for even there a cry is the first utterance;
and searching about, she findeth, under an overhanging rock, or within
a clump of bushes, or, it may be, betwixt grey stones on the side of a hill,
or in any other sheltered and unexpected spot, a little child. This she
taketh tenderly, and beareth home with joy, calling out, "Mother,
mother"—if so be that her mother lives—"I have got a baby—I have
found a child!" All the household gathers round to see;—"*Where is it?
What is it like? Where did you find it?*" and such-like questions, abounding.
And thereupon she relates the whole story of the discovery; for by the
circumstances, such as season of the year, time of the day, condition of
the air, and such like, and, especially, the peculiar and never-repeated
aspect of the heavens and earth at the time, and the nature of the place
of shelter wherein it is found, is determined, or at least indicated, the
nature of the child thus discovered. Therefore, at certain seasons, and
in certain states of the weather, according, in part, to their own fancy,
the young women go out to look for children. They generally avoid

seeking them, though they cannot help sometimes finding them, in places and with circumstances uncongenial to their peculiar likings. But no sooner is a child found, than its claim for protection and nurture obliterates all feeling of choice in the matter. Chiefly, however, in the season of summer, which lasts so long, coming as it does after such long intervals; and mostly in the warm evenings, about the middle of twilight; and principally in the woods and along the river banks, do the maidens go looking for children, just as children look for flowers. And ever as the child grows, yea, more and more as he advances in years, will his face indicate to those who understand the spirit of nature, and her utterances in the face of the world, the nature of the place of his birth, and the other circumstances thereof; whether a clear morning sun guided his mother to the nook whence issued the boy's low cry; or at eve the lonely maiden (for the same woman never finds a second, at least while the first lives) discovers the girl by the glimmer of her white skin, lying in a nest like that of the lark, amid long encircling grasses, and the upward gazing eyes of the lowly daisies; whether the storm bowed the forest trees around, or the still frost fixed in silence the else flowing and babbling stream.

After they grow up, the men and women are but little together. There is this peculiar difference between them, which likewise distinguishes the women from those of the earth. The men alone have arms; the women have only wings. Resplendent wings are they, wherein they can shroud themselves from head to foot in a panoply of glistering glory. By these wings alone, it may frequently be judged in what seasons, and under what aspects they were born. From those that came in winter, go great white wings, white as snow; the edge of every feather shining like the sheen of silver, so that they flash and glitter like frost in the sun. But underneath, they are tinged with a faint pink or rose-colour. Those born in spring have wings of a brilliant green, green as grass; and towards the edges the feathers are enamelled like the surface of the grass-blades. These again are white within. Those that are born in summer have wings of a deep rose-colour, lined with pale gold. And those born in autumn have purple wings, with a rich brown on the inside. But these colours are modified and altered in all varieties, corresponding to the mood of the day and hour, as well as the season of the year; and sometimes I found the various colours so intermingled, that I could not determine even the season, though doubtless the hieroglyphic could be deciphered by more experienced eyes. One splendour, in particular, I remember—wings of deep carmine, with an inner down of warm grey, around a form of brilliant whiteness. She had been found as the sun went down through a low sea-fog, casting crimson along a broad sea-path into a little cave on the shore, where a bathing maiden saw her lying.

But though I speak of sun and fog, and sea and shore, the world there is in some respects very different from the earth whereon men live. For instance, the waters reflect no forms. To the unaccustomed eye they appear, if undisturbed, like the surface of a dark metal, only that the latter would reflect indistinctly, whereas they reflect not at all, except light which falls immediately upon them. This has a great effect in causing the landscapes to differ from those on the earth. On the stillest evening, no tall ship on the sea sends a long wavering reflection almost to the feet of him on the shore; the face of no maiden brightens at its own beauty in a still forest-well. The sun and moon alone make a glitter on the surface. The sea is like a sea of death, ready to ingulf and never to reveal: a visible shadow of oblivion. Yet the women sport in its waters like gorgeous sea-birds. The men more rarely enter them. But, on the contrary, the sky reflects everything beneath it, as if it were built of water like ours. Of course, from its concavity there is some distortion of the reflected objects; yet wondrous combinations of form are often to be seen in the overhanging depth. And then it is not shaped so much like a round dome as the sky of the earth, but, more of an egg-shape, rises to a great towering height in the middle, appearing far more lofty than the other. When the stars come out at night, it shows a mighty cupola, "fretted with golden fires," wherein there is room for all tempests to rush and rave.

One evening in early summer, I stood with a group of men and women on a steep rock that overhung the sea. They were all questioning me about my world and the ways thereof. In making reply to one of their questions, I was compelled to say that children are not born in the Earth as with them. Upon this I was assailed with a whole battery of inquiries, which at first I tried to avoid; but, at last, I was compelled, in the vaguest manner I could invent, to make some approach to the subject in question. Immediately a dim notion of what I meant, seemed to dawn in the minds of most of the women. Some of them folded their great wings all around them, as they generally do when in the least offended, and stood erect and motionless. One spread out her rosy pinions, and flashed from the promontory into the gulf at its foot. A great light shone in the eyes of one maiden, who turned and walked slowly away, with her purple and white wings half dispread behind her. She was found, the next morning, dead beneath a withered tree on a bare hill-side, some miles inland. They buried her where she lay, as is their custom; for, before they die, they instinctively search for a spot like the place of their birth, and having found one that satisfies them, they lie down, fold their wings around them, if they be women, or cross their arms over their breasts, if they are men, just as if they were going to sleep; and so sleep indeed. The sign or cause of coming death is an indescribable longing for something, they know not what, which seizes them, and drives them into solitude, consuming them within, till the body fails. When a youth and a maiden look too deep into each other's eyes, this longing seizes and possesses them; but instead of drawing nearer to each other, they wander away, each alone, into solitary places, and die of their desire. But it seems to me, that thereafter they are born babes upon our earth; where, if, when grown, they find each other, it goes well with them; if not, it will seem to go ill. But of this I know nothing. When I told them that the women on the Earth had not wings like them, but arms, they stared, and said how bold and masculine they must look; not knowing that their wings, glorious as they are, are but undeveloped arms.

But see the power of this book, that, while recounting what I can recall of its contents, I write as if myself had visited the far-off planet, learned its ways and appearances, and conversed with its men and women. And so, while writing, it seemed to me that I had.

The book goes on with the story of a maiden, who, born at the close of autumn, and living in a long, to her endless winter, set out at last to find the regions of spring; for, as in our earth, the seasons are divided over the globe. It begins something like this:

> She watched them dying for many a day,
> Dropping from off the old trees away,
> One by one; or else in a shower
> Crowding over the withered flower.
> For as if they had done some grievous wrong,
> The sun, that had nursed them and loved them so long,
> Grew weary of loving, and, turning back,
> Hastened away on his southern track;
> And helplessly hung each shrivelled leaf,
> Faded away with an idle grief.
> And the gusts of wind, sad Autumn's sighs,
> Mournfully swept through their families;
> Casting away with a helpless moan
> All that he yet might call his own,
> As the child, when his bird is gone for ever,
> Flingeth the cage on the wandering river.
> And the giant trees, as bare as Death,
> Slowly bowed to the great Wind's breath;
> And groaned with trying to keep from groaning
> Amidst the young trees bending and moaning.
> And the ancient planet's mighty sea
> Was heaving and falling most restlessly,
> And the tops of the waves were broken and white,
> Tossing about to ease their might;
> And the river was striving to reach the main,
> And the ripple was hurrying back again.
> Nature lived in sadness now;
> Sadness lived on the maiden's brow,
> As she watched, with a fixed, half-conscious eye,
> One lonely leaf that trembled on high,
> Till it dropped at last from the desolate bough—
> Sorrow, oh, sorrow! 'tis winter now.
> And her tears gushed forth, though it was but a leaf,
> For little will loose the swollen fountain of grief:
> When up to the lip the water goes,
> It needs but a drop, and it overflows.
>
> Oh! many and many a dreary year
> Must pass away ere the buds appear;
> Many a night of darksome sorrow
> Yield to the light of a joyless morrow,
> Ere birds again, on the clothed trees,
> Shall fill the branches with melodies.
> She will dream of meadows with wakeful streams;
> Of wavy grass in the sunny beams;
> Of hidden wells that soundless spring,

Hoarding their joy as a holy thing;
Of founts that tell it all day long
To the listening woods, with exultant song;
She will dream of evenings that die into nights,
Where each sense is filled with its own delights,
And the soul is still as the vaulted sky,
Lulled with an inner harmony;
And the flowers give out to the dewy night,
Changed into perfume, the gathered light;
And the darkness sinks upon all their host,
Till the sun sail up on the eastern coast—
She will wake and see the branches bare,
Weaving a net in the frozen air.

The story goes on to tell how, at last, weary with wintriness, she travelled towards the southern regions of her globe, to meet the spring on its slow way northwards; and how, after many sad adventures, many disappointed hopes, and many tears, bitter and fruitless, she found at last, one stormy afternoon, in a leafless forest, a single snowdrop growing betwixt the borders of the winter and spring. She lay down beside it and died. I almost believe that a child, pale and peaceful as a snowdrop, was born in the Earth within a fixed season from that stormy afternoon.

CHAPTER XIII

I saw a ship sailing upon the sea,
Deeply laden as ship could be;
But not so deep as in love I am,
For I care not whether I sink or swim.
                    OLD BALLAD

But Love is such a Mystery
  I cannot find it out:
For when I think I'm best resolv'd,
  I then am in most doubt.
                    SIR JOHN SUCKLING.

ONE STORY I will try to reproduce. But, alas! it is like trying to reconstruct a forest out of broken branches and withered leaves. In the fairy book, everything was just as it should be, though whether in words or something else, I cannot tell. It glowed and flashed the thoughts upon the soul, with such a power that the medium disappeared from the consciousness, and it was occupied only with the things themselves. My representation of it must resemble a translation from a rich and powerful language, capable of embodying the thoughts of a splendidly developed people, into the meagre and half-articulate speech of a savage tribe. Of course, while I read it, I was Cosmo, and his history was mine. Yet, all the time, I seemed to have a kind of double consciousness, and the story a double meaning. Sometimes it seemed only to represent a simple story of ordinary life, perhaps almost of universal life; wherein two souls, loving each other and longing to come nearer, do, after all, but behold each other as in a glass darkly.

As through the hard rock go the branching silver veins; as into the solid land run the creeks and gulfs from the unresting sea; as the lights and influences of the upper worlds sink silently through the earth's atmosphere; so doth Faerie invade the world of men, and sometimes startle the common eye with an association as of cause and effect, when between the two no connecting links can be traced.

Cosmo von Wehrstahl was a student at the University of Prague. Though of a noble family, he was poor, and prided himself upon the independence that poverty gives; for what will not a man pride himself upon, when he cannot get rid of it? A favourite with his fellow students, he yet had no companions; and none of them had ever crossed the threshold of his lodging in the top of one of the highest houses in the old town. Indeed, the secret of much of that complaisance which recommended him to his fellows, was the thought of his unknown retreat, whither in the evening he could betake himself and indulge undisturbed in his own studies and reveries. These studies, besides those subjects necessary to his course at the University, embraced some less commonly known and approved; for in a secret drawer lay the works of Albertus Magnus and Cornelius Agrippa, along with others less read and more abstruse. As yet, however, he had followed these researches only from curiosity, and had turned them to no practical purpose.

His lodging consisted of one large low-ceiled room, singularly bare of furniture; for besides a couple of wooden chairs, a couch which served for dreaming on both by day and night, and a great press of black oak, there was very little in the room that could be called furniture. But curious instruments were heaped in the corners; and in one stood a skeleton, half-leaning against the wall, half-supported by a string about its neck. One of its hands, all of fingers, rested on the heavy pommel of a great sword that stood beside it. Various weapons were scattered about over the floor. The walls were utterly bare of adornment; for the few strange things, such as a large dried bat with its wings dispread, the skin of a porcupine, and a stuffed sea-mouse, could hardly be reckoned as such. But although his fancy delighted in vagaries like these, he indulged his imagination with far different fare. His mind had never yet been filled with an absorbing passion; but it lay like a still twilight open to any wind, whether the low breath that wafts but odours, or the storm that bows the great trees till they strain and creak. He saw everything as through a rose-coloured glass. When he looked from his window on the street below, not a maiden passed, but she moved as in a story, and drew his thoughts after her till she disappeared in the vista. When he walked in the streets, he always felt as if reading a tale, into which he sought to weave every face of interest that went by; and every sweet voice swept his soul as with the wing of a passing angel. He was in fact a poet without words; the more absorbed and endangered, that the springing waters were dammed back into his soul, where, finding no utterance, they grew, and swelled, and undermined. He used to lie on his hard couch, and read a tale or a poem, till the book dropped from his hand; but he dreamed on, he knew not whether awake or asleep, until the opposite roof grew upon his sense, and turned golden in the sunrise. Then he arose too; and the impulses of vigorous youth kept him ever active, either in study or in sport, until again the close of the day left him free; and the world of night, which had lain drowned in the cataract of the day, rose up in his soul, with all its stars, and dim-seen phantom shapes. But this could hardly last long. Some one form must sooner or later step within the charmed circle, enter the house of life, and compel the bewildered magician to kneel and worship.

One afternoon, towards dusk, he was wandering dreamily in one of the principal streets, when a fellow student roused him by a slap on the shoulder, and asked him to accompany him into a little back alley to look at some old armour which he had taken a fancy to possess. Cosmo was considered an authority in every matter pertaining to arms, ancient or modern. In the use of weapons, none of the students could come near him; and his practical acquaintance with some had principally contributed to establish his authority in reference to all. He accompanied him willingly. They entered a narrow alley, and thence a dirty little court, where a low arched door admitted them into a hetero-geneous assemblage of everything musty, and dusty, and old, that could well be imagined. His verdict on the armour was satisfactory, and his companion at once concluded the purchase. As they were leaving the place, Cosmo's eye was attracted by an old mirror of an elliptical shape, which leaned against the wall, covered with dust. Around it was some curious carving, which he could see but very indistinctly by the glimmering light which the owner of the shop carried in his hand. It was this carving that attracted his attention; at least so it appeared to him. He left the place, however, with his friend, taking no further notice of it. They walked together to the main street, where they parted and took opposite directions.

No sooner was Cosmo left alone, than the thought of the curious old mirror returned to him. A strong desire to see it more plainly arose within him, and he directed his steps once more towards the shop. The owner opened the door when he knocked, as if he had expected him. He was a little, old, withered man, with a hooked nose, and burning eyes constantly in a slow restless motion, and looking here and there as if after something that eluded them. Pretending to examine several other articles, Cosmo at last approached the mirror, and requested to have it taken down.

"Take it down yourself, master; I cannot reach it," said the old man.

Cosmo took it down carefully, when he saw that the carving was indeed delicate and costly, being both of admirable design and execution; containing withal many devices which seemed to embody some meaning to which he had no clue. This, naturally, in one of his tastes and temperament, increased the interest he felt in the old mirror; so much, indeed, that he now longed to possess it, in order to study its frame at his leisure. He pretended, however, to want it only for use; and saying he feared the plate could be of little service, as it was rather old, he brushed away a little of the dust from its face, expecting to see a dull reflection within. His surprise was great when he found the reflection brilliant, revealing a glass not only uninjured by age, but wondrously clear and perfect (should the whole correspond to this part) even for one newly from the hands of the maker. He asked carelessly what the owner wanted for the thing. The old man replied by mentioning a sum of money far beyond the reach of poor Cosmo, who proceeded to replace the mirror where it had stood before.

"You think the price too high?" said the old man.

"I do not know that it is too much for you to ask," replied Cosmo; "but it is far too much for me to give."

The old man held up his light towards Cosmo's face. "I like your look," said he.

Cosmo could not return the compliment. In fact, now he looked closely at him for the first time, he felt a kind of repugnance to him, mingled with a strange feeling of doubt whether a man or a woman stood before him.

"What is your name?" he continued.

"Cosmo von Wehrstahl."

"Ah, ah! I thought as much. I see your father in you. I knew your father very well, young sir. I dare say in some odd corners of my house, you might find some old things with his crest and cipher upon them still. Well, I like you: you shall have the mirror at the fourth part of what I asked for it; but upon one condition."

"What is that?" said Cosmo; for although the price was still a great deal for him to give, he could just manage it; and the desire to possess the mirror had increased to an altogether unaccountable degree, since it had seemed beyond his reach.

"That if you should ever want to get rid of it again, you will let me have the first offer."

"Certainly," replied Cosmo, with a smile; adding, "a moderate condition indeed."

"On your honour?" insisted the seller.

"On my honour," said the buyer; and the bargain was concluded.

"I will carry it home for you," said the old man, as Cosmo took it in his hands.

"No, no; I will carry it myself," said he; for he had a peculiar dislike to revealing his residence to any one, and more especially to this person, to whom he felt every moment a greater antipathy.

"Just as you please," said the old creature, and muttered to himself as he held his light at the door to show him out of the court: "Sold for the sixth time! I wonder what will be the upshot of it this time. I should think my lady had enough of it by now!"

Cosmo carried his prize carefully home. But all the way he had an uncomfortable feeling that he was watched and dogged. Repeatedly he looked about, but saw nothing to justify his suspicions. Indeed, the streets were too crowded and too ill lighted to expose very readily a careful spy, if such there should be at his heels. He reached his lodging in safety, and leaned his purchase against the wall, rather relieved, strong as he was, to be rid of its weight; then, lighting his pipe, threw himself on the couch, and was soon lapt in the folds of one of his haunting dreams.

He returned home earlier than usual the next day, and fixed the mirror to the wall, over the hearth, at one end of his long room. He then carefully wiped away the dust from its face, and, clear as the water of a sunny spring, the mirror shone out from beneath the envious covering. But his interest was chiefly occupied with the curious carving of the frame. This he cleaned as well as he could with a brush; and then he proceeded to a minute examination of its various parts, in the hope of discovering some index to the intention of the carver. In this, however, he was unsuccessful; and, at length, pausing with some weariness and disappointment, he gazed vacantly for a few moments into the depth of the reflected room. But ere long he said, half aloud: "What a strange thing a mirror is! and what a wondrous affinity exists between it and a man's imagination! For this room of mine, as I behold it in the glass, is the same, and yet not the same. It is not the mere representation of the room I live in, but it looks just as if I were reading about it in a story I like. All its commonness has disappeared. The mirror has lifted it out of the region of fact into the realm of art; and the very representing of it to me has clothed with interest that which was otherwise hard and bare; just as one sees with delight upon the stage the representation of a character from which one would escape in life as from something unendurably wearisome. But is it not rather that art rescues nature from the weary and sated regards of our senses, and the degrading injustice of our anxious every-day life, and, appealing to the imagination, which dwells apart, reveals nature in some degree as she really is, and as she represents herself to the eye of the child, whose every-day life, fearless and unambitious, meets the true import of the wonder-teeming world around him, and rejoices therein without questioning? That skeleton, now—I almost fear it, standing there so still, with eyes only for the unseen, like a watch-tower looking across all the waste of this busy world into the quiet regions of rest beyond. And yet I know every bone and every joint in it as well as my own fist. And that old battle-axe looks as if any moment it might be caught up by a mailed hand, and, borne forth by the mighty arm, go crashing through casque, and skull, and brain, invading the Unknown with yet another bewildered ghost. I should like to live in *that* room if I could only get into it."

Scarcely had the half-moulded words floated from him, as he stood gazing into the mirror, when, striking him as with a flash of amazement that fixed him in his posture, noiseless and unannounced, glided suddenly through the door into the reflected room, with stately motion, yet reluctant and faltering step, the graceful form of a woman, clothed all in white. Her back only was visible as she walked slowly up to the couch in the further end of the room, on which she laid herself wearily, turning towards him a face of unutterable loveliness, in which suffering, and dislike, and a sense of compulsion, strangely mingled with the beauty. He stood without the power of motion for some moments, with his eyes irrecoverably fixed upon her; and even after he was conscious of the ability to move, he could not summon up courage to turn and look on her, face to face, in the veritable chamber in which he stood. At length, with a sudden effort, in which the exercise of the will was so pure, that it seemed involuntary, he turned his face to the couch. It was vacant. In bewilderment, mingled with terror, he turned again to the mirror: there, on the reflected couch, lay the exquisite lady-form. She lay with closed eyes, whence two large tears were just welling from beneath the veiling lids; still as death, save for the convulsive motion of her bosom.

Cosmo himself could not have described what he felt. His emotions were of a kind that destroyed consciousness, and could never be clearly recalled. He could not help standing yet by the mirror, and keeping his eyes fixed on the lady, though he was painfully aware of his rudeness, and feared every moment that she would open hers, and meet his fixed regard. But he was, ere long, a little relieved; for, after a while, her eyelids slowly rose, and her eyes remained uncovered, but unemployed for a time; and when, at length, they began to wander about the room, as if languidly seeking to make some acquaintance with her environment, they were never directed towards him: it seemed nothing but what was in the mirror could affect her vision; and, therefore, if she saw him at all, it could only be his back, which, of necessity, was turned towards her in the glass. The two figures in the mirror could not meet face to face, except he turned and looked at her, present in his room; and, as she was not there, he concluded that if he were to turn towards the part in his room corresponding to that in which she lay, his reflection would either be invisible to her altogether, or at least it must appear to her to gaze vacantly towards her, and no meeting of the eyes would produce the impression of spiritual proximity. By and by her eyes fell upon the skeleton, and he saw her shudder and close them. She did not open them again, but signs of repugnance continued evident on her countenance. Cosmo would have removed the obnoxious thing at once, but he feared to discompose her yet more by the assertion of his presence, which the act would involve. So he stood and watched her. The eyelids yet shrouded the eyes, as a costly case the jewels within; the troubled expression gradually faded from the countenance, leaving only a faint sorrow behind; the features settled into an unchanging expression of rest; and by these signs, and the slow regular motion of her breathing, Cosmo knew that she slept. He could now gaze on her without embarrassment. He saw that her figure, dressed in the simplest robe of white, was worthy of her face; and so harmonious, that either the delicately-moulded foot, or any finger of the equally delicate hand, was an index to the whole. As she lay, her whole form manifested the relaxation of perfect repose. He gazed till he was weary, and at last seated himself near the new-found shrine, and mechanically took up a book, like one who watches by a sick-bed. But his eyes gathered no thoughts from the page before him. His intellect had been stunned by the bold contradiction, to its face, of all its experience, and now lay passive, without assertion, or speculation, or even conscious astonishment; while his imagination sent one wild dream of blessedness after another coursing through his soul. How long he sat he knew not; but at length he roused himself, rose, and, trembling in every portion of his frame, looked again into the mirror. She was gone. The mirror reflected faithfully what his room presented, and nothing more. It stood there like a golden setting whence the central jewel has been stolen away; like a night-sky without the glory of its stars. She had carried with her all the strangeness of the reflected room. It had sunk to the level of the one without. But when the first pangs of his disappointment had passed, Cosmo began to comfort himself with the hope that she might return, perhaps the next evening, at the same hour. Resolving that if she did, she should not at least be scared by the hateful skeleton, he removed that and several other articles of questionable appearance into a recess by the side of the hearth, whence they could not possibly cast any reflection into the mirror; and having made his poor room as tidy as he could, sought the solace of the open sky and of a night wind that had begun to blow; for he could not rest where he was. When he returned, somewhat composed, he could hardly prevail with himself to lie down on his bed; for he could not help feeling as if she had lain upon it; and for him to lie there now would be something like sacrilege. However, weariness prevailed; and laying himself on the couch, dressed as he was, he slept till day.

With a beating heart, beating till he could hardly breathe, he stood in dumb hope before the mirror, on the following evening. Again the reflected room shone as through a purple vapour in the gathering twilight. Everything seemed waiting like himself for a coming splendour to glorify its poor earthliness with the presence of a heavenly joy. And just as the room vibrated with the strokes of the neighboring church bell, announcing the hour of six, in glided the pale beauty, and again laid herself on the couch. Poor Cosmo nearly lost his senses with delight. She was there once more! Her eyes sought the corner where the skeleton had stood, and a faint gleam of satisfaction crossed her face, apparently at seeing it empty. She looked suffering still, but there was less of discomfort expressed in her countenance than there had been the night before. She took more notice of the things about her, and seemed to gaze with some curiosity on the strange apparatus standing here and there in her room. At length, however, drowsiness seemed to overtake her, and again she fell asleep. Resolved not to lose sight of her this time, Cosmo watched the sleeping form. Her slumber was so deep and absorbing, that a fascinating repose seemed to pass contagiously from her to him, as he gazed upon her; and he started as if awaking from a dream, when the lady moved, and, without opening her eyes, rose, and passed from the room with the gait of a somnambulist.

Cosmo was now in a state of extravagant delight. Most men have a secret treasure somewhere. The miser has his golden hoard; the virtuoso his pet ring; the student his rare book; the poet his favourite haunt; the lover his secret drawer; but Cosmo had a mirror with a lovely lady in it. And now that he knew by the skeleton, that she was affected by the things around her, he had a new object in life: he would turn the bare chamber in the mirror into a room such as no lady need disdain to call her own. This he could effect only by furnishing and adorning his. And Cosmo was poor. Yet he possessed accomplishments that could be turned to account; although, hitherto, he had preferred living on his slender allowance, to increasing his means by what his pride considered unworthy of his rank. He was the best swordsman in the University; and now he offered to give lessons on fencing and similar exercises, to such as chose to pay him well for the trouble. His proposal was heard with surprise by the students; but it was eagerly accepted by many; and soon his instructions were not confined to the richer students, but were anxiously sought by many of the young nobility of Prague and its neighbourhood. So that very soon he had a good deal of money at his command. The first thing he did was to remove his apparatus and oddities into a closet in the room. Then he placed his bed and a few other necessaries on each side of the hearth, and parted them from the rest of the room by two screens of Indian fabric. Then he put an elegant couch for the lady to lie upon, in the corner where his bed had formerly stood; and, by degrees, every day adding some article of luxury, converted it, at length, into a rich boudoir.

Every night, about the same time, the lady entered. The first time she saw the new couch, she started with a half-smile; then her face grew very sad, the tears came to her eyes, and she laid herself upon the couch, and pressed her face into the silken cushions, as if to hide from everything. She took notice of each addition and each change as the work proceeded; and a look of acknowledgment, as if she knew that some one was ministering to her, and was grateful for it, mingled with the constant look of suffering. At length, after she had lain down as usual one evening, her eyes fell upon some paintings with which Cosmo had just finished adorning the walls. She rose, and to his great delight, walked across the room, and proceeded to examine them carefully, testifying much pleasure in her looks as she did so. But again the sorrowful, tearful expression returned, and again she buried her face in the pillows of her couch. Gradually, however, her countenance had grown more composed; much of the suffering manifest on her first appearance had vanished, and a kind of quiet, hopeful expression had taken its place; which, however, frequently gave way to an anxious, troubled look, mingled with something of sympathetic pity.

Meantime, how fared Cosmo? As might be expected in one of his temperament, his interest had blossomed into love, and his love—shall I call it *ripened,* or—*withered* into passion? But, alas! he loved a shadow. He could not come near her, could not speak to her, could not hear a sound from those sweet lips, to which his longing eyes would cling like bees to their honey-founts. Ever and anon, he sang to himself:

"I shall die for love of the maiden;"

and ever he looked again, and died not, though his heart seemed ready to break with intensity of life and longing. And the more he did for her, the more he loved her; and he hoped that, although she never appeared to see him, yet she was pleased to think that one unknown would give his life to her. He tried to comfort himself over his separation from her, by thinking that perhaps some day she would see him and make signs to him, and that would satisfy him; "for," thought he, "is not this all that a loving soul can do to enter into communion with another? Nay, how many who love, never come nearer than to behold each other as in a mirror; seem to know and yet never know the inward life; never enter the other soul; and part at last, with but the vaguest notion of the universe on the borders of which they have been hovering for years? If I could but speak to her, and knew that she heard me, I should be satisfied." Once he contemplated painting a picture on the wall, which should, of necessity, convey to the lady a thought of himself; but, though he had some skill with the pencil, he found his hand tremble so much when he began the attempt, that he was forced to give it up.

One evening, as he stood gazing on his treasure, he thought he saw a faint expression of self-consciousness on her countenance, as if she surmised that passionate eyes were fixed upon her. This grew; till at last the red blood rose over her neck, and cheek, and brow. Cosmo's longing to approach her became almost delirious. This night she was dressed in an evening costume, resplendent with diamonds. This could add nothing to her beauty, but it presented it in a new aspect; enabled her loveliness to make a new manifestation of itself in a new embodiment. For essential beauty is infinite; and, as the soul of Nature needs an endless succession of varied forms to embody her loveliness, countless faces of beauty springing forth, not any two the same, at every one of her heart-throbs; so the individual form needs an infinite change of its environments, to enable it to uncover all the phases of its loveliness. Diamonds glittered from amidst her hair, half-hidden in its luxuriance, like stars through dark rain-clouds; and the bracelets on her white arms flashed all the colours of a rainbow of lightnings, as she lifted her snowy hands to cover her burning face. But her beauty shone down all its adornment. "If I might have but one of her feet to kiss," thought Cosmo, "I should be content." Alas! he deceived himself, for passion is never content. Nor did he know that there are *two* ways out of her enchanted house. But, suddenly, as if the pang had been driven into his heart from without, revealing itself first in pain, and afterwards in definite form, the thought darted into his mind, "She has a lover somewhere. Remembered words of his bring the colour on her face now. I am nowhere to her. She lives in another world all day, and all night, after she leaves me. Why does she come and make me love her, till I, a strong man, am too faint to look upon her more?" He looked again, and her face was pale as a lily. A sorrowful compassion seemed to rebuke the glitter of the restless jewels, and the slow tears rose in her eyes. She left her room sooner this evening than was her wont. Cosmo remained alone, with a feeling as if his bosom had been suddenly left empty and hollow, and the weight of the whole world was crushing in its walls. The next evening, for the first time since she began to come, she came not.

And now Cosmo was in wretched plight. Since the thought of a rival had occurred to him, he could not rest for a moment. More than ever he longed to see the lady face to face. He persuaded himself that if he but knew the worst he would be satisfied; for then he could abandon Prague, and find that relief in constant motion, which is the hope of all active minds when invaded by distress. Meantime he waited with unspeakable anxiety for the next night, hoping she would return; but she did not appear. And now he fell really ill. Rallied by his fellow-students on his wretched looks, he ceased to attend the lectures. His engagements were neglected. He cared for nothing. The sky, with the great sun in it, was to him a heartless, burning desert. The men and women in the streets were mere puppets, without motives in themselves, or interest to him. He saw them all as on the ever-changing field of a *camera obscura*. She—she alone and altogether—was his universe, his well of life, his incarnate good. For six evenings she came not. Let his absorbing passion, and the slow fever that was consuming his brain, be his excuse for the resolution which he had taken and begun to execute, before that time had expired.

Reasoning with himself, that it must be by some enchantment connected with the mirror, that the form of the lady was to be seen in it, he determined to attempt to turn to account what he had hitherto studied principally from curiosity. "For," said he to himself, "if a spell can force her presence in that glass (and she came unwillingly at first), may not a stronger spell, such as I know, especially with the aid of her half-presence in the mirror, if ever she appears again, compel her living form to come to me here? If I do her wrong, let love be my excuse.
I want only to know my doom from her own lips." He never doubted, all the time, that she was a real earthly woman; or, rather, that there was a woman, who, somehow or other, threw this reflection of her form into the magic mirror.

He opened his secret drawer, took out his books of magic, lighted his lamp, and read and made notes from midnight till three in the morning, for three successive nights. Then he replaced his books; and the next night went out in quest of the materials necessary for the conjuration. These were not easy to find; for, in love-charms and all incantations of this nature, ingredients are employed scarcely fit to be mentioned, and for the thought even of which, in connection with her, he could only excuse himself on the score of his bitter need. At length he succeeded in procuring all he required; and on the seventh evening from that on which she had last appeared, he found himself prepared for the exercise of unlawful and tyrannical power.

He cleared the center of the room; stooped and drew a circle of red on the floor, around the spot where he stood; wrote in the four quarters mystical signs, and numbers which were all powers of seven or nine; examined the whole ring carefully, to see that no smallest break had occurred in the circumference; and then rose from his bending posture. As he rose, the church clock struck seven; and, just as she had appeared the first time, reluctant, slow, and stately, glided in the lady. Cosmo trembled; and when, turning, she revealed a countenance worn and wan, as with sickness or inward trouble, he grew faint, and felt as if he dared not proceed. But as he gazed on the face and form, which now possessed his whole soul, to the exclusion of other joys and griefs, the longing to speak to her, to know that she heard him, to hear from her one word in return, became so unendurable, that he suddenly and hastily resumed his preparations. Stepping carefully from the circle, he put a small brazier into its center. He then set fire to its contents of charcoal, and while it burned up, opened his window and seated himself, waiting, beside it.

It was a sultry evening. The air was full of thunder. A sense of luxurious depression filled the brain. The sky seemed to have grown heavy, and to compress the air beneath it. A kind of purplish tinge pervaded the atmosphere, and through the open window came the scents of the distant fields, which all the vapors of the city could not quench. Soon the charcoal glowed. Cosmo sprinkled upon it the incense and other substances which he had compounded, and, stepping within the circle, turned his face from the brazier and towards the mirror. Then, fixing his eyes upon the face of the lady, he began with a trembling voice to repeat a powerful incantation. He had not gone far, before the lady grew pale; and then, like a returning wave, the blood washed all its banks with its crimson tide, and she hid her face in her hands. Then he passed to a conjuration stronger yet. The lady rose and walked uneasily to and fro in her room. Another spell; and she seemed seeking with her eyes for some object on which they wished to rest. At length it seemed as if she suddenly espied him; for her eyes fixed themselves full and wide upon his, and she drew gradually, and somewhat unwillingly, close to her side of the mirror, just as if his eyes had fascinated her. Cosmo had never seen her so near before. Now at least, eyes met eyes; but he could not quite understand the expression of hers. They were full of tender entreaty, but there was something more that he could not interpret. Though his heart seemed to labor in his throat, he would allow no delight or agitation to turn him from his task. Looking still in her face, he passed on to the mightiest charm he knew. Suddenly the lady turned and walked out of the door of her reflected chamber. A moment after, she entered his room with veritable presence; and, forgetting all his precautions, he sprang from the charmed circle, and knelt before her. There she stood, the living lady of his passionate visions, alone beside him, in a thundery twilight, and the glow of a magic fire.

"Why," said the lady, with a trembling voice, "didst thou bring a poor maiden through the rainy streets alone?"

"Because I am dying for love of thee; but I only brought thee from the mirror there."

"Ah, the mirror!" and she looked up at it, and shuddered. "Alas! I am but a slave, while that mirror exists. But do not think it was the power of thy spells that drew me; it was thy longing desire to see me, that beat at the door of my heart, till I was forced to yield."

"Canst thou love me then?" said Cosmo, in a voice calm as death, but almost inarticulate with emotion.

"I do not know," she replied sadly; "that I cannot tell, so long as I am bewildered with enchantments. It were indeed a joy too great, to lay my head on thy bosom and weep to death; for I think thou lovest me, though I do not know;—but—"

Cosmo rose from his knees.

"I love thea as—nay, I know not what—for since I have loved thee, there is nothing else."

He seized her hand: she withdrew it.

"No, better not; I am in thy power, and therefore I may not."

She burst into tears, and, kneeling before him in her turn, said—

"Cosmo, if thou lovest me, set me free, even from thyself: break the mirror."

"And shall I see thyself instead?"

"That I cannot tell. I will not deceive thee; we may never meet again."

A fierce struggle arose in Cosmo's bosom. Now she was in his power. She did not dislike him at least; and he could see her when he would. To break the mirror would be to destroy his very life, to banish out of his universe the only glory it possessed. The whole world would be but a prison, if he annihilated the one window that looked into the paradise of love. Not yet pure in love, he hesitated.

With a wail of sorrow, the lady rose to her feet. "Ah! he loves me not; he loves me not even as I love him; and alas! I care more for his love than even for the freedom I ask."

"I will not wait to be willing," cried Cosmo; and sprang to the corner where the great sword stood.

Meantime it had grown very dark; only the embers cast a red glow through the room. He seized the sword by the steel scabbard, and stood before the mirror; but as he heaved a great blow at it with the heavy pommel, the blade slipped halfway out of the scabbard, and the pommel struck the wall above the mirror. At that moment, a terrible clap of thunder seemed to burst in the very room beside them; and ere Cosmo could repeat the blow, he fell senseless on the hearth. When he came to himself, he found that the lady and the mirror had both disappeared. He was seized with a brain fever, which kept him to his couch for weeks.

When he recovered his reason, he began to think what could have become of the mirror. For the lady, he hoped she had found her way back as she came; but as the mirror involved her fate with its own, he was more immediately anxious about that. He could not think she had carried it away. It was much too heavy, even if it had not been too firmly fixed in the wall, for her to remove it. Then again, he remembered the thunder; which made him believe that it was not the lightning, but some other blow that had struck him down. He concluded that, either by supernatural agency, he having exposed himself to the vengeance of the demons in leaving the circle of safety, or in some other mode, the mirror had probably found its way back to its former owner; and, horrible to think of, might have been by this time once more disposed of, delivering up the lady into the power of another man; who, if he used his power no worse than he himself had done, might yet give Cosmo abundant cause to curse the selfish indecision which prevented him from shattering the mirror at once. Indeed, to think that she whom he loved, and who had prayed to him for freedom, should be still at the mercy, in some degree, of the possessor of the mirror, and was at least exposed to his constant observation, was in itself enough to madden a chary lover.

Anxiety to be well retarded his recovery; but at length he was able to creep abroad. He first made his way to the old broker's, pretending to be in search of something else. A laughing sneer on the creature's face convinced him that he knew all about it; but he could not see it amongst his furniture, or get any information out of him as to what had become of it. He expressed the utmost surprise at hearing it had been stolen; a surprise which Cosmo saw at once to be counterfeited; while, at the same time, he fancied that the old wretch was not at all anxious to have it mistaken for genuine. Full of distress, which he concealed as well as he could, he made many searches, but with no avail. Of course he could ask no questions; but he kept his ears awake for any remotest hint that might set him in a direction of search. He never went out without a short heavy hammer of steel about him, that he might shatter the mirror the moment he was made happy by the sight of his lost treasure, if ever that blessed moment should arrive. Whether he should see the lady again, was now a thought altogether secondary, and postponed to the achievement of her freedom. He wandered here and there, like an anxious ghost, pale and haggard; gnawed ever at the heart by the thought of what she might be suffering—all from his fault.

One night, he mingled with a crowd that filled the rooms of one of the most distinguished mansions in the city; for he accepted every invitation, that he might lose no chance, however poor, of obtaining some information that might expedite his discovery. Here he wandered about, listening to every stray word that he could catch, in the hope of a revelation. As he approached some ladies who were talking quietly in a corner, one said to another: "Have you heard of the strange illness of the Princess von Hohenweiss?"

"Yes; she has been ill for more than a year now. It is very sad for so fine a creature to have such a terrible malady. She was better for some weeks lately, but within the last few days, the same attacks have returned, apparently accompanied with more suffering than ever. It is altogether an inexplicable story."

"Is there a story connected with her illness?"

"I have only heard imperfect reports of it; but it is said that she gave offence some eighteen months ago to an old woman who had held an office of trust in the family, and who, after some incoherent threats, disappeared. This peculiar affection followed soon after. But the strangest part of the story is its association with the loss of an antique mirror, which stood in her dressing-room, and of which she constantly made use."

Here the speaker's voice sank to a whisper; and Cosmo, although his very soul sat listening in his ears, could hear no more. He trembled too much to dare to address the ladies, even if it had been advisable to expose himself to their curiosity. The name of the Princess was well known to him, but he had never seen her; except indeed it was she, which now he hardly doubted, who had knelt before him on that dreadful night. Fearful of attracting attention, for, from the weak state of his health, he could not recover an appearance of calmness, he made his way to the open air, and reached his lodgings; glad in this, that he at least knew where she lived, although he never dreamed of approaching her openly, even if he should be happy enough to free her from her hateful bondage. He hoped, too, that as he had unexpectedly learned so much, the other and far more important part might be revealed to him ere long.

*   *   *   *   *

"Have you seen Steinwald lately?"

"No, I have not seen him for some time. He is almost a match for me at the rapier, and I suppose he thinks he needs no more lessons."

"I wonder what has become of him. I want to see him very much. Let me see: the last time I saw him, he was coming out of that old broker's den, to which, if you remember, you accompanied me once, to look at some armour. That is fully three weeks ago."

This hint was enough for Cosmo. Von Steinwald was a man of influence in the court, well known for his reckless habits and fierce passions. The very possibility that the mirror should be in his possession was hell itself to Cosmo. But violent or hasty measures of any sort were most unlikely to succeed. All that he wanted was an opportunity of breaking the fatal glass; and to obtain this, he must bide his time. He revolved many plans in his mind, but without being able to fix upon any.

At length, one evening, as he was passing the house of Von Steinwald, he saw the windows more than usually brilliant. He watched for a while; and seeing that company began to arrive, hastened home, and dressed as richly as he could, in the hope of mingling with the guests unquestioned; in effecting which, there could be no difficulty for a man of his carriage.

*   *   *   *   *

In a lofty, silent chamber, in another part of the city, lay a form more like marble than a living woman. The loveliness of death seemed frozen upon her face, for her lips were rigid, and her eyelids closed. Her long white hands were crossed over her breast, and no breathing disturbed their repose. Beside the dead, men speak in whispers, as if the deepest rest of all could be broken by the sound of a living voice. Just so, though the soul was evidently beyond the reach of all intimations from the senses, the two ladies, who sat beside her, spoke in the gentlest tones of subdued sorrow.

"She has lain so for an hour."

"This cannot last long, I fear."

"How much thinner she has grown within the last few weeks! If she would only speak, and explain what she suffers, it would be better for her. I think she has visions in her trances, but nothing can induce her to refer to them when she is awake."

"Does she ever speak in these trances?"

"I have never heard her; but they say she walks sometimes, and once put the whole household in a terrible fright by disappearing for a whole hour, and returning drenched with rain, and almost dead with exhaustion and fright. But even then she would give no account of what had happened."

A scarce audible murmur from the yet motionless lips of the lady here startled her attendants. After several ineffectual attempts at articulation, the word *"Cosmo!"* burst from her. Then she lay still as before; but only for a moment. With a wild cry, she sprang from the couch erect on the floor, flung her arms above her head, with clasped and straining hands, and, her wide eyes flashing with light, called aloud, with a voice exultant as that of a spirit bursting from a sepulchre, "I am free! I am free! I thank thee!" Then she flung herself on the couch, and sobbed; then rose, and paced wildly up and down the room, with gestures of mingled delight and anxiety. Then turning to her motionless attendants—"Quick, Lisa, my cloak and hood!" Then lower—"I must go to him. Make haste, Lisa! You may come with me, if you will."

In another moment they were in the street, hurrying along towards one of the bridges over the Moldau. The moon was near the zenith, and the streets were almost empty. The Princess soon outstripped her attendant, and was half-way over the bridge, before the other reached it.

"Are you free, lady? The mirror is broken: are you free?"

The words were spoken close beside her, as she hurried on. She turned; and there, leaning on the parapet in a recess of the bridge, stood Cosmo, in a splendid dress, but with a white and quivering face.

"Cosmo!—I am free—and thy servant for ever. I was coming to you now."

"And I to you, for Death made me bold; but I could get no further. Have I atoned at all? Do I love you a little—truly?"

"Ah, I know now that you love me, my Cosmo; but what do you say about death?"

He did not reply. His hand was pressed against his side. She looked more closely: the blood was welling from between the fingers. She flung her arms around him with a faint bitter wail.

When Lisa came up, she found her mistress kneeling above a wan dead face, which smiled on in the spectral moonbeams.

And now I will say no more about these wondrous volumes; though I could tell many a tale out of them, and could, perhaps, vaguely represent some entrancing thoughts of a deeper kind which I found within them. From many a sultry noon till twilight, did I sit in that grand hall, buried and risen again in these old books. And I trust I have carried away in my soul some of the exhalations of their undying leaves. In after hours of deserved or needful sorrow, portions of what I read there have often come to me again, with an unexpected comforting; which was not fruitless, even though the comfort might seem in itself groundless and vain.

CHAPTER XIV

> Your gallery
> Have we pass'd through, not without much content
> In many singularities; but we saw not
> That which my daughter came to look upon,
> The statue of her mother.
>
> *Winter's Tale.*

IT SEEMED TO me strange, that all this time I had heard no music in the fairy palace. I was convinced there must be music in it, but that my sense was as yet too gross to receive the influence of those mysterious motions that beget sound. Sometimes I felt sure, from the way the few figures of which I got such transitory glimpses passed me, or glided into vacancy before me, that they were moving to the law of music; and, in fact, several times I fancied for a moment that I heard a few wondrous tones coming I knew not whence. But they did not last long enough to convince me that I had heard them with the bodily sense. Such as they were, however, they stook strange liberties with me, causing me to burst suddenly into tears, of which there was no presence to make me ashamed, or casting me into a kind of trance of speechless delight, which, passing as suddenly, left me faint and longing for more.

Now, on an evening, before I had been a week in the palace, I was wandering through one lighted arcade and corridor after another. At length I arrived, through a door that closed behind me, in another vast hall of the palace. It was filled with a subdued crimson light; by which I saw that slender pillars of black, built close to walls of white marble, rose to a great height, and then, dividing into innumerable divergent arches, supported a roof, like the walls, of white marble, upon which the arches intersected intricately, forming a fretting of black upon the white, like the network of a skeleton-leaf. The floor was black. Between several pairs of the pillars upon every side, the place of the wall behind was occupied by a crimson curtain of thick silk, hanging in heavy and rich folds. Behind each of these curtains burned a powerful light, and these were the sources of the glow that filled the hall. A peculiar delicious odour pervaded the place. As soon as I entered, the old inspiration seemed to return to me, for I felt a strong impulse to sing; or rather, it seemed as if some one else was singing a song in my soul, which wanted to come forth at my lips, imbodied in my breath. But I kept silence; and feeling somewhat overcome by the red light and the perfume, as well as by the emotion within me, and seeing at one end of the hall a great crimson chair, more like a throne than a chair, beside a table of white marble, I went to it, and, throwing myself in it, gave myself up to a succession of images of bewildering beauty, which passed before my inward eye, in a long and occasionally crowded train. Here I sat for hours, I suppose; till, returning somewhat to myself, I saw that the red light had paled away, and felt a cool gentle breath gliding over my forehead. I rose and left the hall with unsteady steps, finding my way with some difficulty to my own chamber, and faintly remembering, as I went, that only in the marble cave, before I found the sleeping statue, had I ever had as similar experience.

After this, I repaired every morning to the same hall; where I sometimes sat in the chair, and dreamed deliciously, and sometimes walked up and down over the black floor. Sometimes I acted within myself a whole drama, during one of these perambulations; sometimes walked deliberately through the whole epic of a tale; sometimes ventured to sing a song, though with a shrinking fear of I knew not what. I was astonished at the beauty of my own voice as it rang through the place, or rather crept undulating, like a serpent of sound, along the walls and roof of this superb music-hall. Entrancing verses arose within me as of their own accord, chanting themselves to their own melodies, and requiring no addition of music to satisfy the inward sense. But, ever in the pauses of these, when the singing mood was upon me, I seemed to hear something like the distant sound of multitudes of dancers, and felt as if it was the unheard music, moving their rhythmic motion, that within me blossomed in verse and song. I felt, too, that could I but see the dance, I should, from the harmony of complicated movements, not of the dancers in relation to each other merely, but of each dancer individually in the manifested plastic power that moved the consenting harmonious form, understand the whole of the music on the billows of which they floated and swung.

At length, one night, suddenly, when this feeling of dancing came upon me, I bethought me of lifting one of the crimson curtains, and looking if, perchance, behind it there might not be hid some other mystery, which might at least remove a step further the bewilderment of the present one. Nor was I altogether disappointed. I walked to one of the magnificent draperies, lifted a corner, and peeped in. There, burned a great, crimson, globe-shaped light, high in the cubical centre of another hall, which might be larger or less than that in which I stood, for its dimensions were not easily perceived, seeing that floor and roof and walls were entirely of black marble. The roof was supported by the same arrangement of pillars radiating in arches, as that of the first hall; only, here, the pillars and arches were of dark red. But what absorbed my delighted gaze, was an innumerable assembly of white marble statues, of every form, and in multitudinous posture, filling the hall throughout. These stood, in the ruddy glow of the great lamp, upon pedestals of jet black. Around the lamp shone in golden letters, plainly legible from where I stood, the two words—

TOUCH NOT!

There was in all this, however, no solution to the sound of dancing; and now I was aware that the influence on my mind had ceased. I did not go in that evening, for I was weary and faint, but I hoarded up the expectation of entering, as of a great coming joy.

Next night I walked, as on the preceding, through the hall. My mind was filled with pictures and songs, and therewith so much absorbed, that I did not for some time think of looking within the curtain I had last night lifted. When the thought of doing so occurred to me first, I happened to be within a few yards of it. I became conscious at the same moment, that the sound of dancing had been for some time in my ears. I approached the curtain quickly, and, lifting it, entered the black hall. Everything was still as death. I should have concluded that the sound must have proceeded from some other more distant quarter, which conclusion its faintness would, in ordinary circumstances, have necessitated from the first; but there was a something about the statues that caused me still to remain in doubt. As I said, each stood perfectly still upon its black pedestal; but there was about every one a certain air, not of motion, but as if it had just ceased from movement; as if the rest were not altogether of the marbly stillness of thousands of years. It was as if the peculiar atmosphere of each had yet a kind of invisible tremulousness; as if its agitated wavelets had not yet subsided into a perfect calm. I had the suspicion that they had anticipated my appearance, and had sprung, each, from the living joy of the dance, to the death-silence and blackness of its isolated pedestal, just before I entered. I walked across the central hall to the curtain opposite the one I had lifted, and, entering there, found all the appearances similar;

only that the statues were different, and differently grouped. Neither did they produce on my mind that impression—of motion just expired, which I had experienced from the others. I found that behind every one of the crimson curtains was a similar hall, similarly lighted, and similarly occupied.

The next night, I did not allow my thoughts to be absorbed as before with inward images, but crept stealthily along to the furthest curtain in the hall, from behind which, likewise, I had formerly seemed to hear the sound of dancing. I drew aside its edge as suddenly as I could, and, looking in, saw that the utmost stillness pervaded the vast place. I walked in, and passed through it to the other end. There I found that it communicated with a circular corridor, divided from it only by two rows of red columns. This corridor, which was black, with red niches holding statues, ran entirely about the statue-halls, forming a communication between the further ends of them all; further, that is, as regards the central hall of white, whence they all diverged like radii, finding their circumference in the corridor. Round this corridor I now went, entering all the halls, of which there were twelve, and finding them all similarly constructed, but filled with quite various statues, of what seemed both ancient and modern sculpture. After I had simply walked through them, I found myself sufficiently tired to long for rest, and went to my own room.

In the night I dreamed that, walking close by one of the curtains, I was suddenly seized with the desire to enter, and dart in. This time I was too quick for them. All the statues were in motion, statues no longer, but men and women—all shapes of beauty that ever sprang from the brain of the sculptor, mingled in the convolutions of a complicated dance. Passing through them to the further end, I almost started from my sleep on beholding, not taking part in the dance with the others, nor seemingly endued with life like them, but standing in marble coldness and rigidity upon a black pedestal in the extreme left corner—my lady of the cave; the marble beauty who sprang from her tomb or her cradle at the call of my songs. While I gazed in speechless astonishment and admiration, a dark shadow, descending from above like the curtain of a stage, gradually hid her entirely from my view. I felt with a shudder that this shadow was perchance my missing demon, whom I had not seen for days. I awoke with a stifled cry.

Of course, the next evening I began my journey through the halls (for I knew not to which my dream had carried me), in the hope of proving the dream to be a true one, by discovering my marble beauty upon her black pedestal. At length, on reaching the tenth hall, I thought I recognized some of the forms I had seen dancing in my dream; and to my bewilderment, when I arrived at the extreme corner on the left, there stood, the only one I had yet seen, a vacant pedestal. It was exactly in the position occupied, in my dream, by the pedestal on which the white lady stood. Hope beat violently in my heart.

"Now," said I to myself, "if yet another part of the dream would but come true, and I should succeed in surprising these forms in their nightly dance; it might be the rest would follow, and I should see on the pedestal my marble queen. Then surely if my songs sufficed to give her life before, when she lay in the bonds of alabaster, much more would they be sufficient then to give her volition and motion, when she alone of assembled crowds of marble forms, would be standing rigid and cold."

But the difficulty was, to surprise the dancers. I had found that a premeditated attempt at surprise, though executed with the utmost care and rapidity, was of no avail. And, in my dream, it was effected by a sudden thought suddenly executed. I saw, therefore, that there was no plan of operation offering any probability of success, but this: to allow my mind to be occupied with other thoughts, as I wandered around the great centre-hall; and so wait till the impulse to enter one of the others should happen to arise in me just at the moment when I was close to one of the crimson curtains. For I hoped that if I entered any one of the twelve halls at the right moment, that would as it were give me the right of entrance to all the others, seeing they all had communication behind. I would not diminish the hope of the right chance, by supposing it necessary that the desire to enter should awake within me, precisely when I was close to the curtains of the tenth hall.

At first, the impulses to see recurred so continually, in spite of the crowded imagery that kept passing through my mind, that they formed too nearly a continuous chain, for the hope that any one of them would succeed as a surprise. But as I persisted in banishing them, they recurred less and less often; and after two or three, at considerable intervals, had come when the spot where I happened to be was unsuitable, the hope strengthened, that soon one might arise just at the right moment; namely, when, in walking round the hall, I should be close to one of the curtains.

At length the right moment and the impulse coincided. I darted into the ninth hall. It was full of the most exquisite moving forms. The whole space wavered and swam with the involutions of an intricate dance. It seemed to break suddenly as I entered, and all made one or two bounds toward their pedestals; but, apparently on finding that they were thoroughly overtaken, they returned to their employment (for it seemed with them earnest enough to be called such) without further heeding me. Somewhat impeded by the floating crowd, I made what haste I could towards the bottom of the hall; whence, entering the corridor, I turned towards the tenth. I soon arrived at the corner I wanted to reach, for the corridor was comparatively empty; but, although the dancers here, after a little confusion, altogether dis-regarded my presence, I was dismayed at beholding, even yet, a vacant pedestal. But I had a conviction that she was near me. And as I looked at the pedestal, I thought I saw upon it, vaguely revealed as if through overlapping folds of drapery, the indistinct outlines of white feet. Yet there was no sign of drapery or concealing shadow whatever. But I remembered the descending shadow in my dream. And I hoped still in the power of my songs; thinking that what could dispel alabaster, might likewise be capable of dispelling what concealed my beauty now, even if it were the demon whose darkness had overshadowed all my life.

CHAPTER XV

Alexander. When will you finish Campaspe?
Apelles. Never finish : for always in absolute beauty there is somewhat above art.

LYLY'S *Campaspe.*

AND NOW, WHAT song should I sing to unveil my Isis, if indeed she was present unseen? I hurried away to the white hall of Phantasy, heedless of the innumerable forms of beauty that crowded my way: these might cross my eyes, but the unseen filled my brain. I wandered long, up and down the silent space: no songs came. My soul was not still enough for songs. Only in the silence and darkness of the soul's night, do those stars of the inward firmament sink to its lower surface from the singing realms beyond, and shine upon the conscious spirit. Here all effort was unavailing. If they came not, they could not be found.

Next night, it was just the same. I walked through the red glimmer of the silent hall; but lonely as there I walked, as lonely trod my soul up and down the halls of the brain. At last I entered one of the statue-halls. The dance had just commenced, and I was delighted to find that I was free of their assembly. I walked on till I came to the sacred corner. There I found the pedestal just as I had left it, with the faint glimmer as of white feet still resting on the dead black. As soon as I saw it, I seemed to feel a presence which longed to become visible; and, as it were, called to me to gift it with self-manifestation, that it might shine on me. The power of song came to me. But the moment my voice, though I sang low and soft, stirred the air of the hall, the dancers started; the quick interweaving crowd shook, lost its form, divided; each figure sprang to its pedestal, and stood a self-evolving life no more, but a rigid, life-like, marble shape, with the whole form composed into the expression of a single state or act. Silence rolled like a spiritual thunder through the grand space. My song had ceased, scared at its own influences. But I saw in the hand of one of the statues close by me, a harp whose chords yet quivered. I remembered that as she bounded past me, her harp had brushed against my arm; so the spell of the marble had not infolded it. I sprang to her, and with a gesture of entreaty, laid my hand on the harp. The marble hand, probably from its contact with the uncharmed harp, had strength enough to relax its hold, and yield the harp to me. No other motion indicated life.

Instinctively I struck the chords and sang. And not to break upon the record of my song, I mention here, that as I sang the first four lines, the loveliest feet became clear upon the black pedestal; and ever as I sang, it was as if a veil were being lifted up from before the form, but an invisible veil, so that the statue appeared to grow before me, not so much by evolution, as by infinitesimal degrees of added height. And, while I sang, I did not feel that I stood by a statue, as indeed it appeared to be, but that a real woman-soul was revealing itself by successive stages of imbodiment, and consequent manifestation and expression.

> Feet of beauty, firmly planting
>   Arches white on rosy heel!
> Whence the life-spring, throbbing, panting,
>   Pulses upward to reveal!
> Fairest things know least despising;
>   Foot and earth meet tenderly:
> 'Tis the woman, resting, rising
>   Upward to sublimity.
>
> Rise the limbs, sedately sloping,
>   Strong and gentle, full and free;
> Soft and slow, like certain hoping,
>   Drawing nigh the broad firm knee.
> Up to speech! As up to roses
>   Pants the life from leaf to flower,
> So each blending change discloses,
>   Nearer still, expression's power.
>
> Lo! fair sweeps, white surges, twining
>   Up and outward fearlessly!
> Temple columns, close combining,
>   Lift a holy mystery.
> Heart of mine! what strange surprises
>   Mount aloft on such a stair!
> Some great vision upward rises,
>   Curving, bending, floating fair.
>
> Bands and sweeps, and hill and hollow
>   Lead my fascinated eye;
> Some apocalypse will follow,
>   Some new word of deity.
> Zoned unseen, and outward swelling,
>   With new thoughts and wonders rife,
> Queenly majesty foretelling,
>   See the expanding house of life!
>
> Sudden heaving, unforbidden
>   Sighs eternal, still the same—
> Mounts of snow have summits hidden
>   In the mists of uttered flame.
> But the spirit, dawning nearly,
>   Finds no speech for earnest pain;
> Finds a soundless sighing merely—
>   Builds its stairs, and mounts again.
>
> Heart, the queen, with secret hoping,
>   Sendeth out her waiting pair;
> Hands, blind hands, half blindly groping,
>   Half inclasping visions rare;
> And the great arms, heartways bending;
>   Might of Beauty, drawing home;
> There returning, and re-blending,
>   Where from roots of love they roam.

Build thy slopes of radiance beamy,
  Spirit, fair with womanhood!
Tower thy precipice, white-gleamy,
  Climb unto the hour of good.
Dumb space will be rent asunder,
  Now the shining column stands
Ready to be crowned with wonder
  By the builder's joyous hands.

All the lines abroad are spreading,
  Like a fountain's failing race
Lo, the chin, first feature, treading,
  Airy foot to rest the face!
Speech is nigh; oh, see the blushing
  Sweet approach of lip and breath!
Round the mouth dim silence, hushing,
  Waits to die ecstatic death.

Span across in treble curving,
  Bow of promise, upper lip!
Set them free, with gracious swerving;
  Let the wing-words float and dip.
Dumb art thou? O Love immortal,
  More than words thy speech must be;
Childless yet the tender portal
  Of the home of melody.

Now the nostrils open fearless,
  Proud in calm unconsciousness.
Sure it must be something peerless
  That the great Pan would express!
Deepens, crowds some meaning tender,
  In the pure, dear lady-face.
Lo, a blinding burst of splendour!—
  'Tis the free soul's issuing grace.

Two calm lakes of molten glory
  Circling round unfathomed deeps!
Lightning-flashes, transitory,
  Cross the gulfs where darkness sleeps.
This the gate, at last, of gladness,
  To the outward-striving *me:*
In a rain of light and sadness,
  Out its loves and longings flee!

With a presence I am smitten
  Dumb, with a foreknown surprise;
Presence greater yet than written.
  Even in the glorious eyes.
Through the gulfs, with inward gazes,
  I may look till I am lost;
Wandering deep in spirit-mazes,
  In a sea without a coast.

Windows open to the glorious!
  Time and space, oh, far beyond!

Woman, ah! thou art victorious,
   And I perish, overfond.
Springs aloft the yet Unspoken
   In the forehead's endless grace,
Full of silences unbroken;
   Infinite, unfeatured face.

Domes above, the mount of wonder,
   Height and hollow wrapt in night;
Hiding in its caverns under
   Woman-nations in their might.
Passing forms, the highest Human
   Faints away to the Divine:
Features none, of man or woman,
   Can unveil the holiest shine.

Sideways, grooved porches only
   Visible to passing eye,
Stand the silent, doorless, lonely
   Entrance-gates of melody.
But all sounds fly in as boldly,
   Groan and song, and kiss and cry,
At their galleries, lifted coldly,
   Darkly, 'twixt the earth and sky.

Beauty, thou art spent, thou knowest:
   So, in faint, half-glad despair,
From the summit thou o'erflowest
   In a fall of torrent hair;
Hiding what thou hast created
   In a half-transparent shroud:
Thus, with glory soft-abated,
   Shines the moon through vapoury cloud.

CHAPTER XVI

Selbst der Styx, der neunfach sie umwindet,
   Wehrt die Rückkehr Ceres Tochter nicht:
Nach dem Apfel greift sie, und es bindet
   Ewig sie des Orkus Pflicht.
         SCHILLER.—*Das Ideal und das Leben.*

Ev'n the Styx, which ninefold her infoldeth,
   Hems not Ceres' daughter in its flow;
But she grasps the apple—ever holdeth
   Her, sad Orcus, down below.

EVER AS I SANG, the veil was uplifted; ever as I sang, the signs of life grew; till, when the eyes dawned upon me, it was with that sunrise of splendour which my feeble song attempted to re-imbody. The wonder is, that I was not altogether overcome, but was able to complete my song as the unseen veil continued to rise. This ability came solely from the state of mental elevation in which I found myself. Only because uplifted in song, was I able to endure the blaze of the dawn. But I cannot tell whether she looked more of statue or more of woman; she seemed removed into that region of phantasy where all is intensely vivid, but nothing clearly defined. At last, as I sang of her descending hair, the glow of soul faded away, like a dying sunset. A lamp within had been extinguished, and the house of life shone blank in a winter morn. She was a statue once more—but visible, and that was much gained. Yet the revulsion from hope and fruition was such, that, unable to restrain myself, I sprang to her, and, in defiance of the law of the place, flung my arms around her, as if I would tear her from the grasp of a visible Death, and lifted her from the pedestal down to my heart. But no sooner had her feet ceased to be in contact with the black pedestal, than she shuddered and trembled all over; then, writhing from my arms, before I could tighten their hold, she sprang into the corridor, with the reproachful cry, "You should not have touched me!" darted behind one of the exterior pillars of the circle, and disappeared. I followed almost as fast; but ere I could reach the pillar, the sound of a closing door, the saddest of all sounds sometimes, fell on my ear; and, arriving at the spot where she had vanished, I saw, lighted by a pale yellow lamp which hung above it, a heavy, rough door, altogether unlike any others I had seen in the palace; for they were all of ebony, or ivory, or covered with silver-plates, or of some odorous wood, and very ornate; whereas this seemed of old oak, with heavy nails and iron studs. Notwithstanding the precipitation of my pursuit, I could not help reading, in silver letters beneath the lamp: *"No one enters here without the leave of the Queen."* But what was the Queen to me, when I followed my white lady? I dashed the door to the wall, and sprang through. Lo! I stood on a waste windy hill. Great stones like tomb-stones stood all about me. No door, no palace was to be seen. A white figure gleamed past me, wringing her hands, and crying, "Ah! you should have sung to me; you should have sung to me!" and disappeared behind one of the stones. I followed. A cold gust of wind met me from behind the stone; and when I looked, I saw nothing but a great hole in the earth, into which I could find no way of entering. Had she fallen in? I could not tell. I must wait for the daylight. I sat down and wept, for there was no help.

CHAPTER XVII

Anfangs wollt 'ich fast verzagen,
　Und ich glaubt' ich trüg' es nie,
Und ich hab' es doch getragen,—
　Aber fragt mich nur nicht: wie?
　　　　　HEINE.

First, I thought, almost despairing,
　This must crush my spirit now;
Yet I bore it, and am bearing—
　Only do not ask me how.

WHEN THE DAYLIGHT came, it brought the possibility of action, but with it little of consolation. With the first visible increase of light, I gazed into the chasm, but could not, for more than an hour, see sufficiently well to discover its nature. At last I saw it was almost a perpendicular opening, like a roughly excavated well, only very large. I could perceive no bottom; and it was not till the sun actually rose, that I discovered a sort of natural staircase, in many parts little more than suggested, which led round and round the gulf, descending spirally into the abyss. I saw at once that this was my path; and without a moment's hesitation, glad to quit the sunlight, which stared at me most heartlessly, I commenced my tortuous descent. It was very difficult. In some parts I had to cling to the rocks like a bat. In one place, I dropped from the track down upon the next returning spire of the stair; which being broad in this particular portion, and standing out from the wall at right angles, received me upon my feet safe, though somewhat stupified by the shock. After descending a great way, I found the stair ended at a narrow opening which entered the rock horizontally. Into this I crept, and, having entered, had just room to turn round. I put my head out into the shaft by which I had come down, and surveyed the course of my descent. Looking up, I saw the stars; although the sun must by this time have been high in the heavens. Looking below, I saw that the sides of the shaft went sheer down, smooth as glass; and far beneath me, I saw the reflection of the same stars I had seen in the heavens when I looked up. I turned again, and crept inwards some distance, when the passage widened, and I was at length able to stand and walk upright. Wider and loftier grew the way; new paths branched off on every side; great open halls appeared; till at last I found myself wandering on through an underground country, in which the sky was of rock, and instead of trees and flowers, there were only fantastic rocks and stones. And ever as I went, darker grew my thoughts, till at last I had no hope whatever of finding the white lady: I no longer called her to myself *my* white lady. Wherever a choice was necessary, I always chose the path which seemed to lead downwards.

At length I began to find that these regions were inhabited. From behind a rock a peal of harsh grating laughter, full of evil humour, rang through my ears, and, looking round, I saw a queer, goblin creature, with a great head and ridiculous features, just such as those described, in German histories and travels, as Kobolds. "What do you want with me?" I said. He pointed at me with a long forefinger, very thick at the root, and sharpened to a point, and answered, "He! he! he! what do *you* want here?" Then, changing his tone, he continued, with mock humility—"Honoured sir, vouchsafe to withdraw from thy slaves the lustre of thy august presence, for thy slaves cannot support its brightness." A second appeared, and struck in: "You are so big, you keep the sun from us. We can't see for you, and we're so cold." Thereupon arose, on all sides, the most terrific uproar of laughter, from voices like those of children in volume, but scrannel and harsh as those of decrepit age, though, unfortunately, without its weakness. The whole pandemonium of fairy devils, of all varieties of fantastic ugliness, both in form and features, and of all sizes from one to four feet, seemed to have suddenly assembled about me. At length, after a great babble of talk among themselves, in a language unknown to me, and after seemingly endless gesticulation, consultation, elbow-nudging, and unmitigated peals of laughter, they formed into a circle about one of their number, who scrambled upon a stone, and, much to my surprise, and somewhat to my dismay, began to sing, in a voice corresponding in its nature to his talking one, from beginning to end, the song with which I had brought the light into the eyes of the white lady. He sang the same air too; and, all the time, maintained a face of mock entreaty and worship; accompanying the song with the travestied gestures of one playing on the lute. The whole assembly kept silence, except at the close of every verse, when they roared, and danced, and shouted with laughter, and flung themselves on the ground, in real or pretended convulsions of delight. When he had finished, the singer threw himself from the top of the stone, turning heels over head several times in his descent; and when he did alight, it was on the top of his head, on which he hopped about, making the most grotesque gesticulations with his legs in the air. Inexpressible laughter followed, which broke up in a shower of tiny stones from innumerable hands. They could not materially injure me, although they cut me on the head and face. I attempted to run away, but they all rushed upon me, and, laying hold of every part that afforded a grasp, held me tight. Crowding about me like bees, they shouted an insect-swarm of exasperating speeches up into my face, among which the most frequently recurring were—"You shan't have her; you shan't have her; he! he! he! She's for a better man; she's for a better man; how he'll kiss her! how he'll kiss her!"

The galvanic torrent of this battery of malevolence stung to life within me a spark of nobleness, and I said aloud, "Well, if he is a better man, let him have her."

They instantly let go their hold of me, and fell back a step or two, with a whole broadside of grunts and humphs, as of unexpected and disappointed approbation. I made a step or two forward, and a lane was instantly opened for me through the midst of the grinning little antics, who bowed most politely to me on every side as I passed. After I had gone a few yards, I looked back, and saw them all standing quite still, looking after me, like a great school of boys; till suddenly one turned round, and with a loud whoop, rushed into the midst of the others. In an instant, the whole was one writhing and tumbling heap of contortion, reminding me of the live pyramids of intertwined snakes of which travellers make report. As soon as one was worked out of the mass, he bounded off a few paces, and then, with a somerset and a run, threw himself gyrating into the air, and descended with all his weight on the summit of the heaving and struggling chaos of fantastic figures. I left them still busy at this fierce and apparently aimless amusement. And as I went, I sang—

> "If a nobler waits for thee,
>   I will weep aside;
> It is well that thou should'st be,
>   Of the nobler, bride.
>
> "For if love builds up the home,
>   Where the heart is free,

Homeless yet the heart must roam,
That has not found thee.

"One must suffer: I, for her,
Yield in her my part.
Take her, thou art worthier—
Still! be still, my heart!

"Gift ungotten! largess high
Of a frustrate will!
But to yield it lovingly,
Is a something still."

Then a little song arose of itself in my soul; and I felt for the moment, while it sang sadly within me, as if I was once more walking up and down the white hall of Phantasy in the Fairy Palace. But this lasted no longer than the song, as will be seen.

"Do not vex thy violet
Perfume to afford;
Else no odour thou wilt get
From its little hoard.

"In thy lady's gracious eyes
Look not thou too long;
Else from them the glory flies,
And thou dost her wrong.

"Come not thou too near the maid,
Clasp her not too wild;
Else the splendour is allayed,
And thy heart beguiled."

A crash of laughter, more discordant and deriding than any I had yet heard, invaded my ears. Looking on in the direction of the sound, I saw a little elderly woman, much taller, however, than the goblins I had just left, seated upon a stone by the side of the path. She rose, as I drew near, and came forward to meet me. She was very plain and commonplace in appearance, without being hideously ugly. Looking up in my face with a stupid sneer, she said: "Isn't it a pity you haven't a pretty girl to walk all alone with you through this sweet country? How different everything would look! wouldn't it? Strange that one can never have what one would like best! How the roses would bloom and all that, even in this infernal hole! wouldn't they, Anodos? Her eyes would light up the old cave, wouldn't they?"

"That depends on who the pretty girl should be," replied I.

"Not so very much matter that," she answered; "look here."

I had turned to go away as I gave my reply, but now I stopped and looked at her. As a rough unsightly bud might suddenly blossom into the most lovely flower; or rather, as a sunbeam bursts through a shapeless cloud, and transfigures the earth; so burst a face of resplendent beauty, as it were *through* the unsightly visage of the woman, destroying it with light as it dawned through it. A summer sky rose above me, grey with heat; across a shining slumberous landscape, looked from afar the peaks of snow-capped mountains; and down from a great rock beside me, fell a sheet of water mad with its own delight.

"Stay with me," she said, lifting up her exquisite face, and looking full in mine.

I drew back. Again the infernal laugh grated upon my ears; again the rocks closed in around me, and the ugly woman looked at me with wicked, mocking hazel eyes.

"You shall have your reward," said she. "You shall see your white lady again."

"That lies not with you," I replied, and turned and left her.

She followed me with shriek upon shriek of laughter, as I went on my way.

I may mention here, that although there was always light enough to see my path and a few yards on every side of me, I never could find out the source of this sad sepulchral illumination.

CHAPTER XVIII

Im Sausen des Windes, im Brausen des Meers,
Und im Seufzen der eigenen Brust.

HEINE.

In the wind's uproar, the sea's raging grim,
And the sighs that are born in him.

Ja, est wird zwar ein anderes Zeitalter kommen, wo es Licht wird, und wo der Mensch aus erhabnen Träumen erwacht, und die Träume—wieder findet, weil er nichts verlor als den Schlaf."

JEAN PAUL—*Hesperus.*

From dreams of bliss shall men awake
  One day, but not to weep:
The dreams remain; they only break
  The mirror of the sleep.

HOW I GOT through this dreary part of my travels, I do not know. I do not think I was upheld by the hope that any moment the light might break in upon me; for I scarcely thought about that. I went on with a dull endurance, varied by moments of uncontrollable sadness; for more and more the conviction grew upon me that I should never see the white lady again. It may seem strange that one with whom I had held so little communion, should have so engrossed my thoughts; but benefits conferred awaken love in some minds, as surely as benefits received in others. Besides being delighted and proud that *my* songs had called the beautiful creature to life, the same fact caused me to feel a tenderness unspeakable for her, accompanied with a kind of feeling of property in her; for so the goblin Selfishness would reward the angel Love. When to all this is added, an overpowering sense of her beauty, and an unquestioning conviction that this was a true index to inward loveliness, it may be understood how it came to pass that my imagination filled my whole soul with the play of its own multitudinous colours and harmonies around the form which yet stood, a gracious marble radiance, in the midst of *its* white hall of phantasy. The time passed by unheeded; for my thoughts were busy. Perhaps this was also in part the cause of my needing no food, and never thinking how I should find any, during this subterranean part of my travels. How long they endured I could not tell, for I had no means of measuring time; and when I looked back, there was such a discrepancy between the decisions of my imagination and my judgment, as to the length of time that had passed, that I was bewildered and gave up all attempts to arrive at any conclusion on the point.

A grey mist continually gathered behind me. When I looked back towards the past, this mist was the medium through which my eyes had to strain for a vision of what had gone by; and the form of the white lady had receded into an unknown region. At length the country of rock began to close again around me, gradually and slowly narrowing, till I found myself walking in a gallery of rock once more, both sides of which I could touch with my outstretched hands. It narrowed yet, until I was forced to move carefully, in order to avoid striking against the projecting pieces of rock. The roof sank lower and lower, until I was compelled, first to stoop, and then to creep on my hands and knees. It recalled terrible dreams of childhood; but I was not much afraid, because I felt sure that this was my path, and my only hope of leaving Fairy Land, of which I was now almost weary.

At length, on getting past an abrupt turn in the passage, through which I had to force myself, I saw, a few yards ahead of me, the long-forgotten daylight shining through a small opening, to which the path, if path it could now be called, led me. With great difficulty I accomplished these last few yards, and came forth to the day. I stood on the shore of a wintry sea, with a wintry sun just a few feet above its horizon-edge. It was bare, and waste, and grey. Hundreds of hopeless waves rushed constantly shorewards, falling exhausted upon a beach of great loose stones, that seemed to stretch miles and miles in both directions. There was nothing for the eye but mingling shades of grey; nothing for the ear but the rush of the coming, the roar of the breaking, and the moan of the retreating wave. No rock lifted up a sheltering severity above the dreariness around; even that from which I had myself emerged rose scarcely a foot above the opening by which I had reached the dismal day, more dismal even than the tomb I had left. A cold, death-like wind swept across the shore, seeming to issue from a pale mouth of cloud upon the horizon. Sign of life was nowhere visible. I wandered over the stones, up and down the beach, a human embodiment of the nature around me. The wind increased; its keen waves flowed through my soul; the foam rushed higher up the stones; a few dead stars began to gleam in the east; the sound of the waves grew louder and yet more despairing. A dark curtain of cloud was lifted up, and a pale blue rent shone between its foot and the edge of the sea, out from which rushed an icy storm of frozen wind, that tore the waters into spray as it passed, and flung the billows in raving heaps upon the desolate shore. I could bear it no longer.

"I will not be tortured to death," I cried; "I will meet it half-way. The life within me is yet enough to bear me up to the face of Death, and then I die unconquered."

Before it had grown so dark, I had observed, though without any particular interest, that on one part of the shore a low platform of rock seemed to run out far into the midst of the breaking waters. Towards this I now went, scrambling over smooth stones, to which scarce even a particle of sea-weed clung; and having found it, I got on it, and followed its direction, as near as I could guess, out into the tumbling chaos. I could hardly keep my feet against the wind and sea. The waves repeatedly all but swept me off my path; but I kept on my way, till I reached the end of the low promontory, which, in the fall of the waves, rose a good many feet above the surface, and, in their rise, was covered with their waters. I stood one moment, and gazed into the heaving abyss beneath me; then plunged headlong into the mounting wave below. A blessing, like the kiss of a mother, seemed to alight on my soul; a calm, deeper than that which accompanies a hope deferred, bathed my spirit. I sank far in the waters, and sought not to return. I felt as if once more the great arms of the beech-tree were around me, soothing me after the miseries I had passed through, and telling me, like a little sick child, that I should be better to-morrow. The waters of themselves lifted me, as with loving arms, to the surface. I breathed again, but did not unclose my eyes. I would not look on the wintry sea, and the pitiless grey sky. Thus I floated, till something gently touched me. It was a little boat floating beside me. How it came there I could not tell; but it rose and sank on the waters, and kept touching me in its fall, as if with a human will to let me know that help was by me. It was a little gay-coloured boat, seemingly covered with glistering scales like those of a fish, all of brilliant rainbow hues. I scrambled into it, and lay down in the bottom, with a sense of exquisite repose. Then I drew over me a rich, heavy, purple cloth that was beside me; and, lying still, knew, by the sound of the waters, that my little bark was fleeting rapidly onwards. Finding, however, none of that stormy motion which the sea had manifested when I beheld it from the shore, I opened my eyes; and, looking first up, saw above me the deep violet sky of a warm southern night; and then, lifting my head, saw that I was sailing fast upon a summer sea, in the last border of a southern twilight. The aureole of the sun yet shot the extreme faint tips of its longest rays above the horizon-waves, and withdrew them not. It was a perpetual twilight. The stars, great and earnest, like children's eyes, bent down lovingly towards the waters; and the reflected stars within seemed to float up, as if longing to meet their embraces. But when I looked down, a new wonder met my view. For, vaguely revealed beneath the wave, I floated above my whole Past. The fields of my childhood flitted by; the halls of my youthful labours; the streets of great cities where I head dwelt; and the assemblies of men and women wherein I had wearied myself seeking for rest. But so indistinct were the visions, that sometimes I thought that I was sailing on a shallow sea, and that strange rocks and forests of sea-plants beguiled my eye, sufficiently to be transformed, by the magic of the phantasy, into well-known objects and regions. Yet, at times, a beloved form seemed to lie close beneath me in sleep; and the eyelids would tremble as if about to forsake the conscious eye; and the arms would heave upwards, as if in dreams they sought for a satisfying presence. But these motions might come only from the heaving of the waters between those forms and me. Soon I fell asleep, overcome with fatigue and delight. In dreams of unspeakable joy—of restored friendships; of revived embraces; of love which said it had never died; of faces that had vanished long ago, yet said with smiling lips that they knew nothing of the grave; of pardons implored, and granted with such bursting floods of love, that I was almost glad I had sinned—thus I passed through this wondrous twilight. I awoke with the feeling that I had been kissed and loved to my heart's content; and found that my boat was floating motionless by the grassy shore of a little island.

CHAPTER XIX

In stiller Ruhe, in wechselloser Einfalt führ ich ununterbrochen das Bewusst-
seyn der ganzen Menschheit in mir.
                                        Schleiermacher—*Monologen.*

In still rest, in changeless simplicity, I bear, uninterrupted, the consciousness of
the whole of Humanity within me.

———

—such a sweetness, such a grace
   In all thy speech appear,
That what to th' eye a beauteous face,
   That thy tongue is to the ear.
                                        Cowley.

THE WATER WAS deep to the very edge; and I sprang from the little boat upon a soft grassy turf. The island seemed rich with a profusion of all grasses and low flowers. All delicate lowly things were most plentiful; but no trees rose skywards; not even a bush overtopped the tall grasses, except in one place near the cottage I am about to describe, where a few plants of the gum-cistus, which drops every night all the blossoms that the day brings forth, formed a kind of natural arbour. The whole island lay open to the sky and sea. It rose nowhere more than a few feet above the level of the waters, which flowed deep all around its border. Here there seemed to be neither tide nor storm. A sense of persistent calm and fulness arose in the mind at the sight of the slow, pulse-like rise and fall of the deep, clear, unrippled waters against the bank of the island, for shore it could hardly be called, being so much more like the edge of a full, solemn river. As I walked over the grass towards the cottage, which stood at a little distance from the bank, all the flowers of childhood looked at me with perfect child-eyes out of the grass. My heart, softened by the dreams through which it had passed, overflowed in a sad, tender love towards them. They looked to me like children impregnably fortified in a helpless confidence. The sun stood half way down the western sky, shining very soft and golden; and there grew a second world of shadows amidst the world of grasses and wild flowers.

The cottage was square, with low walls, and a high pyramidal roof thatched with long reeds, of which the withered blossoms hung over all the eaves. It is noticeable that most of the buildings I saw in Fairy Land were cottages. There was no path to a door, nor, indeed, was there any track worn by footsteps in the island. The cottage rose right out of the smooth turf. It had no windows that I could see; but there was a door in the centre of the side facing me, up to which I went. I knocked, and the sweetest voice I had ever heard said, "Come in." I entered. A bright fire was burning on a hearth in the centre of the earthen floor, and the smoke found its way out at an opening in the centre of the pyramidal roof. Over the fire hung a little pot, and over the pot bent a woman-face, the most wonderful, I thought, that I had ever beheld. For it was older than any countenance I had ever looked upon. There was not a spot in which a wrinkle could lie, where a wrinkle lay not. And the skin was ancient and brown, like old parchment. The woman's form was tall and spare: and when she stood up to welcome me, I saw that she was straight as an arrow. Could that voice of sweetness have issued from those lips of age? Mild as they were, could they be the portals whence flowed such melody? But the moment I saw her eyes, I no longer wondered at her voice: they were absolutely young—those of a woman of five-and-twenty, large, and of a clear grey. Wrinkles had beset them all about; the eyelids themselves were old, and heavy, and worn; but the eyes were very incarnations of soft light. She held out her hand to me, and the voice of sweetness again greeted me, with the single word, "Welcome." She set an old wooden chair for me, near the fire, and went on with her cooking. A wondrous sense of refuge and repose came upon me. I felt like a boy who has got home from school, miles across the hills, through a heavy storm of wind and snow. Almost, as I gazed on her, I sprang from my seat to kiss those old lips. And when, having finished her cooking, she brought some of the dish she had prepared, and set it on a little table by me, covered with a snow-white cloth, I could not help laying my head on her bosom, and bursting into happy tears. She put her arms round me, saying, "Poor child; poor child!"

As I continued to weep, she gently disengaged herself; and, taking a spoon, put some of the food (I did not know what it was) to my lips, entreating me most endearingly to swallow it. To please her, I made an effort, and succeeded. She went on feeding me like a baby, with one arm round me, till I looked up in her face and smiled; then she gave me the spoon, and told me to eat, for it would do me good. I obeyed her, and found myself wonderfully refreshed. Then she drew near the fire an old-fashioned couch that was in the cottage, and making me lie down upon it, sat at my feet, and began to sing. Amazing store of old ballads rippled from her lips, over the pebbles of ancient tunes; and the voice that sang was sweet as the voice of a tuneful maiden that singeth ever

from very fulness of song. The songs were almost all sad, but with a
sound of comfort. One I can faintly recall. It was something like this:

> Sir Aglovaile through the churchyard rode;
>   *Sing, All alone I lie:*
> Little recked he where'er he yode.
>   *All alone, up in the sky.*
>
> Swerved his courser, and plunged with fear;
>   *All alone I lie:*
> His cry might have wakened the dead men near,
>   *All alone, up in the sky.*
>
> The very dead that lay at his feet,
> Lapt in the mouldy winding-sheet.
>
> But he curbed him and spurred him, until he stood
> Still in his place, like a horse of wood,
>
> With nostrils uplift, and eyes wide and wan;
> But the sweat in streams from his fetlocks ran.
>
> A ghost grew out of the shadowy air,
> And sat in the midst of her moony hair.
>
> In her gleamy hair she sat and wept;
> In the dreamful moon they lay and slept;
>
> The shadows above, and the bodies below,
> Lay and slept in the moonbeams slow.
>
> And she sang, like the moan of an autumn wind
> Over the stubble left behind:
>
> > *Alas, how easily things go wrong!*
> > *A sigh too much, or a kiss too long,*
> > *And there follows a mist and a weeping rain,*
> > *And life is never the same again.*
> >
> > *Alas, how hardly things go right!*
> > *'Tis hard to watch in a summer night;*
> > *For the sigh will come, and the kiss will stay,*
> > *And the summer night is a winter day.*
>
> "Oh, lovely ghost, my heart is woe,
> "To see thee weeping and wailing so.
>
> "Oh, lovely ghost," said the fearless knight,
> "Can the sword of a warrior set it right?
>
> "Or prayer of bedesman, praying mild,
> "As a cup of water a feverish child,
>
> "Soothe thee at last, in dreamless mood,
> "To sleep the sleep a dead lady should?

"Thine eyes they fill me with longing sore,
"As if I had known thee for evermore.

"Oh, lovely ghost, I could leave the day,
"To sit with thee in the moon away,

"If thou wouldst trust me, and lay thy head
"To rest on a bosom that is not dead."

The lady sprang up with a strange ghost cry,
And she flung her white ghost-arms on high;

And she laughed a laugh that was not gay,
And it lengthened out till it died away;

And the dead beneath turned and moaned,
And the yew-trees above they shuddered and groaned.

"Will he love me twice with a love that is vain?
"Will he kill the poor ghost yet again?

"I thought thou wert good; but I said, and wept:
"'Can I have dreamed who have not slept?'

"And I knew, alas! or ever I would,
"Whether I dreamed, or thou wert good.

"When my baby died, my brain grew wild.
"I awoke, and found I was with my child."

"If thou art the ghost of my Adelaide,
"How is it? Thou wert but a village maid,

"And thou seemest an angel lady white,
"Though thin, and wan, and past delight."

The lady smiled a flickering smile,
And she pressed her temples hard the while:

"Thou seest that Death for a woman can
"Do more than knighthood for a man."

"But show me the child thou callest mine.
"Is she out to-night in the ghost's sunshine?"

"In St. Peter's Church she is playing on,
"At hide-and-seek, with Apostle John.

"When the moonbeams right through the window go,
"Where the twelve are standing in glorious show,

"She says the rest of them do not stir,
"But one comes down to play with her.

"Then I can go where I list, and weep.
"For good St. John my child will keep."

"Thy beauty filleth the very air.
"Never saw I a woman so fair."

"Come, if thou darest, and sit by my side;
"But do not touch me, or woe will betide.

"Alas I am weak: I well might know
"This gladness betokens some further woe.

"Yet come. It will come. I will bear it. I can.
"For thou lovest me yet—though but as a man."

The knight dismounted in earnest speed;
Away through the tombstones thundered the steed,

And fell by the outer wall, and died.
But the knight he kneeled by the lady's side;

Kneeled beside her in wondrous bliss,
Rapt in an everlasting kiss:

Though never his lips come the lady nigh,
And his eyes alone on her beauty lie.

All the night long, till the cock crew loud,
He kneeled by the lady, lapt in her shroud.

And what they said, I may not say:
Dead night was sweeter than living day.

How she made him so blissful glad
Who made her and found her so ghostly sad,

I may not tell; but it needs no touch
To make them blessed who love so much.

"Come every night, my ghost, to me;
"And one night I will come to thee.

"'Tis good to have a ghostly wife:
"She will not tremble at clang of strife;

"She will only hearken, amid the din,
"Behind the door, if he cometh in."

And this is how Sir Aglovaile
Often walked in the moonlight pale.

And oft when the crescent but thinned the gloom,
Full orbéd moonlight filled his room;

And through beneath his chamber door
Fell a ghostly gleam on the outer floor;

"'But show me the child thou callest mine.'"

ARTHUR HUGHES

And they that passed, in fear averred
That murmured words they often heard.

'Twas then that the eastern crescent shone
Through the chancel window, and good St. John

Played with the ghost-child all the night,
And the mother was free till the morning light,

And sped through the dawning night, to stay
With Aglovaile till the break of day.

And their love was a rapture, lone and high,
And dumb as the moon in the topmost sky.

One night Sir Aglovaile, weary, slept,
And dreamed a dream wherein he wept.

A warrior he was, not often wept he,
But this night he wept full bitterly.

He woke—beside him the ghost-girl shone
Out of the dark: 'twas the eve of St. John.

He had dreamed a dream of a still, dark wood,
Where the maiden of old beside him stood;

But a mist came down, and caught her away,
And he sought her in vain through the pathless day,

Till he wept with the grief that can do no more,
And thought he had dreamt the dream before.

From bursting heart the weeping flowed on;
And lo! beside him the ghost-girl shone;

Shone like the light on a harbour's breast,
Over the sea of his dream's unrest;

Shone like the wondrous, nameless boon,
That the heart seeks ever, night or noon:

Warnings forgotten, when needed most,
He clasped to his bosom the radiant ghost.

She wailed aloud, and faded, and sank.
With upturn'd white face, cold and blank,

In his arms lay the corpse of the maiden pale,
And she came no more to Sir Aglovaile.

Only a voice, when winds were wild,
Sobbed and wailed like a chidden child,

Alas, how easily things go wrong!
A sigh too much, or a kiss too long,

And there follows a mist and a weeping rain,
And life is never the same again.

This was one of the simplest of her songs, which, perhaps, is the cause of my being able to remember it better than most of the others.

While she sung, I was in Elysium, with the sense of a rich soul upholding, embracing, and overhanging mine, full of all plenty and bounty. I felt as if she could give me everything I wanted; as if I should never wish to leave her, but would be content to be sung to and fed by her, day after day, as years rolled by. At last I fell asleep while she sang.

When I awoke, I knew not whether it was night or day. The fire had sunk to a few red embers, which just gave light enough to show me the woman standing a few feet from me, with her back towards me, facing the door by which I had entered. She was weeping, but very gently and plentifully. The tears seemed to come freely from her heart. Thus she stood for a few minutes; then, slowly turning at right angles to her former position, she faced another of the four sides of the cottage. I now observed for the first time, that here was a door likewise; and that, indeed, there was one in the centre of every side of the cottage. When she looked towards this second door, her tears ceased to flow, but sighs took their place. She often closed her eyes as she stood; and every time she closed her eyes, a gentle sigh seemed to be born in her heart and to escape at her lips. But when her eyes were open, her sighs were deep and very sad, and shook her whole frame. Then she turned towards the third door, and a cry as of fear or suppressed pain broke from her; but she seemed to hearten herself against the dismay, and to front it steadily; for, although I often heard a slight cry and sometimes a moan, yet she never moved or bent her head, and I felt sure that her eyes never closed. Then she turned to the fourth door, and I saw her shudder, and then stand still as a statue; till at last she turned towards me and approached the fire. I saw that her face was white as death. But she gave one look upwards, and smiled the sweetest, most child-innocent smile; then heaped fresh wood on the fire, and, sitting down by the blaze, drew her wheel near her, and began to spin. While she spun, she murmured a low strange song, to which the hum of the wheel made a kind of infinite symphony. At length, she paused in her spinning and singing, and glanced towards me, like a mother who looks whether or not her child gives signs of waking. She smiled when she saw that my eyes were open. I asked her whether it was day yet. She answered, "It is always day here, so long as I keep my fire burning."

I felt wonderfully refreshed; and a great desire to see more of the island awoke within me. I rose, and saying that I wished to look about me, went towards the door by which I had entered.

"Stay a moment," said my hostess, with some trepidation in her voice. "Listen to me. You will not see what you expect when you go out of that door. Only remember this: whenever you wish to come back to me, enter wherever you see this mark."

She held up her left hand between me and the fire. Upon the palm, which appeared almost transparent, I saw, in dark red, a mark like this ～ , which I took care to fix in my mind.

She then kissed me, and bade me good-bye with a solemnity that awed me; and bewildered me too, seeing I was only going out for a little ramble in an island, which I did not believe larger than could easily be compassed in a few hours' walk at most. As I went she resumed her spinning.

I opened the door, and stepped out. The moment my foot touched the smooth sward, I seemed to issue from the door of an old barn on my father's estate, where, in the hot afternoons, I used to go and lie amongst the straw, and read. It seemed to me now that I had been asleep there. At a little distance in the field, I saw two of my brothers at play. The moment they caught sight of me, they called out to me to come and join them, which I did; and we played together as we had done years ago, till the red sun went down in the west, and the grey fog began to rise from the river. Then we went home together with a strange happiness. As we went, we heard the continually renewed larum of a landrail in the long grass. One of my brothers and I separated to a little distance, and each commenced running towards the part whence the sound appeared to come, in the hope of approaching the spot where the bird was, and so getting at least a sight of it, if we should not be able to capture the little creature. My father's voice recalled us from trampling down the rich long grass, soon to be cut down and laid aside for winter. I had quite forgotten all about Fairy Land, and the wonderful old woman, and the curious red mark.

My favourite brother and I shared the same bed. Some childish dispute arose between us; and our last words, ere we fell asleep, were not of kindness, notwithstanding the pleasures of the day. When I woke in the morning, I missed him. He had risen early, and had gone to bathe in the river. In another hour, he was brought home drowned. Alas! alas! if we had only gone to sleep as usual, the one with his arm about the other! Amidst the horror of the moment, a strange conviction flashed across my mind, that I had gone through the very same once before.

I rushed out of the house, I knew not why, sobbing and crying bitterly. I ran through the fields in aimless distress, till, passing the old barn, I caught sight of a red mark on the door. The merest trifles sometimes rivet the attention in the deepest misery; the intellect has so little to do with grief. I went up to look at this mark, which I did not remember ever to have seen before. As I looked at it, I thought I would go in and lie down amongst the straw, for I was very weary with running about and weeping. I opened the door; and there in the cottage sat the old woman as I had left her, at her spinning-wheel.

"I did not expect you quite so soon," she said, as I shut the door behind me. I went up to the couch, and threw myself on it with that fatigue wherewith one awakes from a feverish dream of hopeless grief.

The old woman sang:

> "The great sun, benighted,
>   May faint from the sky;
> But love, once uplighted,
>   Will never more die.

"Form, with its brightness,
From eyes will depart:
It walketh, in whiteness,
The halls of the heart."

Ere she had ceased singing, my courage had returned. I started from the couch, and, without taking leave of the old woman, opened the door of Sighs, and sprang into what should appear.

I stood in a lordly hall, where, by a blazing fire on the hearth, sat a lady, waiting, I knew, for some one long desired. A mirror was near me, but I saw that my form had no place within its depths, so I feared not that I should be seen. The lady wonderfully resembled my marble lady, but was altogether of the daughters of men, and I could not tell whether or not it was she. It was not for me she waited. The tramp of a great horse rang through the court without. It ceased, and the clang of armour told that the rider alighted, and the sound of his ringing heels approached the hall. The door opened; but the lady waited, for she would meet her lord alone. He strode in: she flew like a home-bound dove into his arms, and nestled on the hard steel. It was the knight of the soiled armour. But now the armour shone like polished glass; and, strange to tell, though the mirror reflected not my form, I saw a dim shadow of myself in the shining steel.

"O my beloved, thou art come, and I am blessed."

Her soft fingers speedily overcame the hard clasp of his helmet; one by one she undid the buckles of his armour; and she toiled under the weight of the mail, as she *would* carry it aside. Then she unclasped his greaves, and unbuckled his spurs; and once more she sprang into his arms, and laid her head where she could now feel the beating of his heart. Then she disengaged herself from his embrace, and, moving back a step or two, gazed at him. He stood there a mighty form, crowned with a noble head, where all sadness had disappeared, or had been absorbed in solemn purpose. Yet I suppose that he looked more thoughtful than the lady had expected to see him, for she did not renew her caresses, although his face glowed with love, and the few words he spoke were as mighty deeds for strength; but she led him towards the hearth, and seated him in an ancient chair, and set wine before him, and sat at his feet.

"I am sad," he said, "when I think of the youth whom I met twice in the forests of Fairy Land; and who, you say, twice, with his songs, roused you from the death-sleep of an evil enchantment. There was something noble in him, but it was a nobleness of thought, and not of deed. He may yet perish of vile fear."

"Ah!" returned the lady, "you saved him once; and for that I thank you; for may I not say that I somewhat loved him? But tell me how you fared, when you struck your battle-axe into the ash-tree, and he came and found you; for so much of the story you had told me, when the beggar-child came and took you away."

"As soon as I saw him," rejoined the knight, "I knew that earthly arms availed not against such as he; and that my soul must meet him in its naked strength. So I unclasped my helm, and flung it on the ground;

and, holding my good axe yet in my hand, gazed at him with steady eyes. On he came, a horror indeed, but I did not flinch. Endurance must conquer, where force could not reach. He came nearer and nearer, till the ghastly face was close to mine. A shudder as of death ran through me; but I think I did not move, for he seemed to quail, and retreated. As soon as he gave back, I struck one more sturdy blow on the stem of his tree, that the forest rang; and then looked at him again. He writhed and grinned with rage and apparent pain, and again approached me, but retreated sooner than before. I heeded him no more, but hewed with a will at the tree, till the trunk creaked, and the head bowed, and with a crash it fell to the earth. Then I looked up from my labour, and, lo! the spectre had vanished, and I saw him no more; nor ever in my wanderings have I heard of him again."

"Well struck! well withstood! my hero," said the lady.

"But," said the knight, somewhat troubled, "dost thou love the youth still?"

"Ah!" she replied, "how can I help it? He woke me from worse than death; he loved me. I had never been for thee, if he had not sought me first. But I love him not as I love thee. He was but the moon of my night; thou art the sun of my day, O beloved."

"Thou art right," returned the noble man. "It were hard, indeed, not to have some love in return for such a gift as he hath given thee. I, too, owe him more than words can speak."

Humbled before them, with an aching and desolate heart, I yet could not restrain my words:

"Let me, then, be the moon of thy night still, O woman! And when the day is beclouded, as the fairest days will be, let some song of mine comfort thee, as an old, withered, half-forgotten thing, that belongs to an ancient mournful hour of uncompleted birth, which yet was beautiful in its time."

They sat silent, and I almost thought they were listening. The colour of the lady's eyes grew deeper and deeper; the slow tears grew, and filled them, and overflowed. They rose, and passed, hand in hand, close to where I stood; and each looked towards me in passing. Then they disappeared through a door which closed behind them; but, ere it closed, I saw that the room into which it opened was a rich chamber, hung with gorgeous arras. I stood with an ocean of sighs frozen in my bosom. I could remain no longer. She was near me, and I could not see her; near me in the arms of one loved better than I, and I would not see her, and I would not be by her. But how to escape from the nearness of the best beloved? I had not this time forgotten the mark; for the fact that I could not enter the sphere of these living beings kept me aware that, for me, I moved in a vision, while they moved in life. I looked all about for the mark, but could see it nowhere; for I avoided looking just where it was. There the dull red cipher glowed, on the very door of their secret chamber. Struck with agony, I dashed it open, and fell at the feet of the ancient woman, who still spun on, the whole dissolved ocean of my sighs bursting from me in a storm of tearless sobs. Whether I fainted or slept, I do not know; but, as I returned to consciousness, before I seemed to have power to move, I heard the woman singing, and could distinguish the words:

"O light of dead and of dying days!
   O Love! in thy glory go,
 In a rosy mist and a moony maze,
   O'er the pathless peaks of snow.

"But what is left for the cold grey soul,
   That moans like a wounded dove?
 One wine is left in the broken bowl—
   'Tis—*To love, and love, and love.*"

Now I could weep. When she saw me weeping, she sang:

"Better to sit at the waters' birth,
   Than a sea of waves to win;
 To live in the love that floweth forth,
   Than the love that cometh in.

"Be thy heart a well of love, my child,
   Flowing, and free, and sure;
 For a cistern of love, though undefiled,
   Keeps not the spirit pure."

I rose from the earth, loving the white lady as I had never loved her before.

Then I walked up to the door of Dismay, and opened it, and went out. And lo! I came forth upon a crowded street, where men and women went to and fro in multitudes. I knew it well; and, turning to one hand, walked sadly along the pavement. Suddenly I saw approaching me, a little way off, a form well known to me (*well-known!*—alas, how weak the word!) in the years when I thought my boyhood was left behind, and shortly before I entered the realm of Fairy Land. Wrong and Sorrow had gone together, hand-in-hand, as it is well they do. Unchangeably dear was that face. It lay in my heart as a child lies in its own white bed; but I could not meet her.

"Anything but that," I said; and, turning aside, sprang up the steps to a door, on which I fancied I saw the mystic sign. I entered—not the mysterious cottage, but her home. I rushed wildly on, and stood by the door of her room.

"She is out," I said, "I will see the old room once more."

I opened the door gently, and stood in a great solemn church. A deep-toned bell, whose sounds throbbed and echoed and swam through the empty building, struck the hour of midnight. The moon shone through the windows of the clerestory, and enough of the ghostly radiance was diffused through the church to let me see, walking with a stately, yet somewhat trailing and stumbling step, down the opposite aisle, for I stood in one of the transepts, a figure dressed in a white robe, whether for the night, or for that longer night which lies too deep for the day, I could not tell. Was it she? and was this her chamber? I crossed the church, and followed. The figure stopped, seemed to ascend as it were a high bed, and lay down. I reached the place where it lay, glimmering white. The bed was a tomb. The light was too ghostly to see clearly, but I passed my hand over the face and the hands and the feet, which were all bare. They were cold—they were marble, but I knew them. It grew dark. I turned to retrace my steps, but found, ere long, that I had wandered into what seemed a little chapel. I groped about, seeking the door. Everything I touched belonged to the dead. My hands fell on the cold effigy of a knight who lay with his legs crossed and his sword broken beside him. He lay in his noble rest, and I lived on in ignoble strife. I felt for the left hand and a certain finger; I found there the ring I knew: he was one of my own ancestors. I was in the chapel over the burial-vault of my race. I called aloud: "If any of the dead are moving here, let them take pity upon me, for I, alas! am still alive; and let some dead woman comfort me, for I am a stranger in the land of the dead, and see no light." A warm kiss alighted on my lips through the dark. And I said, "The dead kiss well; I will not be afraid." And a great hand was reached out of the dark, and grasped mine for a moment, mightily and tenderly. I said to myself: "The veil between, though very dark, is very thin."

Groping my way further, I stumbled over the heavy stone that covered the entrance of the vault: and, in stumbling, descried upon the stone the mark, glowing in red fire. I caught the great ring. All my efforts could not have moved the huge slab; but it opened the door of the cottage, and I threw myself once more, pale and speechless, on the couch beside the ancient dame. She sang once more:—

> "Thou dreamest: on a rock thou art,
>   High o'er the broken wave;
> Thou fallest with a fearful start,
>   But not into thy grave;
> For, waking in the morning's light,
> Thou smilest at the vanished night.
>
> "So wilt thou sink, all pale and dumb,
>   Into the fainting gloom;
> But ere the coming terrors come,
>   Thou wak'st—where is the tomb?
> Thou wak'st—the dead ones smile above,
> With hovering arms of sleepless love."

She paused; then sang again:

> "We weep for gladness, weep for grief;
>   The tears they are the same;
> We sigh for longing, and relief;
>   The sighs have but one name.
>
> "And mingled in the dying strife,
>   Are moans that are not sad;
> The pangs of death are throbs of life,
>   Its sighs are sometimes glad.
>
> "The face is very strange and white:
>   It is Earth's only spot
> That feebly flickers back the light
>   The living seeth not."

I fell asleep, and slept a dreamless sleep, for I know not how long. When I awoke, I found that my hostess had moved from where she had been sitting, and now sat between me and the fourth door. I guessed that her design was to prevent my entering there. I sprang from the couch, and darted past her to the door. I opened it at once and went out. All I remember is a cry of distress from the woman: "Don't go there, my child! Don't go there!" But I was gone.

I knew nothing more; or, if I did, I had forgot it all when I awoke to consciousness, lying on the floor of the cottage, with my head in the lap of the woman, who was weeping over me, and stroking my hair with both hands, talking to me as a mother might talk to a sick and sleeping, or a dead child. As soon as I looked up and saw her, she smiled through her tears; smiled with withered face and young eyes, till her countenance was irradiated with the light of the smile. Then she bathed my head and face and hands in an icy cold, colourless liquid, which smelt a little of damp earth. Immediately I was able to sit up. She rose and put some food before me. When I had eaten, she said:

"Listen to me, my child. You must leave me directly!"

"Leave you!" I said. "I am so happy with you. I never was so happy in my life."

"But you must go," she rejoined sadly. "Listen! What do you hear?"

"I hear the sound as of a great throbbing of water."

"Ah! you do hear it? Well, I had to go through that door—the door of the Timeless" (and she shuddered as she pointed to the fourth door)— "to find you; for if I had not gone, you would never have entered again; and because I went, the waters around my cottage will rise and rise, and flow and come, till they build a great firmament of waters over my dwelling. But as long as I keep my fire burning, they cannot enter. I have fuel enough for years; and after one year they will sink away again, and be just as they were before you came. I have not been buried for a hundred years now." And she smiled and wept.

"Alas! alas!" I cried. "I have brought this evil on the best and kindest of friends, who has filled my heart with great gifts."

"Do not think of that," she rejoined. "I can bear it very well. You will come back to me some day, I know. But I beg you, for my sake, my dear child, to do one thing. In whatever sorrow you may be, however inconsolable and irremediable it may appear, believe me that the old woman in the cottage with the young eyes," (and she smiled), "knows something, though she must not always tell it, that would quite satisfy you about it, even in the worst moments of your distress. Now you must go."

"But how can I go, if the waters are all about, and if the doors all lead into other regions and other worlds?"

"This is not an island," she replied; "but is joined to the land by a narrow neck; and for the door, I will lead you myself through the right one."

She took my hand, and led me through the third door; whereupon I found myself standing in the deep grassy turf on which I had landed from the little boat, but upon the opposite side of the cottage. She pointed out the direction I must take, to find the isthmus and escape the rising waters.

Then putting her arms around me, she held me to her bosom; and as I kissed her, I felt as if I were leaving my mother for the first time, and could not help weeping bitterly. At length she gently pushed me away, and with the words, "Go, my son, and do something worth doing," turned back, and entering the cottage, closed the door behind her.

I felt very desolate as I went.

CHAPTER XX

Thou hadst no fame; that which thou didst like good
Was but thy appetite that swayed thy blood
For that time to the best; for as a blast
That through a house comes, usually doth cast
Things out of order, yet by chance may come
And blow some one thing to his proper room,
So did thy appetite, and not thy zeal,
Sway thee by chance to do some one thing well.
               FLETCHER'S *Faithful Shepherdess.*

———

The noble hart that harbours vertuous thought,
And is with childe of glorious great intent,
Can never rest, untill it forth have brought
Th' eternall brood of glorie excellent.
               SPENSER.—*The Faerie Queene.*

I HAD NOT gone very far before I felt that the turf beneath my feet was soaked with the rising waters. But I reached the isthmus in safety. It was rocky, and so much higher than the level of the peninsula, that I had plenty of time to cross. I saw on each side of me the water rising rapidly, altogether without wind, or violent motion, or broken waves, but as if a slow strong fire were glowing beneath it. Ascending a steep acclivity, I found myself at last in an open, rocky country. After travelling for some hours, as nearly in a straight line as I could, I arrived at a lonely tower, built on the top of a little hill, which overlooked the whole neighbouring country. As I approached, I heard the clang of an anvil; and so rapid were the blows, that I despaired of making myself heard till a pause in the work should ensue. It was some minutes before a cessation took place; but when it did, I knocked loudly, and had not long to wait; for, a moment after, the door was partly opened by a noble-looking youth, half-undressed, glowing with heat, and begrimed with the blackness of the forge. In one hand he held a sword, so lately from the furnace that it yet shone with a dull fire. As soon as he saw me, he threw the door wide open, and standing aside, invited me very cordially to enter. I did so; when he shut and bolted the door most carefully, and then led the way inwards. He brought me into a rude hall, which seemed to occupy almost the whole of the ground floor of the little tower, and which I saw was now being used as a workshop. A huge fire roared on the hearth, beside which was an anvil. By the anvil stood, in similar undress, and in a waiting attitude, hammer in hand, a second youth, tall as the former, but far more slightly built. Reversing the usual course of perception in such meetings, I thought them, at first sight, very unlike; and, at the second glance, knew that they were brothers. The former, and apparently the elder, was muscular and dark, with curling hair, and large hazel eyes, which sometimes grew wondrously soft. The second was slender and fair, yet with a countenance like an eagle, and an eye which, though pale blue, shone with an almost fierce expression. He stood erect, as if looking from a lofty mountain crag, over a vast plain outstretched below. As soon as we entered the hall, the elder turned to me, and I saw that a glow of satisfaction shone on both their faces. To my surprise and great pleasure, he addressed me thus:

"Brother, will you sit by the fire and rest, till we finish this part of our work?"

I signified my assent; and, resolved to await any disclosure they might be inclined to make, seated myself in silence near the hearth.

The elder brother then laid the sword in the fire, covered it well over, and when it had attained a sufficient degree of heat, drew it out and laid it on the anvil, moving it carefully about, while the younger, with a succession of quick smart blows, appeared either to be welding it, or hammering one part of it to a consenting shape with the rest. Having finished, they laid it carefully in the fire; and, when it was very hot indeed, plunged it into a vessel full of some liquid, whence a blue flame sprang upwards, as the glowing steel entered. There they left it; and, drawing two stools to the fire, sat down, one on each side of me.

"We are very glad to see you, brother. We have been expecting you for some days," said the dark-haired youth.

"I am proud to be called your brother," I rejoined; "and you will not think I refuse the name, if I desire to know why you honour me with it?"

"Ah! then he does not know about it," said the younger. "We thought you had known of the bond betwixt us, and the work we have to do together. You must tell him, brother, from the first."

So the elder began:

"Our father is king of this country. Before we were born, three giant brothers had appeared in the land. No one knew exactly when, and no one had the least idea whence they came. They took possession of a ruined castle that had stood unchanged and unoccupied within the memory of any of the country people. The vaults of this castle had remained uninjured by time, and these, I presume, they made use of at first. They were rarely seen, and never offered the least injury to any one; so that they were regarded in the neighbourhood as at least perfectly harmless, if not rather benevolent beings. But it began to be observed, that the old castle had assumed somehow or other, no one knew when or how, a somewhat different look from what it used to have. Not only were several breaches in the lower part of the walls built up, but actually some of the battlements which yet stood, had been repaired, apparently to prevent them from falling into worse decay, while the more important parts were being restored. Of course, every one supposed the giants must have a hand in the work, but no one ever saw them engaged in it. The peasants became yet more uneasy, after one, who had concealed himself, and watched all night, in the neighbourhood of the castle, reported that he had seen, in full moonlight, the three huge giants working with might and main, all night long, restoring to their former position some massive stones, formerly steps of a grand turnpike stair, a great portion of which had long since fallen, along with part of the wall of the round tower in which it had been built. This wall they were completing, foot by foot, along with the stair. But the people said they had no just pretext for interfering: although the real reason for letting the giants alone was, that everybody was far too much afraid of them to interrupt them.

"At length, with the help of a neighbouring quarry, the whole of the external wall of the castle was finished. And now the country folks were in greater fear than before. But for several years the giants remained very peaceful. The reason of this was afterwards supposed to be the fact, that they were distantly related to several good people in the country; for, as long as these lived, they remained quiet; but as soon as they were all dead the real nature of the giants broke out. Having completed the outside of their castle, they proceeded, by spoiling the country houses around them, to make a quite luxurious provision for their comfort within. Affairs reached such a pass, that the news of their robberies came to my father's ears; but he, alas; was so crippled in his resources, by a war he was carrying on with a neighbouring prince, that he could only spare a very few men, to attempt the capture of their stronghold. Upon these the giants issued in the night, and slew every man of them. And now, grown bolder by success and impunity, they no longer confined their depredations to property, but began to seize the persons of their distinguished neighbours, knights and ladies, and hold them in durance, the misery of which was heightened by all manner of indignity, until they were redeemed by their friends, at an exorbitant ransom. Many knights have adventured their overthrow, but to their own instead; for they have all been slain, or captured, or forced to make a hasty retreat. To crown their enormities, if any man now attempts their destruction, they, immediately upon his defeat, put one or more of their captives to a shameful death, on a turret in sight of all passers-by; so that they have been much less molested of late; and we, although we have burned, for years, to attack these demons and destroy them, dared not, for the sake of their captives, risk the adventure, before we should have reached at least our earliest manhood. Now, however, we are preparing for the attempt; and the grounds of this preparation are these. Having only the resolution, and not the experience, necessary for the undertaking, we went and consulted a lonely woman of wisdom, who lives not very far from here, in the direction of the quarter from which you have come. She received us most kindly, and gave us what seems to be the best of advice. She first inquired what experience we had had in arms. We told her we had been well exercised from our boyhood, and for some years had kept ourselves in constant practice, with a view to this necessity.

"'But you have not actually fought for life and death?' said she.

"We were forced to confess we had not.

"'So much the better in some respects,' she replied. 'Now, listen to me. Go first and work with an armourer, for as long time as you find needful to obtain a knowledge of his craft; which will not be long, seeing your hearts will be all in the work. Then go to some lonely tower, you two alone. Receive no visits from man or woman. There forge for yourselves every piece of armour that you wish to wear, or to use, in your coming encounter. And keep up your exercises. As, however, two of you can be no match for the three giants, I will find you, if I can, a third brother, who will take on himself the third share of the fight, and the preparation. Indeed, I have already seen one who will, I think, be the very man for your fellowship; but it will be some time before he comes to me. He is wandering now without an aim. I will show him to you in a glass, and, when he comes, you will know him at once. If he will share your endeavours, you must teach him all you know, and he will repay you well, in present song, and in future deeds.'

"She opened the door of a curious old cabinet that stood in the room. On the inside of this door was an oval convex mirror. Looking in it for some time, we at length saw reflected the place where we stood, and the old dame seated in her chair. Our forms were not reflected. But at the feet of the dame, lay a young man, yourself, weeping.

"'Surely this youth will not serve our ends,' said I, 'for he weeps.'

"The old woman smiled. 'Past tears are present strength,' said she.

"'Oh!' said my brother, 'I saw you weep once over an eagle you shot.'

"'That was because it was so like you, brother,' I replied; 'but indeed, this youth may have better cause for tears than that—I was wrong.'

"'Wait a while,' said the woman; 'if I mistake not, he will make you weep till your tears are dry for ever. Tears are the only cure for weeping. And you may have need of the cure, before you go forth to fight the giants. You must wait for him, in your tower, till he comes.'

"Now, if you will join us, we will soon teach you to make your armour; and we will fight together, and work together, and love each other as never three loved before. And you will sing to us, willyou not?"

"That I will, when I can," I answered; "but it is only at times that the power of song comes upon me. For that I must wait; but I have a feeling that if I work well, song will not be far off to enliven the labour."

This was all the compact made: the brothers required nothing more, and I did not think of giving anything more. I rose, and threw off my upper garments.

"I know the uses of the sword," I said. "I am ashamed of my white hands beside yours so nobly soiled and hard; but that shame will soon be wiped away."

"No, no; we will not work to-day. Rest is as needful as toil. Bring the wine, brother; it is your turn to serve to-day."

The younger brother soon covered a table with rough viands, but good wine; and we ate and drank heartily, beside our work. Before the meal was over, I had learned all their story. Each had something in his heart which made the conviction, that he would victoriously perish in the coming conflict, a real sorrow to him. Otherwise they thought they would have lived enough. The causes of their trouble were respectively these:—

While they wrought with an armourer, in a city famed for workmanship in steel and silver, the elder had fallen in love with a lady as far
beneath him in real rank, as she was above the station he had as
apprentice to an armourer. Nor did he seek to further his suit by
discovering himself; but there was simply so much manhood about him,
that no one ever thought of rank when in his company. This is what his
brother said about it. The lady could not help loving him in return. He
told her when he left her, that he had a perilous adventure before him,
and that when it was achieved, she would either see him return to claim
her, or hear that he had died with honour. The younger brother's grief
arose from the fact, that, if they were both slain, his old father, the king,
would be childless. His love for his father was so exceeding, that to one
unable to sympathize with it, it would have appeared extravagant. Both
loved him equally at heart; but the love of the younger had been more
developed, because his thoughts and anxieties had not been otherwise
occupied. When at home, he had been his constant companion; and, of
late, had ministered to the infirmities of his growing age. The youth was
never weary of listening to the tales of his sire's youthful adventures;
and had not yet in the smallest degree lost the conviction, that his father
was the greatest man in the world. The grandest triumph possible to his
conception was, to return to his father, laden with the spoils of one of
the hated giants. But they both were in some dread, lest the thought of
the loneliness of these two might occur to them, in the moment when
decision was most necessary, and disturb, in some degree, the self-
possession requisite for the success of their attempt. For, as I have said,
they were yet untried in actual conflict. "Now," thought I, "I see to what
the powers of my gift must minister." For my own part, I did not dread
death, for I had nothing to care to live for; but I dreaded the encounter
because of the responsibility connected with it. I resolved however to
work hard, and thus grow cool, and quick, and forceful.

   The time passed away in work and song, in talk and ramble, in
friendly fight and brotherly aid. I would not forge for myself armour of
heavy mail like theirs, for I was not so powerful as they, and depended
more for any success I might secure, upon nimbleness of motion,
certainty of eye, and ready response of hand. Therefore I began to
make for myself a shirt of steel plates and rings; which work, while
more troublesome, was better suited to me than the heavier labour.
Much assistance did the brothers give me, even after, by their
instructions, I was able to make some progress alone. Their work was in
a moment abandoned, to render any required aid to mine. As the old
woman had promised, I tried to repay them with song; and many were
the tears they both shed, over my ballads and dirges. The songs they
liked best to hear were two which I made for them. They were not half
so good as many others I knew, especially some I had learned from the
wise woman in the cottage; but what comes nearest to our needs we like
the best.

                                    I
                        The king sat on his throne,
                         Glowing in gold and red;

"The time passed away in work and song."

ARTHUR HUGHES

The crown in his right hand shone,
   And the grey hairs crowned his head.

His only son walks in,
   And in walls of steel he stands:
Make me, O father, strong to win,
   "With the blessing of holy hands."

He knelt before his sire,
   Who blessed him with feeble smile;
His eyes shone out with a kingly fire,
   But his old lips quivered the while.

"Go to the fight, my son,
   "Bring back the giant's head;
"And the crown with which my brows have done,
   "Shall glitter on thine instead."

"My father, I seek no crown,
   "But unspoken praise from thee;
"For thy people's good, and thy renown,
   "I will die to set them free."

The king sat down and waited there,
   And rose not, night nor day;
Till a sound of shouting filled the air,
   And cries of a sore dismay,

Then like a king he sat once more,
   With the crown upon his head;
And up to the throne the people bore
   A mighty giant dead.

And up to the throne the people bore
   A pale and lifeless boy.
The king rose up like a prophet of yore,
   In a lofty, deathlike joy.

He put the crown on the chilly brow:
   "Thou should'st have reigned with me;
"But Death is the king of both, and now
   "I go to obey with thee.

"Surely some good in me there lay,
   "To beget the noble one."
The old man smiled like a winter day,
   And fell beside his son.

II

"O lady, thy lover is dead," they cried;
   "He is dead, but hath slain the foe;
"He hath left his name to be magnified
   "In a song of wonder and woe."

"Alas! I am well repaid," said she,
   "With a pain that stings like joy;

"For I feared, from his tenderness to me,
"That he was but a feeble boy.

"Now I shall hold my head on high,
"The queen among my kind.
"If ye hear a sound, 'tis only a sigh
"For a glory left behind."

The first three times I sang these songs, they both wept passionately. But after the third time, they wept no more. Their eyes shone, and their faces grew pale, but they never wept at any of my songs again.

CHAPTER XXI

I put my life in my hands.
The Book of Judges.

AT LENGTH, WITH much toil and equal delight, our armour was finished. We armed each other, and tested the strength of the defence, with many blows of loving force. I was inferior in strength to both my brothers, but a little more agile than either; and upon this agility, joined to precision in hitting with the point of my weapon, I grounded my hopes of success in the ensuing combat. I likewise laboured to develope yet more the keenness of sight with which I was naturally gifted; and, from the remarks of my companions, I soon learned that my endeavours were not in vain.

The morning arrived on which we had determined to make the attempt, and succeed or perish—perhaps both. We had resolved to fight on foot; knowing that the mishap of many of the knights who had made the attempt, had resulted from the fright of their horses at the appearance of the giants; and believing with Sir Gawain, that, though mare's sons might be false to us, the earth would never prove a traitor. But most of our preparations were, in their immediate aim at least, frustrated.

We rose, that fatal morning, by day-break. We had rested from all labour the day before, and now were fresh as the lark. We bathed in cold spring water, and dressed ourselves in clean garments, with a sense of preparation, as for a solemn festivity. When we had broken our fast, I took an old lyre, which I had found in the tower and had myself repaired, and sung for the last time the two ballads of which I have said so much already. I followed them with this, for a closing song:—

Oh, well for him who breaks his dream
With the blow that ends the strife;
And, waking, knows the peace that flows
Around the pain of life!

We are dead, my brothers! Our bodies clasp,
As an armour, our souls about;

This hand is the battle-axe I grasp,
  And this my hammer stout.

Fear not, my brothers, for we are dead;
  No noise can break our rest;
The calm of the grave is about the head,
  And the heart heaves not the breast.

And our life we throw to our people back,
  To live with, a further store;
We leave it them, that there be no lack
  In the land where we live no more.

Oh, well for him who breaks his dream
  With the blow that ends the strife;
And, waking, knows the peace that flows
  Around the noise of life!

As the last few tones of the instrument were following, like a dirge, the death of the song, we all sprang to our feet. For, through one of the little windows of the tower, towards which I had looked as I sang, I saw, suddenly rising over the edge of the slope on which our tower stood, three enormous heads. The brothers knew at once, by my looks, what caused my sudden movement. We were utterly unarmed, and there was no time to arm. But we seemed to adopt the same resolution simultaneously; for each caught up his favourite weapon, and, leaving his defence behind, sprang to the door. I snatched up a long rapier, abruptly, but very finely pointed, in my sword-hand, and in the other a sabre; the elder brother seized his heavy battle-axe; and the younger, a great, two-handed sword, which he wielded in one hand, like a feather. We had just time to get clear of the tower, embrace and say good-bye, and part to some little distance, that we might not incumber each other's motions, ere the triple giant-brotherhood drew near to attack us. They were about twice our height, and armed to the teeth. Through the visors of their helmets, their monstrous eyes shone with a horrible ferocity. I was in the middle position, and the middle giant approached me. My eyes were busy with his armour, and I was not a moment in settling my mode of attack. I saw that his body-armour was somewhat clumsily made, and that the overlapping in the lower part had more play than necessary; and I hoped that, in a fortunate moment, some joint would open a little, in a visible and accessible part. I stood till he came near enough to aim a blow at me with the mace, which has been, in all ages, the favourite weapon of giants, when, of course, I leaped aside, and let the blow fall upon the spot where I had been standing. I expected this would strain the joints of his armour yet more. Full of fury, he made at me again; but I kept him busy, constantly eluding his blows, and hoping thus to fatigue him. He did not seem to fear any assault from me, and I attempted none as yet; but while I watched his motions in order to avoid his blows, I, at the same time, kept equal watch upon those joints of his armour, through some of which I hoped to reach his life. At length, as if somewhat fatigued, he paused a moment, and drew himself slightly up; I bounded forward, foot and hand, ran my rapier right through to the armour of his back, let go the hilt, and passing under his right arm, turned as he fell, and flew at him with my sabre. At one happy blow, I divided the band of his helmet, which fell off, and allowed me, with a second cut across the eyes, to blind him quite; after which I clove his head, and turned, uninjured, to see how my brothers had fared. Both the giants were down, but so were my brothers. I flew first to the one and then to the other couple. Both pairs of combatants were dead, and yet locked together, as in the death struggle. The elder had buried his battle-axe in the body of his foe, and had fallen beneath him as he fell. The giant had strangled him in his own death-agonies. The younger had nearly hewn off the leg of his enemy; and, grappled with in the act, had, while they rolled together on the earth, found for his dagger a passage betwixt the gorget and cuirass of the giant, and stabbed him mortally in the throat. The blood from the giant's throat was yet pouring over the hand of his foe, which still grasped the hilt of the dagger sheathed in the wound. They lay silent. I, the least worthy, remained the sole survivor in the lists.

As I stood exhausted amidst the dead, after the first worthy deed of my life, I suddenly looked behind me, and there lay the Shadow, black in the sunshine. I went into the lonely tower, and there lay the useless armour of the noble youths—supine as they. Ah, how sad it looked! It was a glorious death, but it was death. My songs could not comfort me now. I was almost ashamed that I was alive, when they, the true-hearted, were no more. And yet I breathed freer to think that I had gone through the trial, and had not failed. And perhaps I may be forgiven, if some feelings of pride arose in my bosom, when I looked down on the mighty form, that lay dead by my hand.

"After all, however," I said to myself, and my heart sank, "it was only skill. Your giant was but a blunderer."

I left the bodies of friends and foes, peaceful enough when the death-fight was over, and hastening to the country below, roused the peasants. They came with shouting and gladness, bringing waggons to carry the bodies. I resolved to take the princes home to their father, each as he lay, in the arms of his country's foe. But first I searched the giants, and found the keys of their castle, to which I repaired, followed by a great company of the people. It was a place of wonderful strength. I released the prisoners, knights and ladies, all in a sad condition, from the cruelties and neglects of the giants. It humbled me to see them crowding round me with thanks, when in truth the glorious brothers, lying dead by their lonely tower, were those to whom the thanks belonged. I had but aided in carrying out the thought born in their brain, and uttered in visible form before ever I laid hold thereupon. Yet I did count myself happy to have been chosen for their brother in this great deed.

After a few hours spent in refreshing and clothing the prisoners, we all commenced our journey towards the capital. This was slow at first; but, as the strength and spirits of the prisoners returned, it became more rapid; and in three days we reached the palace of the king. As we entered the city gates, with the huge bulks lying each on a waggon drawn by horses, and two of them inextricably intertwined with the

dead bodies of their princes, the people raised a shout and then a cry,
and followed in multitudes the solemn procession.

I will not attempt to describe the behaviour of the grand old king. Joy
and pride in his sons overcame his sorrow at their loss. On me he
heaped every kindness that heart coud devise or hand execute. He used
to sit and question me, night after night, about everything that was in
any way connected with them and their preparations. Our mode of life,
and relation to each other, during the time we spent together, was a
constant theme. He entered into the minutest details of the construction of the armour, even to a peculiar made of riveting some of the
plates, with unwearying interest. This armour I had intended to beg of
the king, as my sole memorials of the contest; but, when I saw the
delight he took in contemplating it, and the consolation it appeared to
afford him in his sorrow, I could not ask for it; but, at his request, left
my own, weapons and all, to be joined with theirs in a trophy, erected in
the grand square of the palace. The king, with gorgeous ceremony,
dubbed me knight with his own old hand, in which trembled the sword
of his youth.

During the short time I remained, my company was, naturally, much
courted by the young nobles. I was in a constant round of gaiety and
diversion, notwithstanding that the court was in mourning. For the
country was so rejoiced at the death of the giants, and so many of their
lost friends had been restored to the nobility and men of wealth, that
the gladness surpassed the grief. "Ye have indeed left your lives to your
people, my great brothers!" I said.

But I was ever and ever haunted by the old shadow, which I had not
seen all the time that I was at work in the tower. Even in the society of
the ladies of the court, who seemed to think it only their duty to make
my stay there as pleasant to me as possible, I could not help being
conscious of its presence, although it might not be annoying me at the
time. At length, somewhat weary of uninterrupted pleasure, and
nowise strengthened thereby, either in body or mind, I put on a
splendid suit of armour of steel inlaid with silver, which the old King
had given me, and, mounting the horse on which it had been brought
to me, took my leave of the palace, to visit the distant city in which the
lady dwelt, whom the elder prince had loved. I anticipated a sore task,
in conveying to her the news of his glorious fate; but this trial was
spared me, in a manner as strange as anything that had happened to
me in Fairy Land.

CHAPTER XXII

Niemand hat meine Gestalt als der *Ich.*
Schoppe, in JEAN PAUL'S *Titan.*

No one has my form but the *I.*

"In three days we reached the palace of the king."

ARTHUR HUGHES

Joy's a subtil elf.
I think man's happiest when he forgets himself.
CYRIL TOURNEUR.—*The Revenger's Tragedy.*

ON THE THIRD day of my journey, I was riding gently along a road,
apparently little frequented, to judge from the grass that grew upon it.
I was approaching a forest. Everywhere in Fairy Land, forests are the
places where one may most certainly expect adventures. As I drew near,
a youth, unarmed, gentle, and beautiful, who had just cut a branch
from a yew growing on the skirts of the wood, evidently to make
himself a bow, met me, and thus accosted me:
"Sir knight, be careful as thou ridest through this forest; for it is said
to be strangely enchanted, in a sort which even those who have been
witnesses of its enchantment, can hardly describe."
I thanked him for his advice, which I promised to follow, and rode
on. But the moment I entered the wood, it seemed to me that, if
enchantment there was, it must be of a good kind; for the Shadow,
which had been more than usually dark and distressing, since I had set
out on this journey, suddenly disappeared. I felt a wonderful elevation
of spirits, and began to reflect on my past life, and especially on my
combat with the giants, with such satisfaction, that I had actually to
remind myself, that I had only killed one of them; and that, but for the
brothers, I should never have had the idea of attacking them, not to
mention the smallest power of standing to it. Still I rejoiced, and
counted myself amongst the glorious knights of old; having even the
unspeakable presumption—my shame and self-condemnation at the
memory of it are such, that I write it as the only and sorest penance I
can perform—to think of myself (will the world believe it?) as side by
side with Sir Galahad! Scarcely had the thought been born in my mind,
when, approaching me from the left, through the trees, I espied a
resplendent knight of mighty size, whose armour seemed to shine of
itself, without the sun. When he drew near, I was astonished to see that
this armour was like my own; nay, I could trace, line for line, the
correspondence of the inlaid silver to the device on my own. His horse,
too, was like mine in colour, form, and motion; save that, like his rider,
he was greater and fiercer than his counterpart. The knight rode with
beaver up. As he halted right opposite to me in the narrow path,
barring my way, I saw the reflection of my countenance in the centre
plate of shining steel on his breastplate. Above it rose the same face—
his face—only, as I have said, larger and fiercer. I was bewildered. I
could not help feeling some admiration of him, but it was mingled with
a dim conviction that he was evil, and that I ought to fight with him.
"Let me pass," I said.
"When I will," he replied.
Something within me said: "Spear in rest, and ride at him! else thou
art for ever a slave."
I tried, but my arm trembled so much, that I could not couch my
lance. To tell the truth, I, who had overcome the giant, shook like a
coward before this knight. He gave a scornful laugh, that echoed
through the wood, turned his horse, and said, without looking round,
"Follow me."

I obeyed, abashed and stupified. How long he led, and how long I followed, I cannot tell. "I never knew misery before," I said to myself. "Would that I had at least struck him, and had had my death-blow in return! Why, then, do I not call to him to wheel and defend himself? Alas! I know not why, but I cannot. One look from him would cow me like a beaten hound." I followed, and was silent.

At length we came to a dreary square tower, in the middle of a dense forest. It looked as if scarce a tree had been cut down to make room for it. Across the very door, diagonally, grew the stem of a tree, so large that there was just room to squeeze past it in order to enter. One miserable square hole in the roof was the only visible suggestion of a window. Turret or battlement, or projecting masonry of any kind, it had none. Clear and smooth and massy, it rose from its base, and ended with a line straight and unbroken. The roof, carried to a centre from each of the four walls, rose slightly to the point where the rafters met. Round the base lay several little heaps of either bits of broken branches, withered and peeled, or half-whitened bones; I could not distinguish which. As I approached, the ground sounded hollow beneath my horse's hoofs. The knight took a great key from his pocket, and reaching past the stem of the tree, with some difficulty opened the door. "Dismount;" he commanded. I obeyed. He turned my horse's head away from the tower, gave him a terrible blow with the flat side of his sword, and sent him madly tearing through the forest.

"Now," said he, "enter, and take your companion with you."

I looked round: knight and horse had vanished, and behind me lay the horrible shadow. I entered, for I could not help myself; and the shadow followed me. I had a terrible conviction that the knight and he were one. The door closed behind me.

Now I was indeed in pitiful plight. There was literally nothing in the tower but my shadow and me. The walls rose right up to the roof; in which, as I had seen from without, there was one little square opening. This I now knew to be the only window the tower possessed. I sat down on the floor, in listless wretchedness. I think I must have fallen asleep, and have slept for hours; for I suddenly became aware of existence, in observing that the moon was shining through the hole in the roof. As she rose higher and higher, her light crept down the wall over me, till at last it shone right upon my head. Instantaneously the walls of the tower seemed to vanish away like a mist. I sat beneath a beech, on the edge of a forest, and the open country lay, in the moonlight, for miles and miles around me, spotted with glimmering houses and spires and towers. I thought with myself, "Oh, joy! it was only a dream; the horrible narrow waste is gone, and I wake beneath a beech-tree, perhaps one that loves me, and I can go where I will." I rose, as I thought, and walked about, and did what I would, but ever kept near the tree; for always, and, of course, since my meeting with the woman of the beech-tree far more than ever, I loved that tree. So the night wore on. I waited for the sun to rise, before I could venture to renew my journey. But as soon as the first faint light of the dawn appeared, instead of shining upon me from the eye of the morning, it stole like a fainting ghost through the little square hole above my head; and the walls came out as the light grew, and the glorious night was swallowed up of the hateful day. The long dreary day passed. My shadow lay black on the floor. I felt no hunger, no need of food. The night came. The moon shone. I watched her light slowly descending the wall, as I might have watched, adown the sky, the long, swift approach of a helping angel. Her rays touched me, and I was free. Thus night after night passed away. I should have died but for this. Every night the conviction returned, that I was free. Every morning I sat wretchedly disconsolate. At length when the course of the moon no longer permitted her beams to touch me, the night was dreary as the day. When I slept, I was somewhat consoled by my dreams; but all the time I dreamed, I knew that I was only dreaming. But one night, at length, the moon, a mere shred of pallour, scattered a few thin ghostly rays upon me; and I think I fell asleep and dreamed, I sat in an autumn night, before the vintage, on a hill overlooking my own castle. My heart sprang with joy. Oh, to be a child again, innocent, fearless, without shame or desire! I walked down to the castle. All were in consternation at my absence. My sisters were weeping for my loss. They sprang up and clung to me, with incoherent cries, as I entered. My old friends came flocking round me. A grey light shone on the roof of the hall. It was the light of the dawn shining through the square window of my tower. More earnestly than ever, I longed for freedom after this dream; more drearily than ever, crept on the next wretched day. I measured by the sunbeams, caught through the little window in the trap of my tower, how it went by, waiting only for the dreams of the night.

About noon, I started as if something foreign to all my senses and all my experience, had suddenly invaded me; yet it was only the voice of a woman singing. My whole frame quivered with joy, surprise, and the sensation of the unforeseen. Like a living soul, like an incarnation of Nature, the song entered my prison-house. Each tone folded its wings, and laid itself, like a caressing bird, upon my heart. It bathed me like a sea; inwrapt me like an odorous vapour; entered my soul like a long draught of clear spring-water; shone upon me like essential sunlight; soothed me like a mother's voice and hand. Yet, as the clearest forest-well tastes sometimes of the bitterness of decayed leaves, so to my weary, prisoned heart, its cheerfulness had a sting of cold, and its tenderness unmanned me with the faintness of long-departed joys. I wept half-bitterly, half-luxuriously; but not long. I dashed away the tears, ashamed of a weakness which I thought I had abandoned. Ere I knew, I had walked to the door, and seated myself with my ear against it, in order to catch every syllable of the revelation from the unseen outer world. And now I heard each word distinctly. The singer seemed to be standing or sitting near the tower, for the sounds indicated no change of place. The song was something like this:—

> The sun, like a golden knot on high,
> Gathers the glories of the sky,
> And binds them into a shining tent,
> Roofing the world with the firmament.
> And through the pavilion the rich winds blow,
> And through the pavilion the waters go.

And the birds for joy, and the trees for prayer,
Bowing their heads in the sunny air,
And for thoughts, the gently talking springs,
That come from the centre with secret things—
All make a music, gentle and strong,
Bound by the heart into one sweet song.
And amidst them all, the mother Earth
Sits with the children of her birth;
She tendeth them all, as a mother hen
Her little ones round her, twelve or ten:
Oft she sitteth, with hands on knee,
Idle with love for her family.
Go forth to her from the dark and the dust,
And weep beside her, if weep thou must;
If she may not hold thee to her breast,
Like a weary infant, that cries for rest
At least she will press thee to her knee,
And tell a low, sweet tale to thee,
Till the hue to thy cheek, and the light to thine eye,
Strength to thy limbs, and courage high
To thy fainting heart, return amain,
And away to work thou goest again.
From the narrow desert, O man of pride,
Come into the house, so high and wide.

Hardly knowing what I did, I opened the door. Why had I not done so before? I do not know.

At first I could see no one; but when I had forced myself past the tree which grew across the entrance, I saw, seated on the ground, and leaning against the tree, with her back to my prison, a beautiful woman. Her countenance seemed known to me, and yet unknown. She looked up at me and smiled, when I made my appearance.

"Ah! were you the prisoner there? I am very glad I have wiled you out."

"Do you know me then?"

"Do you not know me? But you hurt me, and that, I suppose, makes it easy for a man to forget. You broke my globe. Yet I thank you. Perhaps I owe you many thanks for breaking it. I took the pieces, all black, and wet with crying over them, to the Fairy Queen. There was no music and no light in them now. But she took them from me, and laid them aside; and made me go to sleep in a great hall of white, with black pillars, and many red curtains. When I woke in the morning, I went to her, hoping to have my globe again, whole and sound; but she sent me away without it, and I have not seen it since. Nor do I care for it now. I have something so much better. I do not need the globe to play to me; for I can sing. I could not sing at all before. Now I go about everywhere through Fairy Land, singing till my heart is like to break, just like my globe, for very joy at my own songs. And wherever I go, my songs do good, and deliver people. And now I have delivered you, and I am so happy."

She ceased, and the tears came into her eyes.

All this time, I had been gazing at her; and now fully recognized the face of the child, glorified in the countenance of the woman. I was ashamed and humbled before her; but a great weight was lifted from my thoughts. I knelt before her, and thanked her, and begged her to forgive me.

"Rise, rise," she said; "I have nothing to forgive; I thank you. But now I must be gone, for I do not know how many may be waiting for me, here and there, through the dark forests; and they cannot come out till I come."

She rose, and with a smile and a farewell, turned and left me. I dared not ask her to stay; in fact, I could hardly speak to her. Between her and me, there was a great gulf. She was uplifted by sorrow and well-doing, into a region I could hardly hope ever to enter. I watched her departure, as one watches a sunset. She went like a radiance through the dark wood, which was henceforth bright to me, from simply knowing that such a creature was in it. She was bearing the sun to the unsunned spots. The light and the music of her broken globe were now in her heart and her brain. As she went, she sang; and I caught these few words of her song; and the tones seemed to linger and wind about the trees after she had disappeared:—

> Thou goest thine, and I go mine—
>   Many ways we wend;
> Many days, and many ways,
>   Ending in one end.
>
> Many a wrong, and its curing song;
>   Many a road, and many an inn;
> Room to roam, but only one home
>   For all the world to win.

And so she vanished. With a sad heart, soothed by humility, and the knowledge of her peace and gladness, I bethought me what now I should do. First, I must leave the tower far behind me, lest, in some evil moment, I might be once more caged within its horrible walls. But it was ill walking in my heavy armour; and besides I had now no right to the golden spurs and the resplendent mail, fitly dulled with long neglect. I might do for a squire; but I honoured knighthood too highly, to call myself any longer one of the noble brotherhood. I stripped off all my armour, piled it under the tree, just where the lady had been seated, and took my unknown way, eastward through the woods. Of all my weapons, I carried only a short axe in my hand. Then first I knew the delight of being lowly; of saying to myself, "I am what I am, nothing more." "I have failed," I said; "I have lost myself—would it had been my shadow." I looked round: the shadow was nowhere to be seen. Ere long, I learned that it was not myself, but only my shadow, that I had lost. I learned that it is better, a thousand-fold, for a proud man to fail and be humbled, than to hold up his head in his pride and fancied innocence. I learned that he that will be hero, will barely be a man; that he that will be nothing but a doer of his work, is sure of his manhood. In nothing was my ideal lowered, or dimmed, or grown less precious; I only saw it too plainly, to set myself for a moment beside it. Indeed, my ideal soon became my life; whereas, formerly, my life had consisted in a vain attempt to behold, if not my ideal in myself, at least myself in my ideal. Now, however, I took, at first, what perhaps was a mistaken pleasure, in despising and degrading myself. Another self seemed to arise, like a white spirit from a dead man, from the dumb and trampled self of the past. Doubtless, this self must again die and be buried, and again, from its tomb, spring a winged child; but of this my history as yet bears not the record. Self will come to life even in the slaying of self; but there is ever something deeper and stronger than it, which will emerge at last from the unknown abyss of the soul: will it be as a solemn gloom, burning with eyes? or a clear morning after the rain? or a smiling child, that finds itself nowhere, and everywhere?

CHAPTER XXIII

High erected thought, seated in a heart of courtesy.
                                        SIR PHILIP SIDNEY.

———————

A sweet attractive kinde of grace,
    A full assurance given by lookes,
Continuall comfort in a face,
    The lineaments of Gospell bookes.
                        SPENSER, on *Sir Philip Sidney*.

I HAD NOT gone far, for I had but just lost sight of the hated tower, when a voice of another sort, sounding near or far, as the trees permitted or intercepted its passage, reached me. It was a full, deep, manly voice, but withal clear and melodious. Now it burst on the ear with a sudden swell, and anon, dying away as suddenly, seemed to come to me across a great space. Nevertheless, it drew nearer; till, at last, I could distinguish the words of the song, and get transient glimpses of the singer, between the columns of the trees. He came nearer, dawning upon me like a growing thought. He was a knight, armed from head to heel, mounted upon a strange-looking beast, whose form I could not understand. The words which I heard him sing were like these:—

Heart be stout,
    And eye be true;
Good blade out!
    And ill shall rue.

Courage, horse!
    Thou lackst no skill;
Well thy force
    Hath matched my will.

For the foe,
    With fiery breath,

At a blow,
  Is still in death.

Gently, horse!
  Tread fearlessly;
'Tis his corse
  That burdens thee.

The sun's eye
  Is fierce at noon;
Thou and I
  Will rest full soon.

And new strength
  New work will meet;
Till, at length,
  Long rest is sweet.

And now horse and rider had arrived near enough for me to see, fastened by the long neck to the hinder part of the saddle, and trailing its hideous length on the ground behind, the body of a great dragon. It was no wonder that, with such a drag at his heels, the horse could make but slow progress, notwithstanding his evident dismay. The horrid, serpent-like head, with its black tongue, forked with red, hanging out of its jaws, dangled against the horse's side. Its neck was covered with long blue hair; its sides with scales of green and gold. Its back was of corrugated skin, of a purple hue. Its belly was similar in nature, but its colour was leaden, dashed with blotches of livid blue. Its skinny, batlike wings and its tail were of a dull grey. It was strange to see how so many gorgeous colours, so many curving lines, and such beautiful things as wings and hair and scales, combined to form the horrible creature, intense in ugliness.

The knight was passing me with a salutation; but, as I walked towards him, he reined up, and I stood by his stirrup. When I came near him, I saw, to my surprise and pleasure likewise, although a sudden pain, like a birth of fire, sprang up in my heart, that it was the knight of the soiled armour, whom I knew before, and whom I had seen in the vision, with the lady of the marble. But I could have thrown my arms around him, because she loved him. This discovery only strengthened the resolution I had formed, before I recognised him, of offering myself to the knight, to wait upon him as a squire, for he seemed to be unattended. I made my request in as few words as possible. He hesitated for a moment, and looked at me thoughtfully. I saw that he suspected who I was, but that he continued uncertain of his suspicion. No doubt he was soon convinced of its truth; but all the time I was with him, not a word crossed his lips with reference to what he evidently concluded I wished to leave unnoticed, if not to keep concealed.

"Squire and knight should be friends," said he: "can you take me by the hand?" And he held out the great gauntleted right hand. I grasped it willing and strongly. Not a word more was said. The knight gave the sign to his horse, which again began his slow march, and I walked beside and a little behind.

"Trailing its hideous length on the ground behind, the
body of a great dragon."

Arthur Hughes

We had not gone very far before we arrived at a little cottage; from which, as we drew near, a woman rushed out with the cry:

"My child! my child! have you found my child?"

"I have found her," replied the knight, "but she is sorely hurt. I was forced to leave her with the hermit, as I returned. You will find her there, and I think she will get better. You see I have brought you a present. This wretch will not hurt you again." And he undid the creature's neck, and flung the frightful burden down by the cottage-door.

The woman was now almost out of sight in the wood; but the husband stood at the door, with speechless thanks in his face.

"You must bury the monster," said the knight. "If I had arrived a moment later, I should have been too late. But now you need not fear, for such a creature as this very rarely appears, in the same part, twice during a life-time."

"Will you not dismount and rest you, Sir Knight?" said the peasant, who had, by this time, recovered himself a little.

"That I will, thankfully," said he; and, dismounting, he gave the reins to me, and told me to unbridle the horse, and lead him into the shade. "You need not tie him up," he added; "he will not run away."

When I returned, after obeying his orders, and entered the cottage, I saw the knight seated, without his helmet, and talking most familiarly with the simple host. I stood at the open door for a moment, and, gazing at him, inwardly justified the white lady in preferring him to me. A nobler countenance I never saw. Loving-kindness beamed from every line of his face. It seemed as if he would repay himself for the late arduous combat, by indulging in all the gentleness of a womanly heart. But when the talk ceased for a moment, he seemed to fall into a reverie. Then the exquisite curves of the upper lip vanished. The lip was lengthened and compressed at the same moment. You could have told that, within the lips, the teeth were firmly closed. The whole face grew stern and determined, all but fierce; only the eyes burned on like a holy sacrifice, uplift on a granite rock.

The woman entered, with her mangled child in her arms. She was pale as her little burden. She gazed, with a wild love and despairing tenderness, on the still, all but dead face, white and clear from loss of blood and terror.

The knight rose. The light that had been confined to his eyes, now shone from his whole countenance. He took the little thing in his arms, and, with the mother's help, undressed her, and looked to her wounds. The tears flowed down his face as he did so. With tender hands he bound them up, kissed the pale cheek, and gave her back to her mother. When he went home, all his tale would be of the grief and joy of the parents; while to me, who had looked on, the gracious countenance of the armed man, beaming from the panoply of steel, over the seemingly dead child, while the powerful hands turned it and shifted it, and bound it, if possible even more gently than the mother's, formed the centre of the story.

After we had partaken of the best they could give us, the knight took his leave, with a few parting instructions to the mother, as to how she should treat the child.

I brought the knight his steed, held the stirrup while he mounted, and then followed him through the wood. The horse, delighted to be free of his hideous load, bounded beneath the weight of man and armour, and could hardly be restrained from galloping on. But the knight made him time his powers to mine, and so we went on for an hour or two. Then the knight dismounted, and compelled me to get into the saddle, saying: "Knight and squire must share the labour."

Holding by the stirrup, he walked along by my side, heavily clad as he was, with apparent ease. As we went, he led a conversation, in which I took what humble part my sense of my condition would permit me.

"Somehow or other," said he, "notwithstanding the beauty of this country of Faerie, in which we are, there is much that is wrong in it. If there are great splendours, there are corresponding horrors; heights and depths; beautiful women and awful fiends; noble men and weaklings. All a man has to do, is to better what he can. And if he will settle it with himself, that even renown and success are in themselves of no great value, and be content to be defeated, if so be that the fault is not his; and so go to his work with a cool brain and a strong will, he will get it done; and fare none the worse in the end, that he was not burdened with provision and precaution."

"But he will not always come off well," I ventured to say.

"Perhaps not," rejoined the knight, "in the individual act; but the result of his lifetime will content him."

"So it will fare with you, doubtless," thought I; "but for me——"

Venturing to resume the conversation after a pause, I said, hesitatingly:

"May I ask for what the little beggar-girl wanted your aid, when she came to your castle to find you?"

He looked at me for a moment in silence, and then said:—

"I cannot help wondering how you know of that; but there is something about you quite strange enough to entitle you to the privilege of the country; namely, to go unquestioned. I, however, being only a man, such as you see me, am ready to tell you anything you like to ask me, as far as I can. The little beggar-girl came into the hall where I was sitting, and told me a very curious story, which I can only recollect very vaguely, it was so peculiar. What I can recall is, that she was sent to gather wings. As soon as she had gathered a pair of wings for herself, she was to fly away, she said, to the country she came from; but where that was, she could give no information. She said she had to beg her wings from the butterflies and moths; and whenever she begged, no one refused her. But she needed a great many of the wings of butterflies and moths to make a pair for her; and so she had to wander about day after day, looking for butterflies, and night after night, looking for moths; and then she begged for their wings. But the day before, she had come into a part of the forest, she said, where there were multitudes of splendid butterflies flitting about, with wings which were just fit to make the eyes in the shoulders of hers; and she knew she could have as many of them as she liked for the asking; but as soon as she began to beg, there came a great creature right up to her, and threw her down, and walked over to her. When she got up, she saw the wood was full of these beings stalking about, and seeming to have nothing to do with each other. As soon as ever she began to beg, one of them walked over her; till at last, in dismay, and in growing horror of the senseless creatures, she had run away to look for somebody to help her. I asked her what they were like. She said, like great men, made of wood, without knee or elbow-joints, and without any noses or mouths or eyes in their faces. I laughed at the little maiden, thinking she was making child's game of me; but, although she burst out laughing too, she persisted in asserting the truth of her story.

"'Only come, knight, come and see; I will lead you.'

"So I armed myself, to be ready for anything that might happen, and followed the child; for, though I could make nothing of her story, I could see she was a little human being in need of some help or other. As she walked before me, I looked attentively at her. Whether or not it was from being so often knocked down and walked over, I could not tell, but her clothes were very much torn, and in several places her white skin was peeping through. I thought she was humpbacked; but on looking more closely, I saw, through the tatters of her frock—do not laugh at me—a bunch on each shoulder, of the most gorgeous colours. Looking yet more closely, I saw that they were of the shape of folded wings, and were made of all kinds of butterfly-wings and moth-wings, crowded together like the feathers on the individual butterfly pinion; but, like them, most beautifully arranged, and producing a perfect harmony of colour and shade. I could now more easily believe the rest of her story; especially as I saw, every now and then, a certain heaving motion in the wings, as if they longed to be uplifted and outspread. But beneath her scanty garments complete wings could not be concealed, and indeed, from her own story, they were yet unfinished.

"After walking for two or three hours, (how the little girl found her way, I could not imagine) we came to a part of the forest, the very air of which was quivering with the motions of multitudes of resplendent butterflies; as gorgeous in colour, as if the eyes of peacock's feathers had taken to flight, but of infinite variety of hue and form, only that the appearance of some kind of eye on each wing predominated. 'There they are, there they are!' cried the child, in a tone of victory mingled with terror. Except for this tone, I should have thought she referred to the butterflies, for I could see nothing else. But at that moment an enormous butterfly, whose wings had great eyes of blue surrounded by confused cloudy heaps of more dingy colouring, just like a break in the clouds on a stormy day towards evening, settled near us. The child instantly began murmuring: 'Butterfly, butterfly, give me your wings;' when, the moment after she fell to the ground, and began crying as if hurt. I drew my sword and heaved a great blow in the direction in which the child had fallen. It struck something, and instantly the most grotesque imitation of a man became visible. You see this Fairy Land is full of oddities and all sorts of incredibly ridiculous things, which a man is compelled to meet and treat as real existences, although all the time he feels foolish for doing so. This being, if being it could be called, was like a block of wood roughly hewn into the mere outlines of a man; and hardly so, for it had but head, body, legs, and arms—the head without a face, and the limbs utterly formless. I had hewn off one of its legs, but the two portions moved on as best they could, quite independent of each other; so that I had done no good. I ran after it, and clove it in twain from the head downwards; but it could not be convinced that its vocation was not to walk over people; for, as soon as the little girl began her begging again, all three parts came bustling up; and if I had not interposed my weight between her and them, she would have been trampled again under them. I saw that something else must be done. If the wood was full of the creatures, it would be an endless work to chop them so small that they could do no injury; and then, besides, the parts would be so numerous, that the butterflies would be in danger from the drift of flying chips. I served this one so, however; and then told the girl to beg again, and point out the direction in which one was coming. I was glad to find, however, that I could now see him myself, and wondered how they could have been invisible before. I would not allow him to walk over the child; but while I kept him off, and she began begging again, another appeared; and it was all I could do, from the weight of my armour, to protect her from the stupid, persevering efforts of the two. But suddenly the right plan occurred to me. I tripped one of them up, and, taking him by the legs, set him up on his head, with his heels against a tree. I was delighted to find he could not move. Meantime the poor child was walked over by the other, but it was for the last time. Whenever one appeared, I followed the same plan—tripped him up and set him on his head; and so the little beggar was able to gather her wings without any trouble, which occupation she continued for several hours in my company."

"What became of her?" I asked.

"I took her home with me to my castle, and she told me all her story; but it seemed to me, all the time, as if I were hearing a child talk in its sleep. I could not arrange her story in my mind at all, although it seemed to leave hers in some certain order of its own. My wife——"

Here the Knight checked himself, and said no more. Neither did I urge the conversation farther.

Thus we journeyed for several days, resting at night in such shelter as we could get; and when no better was to be had, lying in the forest under some tree, on a couch of old leaves.

I loved the knight more and more. I believe never squire served his master with more care and joyfulness than I. I tended his horse; I cleaned his armour; my skill in the craft enabled me to repair it when necessary; I watched his needs; and was well repaid, for all, by the love itself which I bore him.

"This," I said to myself, "is a true man. I will serve him, and give him all worship, seeing in him the embodiment of what I would fain become. If I cannot be noble myself, I will yet be servant to his nobleness." He, in return, soon showed me such signs of friendship and respect, as made my heart glad; and I felt that, after all, mine would be no lost life, if I might wait on him to the world's end, although no smile but his should greet me, and no one but him should say, "Well done! he was a good servant!" at last. But I burned to do something more for him than the ordinary routine of a squire's duty permitted.

One afternoon, we began to observe an appearance of roads in the wood. Branches had been cut down, and openings made, where footsteps had worn no path below. These indications increased as we passed on; till, at length, we came into a long, narrow avenue, formed by felling the trees in its line, as the remaining roots evidenced. At some little distance, on both hands, we observed signs of similar avenues, which appeared to converge with ours, towards one spot. Along these, we indistinctly saw several forms moving, which seemed, with ourselves, to approach the common centre. Our path brought us, at last, up to a wall of yew trees, growing close together, and intertwining their branches so, that nothing could be seen beyond it. An opening was cut in it like a door, and all the wall was trimmed smooth and perpendicular. The knight dismounted, and waited till I had provided for his horse's comfort; upon which we entered the place together.

It was a great space, bare of trees, and enclosed by four walls of yew, similar to that through which we had entered. These trees grew to a very great height, and did not divide from each other till close to the top, where their summits formed a row of conical battlements all around the walls. The space contained was a parallelogram of great length. Along each of the two longer sides of the interior, were ranged three ranks of men, in white robes, standing silent and solemn, each with a sword by his side, although the rest of his costume and bearing was more priestly than soldierly. For some distance inwards, the space between these opposite rows was filled with a company of men and women and children, in holiday attire. The looks of all were directed inwards, towards the further end. Far beyond the crowd, in a long avenue, seeming to narrow in the distance, went the long rows of the white-robed men. On what the attention of the multitude was fixed, we could not tell, for the sun had set before we arrived, and it was growing dark within. It grew darker and darker. The multitude waited in silence. The stars began to shine down into the enclosure, and they grew brighter and larger every moment. A wind arose, and swayed the pinnacle of the tree-tops; and made a strange sound, half like music, half like moaning, through the close branches and leaves of the tree-walls. A young girl who stood beside me, clothed in the same dress as the priests, bowed her head, and grew pale with awe.

The knight whispered to me, "How solemn it is! Surely they wait to hear the voice of a prophet. There is something good near!"

But I, though somewhat shaken by the feeling expressed by my master, yet had an unaccountable conviction that here was something bad. So I resolved to be keenly on the watch for what should follow.

Suddenly a great star, like a sun, appeared high in the air over the temple, illuminating it throughout; and a great song arose from the men in white, which went rolling round and round the building, now receding to the end, and now approaching, down the other side, the place where we stood. For some of the singers were regularly ceasing, and the next to them as regularly taking up the song; so that it crept onwards, with gradations produced by changes which could not themselves be detected, for only a few of those who were singing ceased at the same moment. The song paused; and I saw a company of six of the white-robed men walk up the centre of the human avenue, surrounding a youth gorgeously attired beneath his robe of white, and wearing a chaplet of flowers on his head. I followed them closely, with my keenest observation; and, by accompanying their slow progress with my eyes, I was able to perceive more clearly what took place when they arrived at the other end. I knew that my sight was so much more keen than that of most people, that I had good reason to suppose I should see more than the rest could, at such a distance. At the farther end, a throne stood upon a platform, high above the heads of the surrounding priests. To this platform I saw the company begin to ascend, apparently by an inclined plane of gentle slope. The throne itself was elevated again, on a kind of square pedestal, to the top of which led a flight of steps. On the throne sat a majestic-looking figure, whose posture seemed to indicate a mixture of pride and benignity, as he looked down on the multitude below. The company ascended to the foot of the throne, where they all kneeled for some minutes; then they rose and passed round to the side of the pedestal upon which the throne stood. Here they crowded close behind the youth, putting him in the foremost place; and one of them opened a door in the pedestal, for the youth to enter. I was sure I saw him shrink back, and those crowding behind push him in. Then, again, arose a burst of song from the multitude in white, which lasted some time. When it ceased, a new company of seven commenced its march up the centre. As they advanced, I looked up at my master: his noble countenance was full of reverence and awe. Incapable of evil himself, he could scarcely suspect it in another, much less in a multitude such as this, and surrounded with such appearances of solemnity. I was certain it was the really grand accompaniments that overcame him; that the stars overhead, the dark towering tops of the yew-trees, and the wind that, like an unseen spirit, sighed through their branches, bowed his spirit to the belief, that in all these ceremonies lay some great mystical meaning, which, his humility told him, his ignorance prevented him from understanding.

More convinced than before, that there was evil here, I could not endure that my master should be deceived; that one like him, so pure and noble, should respect what, if my suspicions were true, was worse than the ordinary deceptions of priestcraft. I could not tell how far he might be led to countenance, and otherwise support their doings, before he should find cause to repent bitterly of his error. I watched the new procession yet more keenly, if possible, than the former. This time, the central figure was a girl; and, at the close, I observed, yet more indubitably, the shrinking back, and the crowding push. What happened to the victims, I never learned; but I had learned enough, and I could bear it no longer. I stooped, and whispered to the young girl who stood by me, to lend me her white garment. I wanted it, that I might not be entirely out of keeping with the solemnity, but might have at least this help to passing unquestioned. She looked up, half-amused and half-bewildered, as if doubting whether I was in earnest or not. But in her perplexity, she permitted me to unfasten it, and slip it down from her shoulders. I easily got possession of it; and, sinking down on my knees in the crowd, I rose apparently in the habit of one of the worshippers.

Giving my battle-axe to the girl, to hold in pledge for the return of her stole, for I wished to test the matter unarmed, and, if it was a man that sat upon the throne, to attack him with hands bare, as I supposed his must be, I made my way through the crowd to the front, while the singing yet continued, desirous of reaching the platform while it was unoccupied by any of the priests. I was permitted to walk up the long avenue of white robes unmolested, though I saw questioning looks in many of the faces as I passed. I presume my coolness aided my passage; for I felt quite indifferent as to my own fate; not feeling, after the late events of my history, that I was at all worth taking care of; and enjoying, perhaps, something of an evil satisfaction, in the revenge I was thus taking upon the self which had fooled me so long. When I arrived on the platform, the song had just ceased, and I felt as if all were looking towards me. But instead of kneeling at its foot, I walked right up the stairs to the throne, laid hold of a great wooden image that seemed to sit upon it, and tried to hurl it from its seat. In this I failed at first, for I found it firmly fixed. But in dread lest, the first shock of amazement passing away, the guards would rush upon me before I had effected my purpose, I strained with all my might; and, with a noise as of the cracking, and breaking, and tearing of rotten wood, something gave way, and I hurled the image down the steps. Its displacement revealed a great hole in the throne, like the hollow of a decayed tree, going down apparently a great way. But I had no time to examine it, for as I looked into it, up out of it rushed a great brute like a wolf, but twice the size, and tumbled me headlong with itself, down the steps of the throne. As we fell, however, I caught it by the throat, and the moment we reached the platform, a struggle commenced, in which I soon got uppermost, with my hand upon its throat, and knee upon its heart. But now arose a wild cry of wrath and revenge and rescue. A universal hiss of steel, as every sword was swept from its scabbard, seemed to tear the very air in shreds. I heard the rush of hundreds towards the platform on which I knelt. I only tightened my grasp of the brute's throat. His eyes were already starting from his head, and his tongue was hanging out. My anxious hope was, that, even after they had killed me, they would be unable to undo my gripe of his throat, before the monster was past breathing. I therefore threw all my will, and force, and purpose, into the grasping hand. I remember no blow. A faintness came over me, and my consciousness departed.

CHAPTER XXIV

We are ne'er like angels till our passions die.

DECKAR.

This wretched *Inn*, where we scarce stay to bait,
    We call our *Dwelling-Place:*
    We call one *Step* a *Race:*
But angels in their full enlightened state,
Angels, who *Live*, and know what 'tis to *Be*,
Who all the nonsense of our language see,

Who speak *things,* and our *words,* their ill-drawn *pictures,* scorn,
When we, by a foolish figure, say,
Behold an old man dead! then they
Speak properly, and cry, *Behold a man-child born!*

COWLEY.

I WAS DEAD, and right content. I lay in my coffin, with my hands folded in peace. The knight, and the lady I loved, wept over me. Her tears fell on my face.

"Ah!" said the knight, "I rushed amongst them like a madman. I hewed them down like brushwood. Their swords battered on me like hail, but hurt me not. I cut a lane through to my friend. He was dead. But he had throttled the monster, and I had to cut the handful out of its throat, before I could disengage and carry off his body. They dared not molest me as I brought him back."

"He has died well," said the lady.

My spirit rejoiced. They left me to my repose. I felt as if a cool hand had been laid upon my heart, and had stilled it. My soul was like a summer evening, after a heavy fall of rain, when the drops are yet glistening on the trees in the last rays of the down-going sun, and the wind of the twilight has begun to blow. The hot fever of life had gone by, and I breathed the clear mountain-air of the land of Death. I had never dreamed of such blessedness. It was not that I had in any way ceased to be what I had been. The very fact that anything can die, implies the existence of something that cannot die; which must either take to itself another form, as when the seed that is sown dies, and arises again; or, in conscious existence, may perhaps, continue to lead a purely spiritual life. If my passions were dead, the souls of the passions, those essential mysteries of the spirit which had imbodied themselves in the passions, and had given to them all their glory and wonderment, yet lived, yet glowed, with a pure, undying fire. They rose above their vanishing earthly garments, and disclosed themselves angels of light. But oh, how beautiful beyond the old form! I lay thus for a time, and lived as it were an unradiating existence; my soul a motionless lake, that received all things and gave nothing back; satisfied in still contemplation, and spiritual consciousness.

Ere long, they bore me to my grave. Never tired child lay down in his white bed, and heard the sound of his playthings being laid aside for the night, with a more luxurious satisfaction of repose than I knew, when I felt the coffin settle on the firm earth, and heard the sound of the falling mould upon its lid. It has not the same hollow rattle within the coffin, that it sends up to the edge of the grave. They buried me in no graveyard. They loved me too much for that, I thank them; but they laid me in the grounds of their own castle, amid many trees; where, as it was spring-time, were growing primroses, and blue bells, and all the families of the woods.

Now that I lay in her bosom, the whole earth, and each of her many births, was as a body to me, at my will. I seemed to feel the great heart of the mother beating into mine, and feeding me with her own life, her own essential being and nature. I heard the footsteps of my friends above, and they sent a thrill through my heart. I knew that the helpers had gone, and that the knight and the lady remained, and spoke low, gentle, tearful words of him who lay beneath the yet wounded sod. I rose into a single large primrose that grew by the edge of the grave, and from the window of its humble, trusting face, looked full in the countenance of the lady. I felt that I could manifest myself in the primrose; that it said a part of what I wanted to say; just as in the old time, I had used to betake myself to a song for the same end. The flower caught her eye. She stooped and plucked it, saying, "Oh, you beautiful creature!" and, lightly kissing it, put it in her bosom. It was the first kiss she had ever given me. But the flower soon began to wither, and I forsook it.

It was evening. The sun was below the horizon; but his rosy beams yet illuminated a feathery cloud, that floated high above the world. I arose. I reached the cloud; and, throwing myself upon it, floated with it in sight of the sinking sun. He sank, and the cloud grew grey; but the greyness touched not my heart. It carried its rose-hue within; for now I could love without needing to be loved again. The moon came gliding up with all the past in her wan face. She changed my couch into a ghostly pallor, and threw all the earth below as to the bottom of a pale sea of dreams. But she could not make me sad. I knew now, that it is by loving, and not by being loved, that one can come nearest the soul of another; yea, that, where two love, it is the loving of each other, and not the being beloved by each other, that originates and perfects and assures their blessedness. I knew that love gives to him that loveth, power over any soul beloved, even if that soul know him not, bringing him inwardly close to that spirit; a power that cannot be but for good; for in proportion as selfishness intrudes, the love ceases, and the power which springs therefrom dies. Yet all love will, one day, meet with its return. All true love will, one day, behold its own image in the eyes of the beloved, and be humbly glad. This is possible in the realms of lofty Death. "Ah! my friends," thought I, "how I will tend you, and wait upon you, and haunt you with my love."

My floating chariot bore me over a great city. Its faint dull sound steamed up into the air—a sound—how composed? "How many hopeless cries," thought I, "and how many mad shouts go to make up the tumult, here so faint where I float in eternal peace, knowing that they will one day be stilled in the surrounding calm, and that despair dies into infinite hope, and that the seeming impossible there, is the law here! But, O pale-faced women, and gloomy-browed men, and forgotten children, how I will wait on you, and minister to you, and, putting my arms about you in the dark, think hope unto your hearts, when you fancy no one is near! Soon as my senses have all come back, and have grown accustomed to this new blessed life, I will be among you, with the love that healeth."

With this, a pang and a terrible shudder went through me; a writhing as of death convulsed me; and I became once again conscious of a more limited, even a bodily and earthly life.

CHAPTER XXV

Unser Leben ist kein Traum, aber es soll und wird vielleicht einer werden.
                                                          NOVALIS.

Our life is no dream; but it ought to become one, and perhaps will.

And on the ground, which is my modres gate,
I knocke with my staf, erlich and late,
And say to hire, Leve mother, let me in.
                    CHAUCER.—*The Pardoneres Tale.*

SINKING FROM SUCH a state of ideal bliss, into the world of shadows which again closed around and infolded me, my first dread was, not unnaturally, that my own shadow had found me again, and that my torture had commenced anew. It was a sad revulsion of feeling. This, indeed, seemed to correspond to what we think death is, before we die. Yet I felt within me a power of calm endurance to which I had hitherto been a stranger. For, in truth, that I should be able if only to think such things as I had been thinking, was an unspeakable delight. An hour of such peace made the turmoil of a life-time worth striving through.

I found myself lying in the open air, in the early morning, before sunrise. Over me rose the summer heaven, expectant of the sun. The clouds already saw him, coming from afar; and soon every dew-drop would rejoice in his individual presence within it. I lay motionless for a few minutes; and then slowly rose and looked about me. I was on the summit of a little hill; a valley lay beneath, and a range of mountains closed up the view upon that side. But,to my horror, across the valley, and up the height of the opposing mountains, stretched, from my very feet, a hugely expanding shade. There it lay, long and large, dark and mighty. I turned away with a sick despair; when, lo! I beheld the sun just lifting his head above the eastern hill, and the shadow that fell from me, lay only where his beams fell not. I danced for joy. It was only the natural shadow, that goes with every man who walks in the sun. As he arose, higher and higher, the shadow-head sank down the side of the opposite hill, and crept in acrss the valley towards my feet.

Now that I was so joyously delivered from this fear, I saw and recognized the country around me. In the valley below, lay my own castle, and the haunts of my childhood were all about me. I hastened home. My sisters received me with unspeakable joy; but I suppose they observed some change in me, for a kind of respect, with a slight touch of awe in it, mingled with their joy, and made me ashamed. They had been in great distress about me. On the morning of my disappearance, they had found the floor of my room flooded; and, all that day, a wondrous and nearly impervious mist had hung about the castle and grounds. I had been gone, they told me, twenty-one days. To me it seemed twenty-one years. Nor could I yet feel quite secure in my new experiences. When, at night, I lay down once more in my own bed, I did not feel at all sure that when I awoke, I should not find myself in some mysterious region of Fairy Land. My dreams were incessant and perturbed; but when I did awake, I saw clearly that I was in my own home.

My mind soon grew calm; and I began the duties of my new position, somewhat instructed, I hoped, by the adventures that had befallen me in Fairy Land. Could I translate the experience of my travels there, into common life? This was the question. Or must I live it all over again, and learn it all over again, in the other forms that belong to the world of men, whose experience yet runs parallel to that of Fairy Land? These questions I cannot yet answer. But I fear.

Even yet, I find myself looking round sometimes with anxiety, to see whether my shadow falls right away from the sun or no. I have never yet discovered any inclination to either side. And if I am not unfrequently sad, I yet cast no more of a shade on the earth, than most men who have lived in it as long as I. I have a strange feeling sometimes, that I am a ghost, sent into the world to minister to my fellow-men, or, rather, to repair the wrongs I have already done. May the world be brighter for me, at least in those portions of it, where my darkness falls not.

Thus I, who set out to find my Ideal, came back rejoicing that I had lost my Shadow.

When the thought of the blessedness I experienced, after my death in Fairy Land, is too high for me to lay hold upon it and hope in it, I often think of the wise woman in the cottage, and of her solemn assurance that she knew something too good to be told. When I am oppressed by any sorrow or real perplexity, I often feel as if I had only left her cottage for a time, and would soon return out of the vision, into it again. Sometimes, on such occasions, I find myself, unconsciously almost, looking about for the mystic mark of red, with the vague hope of entering her door, and being comforted by her wise tenderness. I then console myself by saying: "I have come through the door of Dismay; and the way back from the world into which that has led me, is through my tomb. Upon that the red sign lies, and I shall find it one day, and be glad."

I will end my story with the relation of an incident which befell me a few days ago. I had been with my reapers, and, when they ceased their work at noon, I had lain down under the shadow of a great, ancient beech-tree, that stood on the edge of the field. As I lay, with my eyes closed, I began to listen to the sound of the leaves overhead. At first, they made sweet inarticulate music alone; but, by and by, the sound seemed to begin to take shape, and to be gradually moulding itself into words; till, at last, I seemed able to distinguish these, half-dissolved in a little ocean of circumfluent tones: "A great good is coming—is coming—is coming to thee, Anodos;" and so over and over again. I fancied that the sound reminded me of the voice of the ancient woman, in the cottage that was four-square. I opened my eyes, and, for a moment, almost believed that I saw her face, with its many wrinkles and its young eyes, looking at me from between two hoary branches of the beech overhead. But when I looked more keenly, I saw only twigs and leaves, and the infinite sky, in tiny spots, gazing through between. Yet I know that good is coming to me—that good is always coming; though few have at all times the simplicity and the courage to believe it. What we call evil, is the only and best shape, which, for the person and his condition at the time, could be assumed by the best good. And so, *Farewell.*

The Wood Beyond the World

By William Morris

"And when he awoke it was broad day, calm and bright
and cloudless."

AUBREY BEARDSLEY

The Wood Beyond the World
CHAPTER I

Of Golden Walter and His Father

A WHILE AGO there was a young man dwelling in a great and goodly city by the sea which had to name Langton on Holm. He was but of five and twenty winters, a fair-faced man, yellow-haired, tall and strong; rather wiser than foolisher than young men are mostly wont; a valiant youth, and a kind; not of many words but courteous of speech; no roisterer, nought masterful, but peaceable and knowing how to forbear: in a fray a perilous foe, and a trusty war-fellow. His father, with whom he was dwelling when this tale begins, was a great merchant, richer than a baron of the land, a head-man of the greatest of the Lineages of Langton, and a captain of the Porte; he was of the Lineage of the Goldings, therefore was he called Bartholomew Golden, and his son Golden Walter.

Now ye may well deem that such a youngling as this was looked upon by all as a lucky man without a lack; but there was this flaw in his lot, whereas he had fallen into the toils of love of a woman exceeding fair, and had taken her to wife, she nought unwilling as it seemed. But when they had been wedded some six months he found by manifest tokens, that his fairness was not so much to her but that she must seek to the foulness of one worser than he in all ways; wherefore his rest departed from him, whereas he hated her for her untruth and her hatred of him; yet would the sound of her voice, as she came and went in the house, make his heart beat; and the sight of her stirred desire within him, so that he longed for her to be sweet and kind with him, and deemed that, might it be so, he should forget all the evil gone by. But it was not so; for ever when she saw him, her face changed, and her hatred of him became manifest, and howsoever she were sweet with others, with him she was hard and sour.

So this went on a while till the chambers of his father's house, yea the very streets of the city, became loathsome to him; and yet he called to mind that the world was wide and he but a young man. So on a day as he sat with his father alone, he spake to him and said: "Father, I was on the quays even now, and I looked on the ships that were nigh boun, and thy sign I saw on a tall ship that seemed to me nighest boun. Will it be long ere she sail?"

"Nay," said his father, "that ship, which hight the Katherine, will they warp out of the haven in two days' time. But why askest thou of her?"

"The shortest word is best, father," said Walter, "and this it is, that I would depart in the said ship and see other lands."

"Yea and whither, son?" said the merchant.

"Whither she goeth," said Walter, "for I am ill at ease at home, as thou wottest, father."

The merchant held his peace awhile, and looked hard on his son, for there was strong love between them; but at last he said: "Well, son, maybe it were best for thee; but maybe also we shall not meet again."

"Yet if we do meet, father, then shalt thou see a new man in me."

"Well," said Bartholomew, "at least I know on whom to lay the loss of thee, and when thou art gone, for thou shalt have thine own way herein, she shall no longer abide in my house. Nay, but it were for the strife that should arise thenceforth betwixt her kindred and ours, it should go somewhat worse with her than that."

Said Walter: "I pray thee shame her not more than needs must be, lest, so doing, thou shame both me and thyself also."

Bartholomew held his peace again for a while; then he said: "Goeth she with child, my son?"

Walter reddened, and said: "I wot not; nor of whom the child may be." Then they both sat silent, till Bartholomew spake, saying: "The end of it is, son, that this is Monday, and that thou shalt go aboard in the small hours of Wednesday; and meanwhile I shall look to it that thou go not away empty-handed; the skipper of the Katherine is a good man and true, and knows the seas well; and my servant Robert the Low, who is clerk of the lading, is trustworthy and wise, and as myself in all matters that look towards chaffer. The Katherine is new and stout-builded, and should be lucky, whereas she is under the ward of her who is the saint called upon in the church where thou wert christened, and myself before thee; and thy mother, and my father and mother all lie under the chancel thereof, as thou wottest."

Therewith the elder rose up and went his ways about his business, and there was no more said betwixt him and his son on this matter.

CHAPTER II

Golden Walter Takes Ship to Sail the Seas

WHEN WALTER WENT down to the Katherine next morning, there was the skipper Geoffrey, who did him reverence, and made him all cheer, and showed him his room aboard ship, and the plenteous goods which his father had sent down to the quays already, such haste as he had made. Walter thanked his father's love in his heart, but otherwise took little heed to his affairs, but wore away the time about the haven, gazing listlessly on the ships that were making them ready outward, or unlading, and the mariners and aliens coming and going: and all these were to him as the curious images woven on a tapestry.

At last when he had wellnigh come back again to the Katherine, he saw there a tall ship, which he had scarce noted before, a ship all-boun, which had her boats out, and men sitting to the oars thereof ready to tow her outwards when the hawser should be cast off, and by seeming her mariners were but abiding for some one or other to come aboard.

So Walter stood idly watching the said ship, and as he looked, lo! folk passing him toward the gangway. These were three; first came a dwarf, dark-brown of hue and hideous, with long arms and ears exceeding great and dog-teeth that stuck out like the fangs of a wild beast. He was clad in a rich coat of yellow silk, and bare in his hand a crooked bow, and was girt with a broad sax.

After him came a maiden, young by seeming, of scarce twenty summers; fair of face as a flower; grey-eyed, brown-haired, with lips full and red, slim and gentle of body. Simple was her array, of a short and strait green gown, so that on her right ankle was clear to see an iron ring.

Last of the three was a lady, tall and stately, so radiant of visage and glorious of raiment, that it were hard to say what like she was; for scarce might the eye gaze steady upon her exceeding beauty; yet must every son of Adam who found himself anigh her, lift up his eyes again after he had dropped them, and look again on her, and yet again and yet again. Even so did Walter, and as the three passed by him, it seemed to him as if all the other folk there about had vanished and were nought; nor had he any vision before his eyes of any looking on them, save himself alone. They went over the gangway into the ship, and he saw them go along the deck till they came to the house on the poop, and entered it, and were gone from his sight.

There he stood staring, till little by little the thronging people of the quays came into his eye-shot again; then he saw how the hawser was cast off and the boats fell to tugging the big ship toward the harbour-mouth with hale and how of men. Then the sail fell down from the yard and was sheeted home and filled with the fair wind as the ship's bows ran up on the first green wave outside the haven. Even therewith the shipmen cast abroad a banner, whereon was done in a green field a grim wolf ramping up against a maiden, and so went the ship upon her way.

Walter stood awhile staring at her empty place where the waves ran into the haven-mouth, and then turned aside and toward the Ka-therine; and at first he was minded to go ask shipmaster Geoffrey of what he knew concerning the said ship and her alien wayfarers; but then it came into his mind, that all this was but an imagination or dream of the day, and that he were best to leave it untold to any. So therewith he went his way from the water-side, and through the streets unto his father's house; but when he was but a little way thence, and the door was before him, him-seemed for a moment of time that he beheld those three coming out down the steps of stone and into the street; to wit the dwarf, the maiden, and the stately lady: but when he stood still to abide their coming, and looked toward them, lo! there was nothing before him save the goodly house of Bartholomew Golden, and three children and a cur dog playing about the steps thereof, and about him were four or five passers-by going about their business. Then was he all confused in his mind, and knew not what to make of it, whether those whom he had seemed to see pass aboard ship were but images of a dream, or children of Adam in very flesh.

Howsoever, he entered the house, and found his father in the chamber, and fell to speech with him about their matters; but for all that he loved his father, and worshipped him as a wise and valiant man, yet at that hour he might not hearken the words of his mouth, so much was his mind entangled in the thought of those three, and they were ever before his eyes, as if they had been painted on a table by the best of limners. And of the two women he thought exceeding much, and cast no wyte upon himself for running after the desire of strange women. For he said to himself that he desired not either of the twain; nay, he might not tell which of the twain, the maiden or the stately queen, were clearest to his eyes; but sore he desired to see both of them again, and to know what they were.

So wore the hours till the Wednesday morning, and it was time that he should bid farewell to his father and get aboard ship; but his father led him down to the quays and on to the Katherine, and there Walter embraced him, not without tears and forebodings; for his heart was full. Then presently the old man went aland; the gangway was unshipped, the hawsers cast off; the oars of the towing-boats splashed in the dark water, the sail fell down from the yard, and was sheeted home, and out plunged the Katherine into the misty sea and rolled up the grey slopes, casting abroad her ancient withal, whereon was beaten the token of Bartholomew Golden, to wit a B and a G to the right and the left, and thereabove a cross and a triangle rising from the midst.

Walter stood on the stern and beheld, yet more with the mind of him than with his eyes; for it all seemed but the double of what the other ship had done; and he thought of it as if the twain were as beads strung on one string and led away by it into the same place, and thence to go in the like order, and so on again and again, and never to draw nigher to each other.

CHAPTER III

Walter Heareth Tidings of the Death of His Father

FAST SAILED THE Katherine over the seas, and nought befell to tell of, either to herself or her crew. She came to one cheaping-town and then to another, and so on to a third and a fourth; and at each was buying and selling after the manner of chapmen; and Walter not only looked on the doings of his father's folk, but lent a hand, what he might, to help them in all matters, whether it were in seaman's craft, or in chaffer. And the further he went and the longer the time wore, the more he was eased of his old trouble wherein his wife and her treason had to do.

But as for the other trouble, to wit his desire and longing to come up with those three, it yet flickered before him; and though he had not seen them again as one sees people in the streets, and as if he might touch them if he would, yet were their images often before his mind's eye; and yet, as time wore, not so often, not so troublously; and forsooth both to those about him and to himself, he seemed as a man well healed of his melancholy mood.

Now they left that fourth stead, and sailed over the seas and came to a fifth, a very great and fair city, which they had made more than seven months from Langton on Holm; and by this time was Walter taking heed and joyance in such things as were toward in that fair city, so far from his kindred, and especially he looked on the fair women there, and desired them, and loved them; but lightly, as befalleth young men.

Now this was the last country whereto the Katherine was boun; so there they abode some ten months in daily chaffer, and in pleasuring them in beholding all that there was of rare and goodly, and making merry with the merchants and the towns-folk, and the country-folk beyond the gates, and Walter was grown as busy and gay as a strong young man is like to be, and was as one who would fain be of some account amongst his own folk.

But at the end of this while, it befell on a day, as he was leaving his hostel for his booth in the market, and had the door in his hand, there stood before him three mariners in the guise of his own country, and with them was one of clerkly aspect, whom he knew at once for his father's scrivener, Arnold Penstrong by name; and when Walter saw him his heart failed him and he cried out: "Arnold, what tidings? Is all well with the folk at Langton?"

Said Arnold: "Evil tidings are come with me; matters are ill with thy folk; for I may not hide that thy father, Bartholomew Golden, is dead, God rest his soul."

At that word it was to Walter as if all that trouble which but now had sat so light upon him, was once again fresh and heavy, and that his past life of the last few months had never been; and it was to him as if he saw his father lying dead on his bed, and heard the folk lamenting about the house. He held his peace awhile, and then he said in a voice of an angry man: "What, Arnold! and did he die in his bed, or how? for he was neither old nor ailing when we parted."

Said Arnold: "Yea, in his bed he died: but first he was somewhat sword-bitten."

"Yea, and how?" quoth Walter.

Said Arnold: "When thou wert gone, in a few days' wearing, thy father sent thy wife out of his house back to her kindred of the Reddings with no honour, and yet with no such shame as might have been, without blame to us of those who knew the tale of thee and her; which, God-a-mercy, will be pretty much the whole of the city.

"Nevertheless, the Reddings took it amiss, and would have a mote with us Goldings to talk of booting. By ill-luck we yea-said that for the saving of the city's peace. But what betid? We met in our Gild-hall, and there befell the talk between us; and in that talk certain words could not be hidden, though they were none too seemly nor too meek. And the said words once spoken drew forth the whetted steel; and there then was the hewing and thrusting! Two of ours were slain outright on the floor, and four of theirs, and many were hurt on either side. Of these was thy father, for as thou mayst well deem, he was nought backward in the fray; but despite his hurts, two in the side and one on the arm, he went home on his own feet, and we deemed that we had come to our above. But well-a-way! it was an evil victory, whereas in ten days he died of his hurts. God have his soul! But now, my master, thou mayst well wot that I am not come to tell thee this only, but moreover to bear the word of the kindred, to wit that thou come back with me straightway in the swift cutter which hath borne me and the tidings; and thou mayst look to it, that though she be swift and light, she is a keel full weatherly."

Then said Walter: "This is a bidding of war. Come back will I, and the Reddings shall wot of my coming. Are ye all-boun?"

"Yea," said Arnold, "we may up anchor this very day, or to-morrow morn at latest. But what aileth thee, master, that thou starest so wild over my shoulder? I pray thee take it not so much to heart! Ever it is the wont of fathers to depart this world before their sons."

But Walter's visage from wrathful red had become pale, and he pointed up street, and cried out: "Look! dost thou see?"

"See what, master?" quoth Arnold: "what! here cometh an ape in gay raiment; belike the beast of some jongleur. Nay, by God's wounds! 'tis a man, though he be exceeding mis-shapen like a very devil. Yea and now there cometh a pretty maid going as if she were of his meney; and lo! here, a most goodly and noble lady! Yea, I see; and doubtless she owneth both the two, and is of the greatest of the folk of this fair city; for on the maiden's ankle I saw an iron ring, which betokeneth thralldom amongst these aliens. But this is strange! for notest thou not how the folk in the street heed not this quaint show; nay not even the stately lady, though she be as lovely as a goddess of the gentiles, and beareth on her gems that would buy Langton twice over; surely they must be over-wont to strange and gallant sights. But now, master, but now!"

"Yea, what is it?" said Walter.

"Why, master, they should not yet be gone out of eyeshot, yet gone they are. What is become of them, are they sunk into the earth?"

"Tush, man!" said Walter, looking not on Arnold, but still staring down the street; "they have gone into some house while thine eyes were turned from them a moment."

"Nay, master, nay," said Arnold, "mine eyes were not off them one instant of time."

"Well," said Walter, somewhat snappishly, "they are gone now, and what have we to do to heed such toys, we with all this grief and strife on our hands? Now would I be alone to turn the matter of thine errand over in my mind. Meantime do thou tell the shipmaster Geoffrey and our other folk of these tidings, and thereafter get thee all ready; and come hither to me before sunrise to-morrow, and I shall be ready for my part; and so sail we back to Langton."

Therewith he turned him back into the house, and the others went their ways; but Walter sat alone in his chamber a long while, and pondered these things in his mind. And whiles he made up his mind that he would think no more of the vision of those three, but would fare back to Langton, and enter into the strife with the Reddings and quell them, or die else. But lo, when he was quite steady in this doom, and his heart was lightened thereby, he found that he thought no more of the Reddings and their strife, but as matters that were passed and done with, and that now he was thinking and devising if by any means he might find out in what land dwelt those three. And then again he strove to put that from him, saying that what he had seen was but meet for one brainsick, and a dreamer of dreams. But furthermore he thought, Yea, and was Arnold, who this last time had seen the images of those three, a dreamer of waking dreams? for he was nought wonted in such wise; then thought he: At least I am well content that he spake to me of their likeness, not I to him; for so I may tell that there was at least something before my eyes which grew not out of mine own brain. And yet again, why should I follow them; and what should I get by it; and indeed how shall I set about it?

Thus he turned the matter over and over; and at last, seeing that if he grew no foolisher over it, he grew no wiser, he became weary thereof, and bestirred him, and saw to the trussing up of his goods, and made all ready for his departure, and so wore the day and slept at nightfall; and at daybreak comes Arnold to lead him to their keel, which hight the Bartholomew. He tarried nought, and with few farewells went aboard ship, and an hour after they were in the open sea with the ship's head turned toward Langton on Holm.

CHAPTER IV

Storm Befalls the Bartholomew, and She Is Driven off Her Course

NOW SWIFT SAILED the Bartholomew for four weeks toward the northwest with a fair wind, and all was well with ship and crew. Then the wind died out on even of a day, so that the ship scarce made way at all, though she rolled in a great swell of the sea, so great, that it seemed to ridge all the main athwart. Moreover down in the west was a great bank of cloud huddled up in haze, whereas for twenty days past the sky had been clear, save for a few bright white clouds flying before the wind. Now the shipmaster, a man right cunning in his craft, looked long on sea and sky, and then turned and bade the mariners take in sail and be right heedful. And when Walter asked him what he looked for, and wherefore he spake not to him thereof, he said surlily: "Why should I tell thee what any fool can see without telling, to wit that there is weather to hand?"

So they abode what should befall, and Walter went to his room to sleep away the uneasy while, for the night was now fallen; and he knew no more till he was waked up by great hubbub and clamour of the shipmen, and the whipping of ropes, and thunder of flapping sails, and the tossing and weltering of the ship withal. But, being a very stouthearted young man, he lay still in his room, partly because he was a landsman, and had no mind to tumble about amongst the shipmen and hinder them; and withal he said to himself: What matter whether I go down to the bottom of the sea, or come back to Langton, since either way my life or my death will take away from me the fulfilment of desire? Yet soothly if there hath been a shift of wind, that is not so ill; for then shall we be driven to other lands, and so at the least our homecoming shall be delayed, and other tidings may hap amidst of our tarrying. So let all be as it will.

So in a little while, in spite of the ship's wallowing and the tumult of the wind and waves, he fell asleep again, and woke no more till it was full daylight, and there was the shipmaster standing in the door of his room, the sea-water all streaming from his wet-weather raiment. He said to Walter: "Young master, the sele of the day to thee! For by good hap we have gotten into another day. Now I shall tell thee that we have striven to beat, so as not to be driven off our course, but all would not avail, wherefore for these three hours we have been running before the wind; but, fair sir, so big hath been the sea that but for our ship being of the stoutest, and our men all yare, we had all grown exceeding wise concerning the ground of the mid-main. Praise be to St. Nicholas and all Hallows! for though ye shall presently look upon a new sea, and maybe a new land to boot, yet is that better than looking on the ugly things down below."

"Is all well with ship and crew then?" said Walter.

"Yea forsooth," said the shipmaster; "verily the Bartholomew is the darling of Oak Woods; come up and look at it, how she is dealing with wind and waves all free from fear."

So Walter did on his foul-weather raiment, and went up on to the quarter-deck, and there indeed was a change of days; for the sea was dark and tumbling mountain-high, and the white-horses were running down the valleys thereof, and the clouds drave low over all, and bore a scud of rain along with them; and though there was but a rag of sail on her, the ship flew before the wind, rolling a great wash of water from bulwark to bulwark.

Walter stood looking on it all awhile, holding on by a stay-rope, and saying to himself that it was well that they were driving so fast toward new things.

Then the shipmaster came up to him and clapped him on the shoulder and said: "Well, shipmate, cheer up! and now come below again and eat some meat, and drink a cup with me."

So Walter went down and ate and drank, and his heart was lighter than it had been since he had heard of his father's death, and the feud awaiting him at home, which forsooth he had deemed would stay his wanderings a weary while, and therewithal his hopes. But now it seemed as if he needs must wander, would he, would he not; and so it was that even this fed his hope; so sore his heart clung to that desire of his to seek home to those three that seemed to call him unto them.

CHAPTER V

Now They Come to a New Land

THREE DAYS THEY drave before the wind, and on the fourth the clouds lifted, the sun shone out and the offing was clear; the wind had much abated, though it still blew a breeze, and was a head wind for sailing toward the country of Langton. So then the master said that, since they were bewildered, and the wind so ill to deal with, it were best to go still before the wind that they might make some land and get knowledge of their whereabouts from the folk thereof. Withal he said that he deemed the land not to be very far distant.

So did they, and sailed on pleasantly enough, for the weather kept on mending, and the wind fell till it was but a light breeze, yet still foul for Langton.

So wore three days, and on the eve of the third, the man from the topmast cried out that he saw land ahead; and so did they all before the sun was quite set, though it were but a cloud no bigger than a man's hand.

When night fell they struck not sail, but went forth toward the land fair and softly; for it was early summer, so that the nights were neither long nor dark.

But when it was broad daylight, they opened a land, a long shore of rocks and mountains, and nought else that they could see at first. Nevertheless as day wore and they drew nigher, first they saw how the mountains fell away from the sea, and were behind a long wall of sheer cliff; and coming nigher yet, they beheld a green plain going up after a little in green bents and slopes to the feet of the said cliff-wall.

No city nor haven did they see there, not even when they were far nigher to the land; nevertheless, whereas they hankered for the peace of the green earth after all the tossing and unrest of the sea, and whereas also they doubted not to find at the least good and fresh water, and belike other bait in the plain under the mountains, they still sailed on not unmerrily; so that by nightfall they cast anchor in five-fathom water hard by the shore.

Next morning they found that they were lying a little way off the mouth of a river not right great; so they put out their boats and towed the ship up into the said river, and when they had gone up it for a mile or thereabouts they found the sea water failed, for little was the ebb and flow of the tide on that coast. Then was the river deep and clear, running between smooth grassy land like to meadows. Also on their left board they saw presently three head of neat cattle going, as if in a meadow of a homestead in their own land, and a few sheep; and thereafter, about a bow-draught from the river, they saw a little house of wood and straw-thatch under a wooded mound, and with orchard trees about it. They wondered little thereat, for they knew no cause why that land should not be builded, though it were in the far outlands. However, they drew their ship up to the bank, thinking that they would at least abide awhile and ask tidings and have some refreshing of the green plain, which was so lovely and pleasant.

But while they were busied herein they saw a man come out of the house, and down to the river to meet them; and they soon saw that he was tall and old, long-hoary of hair and beard, and clad mostly in the skins of beasts.

He drew nigh without any fear or mistrust, and coming close to them gave them the sele of the day in a kindly and pleasant voice. The shipmaster greeted him in his turn, and said withal: "Old man, art thou the king of this country?"

The elder laughed; "It hath had none other a long while," said he; "and at least there is no other son of Adam here to gainsay."

"Thou art alone here then?" said the master.

"Yea," said the old man; "save for the beasts of the field and the wood, and the creeping things, and fowl. Wherefore it is sweet to me to hear your voices."

Said the master: "Where be the other houses of the town?"

The old man laughed. Said he: "When I said that I was alone, I meant that I was alone in the land and not only alone in this stead. There is no house save this betwixt the sea and the dwellings of the Bears, over the cliff-wall yonder, yet and a long way over it."

"Yea," quoth the shipmaster grinning, "and be the bears of thy country so manlike, that they dwell in builded houses?"

The old man shook his head. "Sir," said he, "as to their bodily fashion, it is altogether manlike, save that they be one and all higher and bigger than most. For they be bears only in name; they be a nation of half wild men; for I have been told by them that there be many more than that tribe whose folk I have seen, and that they spread wide about behind these mountains from east to west. Now, sir, as to their souls and understandings I warrant them not; for miscreants they be, trowing neither in God nor his hallows."

Said the master: "Trow they in Mahound then?"

"Nay," said the elder, "I wot not for sure that they have so much as a false God; though I have it from them that they worship a certain woman with mickle worship."

Then spake Walter: "Yea, good sir, and how knowest thou that? dost thou deal with them at all?"

Said the old man: "Whiles some of that folk come hither and have of me what I can spare; a calf or two, or a half-dozen of lambs or hoggets; or a skin of wine or cyder of mine own making: and they give me in return such things as I can use, as skins of hart and bear and other peltries; for now I am old, I can but little of the hunting hereabout. Whiles, also, they bring little lumps of pure copper, and would give me gold also, but it is of little use in this lonely land. Sooth to say, to me they are not masterful or rough-handed; but glad am I that they have been here but of late, and are not like to come again this while; for terrible they are of aspect, and whereas ye be aliens, belike they would not hold their hands from off you; and moreover ye have weapons and other matters which they would covet sorely."

Quoth the master: "Since thou dealest with these wild men, will ye not deal with us in chaffer? For whereas we are come from long travel, we hanker after fresh victual, and here aboard are many things which were for thine avail."

Said the old man: "All that I have is yours, so that ye do but leave me enough till my next ingathering: of wine and cyder, such as it is, I have plenty for your service; ye may drink it till it is all gone, if ye will: a little corn and meal I have, but not much; yet are ye welcome thereto, since the standing corn in my garth is done blossoming, and I have other meat. Cheeses have I and dried fish; take what ye will thereof. But as to my neat and sheep, if ye have sore need of any, and will have them, I may not say you nay: but I pray you if ye may do without them, not to take my milch-beasts or their engenderers; for, as ye have heard me say, the Bear-folk have been here but of late, and they have had of me all I might spare: but now let me tell you, if ye long after flesh-meat, that there is venison of hart and hind, yea, and of buck and doe, to be had on this plain, and about the little woods at the feet of the rock-wall yonder: neither are they exceeding wild; for since I may not take them, I scare them not, and no other man do they see to hurt them; for the Bear-folk come straight to my house, and fare straight home thence. But I will lead you the nighest way to where the venison is easiest to be gotten. As to the wares in your ship, if ye will give me aught I will take it with a good will; and chiefly if ye have a fair knife or two and a roll of linen cloth, that were a good refreshment to me. But in any case what I have to give is free to you and welcome."

The shipmaster laughed: "Friend," said he, "we can thee mickle thanks for all that thou biddest us. And wot well that we be no lifters or sea-thieves to take thy livelihood from thee. So to-morrow, if thou wilt, we will go with thee and upraise the hunt, and meanwhile we will come aland, and walk on the green grass, and water our ship with thy good fresh water."

So the old carle went back to his house to make them ready what cheer he might, and the shipmen, who were twenty and one, all told, what with the mariners and Arnold and Walter's servants, went ashore, all but two who watched the ship and abode their turn. They went well-weaponed, for both the master and Walter deemed wariness wisdom, lest all might not be so good as it seemed. They took of their sail-cloths ashore, and tilted them in on the meadow betwixt the house and the ship, and the carle brought them what he had for their avail, of fresh fruits, and cheeses, and milk, and wine, and cyder, and honey, and there they feasted nowise ill, and were right fain.

CHAPTER VI

The Old Man Tells Walter of Himself. Walter Sees a Shard in the Cliff-wall

BUT WHEN THEY had done their meat and drink the master and the shipmen went about the watering of the ship, and the others strayed off along the meadow, so that presently Walter was left alone with the carle, and fell to speech with him and said: "Father, meseemeth thou shouldest have some strange tale to tell, and as yet we have asked thee of nought save meat for our bellies: now if I ask thee concerning thy life, and how thou camest hither, and abided here, wilt thou tell me aught?"

The old man smiled on him and said: "Son, my tale were long to tell; and mayhappen concerning much thereof my memory should fail me; and withal there is grief therein, which I were loth to awaken: nevertheless if thou ask, I will answer as I may, and in any case will tell thee nought save the truth."

Said Walter: "Well then, hast thou been long here?"

"Yea," said the carle, "since I was a young man, and a stalwarth knight."

Said Walter: "This house, didst thou build it, and raise these garths, and plant orchard and vineyard, and gather together the neat and the sheep, or did some other do all this for thee?"

Said the carle: "I did none of all this; there was one here before me, and I entered into his inheritance, as though this were a lordly manor, with a fair castle thereon, and all well stocked and plenished."

Said Walter: "Didst thou find thy foregoer alive here?"

"Yea," said the elder, "yet he lived but for a little while after I came to him."

He was silent a while, and then he said: "I slew him: even so would he have it, though I bade him a better lot."

Said Walter: "Didst thou come hither of thine own will?"

"Mayhappen," said the carle; "who knoweth? Now have I no will to do either this or that. It is wont that maketh me do, or refrain."

Said Walter: "Tell me this; why didst thou slay the man? did he any scathe to thee?"

Said the elder: "When I slew him, I deemed that he was doing me all scathe: but now I know that it was not so. Thus it was: I would needs go where he had been before, and he stood in the path against me; and I overthrew him, and went on the way I would."

"What came thereof?" said Walter.

"Evil came of it," said the carle.

Then was Walter silent a while, and the old man spake nothing; but there came a smile in his face that was both sly and somewhat sad. Walter looked on him and said: "Was it from hence that thou wouldst go that road?"

"Yea," said the carle.

Said Walter: "And now wilt thou tell me what that road was; whither it went and whereto it led, that thou must needs wend it, though thy first stride were over a dead man?"

"I will not tell thee," said the carle.

Then they held their peace, both of them, and thereafter got on to other talk of no import.

So wore the day till night came; and they slept safely, and on the morrow after they had broken their fast, the more part of them set off with the carle to the hunting, and they went, all of them, a three hours' faring towards the foot of the cliffs, which was all grown over with coppice, hazel and thorn, with here and there a big oak or ash-tree; there it was, said the old man, where the venison was most and best.

Of their hunting need nought be said, saving that when the carle had put them on the track of the deer and shown them what to do, he came back again with Walter, who had no great lust for the hunting, and sorely longed to have some more talk with the said carle. He for his part seemed nought loth thereto, and so led Walter to a mound or hillock amidst the clear of the plain, whence all was to be seen save where the wood covered it; but just before where they now lay down there was no wood, save low bushes, betwixt them and the rock-wall; and Walter noted that whereas otherwhere, save in one place whereto their eyes were turned, the cliffs seemed wellnigh or quite sheer, or indeed in some places beetling over, in that said place they fell away from each other on either side; and before this sinking was a slope or scree, that went gently up toward the sinking of the wall. Walter looked long and earnestly at this place, and spake nought, till the carle said: "What! thou hast found something before thee to look on. What is it then?"

Quoth Walter: "Some would say that where yonder slopes run together up towards that sinking in the cliff-wall there will be a pass into the country beyond."

The carle smiled and said: "Yea, son; nor, so saying, would they err; for that is the pass into the Bear-country, whereby those huge men come down to chaffer with me."

"Yea," said Walter; and therewith he turned him a little, and scanned the rock-wall, and saw how a few miles from that pass it turned somewhat sharply toward the sea, narrowing the plain much there, till it made a bight, the face whereof looked wellnigh north, instead of west, as did the more part of the wall. And in the midst of that northern-looking bight was a dark place which seemed to Walter like a downright shard in the cliff. For the face of the wall was of a bleak grey, and it was but little furrowed.

So then Walter spake: "Lo, old friend, there yonder is again a place that meseemeth is a pass; whereunto doth that one lead?" And he pointed to it: but the old man did not follow the pointing of his finger, but, looking down on the ground, answered confusedly, and said:

"Maybe: I wot not. I deem that it also leadeth into the Bear-country by a roundabout road. It leadeth into the far land."

Walter answered nought: for a strange thought had come uppermost in his mind, that the carle knew far more than he would say of that pass, and that he himself might be led thereby to find the wondrous three. He caught his breath hardly, and his heart knocked against his ribs; but he refrained from speaking for a long while; but at last he spake in a sharp hard voice, which he scarce knew for his own: "Father, tell me, I adjure thee by God and All-hallows, was is through yonder shard that the road lay, when thou must needs make thy first stride over a dead man?"

The old man spake not a while, then he raised his head, and looked Walter full in the eyes, and said in a steady voice: "NO, IT WAS NOT." Thereafter they sat looking at each other a while; but at last Walter turned his eyes away, but knew not what they beheld nor where he was, but he was as one in a swoon. For he knew full well that the carle had lied to him, and that he might as well have said aye as no, and told him, that it verily was by that same shard that he had stridden over a dead man. Nevertheless he made as little semblance thereof as he might, and presently came to himself, and fell to talking of other matters, that had nought to do with the adventures of the land. But after a while he spake suddenly, and said: "My master, I was thinking of a thing."

"Yea, of what?" said the carle.

"Of this," said Walter; "that here in this land be strange adventures toward, and that if we, and I in especial, were to turn our backs on them, and go home with nothing done, it were pity of our lives: for all will be dull and deedless there. I was deeming it were good if we tried the adventure."

"What adventure?" said the old man, rising up on his elbow and staring sternly on him.

Said Walter: "The wending yonder pass to the eastward, whereby the

huge men come to thee from out of the Bear-country; that we might see
what should come thereof."

The carle leaned back again, and smiled and shook his head, and
spake: "That adventure were speedily proven: death would come of it,
my son."

"Yea, and how?" said Walter.

The carle said: "The big men would take thee, and offer thee up as a
blood-offering to that woman, who is their Mawmet. And if ye go all,
then shall they do the like with all of you."

Said Walter: "Is that sure?"

"Dead sure," said the carle.

"How knowest thou this?" said Walter.

"I have been there myself," said the carle.

"Yea," said Walter, "but thou camest away whole."

"Art thou sure thereof?" said the carle.

"Thou art alive yet, old man," said Walter, "for I have seen thee eat
thy meat, which ghosts use not to do." And he laughed.

But the old man answered soberly: "If I escaped, it was by this, that
another woman saved me, and not often shall that befall. Nor wholly
was I saved; my body escaped forsooth. But where is my soul? Where is
my heart, and my life? Young man, I rede thee, try no such adventure;
but go home to thy kindred if thou canst. Moreover, wouldst thou fare
alone? The others shall hinder thee."

Said Walter: "I am the master; they shall do as I bid them: besides,
they will be well pleased to share my goods amongst them if I give them
a writing to clear them of all charges which might be brought against
them."

"My son! my son!" said the carle, "I pray thee go not to thy death!"

Walter heard him silently, but as if he were persuaded to refrain; and
then the old man fell to, and told him much concerning this Bear-folk
and their customs, speaking very freely of them; but Walter's ears were
scarce open to this talk: whereas he deemed that he should have nought
to do with those wild men; and he durst not ask again concerning the
country whereto led the pass on the northward.

CHAPTER VII

Walter Comes to the Shard in the Rock-wall

As THEY WERE in converse thus, they heard the hunters blowing on
their horns all together; whereon the old man arose, and said: "I deem
by the blowing that the hunt will be over and done, and that they be
blowing on their fellows who have gone scatter-meal about the wood. It
is now some five hours after noon, and thy men will be getting back with
their venison, and will be fainest of the victuals they have caught;
therefore will I hasten on before, and get ready fire and water and
other matters for the cooking. Wilt thou come with me, young master,
or abide thy men here?"

Walter said lightly: "I will rest and abide them here; since I cannot fail to see them hence as they go on their ways to thine house. And it may be well that I be at hand to command them and forbid, and put some order amongst them, for rough playmates they be, some of them, and now all heated with the hunting and the joy of the green earth." Thus he spoke, as if nought were toward save supper and bed; but inwardly hope and fear were contending in him, and again his heart beat so hard, that he deemed that the carle must surely hear it. But the old man took him but according to his outward seeming, and nodded his head, and went away quietly toward his house.

When he had been gone a little, Walter rose up heedfully; he had with him a scrip wherein was some cheese and hard-fish, and a little flasket of wine; a short bow he had with him, and a quiver of arrows; and he was girt with a strong and good sword, and a wood-knife withal. He looked to all this gear that it was nought amiss, and then speedily went down off the mound, and when he was come down, he found that it covered him from men coming out of the wood, if he went straight thence to that shard of the rock-wall where was the pass that led southward.

Now it is no nay that thitherward he turned, and went wisely, lest the carle should make a backward cast, and see him, or lest any straggler of his own folk might happen upon him.

For to say sooth, he deemed that did they wind him, they would be like to let him of his journey. He had noted the bearings of the cliffs nigh the shard, and whereas he could see their heads everywhere except from the depths of the thicket, he was not like to go astray.

He had made no great way ere he heard the horns blowing all together again in one place, and looking thitherward through the leafy boughs (for he was now amidst of a thicket) he saw his men thronging the mound, and had no doubt therefore that they were blowing on him; but being well under cover he heeded it nought, and lying still a little, saw them go down off the mound and go all of them toward the carle's house, still blowing as they went, but not faring scatter-meal. Wherefore it was clear that they were nought troubled about him.

So he went on his way to the shard; and there is nothing to say of his journey till he got before it with the last of the clear day, and entered it straightway. It was in sooth a downright breach or cleft in the rock-wall, and there was no hill or bent leading up to it, nothing but a tumble of stones before it, which was somewhat uneasy going, yet needed nought but labour to overcome it, and when he had got over this, and was in the very pass itself, he found it no ill going: forsooth at first it was little worse than a rough road betwixt two great stony slopes, though a little trickle of water ran down amidst of it. So, though it was so nigh nightfall, yet Walter pressed on, yea, and long after the very night was come. For the moon rose wide and bright a little after nightfall. But at last he had gone so long, and was so wearied, that he deemed it nought but wisdom to rest him, and so lay down on a piece of greensward betwixt the stones, when he had eaten a morsel out of his satchel, and drunk of the water out of the stream. There as he lay, if he had any doubt of peril, his weariness soon made it all one to him, for presently he was sleeping as soundly as any man in Langton on Holm.

CHAPTER VIII

Walter Wends the Waste

DAY WAS YET young when he awoke: he leapt to his feet, and went down to the stream and drank of its waters, and washed the night off him in a pool thereof, and then set forth on his way again. When he had gone some three hours, the road, which had been going up all the way, but somewhat gently, grew steeper, and the bent on either side lowered, and lowered, till it sank at last altogether, and then was he on a rough mountain-neck with little grass, and no water; save that now and again was a soft place with a flow amidst of it, and such places he must needs fetch a compass about, lest he be mired. He gave himself but little rest, eating what he needs must as he went. The day was bright and calm, so that the sun was never hidden, and he steered by it due south. All that day he went, and found no more change in that huge neck, save that whiles it was more and whiles less steep. A little before nightfall he happened on a shallow pool some twenty yards over; and he deemed it good to rest there, since there was water for his avail, though he might have made somewhat more out of the tail end of the day.

When dawn came again he awoke and arose, nor spent much time over his breakfast; but pressed on all he might; and now he said to himself, that whatsoever other peril were athwart his way, he was out of the danger of the chase of his own folk.

All this while he had seen no four-footed beast, save now and again a hill-fox, and once some outlandish kind of hare; and of fowl but very few: a crow or two, a long-winged hawk, and twice an eagle high up aloft.

Again, the third night, he slept in the stony wilderness, which still led him up and up. Only toward the end of the day, himseemed that it had been less steep for a long while: otherwise nought was changed, on all sides it was nought but the endless neck, wherefrom nought could be seen, but some other part of itself. This fourth night withal he found no water whereby he might rest, so that he awoke parched, and longing to drink just when the dawn was at its coldest.

But on the fifth morrow the ground rose but little, and at last, when he had been going wearily a long while, and now, hard on noontide, his thirst grieved him sorely, he came on a spring welling out from under a high rock, the water wherefrom trickled feebly away. So eager was he to drink, that at first he heeded nought else; but when his thirst was fully quenched his eyes caught sight of the stream which flowed from the well, and he gave a shout, for lo! it was running south. Wherefore it was with a merry heart that he went on, and as he went, came on more streams, all running south or thereabouts. He hastened on all he might, but in despite of all the speed he made, and that he felt the land now going down southward, night overtook him in that same wilderness. Yet when he stayed at last for sheer weariness, he lay down in what he deemed by the moonlight to be a shallow valley, with a ridge at the southern end thereof.

He slept long, and when he awoke the sun was high in the heavens, and never was brighter or clearer morning on the earth than was that. He arose and ate of what little was yet left him, and drank of the water of a stream which he had followed the evening before, and beside which he had laid him down; and then set forth again with no great hope to come on new tidings that day. But yet when he was fairly afoot, himseemed that there was something new in the air which he breathed, that was soft and bore sweet scents home to him; whereas heretofore, and that especially for the last three or four days, it had been harsh and void, like the face of the desert itself.

So on he went, and presently was mounting the ridge aforesaid, and, as oft happens when one climbs a steep place, he kept his eyes on the ground, till he felt he was on the top of the ridge. Then he stopped to take breath, and raised his head and looked, and lo! he was verily on the brow of the great mountain-neck, and down below him was the hanging of the great hill-slopes, which fell down, not slowly, as those he had been those days a-mounting, but speedily enough, though with little of broken places or sheer cliffs. But beyond this last of the desert there was before him a lovely land of wooded hills, green plains, and little valleys, stretching out far and wide, till it ended at last in great blue mountains and white snowy peaks beyond them.

Then for very surprise of joy his spirit wavered, and he felt faint and dizzy, so that he was fain to sit down a while and cover his face with his hands. Presently he came to his sober mind again, and stood up and looked forth keenly, and saw no sign of any dwelling of man. But he said to himself that that might well be because the good and well-grassed land was still so far off, and that he might yet look to find men and their dwellings when he had left the mountain wilderness quite behind him. So therewith he fell to going his ways down the mountain, and lost little time therein, whereas he now had his livelihood to look to.

CHAPTER IX

Walter Happeneth on the First of Those Three Creatures

WHAT WITH ONE thing, what with another, as his having to turn out of his way for sheer rocks, or for slopes so steep that he might not try the peril of them, and again for bogs impassable, he was fully three days more before he had quite come out of the stony waste, and by that time, though he had never lacked water, his scanty victual was quite done, for all his careful husbandry thereof. But this troubled him little, whereas he looked to find wild fruits here and there, and to shoot some small deer, as hare or coney, and make a shift to cook the same, since he had with him flint and fire-steel. Moreover the further he went, the surer he was that he should soon come across a dwelling, so smooth and fair as everything looked before him. And he had scant fear, save that he might happen on men who should enthrall him.

But when he was come down past the first green slopes, he was so worn, that he said to himself that rest was better than meat, so little as he had slept for the last three days; so he laid him down under an ash-tree by a stream-side, nor asked what was o'clock, but had his fill of sleep, and even when he awoke in the fresh morning was little fain of rising, but lay betwixt sleeping and waking for some three hours more; then he arose, and went further down the next green bent, yet somewhat slowly because of his hunger-weakness. And the scent of that fair land came up to him like the odour of one great nosegay.

So he came to where the land was level, and there were many trees, as oak and ash, and sweet-chestnut and wych-elm, and hornbeam and quicken-tree, not growing in a close wood or tangled thicket, but set as though in order on the flowery greensward, even as it might be in a great king's park.

So came he to a big bird-cherry, whereof many boughs hung low down laden with fruit: his belly rejoiced at the sight, and he caught hold of a bough, and fell to plucking and eating. But whiles he was amidst of this, he heard suddenly, close anigh him, a strange noise of roaring and braying, not very great, but exceeding fierce and terrible, and not like to the voice of any beast that he knew. As has been aforesaid, Walter was no faint-heart; but what with the weakness of his travail and hunger, what with the strangeness of his adventure and his loneliness, his spirit failed him; he turned round towards the noise, his knees shook and he trembled: this way and that he looked, and then gave a great cry and tumbled down in a swoon; for close before him, at his very feet, was the dwarf whose image he had seen before, clad in his yellow coat, and grinning up at him from his hideous hairy countenance.

How long he lay there as one dead, he knew not, but when he woke again there was the dwarf sitting on his hams close by him. And when he lifted up his head, the dwarf sent out that fearful harsh voice again; but this time Walter could make out words therein, and knew that the creature spoke and said:

"How now! What art thou? Whence comest? What wantest?"

Walter sat up and said: "I am a man; I hight Golden Walter; I come from Langton; I want victual."

Said the dwarf, writhing his face grievously, and laughing forsooth: "I know it all: I asked thee to see what wise thou wouldst lie. I was sent forth to look for thee; and I have brought thee loathsome bread with me, such as ye aliens must needs eat: take it!"

Therewith he drew a loaf from a satchel which he bore, and thrust it towards Walter, who took it somewhat doubtfully for all his hunger.

The dwarf yelled at him: "Art thou dainty, alien? Wouldst thou have flesh? Well, give me thy bow and an arrow or two, since thou art lazy-sick, and I will get thee a coney or a hare, or a quail maybe. Ah, I forgot; thou art dainty, and wilt not eat flesh as I do, blood and all together, but must needs half burn it in the fire, or mar it with hot water; as they say my Lady does: or as the Wretch, the Thing does; I know that, for I have seen It eating."

"Nay," said Walter, "this sufficeth;" and he fell to eating the bread, which was sweet between his teeth. Then when he had eaten a while, for hunger compelled him, he said to the dwarf: "But what meanest thou by the Wretch and the Thing? And what Lady is thy Lady?"

The creature let out another wordless roar as of furious anger; and then the words came: "It hath a face white and red, like to thine; and hands white as thine, yea, but whiter; and the like it is underneath its raiment, only whiter still: for I have seen It—yes, I have seen It; ah yes and yes and yes."

And therewith his words ran into gibber and yelling, and he rolled about and smote at the grass: but in a while he grew quiet again and sat still, and then fell to laughing horribly again, and then said: "But thou, fool, wilt think It fair if thou fallest into Its hands, and wilt repent it thereafter, as I did. Oh, the mocking and gibes of It, and the tears and shrieks of It; and the knife! What! sayest thou of my Lady?—What Lady? O alien, what other Lady is there? And what shall I tell thee of her? it is like that she made me, as she made the Bear men. But she made not the Wretch, the Thing; and she hateth It sorely, as I do. And some day to come—"

Thereat he brake off and fell to wordless yelling a long while, and thereafter spake all panting: "Now I have told thee overmuch, and O if my Lady come to hear thereof. Now I will go."

And therewith he took out two more loaves from his wallet, and tossed them to Walter, and so turned and went his ways; whiles walking upright, as Walter had seen his image on the quay of Langton; whiles bounding and rolling like a ball thrown by a lad; whiles scuttling along on all-fours like an evil beast, and ever and anon giving forth that harsh and evil cry.

Walter sat a while after he was out of sight, so stricken with horror and loathing and a fear of he knew not what, that he might not move. Then he plucked up a heart, and looked to his weapons and put the other loaves into his scrip.

Then he arose and went his ways wondering, yea and dreading, what kind of creature he should next fall in with. For soothly it seemed to him that it would be worse than death if they were all such as this one; and that if it were so, he must needs slay and be slain.

CHAPTER X

Walter Happeneth on Another Creature in the Strange Land

BUT AS HE went on through the fair and sweet land so bright and sun-litten, and he now rested and fed, the horror and fear ran off from him, and he wandered on merrily, neither did aught befall him save the coming of night, when he laid him down under a great spreading oak with his drawn sword ready to hand, and fell asleep at once, and woke not till the sun was high.

Then he arose and went on his way again; and the land was no worser than yesterday; but even better, it might be; the greensward more flowery, the oaks and chestnuts greater. Deer of diverse kinds he saw, and might easily have got his meat thereof; but he meddled not with them since he had his bread, and was timorous of lighting a fire. Withal he doubted little of having some entertainment; and that, might be, nought evil; since even that fearful dwarf had been courteous to him after his kind, and had done him good and not harm. But of the happening on the Wretch and the Thing, whereof the dwarf spake, he was yet somewhat afeard.

After he had gone a while and whenas the summer morn was at its brightest, he saw a little way ahead a grey rock rising up from amidst of a ring of oak-trees; so he turned thither straightway; for in this plain-land he had seen no rocks heretofore; and as he went he saw that there was a fountain gushing out from under the rock, which ran thence in a fair little stream. And when he had the rock and the fountain and the stream clear before him, lo! a child of Adam sitting beside the fountain under the shadow of the rock. He drew a little nigher, and then he saw that it was a woman, clad in green like the sward whereon she lay. She was playing with the welling out of the water, and she had trussed up her sleeves to the shoulder that she might thrust her bare arms therein. Her shoes of black leather lay on the grass beside her, and her feet and legs yet shone with the brook.

Belike amidst the splashing and clatter of the water she did not hear him drawing nigh, so that he was close to her before she lifted up her face and saw him, and he beheld her, that it was the maiden of the thrice-seen pageant. She reddened when she saw him, and hastily covered up her legs with her gown-skirt, and drew down the sleeves over her arms, but otherwise stirred not. As for him, he stood still, striving to speak to her; but no word might he bring out, and his heart beat sorely.

But the maiden spake to him in a clear sweet voice, wherein was now no trouble: "Thou art an alien, art thou not? For I have not seen thee before."

"Yea," he said, "I am an alien; wilt thou be good to me?"

She said: "And why not? I was afraid at first, for I thought it had been the King's Son. I looked to see none other; for of goodly men he has been the only one here in the land this long while, till thy coming."

He said: "Didst thou look for my coming at about this time?"

"O nay," she said; "how might I?"

Said Walter: "I wot not; but the other man seemed to be looking for me, and knew of me, and he brought me bread to eat."

She looked on him anxiously, and grew somewhat pale, as she said: "What other one?"

Now Walter did not know what the dwarf might be to her, fellow-servant or what not, so he would not show his loathing of him; but answered wisely: "The little man in the yellow raiment."

But when she heard that word, she went suddenly very pale, and leaned her head aback, and beat the air with her hands; but said presently in a faint voice: "I pray thee talk not of that one while I am by, nor even think of him, if thou mayest forbear."

He spake not, and she was a little while before she came to herself again; then she opened her eyes, and looked upon Walter and smiled kindly on him, as though to ask his pardon for having scared him. Then she rose up in her place, and stood before him; and they were nigh together, for the stream betwixt them was little.

But he still looked anxiously upon her and said: "Have I hurt thee? I pray thy pardon."

She looked on him more sweetly still, and said: "O nay; thou wouldst not hurt me, thou!"

Then she blushed very red, and he in like wise; but afterwards she turned pale, and laid a hand on her breast, and Walter cried out hastily: "O me! I have hurt thee again. Wherein have I done amiss?"

"In nought, in nought," she said; "but I am troubled, I wot not wherefore; some thought hath taken hold of me, and I know it not. Mayhappen in a little while I shall know what troubles me. Now I bid thee depart from me a little, and I will abide here; and when thou comest back, it will either be that I have found it out or not; and in either case I will tell thee."

She spoke earnestly to him; but he said: "How long shall I abide away?"

Her face was troubled as she answered him: "For no long while."

He smiled on her and turned away, and went a space to the other side of the oak-trees, whence she was still within eye-shot. There he abode until the time seemed long to him; but he schooled himself and forbore; for he said: Lest she send me away again. So he abided until again the time seemed long to him, and she called not to him: but once again he forbore to go; then at last he arose, and his heart beat and he trembled, and he walked back again speedily, and came to the maiden, who was still standing by the rock of the spring, her arms hanging down, her eyes downcast. She looked up at him as he drew nigh, and her face changed with eagerness as she said: "I am glad thou art come back, though it be no long while since thy departure" (sooth to say it was scarce half an hour in all). "Nevertheless I have been thinking many things, and thereof will I now tell thee."

He said: "Maiden, there is a river betwixt us, though it be no big one. Shall I not stride over, and come to thee, that we may sit down together side by side on the green grass?"

"Nay," she said, "not yet; tarry a while till I have told thee of matters. I must now tell thee of my thoughts in order."

Her colour went and came now, and she plaited the folds of her gown with restless fingers. At last she said: "Now the first thing is this; that though thou hast seen me first only within this hour, thou hast set thine heart upon me to have me for thy speech-friend and thy darling. And if this be not so, then is all my speech, yea and all my hope, come to an end at once."

"O yea!" said Walter, "even so it is: but how thou hast found this out I wot not; since now for the first time I say it, that thou art indeed my love, and my dear and my darling."

"Hush," she said, "hush! lest the wood have ears, and thy speech is loud: abide, and I shall tell thee how I know it. Whether this thy love shall outlast the first time that thou holdest my body in thine arms, I wot not, nor dost thou. But sore is my hope that it may be so; for I also, though it be but scarce an hour since I set eyes on thee, have cast mine eyes on thee to have thee for my love and my darling, and my speech-friend. And this is how I wot that thou lovest me, my friend. Now is all this dear and joyful, and overflows my heart with sweetness. But now must I tell thee of the fear and the evil which lieth behind it."

Then Walter stretched out his hands to her, and cried out: "Yea, yea! But whatever evil entangle us, now we both know these two things, to wit, that thou lovest me, and I thee, wilt thou not come hither, that I may cast mine arms about thee, and kiss thee, if not thy kind lips or thy friendly face at all, yet at least thy dear hand: yea, that I may touch thy body in some wise?"

She looked on him steadily, and said softly: "Nay, this above all things must not be; and that it may not be is a part of the evil which entangles us. But hearken, friend, once again I tell thee that thy voice is over loud in this wilderness fruitful of evil. Now I have told thee, indeed, of two things whereof we both wot, and thou wottest not. Yet this were better, that thou pledge thy word not to touch so much as one of my hands, and that we go together a little way hence away from these tumbled stones, and sit down upon the open greensward; whereas here is cover if there be spying abroad."

Again, as she spoke, she turned very pale; but Walter said: "Since it must be so, I pledge thee my word to thee as I love thee."

And therewith she knelt down, and did on her foot-gear, and then sprang lightly over the rivulet; and then the twain of them went side by side some half a furlong thence, and sat down, shadowed by the boughs of a slim quicken-tree growing up out of the greensward, whereon for a good space around was neither bush nor brake.

There began the maiden to talk soberly, and said: "This is what I must needs say to thee now, that thou art come into a land perilous for any one that loveth aught of good; from which, forsooth, I were fain that thou wert gotten away safely, even though I should die of longing for thee. As for myself, my peril is, in a measure, less than thine; I mean the peril of death. But lo, thou, this iron on my foot is token that I am a thrall, and thou knowest in what wise thralls must pay for transgressions. Furthermore, of what I am, and how I came hither, time would fail me to tell; but somewhile, maybe, I shall tell thee. I serve an evil mistress, of whom I may say that scarce I wot if she be a woman or not; but by some creatures is she accounted for a god, and as a god is heried; and surely never god was crueller nor colder than she. Me she hateth sorely; yet if she hated me little or nought, small were the gain to me if it were her pleasure to deal hardly by me. But as things now are, and are like to be, it would not be for her pleasure, but for her pain and loss, to make an end of me, therefore, as I said e'en now, my mere life is not in peril with her; unless, perchance, some sudden passion get the better of her, and she slay me, and repent of it thereafter. For so it is, that if it be the least evil of her conditions that she is wanton, at least wanton she is to the letter. Many a time hath she cast the net for the catching of some goodly young man; and her latest prey (save it be thou) is the young man whom I named, when first I saw thee, by the name of the King's Son. He is with us yet, and I fear him; for of late hath he wearied of her, though it is but plain truth to say of her, that she is the wonder of all Beauties of the World. He hath wearied of her, I say, and hath cast his eyes upon me, and if I were heedless, he would betray me to the uttermost of the wrath of my mistress. For needs must I say of him,

though he be a goodly man, and now fallen into thralldom, that he hath
no bowels of compassion; but is a dastard, who for an hour's pleasure
would undo me, and thereafter would stand by smiling and taking my
mistress's pardon with good cheer, while for me would be no pardon.
Seest thou, therefore, how it is with me between these two cruel fools?
And moreover there are others of whom I will not even speak to thee."

And therewith she put her hands before her face, and wept, and
murmured: "Who shall deliver me from this death in life?"

But Walter cried out: "For what else am I come hither, I, I?"

And it was a near thing that he did not take her in his arms, but he
remembered his pledged word, and drew aback from her in terror,
whereas he had an inkling of why she would not suffer it; and he wept
with her.

But suddenly the Maid left weeping, and said in a changed voice:
"Friend, whereas thou speakest of delivering me, it is more like that I
shall deliver thee. And now I pray thy pardon for thus grieving thee
with my grief, and that more especially because thou mayst not solace
thy grief with kisses and caresses; but so it was, that for once I was
smitten by the thought of the anguish of this land, and the joy of all the
world besides."

Therewith she caught her breath in a half-sob, but refrained her and
went on: "Now dear friend and darling, take good heed to all that I
shall say to thee, whereas thou must do after the teaching of my words.
And first, I deem by the monster having met thee at the gates of the
land, and refreshed thee, that the Mistress hath looked for thy coming;
nay, by thy coming hither at all, that she hath cast her net and caught
thee. Hast thou noted aught that might seem to make this more like?"

Said Walter: "Three times in full daylight have I seen go past me the
images of the monster and thee and a glorious lady, even as if ye were
alive."

And therewith he told her in few words how it had gone with him
since that day on the quay at Langton.

She said: "Then it is no longer perhaps, but certain, that thou art her
latest catch; and even so I deemed from the first: and, dear friend, this
is why I have not suffered thee to kiss or caress me, so sore as I longed
for thee. For the Mistress will have thee for her only, and hath lured
thee hither for nought else; and she is wise in wizardry (even as some
deal am I), and wert thou to touch me with hand or mouth on my naked
flesh, yea, or were it even my raiment, then would she scent the savour
of thy love upon me, and then, though it may be she would spare thee,
she would not spare me."

Then was she silent a little, and seemed very downcast, and Walter
held his peace from grief and confusion and helplessness; for of
wizardry he knew nought.

At last the Maid spake again, and said: "Nevertheless we will not die
redeless. Now thou must look to this, that from henceforward it is thee,
and not the King's Son, whom she desireth, and that so much the more
that she hath not set eyes on thee. Remember this, whatsoever her
seeming may be to thee. Now, therefore, shall the King's Son be free,
though he know it not, to cast his love on whomso he will; and, in a way,
I also shall be free to yeasay him. Though, forsooth, so fulfilled is she

with malice and spite, that even then she may turn round on me to punish me for doing that which she would have me do. Now let me think of it."

Then was she silent a good while, and spoke at last: "Yea, all things are perilous, and a perilous rede I have thought of, whereof I will not tell thee as yet; so waste not the short while by asking me. At least the worst will be no worse than what shall come if we strive not against it. And now, my friend, amongst perils it is growing more and more perilous that we twain should be longer together. But I would say one thing yet; and maybe another thereafter. Thou hast cast thy love upon one who will be true to thee, whatsoever may befall; yet is she a guileful creature, and might not help it her life long, and now for thy very sake must needs be more guileful now than ever before. And as for me, the guileful, my love have I cast upon a lovely man, and one true and simple, and a stout-heart; but at such a pinch is he, that if he withstand all temptation, his withstanding may belike undo both him and me. Therefore swear we both of us, that by both of us shall all guile and all falling away be forgiven on the day when we shall be free to love each the other as our hearts will."

Walter cried out: "O love, I swear it indeed! thou art my Hallow, and I will swear it as on the relics of a Hallow; on thy hands and thy feet I swear it."

The words seemed to her a dear caress; and she laughed, and blushed, and looked full kindly on him; and then her face grew solemn, and she said: "On thy life I swear it!"

Then she said: "Now is there nought for thee to do but to go hence straight to the Golden House, which is my Mistress's house, and the only house in this land (save one which I may not see), and lieth southward no long way. How she will deal with thee, I wot not; but all I have said of her and thee and the King's Son is true. Therefore I say to thee, be wary and cold at heart, whatsoever outward semblance thou mayst make. If thou have to yield thee to her, then yield rather late than early, so as to gain time. Yet not so late as to seem shamed in yielding for fear's sake. Hold fast to thy life, my friend, for in warding that, thou wardest me from grief without remedy. Thou wilt see me ere long; it may be tomorrow, it may be some days hence. But forget not, that what I may do, that I am doing. Take heed also that thou pay no more heed to me, or rather less, than if thou wert meeting a maiden of no account in the streets of thine own town. O my love! barren is this first farewell, as was our first meeting; but surely shall there be another meeting better than the first, and the last farewell may be long and long yet."

Therewith she stood up, and he knelt before her a little while without any word, and then arose and went his ways; but when he had gone a space he turned about, and saw her still standing in the same place; she stayed a moment when she saw him turn, and then herself turned about.

So he departed through the fair land, and his heart was full with hope and fear as he went.

CHAPTER XI

Walter Happeneth on the Mistress

IT WAS BUT a little after noon when Walter left the Maid behind: he steered south by the sun, as the Maid had bidden him, and went swiftly; for, as a good knight wending to battle, the time seemed long to him till he should meet the foe.

So an hour before sunset he saw something white and gay gleaming through the boles of the oak-trees, and presently there was clear before him a most goodly house builded of white marble, carved all about with knots and imagery, and the carven folk were all painted of their lively colours, whether it were their raiment or their flesh, and the housings wherein they stood all done with gold and fair hues. Gay were the windows of the house; and there was a pillared porch before the great door, with images betwixt the pillars both of men and beasts: and when Walter looked up to the roof of the house, he saw that it gleamed and shone; for all the tiles were of yellow metal, which he deemed to be of very gold.

All this he saw as he went, and tarried not to gaze upon it; for he said, Belike there will be time for me to look on all this before I die. But he said also, that, though the house was not of the greatest, it was beyond compare of all houses of the world.

Now he entered it by the porch, and came into a hall many-pillared, and vaulted over, the walls painted with gold and ultramarine, the floor dark, and spangled with many colours, and the windows glazed with knots and pictures. Midmost thereof was a fountain of gold, whence the water ran two ways in gold-lined runnels, spanned twice with little bridges of silver. Long was that hall, and now not very light, so that Walter was come past the fountain before he saw any folk therein: then he looked up toward the high-seat, and him-seemed that a great light shone thence, and dazzled his eyes; and he went on a little way, and then fell on his knees; for there before him on the high-seat sat that wondrous Lady, whose lively image had been shown to him thrice before; and she was clad in gold and jewels, as he had erst seen her. But now she was not alone; for by her side sat a young man, goodly enough, so far as Walter might see him, and most richly clad, with a jewelled sword by his side, and a chaplet of gems on his head. They held each other by the hand, and seemed to be in dear converse together; but they spake softly, so that Walter might not hear what they said, till at last the man spake aloud to the Lady: "Seest thou not that there is a man in the hall?"

"Yea," she said, "I see him yonder, kneeling on his knees; let him come nigher and give some account of himself."

So Walter stood up and drew nigh, and stood there, all shamefaced and confused, looking on those twain, and wondering at the beauty of the Lady. As for the man, who was slim, and black-haired, and straight-featured, for all his goodliness Walter accounted him little, and nowise deemed him to look chieftain-like.

Now the Lady spake not to Walter any more than erst; but at last the man said: "Why doest thou not kneel as thou didst erewhile?"

Walter was on the point of giving him back a fierce answer; but the Lady spake and said: "Nay, friend, it matters not whether he kneel or stand; but he may say, if he will, what he would have of me, and wherefore he is come hither."

Then spake Walter, for as wroth and ashamed as he was: "Lady, I have strayed into this land, and have come to thine house as I suppose, and if I be not welcome, I may well depart straightway, and seek a way out of thy land, if thou wouldst drive me thence, as well as out of thine house."

Thereat the Lady turned and looked on him, and when her eyes met his, he felt a pang of fear and desire mingled shoot through his heart. This time she spoke to him; but coldly, without either wrath or any thought of him: "New-comer," she said, "I have not bidden thee hither; but here mayst thou abide a while if thou wilt; nevertheless, take heed that here is no King's Court. There is, forsooth, a folk that serveth me (or, it may be, more than one), of whom thou wert best to know nought. Of others I have but two servants, whom thou wilt see; and the one is a strange creature, who should scare thee or scathe thee with a good will, but of a good will shall serve nought save me; the other is a woman, a thrall, of little avail, save that, being compelled, she will work woman's service for me, but whom none else shall compel. . . Yea, but what is all this to thee; or to me that I should tell it to thee? I will not drive thee away; but if thine entertainment please thee not, make no plaint thereof to me, but depart at thy will. Now is this talk betwixt us overlong, since, as thou seest, I and this King's Son are in converse together. Art thou a King's Son?"

"Nay, Lady," said Walter, "I am but of the sons of the merchants."

"It matters not," she said; "go thy ways into one of the chambers."

And straightway she fell a-talking to the man who sat beside her concerning the singing of the birds beneath her window in the morning; and of how she had bathed her that day in a pool of the woodlands, when she had been heated with hunting, and so forth; and all as if there had been none there save her and the King's Son.

But Walter departed all ashamed, as though he had been a poor man thrust away from a rich kinsman's door; and he said to himself that this woman was hateful, and nought love-worthy, and that she was little like to tempt him, despite all the fairness of her body.

No one else he saw in the house that even; he found meat and drink duly served on a fair table, and thereafter he came on a goodly bed, and all things needful, but no child of Adam to do him service, or bid him welcome or warning. Nevertheless he ate, and drank, and slept, and put off thought of all these things till the morrow, all the more as he hoped to see the kind maiden some time betwixt sunrise and sunset on that new day.

CHAPTER XII

The Wearing of Four Days in the Wood Beyond the World

HE AROSE BETIMES, but found no one to greet him, neither was there any sound of folk moving within the fair house; so he but broke his fast, and then went forth and wandered amongst the trees, till he found him a stream to bathe in, and after he had washed the night off him he lay down under a tree thereby for a while, but soon turned back toward the house, lest perchance the Maid should come thither and he should miss her.

It should be said that half a bow-shot from the house on that side (i.e. due north thereof) was a little hazel-brake, and round about it the trees were smaller of kind than the oaks and chestnuts he had passed through before, being mostly of birch and quicken-beam and young ash, with small wood betwixt them; so now he passed through the thicket, and, coming to the edge thereof, beheld the Lady and the King's Son walking together hand in hand, full lovingly by seeming.

He deemed it unmeet to draw back and hide him, so he went forth past them toward the house. The King's Son scowled on him as he passed, but the Lady, over whose beauteous face flickered the joyous morning smiles, took no more heed of him than if he had been one of the trees of the wood. But she had been so high and disdainful with him the evening before, that he thought little of that. The twain went on, skirting the hazel-copse, and he could not choose but turn his eyes on them, so sorely did the Lady's beauty draw them. Then befell another thing; for behind them the boughs of the hazels parted, and there stood that little evil thing, he or another of his kind; for he was quite unclad save by his fell of yellowy-brown hair, and that he was girt with a leathern girdle, wherein was stuck an ugly two-edged knife: he stood upright a moment, and cast his eyes at Walter and grinned, but not as if he knew him; and scarce could Walter say whether it were the one he had seen, or another: then he cast himself down on his belly, and fell to creeping through the long grass like a serpent, following the footsteps of the Lady and her lover; and now, as he crept, Walter deemed, in his loathing, that the creature was liker to a ferret than aught else. He crept on marvellous swiftly, and was soon clean out of sight. But Walter stood staring after him for a while, and then lay down by the copse-side, that he might watch the house and the entry thereof; for he thought, now perchance presently will the kind maiden come hither to comfort me with a word or two. But hour passed by hour, and still she came not; and still he lay there, and thought of the Maid, and longed for her kindness and wisdom, till he could not refrain his tears, and wept for the lack of her. Then he arose, and went and sat in the porch, and was very downcast of mood.

But as he sat there, back comes the Lady again, the King's Son leading her by the hand; they entered the porch, and she passed by him so close that the odour of her raiment filled all the air about him, and the sleekness of her side nigh touched him, so that he could not fail to note that her garments were somewhat disarrayed, and that she kept her right hand (for her left the King's Son held) to her bosom to hold the cloth together there, whereas the rich raiment had been torn off from her right shoulder. As they passed by him, the King's Son once more scowled on him, wordless, but even more fiercely than before; and again the Lady heeded him nought.

After they had gone on a while, he entered the hall, and found it empty from end to end, and no sound in it save the tinkling of the fountain; but there was victual set on the board. He ate and drank thereof to keep life lusty within him, and then went out again to the wood-side to watch and to long; and the time hung heavy on his hands because of the lack of the fair Maiden.

He was of mind not to go into the house to his rest that night, but to sleep under the boughs of the forest. But a little after sunset he saw a bright-clad image moving amidst the carven images of the porch, and the King's Son came forth and went straight to him, and said: "Thou art to enter the house, and go into thy chamber forthwith, and by no means to go forth of it betwixt sunset and sunrise. My Lady will not away with thy prowling round the house in the night-tide."

Therewith he turned away, and went into the house again; and Walter followed him soberly, remembering how the Maid had bidden him forbear. So he went to his chamber, and slept.

But amidst of the night he awoke and deemed that he heard a voice not far off, so he crept out of his bed and peered around, lest, perchance, the Maid had come to speak with him; but his chamber was dusk and empty: then he went to the window and looked out, and saw the moon shining bright and white upon the greensward. And lo! the Lady walking with the King's Son, and he clad in thin and wanton raiment, but she in nought else save what God had given her of long, crispy yellow hair. Then was Walter ashamed to look on her, seeing that there was a man with her, and gat him back to his bed; but yet a long while ere he slept again he had the image before his eyes of the fair woman on the dewy moonlit grass.

The next day matters went much the same way, and the next also, save that his sorrow was increased, and he sickened sorely of hope deferred. On the fourth day also the forenoon wore as erst; but in the heat of the afternoon Walter sought to the hazel-copse, and laid him down there hard by a little clearing thereof, and slept from very weariness of grief. There, after a while, he woke with words still hanging in his ears, and he knew at once that it was they twain talking together.

The King's Son had just done his say, and now it was the Lady beginning in her honey-sweet voice, low but strong, wherein even was a little of huskiness; she said: "Otto, belike it were well to have a little patience, till we find out what the man is, and whence he cometh; it will always be easy to rid us of him; it is but a word to our Dwarf-king, and it will be done in a few minutes."

"Patience!" said the King's Son, angrily; "I wot not how to have patience with him; for I can see of him that he is rude and violent and headstrong, and a low-born wily one. Forsooth, he had patience enough with me the other even, when I rated him in, like the dog that he is, and he had no manhood to say one word to me. Soothly, as he followed after me, I had a mind to turn about and deal him a buffet on the face, to see if I could but draw one angry word from him."

The Lady laughed, and said: "Well, Otto, I know not; that which thou deemest dastardy in him may be but prudence and wisdom, and he an alien, far from his friends and nigh to his foes. Perchance we shall yet try him what he is. Meanwhile, I rede thee try him not with buffets, save he be weaponless and with bounden hands; or else I deem that but a little while shalt thou be fain of thy blow."

Now when Walter heard her words and the voice wherein they were said, he might not forbear being stirred by them, and to him, all lonely there, they seemed friendly.

But he lay still, and the King's Son answered the Lady and said: "I know not what is in thine heart concerning this runagate, that thou shouldst bemock me with his valiancy, whereof thou knowest nought. If thou deem me unworthy of thee, send me back safe to my father's country; I may look to have worship there; yea, and the love of fair women belike."

Therewith it seemed as if he had put forth his hand to the Lady to caress her, for she said: "Nay, lay not thine hand on my shoulder, for to-day and now it is not the hand of love, but of pride and folly, and would-be mastery. Nay, neither shalt thou rise up and leave me until thy mood is softer and kinder to me."

Then was there silence betwixt them a while, and thereafter the King's Son spake in a wheedling voice: "My goddess, I pray thee pardon me! But canst thou wonder that I fear thy wearying of me, and am therefore peevish and jealous? thou so far above the Queens of the World, and I a poor youth that without thee were nothing!"

She answered nought, and he went on again: "Was it not so, O goddess, that this man of the sons of the merchants was little heedful of thee, and thy loveliness and thy majesty?"

She laughed and said: "Maybe he deemed not that he had much to gain of us, seeing thee sitting by our side, and whereas we spake to him coldly and sternly and disdainfully. Withal, the poor youth was dazzled and shamefaced before us; that we could see in the eyes and the mien of him."

Now this she spoke so kindly and sweetly, that again was Walter all stirred thereat; and it came into his mind that it might be she knew he was anigh and hearing her, and that she spake as much for him as for the King's Son: but that one answered: "Lady, didst thou not see somewhat else in his eyes, to wit, that they had but of late looked on some fair woman other than thee? As for me, I deem it not so unlike that on the way to thine hall he may have fallen in with thy Maid."

He spoke in a faltering voice, as if shrinking from some storm that might come. And forsooth the Lady's voice was changed as she answered, though there was no outward heat in it; rather it was sharp and eager and cold at once. She said: "Yea, that is not ill thought of; but we may not always keep our thrall in mind. If it be so as thou deemest, we shall come to know it most like when we next fall in with her; or if she hath been shy this time, then shall she pay the heavier for it; for we will question her by the Fountain in the Hall as to what betid by the Fountain of the Rock."

Spake the King's Son, faltering yet more: "Lady, were it not better to question the man himself? the Maid is stout-hearted, and will not be speedily quelled into a true tale; whereas the man I deem of no account."

"No, no," said the Lady sharply, "it shall not be."

Then was she silent a while; and then she said: "How if the man should prove to be our master?"

"Nay, our Lady," said the King's Son, "thou art jesting with me; thou and thy might and thy wisdom, and all that thy wisdom may command, to be over-mastered by a gangrel churl!"

"But how if I will not have it command, King's Son?" said the Lady. "I tell thee I know thine heart, but thou knowest not mine. But be at peace! For since thou hast prayed for this woman—nay, not with thy words, I wot, but with thy trembling hands, and thine anxious eyes, and knitted brow—I say, since thou hast prayed for her so earnestly, she shall escape this time. But whether it will be to her gain in the long run, I misdoubt me. See thou to that, Otto! thou who hast held me in thine arms so oft. And now thou mayest depart if thou wilt."

It seemed to Walter as if the King's Son were dumbfoundered at her words: he answered nought, and presently he rose from the ground, and went his ways slowly toward the house. The Lady lay there a little while, and then went her ways also; but turned away from the house toward the wood at the other end thereof, whereby Walter had first come thither.

As for Walter, he was confused in mind and shaken in spirit; and withal he seemed to see guile and cruel deeds under the talk of those two, and waxed wrathful thereat. Yet he said to himself, that nought might he do, but was as one bound hand and foot, till he had seen the Maid again.

CHAPTER XIII

Now Is the Hunt Up

NEXT MORNING WAS he up betimes, but he was cast down and heavy of heart, not looking for aught else to betide than had betid those last four days. But otherwise it fell out; for when he came down into the hall, there was the Lady sitting on the high-seat all alone, clad but in a coat of white linen; and she turned her head when she heard his footsteps, and looked on him, and greeted him, and said: "Come hither, guest."

So he went and stood before her, and she said: "Though as yet thou hast had no welcome here, and no honour, it hath not entered into thine heart to flee from us; and to say sooth, that is well for thee, for flee away from our hand thou mightest not, nor mightest thou depart without our furtherance. But for this we can thee thank, that thou hast abided here our bidding, and eaten thine heart through the heavy wearing of four days, and made no plaint. Yet I cannot deem thee a dastard; thou so well knit and shapely of body, so clear-eyed and bold of visage. Wherefore now I ask thee, art thou willing to do me service, thereby to earn thy guesting?"

Walter answered her, somewhat faltering at first, for he was astonished at the change which had come over her; for now she spoke to him in friendly wise, though indeed as a great lady would speak to a young man ready to serve her in all honour. Said he: "Lady, I can thank thee humbly and heartily in that thou biddest me do thee service; for these days past I have loathed the emptiness of the hours, and nought better could I ask for than to serve so glorious a Mistress in all honour."

She frowned somewhat, and said: "Thou shalt not call me Mistress; there is but one who so calleth me, that is my thrall; and thou art none such. Thou shalt call me Lady, and I shall be well pleased that thou be my squire, and for this present thou shalt serve me in the hunting. So get thy gear; take thy bow and arrows, and gird thee to thy sword. For in this fair land may one find beasts more perilous than be buck or hart. I go now to array me; we will depart while the day is yet young; for so make we the summer day the fairest."

He made obeisance to her, and she arose and went to her chamber, and Walter dight himself, and then abode her in the porch; and in less than an hour she came out of the hall, and Walter's heart beat when he saw that the Maid followed her hard at heel, and scarce might he school his eyes not to gaze over-eagerly at his dear friend. She was clad even as she was before, and was changed in no wise, save that love troubled her face when she first beheld him, and she had much ado to master it: howbeit the Mistress heeded not the trouble of her, or made no semblance of heeding it, till the Maiden's face was all according to its wont.

But this Walter found strange, that after all that disdain of the Maid's thralldom which he had heard of the Mistress, and after all the threats against her, now was the Mistress become mild and debonaire to her, as a good lady to her good maiden. When Walter bowed the knee to her, she turned unto the Maid, and said: "Look thou, my Maid, at this fair new Squire that I have gotten! Will not he be valiant in the greenwood? And see whether he be well shapen or not. Doth he not touch thine heart, when thou thinkest of all the woe, and fear, and trouble of the World beyond the Wood, which he hath escaped, to dwell in this little land peaceably, and well-beloved both by the Mistress and the Maid? And thou, my Squire, look a little at this fair slim Maiden, and say if she pleaseth thee not: didst thou deem that we had any thing so fair in this lonely place?"

Frank and kind was the smile on her radiant visage, nor did she seem to note any whit the trouble on Walter's face, nor how he strove to keep his eyes from the Maid. As for her, she had so wholly mastered her countenance, that belike she used her face guilefully, for she stood as one humble but happy, with a smile on her face, blushing, and with her head hung down as if shamefaced before a goodly young man, a stranger.

But the Lady looked upon her kindly and said: "Come hither, child, and fear not this frank and free young man, who belike feareth thee a little, and full certainly feareth me; and yet only after the manner of men."

And therewith she took the Maid by the hand and drew her to her, and pressed her to her bosom, and kissed her cheeks and her lips, and undid the lacing of her gown and bared a shoulder of her, and swept away her skirt from her feet; and then turned to Walter and said: "Lo thou, Squire! is not this a lovely thing to have grown up amongst our rough oak-boles? What! art thou looking at the iron ring there? It is nought, save a token that she is mine, and that I may not be without her."

Then she took the Maid by the shoulders and turned her about as in sport, and said: "Go thou now, and bring hither the good grey ones; for needs must we bring home some venison to-day, whereas this stout warrior may not feed on nought save manchets and honey."

So the Maid went her way, taking care, as Walter deemed, to give no side glance to him. But he stood there shamefaced, so confused with all this open-hearted kindness of the great Lady and with the fresh sight of the darling beauty of the Maid, that he went nigh to thinking that all he had heard since he had come to the porch of the house that first time was but a dream of evil.

But while he stood pondering these matters, and staring before him as one mazed, the Lady laughed out in his face, and touched him on the arm and said: "Ah, our Squire, is it so that now thou hast seen my Maid thou wouldst with a good will abide behind to talk with her? But call to mind thy word pledged to me e'en now! And moreover I tell thee this for thy behoof now she is out of ear-shot, that I will above all things take thee away to-day: for there be other eyes, and they nought uncomely, that look at whiles on my fair-ankled thrall; and who knows but the swords might be out if I take not the better heed, and give thee not every whit of thy will."

As she spoke and moved forward, he turned a little, so that now the edge of that hazel-coppice was within his eye-shot, and he deemed that once more he saw the yellow-brown evil thing crawling forth from the thicket; then, turning suddenly on the Lady, he met her eyes, and seemed in one moment of time to find a far other look in them than that of frankness and kindness; though in a flash they changed back again, and she said merrily and sweetly: "So, so, Sir Squire, now art thou awake again, and mayest for a little while look on me."

Now it came into his head, with that look of hers, all that might befall him and the Maid if he mastered not his passion, nor did what he might to dissemble; so he bent the knee to her, and spoke boldly to her in her own vein, and said: "Nay, most gracious of ladies, never would I abide behind to-day since thou farest afield. But if my speech be hampered, or mine eyes stray, is it not because my mind is confused by thy beauty, and the honey of kind words which floweth from thy mouth?"

She laughed outright at his word, but not disdainfully, and said: "This is well spoken, Squire, and even what a squire should say to his liege lady, when the sun is up on a fair morning, and she and he and all the world are glad."

She stood quite near him as she spoke, her hand was on his shoulder, and her eyes shone and sparkled. Sooth to say, that excusing of his confusion was like enough in seeming to the truth; for sure never creature was fashioned fairer than she: clad she was for the greenwood as the hunting-goddess of the Gentiles, with her green gown gathered unto her girdle, and sandals on her feet; a bow in her hand and a quiver at her back: she was taller and bigger of fashion than the dear Maiden, whiter of flesh, and more glorious, and brighter of hair; as a flower of flowers for fairness and fragrance.

She said: "Thou art verily a fair squire before the hunt is up, and if thou be as good in the hunting, all will be better than well, and the guest will be welcome. But lo! here cometh our Maid with the good grey ones. Go meet her, and we will tarry no longer than for thy taking the leash in hand."

So Walter looked, and saw the Maid coming with two couple of great hounds in the leash straining against her as she came along. He ran lightly to meet her, wondering if he should have a look, or a half-whisper from her; but she let him take the white thongs from her hand, with the same half-smile of shamefacedness still set on her face, and, going past him, came softly up to the Lady, swaying like a willow-branch in the wind, and stood before her, with her arms hanging down by her sides. Then the Lady turned to her, and said: "Look to thyself, our Maid, while we are away. This fair young man thou needest not to fear indeed, for he is good and leal; but what thou shalt do with the King's Son I wot not. He is a hot lover forsooth, but a hard man; and whiles evil is his mood, and perilous both to thee and me. And if thou do his will, it shall be ill for thee; and if thou do it not, take heed of him, and let me, and me only, come between his wrath and thee. I may do somewhat for thee. Even yesterday he was instant with me to have thee chastised after the manner of thralls; but I bade him keep silence of such words, and jeered him and mocked him, till he went away from me peevish and in anger. So look to it that thou fall not into any trap of his contrivance."

Then the Maid cast herself at the Mistress's feet, and kissed and embraced them; and as she rose up, the Lady laid her hand lightly on her head, and then, turning to Walter, cried out: "Now, Squire, let us leave all these troubles and wiles and desires behind us, and flit through the merry green-wood like the Gentiles of old days."

And therewith she drew up the laps of her gown till the whiteness of her knees was seen, and set off swiftly toward the wood that lay south of the house, and Walter followed, marvelling at her goodliness; nor durst he cast a look backward to the Maiden, for he knew that she desired him, and it was her only that he looked to for his deliverance from this house of guile and lies.

CHAPTER XIV

The Hunting of the Hart

As THEY WENT, they found a change in the land, which grew emptier of big and wide-spreading trees, and more beset with thickets. From one of these they roused a hart, and Walter let slip his hounds thereafter, and he and the Lady followed running. Exceeding swift was she, and well-breathed withal, so that Walter wondered at her; and eager she was in the chase as the very hounds, heeding nothing the scratching of briars or the whipping of stiff twigs as she sped on. But for all their eager hunting, the quarry outran both dogs and folk, and gat him into a great thicket, amidmost whereof was a wide plash of water. Into the thicket they followed him, but he took to the water under their eyes and made land on the other side; and because of the tangle of underwood, he swam across much faster than they might have any hope to come round on him; and so were the hunters left undone for that time.

So the Lady cast herself down on the green grass anigh the water, while Walter blew the hounds in and coupled them up; then he turned round to her, and lo! she was weeping for despite that they had lost the quarry; and again did Walter wonder that so little a matter should raise a passion of tears in her. He durst not ask what ailed her, or proffer her solace, but was not ill apaid by beholding her loveliness as she lay.

Presently she raised up her head and turned to Walter, and spake to him angrily and said: "Squire, why dost thou stand staring at me like a fool?"

"Yea, Lady," he said; "but the sight of thee maketh me foolish to do aught else but to look on thee."

She said, in a peevish voice: "Tush, Squire, the day is too far spent for soft and courtly speeches; what was good there is nought so good here. Withal, I know more of thine heart than thou deemest."

Walter hung down his head and reddened, and she looked on him, and her face changed, and she smiled and said, kindly this time: "Look ye, Squire, I am hot and weary, and ill-content; but presently it will be better with me; for my knees have been telling my shoulders that the cold water of this little lake will be sweet and pleasant this summer noonday, and that I shall forget my foil when I have taken my pleasure therein. Wherefore, go thou with thine hounds without the thicket and there abide my coming. And I bid thee look not aback as thou goest, for therein were peril to thee: I shall not keep thee tarrying long alone."

He bowed his head to her, and turned and went his ways. And now, when he was a little space away from her, he deemed her indeed a marvel of women, and wellnigh forgat all his doubts and fears concerning her, whether she were a fair image fashioned out of lies and guile, or it might be but an evil thing in the shape of a goodly woman. Forsooth, when he saw her caressing the dear and friendly Maid, his heart all turned against her, despite what his eyes and his ears told his mind, and she seemed like as it were a serpent enfolding the simplicity of the body which he loved.

But now it was all changed, and he lay on the grass and longed for her coming; which was delayed for somewhat more than an hour. Then she came back to him, smiling and fresh and cheerful, her green gown let down to her heels.

He sprang up to meet her, and she came close to him, and spake from a laughing face: "Squire, hast thou no meat in thy wallet? For, meseemeth, I fed thee when thou wert hungry the other day; do thou now the same by me."

He smiled, and louted to her, and took his wallet and brought out thence bread and flesh and wine, and spread them all out before her on the green grass, and then stood by humbly before her. But she said: "Nay, my Squire, sit down by me and eat with me, for to-day are we both hunters together."

So he sat down by her trembling, but neither for awe of her greatness, nor for fear and horror of her guile and sorcery.

A while they sat there together after they had done their meat, and the Lady fell a-talking with Walter concerning the parts of the earth, and the manners of men, and of his journeyings to and fro.

At last she said: "Thou hast told me much and answered all my questions wisely, and as my good Squire should, and that pleaseth me. But now tell me of the city wherein thou wert born and bred; a city whereof thou hast hitherto told me nought."

"Lady," he said, "it is a fair and a great city, and to many it seemeth lovely. But I have left it, and now it is nothing to me."

"Hast thou not kindred there?" said she.

"Yea," said he, "and foemen withal; and a false woman waylayeth my life there."

"And what was she?" said the Lady.

Said Walter: "She was but my wife."

"Was she fair?" said the Lady.

Walter looked on her a while, and then said: "I was going to say that she was wellnigh as fair as thou; but that may scarce be. Yet was she very fair. But now, kind and gracious Lady, I will say this word to thee: I marvel that thou askest so many things concerning the city of Langton on Holm, where I was born, and where are my kindred yet; for meseemeth that thou knowest it thyself."

"I know it, I?" said the Lady.

"What, then! thou knowest it not?" said Walter.

Spake the Lady, and some of her old disdain was in her words: "Dost thou deem that I wander about the world and its cheaping-steads like one of the chapmen? Nay, I dwell in the Wood beyond the World, and nowhere else. What hath put this word into thy mouth?"

He said: "Pardon me, Lady, if I have misdone; but thus it was: Mine own eyes beheld thee going down the quays of our city, and thence a ship-board, and the ship sailed out of the haven. And first of all went a strange dwarf, whom I have seen here, and then thy Maid; and then went thy gracious and lovely body."

The Lady's face changed as he spoke, and she turned red and then pale, and set her teeth; but she refrained her, and said: "Squire, I see of thee that thou art no liar, nor light of wit, therefore I suppose that thou hast verily seen some appearance of me; but never have I been in Langton, nor thought thereof, nor known that such a stead there was until thou namedst it e'en now. Wherefore, I deem that an enemy hath cast the shadow of me on the air of that land."

"Yea, my Lady," said Walter; "and what enemy mightest thou have to have done this?"

She was slow of answer, but spake at last from a quivering mouth of anger: "Knowest thou not the saw, that a man's foes are they of his own house? If I find out for a truth who hath done this, the said enemy shall have an evil hour with me."

Again she was silent, and she clenched her hands and strained her limbs in the heat of her anger; so that Walter was afraid of her, and all his misgivings came back to his heart again, and he repented that he had told her so much. But in a little while all that trouble and wrath seemed to flow off her, and again was she of good cheer, and kind and sweet to him; and she said: "But in sooth, however it may be, I thank thee, my Squire and friend, for telling me hereof. And surely no wyte do I lay on thee. And, moreover, is it not this vision which hath brought thee hither?"

"So it is, Lady," said he.

"Then have we to thank it," said the Lady, "and thou art welcome to our land."

And therewith she held out her hand to him, and he took it on his knees and kissed it; and then it was as if a red-hot iron had run through his heart, and he felt faint, and bowed down his head. But he held her hand yet, and kissed it many times, and the wrist and the arm, and knew not where he was.

But she drew a little away from him, and arose and said: "Now is the day wearing, and if we are to bear back any venison we must buckle to the work. So arise, Squire, and take the hounds and come with me; for not far off is a little thicket which mostly harbours foison of deer, great and small. Let us come our ways."

CHAPTER XV

The Slaying of the Quarry

So THEY WALKED on quietly thence some half a mile, and ever the Lady would have Walter to walk by her side, and not follow a little behind her, as was meet for a servant to do; and she touched his hand at whiles as she showed him beast and fowl and tree, and the sweetness of her body overcame him, so that for a while he thought of nothing save her.

Now when they were come to the thicket-side, she turned to him and said: "Squire, I am no ill woodman, so that thou mayst trust me that we shall not be brought to shame the second time; and I shall do sagely: so nock an arrow to thy bow, and abide me here, and stir not hence; for I shall enter this thicket without the hounds, and arouse the quarry for thee; and see that thou be brisk and clean-shooting, and then shalt thou have a reward of me."

Therewith she drew up her skirts through her girdle again, took her bent bow in her hand, and drew an arrow out of the quiver, and stepped lightly into the thicket, leaving him longing for the sight of her, as he hearkened to the tread of her feet on the dry leaves, and the rustling of the brake as she thrust through it.

Thus he stood for a few minutes, and then he heard a kind of gibbering cry without words, yet as of a woman, coming from the thicket, and while his heart was yet gathering the thought that something had gone amiss, he glided swiftly, but with little stir, into the brake.

He had gone but a little way ere he saw the Lady standing there in a narrow clearing, her face pale as death, her knees cleaving together, her body swaying and tottering, her hands hanging down, and the bow and arrow fallen to the ground; and ten yards before her a great-headed yellow creature crouching flat to the earth and slowly drawing nigher.

He stopped short; one arrow was already notched to the string, and another hung loose to the lesser fingers of his string-hand. He raised his right hand, and drew and loosed in a twinkling; the shaft flew close to the Lady's side, and straightway all the wood rung with a huge roar, as the yellow lion turned about to bite at the shaft which had sunk deep into him behind the shoulder, as if a bolt out of the heavens had smitten him. But straightway had Walter loosed again, and then, throwing down his bow, he ran forward with his drawn sword gleaming in his hand, while the lion weltered and rolled, but had no might to move forward. Then Walter went up to him warily and thrust him through to the heart, and leapt aback, lest the beast might yet have life in him to smite; but he left his struggling, his huge voice died out, and he lay there moveless before the hunter.

Walter abode a little, facing him, and then turned about to the Lady, and she had fallen down in a heap whereas she stood, and lay there all huddled up and voiceless. So he knelt down by her, and lifted up her head, and bade her arise, for the foe was slain. And after a little she stretched out her limbs, and turned about on the grass, and seemed to sleep, and the colour came into her face again, and it grew soft and a little smiling. Thus she lay awhile, and Walter sat by her watching her, till at last she opened her eyes and sat up, and knew him, and smiling on him said: "What hath befallen, Squire, that I have slept and dreamed?"

He answered nothing, till her memory came back to her, and then she arose, trembling and pale, and said: "Let us leave this wood, for the Enemy is therein."

And she hastened away before him till they came out at the thicket-side whereas the hounds had been left, and they were standing there uneasy and whining; so Walter coupled them, while the Lady stayed not, but went away swiftly homeward, and Walter followed.

At last she stayed her swift feet, and turned round on Walter, and said: "Squire, come hither."

So did he, and she said: "I am weary again; let us sit under this quicken-tree, and rest us."

So they sat down, and she sat looking between her knees a while; and at last she said: "Why didst thou not bring the lion's hide?"

He said: "Lady, I will go back and flay the beast, and bring on the hide."

And he arose therewith, but she caught him by the skirts and drew him down, and said: "Nay, thou shalt not go; abide with me. Sit down again."

He did so, and she said: "Thou shalt not go from me; for I am afraid: I am not used to looking on the face of death."

She grew pale as she spoke, and set a hand to her breast, and sat so a while without speaking. At last she turned to him smiling, and said: "How was it with the aspect of me when I stood before the peril of the Enemy?" And she laid a hand upon his.

"O gracious one," quoth he, "thou wert, as ever, full lovely, but I feared for thee."

She moved not her hand from his, and she said: "Good and true Squire, I said ere I entered the thicket e'en now that I would reward thee if thou slewest the quarry. He is dead, though thou hast left the skin behind upon the carcase. Ask now thy reward, but take time to think what it shall be."

He felt her hand warm upon his, and drew in the sweet odour of her mingled with the woodland scents under the hot sun of the afternoon, and his heart was clouded with manlike desire of her. And it was a near thing but he had spoken, and craved of her the reward of the freedom of her Maid, and that he might depart with her into other lands; but as his mind wavered betwixt this and that, the Lady, who had been eyeing him keenly, drew her hand away from him; and therewith doubt and fear flowed into his mind, and he refrained him of speech.

Then she laughed merrily and said: "The good Squire is shamefaced; he feareth a lady more than a lion. Will it be a reward to thee if I bid thee to kiss my cheek?"

Therewith she leaned her face toward him, and he kissed her well-favouredly, and then sat gazing on her, wondering what should betide to him on the morrow.

Then she arose and said: "Come, Squire, and let us home; be not abashed, there shall be other rewards hereafter."

So they went their ways quietly; and it was nigh sunset against they entered the house again. Walter looked round for the Maid, but beheld her not; and the Lady said to him: "I go to my chamber, and now is thy service over for this day."

Then she nodded to him friendly and went her ways.

CHAPTER XVI

Of the King's Son and the Maid

BUT AS FOR Walter, he went out of the house again, and fared slowly over the woodlawns till he came to another close thicket or brake; he entered from mere wantonness, or that he might be the more apart and hidden, so as to think over his case. There he lay down under the thick boughs, but could not so herd his thoughts that they would dwell steady in looking into what might come to him within the next days; rather visions of those two women and the monster did but float before him, and fear and desire and the hope of life ran to and fro in his mind.

As he lay thus he heard footsteps drawing near, and he looked between the boughs, and though the sun had just set, he could see close by him a man and a woman going slowly, and they hand in hand; at first he deemed it would be the King's Son and the Lady, but presently he saw that it was the King's Son indeed, but that it was the Maid whom he was holding by the hand. And now he saw of him that his eyes were bright with desire, and of her that she was very pale. Yet when he heard her begin to speak, it was in a steady voice that she said:

"King's Son, thou hast threatened me oft and unkindly, and now thou threatenest me again, and no less unkindly. But whatever were thy need herein before, now is there no more need; for my Mistress, of whom thou wert weary, is now grown weary of thee, and belike will not now reward me for drawing thy love to me, as once she would have done; to wit, before the coming of this stranger. Therefore I say, since I am but a thrall, poor and helpless, betwixt you two mighty ones, I have no choice but to do thy will."

As she spoke she looked all round about her, as one distraught by the anguish of fear. Walter, amidst of his wrath and grief, had wellnigh drawn his sword and rushed out of his lair upon the King's Son. But he deemed it sure that, so doing, he should undo the Maid altogether, and himself also belike, so he refrained him, though it were a hard matter.

The Maid had stayed her feet now close to where Walter lay, some five yards from him only, and he doubted whether she saw him not from where she stood. As to the King's Son, he was so intent upon the Maid, and so greedy of her beauty, that it was not like that he saw anything.

Now moreover Walter looked, and deemed that he beheld something through the grass and bracken on the other side of those two, an ugly brown and yellow body, which, if it were not some beast of the foumart kind, must needs be the monstrous dwarf, or one of his kin; and the flesh crept upon Walter's bones with the horror of him, But the King's Son spoke unto the Maid: "Sweetling, I shall take the gift thou givest me, neither shall I threaten thee any more, howbeit thou givest it not very gladly or graciously."

She smiled on him with her lips alone, for her eyes were wandering and haggard. "My lord," she said, "is not this the manner of women?"

"Well," he said, "I say that I will take thy love even so given. Yet let me hear again that thou lovest not that vile newcomer, and that thou hast not seen him, save this morning along with my Lady. Nay now, thou shalt swear it."

"What shall I swear by?" she said.

Quoth he, "Thou shalt swear by my body;" and therewith he thrust himself close up against her; but she drew her hand from his, and laid it on his breast, and said: "I swear it by thy body."

He smiled on her licorously, and took her by the shoulders, and kissed her face many times, and then stood aloof from her, and said: "Now have I had hansel: but tell me, when shall I come to thee?"

She spoke out clearly: "Within three days at furthest; I will do thee to wit of the day and the hour to-morrow, or the day after."

He kissed her once more, and said: "Forget it not, or the threat holds good."

And therewith he turned about and went his ways toward the house; and Walter saw the yellow-brown thing creeping after him in the gathering dusk.

As for the Maid, she stood for a while without moving, and looking after the King's Son and the creature that followed him. Then she turned about to where Walter lay and lightly put aside the boughs, and Walter leapt up, and they stood face to face. She said softly but eagerly: "Friend, touch me not yet!"

He spake not, but looked on her sternly. She said: "Thou art angry with me?"

Still he spake not; but she said: "Friend, this at least I will pray thee; not to play with life and death; with happiness and misery. Dost thou not remember the oath which we swore each to each but a little while ago? And dost thou deem that I have changed in these few days? Is thy mind concerning thee and me the same as it was? If it be not so, now tell me. For now have I the mind to do as if neither thou nor I are changed to each other, whoever may have kissed mine unwilling lips, or whomsoever thy lips may have kissed. But if thou hast changed, and wilt no longer give me thy love, nor crave mine, then shall this steel" (and she drew a sharp knife from her girdle) "be for the fool and the dastard who hath made thee wroth with me, my friend, and my friend that I deemed I had won. And then let come what will come! But if thou be nought changed, and the oath yet holds then, when a little while hath passed, may we thrust all evil and guile and grief behind us, and long joy shall lie before us, and long life, and all honour in death: if only thou wilt do as I bid thee, O my dear, and my friend, and my first friend!"

He looked on her, and his breast heaved up as all the sweetness of her kind love took hold on him, and his face changed, and the tears filled his eyes and ran over, and rained down before her, and he stretched out his hand toward her.

Then she said exceedingly sweetly: "Now indeed I see that it is well with me, yea, and with thee also. A sore pain it is to me, that not even now may I take thine hand, and cast mine arms about thee, and kiss the lips that love me. But so it has to be. My dear, even so I were fain to stand here long before thee, even if we spake no more word to each other; but abiding here is perilous; for there is ever an evil spy upon my doings, who has now as I deem followed the King's Son to the house, but who will return when he has tracked him home thither: so we must sunder. But belike there is yet time for a word or two: first, the rede which I had thought on for our deliverance is now afoot, though I durst not tell thee thereof, nor have time thereto. But this much shall I tell thee, that whereas great is the craft of my Mistress in wizardry, yet I also have some little craft therein, and this, which she hath not, to change the aspect of folk so utterly that they seem other than they verily are; yea, so that one may have the aspect of another. Now the next thing is this: whatsoever my Mistress may bid thee, do her will therein with no more nay-saying than thou deemest may please her. And the next thing: wheresoever thou mayst meet me, speak not to me, make no sign to me, even when I seem to be all alone, till I stoop down and touch the ring on my ankle with my right hand; but if I do so, then stay thee, without fail, till I speak. The last thing I will say to thee, dear friend, ere we both go our ways, this it is. When we are free, and thou knowest all that I have done, I pray thee deem me not evil and wicked, and be not wroth with me for my deed; whereas thou wottest well that I am not in like plight with other women. I have heard tell that when the knight goeth to the war, and hath overcome his foes by the shearing of swords and guileful tricks, and hath come back home to his own folk, they praise him and bless him, and crown him with flowers, and boast of him before God in the minster for his deliverance of friend and folk and city. Why shouldst thou be worse to me than this? Now is all said, my dear and my friend; farewell, farewell!"

Therewith she turned and went her ways toward the house in all speed, but making somewhat of a compass. And when she was gone, Walter knelt down and kissed the place where her feet had been, and arose thereafter, and made his way toward the house, he also, but slowly, and staying oft on his way.

CHAPTER XVII

Of the House and the Pleasance in the Wood

ON THE MORROW morning Walter loitered a while about the house till the morn was grown old, and then about noon he took his bow and arrows and went into the woods to the northward, to get him some venison. He went somewhat far ere he shot him a fawn, and then he sat him down to rest under the shade of a great chestnut-tree, for it was not far past the hottest of the day. He looked around thence and saw below him a little dale with a pleasant stream running through it, and he bethought him of bathing therein, so he went down and had his pleasure of the water and the willowy banks; for he lay naked a while on the grass by the lip of the water, for joy of the flickering shade, and the little breeze that ran over the down-long ripples of the stream.

Then he did on his raiment, and began to come his ways up the bent, but had scarce gone three steps ere he saw a woman coming towards him from down-stream. His heart came into his mouth when he saw her, for she stooped and reached down her arm, as if she would lay her hand on her ankle, so that at first he deemed it had been the Maid, but at the second eye-shot he saw that it was the Mistress. She stood still and looked on him, so that he deemed she would have him come to her. So he went to meet her, and grew somewhat shamefaced as he drew nigher, and wondered at her, for now was she clad but in one garment of some dark grey silky stuff, embroidered with, as it were, a garland of flowers about the middle, but which was so thin that, as the wind drifted it from side and limb, it had her no more, but for the said garland, than if water were running over her: her face was full of smiling joy and content as she spake to him in a kind, caressing voice, and said: "I give thee good day, good Squire, and well art thou met." And she held out her hand to him. He knelt down before her and kissed it, and abode still upon his kness, and hanging down his head.

But she laughed outright, and stooped down to him, and put her hand to his arms, and raised him up, and said to him: "What is this, my Squire, that thou kneelest to me as to an idol?"

He said faltering: "I wot not; but perchance thou art an idol; and I fear thee."

"What!" she said, "more than yesterday, whenas thou sawest me afraid?"

Said he: "Yea, for that now I see thee unhidden, and meseemeth there hath been none such since the old days of the Gentiles."

She said: "Hast thou not yet bethought thee of a gift to crave of me, a reward for the slaying of mine enemy, and the saving of me from death?"

"O my Lady," he said, "even so much would I have done for any other lady, or, forsooth, for any poor man; for so my manhood would have bidden me. Speak not of gifts to me then. Moreover" (and he reddened therewith, and his voice faltered), "didst thou not give me my sweet reward yesterday? What more durst I ask?"

She held her peace a while, and looked on him keenly; and he reddened under her gaze. Then wrath came into her face, and she reddened and knit her brows, and spake to him in a voice of anger, and said: "Nay, what is this? It is growing in my mind that thou deemest the gift of me unworthy! Thou, an alien, an outcast; one endowed with the little wisdom of the World without the Wood! And here I stand before thee, all glorious in my nakedness, and so fulfilled of wisdom, that I can make this wilderness to any whom I love more full of joy than the kingdoms and cities of the world—and thou!—Ah, but it is the Enemy that hath done this, and made the guileless guileful! Yet will I have the upper hand at least, though thou suffer for it, and I suffer for thee."

Walter stood before her with hanging head, and he put forth his hands as if praying off her anger, and pondered what answer he should make; for now he feared for himself and the Maid; so at last he looked up to her, and said boldly: "Nay, Lady, I know what thy words mean, whereas I remember thy first welcome of me. I wot, forsooth, that thou wouldst call me base-born, and of no account, and unworthy to touch the hem of thy raiment; and that I have been over-bold, and guilty towards thee; and doubtless this is sooth, and I have deserved thine anger: but I will not ask thee to pardon me, for I have done but what I must needs."

She looked on him calmly now, and without any wrath, but rather as if she would read what was written in his inmost heart. Then her face changed into joyousness again, and she smote her palms together, and cried out: "This is but foolish talk; for yesterday did I see thy valiancy, and to-day I have seen thy goodliness; and I say, that though thou mightest not be good enough for a fool woman of the earthly baronage, yet art thou good enough for me, the wise and the mighty, and the lovely. And whereas thou sayest that I gave thee but disdain when first thou camest to us, grudge not against me therefor, because it was done but to prove thee; and now thou art proven."

Then again he knelt down before her, and embraced her knees, and again she raised him up, and let her arm hang down over his shoulder, and her cheek brush his cheek; and she kissed his mouth and said: "Hereby is all forgiven, both thine offence and mine; and now cometh joy and merry days."

Therewith her smiling face grew grave, and she stood before him looking stately and gracious and kind at once, and she took his hand and said: "Thou mightest deem my chamber in the Golden House of the Wood over-queenly, since thou art no masterful man. So now hast thou chosen well the place wherein to meet me to-day, for hard by on the other side of the stream is a bower of pleasance, which, forsooth, not every one who cometh to this land may find; there shall I be to thee as one of the up-country damsels of thine own land, and thou shalt not be abashed."

She sidled up to him as she spoke, and would he, would he not, her sweet voice tickled his very soul with pleasure, and she looked aside on him happy and well-content.

So they crossed the stream by the shallow below the pool wherein Walter had bathed, and within a little they came upon a tall fence of flake-hurdles, and a simple gate therein. The Lady opened the same, and they entered thereby into a close all planted as a most fair garden, with hedges of rose and woodbine, and with linden-trees a-blossom, and long ways of green grass betwixt borders of lilies and clove-gilliflowers, and other sweet garland-flowers. And a branch of the stream which they had crossed erewhile wandered through that garden; and in the midst was a little house built of post and pan, and thatched with yellow straw, as if it were new done.

Then Walter looked this way and that, and wondered at first, and tried to think in his mind what should come next, and how matters would go with him; but his thought would not dwell steady on any other matter than the beauty of the Lady amidst the beauty of the garden; and withal she was now grown so sweet and kind, and even somewhat timid and shy with him, that scarce did he know whose hand he held, or whose fragrant bosom and sleek side went so close to him.

So they wandered here and there through the waning of the day, and when they entered at last into the cool dusk house, then they loved and played together, as if they were a pair of lovers guileless, with no fear for the morrow, and no seeds of enmity and death sown betwixt them.

CHAPTER XVIII

The Maid Gives Walter Tryst

NOW, ON THE morrow, when Walter was awake, he found there was no one lying beside him, and the day was no longer very young; so he arose, and went through the garden from end to end, and all about, and there was none there; and albeit that he dreaded to meet the Lady there, yet was he sad at heart and fearful of what might betide. Howsoever, he found the gate whereby they had entered yesterday, and he went out into the little dale; but when he had gone a step or two he turned about, and could see neither garden nor fence, nor any sign of what he had seen thereof but lately. He knit his brow and stood still to think of it, and his heart grew the heavier thereby; but presently he went his ways and crossed the stream, but had scarce come up on to the grass on the further side, ere he saw a woman coming to meet him, and at first, full as he was of the tide of yesterday and the wondrous garden, deemed that it would be the Lady; but the woman stayed her feet, and, stooping, laid a hand on her right ankle, and he saw that it was the Maid. He drew anigh to her, and saw that she was nought so sad of countenance as the last time she had met him, but flushed of cheek and bright-eyed.

As he came up to her she made a step or two to meet him, holding out her two hands, and then refrained her, and said smiling: "Ah, friend, belike this shall be the last time that I shall say to thee, touch me not, nay, not so much as my hand, or if it were but the hem of my raiment."

The joy grew up in his heart, and he gazed on her fondly, and said: "Why, what hath befallen of late?"

"O friend," she began, "this hath befallen."

But as he looked on her, the smile died from her face, and she became deadly pale to the very lips; she looked askance to her left side, whereas ran the stream; and Walter followed her eyes, and deemed for one instant that he saw the misshapen yellow visage of the dwarf peering round from a grey rock, but the next there was nothing. Then the Maid, though she were as pale as death, went on in a clear, steady, hard voice, wherein was no joy or kindness, keeping her face to Walter and her back to the stream: "This hath befallen, friend, that there is no longer any need to refrain thy love nor mine; therefore I say to thee, come to my chamber (and it is the red chamber over against thine, though thou knewest it not) an hour before this next midnight, and then thy sorrow and mine shall be at an end: and now I must needs depart. Follow me not, but remember!"

And therewith she turned about and fled like the wind down the stream.

But Walter stood wondering, and knew not what to make of it, whether it were for good or ill: for he knew now that she had paled and been seized with terror because of the upheaving of the ugly head; and yet she had seemed to speak out the very thing she had to say. Howsoever it were, he spake aloud to himself: Whatever comes, I will keep tryst with her.

Then he drew his sword, and turned this way and that, looking all about if he might see any sign of the Evil Thing; but nought might his eyes behold, save the grass, and the stream, and the bushes of the dale. So then, still holding his naked sword in his hand, he clomb the bent out of the dale; for that was the only way he knew to the Golden House; and when he came to the top, and the summer breeze blew in his face, and he looked down a fair green slope beset with goodly oaks and chestnuts, he was refreshed with the life of the earth, and he felt the good sword in his fist, and knew that there was might and longing in him, and the world seemed open unto him.

So he smiled, if it were somewhat grimly, and sheathed his sword and went on toward the house.

CHAPTER XIX

Walter Goes to Fetch Home the Lion's Hide

HE ENTERED THE cool dusk through the porch, and, looking down the pillared hall, saw beyond the fountain a gleam of gold, and when he came past the said fountain he looked up to the high-seat, and lo! the Lady sitting there clad in her queenly raiment. She called to him, and he came; and she hailed him, and spake graciously and calmly, yet as if she knew nought of him save as the leal servant of her, a high Lady.

"Squire," she said, "we have deemed it meet to have the hide of the servant of the Enemy, the lion to wit, whom thou slewest yesterday, for a carpet to our feet; wherefore go now, take thy wood-knife, and flay the beast, and bring me home his skin. This shall be all thy service for this day, so mayst thou do it at thine own leisure, and not weary thyself. May good go with thee."

He bent the knee before her, and she smiled on him graciously, but reached out no hand for him to kiss, and heeded him but little. Wherefore, in spite of himself, and though he knew somewhat of her guile, he could not help marvelling that this should be she who had lain in his arms night-long but of late.

Howso that might be, he took his way toward the thicket where he had slain the lion, and came thither by then it was afternoon, at the hottest of the day. So he entered therein, and came to the very place whereas the Lady had lain, when she fell down before the terror of the lion; and there was the mark of her body on the grass where she had lain that while, like as it were the form of a hare. But when Walter went on to where he had slain that great beast, lo! he was gone, and there was no sign of him; but there were Walter's own foot-prints, and the two shafts which he had shot, one feathered red, and one blue. He said at first: Belike someone hath been here, and hath had the carcase away. Then he laughed in very despite, and said: How may that be, since there are no signs of dragging away of so huge a body, and no blood or fur on the grass if they had cut him up, and moreover no trampling of feet, as if there had been many men at the deed. Then was he all abashed, and again laughed in scorn of himself, and said: Forsooth I deemed I had done manly; but now forsooth I shot nought, and nought there was before the sword of my father's son. And what may I deem now, but that this is a land of mere lies, and that there is nought real and alive therein save me. Yea, belike even these trees and the green grass will presently depart from me, and leave me falling down through the clouds.

Therewith he turned away, and gat him to the road that led to the Golden House, wondering what next should befall him, and going slowly as he pondered his case. So came he to that first thicket where they had lost their quarry by water; so he entered the same, musing, and bathed him in the pool that was therein, after he had wandered about it awhile, and found nothing new.

So again he set him to the homeward road, when the day was now waning, and it was near sunset that he was come nigh unto the house, though it was hidden from him as then by a low bent that rose before him; and there he abode and looked about him.

Now as he looked, over the said bent came the figure of a woman, who stayed on the brow thereof and looked all about her, and then ran swiftly down to meet Walter, who saw at once that it was the Maid.

She made no stay then till she was but three paces from him, and then she stooped down and made the sign to him, and then spake to him breathlessly, and said: "Hearken! but speak not till I have done: I bade thee to-night's meeting because I saw that there was one anigh whom I must needs beguile. But by thine oath, and thy love, and all that thou art, I adjure thee come not unto me this night as I bade thee! but be hidden in the hazel-copse outside the house, as it draws toward midnight, and abide me there. Dost thou hearken, and wilt thou? Say yes or no in haste, for I may not tarry a moment of time. Who knoweth what is behind me?"

"Yes," said Walter hastily; "but friend and love—"

"No more," she said; "hope the best;" and turning from him she ran away swiftly, not by the way she had come, but sideways, as though to reach the house by fetching a compass.

But Walter went slowly on his way, thinking within himself that now at that present moment there was nought for it but to refrain him from doing, and to let others do; yet deemed he that it was little manly to be as the pawn upon the board, pushed about by the will of others.

Then, as he went, he bethought him of the Maiden's face and aspect, as she came running to him, and stood before him for that minute; and all eagerness he saw in her, and sore love of him, and distress of soul, all blent together.

So came he to the brow of the bent whence he could see lying before him, scarce more than a bow-shot away, the Golden House, now gilded again and reddened by the setting sun. And even therewith came a gay image toward him, flashing back the level rays from gold and steel and silver; and lo! there was come the King's Son. They met presently, and the King's Son turned to go beside him, and said merrily: "I give thee good even, my Lady's Squire! I owe thee something of courtesy, whereas it is by thy means that I shall be made happy, both to-night, and to-morrow, and many to-morrows; and sooth it is, that but little courtesy have I done thee hitherto."

His face was full of joy, and the eyes of him shone with gladness. He was a goodly man, but to Walter he seemed an ill one; and he hated him so much, that he found it no easy matter to answer him; but he refrained himself, and said: "I can thee thank, King's Son; and good it is that someone is happy in this strange land."

"Art thou not happy then, Squire of my Lady?" said the other.

Walter had no mind to show this man his heart, nay, nor even a corner thereof; for he deemed him any enemy. So he smiled sweetly and somewhat foolishly, as a man luckily in love, and said: "O yea, yea, why should I not be so? How might I be otherwise?"

"Yea then," said the King's Son, "why didst thou say that thou wert glad someone is happy? Who is unhappy, deemest thou?" and he looked on him keenly.

Walter answered slowly: "Said I so? I suppose then that I was thinking of thee; for when first I saw thee, yea, and afterwards, thou didst seem heavy-hearted and ill-content."

The face of the King's Son cleared at this word, and he said: "Yea, so it was; for look you, both ways it was: I was unfree, and I had sown the true desire of my heart whereas it waxed not. But now I am on the brink and verge of freedom, and presently shall my desire be blossomed. Nay now, Squire, I deem thee a good fellow, though it may be somewhat of a fool; so I will no more speak riddles to thee. Thus it is: the Maid hath promised me all mine asking, and is mine; and in two or three days, by her helping also, I shall see the world again."

Quoth Walter, smiling askance on him: "And the Lady? what shall she say to this matter?"

The King's Son reddened, but smiled falsely enough, and said: "Sir Squire, thou knowest enough not to need to ask this. Why should I tell thee that she accounteth more of thy little finger than of my whole body? Now I tell thee hereof freely; first, because this my fruition of love, and my freeing from thralldom, is, in a way, of thy doing. For thou art become my supplanter, and hast taken thy place with yonder lovely tyrant. Fear not for me! she will let me go. As for thyself, see thou to it! But again I tell thee hereof because my heart is light and full of joy, and telling thee will pleasure me, and cannot do me any harm. For if thou say: How if I carry the tale to my Lady? I answer, thou wilt not. For I know that thine heart hath been somewhat set on the jewel that my hand holdeth; and thou knowest well on whose head the Lady's wrath would fall, and that would be neither thine nor mine."

"Thou sayest sooth," said Walter; "neither is treason my wont."

So they walked on silently a while, and then Walter said: "But how if the Maiden had nay-said thee; what hadst thou done then?"

"By the heavens!" said the King's Son fiercely, "she should have paid for her nay-say; then would I—" But he broke off, and said quietly, yet somewhat doggedly: "Why talk of what might have been? She gave me her yea-say pleasantly and sweetly."

Now Walter knew that the man lied, so he held his peace thereon; but presently he said: "When thou art free wilt thou go to thine own land again?"

"Yea," said the King's Son; "she will lead me thither."

"And wilt thou make her thy lady and queen when thou comest to thy father's land?" said Walter.

The King's Son knit his brow, and said: "When I am in mine own land I may do with her what I will; but I look for it that I shall do no otherwise with her than that she shall be well-content."

Then the talk between them dropped, and the King's Son turned off toward the wood, singing and joyous; but Walter went soberly toward the house. Forsooth he was not greatly cast down, for besides that he knew that the King's Son was false, he deemed that under this double tryst lay something which was a-doing in his own behalf. Yet was he eager and troubled, if not down-hearted, and his soul was cast about betwixt hope and fear.

CHAPTER XX

Walter Is Bidden to Another Tryst

So CAME HE into the pillared hall, and there he found the Lady walking to and fro by the high-seat; and when he drew nigh she turned on him, and said in a voice rather eager than angry: "What hast thou done, Squire? Why art thou come before me?"

He was abashed, and bowed before her and said: "O gracious Lady, thou badest me service, and I have been about it."

She said: "Tell me then, tell me, what hath betided?"

"Lady," said he, "when I entered the thicket of thy swooning I found there no carcase of the lion, nor any sign of the dragging away of him."

She looked full in his face for a little, and then went to her chair, and sat down therein; and in a little while spake to him in a softer voice, and said: "Did I not tell thee that some enemy had done that unto me? and lo! now thou seest that so it is."

Then was she silent again, and knit her brows and set her teeth; and thereafter she spake harshly and fiercely: "But I will overcome her, and make her days evil, but keep death away from her, that she may die many times over; and know all the sickness of the heart, when foes be nigh, and friends afar, and there is none to deliver!"

Her eyes flashed, and her face was dark with anger; but she turned and caught Walter's eyes, and the sternness of his face, and she softened at once, and said: "But thou! this hath little to do with thee; and now to thee I speak: Now cometh even and night. Go thou to thy chamber, and there shalt thou find raiment worthy of thee, what thou now art, and what thou shalt be; do on the same, and make thyself most goodly, and then come thou hither and eat and drink with me, and afterwards depart whither thou wilt, till the night has worn to its midmost; and then come thou to my chamber, to wit, through the ivory door in the gallery above; and then and there shall I tell thee a thing, and it shall be for the weal both of thee and of me, but for the grief and woe of the Enemy."

Therewith she reached her hand to him, and he kissed it, and departed and came to his chamber, and found raiment therebefore rich beyond measure; and he wondered if any new snare lay therein: yet if there were, he saw no way whereby he might escape it, so he did it on, and became as the most glorious of kings, and yet lovelier than any king of the world.

Sithence he went his way into the pillared hall, when it was now night, and without the moon was up, and the trees of the wood as still as images. But within the hall shone bright with many candles, and the fountain glittered in the light of them, as it ran tinkling sweetly into the little stream; and the silvern bridges gleamed, and the pillars shone all round about.

And there on the dais was a table dight most royally, and the Lady sitting thereat, clad in her most glorious array, and behind her the Maid standing humbly, yet clad in precious web of shimmering gold, but with feet unshod, and the iron ring upon her ankle.

So Walter came his ways to the high-seat, and the Lady rose and greeted him, and took him by the hands, and kissed him on either cheek, and sat him down beside her. So they fell to their meat, and the Maid served them; but the Lady took no more heed of her than if she were one of the pillars of the hall; but Walter she caressed oft with sweet words, and the touch of her hand, making him drink out of her cup and eat out of her dish. As to him, he was bashful by seeming, but verily fearful; he took the Lady's caresses with what grace he might, and durst not so much as glance at her Maid. Long indeed seemed that banquet to him, and longer yet endured the weariness of his abiding there, kind to his foe and unkind to his friend; for after the banquet they still sat a while, and the Lady talked much to Walter about many things of the ways of the world, and he answered what he might, distraught as he was with the thought of those two trysts which he had to deal with.

At last spake the Lady and said: "Now must I leave thee for a little, and thou wottest where and how we shall meet next; and meanwhile disport thee as thou wilt, so that thou weary not thyself, for I love to see thee joyous."

Then she arose stately and grand; but she kissed Walter on the mouth ere she turned to go out of the hall. The Maid followed her; but or ever she was quite gone, she stooped and made that sign, and looked over her shoulder at Walter, as if in entreaty to him, and there was fear and anguish in her face; but he nodded his head to her in yea-say of the tryst in the hazel-copse, and in a trice she was gone.

Walter went down the hall, and forth into the early night; but in the jaws of the porch he came up against the King's Son, who, gazing at his attire glittering with all its gems in the moonlight, laughed out, and said: "Now may it be seen how thou art risen in degree above me, whereas I am but a king's son, and that a king of a far country; whereas thou art a king of kings, or shalt be this night, yea, and of this very country wherein we both are."

Now Walter saw the mock which lay under his words; but he kept back his wrath, and answered: "Fair sir, art thou as well contented with thy lot as when the sun went down? Hast thou no doubt or fear? Will the Maid verily keep tryst with thee, or hath she given thee yea-say but to escape thee this time? Or, again, may she not turn to the Lady and appeal to her against thee?"

Now when he had spoken these words, he repented thereof, and feared for himself and the Maid, lest he had stirred some misgiving in that young man's foolish heart. But the King's Son did but laugh, and answered nought but to Walter's last words, and said: "Yea, yea! this word of thine showeth how little thou wottest of that which lieth betwixt my darling and thine. Doth the lamb appeal from the shepherd to the wolf? Even so shall the Maid appeal from me to thy Lady. What! ask thy Lady at thy leisure what her wont hath been with her thrall; she shall think it a fair tale to tell thee thereof. But thereof is my Maid all whole now by reason of her wisdom in leechcraft, or somewhat more. And now I tell thee again, that the beforesaid Maid must needs do my will; for if I be the deep sea, and I deem not so ill of myself, that other one is the devil; as belike thou shalt find out for thyself later on. Yea, all is well with me, and more than well."

And therewith he swung merrily into the litten hall. But Walter went out into the moonlit night, and wandered about for an hour or more, and stole warily into the hall and thence into his own chamber. There he did off that royal array, and did his own raiment upon him; he girt him with sword and knife, took his bow and quiver, and stole down and out again, even as he had come in. Then he fetched a compass, and came down into the hazel-coppice from the north, and lay hidden there while the night wore, till he deemed it would lack but little of midnight.

CHAPTER XXI

Walter and the Maid Flee from the Golden House

THERE HE ABODE amidst the hazels, hearkening every littlest sound; and the sounds were nought but the night voices of the wood, till suddenly there burst forth from the house a great wailing cry. Walter's heart came up into his mouth, but he had no time to do aught, for following hard on the cry came the sound of light feet close to him, the boughs were thrust aside, and there was come the Maid, and she but in her white coat, and barefoot. And then first he felt the sweetness of her flesh on his, for she caught him by the hand and said breathlessly: "Now, now! there may yet be time, or even too much, it may be. For the saving of breath ask me no questions, but come!"

He dallied not, but went as she led, and they were light-foot, both of them.

They went the same way, due south to wit, whereby he had gone a-hunting with the Lady; and whiles they ran and whiles they walked; but so fast they went, that by grey of the dawn they were come as far as that coppice or thicket of the Lion; and still they hastened onward, and but little had the Maid spoken, save here and there a word to hearten up Walter, and here and there a shy word of endearment. At last the dawn grew into early day, and as they came over the brow of a bent, they looked down over a plain-land whereas the trees grew scatter-meal, and beyond the plain rose up the land into long green hills, and over those again were blue mountains great and far away.

Then spake the Maid: "Over yonder lie the outlying mountains of the Bears, and through them we needs must pass, to our great peril. Nay, friend," she said, as he handled his sword-hilt, "it must be patience and wisdom to bring us through, and not the fallow blade of one man, though he be a good one. But look! below there runs a stream through the first of the plain, and I see nought for it but we must now rest our bodies. Moreover I have a tale to tell thee which is burning my heart; for maybe there will be a pardon to ask of thee moreover; wherefore I fear thee."

Quoth Walter: "How may that be?"

She answered him not, but took his hand and led him down the bent. But he said: "Thou sayest, rest; but are we now out of all peril of the chase?"

She said: "I cannot tell till I know what hath befallen her. If she be not to hand to set on her trackers, they will scarce happen on us now; if it be not for that one."

And she shuddered, and he felt her hand change as he held it.

Then she said: "But peril or no peril, needs must we rest; for I tell thee again, what I have to say to thee burneth my bosom for fear of thee, so that I can go no further until I have told thee."

Then he said: "I wot not of this Queen and her mightiness and her servants. I will ask thereof later. But besides the others, is there not the King's Son, he who loves thee so unworthily?"

She paled somewhat, and said: "As for him, there had been nought for thee to fear in him, save his treason: but now shall he neither love nor hate any more; he died last midnight."

"Yea, and how?" said Walter.

"Nay," she said, "let me tell my tale all together once for all, lest thou blame me overmuch. But first we will wash us and comfort us as best we may, and then amidst our resting shall the word be said."

By then were they come down to the stream-side, which ran fair in pools and stickles amidst rocks and sandy banks. She said: "There behind the great grey rock is my bath, friend; and here is thine; and lo! the uprising of the sun!"

So she went her ways to the said rock, and he bathed him, and washed the night off him, and by then he was clad again she came back fresh and sweet from the water, and with her lap full of cherries from a wilding which overhung her bath. So they sat down together on the green grass above the sand, and ate the breakfast of the wilderness: and Walter was full of content as he watched her, and beheld her sweetness and her loveliness; yet were they, either of them, somewhat shy and shamefaced each with the other; so that he did but kiss her hands once and again, and though she shrank not from him, yet had she no boldness to cast herself into his arms.

CHAPTER XXII

Of the Dwarf and the Pardon

NOW SHE BEGAN to say: "My friend, now shall I tell thee what I have done for thee and me; and if thou have a mind to blame me, and punish me, yet remember first, that what I have done has been for thee and our hope of happy life. Well, I shall tell thee—"

But therewithal her speech failed her; and, springing up, she faced the bent and pointed with her finger, and she all deadly pale, and shaking so that she might scarce stand, and might speak no word, though a feeble gibbering came from her mouth.

Walter leapt up and put his arm about her, and looked whitherward she pointed, and at first saw nought; and then nought but a brown and yellow rock rolling down the bent: and then at last he saw that it was the Evil Thing which had met him when first he came into that land; and now it stood upright, and he could see that it was clad in a coat of yellow samite.

Then Walter stooped down and gat his bow into his hand, and stood before the Maid, while he nocked an arrow. But the monster made ready his tackle while Walter was stooping down, and or ever he could loose, his bow-string twanged, and an arrow flew forth and grazed the Maid's arm above the elbow, so that the blood ran, and the Dwarf gave forth a harsh and horrible cry. Then flew Walter's shaft, and true was it aimed, so that it smote the monster full on the breast, but fell down from him as if he were made of stone. Then the creature set up his horrible cry again, and loosed withal, and Walter deemed that he had smitten the Maid, for she fell down in a heap behind him. Then waxed Walter wood-wroth, and cast down his bow and drew his sword, and strode forward towards the bent against the Dwarf. But he roared out again, and there were words in his roar, and he said: "Fool! thou shalt go free if thou wilt give up the Enemy?"

"And who," said Walter, "is the Enemy?"

Yelled the Dwarf: "She, the pink and white thing lying there; she is not dead yet; she is but dying for fear of me. Yea, she hath reason! I could have set the shaft in her heart as easily as scratching her arm; but I need her body alive, that I may wreak me on her."

"What wilt thou do with her?" said Walter; for now he had heard that the Maid was not slain he had waxed wary again, and stood watching his chance.

The Dwarf yelled so at his last word, that no word came from the noise a while, and then he said: "What will I with her? Let me at her, and stand by and look on, and then shalt thou have a strange tale to carry off with thee. For I will let thee go this while."

Said Walter: "But what need to wreak thee? What hath she done to thee?"

"What need! what need!" roared the Dwarf; "have I not told thee that she is the Enemy? And thou askest of what she hath done! of what! Fool, she is the murderer! she hath slain the Lady that was our Lady, and that made us; she whom all we worshipped and adored. O impudent fool!"

Therewith he nocked and loosed another arrow, which would have smitted Walter in the face, but that he lowered his head in the very nick of time; then with a great shout he rushed up the bent, and was on the Dwarf before he could get his sword out, and leaping aloft dealt the creature a stroke amidmost of the crown; and so mightily he smote, that he drave the heavy sword right through to the teeth, so that he fell dead straightway.

Walter stood over him a minute, and when he saw that he moved not, he went slowly down to the stream, whereby the Maid yet lay cowering down and quivering all over, and covering her face with her hands. Then he took her by the wrist and said: "Up, Maiden, up! and tell me this tale of the slaying!"

But she shrunk away from him, and looked at him with wild eyes, and said: "What hast thou done with him? Is he gone?"

"He is dead," said Walter; "I have slain him; there lies he with cloven skull on the bent-side: unless, forsooth, he vanish away like the lion I slew! or else, perchance, he will come to life again! And art thou a lie like to the rest of them? let me hear of this slaying."

She rose up, and stood before him trembling, and said: "O, thou art angry with me, and thine anger I cannot bear. Ah, what have I done? Thou hast slain one, and I, maybe, the other; and never had we escaped till both these twain were dead. Ah! thou dost not know! thou dost not know! O me! what shall I do to appease thy wrath!"

He looked on her, and his heart rose to his mouth at the thought of sundering from her. Still he looked on her, and her piteous friendly face melted all his heart; he threw down his sword, and took her by the shoulders, and kissed her face over and over, and strained her to him, so that he felt the sweetness of her bosom. Then he lifted her up like a child, and set her down on the green grass, and went down to the water, and filled his hat therefrom, and came back to her; then he gave her to drink, and bathed her face and her hands, so that the colour came aback to the cheeks and lips of her: and she smiled on him and kissed his hands, and said: "O now thou art kind to me."

"Yea," said he, "and true it is that if thou hast slain, I have done no less, and if thou hast lied, even so have I; and if thou hast played the wanton, as I deem not that thou hast, I full surely have so done. So now thou shalt pardon me, and when thy spirit has come back to thee, thou shalt tell me thy tale in all friendship, and in all loving-kindness will I hearken the same.

Therewith he knelt before her and kissed her feet. But she said: "Yea, yea; what thou willest, that will I do. But first tell me one thing. Hast thou buried this horror and hidden him in the earth?"

He deemed that fear had bewildered her, and that she scarcely yet knew how things had gone. But he said: "Fair sweet friend, I have not done it as yet; but now will I go and do it, if it seem good to thee."

"Yea," she said, "but first must thou smite off his head, and lie it by his buttocks when he is in the earth; or evil things will happen else. This of the burying is no idle matter, I bid thee believe."

"I doubt it not," said he; "surely such malice as was in this one will be hard to slay." And he picked up his sword, and turned to go to the field of deed.

She said: "I must needs go with thee; terror hath so filled my soul, that I durst not abide here without thee."

So they went both together to where the creature lay. The Maid durst not look on the dead monster, but Walter noted that he was girt with a big ungainly sax; so he drew it from the sheath, and there smote off the hideous head of the fiend with his own weapon. Then they twain together laboured the earth, she with Walter's sword, he with the ugly sax, till they had made a grave deep and wide enough; and therein they thrust the creature, and covered him up, weapons and all together.

CHAPTER XXIII

Of the Peaceful Ending of That Wild Day

THEREAFTER WALTER LED the Maid down again, and said to her: "Now, sweetling, shall the story be told."

"Nay, friend," she said, "not here. This place hath been polluted by my craven fear, and the horror of the vile wretch, of whom no words may tell his vileness. Let us hence and onward. Thou seest I have once more come to life again."

"But," said he, "thou hast been hurt by the Dwarf's arrow."

She laughed, and said: "Had I never had greater hurt from them than that, little had been the tale thereof: yet whereas thou lookest dolorous about it, we will speedily heal it."

Therewith she sought about, and found nigh the streamside certain herbs; and she spake words over them, and bade Walter lay them on the wound, which, forsooth, was of the least, and he did so, and bound a strip of his shirt about her arm; and then would she set forth. But he said: "Thou art all unshod; and but if that be seen to, our journey shall be stayed by thy foot-soreness: I may make a shift to fashion thee brogues."

She said: "I may well go barefoot. And in any case, I entreat thee that we tarry here no longer, but go away hence, if it be but for a mile."

And she looked piteously on him, so that he might not gainsay her.

So then they crossed the stream, and set forward, when amidst all these haps the day was worn to mid-morning. But after they had gone a mile, they sat them down on a knoll under the shadow of a big thorn-tree, within sight of the mountains. Then said Walter: "Now will I cut thee the brogues from the skirt of my buff-coat, which shall be well meet for such work; and meanwhile shalt thou tell me thy tale."

"Thou art kind," she said; "but be kinder yet, and abide my tale till we have done our day's work. For we were best to make no long delay here; because, though thou hast slain the King-dwarf, yet there be others of his kindred, who swarm in some parts of the wood as the rabbits in a warren. Now true it is that they have but little understanding, less, it may be, than the very brute beasts; and that, as I said afore, unless they be set on our slot like to hounds, they shall have no inkling of where to seek us, yet might they happen upon us by mere misadventure. And moreover, friend," quoth she, blushing, "I would beg of thee some little respite; for though I scarce fear thy wrath any more, since thou hast been so kind to me, yet is there shame in that which I have to tell thee. Wherefore, since the fairest of the day is before us, let us use it all we may, and, when thou hast done me my new foot-gear, get us gone forward again."

He kissed her kindly and yea-said her asking: he had already fallen to work on the leather, and in a while had fashioned her the brogues; so she tied them to her feet, and arose with a smile and said: "Now am I hale and strong again, what with the rest, and what with thy loving kindness, and thou shalt see how nimble I shall be to leave this land, for as fair as it is. Since forsooth a land of lies it is, and of grief to the children of Adam."

So they went their ways thence, and fared nimbly indeed, and made no stay till some three hours after noon, when they rested by a thicket-side, where the strawberries grew plenty; they ate thereof what they would: and from a great oak hard by Walter shot him first one culver, and then another, and hung them to his girdle to be for their evening's meat; sithence they went forward again, and nought befell them to tell of, till they were come, whenas it lacked scarce an hour of sunset, to the banks of another river, not right great, but bigger than the last one. There the Maid cast herself down and said: "Friend, no further will thy friend go this even; nay, to say sooth, she cannot. So now we will eat of thy venison, and then shall my tale be, since I no longer delay it; and thereafter shall our slumber be sweet and safe as I deem."

She spake merrily now, and as one who feared nothing, and Walter was much heartened by her words and her voice, and he fell to and made a fire, and a woodland oven in the earth, and sithence dighted his fowl, and baked them after the manner of woodmen. And they ate, both of them, in all love, and in good-liking of life, and were much strengthened by their supper. And when they were done, Walter eked his fire, both against the chill of the midnight and dawning, and for a guard against wild beasts, and by that time night was come, and the moon arisen. Then the Maiden drew up to the fire, and turned to Walter and spake.

CHAPTER XXIV

The Maid Tells of What Had Befallen Her

Now, FRIEND, BY the clear of the moon and this fire-light will I tell what I may and can of my tale. Thus it is: If I be wholly of the race of Adam I wot not; nor can I tell thee how many years old I may be. For there are, as it were, shards or gaps in my life, wherein are but a few things dimly remembered, and doubtless many things forgotten. I remember well when I was a little child, and right happy, and there were people about me whom I loved, and who loved me. It was not in this land; but all things were lovely there; the year's beginning, the happy mid-year, the year's waning, the year's ending, and then again its beginning. That passed away, and then for a while is more than dimness, for nought I remember save that I was. Thereafter I remember again, and am a young maiden, and I know some things, and long to know more. I am nowise happy; I am amongst people who bid me go, and I go; and do this, and I do it: none loveth me, none tormenteth me; but I wear my heart in longing for I scarce know what. Neither then am I in this land, but in a land that I love not, and a house that is big and stately, but nought lovely. Then is a dim time again, and sithence a time not right clear; an evil time, wherein I am older, well-nigh grown to womanhood. There are a many folk about me, and they foul, and greedy, and hard; and my spirit is fierce, but my body feeble; and I am set to tasks that I would not do, by them that are unwiser than I; and smitten I am by them that are less valiant than I; and I know lack, and stripes, and divers misery. But all that is now become but a dim picture to me, save that amongst all these unfriends is a friend to me; an old woman, who telleth me sweet tales of other life, wherein all is high and goodly, or at the least valiant and doughty, and she setteth hope in my heart and learneth me, and maketh me to know much . . . O much . . . so that at last I am grown wise, and wise to be mighty if I durst. Yet am I nought in this land all this while, but, as meseemeth, in a great and a foul city.

"And then, as it were, I fall asleep; and in my sleep is nought, save here and there a wild dream, somedeal lovely, somedeal hideous: but of this dream is my Mistress a part, and the monster, withal, whose head thou didst cleave to-day. But when I am awaken from it, then am I verily in this land, and myself, as thou seest me to-day. And the first part of my life here is this, that I am in the pillared hall yonder, half-clad and with bound hands; and the Dwarf leadeth me to the Lady, and I hear his horrible croak as he sayeth: 'Lady, will this one do?' and then the sweet voice of the Lady saying: 'This one will do; thou shalt have thy reward: now, set thou the token upon her.' Then I remember the Dwarf dragging me away, and my heart sinking for fear of him; but for that time he did me no more harm than the rivetting upon my leg this iron ring here thou seest.

"So from that time forward I have lived in this land, and been the thrall of the Lady; and I remember my life here day by day, and no part of it has fallen into the dimness of dreams. Thereof will I tell thee but little: but this I will tell thee, that in spite of my past dreams, or it may be because of them, I had not lost the wisdom which the old woman had erst learned me, and for more wisdom I longed. Maybe this longing shall now make both thee and me happy, but for the passing time it brought me grief. For at first my Mistress was indeed wayward with me, but as any great lady might be with her bought thrall, whiles caressing me, and whiles chastising me, as her mood went; but she seemed not to be cruel of malice, or with any set purpose. But so it was (rather little by little than by any great sudden uncovering of my intent), that she came to know that I also had some of the wisdom whereby she lived her queenly life. That was about two years after I was first her thrall, and three weary years have gone by since she began to see in me the enemy of her days. Now why or wherefore I know not, but it seemeth that it would not avail her to slay me outright, or suffer me to die; but nought withheld her from piling up griefs and miseries on my head. At last she set her servant, the Dwarf, upon me, even he whose head thou clavest to-day. Many things I bore from him whereof it were unseemly for my tongue to tell before thee; but the time came when he exceeded, and I could bear no more; and then I showed him this sharp knife (where-with I would have thrust me through to the heart if thou hadst not pardoned me e'en now), and I told him that if he forbore me not, I would slay, not him, but myself; and this he might not away with because of the commandment of the Lady, who had given him the word that in any case I must be kept living. And her hand, withal, fear held somewhat hereafter. Yet was there need to me of all my wisdom; for with all this her hatred grew, and whiles raged within her so furiously that it overmastered her fear, and at such times she would have put me to death if I had not escaped her by some turn of my lore.

"Now further, I shall tell thee that somewhat more than a year ago hither to this land came the King's Son, the second goodly man, as thou art the third, whom her sorceries have drawn hither since I have dwelt here. Forsooth, when he first came, he seemed to us, to me, and yet more to my Lady, to be as beautiful as an angel, and sorely she loved him; and he her, after his fashion: but he was light-minded, and cold-hearted, and in a while he must needs turn his eyes upon me, and offer me his love, which was but foul and unkind as it turned out; for when I nay-said him, as maybe I had not done save for fear of my Mistress, he had no pity upon me, but spared not to lead me into the trap of her wrath, and leave me without help, or a good word. But, O friend, in spite of all grief and anguish, I learned still, and waxed wise, and wiser, abiding the day of my deliverance, which has come, and thou art come."

Therewith she took Walter's hands and kissed them; but he kissed her face, and her tears wet her lips. Then she went on: "But sithence, months ago, the Lady began to weary of this dastard, despite of his beauty; and then it was thy turn to be swept into her net; I partly guess how. For on a day in broad daylight, as I was serving my Mistress in the hall, and the Evil Thing, whose head is now cloven, was lying across the threshold of the door, as it were a dream fell upon me, though I strove to cast it off for fear of chastisement; for the pillared hall wavered, and vanished from my sight, and my feet were treading a rough stone pavement instead of the marble wonder of the hall, and there was the scent of the salt sea and of the tackle of ships, and behind me were tall houses, and before me the ships indeed, with their ropes beating and their sails flapping and their masts wavering; and in mine ears was the hale and how of mariners; things that I had seen and heard in the dimness of my life gone by.

"And there was I, and the Dwarf before me, and the Lady after me, going over the gangway aboard of a tall ship, and she gathered way and was gotten out of the haven, and straightway I saw the mariners cast abroad their ancient."

Quoth Walter: "What then! Sawest thou the blazon thereon, of a wolf-like beast ramping up against a maiden? And that might well have been thou."

She said: "Yea, so it was; but refrain thee, that I may tell on my tale! The ship and the sea vanished away, but I was not back in the hall of the Golden House; and again were we three in the street of the self-same town which we had but just left; but somewhat dim was my vision thereof, and I saw little save the door of a goodly house before me, and speedily it died out, and we were again in the pillared hall, wherein my thralldom was made manifest."

"Maiden," said Walter, "one question I would ask thee; to wit, didst thou see me on the quay by the ships?"

"Nay," she said, "there were many folk about, but they were all as images of the aliens to me. Now hearken further: three months thereafter came the dream upon me again, when we were all three together in the Pillared Hall; and again was the vision somewhat dim. Once more we were in the street of a busy town, but all unlike to that other one, and there were men standing together on our right hands by the door of a house.

"Yea, yea," quoth Walter; "and, forsooth, one of them was who but I."

"Refrain thee, beloved!" she said; "for my tale draweth to its ending, and I would have thee hearken heedfully: for maybe thou shalt once again deem my deed past pardon. Some twenty days after this last dream, I had some leisure from my Mistress's service, so I went to disport me by the Well of the Oak-tree (or forsooth she might have set in my mind the thought of going there, that I might meet thee and give her some occasion against me); and I sat thereby, nowise loving the earth, but sick at heart, because of the late King's Son had been more than ever instant with me to yield him my body, threatening me else with casting me into all that the worst could do to me of torments and shames day by day. I say my heart failed me, and I was wellnigh brought to the point of yea-saying his desires, that I might take the chance of something befalling me that were less bad than the worst. But here must I tell thee a thing, and pray thee to take it to heart. This, more than aught else, had given me strength to nay-say that dastard, that my wisdom both hath been, and now is, the wisdom of a wise maid, and not of a woman, and all the might thereof shall I lose with my maidenhead. Evil wilt thou think of me then, for all I was tried so sore, that I was at point to cast it all away, so wretchedly as I shrank from the horror of the Lady's wrath.

"But there as I sat pondering these things, I saw a man coming, and thought no otherwise thereof but that it was the King's Son, till I saw the stranger drawing near, and his golden hair, and his grey eyes; and then I heard his voice, and his kindness pierced my heart, and I knew that my friend had come to see me; and O, friend, these tears are for the sweetness of that past hour!"

Said Walter: "I came to see my friend, I also. Now have I noted what thou badest me; and I will forbear all as thou commandest me, till we be safe out of the desert and far away from all evil things; but wilt thou ban me from all caresses?"

She laughed amidst of her tears, and said: "O, nay, poor lad, if thou wilt be but wise."

Then she leaned toward him, and took his face betwixt her hands and kissed him oft, and the tears started in his eyes for love and pity of her.

Then she said: "Alas, friend! even yet mayst thou doom me guilty, and all thy love may turn away from me, when I have told thee all that I have done for the sake of thee and me. O, if then there might be some chastisement for the guilty woman, and not mere sundering!"

"Fear nothing, sweetling," said he; "for indeed I deem that already I know partly what thou hast done."

She sighed, and said: "I will tell thee next, that I banned thy kissing and caressing of me till to-day because I knew that my Mistress would surely know if a man, if thou, hadst so much as touched a finger of mine in love. It was to try me herein that on the morning of the hunting she kissed and embraced me, till I almost died thereof, and showed thee my shoulder and my limbs; and to try thee withal, if thine eye should glister or thy cheek flush thereat; for indeed she was raging in jealousy of thee. Next, my friend, even whiles we were talking together at the Well of the Rock, I was pondering on what we should do to escape from this land of lies. Maybe thou wilt say: Why didst thou not take my hand and flee with me as we fled to-day? Friend, it is most true, that were she not dead we had not escaped thus far. For her trackers would have followed us, set on by her, and brought us back to an evil fate. Therefore I tell thee that from the first I did plot the death of those two, the Dwarf and the Mistress. For no otherwise mightest thou live, or I escape from death in life. But as to the dastard who threatened me with a thrall's pains, I heeded him nought to live or die, for well I knew that thy valiant sword, yea, or thy bare hands, would speedily tame him. Now first I knew that I must make a show of yielding to the King's Son; and somewhat how I did therein, thou knowest. But no night and no time did I give him to bed me, till after I had met thee as thou wentest to the Golden House, before the adventure of fetching the lion's skin; and up to that time I had scarce known what to do, save ever to bid thee, with sore grief and pain, to yield thee to the wicked woman's desire. But as we spake together there by the stream, and I saw that the Evil Thing (whose head thou clavest e'en now) was spying on us, then amidst the sickness of terror which ever came over me whensoever I thought of him, and much more when I saw him (ah! he is dead now!), it came flashing into my mind how I might destroy my enemy. Therefore I made the Dwarf my messenger to her, by bidding thee to my bed in such wise that he might hear it. And wot thou well, that he speedily carried her the tidings. Meanwhile I hastened to lie to the King's Son, and all privily bade him come to me and not thee. And thereafter, by dint of waiting and watching, and taking the only chance that there was, I met thee as thou camest back from fetching the skin of the lion that never was, and gave thee that warning, or else had we been undone indeed."

Said Walter: "Was the lion of her making or of thine then?"

She said: "Of hers: why should I deal with such a matter?"

"Yea," said Walter, "but she verily swooned, and she was verily wroth with the Enemy."

The Maid smiled, and said: "If her lie was not like very sooth, then had she not been the crafts-master that I knew her: one may lie otherwise than with the tongue alone: yet indeed her wrath against the Enemy was nought feigned; for the Enemy was even I, and in these latter days never did her wrath leave me. But to go on with my tale.

"Now doubt thou not, that, when thou camest into the hall yester eve, the Mistress knew of thy counterfeit tryst with me, and meant nought but death for thee; yet first would she have thee in her arms again, therefore did she make much of thee at table (and that was partly for my torment also), and therefore did she make that tryst with thee, and deemed doubtless that thou wouldst not dare to forgo it, even if thou shouldst go to me thereafter.

"Now I had trained that dastard to me as I have told thee, but I gave him a sleepy draught, so that when I came to the bed he might not move toward me nor open his eyes: but I lay down beside him, so that the Lady might know that my body had been there; for well had she wotted if it had not. Then as there I lay I cast over him thy shape, so that none might have known but that thou wert lying by my side, and there, trembling, I abode what should befall. Thus I passed through the hour whenas thou shouldest have been at her chamber, and the time of my tryst with thee was come as the Mistress would be deeming; so that I looked for her speedily, and my heart wellnigh failed me for fear of her cruelty.

"Presently then I heard a stirring in her chamber, and I slipped from out the bed, and hid me behind the hangings, and was like to die for fear of her; and lo, presently she came stealing in softly, holding a lamp in one hand and a knife in the other. And I tell thee of a sooth that I also had a sharp knife in my hand to defend my life if need were. She held the lamp up above her head before she drew near to the bed-side, and I heard her mutter: 'She is not there then! but she shall be taken.' Then she went up to the bed and stooped over it, and laid her hand on the place where I had lain; and therewith her eyes turned to that false image of thee lying there, and she fell a-trembling and shaking, and the lamp fell to the ground and was quenched (but there was bright moonlight in the room, and still I could see what betid). But she uttered a noise like the low roar of a wild beast, and I saw her arm and hand rise up, and the flashing of the steel beneath the hand, and then down came the hand and the steel, and I went nigh to swooning lest perchance I had wrought over well, and thine image were thy very self. The dastard died without a groan: why should I lament him? I cannot. But the Lady drew him toward her, and snatched the clothes from off his shoulders and breast, and fell a-gibbering sounds mostly without meaning, but broken here and there with words. Then I heard her say: 'I shall forget; I shall forget; and the new days shall come.' Then was there silence of her a little, and thereafter she cried out in a terrible voice: 'O no, no, no! I cannot forget; I cannot forget;' and she raised a great wailing cry that filled all the night with horror (didst thou not hear it?), and caught up the knife from the bed and thrust it into her breast, and fell down a dead heap over the bed and on to the man whom she had slain. And then I thought of thee, and joy smote across my terror; how shall I gainsay it? And I fled away to thee, and I took thine hands in mine, thy dear hands, and we fled away together. Shall we be still together?"

He spoke slowly, and touched her not, and she, forbearing all sobbing and weeping, sat looking wistfully on him. He said: "I think thou hast told me all; and whether thy guile slew her, or her own evil heart, she was slain last night who lay in mine arms the night before. It was ill, and ill done of me, for I loved not her, but thee, and I wished for her death that I might be with thee. Thou wottest this, and still thou lovest me, it may be overweeningly. What have I to say then? If there be any guilt of guile, I also was in the guile; and if there be any guilt of murder, I also was in the murder. Thus we say to each other; and to God and his Hallows we say: 'We two have conspired to slay the woman who tormented one of us, and would have slain the other; and if we have done amiss therein, then shall we two together pay the penalty; for in this have we done as one body and one soul.'"

Therewith he put his arms about her and kissed her, but soberly and friendly, as if he would comfort her. And thereafter he said to her: "Maybe to-morrow, in the sunlight, I will ask thee of this woman, what she verily was; but now let her be. And thou, thou art over-wearied, and I bid thee sleep."

So he went about and gathered of bracken a great heap for her bed, and did his coat thereover, and led her thereto, and she lay down meekly, and smiled and crossed her arms over her bosom, and presently fell asleep. But as for him, he watched by the fire-side till dawn began to glimmer, and then he also laid him down and slept.

CHAPTER XXV

Of the Triumphant Summer Array of the Maid

WHEN THE DAY was bright Walter arose, and met the Maid coming from the river-bank, fresh and rosy from the water. She paled a little when they met face to face, and she shrank from him shyly. But he took her hand and kissed her frankly; and the two were glad, and had no need to tell each other of their joy, though much else they deemed they had to say, could they have found words thereto.

So they came to their fire and sat down, and fell to breakfast; and ere they were done, the Maid said: "My Master, thou seest we be come nigh unto the hill-country, and to-day about sunset, belike, we shall come into the Land of the Bear-folk; and both it is, that there is peril if we fall into their hands, and that we may scarce escape them. Yet I deem that we may deal with the peril by wisdom."

"What is the peril?" said Walter; "I mean, what is the worst of it?"

Said the Maid: "To be offered up in sacrifice to their God."

"But if we escape death at their hands, what then?" said Walter.

"One of two things," said she; "the first that they shall take us into their tribe."

"And will they sunder us in that case?" said Walter.

"Nay," said she.

Walter laughed and said: "Therein is little harm then. But what is the other chance?"

Said she: "That we leave them with their good-will, and come back to one of the lands of Christendom."

Said Walter: "I am not all so sure that this is the better of the two choices, though, forsooth, thou seemest to think so. But tell me now, what like is their God, that they should offer up new-comers to him?"

"Their God is a woman," she said, "and the Mother of their nation and tribes (or so they deem) before the days when they had chieftains and Lords of battle."

"That will be long ago," said he; "how then may she be living now?"

Said the Maid: "Doubtless that woman of yore agone is dead this many and many a year; but they take to them still a new woman, one after other, as they may happen on them, to be in the stead of the Ancient Mother. And to tell thee the very truth right out, she that lieth dead in the Pillared Hall was even the last of these; and now, if they knew it, they lack a God. This shall we tell them."

"Yea, yea!" said Walter, "a goodly welcome shall we have of them then, if we come amongst them with our hands red with the blood of their God!"

She smiled on him and said: "If I come amongst them with the tidings that I have slain her, and they trow therein, without doubt they shall make me Lady and Goddess in her stead."

"This is a strange word," said Walter; "but if so they do, how shall that further us in reaching the kindreds of the world, and the folk of Holy Church?"

She laughed outright, so joyous was she grown, now that she knew that his life was yet to be a part of hers. "Sweetheart," she said, "now I see that thou desirest wholly what I desire; yet in any case, abiding with them would be living and not dying, even as thou hadst it e'en now. But, forsooth, they will not hinder our departure if they deem me their God; they do not look for it, nor desire it, that their God should dwell with them daily. Have no fear." Then she laughed again, and said: "What! thou lookest on me and deemest me to be but a sorry image of a goddess; and me with my scanty coat and bare arms and naked feet! But wait! I know well how to array me when the time cometh. Thou shalt see it! And now, my Master, were it not meet that we took to the road?"

So they arose, and found a ford of the river that took the Maid but to the knee, and so set forth up the greensward of the slopes whereas there were but few trees; so went they faring toward the hill-country.

At the last they were come to the feet of the very hills, and in the hollows betwixt the buttresses of them grew nut and berry trees, and the greensward round about them was both thick and much flowery. There they stayed them and dined, whereas Walter had shot a hare by the way, and they had found a bubbling spring under a grey stone in a bight of the coppice, wherein now the birds were singing their best.

When they had eaten and had rested somewhat, the Maid arose and said: "Now shall the Queen array herself, and seem like a very goddess."

Then she fell to work, while Walter looked on; and she made a garland for her head of eglantine where the roses were the fairest; and with mingled flowers of the summer she wreathed her middle about, and let the garland of them hang down to below her knees; and knots of the flowers she made fast to the skirts of her coat, and did them for arm-rings about her arms, and for anklets and sandals for her feet. Then she set a garland about Walter's head, and then stood a little off from him and set her feet together, and lifted up her arms, and said: "Lo now! am I not as like to the Mother of Summer as if I were clad in silk and gold? and even so shall I be deemed by the folk of the Bear. Come now, thou shalt see how all shall be well."

She laughed joyously; but he might scarce laugh for pity of his love. Then they set forth again, and began to climb the hills, and the hours wore as they went in sweet converse; till at last Walter looked on the Maid, and smiled on her, and said: "One thing I would say to thee, lovely friend, to wit: wert thou clad in silk and gold, thy stately raiment might well suffer a few stains, or here and there a rent maybe; but stately would it be still when the folk of the Bear should come up against thee. But as to this flowery array of thine, in a few hours it shall be all faded and nought. Nay, even now, as I look on thee, the meadow-sweet that hangeth from thy girdle-stead has waxen dull, and welted; and the blossoming eyebright that is for a hem to the little white coat of thee is already forgetting how to be bright and blue. What sayest thou then?"

She laughed at his word, and stood still, and looked back over her shoulder, while with her fingers she dealt with the flowers about her side like to a bird preening his feathers. Then she said: "Is it verily so as thou sayest? Look again!"

So he looked, and wondered; for lo! beneath his eyes the spires of the meadow-sweet grew crisp and clear again, the eyebright blossoms shone once more over the whiteness of her legs; the eglantine roses opened, and all was as fresh and bright as if it were still growing on its own roots.

He wondered, and was even somedeal aghast; but she said: "Dear friend, be not troubled! did I not tell thee that I am wise in hidden lore? But in my wisdom shall be no longer any scathe to any man. And again, this my wisdom, as I told thee erst, shall end on the day whereon I am made all happy. And it is thou that shall wield it all, my Master. Yet must my wisdom needs endure for a little season yet. Let us on then, boldly and happily."

CHAPTER XXVI

They Come to the Folk of the Bears

ON THEY WENT, and before long they were come up on to the down-country, where was scarce a tree, save gnarled and knotty thorn-bushes here and there, but nought else higher than the whin. And here on these upper lands they saw that the pastures were much burnt with the drought, albeit summer was not worn old. Now they went making due south toward the mountains, whose heads they saw from time to time rising deep blue over the bleak greyness of the downland ridges. And so they went, till at last, hard on sunset, after they had climbed long over a high bent, they came to the brow thereof, and, looking down, beheld new tidings.

There was a wide valley below them, greener than the downs which they had come over, and greener yet amidmost, from the watering of a stream which, all beset with willows, wound about the bottom. Sheep and neat were pasturing about the dale, and moreover a long line of smoke was going up straight into the windless heavens from the midst of a ring of little round houses built of turfs, and thatched with reed. And beyond that, toward an eastward-lying bight of the dale, they could see what looked like to a doom-ring of big stones, though there were no rocky places in that land. About the cooking-fire amidst of the houses, and here and there otherwhere, they saw, standing or going to and fro, huge figures of men and women, with children playing about betwixt them.

They stood and gazed down at it for a minute or two, and though all were at peace there, yet to Walter, at least, it seemed strange and awful. He spake softly, as though he would not have his voice reach those men, though they were forsooth, out of ear-shot of anything save a shout: "Are these then the children of the Bear? What shall we do now?"

She said: "Yea, of the Bear they be, though there be other folks of them far and far away to the northward and eastward, near to the borders of the sea. And as to what we shall do, let us go down at once, and peacefully. Indeed, by now there will be no escape from them; for lo you! they have seen us."

Forsooth, some three or four of the big men had turned them toward the bent whereon stood the twain, and were hailing them in huge, rough voices, wherein, howsoever, seemed to be no anger or threat. So the Maid took Walter by the hand, and thus they went down quietly, and the Bear-folk, seeing them, stood all together, facing them, to abide their coming. Walter saw of them, that though they were very tall and bigly made, they were not so far above the stature of men as to be marvels. The carles were long-haired and shaggy of beard, and their hair all red or tawny; their skins, where their naked flesh showed, were burned brown with sun and weather, but to a fair and pleasant brown, nought like to blackamoors. The queans were comely and well-eyed; nor was there anything of fierce or evil-looking about either the carles or the queans, but somewhat grave and solemn of aspect were they. Clad were they all, saving the young men-children, but somewhat scantily, and in nought save sheep-skins or deer-skins.

For weapons they saw amongst them clubs, and spears headed with bone or flint, and ugly axes of big flints set in wooden handles; nor was there, as far as they could see, either now or afterward, any bow amongst them. But some of the young men seemed to have slings done about their shoulders.

Now when they were come but three fathom from them, the Maid lifted up her voice, and spake clearly and sweetly: "Hail, ye folk of the Bears! we have come amongst you, and that for your good and not for your hurt: wherefore we would know if we be welcome."

There was an old man who stood foremost in the midst, clad in a mantle of deer-skins worked very goodly, and with a gold ring on his arm, and a chaplet of blue stones on his head, and he spake: "Little are ye, but so goodly, that if ye were but bigger, we should deem that ye were come from the Gods' House. Yet have I heard, that how mighty soever may the Gods be, and chiefly our God, they be at whiles nought so bigly made as we of the Bears. How this may be, I wot not. But if ye be not of the Gods or their kindred, then are ye mere aliens; and we know not what to do with aliens, save we meet them in battle, or give them to the God, or save we make them children of the Bear. But yet again, ye may be messengers of some folk who would find friendship and alliance with us: in which case ye shall at the least depart in peace, and whiles ye are with us shall be our guests in all good cheer. Now, therefore, we bid you declare the matter unto us."

Then spake the Maid: "Father, it were easy for us to declare what we be unto you here present. But, meseemeth, ye who be gathered round the fire here this evening are less than the whole tale of the children of the Bear."

"So it is, Maiden," said the elder, "that many more children hath the Bear."

"This then we bid you," said the Maid, "that ye send the tokens round and gather your people to you, and when they be assembled in the Doom-ring, then shall we put our errand before you; and according to that, shall ye deal with us."

"Thou hast spoken well," said the elder; "and even so had we bidden you ourselves. To-morrow, before noon, shall ye stand in the Doom-ring in this Dale, and speak with the children of the Bear."

Therewith he turned to his own folk and called out something, whereof those twain knew not the meaning; and there came to him, one after another, six young men, unto each of whom he gave a thing from out his pouch, but what it was Walter might not see, save that it was little and of small account: to each, also, he spake a word or two, and straight they set off running, one after the other, turning toward the bent which was over against that whereby the twain had come into the Dale, and were soon out of sight in the gathering dusk.

Then the elder turned him again to Walter and the Maid, and spake: "Man and woman, whatsoever ye may be, or whatsoever may abide you to-morrow, to-night, ye are welcome guests to us; so we bid you come eat and drink at our fire."

So they sat all together upon the grass round about the embers of the fire, and ate curds and cheese, and drank milk in abundance; and as the night grew on them they quickened the fire, that they might have light.

This wild folk talked merrily amongst themselves, with laughter enough and friendly jests, but to the new-comers they were few-spoken, though, as the twain deemed, for no enmity that they bore them. But this found Walter, that the younger ones, both men and women, seemed to find it a hard matter to keep their eyes off them; and seemed, withal, to gaze on them with somewhat of doubt, or, it might be, of fear.

So when the night was wearing a little, the elder arose and bade the twain to come with him, and led them to a small house or booth, which was amidmost of all, and somewhat bigger than the others, and he did them to wit that they should rest there that night, and bade them sleep in peace and without fear till the morrow. So they entered, and found beds thereon of heather and ling, and they laid them down sweetly, like brother and sister, when they had kissed each other. But they noted that four brisk men lay without the booth, and across the door, with their weapons beside them, so that they must needs look upon themselves as captives.

Then Walter might not refrain him, but spake: "Sweet and dear friend, I have come a long way from the quay at Langton, and the vision of the Dwarf, the Maid, and the Lady; and for this kiss wherewith I have kissed thee e'en now, and the kindness of thine eyes, it was worth the time and the travail. But to-morrow, meseemeth, I shall go no further in this world, though my journey be far longer than from Langton hither. And now may God and All Hallows keep thee amongst this wild folk, whenas I shall be gone from thee."

She laughed low and sweetly, and said: "Dear friend, dost thou speak to me thus mournfully to move me to love thee better? Then is thy labour lost; for no better may I love thee than now I do; and that is with mine whole heart. But keep a good courage, I bid thee; for we be not sundered yet, nor shall we be. Nor do I deem that we shall die here, or to-morrow; but many years hence, after we have known all the sweetness of life. Meanwhile, I bid thee good night, fair friend!"

CHAPTER XXVII

Morning Amongst the Bears

SO WALTER LAID him down and fell asleep, and knew no more till he awoke in bright daylight with the Maid standing over him. She was fresh from the water, for she had been to the river to bathe her, and the sun through the open door fell streaming on her feet close to Walter's pillow. He turned about and cast his arm about them, and caressed them, while she stood smiling upon him; then he arose and looked on her, and said: "How thou art fair and bright this morning! And yet . . . and yet . . . were it not well that thou do off thee all this faded and drooping bravery of leaves and blossoms, that maketh thee look like to a jongleur's damsel on a morrow of Mayday?"

And he gazed ruefully on her.

She laughed on him merrily, and said: "Yea, and belike these others think no better of my attire, or not much better; for yonder they are gathering small wood for the burnt-offering; which, forsooth, shall be thou and I, unless I better it all by means of the wisdom I learned of the old woman, and perfected betwixt the stripes of my Mistress, whom a little while ago thou lovedst somewhat."

And as she spake her eyes sparkled, her cheek flushed, and her limbs and her feet seemed as if they could scarce refrain from dancing for joy. Then Walter knit his brow, and for a moment a thought half-framed was in his mind: Is it so, that she will bewray me and live without me? and he cast his eyes on to the ground. But she said: "Look up, and into mine eyes, friend, and see if there be in them any falseness toward thee! For I know thy thought; I know thy thought. Dost thou not see that my joy and gladness is for the love of thee, and the thought of the rest from trouble that is at hand?"

He looked up, and his eyes met the eyes of her love, and he would have cast his arms about her; but she drew aback and said: "Nay, thou must refrain thee awhile, dear friend, lest these folk cast eyes on us, and deem us over lover-like for what I am to bid them deem me. Abide a while, and then shall all be in me according to thy will. But now I must tell thee that it is not very far from noon, and that the Bears are streaming into the Dale, and already there is an host of men at the Doom-ring, and, as I said, the bale for the burnt-offering is wellnigh dight, whether it be for us, or for some other creature. And now I have to bid thee this, and it will be a thing easy for thee to do, to wit, that thou look as if thou wert of the race of the Gods, and not to blench, or show sign of blenching, whatever betide: to yea-say both my yea-say and my nay-say: and lastly this, which is the only hard thing for thee (but thou hast already done it before somewhat), to look upon me with no masterful eyes of love, nor as if thou wert at once praying me and commanding me; rather thou shalt so demean thee as if thou wert my man all simply, and nowise my master."

"O friend beloved," said Walter, "here at least art thou the master, and I will do all thy bidding, in certain hope or this, that either we shall live together or die together."

But as they spoke, in came the elder, and with him a young maiden, bearing with them their breakfast of curds and cream and strawberries, and he bade them eat. So they ate, and were not unmerry; and the while of their eating the elder talked with them soberly, but not hardly, or with any seeming enmity: and ever his talk gat on to the drought, which was now burning up the down-pastures; and how the grass in the watered dales, which was no wide spread of land, would not hold out much longer unless the God sent them rain. And Walter noted that those two, the elder and the Maid, eyed each other curiously amidst of this talk; the elder intent on what she might say, and if she gave heed to his words; while on her side the Maid answered his speech graciously and pleasantly, but said little that was of any import: nor would she have him fix her eyes, which wandered lightly from this thing to that; nor would her lips grow stern and stable, but ever smiled in answer to the light of her eyes, as she sat there with her face as the very face of the gladness of the summer day.

CHAPTER XXVIII

Of the New God of the Bears

AT LAST THE old man said: "My children, ye shall now come with me unto the Doom-ring of our folk, the Bears of the Southern Dales, and deliver to them your errand; and I beseech you to have pity upon your own bodies, as I have pity on them; on thine especially, Maiden, so fair and bright a creature as thou art; for so it is, that if ye deal us out light and lying words after the manner of dastards, ye shall miss the worship and glory of wending away amidst of the flames, a gift to the God and a hope to the people, and shall be passed by the rods of the folk, until ye faint and fail amongst them, and then shall ye be thrust down into the flow at the Dale's End, and a stone-laden hurdle cast upon you, that we may thenceforth forget your folly."

The Maid now looked full into his eyes, and Walter deemed that the old man shrank before her; but she said: "Thou art old and wise, O great man of the Bears, yet nought I need to learn of thee. Now lead us on our way to the Stead of the Errands."

So the elder brought them along to the Doom-ring at the eastern end of the Dale; and it was now all peopled with those huge men, weaponed after their fashion, and standing up, so that the grey stones thereof but showed a little over their heads. But amidmost of the said Ring was a big stone, fashioned as a chair, whereon sat a very old man, long-hoary and white-bearded, and on either side of him stood a great-limbed woman clad in war-gear, holding, each of them, a long spear, and with a flint-bladed knife in the girdle; and there were no other women in all the Mote.

Then the elder led those twain into the midst of the Mote, and there bade them go up on to a wide, flat-topped stone, six feet above the ground, just over against the ancient chieftain; and they mounted it by a rough stair, and stood there before that folk; Walter in his array of the outward world, which had been fair enough, of crimson cloth and silk, and white linen, but was now travel-stained and worn; and the Maid with nought upon her, save the smock wherein she had fled from the Golden House of the Wood beyond the World, decked with the faded flowers which she had wreathed about her yesterday. Nevertheless, so it was, that those big men eyed her intently, and with somewhat of worship.

Now did Walter, according to her bidding, sink down on his knees beside her, and drawing his sword, hold it before him, as if to keep all interlopers aloof from the Maid. And there was silence in the Mote, and all eyes were fixed on those twain.

At last the old chief arose and spake: "Ye men, here are come a man and a woman, we know not whence; whereas they have given word to our folk who first met them, that they would tell their errand to none save the Mote of the People; which it was their due to do, if they were minded to risk it. For either they be aliens without an errand hither, save, it may be, to beguile us, in which case they shall presently die an evil death; or they have come amongst us that we may give them to the

God with flint-edge and fire; or they have a message to us from some folk or other, on the issue of which lieth life or death. Now shall ye hear what they have to say concerning themselves and their faring hither. But, meseemeth, it shall be the woman who is the chief and hath the words in her mouth; for, lo you! the man kneeleth at her feet, as one who would serve and worship her. Speak out then, woman, and let our warriors hear thee."

Then the Maid lifted up her voice, and spake out clear and shrilling, like to a flute of the best of the minstrels: "Ye men of the Children of the Bear, I would ask you a question, and let the chieftain who sitteth before me answer it."

The old man nodded his head, and she went on: "Tell me, Children of the Bear, how long a time is worn since ye saw the God of your worship made manifest in the body of a woman!"

Said the elder: "Many winters have worn since my father's father was a child, and saw the very God in the bodily form of a woman."

Then she said again: "Did ye rejoice at her coming, and would ye rejoice if once more she came amongst you?"

"Yea," said the old chieftain, "for she gave us gifts, and learned us lore, and came to us in no terrible shape, but as a young woman as goodly as thou."

Then said the Maid: "Now, then, is the day of your gladness come; for the old body is dead, and I am the new body of your God, come amongst you for your welfare."

Then fell a great silence on the Mote, till the old man spake and said: "What shall I say and live? For if thou be verily the God, and I threaten thee, wilt thou not destroy me? But thou hast spoken a great word with a sweet mouth, and hast taken the burden of blood on thy lily hands; and if the Children of the Bear be befooled of light liars, how shall they put the shame off them? Therefore I say, show to us a token; and if thou be the God, this shall be easy to thee; and if thou show it not, then is thy falsehood manifest, and thou shalt dree the weird. For we shall deliver thee into the hands of these women here, who shall thrust thee down into the flow which is hereby, after they have wearied themselves with whipping thee. But thy man that kneeleth at thy feet shall we give to the true God, and he shall go to her by the road of the flint and the fire. Hast thou heard? Then give to us the sign and the token."

She changed countenance no whit at his word; but her eyes were the brighter, and her cheek the fresher; and her feet moved a little, as if they were growing glad before the dance; and she looked out over the Mote, and spake in her clear voice: "Old man, thou needest not to fear for thy words. Forsooth it is not me whom thou threatenest with stripes and a foul death, but some light fool and liar, who is not here. Now hearken! I wot well that ye would have somewhat of me, to wit, that I should send you rain to end this drought, which otherwise seemeth like to lie long upon you: but this rain, I must go into the mountains of the south to fetch it you; therefore shall certain of your warriors bring me on my way, with this my man, up to the great pass of the said mountains, and we shall set out thitherward this very day."

She was silent a while, and all looked on her, but none spake or moved, so that they seemed as images of stone amongst the stones.

Then she spake again and said: "Some would say, men of the Bear, that this were a sign and a token great enough; but I know you, and how stubborn and perverse of heart ye be; and how that the gift not yet within your hand is no gift to you; and the wonder ye see not, your hearts trow not. Therefore look ye upon me as here I stand, I who have come from the fairer country and the greenwood of the lands, and see if I bear not the summer with me, and the heart that maketh increase and the hand that giveth."

Lo then! as she spake, the faded flowers that hung about her gathered life and grew fresh again; the woodbine round her neck and her sleek shoulders knit itself together and embraced her freshly, and cast its scent about her face. The lilies that girded her loins lifted up their heads, and the gold of their tassels fell upon her; the eyebright grew clean blue again upon her smock; the eglantine found its blooms again, and then began to shed the leaves thereof upon her feet; the meadow-weet wreathed amongst it made clear the sweetness of her legs, and the mouse-ear studded her raiment as with gems. There she stood amidst of the blossoms, like a great orient pearl against the fretwork of the goldsmiths, and the breeze that came up the valley from behind bore the sweetness of her fragrance all over the Man-mote.

Then, indeed, the Bears stood up, and shouted and cried and smote on their shields, and tossed their spears aloft. Then the elder rose from his seat, and came up humbly to where she stood, and prayed her to say what she would have done; while the others drew about in knots, but durst not come very nigh to her. She answered the ancient chief, and said, that she would depart presently toward the mountains, whereby she might send them the rain which they lacked, and that thence she would away to the southward for a while; but that they should hear of her, or, it might be, see her, before they who were now of middle age should be gone to their fathers.

Then the old man besought her that they might make her a litter of fragrant green boughs, and so bear her away toward the mountain pass amidst a triumph of the whole folk. But she leapt lightly down from the stone, and walked to and fro on the greensward, while it seemed of her that her feet scarce touched the grass; and she spake to the ancient chief where he still kneeled in worship of her, and said: "Nay; deemest thou of me that I need bearing by men's hands, or that I shall tire at all when I am doing my will, and I, the very heart of the year's increase? So it is, that the going of my feet over your pastures shall make them to thrive, both this year and the coming years: surely will I go afoot."

So they worshipped her the more, and blessed her; and then first of all they brought meat, the daintiest they might, both for her and for Walter. But they would not look on the Maid whiles she ate, or suffer Walter to behold her the while. Afterwards, when they had eaten, some twenty men, weaponed after their fashion, made them ready to wend the Maiden up into the mountains, and anon they set out thitherward all together. Howbeit, the huge men held them ever somewhat aloof from the Maid; and when they came to the resting-place for that night, where there was no house, for it was up amongst the foot-hills before the mountains, then it was a wonder to see how carefully they built up a sleeping-place for her, and tilted it over with their skin-cloaks, and how they watched nightlong about her. But Walter they let sleep peacefully on the grass, a little way aloof from the watchers round the Maid.

CHAPTER XXIX

Walter Strays in the Pass and Is Sundered from the Maid

MORNING CAME, AND they arose and went on their ways, and went all day till the sun was nigh set, and they were come up into the very pass; and in the jaws thereof was an earthen howe. There the Maid bade them stay, and she went up on to the howe, and stood there and spake to them, and said: "O men of the Bear, I give you thanks for your following, and I bless you, and promise you the increase of the earth. But now ye shall turn aback, and leave me to go my ways; and my man with the iron sword shall follow me. Now, maybe, I shall come amongst the Bear-folk again before long, and yet again, and learn them wisdom; but for this time it is enough. And I shall tell you that ye were best to hasten home straightway to your houses in the downland dales, for the weather which I have bidden for you is even now coming forth from the forge of storms in the heart of the mountains. Now this last word I give you, that times are changed since I wore the last shape of God that ye have seen, wherefore a change I command you. If so be aliens come amongst you, I will not that ye send them to me by the flint and the fire; rather, unless they be baleful unto you, and worthy of an evil death, ye shall suffer them to abide with you; ye shall make them become children of the Bears, if they be goodly enough and worthy, and they shall be my children as ye be; otherwise, if they be ill-favoured and weakling, let them live and be thralls to you, but not join with you, man to woman. Now depart ye with my blessing."

Therewith she came down from the mound, and went her ways up the pass so lightly, that it was to Walter, standing amongst the Bears, as if she had vanished away. But the men of that folk abode standing and worshipping their God for a little while, and that while he durst not sunder him from their company. But when they had blessed him and gone on their way backward, he betook him in haste to following the Maid, thinking to find her abiding him in some nook of the pass.

Howsoever, it was now twilight or more, and, for all his haste, dark night overtook him, so that perforce he was stayed amidst the tangle of the mountain ways. And, moreover, ere the night was grown old, the weather came upon him on the back of a great south wind, so that the mountain nooks rattled and roared, and there was the rain and the hail, with thunder and lightning, monstrous and terrible, and all the huge array of a summer storm. So he was driven at last to crouch under a big rock and abide the day.

But not so were his troubles at an end. For under the said rock he fell asleep, and when he awoke it was day indeed; but as to the pass, the way thereby was blind with the driving rain and the lowering lift; so that, though he struggled as well as he might against the storm and the tangle, he made but little way.

And now once more the thought came on him, that the Maid was of the fays, or of some race even mightier; and it came on him now not as erst, with half fear and whole desire, but with a bitter oppression of dread, of loss and misery; so that he began to fear that she had but won his love to leave him and forget him for a new-comer, after the wont of fay-women, as old tales tell.

Two days he battled thus with storm and blindness, and wan hope of his life; for he was growing weak and fordone. But the third morning the storm abated, though the rain yet fell heavily, and he could see his way somewhat as well as feel it: withal he found that now his path was leading him downwards. As it grew dusk, he came down into a grassy valley with a stream running through it to the southward, and the rain was now but little, coming down but in dashes from time to time. So he crept down to the stream-side, and lay amongst the bushes there; and said to himself, that on the morrow he would get him victual, so that he might live to seek his Maiden through the wide world. He was of somewhat better heart: but now that he was laid quiet, and had no more for that present to trouble him about the way, the anguish of his loss fell upon him the keener, and he might not refrain him from lamenting his dear Maiden aloud, as one who deemed himself in the empty wilderness: and thus he lamented for her sweetness and her loveliness, and the kindness of her voice and her speech, and her mirth. Then he fell to crying out concerning the beauty of her shaping, praising the parts of her body, as her face, and her hands, and her shoulders, and her feet, and cursing the evil fate which had sundered him from the friendliness of her, and the peerless fashion of her.

CHAPTER XXX

Now They Meet Again

COMPLAINING THUS-WISE, he fell asleep from sheer weariness, and when he awoke it was broad day, calm and bright and cloudless, with the scent of the earth refreshed going up into the heavens, and the birds singing sweetly in the bushes about him: for the dale whereunto he was now come was a fair and lovely place amidst the shelving slopes of the mountains, a paradise of the wilderness, and nought but pleasant and sweet things were to be seen there, now that the morn was so clear and sunny.

He arose and looked about him, and saw where, a hundred yards aloof, was a thicket of small wood, as thorn and elder and whitebeam, all wreathed about with the bines of wayfaring tree; it hid a bight of the stream, which turned round about it, and betwixt it and Walter was the grass short and thick, and sweet, and all beset with flowers; and he said to himself that it was even such a place as wherein the angels were leading the Blessed in the great painted paradise in the choir of the big church at Langton on Holm. But lo! as he looked he cried aloud for joy, for forth from the thicket on to the flowery grass came one like to an angel from out of the said picture, white-clad and bare-foot, sweet of flesh, with bright eyes and ruddy cheeks; for it was the Maid herself. So he ran to her, and she abode him, holding forth kind hands to him, and smiling, while she wept for joy of the meeting. He threw himself upon her, and spared not to kiss her, her cheeks and her mouth, and her arms and her shoulders, and wheresoever she would suffer it. Till at last she drew aback a little, laughing on him for love, and said: "Forbear now, friend, for it is enough for this time, and tell me how thou hast sped."

"Ill, ill," said he.

"What ails thee?" she said.

"Hunger," he said, "and longing for thee."

"Well," she said, "me thou hast; there is one ill quenched; take my hand, and we will see to the other one."

So he took her hand, and to hold it seemed to him sweet beyond measure. But he looked up, and saw a little blue smoke going up into the air from beyond the thicket; and he laughed, for he was weak with hunger, and he said: "Who is at the cooking yonder?"

"Thou shalt see," she said; and led him therewith into the said thicket and through it, and lo! a fair little grassy place, full of flowers, betwixt the bushes and the bight of the stream; and on the little sandy ere, just off the greensward, was a fire of sticks, and beside it two trouts lying, fat and red-flecked.

"Here is the breakfast," said she; "when it was time to wash the night off me e'en now, I went down the strand here into the rippling shallow, and saw the bank below it, where the water draws together yonder, and deepens, that it seemed like to hold fish; and whereas I looked to meet thee presently, I groped the bank for them, going softly; and lo thou! Help me now, that we cook them."

So they roasted them on the red embers, and fell to and ate well, both of them, and drank of the water of the stream out of each other's hollow hands; and that feast seemed glorious to them, such gladness went with it.

But when they were done with their meat, Walter said to the Maid: "And how didst thou know that thou shouldst see me presently?"

She said, looking on him wistfully: "This needed no wizardry. I lay not so far from thee last night, but that I heard thy voice and knew it."

Said he, "Why didst thou not come to me then, since thou heardest me bemoaning thee?"

She cast her eyes down, and plucked at the flowers and grass, and said: "It was dear to hear thee praising me; I knew not before that I was so sore desired, or that thou hadst taken such note of my body, and found it so dear."

Then she reddened sorely, and said: "I knew not that aught of me had such beauty as thou didst bewail."

And she wept for joy. Then she looked on him and smiled and said: "Wilt thou have the very truth of it? I went close up to thee, and stood there hidden by the bushes and the night. And amidst thy bewailing, I knew that thou wouldst soon fall asleep, and in sooth I out-waked thee."

Then was she silent again; and he spake not, but looked on her shyly; and she said, reddening yet more: "Furthermore, I must needs tell thee that I feared to go to thee in the dark night, and my heart so yearning towards thee."

And she hung her head adown; but he said: "Is it so indeed, that thou fearest me? Then doth that makes me afraid—afraid of thy nay-say. For I was going to entreat thee, and say to thee: Beloved, we have now gone through many troubles; let us now take a good reward at once, and wed together, here amidst this sweet and pleasant house of the mountains, ere we go further on our way; if indeed we go further at all. For where shall we find any place sweeter or happier than this?"

But she sprang up to her feet, and stood there trembling before him, because of her love; and she said: "Beloved, I have deemed that it were good for us to go seek mankind as they live in the world, and to live amongst them. And as for me, I will tell thee the sooth, to wit, that I long for this sorely. For I feel afraid in the wilderness, and as if I needed help and protection against my Mistress, though she be dead; and I need the comfort of many people, and the throngs of the cities. I cannot forget her: it was but last night that I dreamed (I suppose as the dawn grew a-cold) that I was yet under her head, and she was stripping me for the torment; so that I woke up panting and crying out. I pray thee be not angry with me for telling thee of my desires; for if thou wouldst not have it so, then here will I abide with thee as thy mate, and strive to gather courage."

He rose up and kissed her face, and said: "Nay, I had in sooth no mind to abide here for ever; I meant but that we should feast a while here, and then depart: sooth it is, that if thou dreadest the wilderness, somewhat I dread the city."

She turned pale, and said: "Thou shalt have thy will, my friend, if it must be so. But bethink thee! we be not yet at our journey's end, and may have many things and much strife to endure, before we be at peace and in welfare. Now shall I tell thee—did I not before?—that while I am a maid untouched, my wisdom, and some deal of might, abideth with me, and only so long. Therefore I entreat thee, let us go now, side by side, out of this fair valley, even as we are, so that my wisdom and might may help thee at need. For, my friend, I would not that our lives be short, so much of joy as hath now come into them."

"Yea, beloved," he said, "let us on straightway then, and shorten the while that sundereth us."

"Love," she said, "thou shalt pardon me one time for all. But this is to be said, that I know somewhat of the haps that lie a little way ahead of us; partly by my lore, and partly by what I learned of this land of the wild folk whiles thou wert lying asleep that morning."

So they left that pleasant place by the water, and came into the open valley, and went their ways through the pass; and it soon became stony again, as they mounted the bent which went up from out the dale. And when they came to the brow of the said bent, they had a sight of the open country lying fair and joyous in the sunshine, and amidst of it, against the blue hills, the walls and towers of a great city.

Then said the Maid: "O, dear friend, lo you! is not that our abode that lieth yonder, and is so beauteous? Dwell not our friends there, and our protection against uncouth wights, and mere evil things in guileful shapes? O city, I bid thee hail!"

But Walter looked on her, and smiled somewhat; and said: "I rejoice in thy joy. But there be evil things in yonder city also, though they be not fays nor devils, or it is like to no city that I wot of. And in every city shall foes grow up to us without rhyme or reason, and life therein shall be tangled unto us."

"Yea," she said; "but in the wilderness amongst the devils, what was to be done by manly might or valiancy? There hadst thou to fall back upon the guile and wizardry which I had filched from my very foes. But when we come down yonder, then shall thy valiancy prevail to cleave the tangle for us. Or at the least, it shall leave a tale of thee behind, and I shall worship thee."

He laughed, and his face grew brighter: "Mastery mows the meadow," quoth he, "and one man is of little might against many. But I promise thee I shall not be slothful before thee."

CHAPTER XXXI

They Come Upon New Folk

WITH THAT THEY went down from the bent again, and came to where the pass narrowed so much, that they went betwixt a steep wall of rock on either side; but after an hour's going, the said wall gave back suddenly, and, or they were ware almost, they came on another dale like to that which they had left but not so fair, though it was grassy and well watered, and not so big either. But here indeed befell a change to them; for lo! tents and pavilions pitched in the said valley, and amidst of it a throng of men, mostly weaponed, and with horses ready saddled at hand. So they stayed their feet, and Walter's heart failed him, for he said to himself: Who wotteth what these men may be, save that they be aliens? It is most like that we shall be taken as thralls; and then, at the best, we shall be sundered; and that is all one with the worst.

But the Maid, when she saw the horses, and the gay tents, and the pennons fluttering, and the glitter of spears, and gleaming of white armour, smote her palms together for joy, and cried out: "Here now are come the folk of the city for our welcoming, and fair and lovely are they, and of many things shall they be thinking, and a many things shall they do, and we shall be partakers thereof. Come then, and let us meet them, fair friend!"

But Walter said: "Alas! thou knowest not: would that we might flee! But now is it over late; so put we a good face on it, and go to them quietly, as erewhile we did in the Bear-country."

So did they; and there sundered six from the men-at-arms and came to those twain, and made humble obeisance to Walter, but spake no word. Then they made as they would lead them to the others, and the twain went with them wondering, and came into the ring of men-at-arms, and stood before an old hoar knight, armed all, save his head, with most goodly armour, and he also bowed before Walter, but spake no word. Then they took them to the master pavilion, and made signs to them to sit, and they brought them dainty meat and good wine. And the while of their eating arose up a stir about them; and when they were done with their meat, the ancient knight came to them, still bowing in courteous wise, and did them to wit by signs that they should depart:

and when they were without, they saw all the other tents struck, and men beginning to busy them with striking the pavilion, and the others mounted and ranked in good order for the road; and there were two horse-litters before them, wherein they were bidden to mount, Walter in one, and the Maid in the other, and no otherwise might they do. Then presently was a horn blown, and all took to the road together; and Walter saw betwixt the curtains of the litter that men-at-arms rode on either side of him, albeit they had left him his sword by his side.

So they went down the mountain-passes, and before sunset were gotten into the plain; but they made no stay for night-fall, save to eat a morsel and drink a draught, going through the night as men who knew their way well. As they went, Walter wondered what would betide, and if peradventure they also would be for offering them up to their Gods; whereas they were aliens for certain, and belike also Saracens. Moreover there was a cold fear at his heart that he should be sundered from the Maid, whereas their masters now were mighty men of war, holding in their hands that which all men desire, to wit, the manifest beauty of a woman. Yet he strove to think the best of it that he might. And so at last, when the night was far spent, and dawn was at hand, they stayed at a great and mighty gate in a huge wall. There they blew loudly on the horn thrice, and thereafter the gates were opened, and they all passed through into a street, which seemed to Walter in the glimmer to be both great and goodly amongst the abodes of men. Then it was but a little ere they came into a square, wide-spreading, one side whereof Walter took to be the front of a most goodly house. There the doors of the court opened to them or ever the horn might blow, though, forsooth, blow it did loudly three times; all they entered therein, and men came to Walter and signed to him to alight. So did he, and would have tarried to look about for the Maid, but they suffered it not, but led him up a huge stair into a chamber, very great, and but dimly lighted because of its greatness. Then they brought him to a bed dight as fair as might be, and made signs to him to strip and lie therein. Perforce he did so, and then they bore away his raiment, and left him lying there. So he lay there quietly, deeming it no avail for him, a mother-naked man, to seek escape thence; but it was long ere he might sleep, because of his trouble of mind. At last, pure weariness got the better of his hopes and fears, and he fell into slumber just as the dawn was passing into day.

CHAPTER XXXII

Of the New King of the City and Land of Stark-wall

WHEN HE AWOKE again the sun was shining brightly into that chamber, and he looked, and beheld that it was peerless of beauty and riches, amongst all that he had ever seen: the ceiling done with gold and oversea blue; the walls hung with arras of the fairest, though he might not tell what was the history done therein. The chairs and stool were of carven work well be-painted, and amidmost was a great ivory chair under a cloth of estate, of bawdekin of gold and green, much be-pearled; and all the floor was of fine work alexandrine.

He looked on all this, wondering what had befallen him, when lo! there came folk into the chamber, to wit, two serving-men well-bedight, and three old men clad in rich gowns of silk. These came to him and (still by signs, without speech) bade him arise and come with them; and when he bade them look to it that he was naked, and laughed doubt-fully, they neither laughed in answer, nor offered him any raiment, but still would have him arise, and he did so perforce. They brought him with them out of the chamber, and through certain passages pillared and goodly, till they came to a bath as fair as any might be; and there the serving-men washed him carefully and tenderly, the old men looking on the while. When it was done, still they offered not to clothe him, but led him out, and through the passages again, back to the chamber. Only this time he must pass between a double hedge of men, some weaponed, some in peaceful array, but all clad gloriously, and full chieftain-like of aspect, either for valiancy or wisdom.

In the chamber itself was now a concourse of men, of great estate by deeming of their array; but all these were standing orderly in a ring about the ivory chair aforesaid. Now said Walter to himself: Surely all this looks toward the knife and the altar for me; but he kept a stout countenance despite of all.

So they led him up to the ivory chair, and he beheld on either side thereof a bench, and on each was laid a set of raiment from the shirt upwards; but there was much diversity betwixt these arrays. For one was all of robes of peace, glorious and be-gemmed, unmeet for any save a great King; while the other was war-weed, seemly, well-fashioned, but little adorned; nay rather, worn and bestained with weather, and the pelting of the spear-storm.

Now those old men signed to Walter to take which of those raiments he would, and do it on. He looked to the right and the left, and when he had looked on the war-gear, the heart arose in him, and he called to mind the array of the Goldings in the forefront of battle, and he made one step toward the weapons, and laid his hand thereon. Then ran a glad murmur through that concourse, and the old men drew up to him smiling and joyous, and helped him to do them on; and as he took up the helm, he noted that over its broad brown iron sat a golden crown.

So when he was clad and weaponed, girt with a sword, and a steel axe in his hand, the elders showed him to the ivory throne, and he laid the axe on the arm of the chair, and drew forth the sword from the scabbard, and sat him down, and laid the ancient blade across his knees; then he looked about on those great men, and spake: "How long shall we speak no word to each other, or is it so that God hath stricken you dumb?"

Then all they cried out with one voice: "All hail to the King, the King of Battle!"

Spake Walter: "If I be king, will ye do my will as I bid you?"

Answered the elder: "Nought have we will to do, lord, save as thou biddest."

Said Walter: "Thou then, wilt thou answer a question in all truth?"

"Yea, lord," said the elder, "if I may live afterward."

Then said Walter: "The woman that came with me into your Camp of the Mountain, what hath befallen her?"

The elder answered: "Nought hath befallen her, either of good or evil, save that she hath slept and eaten and bathed her. What, then, is the King's pleasure concerning her?"

"That ye bring her hither to me straightway," said Walter.

"Yea," said the elder; "and in what guise shall we bring her hither? shall she be arrayed as a servant, or a great lady?"

Then Walter pondered a while, and spake at last: "Ask her what is her will herein, and as she will have it, so let it be. But set ye another chair beside mine, and lead her thereto. Thou wise old man, send one or two to bring her in hither, but abide thou, for I have a question or two to ask of thee yet. And ye, lords, abide here the coming of my she-fellow, if it weary you not."

So the elder spake to three of the most honourable of the lords, and they went their ways to bring in the Maid.

CHAPTER XXXIII

Concerning the Fashion of King-making in Stark-wall

MEANWHILE THE KING spake to the elder, and said: "Now tell me whereof I am become king, and what is the fashion and cause of the king-making; for wondrous it is to me, whereas I am but an alien amidst or mighty men."

"Lord," said the old man, "thou art become king of a mighty city, which hath under it many other cities and wide lands, and havens by the sea-side, and which lacketh no wealth which men desire. Many wise men dwell therein, and of fools not more than in other lands. A valiant host shall follow thee to battle when needs must thou wend afield; an host not to be withstood, save by the ancient God-folk, if any of them were left upon the earth, as belike none are. And as to the name of our said city, it hight the City of the Stark-wall, or more shortly, Stark-wall. Now as to the fashion of our king-making: If our king dieth and leaveth an heir male, begotten of his body, then is he king after him; but if he die and leave no heir, then send we out a great lord, with knights and sergeants, to that pass of the mountain whereto ye came yesterday; and the first man that cometh unto them, they take and lead to the city, as they did with thee, lord. For we believe and trow that of old time our forefathers came down from the mountains by that same pass, poor and rude, but full of valiancy, before they conquered these lands, and builded the Stark-wall. But now furthermore, when we have gotten the said wanderer, and brought him home to our city, we behold him mother-naked, all the great men of us, both sages and warriors; then if we find him ill-fashioned and counterfeit of his body, we roll him in a great carpet till he dies; or whiles, if he be but a simple man, and without guile, we deliver him for thrall to some artificer amongst us, as a shoemaker, a wright, or what not, and so forget him. But in either case we make as if no such man had come to us, and we send again the lord and his knights to watch the pass; for we say that such an one the Fathers of old time have not sent us. But again, when we have seen to the new-comer that he is well-fashioned of his body, all is not done; for we deem that never would the Fathers send us a dolt or a craven to be our king. Therefore we bid the naked one take to him which he will of these raiments, either the ancient armour, which now thou bearest, lord, or this golden raiment here; and if he take the war-gear, as thou takedst it, King, it is well; but if he take the raiment of peace, then hath he the choice either to be thrall of some goodman of the city or to be proven how wise he may be, and so fare the narrow edge betwixt death and kingship; for if he fall short of his wisdom, then shall he die the death. Thus is thy question answered, King, and praise be to the Fathers that they have sent us one whom none may doubt, either for wisdom or valiancy."

CHAPTER XXXIV

Now Cometh the Maid to the King

THEN ALL THEY bowed before the King, and he spake again: "What is that noise that I hear without, as if it were the rising of the sea on a sandy shore, when the south-west wind is blowing."

Then the elder opened his mouth to answer; but before he might get out the word, there was a stir without the chamberdoor, and the throng parted, and lo! amidst of them came the Maid, and she yet clad in nought save the white coat wherewith she had won through the wilderness, save that on her head was a garland of red roses, and her middle was wreathed with the same. Fresh and fair she was as the dawn of June; her face bright, red-lipped, and clear-eyed, and her cheeks flushed with hope and love. She went straight to Walter where he sat, and lightly put away with her hand the elder who would lead her to the ivory throne beside the King; but she knelt down before him, and laid her hand on his steel-clad knee, and said: "O my lord, now I see that thou hast beguiled me, and that thou wert all along a king-born man coming home to thy realm. But so dear thou hast been to me; and so fair and clear, and so kind withal do thine eyes shine on me from under the grey war-helm, that I will beseech thee not to cast me out utterly, but suffer me to be thy servant and handmaid for a while. Wilt thou not?"

But the King stooped down to her and raised her up, and stood on his feet, and took her hands and kissed them, and set her down beside him, and said to her: "Sweetheart, this is now thy place till the night cometh, even by my side."

So she sat down there meek and valiant, her hands laid in her lap, and her feet one over the other; while the King said: "Lords, this is my beloved, and my spouse. Now, therefore, if ye will have me for King, ye must worship this one for Queen and Lady; or else suffer us both to go our ways in peace."

Then all they that were in the chamber cried out aloud: "The Queen, the Lady! The beloved of our lord!"

And this cry came from their hearts, and not their lips only; for as they looked on her, and the brightness of her beauty, they saw also the meekness of her demeanour, and the high heart of her, and they all fell to loving her. But the young men of them, their cheeks flushed as they beheld her, and their hearts went out to her, and they drew their swords and brandished them aloft, and cried out for her as men made suddenly drunk with love: "The Queen, the Lady, the lovely one!"

CHAPTER XXXV

Of the King of Stark-wall and His Queen

BUT WHILE THIS betid, that murmur without, which is aforesaid, grew louder; and it smote on the King's ear, and he said again to the elder: "Tell us now of that noise withoutward, what is it?"

Said the elder: "If thou, King, and the Queen, wilt but arise and stand in the window, and go forth into the hanging gallery thereof, then shall ye know at once what is this rumour, and therewithal shall ye see a sight meet to rejoice the heart of a king new come into kingship."

So the King arose and took the Maid by the hand, and went to the window and looked forth; and lo! the great square of the place all thronged with folk as thick as they could stand, and the more part of the carles with a weapon in hand, and many armed right gallantly. Then he went out into the gallery with his Queen, still holding her hand, and his lords and wise men stood behind him. Straightway then arose a cry, and a shout of joy and welcome that rent the very heavens, and the great place was all glittering and strange with the tossing up of spears and the brandishing of swords, and the stretching forth of hands.

But the Maid spake softly to King Walter and said: "Here then is the wilderness left behind a long way, and here is warding and protection against the foes of our life and soul. O blessed be thou and thy valiant heart!"

But Walter spake nothing, but stood as one in a dream; and yet, if that might be, his longing toward her increased manifold.

But down below, amidst of the throng, stood two neighbours somewhat anigh to the window; and quoth one to the other: "See thou! the new man in the ancient armour of the Battle of the Waters, bearing the sword that slew the foeman king on the Day of the Doubtful Onset! Surely this is a sign of good-luck to us all."

"Yea," said the second, "he beareth his armour well, and the eyes are bright in the head of him: but hast thou beheld well his she-fellow, and what the like of her is?"

"I see her," said the other, "that she is a fair woman; yet somewhat worse clad than simply. She is in her smock, man, and were it not for the balusters I deem ye should see her barefoot. What is amiss with her?"

"Dost thou not see her," said the second neighbour, "that she is not only a fair woman, but yet more, one of those lovely ones that draw the heart out of a man's body, one may scarce say for why? Surely Stark-wall hath cast a lucky net this time. And as to her raiment, I see of her that she is clad in white and wreathed with roses, but that the flesh of her is so wholly pure and sweet that it maketh all her attire but a part of her body, and halloweth it, so that it hath the semblance of gems. Alas, my friend! let us hope that this Queen will fare abroad unseldom amongst the people."

Thus, then, they spake; but after a while the King and his mate went back into the chamber, and he gave command that the women of the Queen should come and fetch her away, to attire her in royal array. And thither came the fairest of the honourable damsels, and were fain of being her waiting-women. Therewithal the King was unarmed, and dight most gloriously, but still he bore the Sword of the King's Slaying: and sithence were the King and the Queen brought into the great hall of the palace, and they met on the dais, and kissed before the lords and other folk that thronged the hall. There they ate a morsel and drank a cup together, while all beheld them; and then they were brought forth, and a white horse of the goodliest, well bedight, brought for each of them, and thereon they mounted and went their ways together, by the lane which the huge throng made for them, to the great church, for the hallowing and the crowning; and they were led by one squire alone, and he unarmed; for such was the custom of Stark-wall when a new king should be hallowed: so came they to the great church (for that folk was not miscreant, so to say), and they entered it, they two alone, and went into the choir: and when they had stood there a little while wondering at their lot, they heard how the bells fell a-ringing tunefully over their heads; and then drew near the sound of many trumpets blowing together, and thereafter the voices of many folk singing; and then were the great doors thrown open, and the bishop and his priests came into the church with singing and minstrelsy, and thereafter came the whole throng of the folk, and presently the nave of the church was filled by it, as when the water follows the cutting of the dam, and fills up the dyke. Thereafter came the bishop and his mates into the choir, and came up to the King, and gave him and the Queen the kiss of peace. Then was mass sung gloriously; and thereafter was the King anointed and crowned, and great joy was made throughout the church. Afterwards they went back afoot to the palace, they two alone together, with none but the esquire going before to show them the way. And as they went, they passed close beside those two neighbours, whose talk has been told of afore, and the first one, he who had praised the King's war-array, spake and said: "Truly, neighbour, thou art in the right of it; and now the Queen has been dight duly, and hath a crown on her head, and is clad in white samite done all over with pearls, I see her to be of exceeding goodliness; as goodly, maybe, as the Lord King."

Quoth the other: "Unto me she seemeth as she did e'en now; she is clad in white, as then she was, and it is by reason of the pure and sweet flesh of her that the pearls shine out and glow, and by the holiness of her body is her rich attire hallowed; but, forsooth, it seemed to me as she went past as though paradise had come anigh to our city, and that all the air breathed of it. So I say, praise be to God and His Hallows who hath suffered her to dwell amongst us!"

Said the first man: "Forsooth, it is well; but knowest thou at all whence she cometh, and of what lineage she may be?"

"Nay," said the other, "I wot not whence she is; but this I wot full surely, that when she goeth away, they whom she leadeth with her shall be well bestead. Again, of her lineage nought know I; but this I know, that they that come of her, to the twentieth generation, shall bless and praise the memory of her, and hallow her name little less than they hallow the name of the Mother of God."

So spake those two; but the King and Queen came back to the palace, and sat among the lords and at the banquet which was held thereafter, and long was the time of their glory, till the night was far spent and all men must seek to their beds.

CHAPTER XXXVI

Of Walter and the Maid in the Days of the Kingship

LONG IT WAS, indeed, till the women, by the King's command, had brought the Maid to the King's chamber; and he met her, and took her by the shoulders and kissed her, and said: "Art thou not weary, sweetheart? Doth not the city, and the thronging folk, and the watching eyes of the great ones . . . doth it not all lie heavy on thee, as it doth upon me?"

She said: "And where is the city now? is not this the wilderness again, and thou and I alone together therein?"

He gazed at her eagerly, and she reddened, so that her eyes shone light amidst the darkness of the flush of her cheeks.

He spake trembling and softly, and said: "Is it not in one matter better than the wilderness? is not the fear gone, yea, every whit thereof?"

The dark flush had left her face, and she looked on him exceeding sweetly, and spoke steadily and clearly: "Even so it is, beloved." Therewith she set her hand to the girdle that girt her loins, and did it off, and held it out toward him, and said: "Here is the token; this is a maid's girdle, and the woman is ungirt."

So he took the girdle and her hand withal, and cast his arms about her: and amidst the sweetness of their love and their safety, and assured hope of many days of joy, they spake together of the hours when they fared the razor-edge betwixt guile and misery and death, and the sweeter yet it grew to them because of it; and many things she told him ere the dawn, of the evil days bygone, and the dealings of the Mistress with her, tll the grey day stole into the chamber to make manifest her loveliness; which, forsooth, was better even than the deeming of that man amidst the throng whose heart had been so drawn towards her. So they rejoiced together in the new day.

But when the full day was, and Walter arose, he called his thanes and wise men to the council; and first he bade open the prison-doors, and feed the needy and clothe them, and make good cheer to all men, high and low, rich and unrich; and thereafter he took counsel with them on many matters, and they marvelled at his wisdom and the keenness of his wit; and so it was, that some were but half pleased thereat, whereas they saw that their will was like to give way before his in all matters. But the wiser of them rejoiced in him, and looked for good days while his life lasted.

Now of the deeds that he did, and his joys and his griefs, the tale shall tell no more; nor of how he saw Langton again, and his dealings there.

In Stark-wall he dwelt, and reigned a King, well beloved of his folk, sorely feared of their foemen. Strife he had to deal with, at home and abroad; but therein he was not quelled, till he fell asleep fair and softly, when this world had no more of deeds for him to do. Nor may it be said that the needy lamented him; for no needy had he left in his own land. And few foes he left behind to hate him.

As to the Maid, she so waxed in loveliness and kindness, that it was a year's joy for any to have cast eyes upon her in street or on field. All wizardry left her since the day of her wedding; yet of wit and wisdom she had enough left, and to spare; for she needed no going about, and no guile, any more than hard commands, to have her will done. So loved she was by all folk, forsooth, that it was a mere joy for any to go about her errands. To be short, she was the land's increase, and the city's safeguard, and the bliss of the folk.

Somewhat, as the days passed, it misgave her that she had beguiled the Bear-folk to deem her their God; and she considered and thought how she might atone it.

So the second year after they had come to Stark-wall, she went with certain folk to the head of the pass that led down to the Bears; and there she stayed the men-at-arms, and went on further with a two score of husbandmen whom she had redeemed from thralldom in Stark-wall; and when they were hard on the dales of the Bears, she left them there in a certain little dale, with their wains and horses, and seed-corn, and iron tools, and went down all bird-alone to the dwelling of those huge men, unguarded now by sorcery, and trusting in nought but her loveliness and kindness. Clad she was now, as when she fled from the Wood beyond the World, in a short white coat alone, with bare feet and naked arms; but the said coat was now embroidered with the imagery of blossoms in silk and gold, and gems, whereas now her wizardry had departed from her.

So she came to the Bears, and they knew her at once, and worshipped and blessed her, and feared her. But she told them that she had a gift for them, and was come to give it; and therewith she told them of the art of tillage, and bade them learn it; and when they asked her how they should do so, she told them of the men who were abiding them in the mountain dale, and bade the Bears take them for their brothers and sons of the ancient Fathers, and then they should be taught of them. This they behight her to do, and so she led them to where her freedmen lay, whom the Bears received with all joy and loving-kindness, and took them into their folk.

So they went back to their dales together; but the Maid went her ways back to her men-at-arms and the city of Stark-wall.

Thereafter she sent more gifts and messages to the Bears, but never again went herself to see them; for as good a face as she put on it that last time, yet her heart waxed cold with fear, and it almost seemed to her that her Mistress was alive again, and that she was escaping from her and plotting against her once more.

As for the Bears, they throve and multiplied; till at last strife arose great and grim betwixt them and other peoples; for they had become mighty in battle: yea, once and again they met the host of Stark-wall in fight, and overthrew and were overthrown. But that was a long while after the Maid had passed away.

Now of Walter and the Maid is no more to be told, saving that they begat between them goodly sons and fair daughters; whereof came a great lineage in Stark-wall; which lineage was so strong, and endured so long a while, that by then it had died out, folk had clean forgotten their ancient custom of king-making, so that after Walter of Langton there was never another king that came down to them poor and lonely from out of the Mountains of the Bears.

The Master Key

An Electrical Fairy Tale

FOUNDED UPON THE MYSTERIES
OF ELECTRICITY AND THE OPTIMISM
OF ITS DEVOTEES. IT WAS WRITTEN FOR
BOYS, BUT OTHERS MAY READ IT

By L. Frank Baum

Illustrations by F. Y. Cory

To my son
ROBERT STANTON BAUM

Who Knows?

These things are quite improbable, to be sure; but are they impossible?

Our big world rolls over as smoothly as it did centuries ago, without a squeak to show it needs oiling after all these years of revolution. But times change because men change, and because civilization, like John Brown's soul, goes ever marching on.

The impossibilities of yesterday become the accepted facts of today.

Here is a fairy tale founded upon the wonders of electricity and written for children of this generation. Yet when my readers shall have become men and women my story may not seem to their children like a fairy tale at all.

Perhaps one, perhaps two—perhaps several of the Demon's devices will be, by that time, in popular use.

Who knows?

"In wonder all philosophy began; in wonder it all ends;
and admiration fills up the interspace.
But the first wonder is the offspring of ignorance:
the last is the parent of adoration."

COLERIDGE.

The Master Key

CHAPTER I

Rob's Workshop

WHEN ROB became interested in electricity his clear-headed father considered the boy's fancy to be instructive as well as amusing; so he heartily encouraged his son, and Rob never lacked batteries, motors or supplies of any sort that his experiments might require.

He fitted up the little back room in the attic as his workshop, and from thence a network of wires soon ran throughout the house. Not only had every outside door its electric bell, but every window was fitted with a burglar alarm; moreover no one could cross the threshold of any interior room without registering the fact in Rob's workshop. The gas was lighted by an electric fob; a chime, connected with an erratic clock in the boy's room, woke the servants at all hours of the night and caused the cook to give warning; a bell rang whenever the postman dropped a letter into the box; there were bells, bells, bells everywhere, ringing at the right time, the wrong time and all the time. And there were telephones in the different rooms, too, through which Rob could call up the different members of the family just when they did not wish to be disturbed.

His mother and sisters soon came to vote the boy's scientific craze a nuisance; but his father was delighted with these evidences of Rob's skill as an electrician, and insisted that he be allowed perfect freedom in carrying out his ideas.

"Electricity," said the old gentleman, sagely, "is destined to become the motive power of the world. The future advance of civilization will be along electrical lines. Our boy may become a great inventor and astonish the world with his wonderful creations."

"And in the meantime," said the mother, despairingly, "we shall all be electrocuted, or the house burned down by crossed wires, or we shall be blown into eternity by an explosion of chemicals!"

"Nonsense!" ejaculated the proud father. "Rob's storage batteries are not powerful enough to electrocute one or set the house on fire. Do give the boy a chance, Belinda.''

"And his pranks are so humiliating," continued the lady. "When the minister called yesterday and rang the bell a big card appeared on the front door on which was printed the words: 'Busy; Call Again.' Fortunately Helen saw him and let him in, but when I reproved Robert for the act he said he was just trying the sign to see if it would work."

"Exactly! The boy is an inventor already. I shall have one of those cards attached to the door of my private office at once. I tell you, Belinda, our son will be a great man one of these days," said Mr. Joslyn, walking up and down with pompous strides and almost bursting with the pride he took in his young hopeful.

Mrs. Joslyn sighed. She knew remonstrance was useless so long as her husband encouraged the boy, and that she would be wise to bear her cross with fortitude.

Rob also knew his mother's protests would be of no avail; so he continued to revel in electrical processes of all sorts, using the house as an experimental station to test the powers of his productions.

It was in his own room, however,—his "workshop"—that he especially delighted. For not only was it the center of all his numerous "lines" throughout the house, but he had rigged up therein a wonderful array of devices for his own amusement. A trolley car moved around a circular track and stopped regularly at all stations; an engine and train of cars moved jerkily up and down a steep grade and through a tunnel; a windmill was busily pumping water from the dishpan into the copper skillet; a sawmill was in full operation and a host of mechanical blacksmiths, scissors-grinders, carpenters, wood-choppers and millers were connected with a motor which kept them working away at their trades in awkward but persevering fashion.

The room was crossed and recrossed with wires. They crept up the walls, lined the floor, made a grille of the ceiling and would catch an unwary visitor under the chin or above the ankle just when he least expected it. Yet visitors were forbidden in so crowded a room, and even his father declined to go farther than the doorway. As for Rob, he thought he knew all about the wires, and what each one was for; but they puzzled even him, at times, and he was often perplexed to know how to utilize them all.

One day when he had locked himself in to avoid interruption while he planned the electrical illumination of a gorgeous pasteboard palace, he really became confused over the network of wires. He had a "switchboard," to be sure, where he could make and break connections as he chose; but the wires had somehow become mixed, and he could not tell what combinations to use to throw the power on to his miniature electric lights.

So he experimented in a rather haphazard fashion, connecting this and that wire blindly and by guesswork, in the hope that he would strike the right combination. Then he thought the combination might be right and there was a lack of power; so he added other lines of wire to his connections, and still others, until he had employed almost every wire in the room.

Yet it would not work; and after pausing a moment to try to think what was wrong he went at it again, putting this and that line into connection, adding another here and another there, until suddenly, as he made a last change, a quick flash of light almost blinded him, and the switchboard crackled ominously, as if struggling to carry a powerful current.

Rob covered his face at the flash, but finding himself unhurt he took away his hands and with blinking eyes attempted to look at a wonderful radiance which seemed to fill the room, making it many times brighter than the brightest day.

Although at first completely dazzled, he peered before him until he discovered that the light was concentrated near one spot, from which all the glorious rays seemed to scintillate.

He closed his eyes a moment to rest them; then reopening them and shading them somewhat with his hands, he made out the form of a curious Being standing with majesty and composure in the center of the magnificent radiance and looking down upon him!

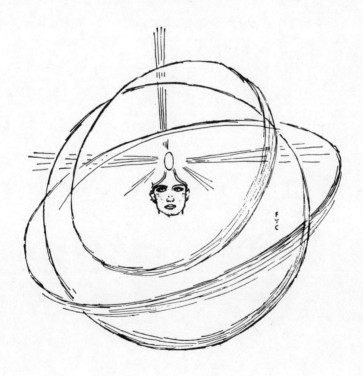

CHAPTER II

The Demon of Electricity

ROB WAS a courageous boy, but a thrill of fear passed over him in spite of his bravest endeavor as he gazed upon the wondrous apparition that confronted him. For several moments he sat as if turned to stone, so motionless was he; but his eyes were nevertheless fastened upon the Being and devouring every detail of his appearance.

And how strange an appearance he presented!

His jacket was a wavering mass of white light, edged with braid of red flames that shot little tongues in all directions. The buttons blazed in golden fire. His trousers had a bluish, incandescent color, with glowing stripes of crimson braid. His vest was gorgeous with all the colors of the rainbow blended into a flashing, resplendent mass. In feature he was most majestic, and his eyes held the soft but penetrating brilliance of electric lights.

It was hard to meet the gaze of those searching eyes, but Rob did it, and at once the splendid apparition bowed and said in a low, clear voice:

"I am here."

"I know that," answered the boy, trembling, "but *why* are you here?"

"Because you have touched the Master Key of Electricity, and I must obey the laws of nature that compel me to respond to your summons."

"I—I didn't know I touched the Master Key," faltered the boy.

"I understand that. You did it unconsciously. No one in the world has ever done it before, for Nature has hitherto kept the secret safe locked within her bosom."

Rob took time to wonder at this statement.

"Then who are you?" he inquired, at length.

"The Demon of Electricity," was the solemn answer.

"Good gracious!" exclaimed Rob, "a demon!"

"Certainly. I am, in truth, the Slave of the Master Key, and am forced to obey the commands of any one who is wise and brave enough—or, as in your own case, fortunate and foolhardy enough—to touch it."

"I—I've never guessed there was such a thing as a Master Key, or—or a Demon of Electricity, and—and I'm awfully sorry I—I called you up!"

stammered the boy, abashed by the imposing appearance of his companion.

The Demon actually smiled at this speech,—a smile that was almost reassuring.

"I am not sorry," he said, in kindlier tone, "for it is not much pleasure waiting century after century for some one to command my services. I have often thought my existence uncalled for, since you Earth people are so stupid and ignorant that you seem unlikely ever to master the secret of electrical power."

"Oh, we have some great masters among us!" cried Rob, rather nettled at this statement. "Now, there's Edison—"

"Edison!" exclaimed the Demon, with a faint sneer; "what does he know?"

"Lots of things," declared the boy. "He's invented no end of wonderful electrical things."

"You are wrong to call them wonderful," replied the Demon, lightly. "He really knows little more than yourself about the laws that control electricity. His inventions are trifling things in comparison with the really wonderful results to be obtained by one who would actually know how to direct the electric powers instead of groping blindly after insignificant effects. Why, I've stood for months by Edison's elbow, hoping and longing for him to touch the Master Key; but I can see plainly he will never accomplish it."

"Then there's Tesla," said the boy.

The Demon laughed.

"There is Tesla, to be sure," he said. "But what of him?"

"Why, he's discovered a powerful light," the Demon gave an amused chuckle, "and he's in communication with the people in Mars."

"What people?"

"Why, the people who live there."

"There are none."

This quiet statement almost took Rob's breath away, and caused him to stare hard at his visitor.

"It's generally thought," he resumed, in an annoyed tone, "that Mars has inhabitants who are far in advance of ourselves in civilization. Many scientific men think the people of Mars have been trying to signal us for years, only we don't understand their signals. And great novelists have written about the Martians and their wonderful civilization, and—"

"And they all know as much about that little planet as you do yourself," interrupted the Demon, impatiently. "The trouble with you Earth people is that you delight in guessing about what you can not know. Now I happen to know all about Mars, because I can traverse all space and have had ample leisure to investigate the different planets. Mars is not peopled at all, nor is any other of the planets you recognize in the heavens. Some contain low orders of beasts, to be sure, but Earth alone has an intelligent, thinking, reasoning population, and your scientists and novelists would do better trying to comprehend their own planet than in groping through space to unravel the mysteries of barren and unimportant worlds."

Rob listened to this with surprise and disappointment; but he reflected that the Demon ought to know what he was talking about, so he did not venture to contradict him.

"It is really astonishing," continued the Apparition, "how little you people have learned about electricity. It is an Earth element that has existed since the Earth itself was formed, and if you but understood its proper use humanity would be marvelously benefited in many ways."

"We are, already," protested Rob; "our discoveries in electricity have enabled us to live much more conveniently."

"Then imagine your condition were you able fully to control this great element," replied the other, gravely. "The weaknesses and privations of mankind would be converted into power and luxury."

"That's true, Mr.—Mr.—Demon," said the boy. "Excuse me if I don't get your name right, but I understood you to say you are a demon."

"Certainly. The Demon of Electricity."

"But electricity is a good thing, you know, and—and—"

"Well?"

"I've always understood that demons were bad things," added Rob, boldly.

"Not necessarily," returned his visitor. "If you will take the trouble to consult your dictionary, you will find that demons may be either good or bad, like any other class of beings. Originally all demons were good, yet of late years people have come to consider all demons evil. I do not know why. Should you read Hesiod you will find he says:

> 'Soon was a world of holy demons made,
> Aerial spirits, by great Jove designed
> To be on earth the guardians of mankind.' "

"But Jove was himself a myth," objected Rob, who had been studying mythology.

The Demon shrugged his shoulders.

"Then take the words of Mr. Shakespeare, to whom you all defer," he replied. "Do you not remember that he says:

> 'Thy demon (that's thy spirit which keeps thee) is
> Noble, courageous, high, unmatchable.' "

"Oh, if Shakespeare says it, that's all right," answered the boy. "But it seems you're more like a genius, for you answer the summons of the Master Key of Electricity in the same way Aladdin's genius answered the rubbing of the lamp."

"To be sure. A demon is also a genius; and a genius is a demon," said the Being. "What matters a name? I am here to do your bidding."

CHAPTER III

The Three Gifts

FAMILIARITY WITH any great thing removes our awe of it. The great general is only terrible to the enemy; the great poet is frequently scolded by his wife; the children of the great statesman clamber about his knees with perfect trust and impunity; the great actor who is called before the curtain by admiring audiences is often waylaid at the stage door by his creditors.

So Rob, having conversed for a time with the glorious Demon of Electricity, began to regard him with more composure and less awe, as his eyes grew more and more accustomed to the splendor that at first had well-nigh blinded them.

When the Demon announced himself ready to do the boy's bidding, he frankly replied:

"I am no skilled electrician, as you very well know. My calling you here was an accident. So I don't know how to command you, nor what to ask you to do."

"But I must not take advantage of your ignorance," answered the Demon. "Also, I am quite anxious to utilize this opportunity to show the world what a powerful element electricity really is. So permit me to inform you that, having struck the Master Key, you are at liberty to demand from me three gifts each week for three successive weeks. These gifts, provided they are within the scope of electricity, I will grant."

Rob shook his head regretfully.

"If I were a great electrician I should know what to ask," he said. "But I am too ignorant to take advantage of your kind offer."

"Then," replied the Demon, "I will myself suggest the gifts, and they will be of such a character that the Earth people will learn the possibilities that lie before them and be encouraged to work more intelligently and to persevere in mastering those natural and simple laws which control electricity. For one of the greatest errors they now labor under is that electricity is complicated and hard to understand. It is really the simplest Earth element, lying within easy reach of any one who stretches out his hand to grasp and control its powers."

Rob yawned, for he thought the Demon's speeches were growing rather tiresome. Perhaps the genius noticed this rudeness, for he continued:

"I regret, of course, that you are a boy instead of a grown man, for it will appear singular to your friends that so thoughtless a youth should seemingly have mastered the secrets that have baffled your most learned scientists. But that can not be helped, and presently you will become, through my aid, the most powerful and wonderful personage in all the world."

"Thank you," said Rob, meekly. "It'll be no end of fun."

"Fun!" echoed the Demon, scornfully. "But never mind; I must use the material Fate has provided for me, and make the best of it."

"What will you give me first?" asked the boy, eagerly.

"That requires some thought," returned the Demon, and paused for several moments, while Rob feasted his eyes upon the gorgeous rays of color that flashed and vibrated in every direction and surrounded the figure of his visitor with an intense glow that resembled a halo.

Then the Demon raised his head and said:

"The thing most necessary to man is food to nourish his body. He passes a considerable part of his life in the struggle to procure food, to prepare it properly, and in the act of eating. This is not right. Your body can not be very valuable to you if all your time is required to feed it. I shall, therefore, present you, as my first gift, this box of tablets. Within each tablet are stored certain elements of electricity which are capable of nourishing a human body for a full day. All you need do is to toss one into your mouth each day and swallow it. It will nourish you, satisfy your hunger and build up your health and strength. The ordinary food of mankind is more or less injurious; this is entirely beneficial. Moreover, you may carry enough tablets in your pocket to last for months."

Here he presented Rob the silver box of tablets, and the boy, somewhat nervously, thanked him for the gift.

"The next requirement of man," continued the Demon, "is defense from his enemies. I notice with sorrow that men frequently have wars and kill one another. Also, even in civilized communities, man is in constant danger from highwaymen, cranks and policemen. To defend himself he uses heavy and dangerous guns, with which to destroy his enemies. This is wrong. He has no right to take away what he can not bestow; to destroy what he can not create. To kill a fellow-creature is a horrid crime, even if done in self-defense. Therefore, my second gift to you is this little tube. You may carry it within your pocket. Whenever an enemy threatens you, be it man or beast, simply point the tube and press this button in the handle. An electric current will instantly be directed upon your foe, rendering him wholly unconscious for the period of one hour. During that time you will have opportunity to escape. As for your enemy, after regaining consciousness he will suffer no inconvenience from the encounter beyond a slight headache."

"That's fine!" said Rob, as he took the tube. It was scarcely six inches long, and hollow at one end.

"The busy lives of men," proceeded the Demon, "require them to move about and travel in all directions. Yet to assist them there are only such crude and awkward machines as electric trolleys, cable cars, steam

railways and automobiles. These crawl slowly over the uneven surface of
the earth and frequently get out of order. It has grieved me that men have
not yet discovered what even the birds know: that the atmosphere offers
them swift and easy means of traveling from one part of the earth's
surface to another."

"Some people have tried to build airships," remarked Rob.

"So they have; great, unwieldy machines which offer so much resistance to the air that they are quite useless. A big machine is not needed
to carry one through the air. There are forces in nature which may be
readily used for such purpose. Tell me, what holds you to the Earth, and
makes a stone fall to the ground?"

"Attraction of gravitation," said Rob, promptly.

"Exactly. That is one force I refer to," said the Demon. "The force of
repulsion, which is little known, but just as powerful, is another that
mankind may direct. Then there are the Polar electric forces, attracting
objects toward the north or south poles. You have guessed something of
this by the use of the compass, or electric needle. Opposed to these is
centrifugal electric force, drawing objects from east to west, or in the
opposite direction. This force is created by the whirl of the earth upon
its axis, and is easily utilized, although your scientific men have as yet paid
little attention to it.

"These forces, operating in all directions, absolute and immutable, are
at the disposal of mankind. They will carry you through the atmosphere
wherever and whenever you choose. That is, if you know how to control
them. Now, here is a machine I have myself perfected."

The Demon drew from his pocket something that resembled an open-
faced watch, having a narrow, flexible band attached to it.

"When you wish to travel," said he, "attach this little machine to your
left wrist by means of the band. It is very light and will not be in your way.
On this dial are points marked 'up' and 'down' as well as a perfect
compass. When you desire to rise into the air set the indicator to the word
'up,' using a finger of your right hand to turn it. When you have risen as
high as you wish, set the indicator to the point of the compass you want
to follow and you will be carried by the proper electric force in that
direction. To descend, set the indicator to the word 'down.' Do you
understand?"

"Perfectly!" cried Rob, taking the machine from the Demon with un-
feigned delight. "This is really wonderful, and I'm awfully obliged to
you!"

"Don't mention it," returned the Demon, dryly. "These three gifts you
may amuse yourself with for the next week. It seems hard to entrust such
great scientific discoveries to the discretion of a mere boy; but they are
quite harmless, so if you exercise proper care you can not get into trouble
through their possession. And who knows what benefits to humanity may
result? One week from today, at this hour, I will again appear to you, at
which time you shall receive the second series of electrical gifts."

"I'm not sure," said Rob, "that I shall be able again to make the
connections that will strike the Master Key."

"Probably not," answered the Demon. "Could you accomplish that,
you might command my services forever. But, having once succeeded,

you are entitled to the nine gifts—three each week for three weeks—so
you have no need to call me to do my duty. I shall appear of my own
accord."

"Thank you," murmured the boy.

The Demon bowed and spread his hands in the form of a semi-circle.
An instant later there was a blinding flash, and when Rob recovered from
it and opened his eyes the Demon of Electricity had disappeared.

CHAPTER IV

Testing the Instruments

THERE IS little doubt that had this strange experience befallen a grown man he would have been stricken with a fit of trembling or a sense of apprehension, or even fear, at the thought of having faced the terrible Demon of Electricity, of having struck the Master Key of the world's greatest natural forces, and finding himself possessed of three such wonderful and useful gifts. But a boy takes everything as a matter of course. As the tree of knowledge sprouts and expands within him, shooting out leaf after leaf of practical experience, the succession of surprises dulls his faculty of wonderment. It takes a great deal to startle a boy.

Rob was full of delight at his unexpected good fortune; but he did not stop to consider that there was anything remarkably queer or uncanny in the manner in which it had come to him. His chief sensation was one of pride. He would now be able to surprise those who had made fun of his electrical craze and force them to respect his marvelous powers. He decided to say nothing about the Demon or the accidental striking of the Master Key. In exhibiting to his friends the electrical devices he had acquired it would be "no end of fun" to mark their amazement and leave them to guess how he performed his feats.

So he put his treasures into his pocket, locked his workshop and went downstairs to his room to prepare for dinner.

While brushing his hair he remembered it was no longer necessary for him to eat ordinary food. He was feeling quite hungry at that moment, for he had a boy's ravenous appetite; but, taking the silver box from his pocket, he swallowed a tablet and at once felt his hunger as fully satisfied as if he had partaken of a hearty meal, while at the same time he experienced an exhilarating glow throughout his body and a clearness of brain and gaiety of spirits which filled him with intense gratification.

Still, he entered the dining room when the bell rang and found his father and mother and sisters already assembled there.

"Where have you been all day, Robert?" inquired his mother.

"No need to ask," said Mr. Joslyn, with a laugh. "Fussing over electricity, I'll bet a cookie!"

"I do wish," said the mother, fretfully, "that he would get over that mania. It unfits him for anything else."

"Precisely," returned her husband, dishing the soup; "but it fits him for a great career when he becomes a man. Why shouldn't he spend his summer vacation in pursuit of useful knowledge instead of romping around like ordinary boys?"

"No soup, thank you," said Rob.

"What!" exclaimed his father, looking at him in surprise, "it's your favorite soup."

"I know," said Rob, quietly, "but I don't want any."

"Are you ill, Robert?" asked his mother.

"Never felt better in my life," answered Rob, truthfully.

Yet Mrs. Joslyn looked worried, and when Rob refused the roast, she was really shocked.

"Let me feel your pulse, my poor boy!" she commanded, and wondered to find it so regular.

In fact, Rob's action surprised them all. He sat calmly throughout the meal, eating nothing, but apparently in good health and spirits, while even his sisters regarded him with troubled countenances.

"He's worked too hard, I guess," said Mr. Joslyn, shaking his head sadly.

"Oh, no; I haven't," protested Rob; "but I've decided not to eat anything, hereafter. It's a bad habit, and does more harm than good."

"Wait till breakfast," said sister Helen, with a laugh; "you'll be hungry enough by that time."

However, the boy had no desire for food at breakfast time, either, as the tablet sufficed for an entire day. So he renewed the anxiety of the family by refusing to join them at the table.

"If this goes on," Mr. Joslyn said to his son, when breakfast was finished, "I shall be obliged to send you away for your health."

"I think of making a trip this morning," said Rob, carelessly.

"Where to?"

"Oh, I may go to Boston, or take a run over to Cuba or Jamaica," replied the boy.

"But you can not go so far by yourself," declared his father; "and there is no one to go with you, just now. Nor can I spare the money at present for so expensive a trip."

"Oh, it won't cost anything," replied Rob, with a smile.

Mr. Joslyn looked upon him gravely and sighed. Mrs. Joslyn bent over her son with tears in her eyes and said:

"This electrical nonsense has affected your mind, dear. You must promise me to keep away from that horrid workshop for a time."

"I won't enter it for a week," he answered. "But you needn't worry about me. I haven't been experimenting with electricity all this time for nothing, I can tell you. As for my health, I'm as well and strong as any boy need be, and there's nothing wrong with my head, either. Common folks always think great men are crazy, but Edison and Tesla and I don't pay any attention to that. We've got our discoveries to look after. Now, as I said, I'm going for a little trip in the interests of science. I may be back tonight, or I may be gone several days. Anyhow, I'll be back in a week, and you mustn't worry about me a single minute."

"How are you going?" inquired his father, in the gentle, soothing tone persons use in addressing maniacs.

"Through the air," said Rob.

His father groaned.

"Where's your balloon?" inquired sister Mabel, sarcastically.

"I don't need a balloon," returned the boy. "That's a clumsy way of traveling, at best. I shall go by electric propulsion."

"Good gracious!" cried Mr. Joslyn, and the mother murmured: "My poor boy! my poor boy!"

"As you are my nearest relatives," continued Rob, not noticing these exclamations, "I will allow you to come into the back yard and see me start. You will then understand something of my electrical powers."

They followed him at once, although with unbelieving faces, and on the way Rob clasped the little machine to his left wrist, so that his coat sleeve nearly hid it.

When they reached the lawn at the back of the house Rob kissed them all good-by, much to his sisters' amusement, and turned the indicator of the little instrument to the word "up."

Immediately he began to rise into the air.

"Don't worry about me!" he called down to them. "Good-by!"

Mrs. Joslyn, with a scream of terror, hid her face in her hands.

"He'll break his neck!" cried the astounded father, tipping back his head to look after his departing son.

"Come back! Come back!" shouted the girls to the soaring adventurer.

"I will—some day!" was the far-away answer.

Having risen high enough to pass over the tallest tree or steeple, Rob put the indicator to the east of the compass-dial and at once began moving rapidly in that direction.

The sensation was delightful. He rode as gently as a feather floats, without any exertion at all on his own part; yet he moved so swiftly that he easily distanced a railway train that was speeding in the same direction.

"This is great!" reflected the youth. "Here I am, traveling in fine style, without a penny to pay any one! And I've enough food to last me a month in my coat pocket. This electricity is the proper stuff, after all! And the Demon's a trump, and no mistake. Whee-ee! How small everything looks down below there. The people are bugs, and the houses are soap boxes, and the trees are like clumps of grass. I seem to be passing over a town. Guess I'll drop down a bit, and take in the sights."

He pointed the indicator to the word "down," and at once began dropping through the air. He experienced the sensation one feels while descending in an elevator. When he reached a point just above the town he put the indicator to the zero mark and remained stationary, while he examined the place. But there was nothing to interest him, particularly; so after a brief survey he once more ascended and continued his journey toward the east.

At about two o'clock in the afternoon he reached the city of Boston, and alighting unobserved in a quiet street he walked around for several hours enjoying the sights and wondering what people would think of him if they but knew his remarkable powers. But as he looked just like any other boy no one noticed him in any way.

It was nearly evening, and Rob had wandered down by the wharves to look at the shipping, when his attention was called to an ugly looking bull dog, which ran toward him and began barking ferociously.

"Get out!" said the boy, carelessly, and made a kick at the brute.

The dog uttered a fierce growl and sprang upon him with bared teeth and flashing red eyes. Instantly Rob drew the electric tube from his pocket, pointed it at the dog and pressed the button. Almost at the same moment the dog gave a yelp, rolled over once or twice and lay still.

"I guess that'll settle him," laughed the boy; but just then he heard an angry shout, and looking around saw a policeman running toward him.

"Kill me dog, will ye—eh?" yelled the officer; "well, I'll just run ye in for that same, an' ye'll spend the night in the lockup!" And on he came, with drawn club in one hand and a big revolver in the other.

"You'll have to catch me first," said Rob, still laughing, and to the amazement of the policeman he began rising straight into the air.

"Come down here! Come down, or I'll shoot!" shouted the fellow, flourishing his revolver.

Rob was afraid he would; so, to avoid accidents, he pointed the tube at him and pressed the button. The red-whiskered policeman keeled over quite gracefully and fell across the body of the dog, while Rob continued to mount upward until he was out of sight of those in the streets.

"That was a narrow escape," he thought, breathing more freely. "I hated to paralyze that policeman, but he might have sent a bullet after me. Anyhow, he'll be all right again in an hour, so I needn't worry."

It was beginning to grow dark, and he wondered what he should do next. Had he possessed any money he would have descended to the town and taken a bed at a hotel, but he had left home without a single penny. Fortunately the nights were warm at this season, so he determined to travel all night, that he might reach by morning some place he had never before visited.

Cuba had always interested him, and he judged it ought to lie in a southeasterly direction from Boston. So he set the indicator to that point and began gliding swiftly toward the southeast.

He now remembered that it was twenty-four hours since he had eaten the first electrical tablet. As he rode through the air he consumed another. All hunger at once left him, while he felt the same invigorating sensations as before.

After a time the moon came out, and Rob amused himself gazing at the countless stars in the sky and wondering if the Demon was right when he said the world was the most important of all the planets.

But presently he grew sleepy, and before he realized what was happening he had fallen into a sound and peaceful slumber, while the indicator still pointed to the southeast and he continued to move rapidly through the cool night air.

CHAPTER V

The Cannibal Island

DOUBTLESS THE adventures of the day had tired Rob, for he slept through-out the night as comfortably as if he had been within his own room, lying upon his own bed. When, at last, he opened his eyes and gazed sleepily about him, he found himself over a great body of water, moving along with considerable speed.

"It's the ocean, of course," he said to himself. "I haven't reached Cuba yet."

It is to be regretted that Rob's knowledge of geography was so superficial; for, as he had intended to reach Cuba, he should have taken a course almost southwest from Boston, instead of southeast. The sad result of his ignorance you will presently learn, for during the entire day he continued to travel over a boundless waste of ocean, without the sight of even an island to cheer him.

The sun shone so hot that he regretted he had not brought an umbrella. But he wore a wide-brimmed straw hat, which protected him some-what, and he finally discovered that by rising to a considerable distance above the ocean he avoided the reflection of the sun upon the water and also came within the current of good breeze.

Of course he dared not stop, for there was no place to land; so he calmly continued his journey.

"It may be I've missed Cuba," he thought; "but I can not change my course now, for if I did I might get lost, and never be able to find land again. If I keep on as I am I shall be sure to reach land of some sort, in time, and when I wish to return home I can set the indicator to the northwest and that will take me directly back to Boston."

This was good reasoning, but the rash youth had no idea he was speeding over the ocean, or that he was destined to arrive shortly at the barbarous island of Brava, off the coast of Africa. Yet such was the case; just as the sun sank over the edge of the waves he saw, to his great relief, a large island directly in his path.

He dropped to a lower position in the air, and when he judged himself

364

to be over the center of the island he turned the indicator to zero and stopped short.

The country was beautifully wooded, while pretty brooks sparkled through the rich green foliage of the trees. The island sloped upwards from the sea coast in all directions, rising to a hill that was almost a mountain in the center. There were two open spaces, one on each side of the island, and Rob saw that these spaces were occupied by queer-looking huts built from brushwood and branches of trees. This showed that the island was inhabited, but as Rob had no idea what island it was he wisely determined not to meet the natives until he had discovered what they were like and whether they were disposed to be friendly.

So he moved over the hill, the top of which proved to be a flat, grass-covered plateau about fifty feet in diameter. Finding it could not be easily reached from below, on account of its steep sides, and contained neither men nor animals, he alighted on the hilltop and touched his feet to the earth for the first time in twenty-four hours.

The ride through the air had not tired him in the least; in fact, he felt as fresh and vigorous as if he had been resting throughout the journey. As he walked upon the soft grass of the plateau he felt elated, and compared himself to the explorers of ancient days; for it was evident that civilization had not yet reached this delightful spot.

There was scarcely any twilight in this tropical climate and it grew dark quickly. Within a few minutes the entire island, save where he stood, became dim and indistinct. He ate his daily tablet, and after watching the red glow fade in the western sky and the gray shadows of night settle around him he stretched himself comfortably upon the grass and went to sleep.

The events of the day must have deepened his slumber, for when he awoke the sun was shining almost directly over him, showing that the day was well advanced. He stood up, rubbed the sleep from his eyes and decided he would like a drink of water. From where he stood he could see several little brooks following winding paths through the forest, so he settled upon one that seemed farthest from the brushwood villages, and turning his indicator in that direction soon floated through the air to a sheltered spot upon the bank.

Kneeling down, he enjoyed a long, refreshing drink of the clear water, but as he started to regain his feet a coil of rope was suddenly thrown about him, pinning his arms to his sides and rendering him absolutely helpless.

At the same time his ears were saluted with a wild chattering in an unknown tongue, and he found himself surrounded by a group of natives of hideous appearance. They were nearly naked, and bore spears and heavy clubs as their only weapons. Their hair was long, curly, and thick as bushes, and through their noses and ears were stuck the teeth of sharks and curious metal ornaments.

These creatures had stolen upon Rob so quietly that he had not heard a sound, but now they jabbered loudly, as if much excited.

Finally one fat and somewhat aged native, who seemed to be a chief, came close to Rob and said, in broken English:

"How get here?"

"I flew," said the boy, with a grin.

The chief shook his head, saying:

"No boat come. How white man come?"

"Through the air," replied Rob, who was rather flattered at being called a "man."

The chief looked into the air with a puzzled expression and shook his head again.

"White man lie," he said calmly.

Then he held further conversation with his fellows, after which he turned to Rob and announced:

"Me see white man many times. Come in big boats. White men all bad. Make kill with bang-sticks. We kill white man with club. Then we eat white man. Dead white man good. Live white man bad!"

This did not please Rob at all. The idea of being eaten by savages had never occurred to him as a sequel to his adventures. So he said rather anxiously to the chief:

"Look here, old fellow; do you want to die?"

"Me no die. You die," was the reply.

"You'll die, too, if you eat me," said Rob. "I'm full of poison."

"Poison? Don't know poison," returned the chief, much perplexed to understand him.

"Well, poison will make you sick—awful sick. Then you'll die. I'm full of it; eat it every day for breakfast. It don't hurt white men, you see, but it kills black men quicker than the bang-stick."

The chief listened to this statement carefully, but only understood it in part. After a moment's reflection he declared:

"White man lie. Lie all time. Me eat plenty white man. Never get sick; never die." Then he added, with renewed cheerfulness: "Me eat you, too!"

Before Rob could think of a further protest, his captors caught up the end of the rope and led him away through the forest. He was tightly bound, and one strand of rope ran across the machine on his wrist and pressed it into his flesh until the pain was severe. But he resolved to be brave, whatever happened, so he stumbled along after the savages without a word.

After a brief journey they came to a village, where Rob was thrust into a brushwood hut and thrown upon the ground, still tightly bound.

"We light fire," said the chief. "Then kill little white man. Then eat him."

With this comforting promise he went away and left Rob alone to think the matter over.

"This is tough," reflected the boy, with a groan. "I never expected to feed cannibals. Wish I was at home with mother and dad and the girls. Wish I'd never seen the Demon of Electricity and his wonderful inventions. I was happy enough before I struck that awful Master Key. And now I'll be eaten—with salt and pepper, probably. Wonder if there'll be any gravy. Perhaps they'll boil me, with biscuits, as mother does chickens. Oh-h-h-h-h! It's just awful!"

In the midst of these depressing thoughts he became aware that something was hurting his back. After rolling over he found that he had been lying upon a sharp stone that stuck out of the earth. This gave him an idea. He rolled upon the stone again and began rubbing the rope that bound him against the sharp edge.

Outside he could hear the crackling of fagots and the roar of a newly kindled fire, so he knew he had no time to spare. He wriggled and pushed his body right and left, right and left, sawing away at the rope, until the strain and exertion started the perspiration from every pore.

At length the rope parted, and hastily uncoiling it from his body Rob stood up and rubbed his benumbed muscles and tried to regain his lost breath. He had not freed himself a moment too soon, he found, for hearing a grunt of surprise behind him he turned around and saw a native standing in the door of the hut.

Rob laughed, for he was not a bit afraid of the blacks now. As the native made a rush toward him the boy drew the electric tube from his pocket, pointed it at the foe, and pressed the button. The fellow sank to the earth without even a groan, and lay still.

Then another black entered, followed by the fat chief. When they saw Rob at liberty, and their comrade lying apparently dead, the chief cried out in surprise, using some expressive words in his own language.

"If it's just the same to you, old chap," said Rob, coolly, "I won't be eaten today. You can make a pie of that fellow on the ground."

"No! We eat you," cried the chief, angrily. "You cut rope, but no get away; no boat!"

"I don't need a boat, thank you," said the boy; and then, as the other native sprang forward, he pointed the tube and laid him out beside his first victim.

At this act the chief stood an instant in amazed uncertainty. Then he turned and rushed from the hut.

Laughing with amusement at the waddling, fat figure, Rob followed the chief and found himself standing almost in the center of the native village. A big fire was blazing merrily and the blacks were busy making preparations for a grand feast.

Rob was quickly surrounded by a crowd of the villagers, who chattered fiercely and made threatening motions in his direction; but as the chief cried out to them a warning in the native tongue they kept a respectful distance and contented themselves with brandishing their spears and clubs.

"If any of your fellows come nearer," Rob said to the fat chief, "I'll knock 'em over."

"What you make do?" asked the chief, nervously.

"Watch sharp, and you'll see," answered Rob. Then he made a mocking bow to the circle and continued: "I'm pleased to have met you fellows, and proud to think you like me well enough to want to eat me; but I'm in a bit of a hurry today, so I can't stop to be digested." After which, as the crowd broke into a hum of surprise, he added: "Good-day, black folks!" and quickly turned the indicator of his traveling machine to the word "up."

Slowly he rose into the air, until his heels were just above the gaping blacks; but there he stopped short. With a thrill of fear he glanced at the indicator. It was pointed properly, and he knew at once that something was wrong with the delicate mechanism that controlled it. Probably the pressure of the rope across its face, when he was bound, had put it out of order. There he was, seven feet in the air, but without the power to rise an inch farther.

This short flight, however, had greatly astonished the blacks, who, seeing his body suspended in mid-air, immediately hailed him as a god, and prostrated themselves upon the ground before him.

The fat chief had seen something of white men in his youth, and had learned to mistrust them. So, while he remained as prostrate as the rest, he peeped at Rob with one of his little black eyes and saw that the boy was ill at ease, and seemed both annoyed and frightened.

So he muttered some orders to the man next him, who wriggled along the ground until he had reached a position behind Rob, when he rose and pricked the suspended "god" with the point of his spear.

"Ouch!" yelled the boy; "stop that!"

He twisted his head around, and seeing the black again make a movement with the spear, Rob turned his electric tube upon him and keeled him over like a ten-pin.

The natives, who had looked up at his cry of pain, again prostrated themselves, kicking their toes against the ground in a terrified tattoo at this new evidence of the god's powers.

The situation was growing somewhat strained by this time, and Rob did not know what the savages would decide to do next; so he thought it best to move away from them, since he was unable to rise to a greater height. He turned the indicator towards the south, where a level space appeared between the trees; but instead of taking that direction he moved towards the northeast, a proof that his machine had now become absolutely unreliable. Moreover, he was slowly approaching the fire, which, although it had ceased blazing, was a mass of glowing red embers.

In his excitement he turned the indicator this way and that, trying to change the direction of his flight, but the only result of his endeavor was to carry him directly over the fire, where he came to a full stop.

"Murder! Help! Fire and blazes!" he cried, as he felt the glow of the coals beneath him. "I'll be roasted, after all! Here; help, Fatty, help!"

The fat chief sprang to his feet and came to the rescue. He reached up, caught Rob by the heels, and pulled him down to the ground, away from the fire. But the next moment, as he clung to the boy's feet, they both soared into the air again, and, although now far enough from the fire to escape its heat, the savage, finding himself lifted from the earth, uttered a scream of horror and let go of Rob, to fall head over heels upon the ground.

The other blacks had by this time regained their feet, and now they crowded around their chief and set him upright again.

Rob continued to float in the air, just above their heads, and now abandoned all thoughts of escaping by means of his wrecked traveling machine. But he resolved to regain a foothold upon the earth and take his chances of escape by running rather than flying. So he turned the indicator to the word "down," and very slowly it obeyed, allowing him, to his great relief, to sink gently to the ground.

CHAPTER VI

The Buccaneers

ONCE MORE the blacks formed a circle around our adventurer, who coolly drew his tube and said to the chief:

"Tell your people I'm going to walk away through those trees, and if any one dares to interfere with me I'll paralyze him."

The chief understood enough English to catch his meaning, and repeated the message to his men. Having seen the terrible effect of the electric tube they wisely fell back and allowed the boy to pass.

He marched through their lines with a fine air of dignity, although he was fearful lest some of the blacks should stick a spear into him or bump his head with a warclub. But they were awed by the wonders they had seen and were still inclined to believe him a god, so he was not molested.

When he found himself outside the village he made for the high plateau in the center of the island, where he could be safe from the cannibals while he collected his thoughts. But when he reached the place he found the sides so steep he could not climb them, so he adjusted the indicator to the word "up" and found it had still enough power to support his body while he clambered up the rocks to the level, grass-covered space at the top.

Then, reclining upon his back, he gave himself up to thoughts of how he might escape from his unpleasant predicament.

"Here I am, on a cannibal island, hundreds of miles from civilization, with no way to get back," he reflected. "The family will look for me every day, and finally decide I've broken my neck. The Demon will call upon me when the week is up and won't find me at home; so I'll miss the next three gifts. I don't mind that so much, for they might bring me into worse scrapes than this. But how am I to get away from this beastly island? I'll be eaten, after all, if I don't look out!"

These and similar thoughts occupied him for some time, yet in spite of much planning and thinking he could find no practical means of escape.

At the end of an hour he looked over the edge of the plateau and found it surrounded by a ring of the black cannibals, who had calmly seated themselves to watch his movements.

"Perhaps they intend to starve me into surrender," he thought; "but they won't succeed so long as my tablets hold out. And if, in time, they should starve me, I'll be too thin and tough to make good eating; so I'll get the best of them, anyhow."

Then he again lay down and began to examine his electrical traveling machine. He did not dare take it apart, fearing he might not be able to get it together again, for he knew nothing at all about its construction. But he discovered two little dents on the edge, one on each side, which had evidently been caused by the pressure of the rope.

"If I could get those dents out," he thought, "the machine might work."

He first tried to pry out the edges with his pocket knife, but the attempt resulted in failure. Then, as the sides seemed a little bulged outward by the dents, he placed the machine between two flat stones and pressed them together until the little instrument was nearly round again. The dents remained, to be sure, but he hoped he had removed the pressure upon the works.

There was just one way to discover how well he had succeeded, so he fastened the machine to his wrist and turned the indicator to the word "up."

Slowly he ascended, this time to a height of nearly twenty feet. Then his progress became slower and finally ceased altogether.

"That's a little better," he thought. "Now let's see if it will go side-wise."

He put the indicator to "north-west,"—the direction of home—and very slowly the machine obeyed and carried him away from the plateau and across the island.

The natives saw him go, and springing to their feet began uttering excited shouts and throwing their spears at him. But he was already so high and so far away that they failed to reach him, and the boy continued his journey unharmed.

Once the branches of a tall tree caught him and nearly tipped him over; but he managed to escape others by drawing up his feet. At last he was free of the island and traveling over the ocean again. He was not at all sorry to bid good-by to the cannibal island, but he was worried about the machine, which clearly was not in good working order. The vast ocean was beneath him, and he moved no faster than an ordinary walk.

"At this rate I'll get home some time next year," he grumbled. "However, I suppose I ought to be glad the machine works at all." And he really was glad.

All the afternoon and all the long summer night he moved slowly over the water. It was annoying to go at "a reg'lar jog-trot," as Rob called it, after his former swift flight; but there was no help for it.

Just as dawn was breaking he saw in the distance a small vessel, sailing in the direction he was following, yet scarcely moving for lack of wind. He soon caught up with it, but saw no one on deck, and the craft had a dingy and uncared-for appearance that was not reassuring. But after hovering over it for some time Rob decided to board the ship and rest for a while. He alighted near the bow, where the deck was highest, and was about to explore the place when a man came out of the low cabin and espied him.

This person had a most villainous countenance, and was dark-skinned, black-bearded and dressed in an outlandish, piratical costume. On seeing the boy he gave a loud shout and was immediately joined by four companions, each as disagreeable in appearance as the first.

Rob knew there would be trouble the moment he looked at this evil crew, and when they drew their daggers and pistols and began fiercely shouting in an unknown tongue, the boy sighed and took the electric tube from his coat pocket.

The buccaneers did not notice the movement, but rushed upon him so quickly that he had to press the button at a lively rate. The tube made no noise at all, so it was a strange and remarkable sight to see the pirates suddenly drop to the deck and lie motionless. Indeed, one was so nearly upon him when the electric current struck him that his head, in falling, bumped into Rob's stomach and sent him reeling against the side of the vessel.

He quickly recovered himself, and seeing his enemies were rendered harmless, the boy entered the cabin and examined it curiously. It was dirty and ill-smelling enough, but the corners and spare berths were heaped with merchandise of all kinds which had been taken from those so unlucky as to have met these cruel and desperate men.

After a short inspection of the place he returned to the deck and again seated himself in the bow.

The crippled condition of his traveling machine was now his chief trouble, and although a good breeze had sprung up to fill the sails and the little bark was making fair headway, Rob knew he could never expect to reach home unless he could discover a better mode of conveyance than this.

He unstrapped the machine from his wrist to examine it better, and while holding it carelessly in his hand it slipped and fell with a bang to the deck, striking upon its round edge and rolling quickly past the cabin and out of sight. With a cry of alarm he ran after it, and after much search found it lying against the bulwark near the edge of a scupper hole, where the least jar of the ship would have sent it to the bottom of the ocean. Rob hastily seized his treasure, and upon examining it found the fall had bulged the rim so that the old dents scarcely showed at all. But its original shape was more distorted than ever, and Rob feared he had utterly ruined its delicate mechanism. Should this prove to be true, he might now consider himself a prisoner of this piratical band, the members of which, although temporarily disabled, would soon regain consciousness.

He sat in the bow, sadly thinking of his misfortunes, until he noticed that one of the men began to stir. The effect of the electric shock conveyed by the tube was beginning to wear away, and now the buccaneer sat up, rubbed his head in a bewildered fashion and looked around him. When he saw Rob he gave a shout of rage and drew his knife, but one motion of the electric tube made him cringe and slip away to the cabin, where he remained out of danger.

And now the other four sat up, groaning and muttering in their outlandish speech; but they had no notion of facing Rob's tube a second time, so one by one they joined their leader in the cabin, leaving the boy undisturbed.

By this time the ship had begun to pitch and toss in an uncomfortable fashion, and Rob noticed that the breeze had increased to a gale. There being no one to look after the sails, the vessel was in grave danger of capsizing or breaking her masts. The waves were now running high, too, and Rob began to be worried.

Presently the captain of the pirates stuck his head out of the cabin door, jabbered some unintelligible words and pointed to the sails. The boy nodded, for he understood they wanted to attend to the rigging. So the crew trooped forth, rather fearfully, and began to reef the sails and put the ship into condition to weather the storm.

Rob paid no further attention to them. He looked at his traveling machine rather doubtfully and wondered if he dared risk its power to carry him through the air. Whether he remained in the ship or trusted to the machine, he stood a good chance of dropping into the sea at any moment. So, while he hesitated, he attached the machine to his wrist and leaned over the bulwarks to watch the progress of the storm. He might stay in the ship until it foundered, he thought, and then take his chances with the machine. He decided to wait until a climax arrived.

The climax came the next moment, for while he leaned over the bulwarks the buccaneers stole up behind him and suddenly seized him in their grasp. While two of them held his arms the others searched his pockets, taking from him the electric tube and the silver box containing his tablets. These they carried to the cabin and threw upon the heap of other valuables they had stolen. They did not notice his traveling machine, however, but seeing him now unarmed they began jeering and laughing at him, while the brutal captain relieved his anger by giving the prisoner several malicious kicks.

Rob bore his misfortune meekly, although he was almost ready to cry with grief and disappointment. But when one of the pirates, to inflict further punishment on the boy, came towards him with a heavy strap, he resolved not to await the blow.

Turning the indicator to the word "up" he found, to his joy and relief, that it would yet obey the influence of the power of repulsion. Seeing him rise into the air the fellow made a grab for his foot and held it firmly, while his companions ran to help him. Weight seemed to make no difference in the machine; it lifted the pirate as well as Rob; it lifted another who clung to the first man's leg, and another who clung to him. The other two also caught hold, hoping their united strength would pull him down, and the next minute Rob was soaring through the air with the entire string of five buccaneers dangling from his left leg.

At first the villains were too astounded to speak, but as they realized that they were being carried through the air and away from their ship they broke into loud shouts of dismay, and finally the one who grasped Rob's leg lost his hold and the five plunged downward and splashed into the sea.

Finding the machine disposed to work accurately, Rob left the buccaneers to swim to the ship in the best way they could, while he dropped down to the deck again and recovered from the cabin his box of tablets and the electric tube. The fellows were just scrambling on board when he again escaped, shooting into the air with considerable speed.

Indeed, the instrument now worked better than at any time since he had reached the cannibal island, and the boy was greatly delighted.

The wind at first sent him spinning away to the south, but he continued to rise until he was above the air currents, and the storm raged far beneath him. Then he set the indicator to the northwest and breathlessly waited to see if it would obey. Hurrah! away he sped at a fair rate of speed, while all his anxiety changed to a feeling of sweet contentment.

His success had greatly surprised him, but he concluded that the jar caused by dropping the instrument had relieved the pressure upon the works, and so helped rather than harmed the free action of the electric currents.

While he moved through the air with an easy, gliding motion he watched with much interest the storm raging below. Above his head the sun was peacefully shining and the contrast was strange and impressive. After an hour or so the storm abated, or else he passed away from it, for the deep blue of the ocean again greeted his eyes. He dropped downward until he was about a hundred feet above the water, when he continued his northwesterly course.

But now he regretted having interfered for a moment with the action of the machine, for his progress, instead of being swift as a bird's flight, became slow and jerky, nor was he sure that the damaged machine might not break down altogether at any moment. Yet so far his progress was in the right direction, and he resolved to experiment no further with the instrument, but to let it go as it would, so long as it supported him above the water. However irregular the motion might be, it was sure, if continued, to bring him to land in time, and that was all he cared about just then.

When night fell his slumber was broken and uneasy, for he wakened more than once with a start of fear that the machine had broken and he was falling into the sea. Sometimes he was carried along at a swift pace, and again the machine scarcely worked at all; so his anxiety was excusable.

The following day was one of continued uneasiness for the boy, who began to be harassed by doubts as to whether, after all, he was moving in the right direction. The machine had failed at one time in this respect and it might again. He had lost all confidence in its accuracy.

In spite of these perplexities Rob passed the second night of his uneven flight in profound slumber, being exhausted by the strain and excitement he had undergone. When he awoke at daybreak, he saw, to his profound delight, that he was approaching land.

The rising sun found him passing over a big city, which he knew to be Boston.

He did not stop. The machine was so little to be depended upon that he dared make no halt. But he was obliged to alter the direction from northwest to west, and the result of this slight change was so great a reduction in speed that it was mid-day before he saw beneath him the familiar village in which he lived.

Carefully marking the location of his father's house, he came to a stop directly over it, and a few moments later he managed to land upon the exact spot in the back yard whence he had taken his first successful flight.

CHAPTER VII

The Demon Becomes Angry

WHEN ROB had been hugged and kissed by his mother and sisters, and even Mr. Joslyn had embraced him warmly, he gave them a brief account of his adventures. The story was received with many doubtful looks and much grave shaking of heads, as was quite natural under the circumstances.

"I hope, my dear son," said his father, "that you have now passed through enough dangers to last you a lifetime, so that hereafter you will be contented to remain at home."

"Oh, Robert!" cried his mother, with tears in her loving eyes, "you don't know how we've all worried about you for the past week!"

"A week?" asked Rob, with surprise.

"Yes; it's a week tomorrow morning since you flew into the air and disappeared."

"Then," said the boy, thoughtfully, "I've reached home just in time."

"In time for what?" she asked.

But he did not answer that question. He was thinking of the Demon, and that on the afternoon of this very day he might expect the wise and splendid genius to visit him a second time.

At luncheon, although he did not feel hungry, he joined the family at table and pleased his mother by eating as heartily as of old. He was surprised to find how good the food tasted, and to realize what a pleasure it is to gratify one's sense of taste. The tablets were all right for a journey, he thought, but if he always ate them he would be sure to miss a great deal of enjoyment, since there was no taste to them at all.

At four o'clock he went to his workshop and unlocked the door. Everything was exactly as he had left it, and he looked at his simple electrical devices with some amusement. They seemed tame beside the wonders now in his possession; yet he recollected that his numerous wires had enabled him to strike the Master Key, and therefore should not be despised.

Before long he noticed a quickening in the air, as if it were suddenly surcharged with electric fluid, and the next instant, in a dazzling flash of light, appeared the Demon.

"I am here!" he announced.

"So am I," answered Rob. "But at one time I really thought I should never see you again. I've been—"

"Spare me your history," said the Demon, coldly. "I am aware of your adventures."

"Oh, you are!" said Rob, amazed. "Then you know—"

"I know all about your foolish experiences," interrupted the Demon, "for I have been with you constantly, although I remained invisible."

"Then you know what a jolly time I've had," returned the boy. "But why do you call them foolish experiences?"

"Because they were, abominably foolish!" retorted the Demon, bitterly. "I entrusted to you gifts of rare scientific interest—electrical devices of such utility that their general adoption by mankind would create a new era in earth life. I hoped your use of these devices would convey such hints to electrical engineers that they would quickly comprehend their mechanism and be able to reproduce them in sufficient quantities to supply the world. And how do you treat these marvelous gifts? Why, you carry them to a cannibal island, where even your crude civilization has not yet penetrated!"

"I wanted to astonish the natives," said Rob, grinning.

The Demon uttered an exclamation of anger, and stamped his foot so fiercely that thousands of electric sparks filled the air, to disappear quickly with a hissing, crinkling sound.

"You might have astonished those ignorant natives as easily by showing them an ordinary electric light," he cried, mockingly. "The power of your gifts would have startled the most advanced electricians of the world. Why did you waste them upon barbarians?"

"Really," faltered Rob, who was frightened and awed by the Demon's vehement anger, "I never intended to visit a cannibal island. I meant to go to Cuba."

"Cuba! Is that a center of advanced scientific thought? Why did you not take your marvels to New York or Chicago; or, if you wished to cross the ocean, to Paris or Vienna?"

"I never thought of those places," acknowledged Rob, meekly.

"Then you were foolish, as I said," declared the Demon, in a calmer tone. "Can you not realize that it is better to be considered great by the intelligent thinkers of the earth, than to be taken for a god by stupid cannibals?"

"Oh, yes, of course," said Rob. "I wish now that I had gone to Europe. But you're not the only one who has a kick coming," he continued. "Your flimsy traveling machine was nearly the death of me."

"Ah, it is true," acknowledged the Demon, frankly. "The case was made of too light material. When the rim was bent it pressed against the works and impeded the proper action of the currents. Had you gone to a civilized country such an accident could not have happened; but to avoid possible trouble in the future I have prepared a new instrument, having a stronger case, which I will exchange for the one you now have."

"That's very kind of you," said Rob, eagerly handing his battered machine to the Demon and receiving the new one in return. "Are you sure this will work?"

"It is impossible for you to injure it," answered the other.

"And how about the next three gifts?" inquired the boy, anxiously.

"Before I grant them," replied the Demon, "you must give me a promise to keep away from uncivilized places and to exhibit your acquirements only among people of intelligence."

"All right," agreed the boy; "I'm not anxious to visit that island again, or any other uncivilized country."

"Then I will add to your possessions three gifts, each more precious and important than the three you have already received."

At this announcement Rob began to quiver with excitement, and sat staring eagerly at the Demon, while the latter increased in stature and sparkled and glowed more brilliantly than ever.

CHAPTER VIII

Rob Acquires New Powers

"I HAVE seen the folly of sending you into the world with an offensive instrument, yet with no method of defense," resumed the Demon, presently. "You have knocked over a good many people with that tube during the past week."

"I know," said Rob; "but I couldn't help it. It was the only way I had to protect myself."

"Therefore my next gift shall be this Garment of Protection. You must wear it underneath your clothing. It has power to accumulate and exercise electrical repellent force. Perhaps you do not know what that means, so I will explain more fully. When any missile, such as a bullet, sword or lance, approaches your person, its rush through the air will arouse the repellent force of which I speak, and this force, being more powerful than the projective force, will arrest the flight of the missile and throw it back again. Therefore nothing can touch your person that comes with any degree of force or swiftness, and you will be safe from all ordinary weapons. When wearing this Garment you will find it unnecessary to use the electric tube except on rare occasions. Never allow revenge or animosity to influence your conduct. Men may threaten, but they can not injure you, so you must remember that they do not possess your mighty advantages, and that, because of your strength, you should bear with them patiently."

Rob examined the garment with much curiosity. It glittered like silver, yet was soft and pliable as lamb's wool. Evidently the Demon had prepared it especially for his use, for it was just Rob's size.

"Now," continued the Demon, more gravely, "we approach the subject of an electrical device so truly marvelous that even I am awed when I contemplate the accuracy and perfection of the natural laws which guide it and permit it to exercise its functions. Mankind has as yet conceived nothing like it, for it requires full knowledge of electrical power to understand even its possibilities."

The Being paused, and drew from an inner pocket something resembling a flat metal box. In size it was about four inches by six, and nearly an inch in thickness.

"What is it?" asked Rob, wonderingly.

"It is an automatic Record of Events," answered the Demon.

"I don't understand," said Rob, with hesitation.

"I will explain to you its use," returned the Demon, "although the electrical forces which operate it and the vibratory currents which are the true records must remain unknown to you until your brain has mastered the higher knowledge of electricity. At present the practical side of this invention will be more interesting to you than a review of its scientific construction.

"Suppose you wish to know the principal events that are occurring in Germany at the present moment. You first turn this little wheel at the side until the word 'GERMANY' appears in the slot at the small end. Then open the top cover, which is hinged, and those passing events in which you are interested will appear before your eyes."

The Demon, as he spoke, opened the cover, and, looking within, the boy saw, as in a mirror, a moving picture before him. A regiment of soldiers was marching through the streets of Berlin, and at its head rode a body of horsemen, in the midst of which was the Emperor himself. The people who thronged the sidewalks cheered and waved their hats and handkerchiefs with enthusiasm, while a band of musicians played a German air, which Rob could distinctly hear.

While he gazed, spell-bound, the scene changed, and he looked upon a great warship entering a harbor with flying pennants. The rails were lined with officers and men straining their eyes for the first sight of their beloved "*Vaterland*" after a long foreign cruise, and a ringing cheer, as from a thousand throats, came faintly to Rob's ear.

Again the scene changed, and within a dingy, underground room, hemmed in by walls of stone, and dimly lighted by a flickering lamp, a body of wild-eyed, desperate men were plighting an oath to murder the Emperor and overthrow his government.

"Anarchists?" asked Rob, trembling with excitement.

"Anarchists!" answered the Demon, with a faint sneer, and he shut the cover of the Record with a sudden snap.

"It's wonderful!" cried the boy, with a sigh that was followed by a slight shiver.

"The Record is, indeed, proof within itself of the marvelous possibilities of electricity. Men are now obliged to depend upon newspapers for information; but these can only relate events long after they have occurred. And newspaper statements are often unreliable and sometimes wholly false, while many events of real importance are never printed in their columns. You may guess what an improvement is this automatic Record of Events, which is as reliable as Truth itself. Nothing can be altered or falsified, for the vibratory currents convey the actual events to your vision, even as they happen."

"But suppose," said Rob, "that something important should happen while I'm asleep, or not looking at the box?"

"I have called this a Record," replied the Demon, "and such it really is, although I have shown you only such events as are in process of being recorded. By pressing this spring you may open the opposite cover of the box, where all events of importance that have occurred throughout the world during the previous twenty-four hours will appear before you in succession. You may thus study them at your leisure. The various scenes constitute a register of the world's history, and may be recalled to view as often as you desire."

"It's—it's like knowing everything," murmured Rob, deeply impressed for perhaps the first time in his life.

"It *is* knowing everything," returned the Demon; "and this mighty gift I have decided to entrust to your care. Be very careful as to whom you permit to gaze upon these pictures of passing events, for knowledge may often cause great misery to the human race."

"I'll be careful," promised the boy, as he took the box reverently within his own hands.

"The third and last gift of the present series," resumed the Demon, "is one no less curious than the Record of Events, although it has an entirely different value. It is a Character Marker."

"What's that?" inquired Rob.

"I will explain. Perhaps you know that your fellow-creatures are more or less hypocritical. That is, they try to appear good when they are not, and wise when in reality they are foolish. They tell you they are friendly when they positively hate you, and try to make you believe they are kind when their natures are cruel. This hypocrisy seems to be a human failing. One of your writers has said, with truth, that among civilized people things are seldom what they seem."

"I've heard that," remarked Rob.

"On the other hand," continued the Demon, "some people with fierce countenances are kindly by nature, and many who appear to be evil are in reality honorable and trustworthy. Therefore, that you may judge all your fellow-creatures truly, and know upon whom to depend, I give you the Character Marker. It consists of this pair of spectacles. While you wear them every one you meet will be marked upon the forehead with a letter indicating his or her character. The good will bear the letter 'G,' the evil the letter 'E.' The wise will be marked with a 'W' and the foolish with an 'F.' The kind will show a 'K' upon their foreheads and the cruel a letter 'C.' Thus you may determine by a single look the true natures of all those you encounter."

"And are these, also, electrical in their construction?" asked the boy, as he took the spectacles.

"Certainly. Goodness, wisdom and kindness are natural forces, creating character. For this reason men are not always to blame for bad character, as they acquire it unconsciously. All character sends out certain electrical vibrations, which these spectacles concentrate in their lenses and exhibit to the gaze of their wearer, as I have explained."

"It's a fine idea," said the boy; "who discovered it?"

"It is a fact that has always existed, but is now utilized for the first time."

"Oh!" said Rob.

"With these gifts, and the ones you acquired a week ago, you are now equipped to astound the world and awaken mankind to a realization of the wonders that may be accomplished by natural forces. See that you employ these powers wisely, in the interests of science, and do not forget your promise to exhibit your electrical marvels only to those who are most capable of comprehending them."

"I'll remember," said Rob.

"Then adieu until a week from today, when I will meet you here at this hour and bestow upon you the last three gifts which you are entitled to receive. Good-by!"

"Good-by!" repeated Rob, and in a gorgeous flash of color the Demon disappeared, leaving the boy alone in the room with his new and wonderful possessions.

CHAPTER IX

The Second Journey

By this time you will have gained a fair idea of Rob's character. He is, in truth, a typical American boy, possessing an average intelligence not yet regulated by the balance-wheel of experience. The mysteries of electricity were so attractive to his eager nature that he had devoted considerable time and some study to electrical experiment; but his study was the superficial kind that seeks to master only such details as may be required at the moment. Moreover, he was full of boyish recklessness and irresponsibility and therefore difficult to impress with the dignity of science and the gravity of human existence. Life, to him, was a great theater wherein he saw himself the most interesting if not the most important actor, and so enjoyed the play with unbounded enthusiasm.

Aside from the extraordinary accident which had forced the Electrical Demon into his life, Rob may be considered one of those youngsters who might possibly develop into a brilliant manhood or enter upon an ordinary, humdrum existence, as Fate should determine. Just at present he had no thought beyond the passing hour, nor would he bother himself by attempting to look ahead or plan for the future.

Yet the importance of his electrical possessions and the stern injunction of the Demon to use them wisely had rendered the boy more thoughtful than at any previous time during his brief life, and he became so preoccupied at the dinner table that his father and mother cast many anxious looks in his direction.

Of course Rob was anxious to test his newly acquired powers, and decided to lose no time in starting upon another journey. But he said nothing to any of the family about it, fearing to meet with opposition.

He passed the evening in the sitting room, in company with his father and mother and sisters, and even controlled his impatience to the extent of playing a game of carom with Nell; but he grew so nervous and impatient at last that his sister gave up the game in disgust and left him to his own amusement.

At one time he thought of putting on the electric spectacles and seeing what the real character of each member of his family might be; but a sudden fear took possession of him that he might regret the act forever afterward. They were his nearest and dearest friends on earth, and in his boyish heart he loved them all and believed in their goodness and sincerity. The possibility of finding a bad character mark on any of their familiar faces made him shudder, and he determined then and there never to use the spectacles to view the face of a friend or relative. Had any one, at that moment, been gazing at Rob through the lenses of the wonderful Character Marker, I am sure a big "W" would have been found upon the boy's forehead.

When the family circle broke up, and all retired for the night, Rob kissed his parents and sisters with real affection before going to his own room. But, on reaching his cozy little chamber, instead of preparing for bed Rob clothed himself in the Garment of Repulsion. Then he covered the glittering Garment with his best summer suit of clothes, which effectually concealed it.

He now looked around to see what else he should take, and thought of an umbrella, a raincoat, a book or two to read during the journey, and several things besides; but he ended by leaving them all behind.

"I can't be loaded down with so much truck," he decided; "and I'm going into civilized countries, this time, where I can get anything I need."

However, to prevent a recurrence of the mistake he had previously made, he tore a map of the world and a map of Europe from his geography, and, folding them up, placed them in his pocket. He also took a small compass that had once been a watch-charm, and, finally, the contents of a small iron bank that opened with a combination lock. This represented all his savings, amounting to two dollars and seventeen cents in dimes, nickles and pennies.

"It isn't a fortune," he thought, as he counted it up, "but I didn't need any money the last trip, so perhaps I'll get along somehow. I don't like to tackle dad for more, for he might ask questions and try to keep me at home."

By the time he had finished his preparations and stowed all his electrical belongings in his various pockets, it was nearly midnight and the house was quiet. So Rob stole down stairs in his stocking feet and noiselessly opened the back door.

It was a beautiful July night and, in addition to the light of the full moon, the sky was filled with the radiance of countless thousands of brilliant stars.

After Rob had put on his shoes he unfolded the map, which was plainly visible by the starlight, and marked the direction he must take to cross the Atlantic and reach London, his first stopping place. Then he consulted his compass, put the indicator of his traveling machine to the word "up," and shot swiftly into the air. When he had reached a sufficient height he placed the indicator to a point north of east and, with a steady and remarkably swift flight, began his journey.

"Here goes," he remarked, with a sense of exaltation, "for another week of adventure! I wonder what'll happen between now and next Saturday."

CHAPTER X

How Rob Served a Mighty King

THE NEW traveling machine was a distinct improvement over the old one, for it carried Rob with wonderful speed across the broad Atlantic.

He fell asleep soon after starting, and only wakened when the sun was high in the heavens. But he found himself whirling along at a good rate, with the greenish shimmer of the peaceful ocean waves spread beneath him far beyond his range of vision.

Being in the track of the ocean steamers it was not long before he found himself overtaking a magnificent vessel whose decks were crowded with passengers. He dropped down some distance, to enable him to see these people more plainly, and while he hovered near he could hear the excited exclamations of the passengers, who focused dozens of marine glasses upon his floating form. This inspection somewhat embarrassed him, and having no mind to be stared at he put on additional speed and soon left the steamer far behind him.

About noon the sky clouded over, and Rob feared a rainstorm was approaching. So he rose to a point considerably beyond the clouds, where the air was thin but remarkably pleasant to inhale and the rays of the sun were not so hot as when reflected by the surface of the water.

He could see the dark clouds rolling beneath him like volumes of smoke from a factory chimney, and knew the earth was catching a severe shower of rain; yet he congratulated himself on his foresight in not being burdened with umbrella or raincoat, since his elevated position rendered him secure from rain-clouds.

But, having cut himself off from the earth, there remained nothing to see except the clear sky overhead and the tumbling clouds beneath; so he took from his pocket the Automatic Record of Events, and watched with breathless interest the incidents occurring in different parts of the world. A big battle was being fought in the Philippines, and so fiercely was it contested that Rob watched its progress for hours, with rapt attention. Finally a brave rally by the Americans sent their foes to the cover of the woods, where they scattered in every direction, only to form again in a deep valley hidden by high hills.

"If only I was there," thought Rob, "I could show that captain where to find the rebels and capture them. But I guess the Philippines are rather out of my way, so our soldiers will never know how near they are to a complete victory."

The boy also found considerable amusement in watching the course of an insurrection in Venezuela, where opposing armies of well-armed men preferred to bluster and threaten rather than come to blows.

During the evening he found that an "important event" was Madame Bernhardt's production of a new play, and Rob followed it from beginning to end with great enjoyment, although he felt a bit guilty at not having purchased a ticket.

"But it's a crowded house, anyway," he reflected, "and I'm not taking up a reserved seat or keeping any one else from seeing the show. So where's the harm? Yet it seems to me if these Records get to be common, as the Demon wishes, people will all stay at home and see the shows, and the poor actors'll starve to death."

The thought made him uneasy, and he began, for the first time, to entertain a doubt of the Demon's wisdom in forcing such devices upon humanity.

The clouds had now passed away and the moon sent her rays to turn the edges of the waves into glistening showers of jewels.

Rob closed the lid of the wonderful Record of Events and soon fell into a deep sleep that held him unconscious for many hours.

When he awoke he gave a start of surprise, for beneath him was land. How long it was since he had left the ocean behind him he could not guess, but his first thought was to set the indicator of the traveling machine to zero and to hover over the country until he could determine where he was.

This was no easy matter. He saw green fields, lakes, groves and villages; but these might exist in any country. Being still at a great elevation he descended gradually until he was about twenty feet from the surface of the earth, where he paused near the edge of a small village.

At once a crowd of excited people assembled, shouting to one another and pointing towards him in wonder. In order to be prepared for emergencies Rob had taken the electric tube from his pocket, and now, as he examined the dress and features of the people below, the tube suddenly slipped from his grasp and fell to the ground, where one end stuck slantingly into the soft earth.

A man rushed eagerly towards it, but the next moment he threw up his hands and fell upon his back, unconscious. Others who ran to assist their fallen comrade quickly tumbled into a heap beside him.

It was evident to Rob that the tube had fallen in such a position that the button was being pressed continually and a current of electric fluid issued to shock whoever came near. Not wishing to injure these people he dropped to the ground and drew the tube from the earth, thus releasing the pressure upon the button.

But the villagers had now decided that the boy was their enemy, and no sooner had he touched the ground than a shower of stones and sticks rained about him. Not one reached his body, however, for the Garment of Repulsion stopped their flight and returned them to rattle with more or less force against those who had thrown them—"like regular boomerangs," thought Rob.

To receive their own blows in this fashion seemed so like magic to the simple folk that with roars of fear and pain they ran away in all directions.

"It's no use stopping here," remarked Rob, regretfully, "for I've spoiled my welcome by this accident. I think these people are Irish, by their looks and speech, so I must be somewhere in the Emerald Isle."

He consulted his map and decided upon the general direction he should take to reach England, after which he again rose into the air and before long was passing over the channel towards the shores of England.

Either his map or compass or his calculations proved wrong, for it was high noon before, having changed his direction a half dozen times, he came to the great city of London. He saw at a glance that it would never do to drop into the crowded streets, unless he wanted to become an object of public curiosity; so he looked around for a suitable place to alight.

Near by was a monstrous church that sent a sharp steeple far into the air. Rob examined this spire and saw a narrow opening in the masonry that led to a small room where a chime of bells hung. He crept through the opening and, finding a ladder that connected the belfry with a platform below, began to descend.

There were three ladders, and then a winding flight of narrow, rickety stairs to be passed before Rob finally reached a small room in the body of the church. This room proved to have two doors, one connecting with the auditorium and the other letting into a side street. Both were locked, but Rob pointed the electric tube at the outside door and broke the lock in an instant. Then he walked into the street as composedly as if he had lived all his life in London.

There were plenty of sights to see, you may be sure, and Rob walked around until he was so tired that he was glad to rest upon one of the benches in a beautiful park. Here, half hidden by the trees, he amused himself by looking at the Record of Events.

"London's a great town, and no mistake," he said to himself; "but let's see what the British are doing in South Africa today."

He turned the cylinder to "South Africa," and, opening the lid, at once became interested. An English column, commanded by a brave but stubborn officer, was surrounded by the Boer forces and fighting desperately to avoid capture or annihilation.

"This would be interesting to King Edward," thought the boy. "Guess I'll hunt him up and tell him about it."

A few steps away stood a policeman. Rob approached him and asked: "Where's the king today?"

The officer looked at him with mingled surprise and suspicion.

"'Is Majesty is sojournin' at Marlb'ro 'Ouse, just now," was the reply. "Per'aps you wants to make 'im a wissit," he continued, with lofty sarcasm.

"That's it, exactly," said Rob. "I'm an American, and thought while I was in London I'd drop in on His Royal Highness and say 'hello' to him."

The officer chuckled, as if much amused.

"Hamericans is bloomin' green," he remarked, "so youse can stand for

Hamerican, right enough. No other wissitors is such blarsted fools. But yon's the palace, an' I s'pose 'is Majesty'll give ye a 'ot reception."

"Thanks; I'll look him up," said the boy, and left the officer convulsed with laughter.

He soon knew why. The palace was surrounded by a cordon of the king's own life guards, who admitted no one save those who presented proper credentials.

"There's only one thing to do;" thought Rob, "and that's to walk straight in, as I haven't any friends to give me a regular introduction."

So he boldly advanced to the gate, where he found himself stopped by crossed carbines and a cry of "Halt!"

"Excuse me," said Rob; "I'm in a hurry."

He pushed the carbines aside and marched on. The soldiers made thrusts at him with their weapons, and an officer jabbed at his breast with a glittering sword, but the Garment of Repulsion protected him from these dangers as well as from a hail of bullets that followed his advancing figure.

He reached the entrance of the palace only to face another group of guardsmen and a second order to halt, and as these soldiers were over six feet tall and stood shoulder to shoulder Rob saw that he could not hope to pass them without using his electric tube.

"Stand aside, you fellows!" he ordered.

There was no response. He extended the tube and, as he pressed the button, described a semi-circle with the instrument. Immediately the tall guardsmen toppled over like so many tenpins, and Rob stepped across their bodies and penetrated to the reception room, where a brilliant assemblage awaited, in hushed and anxious groups, for opportunity to obtain audience with the king.

"I hope his Majesty isn't busy," said Rob to a solemn-visaged official who confronted him. "I want to have a little talk with him."

"I—I—ah—beg pardon!" exclaimed the astounded master of ceremonies. "What name, please?"

"Oh, never mind my name," replied Rob, and pushing the gentleman aside he entered the audience chamber of the great king.

King Edward was engaged in earnest consultation with one of his ministers, and after a look of surprise in Rob's direction and a grave bow he bestowed no further attention upon the intruder.

But Rob was not to be baffled now.

"Your Majesty," he interrupted, "I've important news for you. A big fight is taking place in South Africa and your soldiers will probably be cut into mince meat."

The minister strode towards the boy angrily.

"Explain this intrusion!" he cried.

"I have explained. The Boers are having a regular killing-bee. Here! take a look at it yourselves."

He drew the Record from his pocket, and at the movement the minister shrank back as if he suspected it was an infernal machine and might blow his head off; but the king stepped quietly to the boy's side and looked into the box when Rob threw open the lid.

As he comprehended the full wonder of the phenomenon he was observing Edward uttered a low cry of amazement, but thereafter he silently gazed upon the fierce battle that still raged far away upon the African *veld*. Before long his keen eye recognized the troops engaged and realized their imminent danger.

"They'll be utterly annihilated!" he gasped. "What shall we do?"

"Oh, we can't do anything just now," answered Rob. "But it's curious to watch how bravely the poor fellows fight for their lives."

The minister, who by this time was also peering into the box, groaned aloud, and then all three forgot their surroundings in the tragedy they were beholding.

Hemmed in by vastly superior numbers, the English were calmly and stubbornly resisting every inch of advance and selling their lives as dearly as possible. Their leader fell pierced by a hundred bullets, and the king, who had known him from boyhood, passed his hand across his eyes as if to shut out the awful sight. But the fascination of the battle forced him to look again, and the next moment he cried aloud:

"Look there! Look there!"

Over the edge of a line of hills appeared the helmets of a file of English soldiers. They reached the summit, followed by rank after rank, until the hillside was alive with them. And then, with a ringing cheer that came like a faint echo to the ears of the three watchers, they broke into a run and dashed forward to the rescue of their brave comrades. The Boers faltered, gave back, and the next moment fled precipitately, while the exhausted survivors of the courageous band fell sobbing in to the arms of their rescuers.

Rob closed the lid of the Record with a sudden snap that betrayed his deep feeling, and the king pretended to cough behind his handkerchief and stealthily wiped his eyes.

"'Twasn't so bad, after all," remarked the boy, with assumed cheerfulness; "but it looked mighty ticklish for your men at one time."

King Edward regarded the boy curiously, remembering his abrupt entrance and the marvelous device he had exhibited.

"What do you call that?" he asked, pointing at the Record with a finger that trembled slightly from excitement.

"It is a new electrical invention," replied Rob, replacing it in his pocket, "and so constructed that events are reproduced at the exact moment they occur."

"Where can I purchase one?" demanded the king, eagerly.

"They're not for sale," said Rob. "This one of mine is the first that ever happened."

"Oh!"

"I really think," continued the boy, nodding sagely, "that it wouldn't be well to have these Records scattered around. Their use would give some folks unfair advantage over others, you know."

"Certainly."

"I only showed you this battle because I happened to be in London at the time and thought you'd be interested."

"It was very kind of you," said Edward; "but how did you gain admittance?"

"Well, to tell the truth, I was obliged to knock over a few of your tall life-guards. They seem to think you're a good thing and need looking after, like jam in a cupboard."

The king smiled.

"I hope you haven't killed my guards," said he.

"Oh, no; they'll come around all right."

"It is necessary," continued Edward, "that public men be protected from intrusion, no matter how democratic they may be personally. You would probably find it as difficult to approach the President of the United States as the King of England."

"Oh, I'm not complaining," said Rob. "It wasn't much trouble to break through."

"You seem quite young to have mastered such wonderful secrets of Nature," continued the king.

"So I am," replied Rob, modestly; "but these natural forces have really existed since the beginning of the world, and someone was sure to discover them in time." He was quoting the Demon, although unconsciously.

"You are an American, I suppose," said the minister, coming close to Rob and staring him in the face.

"Guessed right the first time," answered the boy, and drawing his Character Marking spectacles from his pocket, he put them on and stared at the minister in turn.

Upon the man's forehead appeared the letter "E."

"Your Majesty," said Rob, "I have here another queer invention. Will you please wear these spectacles for a few moments?"

The king at once put them on.

"They are called Character Markers," continued the boy, "because the lenses catch and concentrate the character vibrations radiating from every human individual and reflect the true character of the person upon his forehead. If a letter 'G' appears, you may be sure his disposition is good; if his forehead is marked with an 'E' his character is evil, and you must beware of treachery."

The king saw the "E" plainly marked upon his minister's forehead, but he said nothing except "Thank you," and returned the spectacles to Rob.

But the minister, who from the first had been ill at ease, now became positively angry.

"Do not believe him, your Majesty!" he cried. "It is a trick, and meant to deceive you."

"I did not accuse you," answered the king, sternly. Then he added: "I wish to be alone with this young gentleman."

The minister left the room with an anxious face and hanging head.

"Now," said Rob, "let's look over the record of the past day and see if that fellow has been up to any mischief."

He turned the cylinder of the Record to "England," and slowly the events of the last twenty-four hours were reproduced, one after the other, upon the polished plate.

Before long the king uttered an exclamation. The Record pictured a small room in which were seated three gentlemen engaged in earnest conversation. One of them was the accused minister.

"Those men," said the king in a low voice, while he pointed out the other two, "are my avowed enemies. This is proof that your wonderful spectacles indicated my minister's character with perfect truth. I am grateful to you for thus putting me upon my guard, for I have trusted the man fully."

"Oh, don't mention it," replied the boy, lightly; "I'm glad to have been of service to you. But it's time for me to go."

"I hope you will favor me with another interview," said the king, "for I am much interested in your electrical inventions. I will instruct my guards to admit you at any time, so you will not be obliged to fight your way in."

"All right. But it really doesn't matter," answered Rob. "It's no trouble at all to knock 'em over."

Then he remembered his manners and bowed low before the king, who seemed to him "a fine fellow and not a bit stuck up." And then he walked calmly from the palace.

The people in the outer room stared at him wonderingly and the officer of the guard saluted the boy respectfully. But Rob only smiled in an amused way as he marched past them with his hands thrust deep into his trousers' pockets and his straw hat tipped jauntily upon the back of his head.

CHAPTER XI

The Man of Science

ROB PASSED the remainder of the day wandering about London and amusing himself by watching the peculiar ways of the people. When it became so dark that there was no danger of his being observed, he rose through the air to the narrow slit in the church tower and lay upon the floor of the little room, with the bells hanging all around him, to pass the night.

He was just falling asleep when a tremendous din and clatter nearly deafened him, and set the whole tower trembling. It was the midnight chime.

Rob clutched his ears tightly, and when the vibrations had died away descended by the ladder to a lower platform. But even here the next hourly chime made his ears ring, and he kept descending from platform to platform until the last half of a restless night was passed in the little room at the bottom of the tower.

When, at daylight, the boy sat up and rubbed his eyes, he said, wearily: "Churches are all right as churches; but as hotels they are rank failures. I ought to have bunked in with my friend, King Edward."

He climbed up the stairs and the ladders again and looked out the little window in the belfry. Then he examined his map of Europe.

"I believe I'll take a run over to Paris," he thought. "I must be home again by Saturday, to meet the Demon, so I'll have to make every day count."

Without waiting for breakfast, since he had eaten a tablet the evening before, he crept through the window and mounted into the fresh morning air until the great city with its broad waterway lay spread out beneath him. Then he sped away to the southeast and, crossing the channel, passed between Amiens and Rouen and reached Paris before ten o'clock.

Near the outskirts of the city appeared a high tower, upon the flat roof of which a man was engaged in adjusting a telescope. Upon seeing Rob, who was passing at no great distance from this tower, the man cried out:

"*Approchez!—Venez ici!*"

Then he waved his hands frantically in the air, and fairly danced with excitement. So the boy laughed and dropped down to the roof where, standing beside the Frenchman, whose eyes were actually protruding from their sockets, he asked, coolly:

"Well, what do you want?"

The other was for a moment speechless. He was a tall, lean man, having a bald head but a thick, iron-gray beard, and his black eyes sparkled brightly from behind a pair of gold-rimmed spectacles. After attentively regarding the boy for a time he said, in broken English:

"But, M'sieur, how can you fly wizout ze—ze machine? I have experiment myself wiz some air-ship; but you—zere is nossing to make go!"

Rob guessed that here was his opportunity to do the Demon a favor by explaining his electrical devices to this new acquaintance, who was evidently a man of science.

"Here is the secret, Professor," he said, and holding out his wrist displayed the traveling machine and explained, as well as he could, the forces that operated it.

The Frenchman, as you may suppose, was greatly astonished, and to show how perfectly the machine worked Rob turned the indicator and rose a short distance above the tower, circling around it before he rejoined the professor on the roof. Then he showed his food tablets, explaining how each was stored with sufficient nourishment for an entire day.

The scientist positively gasped for breath, so powerful was the excitement he experienced at witnessing these marvels.

"Eet is wonderful—grand—magnifique!" he exclaimed.

"But here is something of still greater interest," continued Rob, and taking the Automatic Record of Events from his pocket he allowed the professor to view the remarkable scenes that were being enacted throughout the civilized world.

The Frenchman was now trembling violently, and he implored Rob to tell him where he might obtain similar electrical machines.

"I can't do that," replied the boy, decidedly; "but, having seen these, you may be able to discover their construction for yourself. Now that you know such things to be possible and practical, the hint should be sufficient to enable a shrewd electrician to prepare duplicates of them."

The scientist glared at him with evident disappointment, and Rob continued:

"These are not all the wonders I can exhibit. Here is another electrical device that is, perhaps, the most remarkable of any I possess."

He took the Character Marking spectacles from his pocket and fitted them to his eyes. Then he gave a whistle of surprise and turned his back upon his new friend. He had seen upon the Frenchman's forehead the letters "E" and "C."

"Guess I've struck the wrong sort of scientist, after all!" he muttered, in a disgusted tone.

His companion was quick to prove the accuracy of the Character Marker. Seeing the boy's back turned, he seized a long iron bar that was used to operate the telescope, and struck at Rob so fiercely that had he not worn the Garment of Protection his skull would have been crushed by the blow. As it was, the bar rebounded with a force that sent the murderous

Frenchman sprawling upon the roof, and Rob turned around and laughed at him.

"It won't work, Professor," he said. "I'm proof against assassins. Perhaps you had an idea that when you had killed me you could rob me of my valuable possessions; but they wouldn't be a particle of use to a scoundrel like you, I assure you! Good morning."

Before the surprised and baffled scientist could collect himself sufficiently to reply, the boy was soaring far above his head and searching for a convenient place to alight, that he might investigate the charms of this famed city of Paris.

It was indeed a beautiful place, with many stately buildings lining the shady boulevards. So thronged were the streets that Rob well knew he would soon be the center of a curious crowd should he alight upon them. Already a few sky-gazers had noted the boy moving high in the air, above their heads, and one or two groups stood pointing their fingers at him.

Pausing at length above the imposing structure of the Hotel Anglais, Rob noticed at one of the upper floors an open window, before which was a small iron balcony. Alighting upon this he proceeded to enter, without hesitation, the open window. He heard a shriek and a cry of "*Au voleur!*" and caught sight of a woman's figure as she dashed into an adjoining room, slamming and locking the door behind her.

"I don't know as I blame her," observed Rob, with a smile at the panic he had created. "I s'pose she takes me for a burglar, and thinks I've climbed up the lightning rod."

He soon found the door leading into the hallway and walked down several flights of stairs until he reached the office of the hotel.

"How much do you charge a day?" he inquired, addressing a fat and pompous-looking gentleman behind the desk.

The man looked at him in a surprised way, for he had not heard the boy enter the room. But he said something in French to a waiter who was passing, and the latter came to Rob and made a low bow.

"I speak ze Eengliss ver' fine," he said. "What desire have you?"

"What are your rates by the day?" asked the boy.

"Ten francs, M'sieur."

"How many dollars is that?"

"Dollar Americaine?"

"Yes; United States money."

"Ah, *oui!* Eet is ze two dollar, M'sieur."

"All right; I can stay about a day before I go bankrupt. Give me a room."

"*Certainement,* M'sieur. Have you ze luggage?"

"No; but I'll pay in advance," said Rob, and began counting out his dimes and nickels and pennies, to the unbounded amazement of the waiter, who looked as if he had never seen such coins before.

He carried the money to the fat gentleman, who examined the pieces curiously, and there was a long conference between them before it was decided to accept them in payment for a room for a day. But at this season the hotel was almost empty, and when Rob protested that he had no other money the fat gentleman put the coins into his cash box with a resigned sigh and the waiter showed the boy to a little room at the very top of the building.

Rob washed and brushed the dust from his clothes, after which he sat down and amused himself by viewing the pictures that constantly formed upon the polished plate of the Record of Events.

CHAPTER XII

How Rob Saved a Republic

WHILE FOLLOWING the shifting scenes of the fascinating Record Rob noted an occurrence that caused him to give a low whistle of astonishment and devote several moments to serious thought.

"I believe it's about time I interfered with the politics of this Republic," he said, at last, as he closed the lid of the metal box and restored it to his pocket. "If I don't take a hand there probably won't be a Republic of France very long and, as a good American, I prefer a republic to a monarchy."

Then he walked down-stairs and found his English-speaking waiter.

"Where's President Loubet?" he asked.

"Ze President! Ah, he is wiz his mansion. To be at his residence, M'sieur."

"Where is his residence?"

The waiter began a series of voluble and explicit directions which so confused the boy that he exclaimed:

"Oh, much obliged!" and walked away in disgust.

Gaining the street he approached a gendarme and repeated his question, with no better result than before, for the fellow waved his arms wildly in all directions and roared a volley of incomprehensible French phrases that conveyed no meaning whatever.

"If ever I travel in foreign countries again," said Rob, "I'll learn their lingo in advance. Why doesn't the Demon get up a conversation machine that will speak all languages?"

By dint of much inquiry, however, and after walking several miles following ambiguous directions, he managed to reach the residence of President Loubet. But there he was politely informed that the President was busily engaged in his garden, and would see no one.

"That's all right," said the boy, calmly. "If he's in the garden I'll have no trouble finding him."

Then, to the amazement of the Frenchmen, Rob shot into the air fifty feet or so, from which elevation he overlooked a pretty garden in the rear of the President's mansion. The place was protected from ordinary intrusion by high walls, but Rob descended within the enclosure and walked up to a man who was writing at a small table placed under the spreading branches of a large tree.

"Is this President Loubet?" he inquired, with a bow.

The gentleman looked up.

"My servants were instructed to allow no one to disturb me," he said, speaking in excellent English.

"It isn't their fault; I flew over the wall," returned Rob. "The fact is," he added, hastily, as he noted the President's frown, "I have come to save the Republic; and I haven't much time to waste over a bundle of Frenchmen, either."

The President seemed surprised.

"Your name!" he demanded, sharply.

"Robert Billings Joslyn, United States of America!"

"Your business, Monsieur Joslyn!"

Rob drew the Record from his pocket and placed it upon the table.

"This, sir," said he, "is an electrical device that records all important events. I wish to call your attention to a scene enacted in Paris last evening which may have an effect upon the future history of your country."

He opened the lid, placed the Record so that the President could see clearly, and then watched the changing expressions upon the great man's face; first indifference, then interest, the next moment eagerness and amazement.

"*Mon Dieu!*" he gasped; "the Orleanists!"

Rob nodded.

"Yes; they've worked up a rather pretty plot, haven't they?"

The President did not reply. He was anxiously watching the Record and scribbling notes on a paper beside him. His face was pale and his lips tightly compressed.

Finally he leaned back in his chair and asked:

"Can you reproduce this scene again?"

"Certainly, sir," answered the boy; "as often as you like."

"Will you remain here while I send for my minister of police? It will require but a short time."

"Call him up, then. I'm in something of a hurry myself, but now I've mixed up with this thing I'll see it through."

The President touched a bell and gave an order to his servant. Then he turned to Rob and said, wonderingly:

"You are a boy!"

"That's true, Mr. President," was the answer; "but an American boy, you must remember. That makes a big difference, I assure you."

The President bowed gravely.

"This is your invention?" he asked.

"No; I'm hardly equal to that. But the inventor has made me a present of the Record, and it's the only one in the world."

"It is a marvel," remarked the President, thoughtfully. "More! It is a real miracle. We are living in an age of wonders, my young friend."

"No one knows that better than myself, sir," replied Rob. "But, tell me, can you trust your chief of police?"

"I think so," said the President, slowly; "yet since your invention has shown me that many men I have considered honest are criminally implicated in this royalist plot, I hardly know whom to depend upon."

"Then please wear these spectacles during your interview with the minister of police," said the boy. "You must say nothing, while he is with us, about certain marks that will appear upon his forehead; but when he has gone I will explain those marks so you will understand them."

The President covered his eyes with the spectacles.

"Why," he exclaimed, "I see upon your own brow the letters—"

"Stop, sir!" interrupted Rob, with a blush; "I don't care to know what the letters are, if it's just the same to you."

The President seemed puzzled by this speech, but fortunately the minister of police arrived just then and, under Rob's guidance, the pictured record of the Orleanist plot was reproduced before the startled eyes of the official.

"And now," said the boy, "let us see if any of this foolishness is going on just at present."

He turned to the opposite side of the Record and allowed the President and his minister of police to witness the quick succession of events even as they occurred.

Suddenly the minister cried, "Ha!" and, pointing to the figure of a man disembarking from an English boat at Calais, he said, excitedly:

"That, your Excellency, is the Duke of Orleans, in disguise! I must leave you for a time, that I may issue some necessary orders to my men; but this evening I shall call to confer with you regarding the best mode of suppressing this terrible plot."

When the official had departed, the President removed the spectacles from his eyes and handed them to Rob.

"What did you see?" asked the boy.

"The letters 'G' and 'W'."

"Then you may trust him fully," declared Rob, and explained the construction of the Character Marker to the interested and amazed statesman.

"And now I must go," he continued, "for my stay in your city will be a short one and I want to see all I can."

The President scrawled something on a sheet of paper and signed his name to it, afterward presenting it, with a courteous bow, to his visitor.

"This will enable you to go wherever you please, while in Paris," he said. "I regret my inability to reward you properly for the great service you have rendered my country; but you have my sincerest gratitude, and may command me in any way."

"Oh, that's all right," answered Rob. "I thought it was my duty to warn you, and if you look sharp you'll be able to break up this conspiracy. But I don't want any reward. Good day, sir."

He turned the indicator of his traveling machine and immediately rose into the air, followed by a startled exclamation from the President of France.

Moving leisurely over the city, he selected a deserted thoroughfare to alight in, from whence he wandered unobserved into the beautiful boulevards. These were now brilliantly lighted, and crowds of pleasure seekers thronged them everywhere. Rob experienced a decided sense of relief as he mixed with the gay populace and enjoyed the sights of the splendid city, for it enabled him to forget, for a time, the responsibilities thrust upon him by the possession of the Demon's marvelous electrical devices.

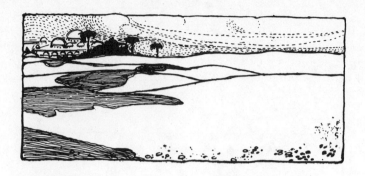

CHAPTER XIII

Rob Loses His Treasures

OUR YOUNG adventurer had intended to pass the night in the little bed at his hotel, but the atmosphere of Paris proved so hot and disagreeable that he decided it would be more enjoyable to sleep while journeying through the cooler air that lay far above the earth's surface. So just as the clocks were striking the midnight hour Rob mounted skyward and turned the indicator of the traveling machine to the east, intending to make the city of Vienna his next stop.

He had risen to a considerable distance, where the air was remarkably fresh and exhilarating, and the relief he experienced from the close and muggy streets of Paris was of such a soothing nature that he presently fell fast asleep. His day in the metropolis had been a busy one, for, like all boys, he had forgotten himself in the delight of sight-seeing and had tired his muscles and exhausted his strength to an unusual degree.

It was about three o'clock in the morning when Rob, moving restlessly in his sleep, accidently touched with his right hand the indicator of the machine which was fastened to his left wrist, setting it a couple of points to the south of east. He was, of course, unaware of the slight alteration in his course, which was destined to prove of serious importance in the near future. For the boy's fatigue induced him to sleep far beyond daybreak, and during this period of unconsciousness he was passing over the face of European countries and approaching the lawless and dangerous dominions of the Orient.

When, at last, he opened his eyes, he was puzzled to determine where he was. Beneath him stretched a vast, sandy plain, and speeding across this he came to a land abounding in luxuriant vegetation.

The centrifugal force which propelled him was evidently, for some reason, greatly accelerated, for the scenery of the country he was crossing glided by him at so rapid a rate of speed that it nearly took his breath away.

"I wonder if I've passed Vienna in the night," he thought. "It ought not to have taken me more than a few hours to reach there from Paris."

Vienna was at that moment fifteen hundred miles behind him; but

Rob's geography had always been his stumbling block at school, and he had not learned to gage the speed of the traveling machine; so he was completely mystified as to his whereabouts.

Presently a village having many queer spires and minarets whisked by him like a flash. Rob became worried, and resolved to slow up at the next sign of habitation.

This was a good resolution, but Turkestan is so thinly settled that before the boy could plan out a course of action he had passed the barren mountain range of Thian-Shan as nimbly as an acrobat leaps a jumping-bar.

"This won't do at all!" he exclaimed, earnestly. "The traveling machine seems to be running away with me, and I'm missing no end of sights by scooting along up here in the clouds."

He turned the indicator to zero, and was relieved to find it obey with customary quickness. In a few moments he had slowed up and stopped, when he found himself suspended above another stretch of sandy plain. Being too high to see the surface of the plain distinctly he dropped down a few hundred feet to a lower level, where he discovered he was surrounded by billows of sand as far as his eye could reach.

"It's a desert, all right," was his comment; "perhaps old Sahara herself."

He started the machine again towards the east, and at a more moderate rate of speed skimmed over the surface of the desert. Before long he noticed a dark spot ahead of him which proved to be a large body of fierce looking men, riding upon dromedaries and slender, spirited horses and armed with long rifles and crookedly shaped simitars.

"Those fellows seem to be looking for trouble," remarked the boy, as he glided over them, "and it wouldn't be exactly healthy for an enemy to get in their way. But I haven't time to stop, so I'm not likely to get mixed up in any rumpus with them."

However, the armed caravan was scarcely out of sight before Rob discovered he was approaching a rich, wooded oasis of the desert, in the midst of which was built the walled city of Yarkand. Not that he had ever heard of the place, or knew its name; for few Europeans and only one American traveler had ever visited it. But he guessed it was a city of some importance from its size and beauty, and resolved to make a stop there.

Above the high walls projected many slender, white minarets, indicating that the inhabitants were either Turks or some race of Mohammedans; so Rob decided to make investigations before trusting himself to their company.

A cluster of tall trees with leafy tops stood a short distance outside the walls, and here the boy landed and sat down to rest in the refreshing shade.

The city seemed as hushed and still as if it were deserted, and before him stretched the vast plain of white, heated sands. He strained his eyes to catch a glimpse of the band of warriors he had passed, but they were moving slowly and had not yet appeared.

The trees that sheltered Rob were the only ones without the city, although many low bushes or shrubs grew scattering over the space between him and the walls. An arched gateway broke the enclosure at his left, but the gates were tightly shut.

Something in the stillness and the intense heat of the mid-day sun made the boy drowsy. He stretched himself upon the ground beneath the dense foliage of the biggest tree and abandoned himself to the languor that was creeping over him.

"I'll wait until that army of the desert arrives," he thought, sleepily. "They either belong in this city or have come to capture it, so I can tell better what to dance when I find out what the band plays."

The next moment he was sound asleep, sprawling upon his back in the shade and slumbering as peacefully as an infant.

And while he lay motionless three men dropped in quick succession from the top of the city wall and hid among the low bushes, crawling noiselessly from one to another and so approaching, by degrees, the little group of trees.

They were Turks, and had been sent by those in authority within the city to climb the tallest tree of the group and discover if the enemy was near. For Rob's conjecture had been correct, and the city of Yarkand awaited, with more or less anxiety, a threatened assault from its hereditary enemies, the Tatars.

The three spies were not less forbidding in appearance than the horde of warriors Rob had passed upon the desert. Their features were coarse and swarthy, and their eyes had a most villainous glare. Old fashioned pistols and double-edged daggers were stuck in their belts and their clothing, though of gorgeous colors, was soiled and neglected.

With all the caution of the American savage these Turks approached the tree, where, to their unbounded amazement, they saw the boy lying asleep. His dress and fairness of skin at once proclaimed him, in their shrewd eyes, a European, and their first thought was to glance around in search of his horse or dromedary. Seeing nothing of the kind near they were much puzzled to account for his presence, and stood looking down at him with evident curiosity.

The sun struck the polished surface of the traveling machine which was attached to Rob's wrist and made the metal glitter like silver. This attracted the eyes of the tallest Turk, who stooped down and stealthily unclasped the band of the machine from the boy's outstretched arm. Then, after a hurried but puzzled examination of the little instrument, he slipped it into the pocket of his jacket.

Rob stirred uneasily in his sleep, and one of the Turks drew a slight but stout rope from his breast and with gentle but deft movement passed it around the boy's wrists and drew them together behind him. The action was not swift enough to arouse the power of repulsion in the Garment of Protection, but it awakened Rob effectually, so that he sat up and stared hard at his captors.

"What are you trying to do, anyhow?" he demanded.

The Turks laughed and said something in their own language. They had no knowledge of English.

"You're only making fools of yourselves," continued the boy, wrathfully. "It's impossible for you to injure me."

The three paid no attention to his words. One of them thrust his hand into Rob's pocket and drew out the electric tube. His ignorance of modern appliances was so great that he did not know enough to push the button. Rob saw him looking down the hollow end of the tube and murmured:

"I wish it would blow your ugly head off!"

But the fellow, thinking the shining metal might be of some value to him, put the tube in his own pocket and then took from the prisoner the silver box of tablets.

Rob writhed and groaned at losing his possessions in this way, and while his hands were fastened behind him tried to feel for and touch the indicator of the traveling machine. When he found that the machine also had been taken, his anger gave way to fear, for he realized he was in a dangerously helpless condition.

The third Turk now drew the Record of Events from the boy's inner pocket. He knew nothing of the springs that opened the lids, so, after a curious glance at it, he secreted the box in the folds of his sash and continued the search of the captive. The Character Marking Spectacles were next abstracted, but the Turk, seeing in them nothing but spectacles, scornfully thrust them back into Rob's pocket, while his comrades laughed at him. The boy was now rifled of seventeen cents in pennies, a broken pocket knife and a lead-pencil, the last article seeming to be highly prized.

After they had secured all the booty they could find, the tall Turk, who seemed the leader of the three, violently kicked at the prisoner with his heavy boot. His surprise was great when the Garment of Repulsion arrested the blow and nearly overthrew the aggressor in turn. Snatching a dagger from his sash, he bounded upon the boy so fiercely that the next instant the enraged Turk found himself lying upon his back three yards away, while his dagger flew through the air and landed deep in the desert sands.

"Keep it up!" cried Rob, bitterly. "I hope you'll enjoy yourself."

The other Turks raised their comrade to his feet, and the three stared at one another in surprise, being unable to understand how a bound prisoner could so effectually defend himself. But at a whispered word from the leader, they drew their long pistols and fired point blank into Rob's face. The volley echoed sharply from the city walls, but as the smoke drifted slowly away the Turks were horrified to see their intended victim laughing at them.

Uttering cries of terror and dismay, the three took to their heels and bounded towards the wall, where a gate quickly opened to receive them, the populace feeling sure the Tatar horde was upon them.

Nor was this guess so very far wrong; for as Rob, sitting disconsolate upon the sand, raised his eyes, he saw across the desert a dark line that marked the approach of the invaders.

Nearer and nearer they came, while Rob watched them and bemoaned the foolish impulse that had led him to fall asleep in an unknown land where he could so easily be overpowered and robbed of his treasures.

"I always suspected these electrical inventions would be my ruin some day," he reflected, sadly; "and now I'm side-tracked and left helpless in this outlandish country, without a single hope of ever getting home again.

They probably won't be able to kill me, unless they find my Garment of Repulsion and strip that off; but I never could cross this terrible desert on foot and, having lost my food tablets, I'd soon starve if I attempted it."

Fortunately, he had eaten one of the tablets just before going to sleep, so there was no danger of immediate starvation. But he was miserable and unhappy, and remained brooding over his cruel fate until a sudden shout caused him to look up.

CHAPTER XIV

Turk and Tatar

THE TATARS had arrived, swiftly and noiselessly, and a dozen of the warriors, still mounted, were surrounding him.

His helpless condition aroused their curiosity, and while some of them hastily cut away his bonds and raised him to his feet, others plied him with questions in their own language. Rob shook his head to indicate that he could not understand; so they led him to the chief—an immense, bearded representative of the tribe of Kara-Khitai, the terrible and relentless Black Tatars of Thibet. The huge frame of this fellow was clothed in flowing robes of cloth-of-gold, braided with jewels, and he sat majestically upon the back of a jet-black camel.

Under ordinary circumstances the stern features and flashing black eyes of this redoubtable warrior would have struck a chill of fear to the boy's heart; but now under the influence of the crushing misfortunes he had experienced, he was able to gaze with indifference upon the terrible visage of the desert chief.

The Tatar seemed not to consider Rob an enemy. Instead, he looked upon him as an ally, since the Turks had bound and robbed him.

Finding it impossible to converse with the chief, Rob took refuge in the sign language. He turned his pockets wrong side out, showed the red welts left upon his wrists by the tight cord, and then shook his fists angrily in the direction of the town.

In return the Tatar nodded gravely and issued an order to his men.

By this time the warriors were busily pitching tents before the walls of Yarkand and making preparations for a formal siege. In obedience to the chieftain's orders, Rob was given a place within one of the tents nearest the wall and supplied with a brace of brass-mounted pistols and a dagger with a sharp, zigzag edge. These were evidently to assist the boy in fighting the Turks, and he was well pleased to have them. His spirits rose considerably when he found he had fallen among friends, although most of his new comrades had such evil faces that it was unnecessary to put on the Character Markers to judge their natures with a fair degree of accuracy.

"I can't be very particular about the company I keep," he thought, "and this gang hasn't tried to murder me, as the rascally Turks did. So for the present I'll stand in with the scowling chief and try to get a shot at the thieves who robbed me. If our side wins I may get a chance to recover some of my property. It's a slim chance, of course, but it's the only hope I have left."

That very evening an opportunity occurred for Rob to win glory in the eyes of his new friends. Just before sundown the gates of the city flew open and a swarm of Turks, mounted upon fleet horses and camels, issued forth and fell upon their enemies. The Tatars, who did not expect the sally, were scarcely able to form an opposing rank when they found themselves engaged in a hand-to-hand conflict, fighting desperately for their lives. In such a battle, however, the Turks were at a disadvantage, for the active Tatars slipped beneath their horses and disabled them, bringing both the animals and their riders to the earth.

At the first onslaught Rob shot his pistol at a Turk and wounded him so severely that he fell from his horse. Instantly the boy seized the bridle and sprang upon the steed's back, and the next moment he had dashed into the thickest part of the fray. Bullets and blows rained upon him from all sides, but the Garment of Repulsion saved him from a single scratch.

When his pistols had been discharged he caught up the broken handle of a spear, and used it as a club, galloping into the ranks of the Turks and belaboring them as hard as he could. The Tatars cheered and followed him, and the Turks were so amazed at his miraculous escape from their bullets that they became terrified, thinking he bore a charmed life and was protected by unseen powers.

This terror helped turn the tide of battle, and before long the enemy was pressed back to the walls and retreated through the gates, which were hastily fastened behind them.

In order to prevent a repetition of this sally the Tatars at once invested the gates, so that if the Turks should open them they were as likely to let their foes in as to oppose them.

While the tents were being moved up Rob had an opportunity to search the battlefield for the bodies of the three Turks who had robbed him, but they were not among the fallen.

"Those fellows were too cowardly to take part in a fair fight," declared the boy; but he was much disappointed, nevertheless, as he felt very helpless without the electric tube or the traveling machine.

The Tatar chief now called Rob to his tent and presented him with a beautiful ring set with a glowing pigeon's-blood ruby, in acknowledgment of his services. This gift made the boy feel very proud, and he said to the chief:

"You're all right, old man, even if you do look like a pirate. If you can manage to capture that city, so I can get my electrical devices back, I'll consider you a trump as long as I live."

The chief thought this speech was intended to express Rob's gratitude, so he bowed solemnly in return.

During the night that followed upon the first engagement of the Turks and Tatars, the boy lay awake trying to devise some plan to capture the city. The walls seemed too high and thick to be either scaled or broken by the Tatars, who had no artillery whatever; and within the walls lay all the fertile part of the oasis, giving the besieged a good supply of water and provisions, while the besiegers were obliged to subsist on what water and food they had brought with them.

Just before dawn Rob left his tent and went out to look at the great wall. The stars gave plenty of light, but the boy was worried to find that, according to Eastern custom, no sentries or guards whatever had been posted and all the Tatars were slumbering soundly.

The city was likewise wrapped in profound silence, but just as Rob was turning away he saw a head project stealthily over the edge of the wall before him, and recognized in the features one of the Turks who had robbed him.

Finding no one awake except the boy the fellow sat upon the edge of the wall, with his feet dangling downward, and grinned wickedly at his former victim. Rob watched him with almost breathless eagerness.

After making many motions that conveyed no meaning whatever, the Turk drew the electric tube from his pocket and pointed his finger first at the boy and then at the instrument, as if inquiring what it was used for. Rob shook his head. The Turk turned the tube over several times and examined it carefully, after which he also shook his head, seeming greatly puzzled.

By this time the boy was fairly trembling with excitement. He longed to recover this valuable weapon, and feared that at any moment the curious Turk would discover its use. He held out his hand toward the tube, and tried to say, by motions, that he would show the fellow how to use it. The man seemed to understand, but he would not let the glittering instrument out of his possession.

Rob was almost in despair, when he happened to notice upon his hand the ruby ring given him by the chief. Drawing the jewel from his finger he made offer, by signs, that he would exchange it for the tube.

The Turk was much pleased with the idea, and nodded his head repeatedly, holding out his hand for the ring. Rob had little confidence in the man's honor, but he was so eager to regain the tube that he decided to trust him. So he threw the ring to the top of the wall, where the Turk caught it skilfully; but when Rob held out his hand for the tube the scoundrel only laughed at him and began to scramble to his feet in order to beat a retreat. Chance, however, foiled this disgraceful treachery, for in his hurry the Turk allowed the tube to slip from his grasp, and it rolled off the wall and fell upon the sand at Rob's very feet.

The robber turned to watch its fall and, filled with sudden anger, the boy grabbed the weapon, pointed it at his enemy, and pressed the button. Down tumbled the Turk, without a cry, and lay motionless at the foot of the wall.

Rob's first thought was to search the pockets of his captive, and to his delight he found and recovered his box of food tablets. The Record of Events and the traveling machine were doubtless in the possession of the other robbers, but Rob did not despair of recovering them, now that he had the tube to aid him.

Day was now breaking, and several of the Tatars appeared and examined the body of the Turk with grunts of surprise, for there was no mark upon him to show how he had been slain. Supposing him to be dead, they tossed him aside and forgot all about him.

Rob had secured his ruby ring again, and going to the chief's tent he showed the jewel to the guard and was at once admitted. The black-bearded chieftain was still reclining upon his pillows, but Rob bowed before him, and by means of signs managed to ask for a band of warriors to assist him in assaulting the town. The chieftain appeared to doubt the wisdom of the enterprise, not being able to understand how the boy could expect to succeed; but he graciously issued the required order, and by the time Rob reached the city gate he found a large group of Tatars gathered to support him, while the entire camp, roused to interest in the proceedings, stood looking on.

Rob cared little for the quarrel between the Turks and Tatars, and under ordinary circumstances would have refused to side with one or the other; but he knew he could not hope to recover his electrical machines unless the city was taken by the band of warriors who had befriended him, so he determined to force an entrance for them.

Without hesitation he walked close to the great gate and shattered its fastenings with the force of the electric current directed upon them from the tube. Then, shouting to his friends the Tatars for assistance, they rushed in a body upon the gate and dashed it open.

The Turks had expected trouble when they heard the fastenings of the huge gate splinter and fall apart, so they had assembled in force before the opening. As the Tatars poured through the gateway in a compact mass they were met by a hail of bullets, spears and arrows, which did fearful execution among them. Many were killed outright, while others fell wounded to be trampled upon by those who pressed on from the rear.

Rob maintained his position in the front rank, but escaped all injury through the possession of the Garment of Repulsion. But he took an active part in the fight and pressed the button of the electric tube again and again, tumbling the enemy into heaps on every side, even the horses and camels falling helplessly before the resistless current of electricity.

The Tatars shouted joyfully as they witnessed this marvelous feat and rushed forward to assist in the slaughter; but the boy motioned them all back. He did not wish any more bloodshed than was necessary, and knew that the heaps of unconscious Turks around him would soon recover.

So he stood alone and faced the enemy, calmly knocking them over as fast as they came near. Two of the Turks managed to creep up behind the boy, and one of them, who wielded an immense simitar with a two-edged blade as sharp as a razor, swung the weapon fiercely to cut off Rob's head. But the repulsive force aroused in the Garment was so terrific that it sent the weapon flying backwards with redoubled swiftness, so that it caught the second Turk at the waist and cut him fairly in two.

Thereafter they all avoided coming near the boy, and in a surprisingly short time the Turkish forces were entirely conquered, all having been reduced to unconsciousness except a few cowards who had run away and hidden in the cellars or garrets of the houses.

The Tatars entered the city with shouts of triumph, and the chief was so delighted that he threw his arms around Rob's neck and embraced him warmly.

Then began the sack of Yarkand, the fierce Tatars plundering the bazaars and houses, stripping them of everything of value they could find.

Rob searched anxiously among the bodies of the unconscious Turks for the two men who had robbed him, but neither could be found. He was more successful later, for in running through the streets he came upon Tatar warriors. He reflected, gloomily, that this did not affect his own position in any way, since he could not escape from the oasis.

Suddenly, on glancing at the crowd, Rob saw something that arrested his attention. A young girl was fastening some article to the wrist of a burly, villainous-looking Turk. The boy saw a glitter that reminded him of the traveling machine, but immediately afterward the man and the girl bent their heads over the fellow's wrist in such a way that Rob could see nothing more.

While the couple were apparently examining the strange device, Rob started to his feet and walked toward them. The crowd fell back at his approach, but the man and the girl were so interested that they did not notice him. He was still several paces away when the girl put out her finger and touched the indicator on the dial.

To Rob's horror and consternation the big Turk began to rise slowly into the air, while a howl of fear burst from the crowd. But the boy made a mighty spring and caught the Turk by his foot, clinging to it with desperate tenacity, while they both mounted steadily upward until they were far above the city of the desert.

The big Turk screamed pitifully at first, and then actually fainted away from fright. Rob was much frightened, on his part, for he knew if his hands slipped from their hold he would fall to his death. Indeed, one hand was slipping already, so he made a frantic clutch and caught firmly hold of the Turk's baggy trousers. Then, slowly and carefully, he drew himself up and seized the leather belt that encircled the man's waist. This firm grip gave him new confidence, and he began to breathe more freely.

He now clung to the body of the Turk with both legs entwined, in the way he was accustomed to cling to a tree-trunk when he climbed after cherries at home. He had conquered his fear of falling, and took time to recover his wits and his strength.

They had now reached such a tremendous height that the city looked like a speck on the desert beneath them. Knowing he must act quickly, Rob seized the dangling left arm of the unconscious Turk and raised it until he could reach the dial of the traveling machine. He feared to unclasp the machine just then, for two reasons: if it slipped from his grasp they would both plunge downward to their death; and he was not sure the machine would work at all if in any other position than fastened to the left wrist.

Rob determined to take no chances, so he left the machine attached to the Turk and turned the indicator to zero and then to "East," for he did not wish to rejoin either his enemies the Turks or his equally undesirable friends the Tatars.

After traveling eastward a few minutes he lost sight of the city altogether; so, still clinging to the body of the Turk, he again turned the indicator and began to descend. When, at last, they landed gently upon a rocky eminence of the Kuen-Lun mountains, the boy's strength was almost exhausted, and his limbs ached with the strain of clinging to the Turk's body.

His first act was to transfer the traveling machine to his own wrist and to see that his other electrical devices were safely bestowed in his pockets. Then he sat upon the rock to rest until the Turk recovered consciousness.

Presently the fellow moved uneasily, rolled over, and then sat up and stared at his surroundings. Perhaps he thought he had been dreaming, for he rubbed his eyes and looked again with mingled surprise and alarm. Then, seeing Rob, he uttered a savage shout and drew his dagger.

Rob smiled and pointed the electric tube at the man, who doubtless recognized its power, for he fell back scowling and trembling.

"This place seems like a good jog from civilization," remarked the boy, as coolly as if his companion could understand what he said; "but as your legs are long and strong you may be able to find your way. It's true you're liable to starve to death, but if you do it will be your own misfortune and not my fault."

The Turk glared at him sullenly, but did not attempt to reply.

Rob took out his box of tablets, ate one of them and offered another to his enemy. The fellow accepted it ungraciously enough, but seeing Rob eat one he decided to follow his example, and consumed the tablet with a queer expression of distrust upon his face.

"Brave man!" cried Rob, laughingly; "you've avoided the pangs of starvation for a time, anyhow, so I can leave you with a clear conscience."

Without more ado he turned the indicator of the traveling machine and mounted into the air, leaving the Turk sitting upon the rocks and staring after him in comical bewilderment.

CHAPTER XV

A Battle with Monsters

Our young adventurer never experienced a more grateful feeling of relief and security than when he found himself once more high in the air, alone, and in undisputed possession of the electrical devices bestowed upon him by the Demon.

The dangers he had passed through since landing at the city of the desert and the desperate chance that alone had permitted him to regain the traveling machine made him shudder at the bare recollection and rendered him more sober and thoughtful than usual.

We who stick closely to the earth's surface can scarcely realize how Rob could travel through the air at such dizzy heights without any fear or concern whatsoever. But he had come to consider the air a veritable refuge. Experience had given him implicit confidence in the powers of the electrical instrument whose unseen forces carried him so swiftly and surely, and while the tiny, watch-like machine was clasped to his wrist he felt himself to be absolutely safe.

Having slipped away from the Turk and attained a fair altitude, he set the indicator at zero and paused long enough to consult his map and decide what direction it was best for him to take. The mischance that had swept him unwittingly over the countries of Europe had also carried him more than half way around the world from his home. Therefore the nearest way to reach America would be to continue traveling to the eastward.

So much time had been consumed at the desert oasis that he felt he must now hasten if he wished to reach home by Saturday afternoon; so, having quickly come to a decision, he turned the indicator and began a swift flight into the east.

For several hours he traveled above the great desert of Gobi, but by noon signs of a more fertile country began to appear, and, dropping to a point nearer the earth, he was able to observe closely the country of the Chinese, with its crowded population and ancient but crude civilization.

Then he came to the Great Wall of China and to mighty Peking, above which he hovered some time, examining it curiously. He really longed to

411

make a stop there, but with his late experiences fresh in his mind he thought it much safer to view the wonderful city from a distance.

Resuming his flight he presently came to the gulf of Laou Tong, whose fair face was freckled with many ships of many nations, and so on to Korea, which seemed to him a land fully a century behind the times.

Night overtook him while speeding across the Sea of Japan, and having a great desire to view the Mikado's famous islands, he put the indicator at zero, and, coming to a full stop, composed himself to sleep until morning, that he might run no chances of being carried beyond his knowledge during the night.

You might suppose it no easy task to sleep suspended in mid-air, yet the magnetic currents controlled by the traveling machine were so evenly balanced that Rob was fully as comfortable as if reposing upon a bed of down. He had become somewhat accustomed to passing the night in the air and now slept remarkably well, having no fear of burglars or fire or other interruptions that dwellers in cities are subject to.

One thing, however, he should have remembered: that he was in an ancient and little known part of the world and reposing above a sea famous in fable as the home of many fierce and terrible creatures; while not far away lay the land of the dragon, the simurg and other ferocious monsters.

Rob may have read of these things in fairy tales and books of travel, but if so they had entirely slipped his mind; so he slumbered peacefully and actually snored a little, I believe, towards morning.

But even as the red sun peeped curiously over the horizon he was awakened by a most unusual disturbance—a succession of hoarse screams and a pounding of the air as from the quickly revolving blades of some huge windmill.

He rubbed his eyes and looked around.

Coming towards him at his right hand was an immense bird, whose body seemed almost as big as that of a horse. Its wide-open, curving beak was set with rows of pointed teeth, and the talons held against its breast and turned threateningly outward were more powerful and dreadful than a tiger's claws.

While, fascinated and horrified, he watched the approach of this feathered monster, a scream sounded just behind him and the next instant the stroke of a mighty wing sent him whirling over and over through the air.

He soon came to a stop, however, and saw that another of the monsters had come upon him from the rear and was now, with its mate, circling closely around him, while both uttered continuously their hoarse, savage cries.

Rob wondered why the Garment of Repulsion had not protected him from the blow of the bird's wing; but, as a matter of fact, it had protected him. For it was not the wing itself but the force of the eddying currents of air that had sent him whirling away from the monster. With the indicator at zero the magnetic currents and the opposing powers of attraction and repulsion were so evenly balanced that any violent atmospheric disturbance affected him in the same way that thistledown is affected by a summer breeze. He had noticed something of this before, but whenever a strong wind was blowing he was accustomed to rise to a position above the air currents. This was the first time he had slept with the indicator at zero.

The huge birds at once renewed their attack, but Rob had now recovered his wits sufficiently to draw the electric tube from his pocket. The first one to dart towards him received the powerful electric current direct from the tube, and fell stunned and fluttering to the surface of the sea, where it floated motionless. Its mate, perhaps warned by this sudden disaster, renewed its circling flight, moving so swiftly that Rob could scarcely follow it, and drawing nearer and nearer every moment to its intended victim. The boy could not turn in the air very quickly, and he feared an attack in the back, mistrusting the saving power of the Garment of Repulsion under such circumstances; so in desperation he pressed his finger upon the button of the tube and whirled the instrument around his head in the opposite direction to that in which the monster was circling. Presently the current and the bird met, and with one last scream the creature tumbled downwards to join its fellow upon the waves, where they lay like two floating islands.

Their presence had left a rank, sickening stench in the surrounding atmosphere, so Rob made haste to resume his journey and was soon moving rapidly eastward.

He could not control a shudder at the recollection of his recent combat, and realized the horror of a meeting with such creatures by one who had no protection from their sharp beaks and talons.

"It's no wonder the Japs draw ugly pictures of those monsters," he thought. "People who live in these parts must pass most of their lives in a tremble."

The sun was now shining brilliantly, and when the beautiful islands of Japan came in sight Rob found that he had recovered his wonted cheerfulness. He moved along slowly, hovering with curious interest over the quaint and picturesque villages and watching the industrious Japanese patiently toiling at their tasks. Just before he reached Tokio he came to a military fort, and for nearly an hour watched the skilful maneuvers of a regiment of soldiers at their morning drill. They were not very big people, compared with other nations, but they seemed alert and well trained, and the boy decided it would require a brave enemy to face them on a field of battle.

Having at length satisfied his curiosity as to Japanese life and customs Rob prepared for his long flight across the Pacific Ocean.

By consulting his map he discovered that should he maintain his course due east, as before, he would arrive at a point in America very near to San Francisco, which suited his plans excellently.

Having found that he moved more swiftly when farthest from the earth's surface, because the air was more rarefied and offered less resistance, Rob mounted upwards until the islands of Japan were mere specks visible through the clear, sunny atmosphere.

Then he began his eastward flight, the broad surface of the Pacific seeming like a blue cloud far beneath him.

CHAPTER XVI

Shipwrecked Mariners

AMPLE PROOF of Rob's careless and restless nature having been frankly placed before the reader in these pages, you will doubtless be surprised when I relate that during the next few hours our young gentleman suffered from a severe attack of homesickness, becoming as gloomy and unhappy in its duration as ever a homesick boy could be.

It may have been because he was just then cut off from all his fellow-creatures and even from the world itself; it may have been because he was satiated with marvels and with the almost absolute control over the powers which the Demon had conferred upon him; or it may have been because he was born and reared a hearty, healthy American boy, with a disposition to battle openly with the world and take his chances equally with his fellows, rather than be placed in such an exclusive position that no one could hope successfully to oppose him.

Perhaps he himself did not know what gave him this horrible attack of "the blues," but the truth is he took out his handkerchief and cried like a baby from very loneliness and misery.

There was no one to see him, thank goodness! and the tears gave him considerable relief. He dried his eyes, made an honest struggle to regain his cheerfulness, and then muttered to himself:

"If I stay up here, like an air-bubble in the sky, I shall certainly go crazy. I suppose there's nothing but water to look at down below, but if I could only sight a ship, or even see a fish jump, it would do me no end of good."

Thereupon he descended until, as the ocean's surface came nearer and nearer, he discovered a tiny island lying almost directly underneath him. It was hardly big enough to make a dot on the biggest map, but a clump of trees grew in the central portion, while around the edges were jagged rocks protecting a sandy beach and a stretch of flower-strewn upland leading to the trees.

It looked very beautiful from Rob's elevated position, and his spirits brightened at once.

"I'll drop down and pick a bouquet," he exclaimed, and a few moments later his feet touched the firm earth of the island.

But before he could gather a dozen of the brilliant flowers a glad shout reached his ears, and, looking up, he saw two men running towards him from the trees.

They were dressed in sailor fashion, but their clothing was reduced to rags and scarcely clung to their brown, skinny bodies. As they advanced they waved their arms wildly in the air and cried in joyful tones:

"A boat! A boat!"

Rob stared at them wonderingly, and had much ado to prevent the poor fellows from hugging him outright, so great was their joy at his appearance. One of them rolled upon the ground, laughing and crying by turns, while the other danced and cut capers until he became so exhausted that he sank down breathless beside his comrade.

"How came you here?" then inquired the boy, in pitying tones.

"We're shipwrecked American sailors from the bark 'Cynthia Jane,' which went down near here over a month ago," answered the smallest and thinnest of the two. "We escaped by clinging to a bit of wreckage and floated to this island, where we have nearly starved to death. Indeed, we now have eaten everything on the island that was eatable, and had your boat arrived a few days later you'd have found us lying dead upon the beach!"

Rob listened to this sad tale with real sympathy.

"But I didn't come here in a boat," said he.

The men sprang to their feet with white, scared faces.

"No boat!" they cried; "are you, too, shipwrecked?"

"No;" he answered. "I flew here through the air." And then he explained to them the wonderful electric traveling machine.

But the sailors had no interest whatever in the relation. Their disappointment was something awful to witness, and one of them laid his head upon his comrade's shoulder and wept with unrestrained grief, so weak and discouraged had they become through suffering.

Suddenly Rob remembered that he could assist them, and took the box of concentrated food tablets from his pocket.

"Eat these," he said, offering one to each of the sailors.

At first they could not understand that these small tablets would be able to allay the pangs of hunger; but when Rob explained their virtues the men ate them greedily. Within a few moments they were so greatly restored to strength and courage that their eyes brightened, their sunken cheeks flushed, and they were able to converse with their benefactor with calmness and intelligence.

Then the boy sat beside them upon the grass and told them the story of his acquaintance with the Demon and of all his adventures since he had come into possession of the wonderful electric contrivances. In his present mood he felt it would be a relief to confide in some one, and so these poor, lonely men were the first to hear his story.

When he related the manner in which he had clung to the Turk while both ascended into the air, the elder of the two sailors listened with rapt attention, and then, after some thought, asked:

"Why couldn't you carry one or both of us to America?"

Rob took time seriously to consider this idea, while the sailors eyed him with eager interest. Finally he said:

"I'm afraid I couldn't support your weight long enough to reach any other land. It's a long journey, and you'd pull my arms out of joint before we'd been up an hour."

Their faces fell at this, but one of them said:

"Why couldn't we swing ourselves over your shoulders with a rope? Our two bodies would balance each other and we are so thin and emaciated that we do not weigh very much."

While considering this suggestion Rob remembered how at one time five pirates had clung to his left leg and been carried some distance through the air.

"Have you a rope?" he asked.

"No," was the answer; "but there are plenty of long, tough vines growing on the island that are just as strong and pliable as ropes."

"Then, if you are willing to run the chances," decided the boy, "I will make the attempt to save you. But I must warn you that in case I find I can not support the weight of your bodies I shall drop one or both of you into the sea."

They looked grave at this prospect, but the biggest one said:

"We would soon meet death from starvation if you left us here on the island; so, as there is at least a chance of our being able to escape in your company I, for one, am willing to risk being drowned. It is easier and quicker than being starved. And, as I'm the heavier, I suppose you'll drop me first."

"Certainly," declared Rob, promptly.

This announcement seemed to be an encouragement to the little sailor, but he said, nervously:

"I hope you'll keep near the water, for I haven't a good head for heights—they always make me dizzy."

"Oh, if you don't want to go," began Rob, "I can easily—"

"But I do! I do! I do!" cried the little man, interrupting him. "I shall die if you leave me behind!"

"Well, then, get your ropes, and we'll do the best we can," said the boy.

They ran to the trees, around the trunks of which were clinging many tendrils of greenish-brown vine which possessed remarkable strength. With their knives they cut a long section of this vine, the ends of which were then tied into loops large enough to permit the sailors to sit in them comfortably. The connecting piece Rob padded with seaweed gathered from the shore, to prevent its cutting into his shoulders.

"Now, then," he said, when all was ready, "take your places."

The sailors squatted in the loops, and Rob swung the vine over his shoulders and turned the indicator of the traveling machine to "up."

As they slowly mounted into the sky the little sailor gave a squeal of terror and clung to the boy's arm; but the other, although seemingly anxious, sat quietly in his place and made no trouble.

"D—d—don't g—g—go so high" stammered the little one, tremblingly; "suppose we should f—f—fall!"

"Well, s'pose we should?" answered Rob, gruffly. "You couldn't drown until you struck the water, so the higher we are the longer you'll live in case of accident."

This phase of the question seemed to comfort the frightened fellow somewhat; but, as he said, he had not a good head for heights, and so continued to tremble in spite of his resolve to be brave.

The weight on Rob's shoulders was not so great as he had feared, the traveling machine seeming to give a certain lightness and buoyancy to everything that came into contact with its wearer.

As soon as he had reached a sufficient elevation to admit of good speed he turned the indicator once more to the east and began moving rapidly through the air, the shipwrecked sailors dangling at either side.

"This is aw—aw—awful!" gasped the little one.

"Say, you shut up!" commanded the boy, angrily. "If your friend was as big a coward as you are I'd drop you both this minute. Let go my arm and keep quiet, if you want to reach land alive."

The fellow whimpered a little, but managed to remain silent for several minutes. Then he gave a sudden twitch and grabbed Rob's arm again.

"S'pose—s'pose the vine should break!" he moaned, a horrified look upon his face.

"I've had about enough of this," said Rob, savagely. "If you haven't any sense you don't deserve to live." He turned the indicator on the dial of the machine and they began to descend rapidly.

The little fellow screamed with fear, but Rob paid no attention to him until the feet of the two suspended sailors were actually dipping into the waves, when he brought their progress to an abrupt halt.

"Wh—wh—what are you g—g—going to do?" gurgled the cowardly sailor.

"I'm going to feed you to the sharks—unless you promise to keep your mouth shut," retorted the boy. "Now, then; decide at once! Which will it be—sharks or silence?"

"I won't say a word—'pon my honor, I won't!" said the sailor, shudder-ingly.

"All right; remember your promise and we'll have no further trouble," remarked Rob, who had hard work to keep from laughing at the man's abject terror.

Once more he ascended and continued the journey, and for several hours they rode along swiftly and silently. Rob's shoulders were begin-ning to ache with the continued tugging of the vine upon them, but the thought that he was saving the lives of two unfortunate fellow-creatures gave him strength and courage to persevere.

Night was falling when they first sighted land; a wild and seemingly uninhabited stretch of the American coast. Rob made no effort to select a landing place, for he was nearly worn out with the strain and anxiety of the journey. He dropped his burden upon the brow of a high bluff overlooking the sea and, casting the vine from his shoulders, fell to the earth exhausted and half fainting.

CHAPTER XVII

The Coast of Oregon

WHEN HE had somewhat recovered, Rob sat up and looked around him. The elder sailor was kneeling in earnest prayer, offering grateful thanks for his escape from suffering and death. The younger one lay upon the ground sobbing and still violently agitated by recollections of the frightful experiences he had undergone. Although he did not show his feelings as plainly as the men, the boy was none the less gratified at having been instrumental in saving the lives of two fellow-beings.

The darkness was by this time rapidly enveloping them, so Rob asked his companions to gather some brushwood and light a fire, which they quickly did. The evening was cool for the time of year, and the heat from the fire was cheering and grateful; so they all lay near the glowing embers and fell fast asleep.

The sound of voices aroused Rob next morning, and on opening his eyes and gazing around he saw several rudely dressed men approaching. The two shipwrecked sailors were still sound asleep.

Rob stood up and waited for the strangers to draw near. They seemed to be fishermen, and were much surprised at finding three people asleep upon the bluff.

"Whar 'n thunder 'd ye come from?" asked the foremost fisherman, in a surprised voice.

"From the sea," replied the boy. "My friends here are shipwrecked sailors from the 'Cynthia Jane.' "

"But how'd ye make out to climb the bluff?" inquired a second fisherman; "no one ever did it afore, as we knows on."

"Oh, that is a long story," replied the boy, evasively.

The two sailors had awakened and now saluted the new-comers. Soon they were exchanging a running fire of questions and answers.

"Where are we?" Rob heard the little sailor ask.

"Coast of Oregon," was the reply. "We're about seven miles from Port Orford by land an' about ten miles by sea."

"Do you live at Port Orford?" inquired the sailor.

"That's what we do, friend; an' if your party wants to join us we'll do our best to make you comf'table, bein' as you're shipwrecked an' need help."

Just then a loud laugh came from another group, where the elder sailor had been trying to explain Rob's method of flying through the air.

"Laugh all you want to," said the sailor, sullenly; "it's true—ev'ry word of it!"

"Mebbe you think it, friend," answered a big, good-natured fisherman; "but it's well known that shipwrecked folks go crazy sometimes, an' imagine strange things. Your mind seems clear enough in other ways, so I advise you to try and forget your dreams about flyin'."

Rob now stepped forward and shook hands with the sailors.

"I see you have found friends," he said to them, "so I will leave you and continue my journey, as I'm in something of a hurry."

Both sailors began to thank him profusely for their rescue, but he cut them short.

"That's all right. Of course I couldn't leave you on that island to starve to death, and I'm glad I was able to bring you away with me."

"But you threatened to drop me into the sea," remarked the little sailor, in a grieved voice.

"So I did," said Rob, laughing; "but I wouldn't have done it for the world—not even to have saved my own life. Good-by!"

He turned the indicator and mounted skyward, to the unbounded amazement of the fishermen, who stared after him with round eyes and wide open mouths.

"This sight will prove to them that the sailors are not crazy," he thought, as he turned to the south and sped away from the bluff. "I suppose those simple fishermen will never forget this wonderful occurrence, and they'll probably make reg'lar heroes of the two men who have crossed the Pacific through the air."

He followed the coast line, keeping but a short distance above the earth, and after an hour's swift flight reached the city of San Francisco.

His shoulders were sore and stiff from the heavy strain upon them of the previous day, and he wished more than once that he had some of his mother's household liniment to rub them with. Yet so great was his delight at reaching once more his native land that all discomforts were speedily forgotten.

Much as he would have enjoyed a day in the great metropolis of the Pacific slope, Rob dared not delay longer than to take a general view of the place, to note its handsome edifices and to wonder at the throng of Chinese inhabiting one section of the town.

These things were much more plainly and quickly viewed by Rob from above than by threading a way through the streets on foot; for he looked down upon the city as a bird does, and covered miles with a single glance.

Having satisfied his curiosity without attempting to alight, he turned to the southeast and followed the peninsula as far as Palo Alto, where he viewed the magnificent buildings of the university. Changing his course to the east, he soon reached Mount Hamilton, and, being attracted by the great tower of the Lick Observatory, he hovered over it until he found he had attracted the excited gaze of its inhabitants, who doubtless observed him very plainly through the big telescope.

But so unreal and seemingly impossible was the sight witnessed by the learned astronomers that they have never ventured to make the incident public, although long after the boy had darted away into the east they argued together concerning the marvelous and incomprehensible vision. Afterward they secretly engrossed the circumstance upon their records, but resolved never to mention it in public, lest their wisdom and veracity should be assailed by the skeptical.

Meantime Rob rose to a higher altitude, and sped swiftly across the great continent. By noon he sighted Chicago, and after a brief inspection of the place from the air determined to devote at least an hour to forming the acquaintance of this most wonderful and cosmopolitan city.

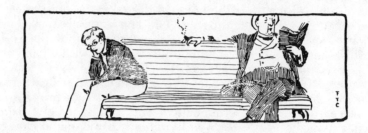

CHAPTER XVIII

A Narrow Escape

THE AUDITORIUM Tower, where "the weather man" sits to flash his reports throughout the country, offered an inviting place for the boy to alight. He dropped quietly upon the roof of the great building and walked down the staircase until he reached the elevators, by means of which he descended to the ground floor without exciting special attention.

The eager rush and hurry of the people crowding the sidewalks impressed Rob with the idea that they were all behind time and were trying hard to catch up. He found it impossible to walk along comfortably without being elbowed and pushed from side to side; so a half hour's sight-seeing under such difficulties tired him greatly. It was a beautiful afternoon, and finding himself upon the Lake Front, Rob hunted up a vacant bench and sat down to rest.

Presently an elderly gentleman with a reserved and dignified appearance and dressed in black took a seat next to the boy and drew a magazine from his pocket. Rob saw that he opened it to an article on "The Progress of Modern Science," in which he seemed greatly interested.

After a time the boy remembered that he was hungry, not having eaten a tablet in more than twenty-four hours. So he took out the silver box and ate one of the small, round disks it contained.

"What are those?" inquired the old gentleman in a soft voice. "You are too young to be taking patent medicines."

"These are not medicines, exactly," answered the boy, with a smile. "They are Concentrated Food Tablets, stored with nourishment by means of electricity. One of them furnishes a person with food for an entire day."

The old gentleman stared at Rob a moment and then laid down his magazine and took the box in his hands, examining the tablets curiously.

"Are these patented?" he asked.

"No," said Rob; "they are unknown to any one but myself."

"I will give you a half million dollars for the recipe to make them," said the gentleman.

"I fear I must refuse your offer," returned Rob, with a laugh.

"I'll make it a million," said the gentleman, coolly.

Rob shook his head.

"Money can't buy the recipe," he said; "for I don't know it myself."

"Couldn't the tablets be chemically analyzed, and the secret discovered?" inquired the other.

"I don't know; but I'm not going to give any one the chance to try," declared the boy, firmly.

The old gentleman picked up his magazine without another word, and resumed his reading.

For amusement Rob took the Record of Events from his pocket and began looking at the scenes reflected from its polished plate.

Presently he became aware that the old gentleman was peering over his shoulder with intense interest. General Funston was just then engaged in capturing the rebel chief, Aguinaldo, and for a few moments both man and boy observed the occurrence with rapt attention. As the scene was replaced by one showing a secret tunnel of the Russian Nihilists, with the conspirators carrying dynamite to a recess underneath the palace of the Czar, the gentleman uttered a long sigh and asked:

"Will you sell that box?"

"No," answered Rob, shortly, and put it back into his pocket.

"I'll give you a million dollars to control the sale in Chicago alone," continued the gentleman, with an eager inflection in his smooth voice.

"You seem quite anxious to get rid of money," remarked Rob, carelessly. "How much are you worth?"

"Personally?"

"Yes."

"Nothing at all, young man. I am not offering you my own money. But with such inventions as you have exhibited I could easily secure millions of capital. Suppose we form a trust, and place them upon the market. We'll capitalize it for a hundred millions, and you can have a quarter of the stock—twenty-five millions. That would keep you from worrying about grocery bills."

"But I wouldn't need groceries if I had the tablets," said Rob, laughing.

"True enough! But you could take life easily and read your newspaper in comfort, without being in any hurry to get down town to business. Twenty-five millions would bring you a cozy little income, if properly invested."

"I don't see why one should read newspapers when the Record of Events shows all that is going on in the world," objected Rob.

"True, true! But what do you say to the proposition?"

"I must decline, with thanks. These inventions are not for sale."

The gentleman sighed and resumed his magazine, in which he became much absorbed.

Rob put on the Character Marking Spectacles and looked at him. The letters "E," "W" and "C" were plainly visible upon the composed, respectable looking brow of his companion.

"Evil, wise and cruel," reflected Rob, as he restored the spectacles to his pocket. "How easily such a man could impose upon people. To look at him one would think that butter wouldn't melt in his mouth!"

He decided to part company with this chance acquaintance and, rising from his seat, strolled leisurely up the walk. A moment later, on looking back, he discovered that the old gentleman had disappeared.

He walked down State Street to the river and back again, amused by the activity displayed in this busy section of the city. But the time he had allowed himself in Chicago had now expired, so he began looking around for some high building from the roof of which he could depart unnoticed.

This was not at all difficult, and selecting one of many stores he ascended by an elevator to the top floor and from there mounted an iron stairway leading to the flat roof. As he climbed this stairway he found himself followed by a pleasant looking young man, who also seemed desirous of viewing the city from the roof.

Annoyed at the inopportune intrusion, Rob's first thought was to go back to the street and try another building; but, upon reflecting that the young man was not likely to remain long and he would soon be alone, he decided to wait. So he walked to the edge of the roof and appeared to be interested in the scenery spread out below him.

"Fine view from here, ain't it?" said the young man, coming up to him and placing his hand carelessly upon the boy's shoulder.

"It is, indeed," replied Rob, leaning over the edge to look into the street.

As he spoke he felt himself gently but firmly pushed from behind and, losing his balance, he plunged headforemost from the roof and whirled through the intervening space toward the sidewalk far below.

Terrified though he was by the sudden disaster, the boy had still wit enough remaining to reach out his right hand and move the indicator of the machine upon his left wrist to the zero mark. Immediately he paused in his fearful flight and presently came to a stop at a distance of less than fifteen feet from the flagstones which had threatened to crush out his life.

As he stared downward, trying to recover his self-possession, he saw the old gentleman he had met on the Lake Front standing just below and looking at him with a half frightened, half curious expression in his eyes.

At once Rob saw through the whole plot to kill him and thus secure possession of his electrical devices. The young man upon the roof who had attempted to push him to his death was a confederate of the innocent appearing old gentleman, it seemed, and the latter had calmly awaited his fall to the pavement to seize the coveted treasures from his dead body. It was an awful idea, and Rob was more frightened than he had ever been before in his life—or ever has been since.

But now the shouts of a vast concourse of amazed spectators reached the boy's ears. He remembered that he was suspended in mid-air over the crowded street of a great city, while thousands of wondering eyes were fixed upon him.

So he quickly set the indicator to the word "up," and mounted skyward until the watchers below could scarcely see him. Then he fled away into the east, even yet shuddering with the horror of his recent escape from death and filled with disgust at the knowledge that there were people who held human life so lightly that they were willing to destroy it to further their own selfish ends.

"And the Demon wants such people as these to possess his electrical devices, which are as powerful to accomplish evil when in wrong hands as they are good!'' thought the boy, resentfully. "This would be a fine world if Electric Tubes and Records of Events and Traveling Machines could be acquired by selfish and unprincipled persons!''

So unnerved was Rob by his recent experiences that he determined to make no more stops. However, he alighted at nightfall in the country, and slept upon the sweet hay in a farmer's barn.

But, early the next morning, before any one else was astir, he resumed his journey, and at precisely ten o'clock of this day, which was Saturday, he completed his flying trip around the world by alighting unobserved upon the well-trimmed lawn of his own home.

CHAPTER XIX

Rob Makes a Resolution

WHEN ROB opened the front door he came face to face with Nell, who gave an exclamation of joy and threw herself into his arms.

"Oh, Rob!" she cried, "I'm so glad you've come. We have all been dreadfully worried about you, and mother—"

"Well, what about mother?" inquired the boy, anxiously, as she paused.

"She's been very ill, Rob; and the doctor said today that unless we heard from you soon he would not be able to save her life. The uncertainty about you is killing her."

Rob stood stock still, all the eager joy of his return frozen into horror at the thought that he had caused his dear mother so much suffering.

"Where is she, Nell?" he asked, brokenly.

"In her room. Come; I'll take you to her."

Rob followed with beating heart, and soon was clasped close to his mother's breast.

"Oh, my boy—my dear boy!" she murmured, and then for very joy and love she was unable to say more, but held him tight and stroked his hair gently and kissed him again and again.

Rob said little, except to promise that he would never again leave home without her full consent and knowledge. But in his mind he contrasted the love and comfort that now surrounded him with the lonely and unnatural life he had been leading and, boy though he was in years, a mighty resolution that would have been creditable to an experienced man took firm root in his heart.

He was obliged to recount all his adventures to his mother and, although he made light of the dangers he had passed through, the story drew many sighs and shudders from her.

When luncheon time arrived he met his father, and Mr. Joslyn took occasion to reprove his son in strong language for running away from home and leaving them filled with anxiety as to his fate. However, when he saw how happy and improved in health his dear wife was at her boy's return, and when he had listened to Rob's manly confession of error and expressions of repentance, he speedily forgave the culprit and treated him as genially as ever.

Of course the whole story had to be repeated, his sisters listening this time with open eyes and ears and admiring their adventurous brother immensely. Even Mr. Joslyn could not help becoming profoundly interested, but he took care not to show any pride he might feel in his son's achievements.

When his father returned to his office Rob went to his own bed-chamber and sat for a long time by the window in deep thought. When at last he aroused himself, he found it was nearly four o'clock.

"The Demon will be here presently," he said, with a thrill of aversion, "and I must be in the workshop to receive him."

Silently he stole to the foot of the attic stairs and then paused to listen. The house seemed very quiet, but he could hear his mother's voice softly humming a cradle song that she had sung to him when he was a baby.

He had been nervous and unsettled and a little fearful until then, but perhaps the sound of his mother's voice gave him courage, for he boldly ascended the stairs and entered the workshop, closing and locking the door behind him.

CHAPTER XX

The Unhappy Fate of the Demon

AGAIN THE atmosphere quickened and pulsed with accumulating vibrations. Again the boy found himself aroused to eager expectancy. There was a whirl in the air; a crackling like distant musketry; a flash of dazzling light—and the Demon stood before him for the third time.

"I give you greetings!" said he, in a voice not unkindly.

"Good afternoon, Mr. Demon," answered the boy, bowing gravely.

"I see you have returned safely from your trip," continued the Apparition, cheerfully, "although at one time I thought you would be unable to escape. Indeed, unless I had knocked that tube from the rascally Turk's hand as he clambered to the top of the wall, I believe you would have been at the Yarkand oasis yet—either dead or alive, as chance might determine."

"Were you there?" asked Rob.

"To be sure. And I recovered the tube for you, without which you would have been helpless. But that is the only time I saw fit to interfere in any way."

"I'm afraid I did not get a chance to give many hints to inventors or scientists," said Rob.

"True, and I have deeply regretted it," replied the Demon. "But your unusual powers caused more astonishment and consternation than you, perhaps, imagined; for many saw you whom you were too busy to notice. As a result several able electricians are now thinking new thoughts along new lines, and some of them may soon give these or similar inventions to the world."

"You are satisfied, then?" asked Rob.

"As to that," returned the Demon, composedly, "I am not. But I have hopes that with the addition of the three marvelous devices I shall present you with today you will succeed in arousing so much popular interest in electrical inventions as to render me wholly satisfied with the result of this experiment."

Rob regarded the brilliant apparition with a solemn face, but made no answer.

429

"No living person," continued the Demon, "has ever before been favored with such comforting devices for the preservation and extension of human life as yourself. You seem quite unappreciative, it is true; but since our connection I have come to realize that you are but an ordinary boy, with many boyish limitations; so I do not condemn your foolish actions too harshly."

"That is kind of you," said Rob.

"To prove my friendliness," pursued the Demon, "I have brought, as the first of today's offerings, this Electro-Magnetic Restorer. You see it is shaped like a thin metal band, and is to be worn upon the brow, clasping at the back of the head. Its virtues surpass those of either the fabulous 'Fountain of Youth,' or the 'Elixir of Life,' so vainly sought for in past ages. For its wearer will instantly become free from any bodily disease or pain and will enjoy perfect health and vigor. In truth, so great are its powers that even the dead may be restored to life, provided the blood has not yet chilled. In presenting you with this appliance, I feel I am bestowing upon you the greatest blessing and most longed-for boon ever bequeathed to suffering humanity."

Here he held the slender, dull-colored metallic band toward the boy.

"Keep it," said Rob.

The Demon started, and gave him an odd look.

"What did you say?" he asked.

"I told you to keep it," answered Rob. "I don't want it."

The Demon staggered back as if he had been struck.

"Don't want it!" he gasped.

"No; I've had enough of your infernal inventions!" cried the boy, with sudden anger.

He unclasped the traveling machine from his wrist and laid it on the table beside the Demon.

"There's the thing that's responsible for most of my troubles," said he, bitterly. "What right has one person to fly through the air while all his fellow-creatures crawl over the earth's surface? And why should I be cut off from all the rest of the world because you have given me this confounded traveling machine? I didn't ask for it, and I won't keep it a moment longer. Give it to some one you hate more than you do me!"

The Demon stared aghast and turned his glittering eyes wonderingly from Rob to the traveling machine and back again, as if to be sure he had heard and seen aright.

"And here are your food tablets," continued the boy, placing the box upon the table. "I've only enjoyed one square meal since you gave them to me. They're all right to preserve life, of course, and answer the purpose for which they were made; but I don't believe nature ever intended us to exist upon such things, or we wouldn't have the sense of taste, which enables us to enjoy natural food. As long as I'm a human being I'm going to eat like a human being, so I've consumed my last Electrical Concentrated Food Tablet—and don't you forget it!"

The Demon sank into a chair, nerveless and limp, but still staring fearfully at the boy.

"And there's another of your unnatural devices," said Rob, putting the Automatic Record of Events upon the table beside the other things.

"What right have you to capture vibrations that radiate from private and secret actions and discover them to others who have no business to know them? This would be a fine world if every body could peep into every one else's affairs, wouldn't it? And here is your Character Marker. Nice thing for a decent person to own, isn't it? Any one who would take advantage of such a sneaking invention as that would be worse than a thief! Oh, I've used them, of course, and I ought to be spanked for having been so mean and underhanded; but I'll never be guilty of looking through them again."

The Demon's face was frowning and indignant. He made a motion to rise, but thought better of it and sank back in his chair.

"As for the Garment of Protection," resumed the boy, after a pause, "I've worn it for the last time, and here it is, at your service. I'll put the Electric Tube with it. Not that these are such very bad things in themselves, but I'll have none of your magical contrivances. I'll say this, however: if all armies were equipped with Electrical Tubes instead of guns and swords the world would be spared a lot of misery and unnecessary bloodshed. Perhaps they will be, in time; but that time hasn't arrived yet."

"You might have hastened it," said the Demon, sternly, "if you had been wise enough to use your powers properly."

"That's just it," answered Rob. "I'm *not* wise enough. Nor is the majority of mankind wise enough to use such inventions as yours unselfishly and for the good of the world. If people were better, and every one had an equal show, it would be different."

For some moments the Demon sat quietly thinking. Finally the frown left his face and he said, with animation:

"I have other inventions, which you may use without any such qualms of conscience. The Electro-Magnetic Restorer I offered you would be a great boon to your race, and could not possibly do harm. And, besides this, I have brought you what I call the Illimitable Communicator. It is a simple electric device which will enable you, wherever you may be, to converse with people in any part of the world, without the use of such crude connections as wires. In fact, you may"—

"Stop!" cried Rob. "It is useless for you to describe it, because I'll have nothing more to do with you or your inventions. I have given them a fair trial, and they've got me into all sorts of trouble and made all my friends miserable. If I was some high-up scientist it would be different; but I'm just a common boy, and I don't want to be anything else."

"But, your duty—" began the Demon.

"My duty I owe to myself and to my family," interrupted Rob. "I have never cultivated science, more than to fool with some simple electrical experiments, so I owe nothing to either science or the Demon of Electricity, so far as I can see."

"But consider," remonstrated the Demon, rising to his feet and speaking in a pleading voice, "consider the years that must elapse before any one else is likely to strike the Master Key! And, in the meanwhile, consider my helpless position, cut off from all interest in the world while I have such wonderful inventions on my hands for the benefit of mankind. If you have no love for science or for the advancement of civilization, *do* have some consideration for your fellow-creatures, and for me!"

"If my fellow-creatures would have as much trouble with your electrical inventions as I had, I am doing them a service by depriving them of your devices," said the boy. "As for yourself, I've no fault to find with you, personally. You're a very decent sort of Demon, and I've no doubt you mean well; but there's something wrong about our present combination, I'm sure. It isn't natural."

The Demon made a gesture of despair.

"Why, oh why did not some intelligent person strike the Master Key!" he moaned.

"That's it!" exclaimed Rob. "I believe that's the root of the whole evil."

"What is?" inquired the Demon, stupidly.

"The fact that an intelligent person did not strike the Master Key. You don't seem to understand. Well, I'll explain. You're the Demon of Electricity, aren't you?"

"I am," said the other, drawing himself up proudly.

"Your mission is to obey the commands of whoever is able to strike the Master Key of Electricity."

"That is true."

"I once read in a book that all things are regulated by exact laws of nature. If that is so you probably owe your existence to those laws." The Demon nodded. "Doubtless it was intended that when mankind became intelligent enough and advanced enough to strike the Master Key, you and all your devices would not only be necessary and acceptable to them, but the world would be prepared for their general use. That seems reasonable, doesn't it?"

"Perhaps so. Yes; it seems reasonable," answered the Demon, thoughtfully.

"Accidents are always liable to happen," continued the boy. "By accident the Master Key was struck long before the world of science was ready for it—or for you. Instead of considering it an accident and paying no attention to it you immediately appeared to me—a mere boy—and offered your services."

"I was very anxious to do something," returned the Demon, evasively. "You've no idea how stupid it is for me to live invisible and unknown, while all the time I have in my possession secrets of untold benefit to the world."

"Well, you'll have to keep cool and bide your time," said Rob. "The world wasn't made in a minute, and while civilization is going on at a pretty good pace, we're not up to the Demon of Electricity yet."

"What shall I do!" groaned the Apparition, wringing his hands miserably; "oh, what shall I do!"

"Go home and lie down," replied Rob, sympathetically. "Take it easy and don't get rattled. Nothing was ever created without a use, they say; so your turn will come some day, sure! I'm sorry for you, old fellow, but it's all your own fault."

"You are right!" exclaimed the Demon, striding up and down the room, and causing thereby such a crackling of electricity in the air that Rob's hair became rigid enough to stand on end. "You are right, and I must wait—wait—wait—patiently and silently—until my bonds are loosed by intelligence rather than chance! It is a dreary fate. But I must wait—I must wait—I must wait!"

"I'm glad you've come to your senses," remarked Rob, drily. "So, if you've nothing more to say—"

"No! I have nothing more to say. There *is* nothing more to say. You and I are two. We should never have met!" retorted the Demon, showing great excitement.

"Oh, I didn't seek your acquaintance," said Rob. "But I've tried to treat you decently, and I've no fault to find with you except that you forgot you were a slave and tried to be a master."

The Demon did not reply. He was busily forcing the various electrical devices that Rob had relinquished into the pockets of his fiery jacket.

Finally he turned with an abrupt movement.

"Good-by!" he cried. "When mortal eyes next behold me they will be those of one fit to command my services! As for you, your days will be passed in obscurity and your name be unknown to fame. Good-by,—forever!"

The room filled with a flash of white light so like a sheet of lightning that the boy went reeling backwards, half stunned and blinded by its dazzling intensity.

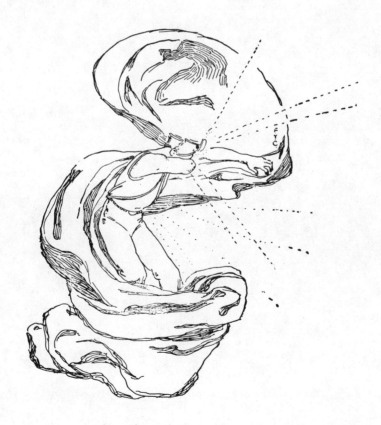

When he recovered himself the Demon of Electricity had disappeared.

Rob's heart was very light as he left the workshop and made his way down the attic stairs.

"Some people might think I was a fool to give up those electrical inventions," he reflected; "but I'm one of those persons who know when they've had enough. It strikes me the fool is the fellow who can't learn a lesson. I've learned mine, all right. It's no fun being a century ahead of the times!"

The Doom That Came to Sarnath

By H. P. Lovecraft

"They had bulging eyes, pouting, flabby lips, and curious
ears, and were without voice."

JOHN D. BATTEN

The Doom That Came to Sarnath

THERE IS IN the land of Mnar a vast still lake that is fed by no stream, and out of which no stream flows. Ten thousand years ago there stood by its shore the mighty city of Sarnath, but Sarnath stands there no more.

It is told that in the immemorial years when the world was young, before ever the men of Sarnath came to the land of Mnar, another city stood beside the lake; the gray stone city of Ib, which was old as the lake itself, and peopled with beings not pleasing to behold. Very old and ugly were these beings, as indeed are most beings of a world yet inchoate and rudely fashioned. It is written on the brick cylinders of Kadatheron that the beings of Ib were in hue as green as the lake and the mists that rise above it; that they had bulging eyes, pouting, flabby lips, and curious ears, and were without voice. It is also written that they descended one night from the moon in a mist; they and the vast still lake and gray stone city Ib. However this may be, it is certain that they worshipped a sea-green stone idol chiseled in the likeness of Bokrug, the great water-lizard; before which they danced horribly when the moon was gibbous. And it is written in the papyrus of Ilarnek, that they one day discovered fire, and thereafter kindled flames on many ceremonial occasions. But not much is written of these beings, because they lived in very ancient times, and man is young, and knows but little of the very ancient living things.

After many eons men came to the land of Mnar, dark shepherd folk with their fleecy flocks, who built Thraa, Ilarnek, and Kadatheron on the winding river Ai. And certain tribes, more hardy than the rest, pushed on to the border of the lake and built Sarnath at a spot where precious metals were found in the earth.

Not far from the gray city of Ib did the wandering tribes lay the first stones of Sarnath, and at the beings of Ib they marveled greatly. But with their marveling was mixed hate, for they thought it not meet that beings of such aspect should walk about the world of men at dusk. Nor did they like the strange sculptures upon the gray monoliths of Ib, for those sculptures lingered so late in the world, even until the coming men, none can tell; unless it was because the land of Mnar is very still, and remote from most other lands, both of waking and of dream.

As the men of Sarnath beheld more of the beings of Ib their hate grew, and it was not less because they found the beings weak, and soft as jelly to the touch of stones and arrows. So one day the young warriors, the slingers and the spearmen and the bowmen, marched against Ib and slew all the inhabitants thereof, pushing the queer bodies into the lake with long spears, because they did not wish to touch them. And because they did not like the gray sculptured monoliths of Ib they cast these also into the lake; wondering from the greatness of the labor how ever the stones were brought from afar, as they must have been, since there is naught like them in the land of Mnar or in the lands adjacent.

Thus of the very ancient city of Ib was nothing spared, save the seagreen stone idol chiseled in the likeness of Bokrug, the water-lizard. This the young warriors took back with them as a symbol of conquest over the old gods and beings of Ib, and as a sign of leadership in Mnar. But on the night after it was set up in the temple, a terrible thing must have happened, for weird lights were seen over the lake, and in the morning the people found the idol gone and the high-priest Taran-Ish lying dead, as from some fear unspeakable. And before he died, Taran-Ish had scrawled upon the altar of chrysolite with coarse shaky strokes the sign of DOOM.

After Taran-Ish there were many high-priests in Sarnath but never was the sea-green stone idol found. And many centuries came and went, wherein Sarnath prospered exceedingly, so that only priests and old women remembered what Taran-Ish had scrawled upon the altar of chrysolite. Betwixt Sarnath and the city of Ilarnek arose a caravan route, and the precious metals from the earth were exchanged for other metals and rare cloths and jewels and books and tools for artificers and all things of luxury that are known to the people who dwell along the winding river Ai and beyond. So Sarnath waxed mighty and learned and beautiful, and sent forth conquering armies to subdue the neighboring cities; and in time there sate upon a throne in Sarnath the kings of all the land of Mnar and of many lands adjacent.

The wonder of the world and the pride of all mankind was Sarnath the magnificent. Of polished desert-quarried marble were its walls, in height three hundred cubits and in breadth seventy-five, so that chariots might pass each other as men drove them along the top. For full five hundred stadia did they run, being open only on the side toward the lake where a green stone sea-wall kept back the waves that rose oddly once a year at the festival of the destroying of Ib. In Sarnath were fifty streets from the lake to the gates of the caravans, and fifty more intersecting them. With onyx were they paved, save those whereon the horses and camels and elephants trod, which were paved with granite. And the gates of Sarnath were as many as the landward ends of the streets, each of bronze, and flanked by the figures of lions and elephants carven from some stone no longer known among men. The houses of Sarnath were of glazed brick and chalcedony, each having its walled garden and crystal lakelet. With strange art were they builded, for no other city had houses like them; and travelers from Thraa and Ilarnket and Kadatheron marveled at the shining domes wherewith they were surrounded.

But more marvelous still were the palaces and the temples, and the gardens made by Zokkar the olden king. There were many palaces, the last of which were mightier than any in Thraa or Ilarnek or Kadatheron. So high were they that one within might sometimes fancy himself beneath only the sky; yet when lighted with torches dipt in the oil of Dother their walls showed vast paintings of kings and armies, of a splendor at once inspiring and stupefying to the beholder. Many were the pillars of the palaces, all of tinted marble, and carven into designs of surpassing beauty. And in most of the palaces the floors were mosaics of beryl and lapis lazuli and sardonyx and carbuncle and other choice materials, so disposed that the beholder might fancy himself walking over beds of the rarest flowers. And there were likewise fountains, which cast scented waters about in pleasing jets arranged with cunning art. Outshining all others was the palace of the kings of Mnar and of the land adjacent. On a pair of golden crouching lions rested the throne, many steps above the gleaming floor. And it was wrought of one piece of ivory, though no man lives who knows whence so vast a piece could have come. In that palace there were also many galleries, and many amphitheaters where lions and men and elephants battled at the pleasure of the kings. Sometimes the amphitheaters were flooded with water conveyed from the lake in mighty aqueducts, and then were enacted stirring sea-fights, or combats betwixt swimmers and deadly marine things.

Lofty and amazing were the seventeen tower-like temples of Sarnath, fashioned of a bright multi-colored stone not known elsewhere. A full thousand cubits high stood the greatest among them, wherein the highpriests dwelt with a magnificence scarce less than that of the kings. On the ground were halls as vast and splendid as those of the palaces; where gathered throngs in worship of Zo-Kalar and Tamash and Lobon, the chief gods of Sarnath, whose incense-enveloped shrines were as the thrones of monarchs. Not like the eikons of other gods were those of Zo-Kalar and Tamash and Lobon. For so close to life were they that one might swear the graceful bearded gods themsleves sate on the ivory thrones. And up unending steps of zircon was the tower-chamber, wherefrom the high-priests looked out over the city and the plains and the lake by day; and at the cryptic moon and significant stars and planets, and their reflections in the lake, at night. Here was done the very secret and ancient rite in detestation of Bokrug, the water-lizard, and here rested the altar of chrysolite which bore the Doom-scrawl of Taran-Ish.

Wonderful likewise were the gardens made by Zokkar the olden king. In the center of Sarnath they lay, covering a great space and encircled by a high wall. And they were surmounted by a mighty dome of glass, through which shone the sun and moon and planets when it was not clear. In summer the gardens were cooled with fresh odorous breezes skilfully wafted by fans, and in winter they were heated with concealed fires, so that in those gardens it was always spring. There ran little streams over bright pebbles, dividing meads of green and gardens of many hues, and spanned by a multitude of bridges. Many were the waterfalls in their courses, and many were the lilied lakelets into which they expanded. Over the streams and lakelets rode white swans, whilst the music of rare birds chimed in with the melody of the waters. In ordered terraces rose the green banks, adorned here and there with bowers of vines and sweet blossoms, and seats and benches of marble and porphyry. And there were many small shrines and temples where one might rest or pray to small gods.

Each year there was celebrated in Sarnath the feast of the destroying of Ib, at which time wine, song, dancing and merriment of every kind abounded. Great honors were then paid to the shades of those who had annihilated the old ancient beings, and the memory of those beings and of their elder gods was derided by dancers and lutanists crowned with roses from the gardens of Zokkar. And the kings would look out over the lake and curse the bones of the dead that lay beneath it.

At first the high-priests liked not these festivals, for there had descended amongst them queer tales of how the sea-green eikon had vanished, and how Taran-Ish had died from fear and left a warning. And they said that from their high tower they sometimes saw lights beneath the waters of the lake. But as many years passed without calamity even the priests laughed and cursed and joined in the orgies of the feasters. Indeed, had they not themselves, in their high tower, often performed the very ancient and secret rite in detestation of Bokrug, the water-lizard? And a thousand years of riches and delight passed over Sarnath, wonder of the world.

Gorgeous beyond thought was the feast of the thousandth year of the destroying of Ib. For a decade had it been talked of in the land of Mnar, and as it drew nigh there came to Sarnath on horses and camels and elephants men from Thraa, Ilarnek, and Kadatheron, and all the cities of Mnar and the lands beyond. Before the marble walls on the appointed night were pitched the pavilions of princes and the tents of travelers. Within the banquet-hall reclined Nargis-Hei, the king, drunken with ancient wine from the vaults of conquered Pnoth, and surrounded by feasting nobles and hurrying slaves. There were eaten many strange delicacies at that feast; peacocks from the distant hills of Implan, heels of camels from the Bnazic desert, nuts and spices from Sydathrian groves, and pearls from wave-washed Mtal dissolved in the vinegar of Thraa. Of sauces there were an untold number, prepared by the subtlest cooks in all Mnar, and suited to the palate of every feaster. But most prized of all the viands were the great fishes from the lake, each of vast size, and served upon golden platters set with rubies and diamonds.

Whilst the king and his nobles feasted within the palace, and viewed the crowning dish as it awaited them on golden platters, others feasted elsewhere. In the tower of the great temple the priests held revels, and in pavilions without the walls the princes of neighboring lands made merry. And it was the high-priest Gnai-Kah who first saw the shadows that descended from the gibbous moon into the lake, and the damnable green mists that arose from the lake to meet the moon and to shroud in a sinister haze the towers and the domes of fated Sarnath. Thereafter those in the towers and without the walls beheld strange lights on the water, and saw that the gray rock Akurion, which was wont to rear high above it near the shore, was almost submerged. And fear grew vaguely yet swiftly, so that the princes of Ilarnek and of far Rokol took down and folded their tents and pavilions and departed, though they scarce knew the reason for their departing.

Then, close to the hour of midnight, all the bronze gates of Sarnath burst open and emptied forth a frenzied throng that blackened the plain, so that all the visiting princes and travelers fled away in fright. For on the faces of this throng was writ a madness born of horror unendurable, and on their tongues were words so terrible that no hearer paused for proof. Men whose eyes were wild with fear shrieked aloud of the sight within the king's banquet-hall, where through the windows were seen no longer the forms of Nargis-Hei and his nobles and slaves, but a horde of indescribable green voiceless things with bulging eyes, pouting, flabby lips, and curious ears; things which danced horribly, bearing in their paws golden platters set with rubies and diamonds and containing uncouth flames. And the princes and travelers, as they fled from the doomed city of Sarnath on horses and camels and elephants, looked again upon the mist-begetting lake and saw the gray rock Akurion was quite submerged. Through all the land of Mnar and the land adjacent spread the tales of those who had fled from Sarnath, and caravans sought that accursed city and its precious metals no more. It was long ere any travelers went thither, and even then only the brave and adventurous young men of yellow hair and blue eyes, who are no kin to the men of Mnar. These men indeed went to the lake to view Sarnath; but though they found the vast still lake itself, and the gray rock Akurion which rears high above it near the shore, they beheld not the wonder of the world and pride of all mankind. Where once had risen walls of three hundred cubits and towers yet higher, now stretched only the marshy shore, and where once had dwelt fifty million of men now crawled the detestable water-lizard. Not even the mines of precious metal remained. DOOM had come to Sarnath.

But half buried in the rushes was spied a curious green idol; an exceedingly ancient idol chiseled in the likeness of Bokrug, the great water-lizard. That idol, enshrined in the high temple at Ilarnek, was subsequently worshipped beneath the gibbous moon throughout the land of Mnar.

Swords of the Purple Kingdom

By Robert E. Howard

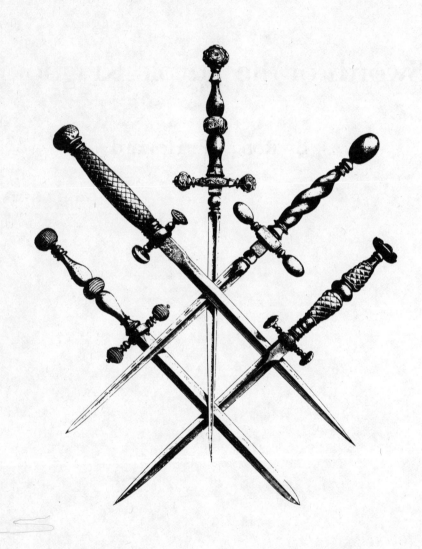

Swords of the Purple Kingdom

I

"Valusia Plots Behind Closed Doors"

A SINISTER QUIET lay like a shroud over the ancient city of Valusia. The heat waves danced from roof to shining roof and shimmered against the smooth marble walls. The purple towers and golden spires were softened in the faint haze. No ringing hoofs on the wide paved streets broke the drowsy silence, and the few pedestrians who appeared did what they had to do hastily and vanished indoors again. The city seemed like a realm of ghosts.

Kull, king of Valusia, drew aside the filmy curtains and gazed over the golden window sill, out over the court with sparkling fountains and trim hedges and pruned trees, over the high wall and at the blank windows of houses which met his glance.

"All Valusia plots behind closed doors, Brule," he grunted.

His companion, a dark-faced, powerful warrior of medium height, grinned hardly. "You are too suspicious, Kull. The heat drives most of them indoors."

"But they plot," reiterated Kull. He was a tall, broad-shouldered barbarian, with the true fighting build: wide shoulders, mighty chest, and lean flanks. Under heavy black brows his cold gray eyes brooded. His features betrayed his birthplace, for Kull the usurper was an Atlantean.

"True, they plot. When did the people ever fail to plot, no matter who held the throne? And they might be excused now, Kull."

"Aye," the giant's brow clouded, "I am an alien. The first barbarian to press the Valusian throne since the beginning of time. When I was a commander of her forces they overlooked the accident of my birth. But now they hurl it into my teeth—by looks and thoughts, at least."

"What do you care? I am an alien also. Aliens rule Valusia now, since the people have grown too weak and degenerate to rule themselves. An Atlantean sits on her throne, backed by all the Picts, the empire's most ancient and powerful allies; her court is filled with foreigners; her armies with barbarian mercenaries; and the Red Slayers—well, they are at least Valusians, but they are men of the mountains who look upon themselves as a different race."

Kull shrugged his shoulders restlessly.

"I know what the people think, and with what aversion and anger the powerful old Valusian families must look on the state of affairs. But

445

what would you have? The empire was worse under Borna, a native Valusian and a direct heir of the old dynasty, than it has been under me. This is the price a nation must pay for decaying: the strong young people come in and take possession, one way or another. I have at least rebuilt the armies, organized the mercenaries and restored Valusia to a measure of her former international greatness. Surely it is better to have one barbarian on the throne holding the crumbling bands together, than to have a hundred thousand riding red-handed through the city streets. Which is what would have happened by now, had it been left to King Borna. The kingdom was splitting under his feet, invasion threatened on all sides, the heathen Grondarians were ready to launch a raid of appalling magnitude—

"Well, I killed Borna with my bare hands that wild night when I rode at the head of the rebels. That bit of ruthlessness won me some enemies, but within six months I had put down anarchy and all counter-rebellions, had welded the nation back into one piece, had broken the back of the Triple Federation, and crushed the power of the Grondarians. Now Valusia dozes in peace and quiet, and between naps plots my overthrow. There has been no famine since my reign, the storehouses are bulging with grain, the trading ships ride heavy with cargo, the merchants' purses are full, the people are fat-bellied—but still they murmur and curse and spit on my shadow. What do they want?"

The Pict grinned savagely and with bitter mirth. "Another Borna! A red-handed tyrant! Forget their ingratitude. You did not seize the kingdom for their sakes, nor do you hold it for their benefit. Well, you have accomplished a lifelong ambition, and you are firmly seated on the throne. Let them murmur and plot. You are king."

Kull nodded grimly. "I am king of this purple kingdom! And until my breath stops and my ghost goes down the long shadow road, I will be king. What now?"

A slave bowed deeply, "Nalissa, daughter of the great house of bora Ballin, desires audience, most high majesty."

A shadow crossed the king's brow. "More supplication in regard to her damnable love affair," he sighed to Brule. "Mayhap you'd better go." To the slave, "Let her enter the presence."

Kull sat in a chair padded with velvet and gazed at Nalissa. She was only some nineteen years of age; and clad in the costly but scanty fashion of Valusian noble ladies, she presented a ravishing picture, the beauty of which even the barbarian king could appreciate. Her skin was a marvelous white, due partly to many baths in milk and wine, but mainly to a heritage of loveliness. Her cheeks were tinted naturally with a delicate pink, and her lips were full and red. Under delicate black brows brooded a pair of deep soft eyes, dark as mystery, and the whole picture was set off by a mass of curly black hair which was partly confined by slim golden band.

Nalissa knelt at the feet of the king, and clasping his sword-hardened fingers in her soft slim hands, she looked up into his eyes; her own eyes luminous and pensive with appeal. Of all the people in the kingdom, Kull preferred not to look into the eyes of Nalissa. He saw there at times a depth of allure and mystery. She knew something of her powers, the spoiled and pampered child of aristocracy, but her full powers she little guessed because of her youth. But Kull, who was wise in the ways of men and women, realized with some uneasiness that with maturity Nalissa was bound to become a terrific power in the court and in the land, either for good or bad.

"But your majesty," she was wailing now, like a child begging for a toy, "please let me marry Dalgar of Farsun. He has become a Valusian citizen, he is high in favor at court, as you yourself say. Why—"

"I have told you," said the king with patience, "it is nothing to me whether you marry Dalgar, Brule, or the devil! But your father does not wish you to marry this Farsunian adventurer and—"

"But you can make him let me!" she cried.

"The house of bora Ballin I number among my staunchest supporters," answered the Atlantean. "And Murom bora Ballin, your father, among my closest friends. When I was a friendless gladiator, he befriended me. He lent me money when I was a common soldier, and he espoused my cause when I struck for the throne. Not to save this right hand of mine would I force him into an action to which he is so violently opposed, or interfere in his family affairs."

Nalissa had not yet learned that some men cannot be moved by feminine wiles. She pleaded, coaxed, and pouted. She kissed Kull's hands, wept on his breast, perched on his knee and argued, all much to his embarrassment, but to no avail. Kull was sincerely sympathetic, but adamant. To all her appeals and blandishments he had one answer: that it was none of his business, that her father knew better what she needed, and that he, Kull, was not going to interfere.

At last Nalissa gave up and left the presence with bowed head and dragging steps. As she emerged from the royal chamber, she met her father coming in. Murom bora Ballin, guessing his daughter's purpose in visiting the king, said nothing to her, but the look he gave her spoke eloquently of punishment to come. The girl climbed miserably into her sedan chair, feeling as if her sorrow was too heavy a load for any one girl to bear. Then her inner nature asserted itself. Her dark eyes smoldered with rebellion, and she spoke a few quick words to the slaves who carried her chair.

Count Murom stood before his king meanwhile, and his features were frozen into a mask of formal deference. Kull noted that expression, and it hurt him. Formality existed between himself and all his subjects and allies except the Pict, Brule; and the ambassador, Ka-nu; but this studied formality was a new thing in Count Murom, and Kull guessed the reason.

"Your daughter was here, Count," he said abruptly.

"Yes, your majesty," the tone was impassive and respectful.

"You probably know why. She wants to marry Dalgar of Farsun."

The count made a stately inclination of his head. "If your majesty so wishes, he has but to say the word." His features froze into harder lines.

Kull, stung, rose and strode across the chamber to the window, where once again he gazed out at the drowsing city. Without turning, he said, "Not for half my kingdom would I interfere with your family affairs, nor force you into a course unpleasant to you."

The count was at his side in an instant, his formality vanished, his fine eyes eloquent. "Your majesty, I have wronged you in my thoughts—I should have known—" He made as if to kneel, but Kull restrained him.

The king grinned. "Be at ease, Count. Your private affairs are your own. I cannot help you, but you can help me. There is conspiracy in the air; I smell danger as in my early youth I sensed the nearness of a tiger in the jungle or a serpent in the high grass."

"My spies have been combing the city, your majesty," said the count, his eyes kindling at the prospect of action. "The people murmur as they will murmur under any ruler—but I have recently come from Ka-nu at the consulate, and he told me to warn you that outside influence and foreign money were at work. He said he knew nothing definite, but his Picts wormed some information from a drunken servant of the Verulian ambassador—vague hints at some coup that government is planning."

Kull grunted. "Verulian trickery is a byword. But Gen Dala, the Verulian ambassador, is the soul of honor."

"So much better a figurehead. If he knows nothing of what his nation plans, so much the better will he serve as a mask for their doings."

"But what would Verulia gain?" asked Kull.

"Gomlah, a distant cousin of King Gorna, took refuge there when you overthrew the old dynasty. With you slain, Valusia would fall to pieces. Her armies would become disorganized, all her allies except the Picts would desert her, the mercenaries whom only you can control would turn against her, and she would be an easy prey for the first powerful nation who might move against her. Then, with Gomlah as an excuse for invasion, as a puppet on Valusia's throne—"

"I see," grunted Kull. "I am better at battle than in council, but I see. So—the first step must be my removal, eh?"

"Yes, your majesty."

Kull smiled and flexed his mighty arms. "After all, this ruling grows dull at times." His fingers caressed the hilt of the great sword which he wore at all times.

"Tu, chief councilor to the king, and Dondal, his nephew," sang out a slave, and two men entered the presence.

Tu, chief councilor, was a portly man of medium height and late middle life, who looked more like a merchant than a councilor. His hair was thin, his face lined, and on his brow rested a look of perpetual suspicion. Tu's years and honors rested heavily on him. Originally of plebian birth, he had won his way by sheer power of craft and intrigue. He had seen three kings come and go before Kull, and the strain told on him.

His nephew Dondal was a slim, foppish youth with keen dark eyes and a pleasant smile. His chief virtue lay in the fact that he kept a discreet tongue in his head and never repeated what he heard at court. For this reason he was admitted into places not even warranted by his close kinship to Tu.

"Just a small matter of state, your majesty," said Tu. "This permit for a new harbor on the western coast. Will your majesty sign?"

Kull signed his name; Tu drew from inside his bosom a signet ring attached to a small chain which he wore around his neck, and affixed the seal. This ring was the royal signature, in effect. No other ring in the world was exactly like it, and Tu wore it about his neck, waking or sleeping. Outside those in the royal chamber at the moment, not four men in the world knew where the ring was kept.

II

Mystery

THE QUIET OF the day had merged almost imperceptibly into the quiet of night. The moon had not yet risen, and the small silver stars gave little light, as if their radiance was strangled by the heat which still rose from the earth.

Along a deserted street a single horse's hoofs clanged hollowly. If eyes watched from the blank windows, they gave no sign that betrayed that anyone knew Dalgar of Farsun was riding through the night and the silence.

The young Farsunian was fully armed, his lithe athletic body was completely encased in light armor, and a morion was on his head. He looked capable of handling the long, slim jewel-hilted sword at his side, and the scarf which crossed his steel-clad breast, with its red rose, detracted nothing from the picture of manhood he presented.

Now as he rode he glanced at a crumpled note in his hand, which, half unfolded, disclosed the following message in the characters of Valusia: "At midnight, my beloved, in the Accursed Gardens beyond the walls. We will fly together."

A dramatic note; Dalgar's handsome lips curved slightly as he read. Well, a little melodrama was pardonable in a young girl, and the youth enjoyed a touch himself. A thrill of ecstasy shook him at the thought of that rendezvous. By dawn he would be far across the Verulian border with his bride-to-be; then let Count Murom bora Ballin rave; let the whole Valusian army follow their tracks. With that much start, he and Nalissa would be in safety. He felt high and romantic; his heart swelled with the foolish heroics of youth. It was hours until midnight, but—he nudged his horse with an armored heel and turned aside to take a shortcut through some dark narrow streets.

"Oh, silver moon and a silver breast—" he hummed under his breath the flaming love songs of the mad, dead poet Ridondo; then his horse snorted and shied. In the shadow of a squalid doorway, a dark bulk moved and groaned.

Drawing his sword, Dalgar slipped from the saddle and bent over he who groaned.

Bending very close, he made out the form of a man. He dragged the body into a comparatively lighter area, noting that he was still breathing. Something warm and sticky adhered to his hand.

The man was portly and apparently old, since his hair was sparse and his beard shot with white. He was clad in the rags of a beggar, but even in the darkness Dalgar could tell that his hands were soft and white under their grime. A nasty gash on the side of his head seeped blood, and his eyes were closed. He groaned from time to time.

Dalgar tore a piece from his sash to staunch the wound, and in so doing, a ring on his finger became entangled in the unkempt beard. He jerked impatiently—the beard came away entirely, disclosing the smooth-shaven, deeply lined face of a man in late middle life. Dalgar cried out and recoiled. He bounded to his feet, bewildered and shocked. A moment he stood, staring down at the groaning man; then the quick rattle of hoofs on a parallel street recalled him to life.

He ran down a side alley and accosted the rider. This man pulled up with a quick motion, reaching for his sword as he did so. The steel-shod hoofs of his steed struck fire from the flagstones as the horse set back on his haunches.

"What now? Oh, it's you, Dalgar."

"Brule!" cried the young Farsunian. "Quick! Tu, the chief councilor, lies in yonder side street, senseless—mayhap murdered!"

The Pict was off his horse in an instant, sword flashing into his hand. He flung the reins over his mount's head and left the steed standing there like a statue while he followed Dalgar on a run.

Together they bent over the stricken councilor while Brule ran an experienced hand over him.

"No fracture, apparently," grunted the Pict. "Can't tell for sure, of course. Was his beard off when you found him?"

"No, I pulled it off accidentally—"

"Then likely this is the work of some thug who knew him not. I'd rather think that. If the man who struck him down knew he was Tu, there's black treachery brewing in Valusia. I told him he'd come to grief prowling around the city disguised this way—but you cannot tell a councilor anything. He insisted that in this manner he learned all that was going on; kept his finger on the empire's pulse, as he said."

"But if it were a cutthroat," said Dalgar, "why did they not rob him? Here is his purse with a few copper coins in it—and who would seek to rob a beggar?"

The Spear-slayer swore. "Right. But who in Valka's name could know he was Tu? He never wore the same disguise twice, and only Dondal and a slave helped him with it. And what did they want, whoever struck him down? Oh well, Valka—he'll die while we stand here jabbering. Help me get him on my horse."

With the chief councilor lolling drunkenly in the saddle, upheld by Brule's steel-sinewed arms, they clattered through the streets to the palace. They were admitted by a wondering guard, and the senseless man was carried to an inner chamber and laid on a couch, where he was showing signs of recovering consciousness, under the ministrations of the slaves and court women.

At last he sat up and gripped his head, groaning. Ka-nu, Pictish amabassador and the craftiest man in the Kingdom, bent over him.

"Tu! Who smote you?"

"I don't know," the councilor was still dazed. "I remember nothing."

"Had you any documents of importance about you?"

"No."

"Did they take anything from you?"

Tu began fumbling at his garments uncertainly; his clouded eyes began to clear, then flared in sudden apprehension. "The ring! The royal signet ring! It is gone!"

Ka-nu smote his fist into his palm and cursed soulfully.

"This comes of carrying the thing with you! I warned you! Quick, Brule, Kelkor—Dalgar; foul treason is afoot! Haste to the king's chamber."

In front of the royal bedchamber, ten of the Red Slayers, men of the king's favorite regiment, stood at guard. To Ka-nu's staccato questions, they answered that the king had retired an hour or so ago, that no one had sought entrance, and that they had heard no sound.

Ka-nu knocked on the door. There was no response. In a panic he pushed against the door. It was locked from within.

"Break that door down!" he screamed, his face white, his voice unnatural with unaccustomed strain.

Two of the Red Slayers, giants in size, hurled their full weight against the door, but it, being of heavy oak braced with bronze bands, held. Brule pushed them away and attacked the massive portal with his sword. Under the heavy blows of the keen edge, wood and metal gave way, and in a few moments Brule shouldered through the shreds and rushed into the room. He halted short with a stifled cry, and, glaring over his shoulder, Ka-nu clutched wildly at his beard. The royal bed was mussed as if it had been slept in, but of the king there was no sign. The room was empty, and only the open window gave hint of any clue.

"Sweep the streets!" roared Ka-nu. "Comb the city! Guard all the gates! Kelkor, rouse out the full force of the Red Slayers. Brule, gather your horsemen and ride them to death if necessary. Haste! Dalgar—"

But the Farsunian was gone. He had suddenly remembered that the hour of midnight approached, and of far more importance to him than the whereabouts of any king was the fact that Nalissa bora Ballin was awaiting him in the Accursed Gardens two miles beyond the city wall.

III

The Sign of the Seal

THAT NIGHT KULL had retired early. As was his custom, he halted outside the door of the royal bedchamber for a few minutes to chat with the guard, his old regimental mates, and exchange a reminiscence or so of the days when he had ridden in the ranks of the Red Slayers. Then, dismissing his attendants, he entered the chamber, flung back the covers of his bed, and prepared to retire. Strange proceedings for a king, no doubt, but Kull had been long used to the rough life of a soldier, and before that he had been a savage tribesman. He had never gotten used to having things done for him, and in the privacy of his bedchamber he would at least attend to himself.

But just as he turned to extinguish the candle which illumined his room, he heard a slight tapping at the window sill. Hand on sword, he crossed the room with the easy, silent tread of a great panther and looked out. The window opened on the inner grounds of the palace; the hedges and trees loomed vaguely in the semi-darkness of the starlight. Fountains glimmered vaguely, and he could not make out the forms of any of the sentries who paced those confines.

But here at his elbow was mystery. Clinging to the vines which covered the wall was a small wizened fellow who looked much like the professional beggars which swarmed the more sordid of the city's streets. He seemed harmless with his thin limbs and monkey face, but Kull regarded him with a scowl.

"I see I shall have to plant sentries at the very foot of my window, or tear these vines down," said the king. "How did you get through the guards?"

The wizened one put his skinny finger across puckered lips for silence; then with a simian-like dexterity, slid a hand through the bars. He silently handed Kull a piece of parchment. The king unrolled it and read: "King Kull: If you value your life, or the welfare of the kingdom, follow this guide to the place where he shall lead you. Tell no one. Let yourself be not seen by the guards. The regiments are honeycombed with treason, and if you are to live and hold the throne, you must do exactly as I say. Trust the bearer of this note implicity." It was signed "Tu, Chief Counciler of Valusia" and was sealed with the royal signet ring.

Kull knit his brows. The thing had an unsavory look—but this was Tu's handwriting—he noted the peculiar, almost imperceptible, quirk in the last letter of Tu's name, which was the councilor's trademark, so to speak. And then the sign of the seal, the seal which could not be duplicated. Kull sighed.

"Very well," he said. "Wait until I arm myself."

Dressed and clad in light chain-mail armor, Kull turned again to the window. He gripped the bars, one in each hand, and cautiously exerting his tremendous strength, felt them give until even his broad shoulders could slip between them. Clambering out, he caught the vines and swung down them with as much ease as was displayed by the small beggar who preceded him.

At the foot of the wall, Kull caught his companion's arm.

"How did you elude the guard?" he whispered.

"To such as accosted me, I showed the sign of the royal seal."

"That will scarcely suffice now," grunted the king. "Follow me; I know their routine."

Some twenty minutes followed of lying in wait behind a hedge or tree until a sentry passed, of dodging quickly into the shadows and making short, stealthy dashes. At last they came to the outer wall. Kull took his guide by the ankles and lifted him until his fingers clutched the top of the wall. Once astride it, the beggar reached down a hand to aid the king; but Kull, with a contemptuous gesture, backed off a few paces, took a short run, and bounding high in the air, caught the parapet with one upflung hand, swinging his great form up across the top of the wall with an almost incredible display of strength and agility.

The next instant the two strangely incongruous figures had dropped down on the opposite side and faded into the gloom.

IV

"Here I Stand at Bay!"

NALISSA, DAUGHTER OF the house of bora Ballin, was nervous and frightened. Upheld by her high hopes and her sincere love, she did not regret her rash actions of the last few hours, but she earnestly wished for the coming of midnight and her lover.

Up to the present, her escapade had been easy. It was not easy for anyone to leave the city after nightfall, but she had ridden away from her father's house just before sundown, telling her mother that she was going to spend the night with a girl friend. It was well for her that women were allowed unusual freedom in the city of Valusia, and were not kept hemmed in seraglios and veritable prison houses as they were in the Eastern empires; a custom which survived the Flood.

Nalissa had ridden boldly through the eastern gate, and then made directly for the Accursed Gardens, two miles east of the city. These Gardens had once been the pleasure resort and country estate of a nobleman, but tales of grim debauches and ghastly rites of devil worship began to get abroad; and finally the people, maddened by the regular disappearance of their children, had descended on the Gardens in a frenzied mob and had hanged the prince to his own portals. Combing the Gardens, the people had found foul things, and in a flood of repulsion and horror had partially destroyed the mansion and the summer houses, the arbors, the grottoes, and the walls. But built of imperishable marble, many of the buildings had resisted both the sledges of the mob and the corrosion of time. Now, deserted for a hundred years, a miniature jungle had sprung up within the crumbling walls and rank vegetation overran the ruins.

Nalissa concealed her steed in a ruined summer house, and seated herself on the cracked marble floor, settling down to wait. At first it was not bad. The gentle summer sunset flooded the land, softening all scenes with its mellow gold. The green sea about her, shot with white gleams which were marble walls and crumbling roofs, intrigued her. But as night fell and the shadows merged, Nalissa grew nervous. The night wind whispered grisly things through the branches and the broad palm leaves and the tall grass, and the stars seemed cold and far away. Legends and tales came back to her, and she fancied that above the throb of her pounding heart she could hear the rustle of unseen black wings and the mutter of fiendish voices.

She prayed for midnight and Dalgar. Had Kull seen her then he would not have thought of her strange deep nature, nor the signs of her great future; he would have seen only a frightened little girl who passionately desired to be taken up and cuddled.

But the thought of leaving never entered her mind.

Time seemed as if it would never pass, but pass it did somehow. At last a faint glow betrayed the rising of the moon, and she knew the hour was closing to midnight.

Then suddenly there came a sound which brought her to her feet, her heart flying into her throat. Somewhere in the supposedly deserted Gardens there crashed into the silence a shout and a clang of steel. A short, hideous scream chilled the blood in her veins; then silence fell in a suffocating shroud.

Dalgar—Dalgar! The thought beat like a hammer in her dazed brain. Her lover had come and had fallen foul of someone—or something.

She stole from her hiding place, one hand over her heart which seemed about to burst through her ribs. She stole along a broken pave, and the whispering palm leaves brushed against her like her ghostly fingers. About her lay a pulsating gulf of shadows, vibrant and alive with nameless evil. There was no sound.

Ahead of her loomed the ruined mansion; then without a sound, two men stepped into her path. She screamed once; then her tongue froze with terror. She tried to flee, but her legs would not work, and before she could move, one of the men had caught her up and tucked her under his arm as if she were a tiny child.

"A woman," he growled in a language which Nalissa barely understood, and which she recognized as Verulian. "Lend me your dagger and I'll—"

"We haven't time now," interposed the other, speaking in the Valusian tongue. "Toss her in there with him, and we'll finish them both together. We must get Phondar here before we kill him; he wants to question him a little."

"Small use," rumbled the Verulian giant, striding after his companion. "He won't talk—I can tell you that—he's opened his mouth only to curse us, since we captured him."

"Nalissa, tucked ignominiously under her captor's arm, was frozen with fear, but her mind was working. Who was this "him" they were going to question and then kill? The thought that it must be Dalgar drove her own fear from her mind, and flooded her soul with a wild and desperate rage. She began to kick and struggle violently and was punished with a resounding smack that brought tears to her eyes and a cry of pain to her lips. She lapsed into a humiliated submission and was presently tossed unceremoniously through a shadowed doorway, to sprawl in a disheveled heap on the floor.

"Hadn't we better tie her?" queried the giant.

"What use? She can't escape. And she can't untie *him*. Hurry up; we've got work to do."

Nalissa sat up and looked timidly about. She was in a small chamber, the corners of which were screened with spider webs. Dust was deep on the floor, and fragments of marble from the crumbling walls littered it. Part of the roof was gone, and the slowly rising moon poured light through the aperture. By its light she saw a form on the floor, close to the wall. She shrank back, her teeth sinking into her lip with horrified anticipation; then she saw with a delirious sensation of relief that the man was too large to be Dalgar. She crawled over to him and looked into his face. He was bound hand and foot and gagged; above the gag, two cold gray eyes looked up into hers.

"King Kull!" Nalissa pressed both hands against her temples while the room reeled to her shocked and astounded gaze. The next instant her slim, strong fingers were at work on the gag. A few minutes of agonized effort, and it came free. Kull stretched his jaws and swore in his own language, considerate, even in that moment, of the girl's tender ears.

"Oh, my lord, how came you here?" The girl was wringing her hands.

"Either my most trusted councilor is a traitor or I am a madman!" growled the giant. "One came to me with a letter in Tu's handwriting, bearing even the royal seal. I followed him, as instructed, through the city and to a gate, the existence of which I had never known. This gate was unguarded and apparently unknown to any but they who plotted against me. Outside the gate, one awaited us with horses, and we came full speed to these damnable gardens. At the outer edge we left the horses, and I was led, like a blind, dumb fool for sacrifice, into this ruined mansion.

"As I came through the door, a great man-net fell on me, entangling my sword arm and binding my limbs, and a dozen rogues sprang on me. Well, mayhap my taking was not so easy as they had thought. Two of them were swinging on my already encumbered right arm so I could not use my sword, but I kicked one in the side and felt his ribs give way, and bursting some of the net's strands with my left hand, I gored another with my dagger. He had his death thereby and screamed like a lost soul as he gave up the ghost.

"But by Valka, there were too many of them. At last they had me stripped of my armor,"—Nalissa saw the king wore only a sort of loincloth—"and bound as you see me. The devil himself could not break these strands; no, scant use to try to untie the knots. One of the men was a seaman, and I know of old the sort of knots they tie. I was a galley slave once, you know."

"But what can I do?" wailed the girl, wringing her hands.

"Take a heavy piece of marble and flake off a sharp sliver," said Kull swiftly. "You must cut these ropes—"

She did as he bid and was rewarded with a long thin piece of stone, the concave edge of which was as keen as a razor with a jagged edge.

"I fear I will cut your skin, sire," she apologized as she began work.

"Cut skin, flesh, and bone, but get me free!" snarled Kull, his eyes blazing. "Trapped like a blind fool! Oh, imbecile that I am! Valka, Honan, and Hotath! But let me get my hands on the rogues—how came you here?"

"Let us talk of that later," said Nalissa rather breathlessly. "Just now there is time for haste."

Silence fell as the girl sawed at the stubborn strands, giving no heed to her own tender hands, which were soon lacerated and bleeding. Slowly strand by strand, the cords gave way; but there were still enough to hold the ordinary man helpless when a heavy step sounded outside the door.

Nalissa froze. A voice spoke, "He is within, Phondar, bound and gagged. With him is some Valusian wench that we caught wandering about the Gardens."

"Then be on watch for some gallant," spoke another voice, whose harsh, grating tones were those of a man accustomed to being obeyed. "Likely she was to meet some fop here. You—"

"No names, no names, good Phondar," broke in a silky Valusian voice. "Remember our agreement; until Gomlah mounts the throne, I am simply—the Masked One."

"Very good," grunted the Verulian. "You have done a good night's work, Masked One. None but you could have done it, for only you knew how to obtain the royal signet. Only you could so closely counterfeit Tu's writing—by the way, did you kill the old fellow?"

"What matter? Tonight, or the day Gomlah mounts the throne, he dies. The matter of most importance is that the king lies helpless in our power."

Kull was racking his brain trying to place the hauntingly familiar voice of the traitor. And Phondar—his face grew grim. A deep conspiracy indeed, if Verulia must send the commander of her royal armies to do her foul work. The king knew Phondar well, and had aforetime entertained him in the palace.

"Go in and bring him out," said Phondar. "We will take him to the old torture chamber. I have questions to ask him."

The door opened, admitting one man: the giant who had captured Nalissa. The door closed behind him and he crossed the room, giving scarcely a glance to the girl who cowered in a corner. He bent over the bound king, took him by leg and shoulder to lift him bodily; there came a sudden loud snap as Kull, throwing all his iron strength into one convulsive wrench, broke the remaining strands which bound him.

He had not been tied long enough for all circulation to be cut off and his strength affected thereby. As a python strikes, his hands shot to the giant's throat; shot and gripped like a steel vise.

The giant went to his knees. One hand flew to the fingers at his throat, the other to his dagger. His fingers sank like steel into Kull's wrist, the dagger flashed from its sheath; then his eyes bulged, his tongue sagged out. The fingers fell away from the king's wrist, and the dagger slipped from a nerveless grip. The Verulian went limp, his throat literally crushed in that terrible grip. Kull, with one terrific wrench, broke his neck and, releasing him, tore the sword from its sheath. Nalissa had picked up the dagger.

The combat had taken only a few flashing seconds and had caused no more noise than might have resulted from a man lifting and shouldering a great weight.

"Hasten!" called Phondar's voice impatiently from beyond the door, and Kull, crouching tigerlike just inside, thought quickly. He knew that there were at least a score of conspirators in the Gardens. He knew also, from the sound of voices, that there were only two or three outside the door at the moment. This room was not a good place to defend. In a moment they would be coming in to see what occasioned the delay. He reached a decision and acted promptly.

He beckoned the girl. "As soon as I have gone through the door, run out likewise and go up the stairs which lead away to the left." She nodded, trembling, and he patted her slim shoulder reassuringly. Then he whirled and flung open the door.

To the men outside, expecting the Verulian giant with the helpless king on his shoulders, appeared an apparition which was dumbfounding in its unexpectedness. Kull stood in the door; Kull, half-naked, crouching like a great human tiger, his teeth bared in a snarl of battle fury, his eyes blazing. His sword blade whirled like a wheel of silver in the moonlight.

Kull saw Phondar, two Verulian soldiers, a slim figure in a black mask—a flashing instant, and then he was among them and the dance of death was on. The Verulian commander went down in the king's first lunge, his head cleft to the teeth in spite of his helmet. The Masked One drew and thrust, his point raking Kull's cheek; one of the soldiers drove at the king with a spear, was parried, and the next instant lay dead across his master. The remaining soldier broke and ran, yelling lustily for his comrades. The Masked One retreated swiftly before the headlong attack of the king, parrying and guarding with an almost uncanny skill. He had not time to launch an attack of his own; before the whirlwind ferocity of Kull's charge he had only time for defense. Kull beat against his blade like a blacksmith on an anvil, and again and again it seemed as though the long Verulian steel must inevitably cleave that masked and hooded head, but always the long slim Valusian sword was in the way, turning the blow by an inch or stopping it within a hair's breadth of the skin, but always just enough.

Then Kull saw the Verulian soldiers running through the foliage and heard the clang of their weapons and their fierce shouts. Caught here in the open, they would get behind him and slit him like a rat. He slashed once more, viciously, at the retreating Valusian, and then, backing away, turned and ran fleetly up the stairs, at the top of which Nalissa already stood.

There he turned at bay. He and the girl stood on a sort of artificial promontory. A stair led up, and a stair had once led down the other way, but now the back stair had long since crumbled away. Kull saw that they were in a cul-de-sac. The walls were cut deep with ornate carvings but— *Well,* thought Kull, *here we die. But here many others die, too.*

The Verulians were gathering at the foot of the stair, under the leadership of the mysterious masked Valusian. Kull took a fresh grip on his sword hilt and flung back his head, an unconscious reversion to days when he had worn a lion-like mane of hair.

Kull had never feared death; he did not fear it now, and, except for one consideration, he would have welcomed the clamor and madness of battle as an old friend, without regrets. This consideration was the girl who stood beside him. As he looked at her trembling form and white face, he reached a sudden decision.

He raised his hand and shouted, "Ho, men of Verulia! Here I stand at bay. Many shall fall before I die. But promise me to release the girl, unharmed, and I will not lift a hand. You may then kill me like a sheep."

Nalissa cried in protest, and the Masked One laughed. "We make no bargains with one already doomed. The girl also must die, and I make no promises to be broken. Up, warriors, and take him!"

They flooded the stair like a black wave of death, swords sparkling like frosty silver in the moonlight. One was far in advance of his fellows, a huge warrior who bore on high a great battle-axe. Moving quicker than Kull had anticipated, this man was on the landing in an instant. Kull rushed in, and the axe descended. He caught the heavy shaft with his left hand and checked the downward rush of the weapon in mid-air—a feat few men could have done—and at the same time struck in from the side with his right, a sweeping hammerlike blow which sent the long sword crunching through armor, muscle, and bone, and left the broken blade wedged in the spinal column.

At the same instant, he released the useless hilt and tore the axe from the nerveless grasp of the dying warrior, who pitched back down the stairs. And Kull laughed shortly and grimly.

The Verulians hesitated on the stair, and, below, the Masked One savagely urged them on. They were inclined to be rebellious.

"Phondar is dead," shouted one. "Shall we take orders from this Valusian? This is a devil and not a man who faces us! Let us save ourselves!"

"Fools!" the Masked One's voice rose in a ferine shriek. "Don't you see that your own safety lies in slaying the king? If you fail tonight, your own government will repudiate you and will aid the Valusians in hunting you down! Up, fools! You will die, some of you, but better for a few to die under the king's axe than for all to die on the gibbet! Let one man retreat down these stairs—that man will I kill!" And the long, slender sword menaced them.

Desperate, afraid of their leader, and recognizing the truth of his words, the score or more of warriors turned their breasts to Kull's steel. As they massed for what must necessarily be the last charge, Nalissa's attention was attracted by a movement at the base of the wall. A shadow detached itself from the rest of the shadows and moved up the sheer face of the wall, climbing like an ape and using the deep carvings for foot and hand holds. This side of the wall was in shadow, and she could not make out the features of the man; moreover, he wore a heavy morion which shaded his face.

Saying nothing to Kull, who stood at the landing, his axe poised, she stole over to the edge of the wall, half concealing herself behind a ruin of what had once been a parapet. Now she could see that the man was in full armor, but still she could not make out his features. Her breath came fast, and she raised the dagger, fighting fiercely to overcome a tendency of nausea.

Now a steel-clad arm hooked up over the edge—she sprang as quickly and silently as a tigress and struck full at the unprotected face suddenly upturned in the moonlight. And even as the dagger fell, and she was unable to check the blow, she screamed, wildly and agonizedly. For in that fleeting second, she recognized the face of her lover, Dalgar of Farsun.

V

The Battle of the Stair

Dalgar, after unceremoniously leaving the distracted presence of Ka-nu, ran to his horse and rode hard for the eastern gate. He had heard Ka-nu give orders to close the gates and let no one out, and he rode like a madman to beat that order. It was a hard matter to get out at night anyway, and Dalgar, having learned that the gates were not guarded tonight by the incorruptible Red Slayers, had planned to bribe his way out. Now he depended upon the audacity of his scheme.

All in a lather of sweat, he halted at the eastern gate and shouted, "Unbolt the gate! I must ride to the Verulian border tonight! Quickly! The king has vanished! Let me through and then guard the gate! In the name of the king!"

Then, as the soldier hesitated, "Haste, fools! The king may be in mortal danger! Hark!"

Far out across the city, chilling hearts with sudden nameless dread, sounded the deep tones of the great bronze Bell of the King, which booms only when the king is in peril. The guards were electrified. They knew Dalgar was high in favor as a visiting noble. They believed what he said, so, under the impetuous blast of his will, they swung the great iron gates wide, and he shot through like a thunderbolt, to vanish instantly in the outer darkness.

As Dalgar rode, he hoped no great harm had come to Kull, for he liked the bluff barbarian far more than he had ever liked any of the sophisticated and bloodless kings of the Seven Empires. Had it been possible, he would have aided in the search. But Nalissa was waiting for him, and already he was late.

As the young nobleman entered the Gardens, he had a peculiar feeling that here in the heart of desolation and loneliness there were many men. An instant later he heard a clash of steel, the sound of many running footsteps, and a fierce shouting in a foreign tongue. Slipping off his horse and drawing his sword, he crept through the underbrush until he came in sight of the ruined mansion. There a strange sight burst upon his vision. At the top of the crumbling staircase stood a half-naked, blood-stained giant whom he recognized as the king of Valusia. By his side stood a girl—a half-stifled cry burst from Dalgar's lips. Nalissa! His nails bit into the palms of his clenched hand. Who were those men in dark clothing who swarmed up the stairs? No matter. They meant death to the girl and to Kull. He heard the king challenge them and offer his life for Nalissa's, and a flood of gratitude engulfed him. Then he noted the deep carvings on the wall nearest him. The next instant he was climbing, to die by the side of the king, protecting the girl he loved.

He had lost sight of Nalissa, and now as he climbed he dared not take the time to look up for her. This was a slippery and treacherous task. He did not see her until he caught hold of the edge to pull himself up; then he heard her scream and saw her hand falling toward his face, gripping a gleam of silver. He ducked and took the blow on his morion; the dagger snapped at the hilt, and Nalissa collapsed in his arms the next moment.

Kull had whirled, axe high, at her scream; now he paused. He recognized the Farsunian, and even in that instant he read between the lines. He knew why the couple were here and grinned with real enjoyment.

A second the charge had halted, as the Verulians had noted the second man on the landing; now they came on again, bounding up the steps in the moonlight, blades gleaming, eyes wild with desperation. Kull met the first with an overhand smash that crushed helmet and skull; then Dalgar was at his side, and his blade licked out and into a Verulian throat. Then began the battle of the stair, since immortalized by singers and poets.

Kull was there to die and to slay before he died. He gave scant thought to defense. His axe played a wheel of death about him, and with each blow there came a crunch of steel and bone, a spurt of blood, a gurgling cry of agony. Bodies choked the wide stair, but still the survivors came, clambering over the gory forms of their comrades.

Dalgar had little opportunity to thrust or cut. He had seen in an instant that his best task lay in protecting Kull, who was a born killer, but who, in his armorless condition, was likely to fall at any instant.

So Dalgar wove a web of steel about the king, bringing into play all the sword skill that was his. Again and again his flashing blade turned a point from Kull's heart; again and again his mail-clad forearm intercepted a blow that else had killed. Twice he took on his own helmet slashes meant for the king's bare head.

It is not easy to guard another man and yourself at the same time. Kull was bleeding from cuts on the face and breast, from a gash above the temple, a stab in the thigh, and a deep wound in the left shoulder; a thrusting pike had rent Dalgar's cuirass and wounded him in the side, and he felt his strength ebbing. A last mad effort of their foes and the Farsunian was overthrown. He fell at Kull's feet, and a dozen points prodded for his life. With a lion-like roar, Kull cleared a space with one mighty sweep of his red axe and stood astride the fallen youth. They closed in—

There burst on Kull's ears a crash of horses' hoofs and the Accursed Gardens were flooded with wild riders, yelling like wolves in the moonlight. A storm of arrows swept the stairs, and men howled, pitching headlong to lie still, or to tear at the cruel, deeply embedded shafts. The few whom Kull's axe and the arrows had left fled down the stairs to be met at the bottom by the whistling curved swords of Brule's Picts. And there they died, fighting to the last, those bold Verulian warriors—cat's-paws for their false king, sent out on a dangerous and foul mission, disowned by the men who sent them out, and branded forever with infamy. But they died like men.

But one did not die there at the foot of the stairs. The Masked One had fled at the first sound of hoofs, and now he shot across the Gardens riding a superb horse. He had almost reached the outer wall when Brule, the Spear-slayer, dashed across his path. There on the promontory, leaning on his bloody axe, Kull saw them fight beneath the moon.

The Masked One had abandoned his defensive tactics. He charged the Pict with reckless courage, and the Spear-slayer met him, horse to horse, man to man, blade to blade. Both were magnificent horsemen. Their steeds, obeying the touch of the bridle, the nudge of the knee, whirled, reared, and spun. But through all their motions, the whistling blades never lost touch of each other. Brule, unlike his tribesmen, used the slim straight sword of Valusia. In reach and speed there was little difference between them, and Kull, watching, again and again caught his breath and bit his lip as it seemed Brule would fall before an unusually vicious thrust.

No crude hacking and slashing for these seasoned warriors. They thrust and countered, parried and thrust again. Then suddenly Brule seemed to lose touch with his opponent's blade—he parried wildly, leaving himself wide open—the Masked One struck heels into his horse's side as he lunged, so that the sword and horse shot forward as one. Brule leaned aside, let the blade glance from the side of his cuirass; his own blade shot straight out, elbow, wrist, hilt, and point making a straight line from his shoulder. The horses crashed together and together they rolled headlong on the sward. But from that tangle of lashing hoofs Brule rose unharmed, while there in the grass lay the Masked One. Brule's sword still transfixing him.

Kull awoke as from a trance; the Picts were howling about like wolves, but he raised his hand for silence. "Enough! You are all heroes! But attend to Dalgar; he is sorely wounded. And when you have finished, you might see to my own wounds. Brule, how came you to find me?"

Brule beckoned Kull to where he stood above the dead Masked One.

"A beggar crone saw you climb the palace wall, and out of curiosity watched where you went. She followed and saw you go through the forgotten gate. I was riding the plain between the wall and these Gardens when I heard the clash of steel. But who can this be?"

"Raise the mask," said Kull. "Whoever it is, it is he who copied Tu's handwriting, who took the signet ring from Tu, and—"

Brule tore the mask away.

"Dondal!" Kull ejaculated. "Tu's nephew! Brule, Tu must never know this. Let him think that Dondal rode with you and died fighting for his king."

Brule seemed stunned. "Dondal! A traitor! Why, many a time I've drunk wine with him and slept it off in one of his beds."

Kull nodded. "I liked Dondal."

Brule cleansed his blade and drove it home in the scabbard with a vicious clank. "Want will make a rogue of any man," he said moodily. "He was deep in debt—Tu was penurious with him. Always maintained that giving young men money was bad for them. Dondal was forced to keep up appearances for his pride's sake, and so fell into the hands of the usurers. Thus Tu is the great traitor, for he drove the boy into treachery by his parsimony—and I could wish Tu's heart had stopped my point instead of his."

So saying, the Pict turned on his heel and strode sombrely away.

Kull turned back to Dalgar, who lay half-senseless while the Pictish warriors dressed his wounds with experienced fingers. Others attended to the king, and while they staunched, cleansed, and bandaged, Nalissa came up to Kull.

"Sire," she held out her small hands, now scratched and stained with dried blood, "will you now have mercy on us—grant my plea if—" her voice caught on a sob—"if Dalgar lives?"

Kull caught her slim shoulders and shook her in his anguish.

"Girl, girl, girl! Ask me anything except something I cannot grant. Ask half my kingdom or my right hand, and it is yours. I will ask Murom to let you marry Dalgar—I will beg him—but I cannot force him."

Tall horsemen were gathering through the Gardens, whose resplendent armor shone smong the half-naked, wolfish Picts. A tall man hurried up, throwing back the vizor of his helmet.

"Father!"

Murom bora Ballin crushed his daughter to his breast with a sob of thanksgiving, and then turned to *his* king.

"Sire, you are sorely wounded!"

Kull shook his head. "Not sorely; at least, not for me, though other men might feel stiff and sore. But yonder lies he who took the death thrusts meant for me; who was my shield and my helmet, and but for whom Valusia had howled for a new king."

Murom whirled toward the prostrate youth.

"Dalgar! Is he dead?"

"Nigh unto it," growled a weary Pict who was still working above him. "But he is steel and whalebone; with any care he should live."

"He came here to meet your daughter and elope with her," said Kull, while Nalissa hung her head. "He crept through the brush and saw me fighting for my life and hers, atop yonder stair. He might have escaped. Nothing barred him. But he climbed the sheer wall to certain death, as it seemed then, and fought by my side as gayly as he ever rode to a feast—and he not even a subject of mine by birth."

Murom's hands clenched and unclenched. His eyes kindled and softened as they bent on his daughter.

"Nalissa," he said softly, drawing the girl into the shelter of his steel-clad arm, "do you still wish to marry this reckless youth?"

Her eyes spoke eloquently enough.

Kull was speaking. "Take him up carefully and bear him to the palace; he shall have the best—"

Murom interposed, "Sire, if I may ask; let him be taken to my castle. There the finest physicians shall attend him and on his recovery—well, if it be your royal pleasure, might we not celebrate the event with a wedding?"

Nalissa screamed with joy, clapped her hands, kissed her father and Kull, and was off to Dalgar's side like a whirlwind.

Murom smiled softly, his aristocratic face alight.

"Out of a night of blood and terror, joy and happiness are born."

The barbarian king grinned and shouldered his stained and notched axe.

"Life is that way, Count; one man's bane is another's bliss."

The Rule of Names

By Ursula K. Le Guin

"It was a long, long time since he had had a real meal."

H. J. FORD

The Rule of Names

MR. UNDERHILL CAME out from under his hill, smiling and breathing hard. Each breath shot out of his nostrils as a double puff of steam, snow-white in the morning sunshine. Mr. Underhill looked up at the bright December sky and smiled wider than ever, showing snow-white teeth. Then he went down to the village.

"Morning, Mr. Underhill," said the villagers as he passed them in the narrow street between houses with conical, overhanging roofs like the fat red caps of toadstools. "Morning, morning!" he replied to each. (It was of course bad luck to wish anyone a *good* morning; a simple statement of the time of day was quite enough, in a place so permeated with Influences as Sattins Island, where a careless adjective might change the weather for a week.) All of them spoke to him, some with affection, some with affectionate disdain. He was all the little island had in the way of a wizard, and so deserved respect—but how could you respect a little fat man of fifty who waddled along with his toes turned in, breathing steam and smiling? He was no great shakes as a workman either. His fireworks were fairly elaborate but his elixirs were weak. Warts he charmed off frequently reappeared after three days; tomatoes he enchanted grew no bigger than canteloupes; and those rare times when a strange ship stopped at Sattins Harbor, Mr. Underhill always stayed under his hill—for fear, he explained, of the evil eye. He was, in other words, a wizard the way walleyed Gan was a carpenter: by default. The villagers made do with badly-hung doors and inefficient spells, for this generation, and relieved their annoyance by treating Mr. Underhill quite familiarly, as a mere fellow-villager. They even asked him to dinner. Once he asked some of them to dinner, and served a splendid repast, with silver, crystal, damask, roast goose, sparkling Andrades '639, and plum pudding with hard sauce; but he was so nervous all through the meal that it took the joy out of it, and besides, everybody was hungry again half an hour afterward. He did not like anyone to visit his cave, not even the anteroom, beyond which in fact nobody had ever got. When he saw people approachingg the hill he always came trotting out to meet them. "Let's sit out here under the pine trees!" he would say, smiling and waving towards the fir grove, or if it was raining, "Let's go have a drink at the inn, eh?" though everybody knew he drank nothing stronger than well-water.

Some of the village children, teased by that locked cave, poked and pried and made raids while Mr. Underhill was away; but the small door that led into the inner chamber was spell-shut, and it seemed for once to be an effective spell. Once a couple of boys, thinking the wizard was over on the West Shore curing Mrs. Ruuna's sick donkey, brought a crowbar and a hatchet up there, but at the first whack of the hatchet on the door there came a roar of wrath from inside, and a cloud of purple steam. Mr. Underhill had got home early. The boys fled. He did not come out, and the boys came to no harm, though they said you couldn't believe what a huge hooting howling hissing horrible bellow that little fat man could make unless you'd heard it.

His business in town this day was three dozen fresh eggs and a pound of liver; also a stop at Seacaptain Fogeno's cottage to renew the seeing-charm on the old man's eyes (quite useless when applied to a case of detached retina, but Mr. Underhill kept trying), and finally a chat with old Goody Guld, the concertina-maker's widow. Mr. Underhill's friends were mostly old people. He was timid with the strong young men of the village, and the girls were shy of him. "He makes me nervous, he smiles so much," they all said, pouting, twisting silky ringlets round a finger. "Nervous" was a newfangled word, and their mothers all replied grimly, "Nervous my foot, silliness is the word for it. Mr. Underhill is a very respectable wizard!"

After leaving Goody Guld, Mr. Underhill passed by the school, which was being held this day out on the common. Since no one on Sattins Island was literate, there were no books to learn to read from and no desks to carve initials on and no blackboards to erase, and in fact no schoolhouse. On rainy days the children met in the loft of the Communal Barn, and got hay in their pants; on sunny days the schoolteacher, Palani, took them anywhere she felt like. Today, surrounded by thirty interested children under twelve and forty uninterested sheep under five, she was teaching an important item on the curriculum: the Rules of Names. Mr. Underhill, smiling shyly, paused to listen and watch. Palani, a plump, pretty girl of twenty, made a charming picture there in the wintry sunlight, sheep and children around her, a leafless oak above her, and behind her the dunes and sea and clear, pale sky. She spoke earnestly, her face flushed pink by wind and words. "Now you know the Rules of Names already, children. There are two, and they're the same on every island in the world. What's one of them?"

"It ain't polite to ask anybody what his name is," shouted a fat, quick boy, interrupted by a little girl shrieking, "You can't never tell your own name to nobody my ma says!"

"Yes, Suba. Yes, Popi dear, don't screech. That's right. You never ask anybody his name. You never tell your own. Now think about that a minute and then tell my why we call our wizard Mr. Underhill." She smiled across the curly heads and the wooly backs at Mr. Underhill, who beamed, and nervously clutched his sack of eggs.

"'Cause he lives under a hill!" said half the children.

"But is it his truename?"

"No!" said the fat boy, echoed by little Popi shrieking, "No!"

"How do you know it's not?"

"'Cause he came here all alone and so there wasn't anybody knew his true name so they couldn't tell, and *he* couldn't—"

"Very good, Suba. Popi, don't shout. That's right. Even a wizard can't tell his true name. When you children are through school and go through the Passage, you'll leave your childnames behind and keep only your truenames, which you must never ask for and never give away. Why is that the rule?"

The children were silent. The sheep bleated gently. Mr. Underhill answered the question: "Because the name is the thing," he said in his shy, soft, husky voice, "and the truename is the true thing. To speak the name is to control the thing. Am I right, Schoolmistress?"

She smiled and curtseyed, evidently a little embarrassed by his participation. And he trotted off towards his hill, clutching his eggs to his bosom. Somehow the minute spent watching Palani and the children had made him very hungry. He locked his inner door behind him with a hasty incantation, but there must have been a leak or two in the spell, for soon the bare anteroom of the cave was rich with the smell of frying eggs and sizzling liver.

The wind that day was light and fresh out of the west, and on it at noon a little boat came skimming the bright waves into Sattins Harbor. Even as it rounded the point a sharp-eyed boy spotted it, and knowing, like every child on the island, every sail and spar of the forty boats of the fishing fleet, he ran down the street calling out "A foreign boat, a foreign boat!" Very seldom was the lonely isle visited by a boat from some equally lonely isle of the East Reach, or an adventurous trader from the Archipelago. By the time the boat was at the pier half the village was there to greet it, and fishermen were following it homewards, and cowherds and clam-diggers and herb-hunters were puffing up and down all the rocky hills, heading towards the harbor.

But Mr. Underhill's door stayed shut.

There was only one man aboard the boat. Old Seacaptain Fogeno, when they told him that, drew down a bristle of white brows over his unseeing eyes. "There's only one kind of man," he said, "that sails the Outer Reach alone. A wizard, or a warlock, or a Mage . . ."

So the villagers were breathless hoping to see for once in their lives a Mage, one of the mighty White Magicians of the rich, towered, crowded inner islands of the Archipelago. They were disappointed, for the voyager was quite young, a handsome black-bearded fellow who hailed them cheerfully from his boat, and leaped ashore like any sailor glad to have made port. He introduced himself at once as a sea-peddlar. But when they told Seacaptain Fogeno that he carried an oaken walking-stick around with him, the old man nodded. "Two wizards in one town," he said. "Bad!" And his mouth snapped shut like an old carp's.

As the stranger could not give them his name, they gave him one right away: Blackbeard. And they gave him plenty of attention. He had a small mixed cargo of cloth and sandals and piswi feathers for trimming cloaks and cheap incense and levity stones and fine herbs and great glass beads from Venway—the usual peddlar's lot. Everyone on Sattins Island came to look, to chat with the voyager, and perhaps to buy something—"Just to remember him by!" cackled Goody Guld, who like all the women and girls of the village was smitten with Blackbeard's bold good looks. All the boys hung round him too, to hear him tell of his voyages to far, strange islands of the Reach or describe the great rich islands of the Archipelago, the Inner Lanes, the roadsteads white with ships, and the golden roofs of Havnor. The men willingly listened to his tales; but some of them wondered why a trader should sail alone, and kept their eyes thoughtfully upon his oaken staff.

But all this time Mr. Underhill stayed under his hill.

"This is the first island I've ever seen that had no wizard," said Blackbeard one evening to Goody Guld, who had invited him and her nephew and Palani in for a cup of rushwash tea. "What do you do when you get a toothache, or the cow goes dry?"

"Why, we've got Mr. Underhill!" said the old woman.

"For what that's worth," muttered her nephew Birt, and then blushed purple and spilled his tea. Birt was a fisherman, a large, brave, wordless young man. He loved the schoolmistress, but the nearest he had come to telling her of his love was to give baskets of fresh mackerel to her father's cook.

"Oh, you do have a wizard?" Blackbeard asked. "Is he invisible?"

"No, he's just very shy," said Palani. "You've only been here a week, you know, and we see so few strangers here. . . ." She also blushed a little, but did not spill her tea.

Blackbeard smiled at her. "He's a good Sattinsman, then, eh?"

"No," said Goody Guld, "no more than you are. Another cup, nevvy? keep it in the cup this time. No, my dear, he came in a little bit of a boat, four years ago was it? just a day after the end of the shad run, I recall, for they was taking up the nets over in East Creek, and Pondi Cowherd broke his leg that very morning—five years ago it must be. No, four. No, five it is, 'twas the year the garlic didn't sprout. So he sails in on a bit of a sloop loaded full up with great chests and boxes and says to Seacaptain Fogeno, who wasn't blind then, though old enough goodness knows to be blind twice over, 'I hear tell,' he says, 'you've got no wizard nor warlock at all, might you be wanting one?' 'Indeed, if the magic's white!' says the Captain, and before you could say cuttlefish Mr. Underhill had settled down in the cave under the hill and was charming the mange off Goody Beltow's cat. Though the fur grew in grey, and 'twas an orange cat. Queer-looking thing it was after that. It died last winter in the cold spell. Goody Beltow took on so at that cat's death, poor thing, worse than when her man was drowned on the Long Banks, the year of the long herring-runs, when nevvy Birt here was but a babe in petticoats." Here Birt spilled his tea again, and Blackbeard grinned, but Goody Guld proceeded undismayed, and talked on till nightfall.

Next day Blackbeard was down at the pier, seeing after the sprung board in his boat which he seemed to take a long time fixing, and as usual drawing the taciturn Sattinsmen into talk. "Now which of these is your wizard's craft?" he asked. "Or has he got one of those the Mages fold up into a walnut shell when they're not using it?"

"Nay," said a stolid fisherman. "She's oop in his cave, under hill."

"He carried the boat he came in up to his cave?"

"Aye. Clear oop. I helped. Heavier as lead she was. Full oop with great boxes, and they full oop with books o'spells, he says. Heavier as lead she was." And the stolid fisherman turned his back, sighing stolidly. Goody Guld's nephew, mending a net nearby, looked up from his work and asked with equal stolidity. "Would ye like to meet Mr. Underhill, maybe?"

Blackbeard returned Birt's look. Clever black eyes met candid blue ones for a long moment; then Blackbeard smiled and said, "Yes. Will you take me up to the hill, Birt?"

"Aye, when I'm done with this," said the fisherman. And when the net was mended, he and the Archipelagan set off up the village street towards the high green hill above it. But as they crossed the common Blackbeard said, "Hold on a while, friend Birt. I have a tale to tell you, before we meet your wizard."

"Tell away," says Birt, sitting down in the shade of a live-oak.

"It's a story that started a hundred years ago, and isn't finished yet—though it soon will be, very soon. . . . In the very heart of the Archipelago, where the islands crowd thick as flies on honey, there's a little isle called Pendor. The sealords of Pendor were mighty men, in the old days of war before the League. Loot and ransom and tribute came pouring into Pendor, and they gathered a great treasure there, long ago. Then from somewhere away out in the West Reach, where dragons breed on the lava isles, came one day a very mighty dragon. Not one of those overgrown lizards most of you Outer Reach folk call dragons, but a big, black, winged, wise, cunning monster, full of strength and subtlety, and like all dragons loving gold and precious stones above all things. He killed the Sealord and his soldiers, and the people of Pendor fled in their ships by night. They all fled away and left the dragon coiled up in Pendor Towers. And there he stayed for a hundred years, dragging his scaly belly over the emeralds and sapphires and coins of gold, coming forth only once in a year or two when he must eat. He'd raid nearby islands for his food. You know what dragons eat?"

Birt nodded and said in a whisper, "Maidens."

"Right," said Blackbeard. "Well, that couldn't be endured forever, nor the thought of his sitting on all that treasure. So after the League grew strong, and the Archipelago wasn't so busy with wars and piracy, it was decided to attack Pendor, drive out the dragon, and get the gold and jewels for the treasury of the League. They're forever wanting money, the League is. So a huge fleet gathered from fifty islands, and seven Mages stood in the prows of the seven strongest ships, and they sailed towards Pendor. . . . They got there. They landed. Nothing stirred. The houses all stood empty, the dishes on the tables full of a hundred years' dust. The bones of the old Sealord and his men lay about in the castle courts and on the stairs. And the Tower rooms reeked of dragon. But there was no dragon. And no treasure, not a diamond the size of a poppyseed, not a single silver bead . . . Knowing that he couldn't stand up to seven Mages, the dragon had skipped out. They tracked him, and found he'd flown to a deserted island up north called Udrath; they followed his trail there, and what did they find? Bones again. His bones—the dragon's. But no treasure. A wizard, some unknown wizard from somewhere, must have met him single-handed, and defeated him—and then made off with the treasure, right under the League's nose!"

The fisherman listened, attentive and expressionless.

"Now that must have been a powerful wizard and a clever one, first to kill a dragon, and second to get off without leaving a trace. The lords and Mages of the Archipelago couldn't track him at all, neither where he'd come from nor where he'd made off to. They were about to give up. That was last spring; I'd been off on a three-year voyage up in the North Reach, and got back about that time. And they asked me to help them find the unknown wizard. That was clever of them. Because I'm not only a wizard myself, as I think some of the oafs here have guessed, but I am also a descendant of the Lords of Pendor. That treasure is mine. It's mine, and knows that it's mine. Those fools of the League couldn't find it, because it's not theirs. It belongs to the House of Pendor, and the great emerald, the star of the board, Inalkil the Greenstone, knows its master. Behold!" Blackbeard raised his oaken staff and cried aloud, "Inalkil!" The tip of the staff began to glow green, a fiery green radiance, a dazzling haze the color of April grass, and at the same moment the staff tipped in the wizard's hand, leaning, slanting till it pointed straight at the side of the hill above them.

"It wasn't so bright a glow, far away in Havnor," Blackbeard murmured, "but the staff pointed true. Inalkil answered when I called. The jewel knows its master. And I know the thief, and I shall conquer him. He's a mighty wizard, who could overcome a dragon. But I am mightier. Do you want to know why, oaf? Because I know his name!"

As Blackbeard's tone got more arrogant, Birt had looked duller and duller, blanker and blanker; but at this he gave a twitch, shut his mouth, and stared at the Archipelagan. "How did you . . . learn it?" he asked very slowly.

Blackbeard grinned, and did not answer.

"Black magic?"

"How else?"

Birt looked pale, and said nothing.

"I am the Sealord of Pendor, oaf, and I will have the gold my fathers won, and the jewels my mothers wore, and the Greenstone! For they are mine. —Now, you can tell your village boobies the whole story after I have defeated this wizard and gone. Wait here. Or you can come and watch, if you're not afraid. You'll never get the chance again to see a great wizard in all his power." Blackbeard turned, and without a backward glance strode off up the hill towards the entrance to the cave.

Very slowly, Birt followed. A good distance from the cave he stopped, sat down under a hawthorn tree, and watched. The Archipelagan had stopped; a stiff, dark figure alone on the green swell of the hill before the gaping cave-mouth, he stood perfectly still. All at once he swung his staff up over his head, and the emerald radiance shone about him as he shouted, "Thief, thief of the Hoard of Pendor, come forth!"

There was a crash, as of dropped crockery, from inside the cave, and a lot of dust came spewing out. Scared, Birt ducked. When he looked again he saw Blackbeard still standing motionless, and at the mouth of the cave, dusty and dishevelled, stood Mr. Underhill. He looked small and pitiful, with his toes turned in as usual, and his little bowlegs in black tights, and no staff—he never had had one, Birt suddenly thought. Mr. Underhill spoke. "Who are you?" he said in his husky little voice.

"I am the Sealord of Pendor, thief, come to claim my treasure!"

At that, Mr. Underhill slowly turned pink, as he always did when people were rude to him. But he then turned something else. He turned yellow. His hair bristled out, he gave a coughing roar—and was a yellow lion leaping down the hill at Blackbeard, white fangs gleaming.

But Blackbeard no longer stood there. A gigantic tiger, color of night and lightning, bounded to meet the lion. . . .

The lion was gone. Below the cave all of a sudden stood a high grove of trees, black in the winter sunshine. The tiger, checking himself in mid-leap just before he entered the shadow of the trees, caught fire in the air, became a tongue of flame lashing out at the dry black branches. . . .

But where the trees had stood a sudden cataract leaped from the hillside, an arch of silvery crashing water, thundering down upon the fire. But the fire was gone. . . .

For just a moment before the fisherman's staring eyes two hills rose— the green one he knew, and a new one, a bare, brown hillock ready to drink up the rushing waterfall. That passed so quickly it made Birt blink, and after blinking he blinked again, and moaned, for what he saw now was a great deal worse. Where the cataract had been there hovered a dragon. Black wings darkened all the hill, steel claws reached groping, and from the dark, scaly, gaping lips fire and steam shot out.

Beneath the monstrous creature stood Blackbeard, laughing.

"Take any shape you please, little Mr. Underhill!" he taunted. "I can match you. But the game grows tiresome. I want to look upon my treasure, upon Inalkil. Now, big dragon, little wizard, take your true shape. I command you by the power of your true name—Yevaud!"

Birt could not move at all, not even to blink. He cowered, staring whether he would or not. He saw the black dragon hang there in the air above Blackbeard. He saw the fire lick like many tongues from the scaly mouth, the steam jet from the red nostrils. He saw Blackbeard's face grow white, white as chalk, and the beard-fringed lips trembling.

"Your name is Yevaud!"

"Yes," said a great, husky, hissing voice. "My truename is Tevaud, and my true shape is this shape."

"But the dragon was killed—they found dragon-bones on Udrath Island—"

"That was another dragon," said the dragon, and then stooped like a hawk, talons outstretched. And Birt shut his eyes.

When he opened them the sky was clear, the hillside empty, except for a reddish-blackish trampled spot, and a few talon-marks in the grass.

Birt the fisherman got to his feet and ran. He ran across the common, scattering sheep to right and left, and straight down the village street to Palani's father's house. Palani was out in the garden weeding the nasturtiums. "Come with me!" Birt gasped. She stared. He grabbed her wrist and dragged her with him. She screeched a little, but did not resist. He ran with her straight to the pier, pushed her into his fishing-sloop the *Queenie,* untied the painter, took up the oars and set off rowing like a demon. The last that Sattins Island saw of him and Palani was the *Queenie's* sail vanishing in the direction of the nearest island westward.

The villagers thought they would never stop talking about it, how Goody Guld's nephew Birt had lost his mind and sailed off with the schoolmistress on the very same day that the peddlar Blackbeard disappeared without a trace, leaving all his feathers and beads behind. But they did stop talking about it, three days later. They had other things to talk about, when Mr. Underhill finally came out of his cave.

Mr. Underhill had decided that since his truename was no longer a secret, he might as well drop his disguise. Walking was a lot harder than flying, and besides, it was a long, long time since he had had a real meal.